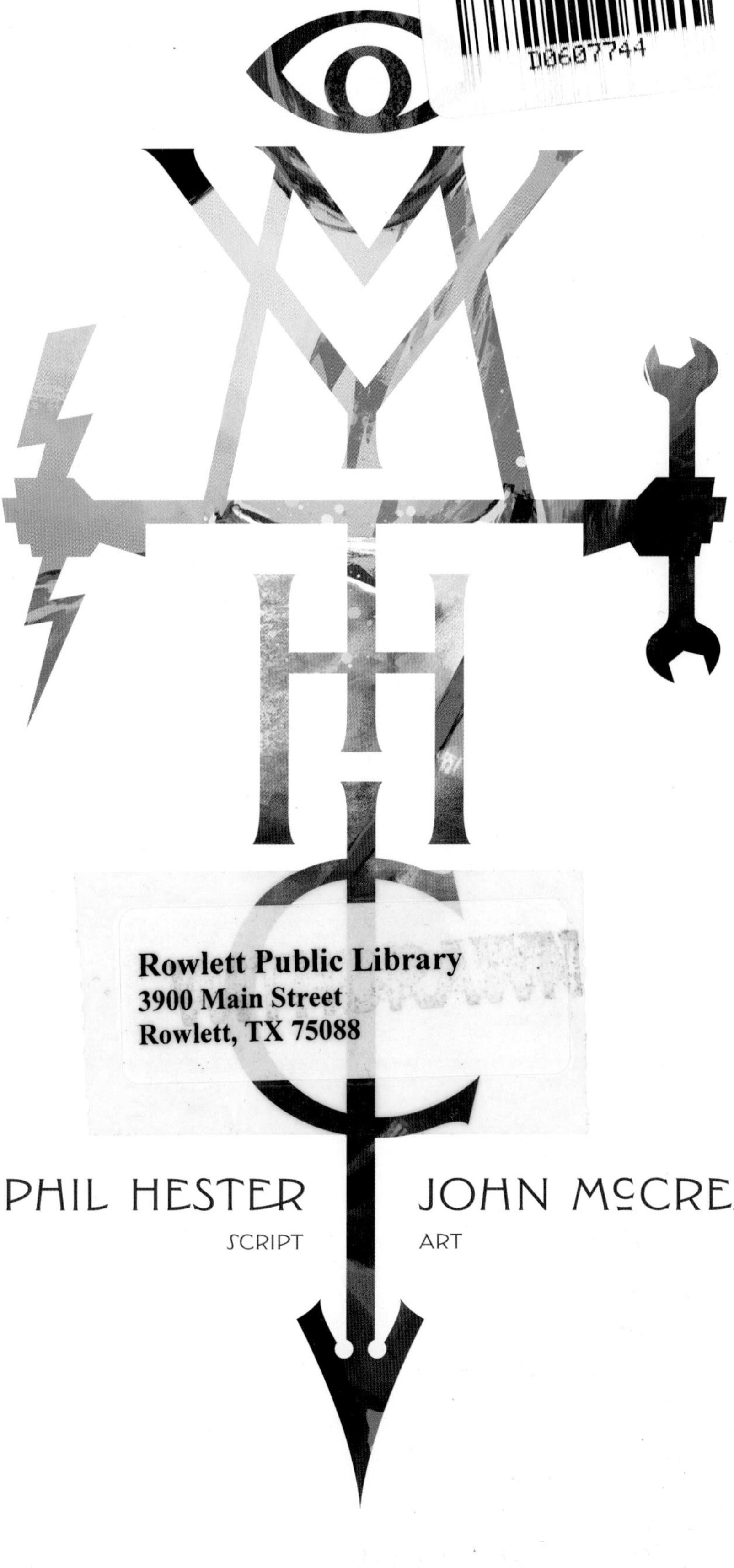

PHIL HESTER
SCRIPT

JOHN McCREA
ART

For Jack Kirby and Stan Lee — Phil

For Rachel, Kirby, Ella, Harvey and Luke – love you all so much! — John

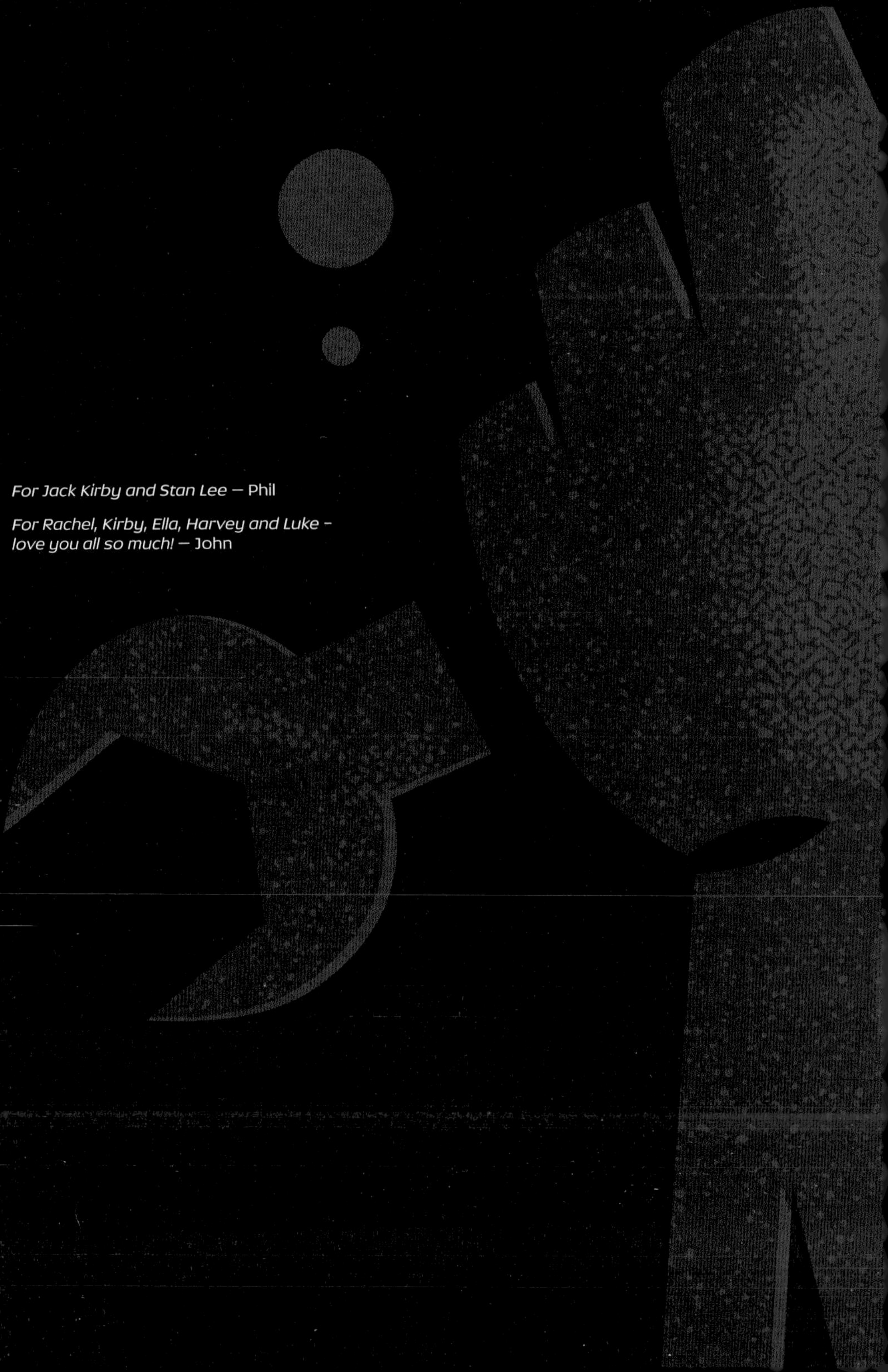

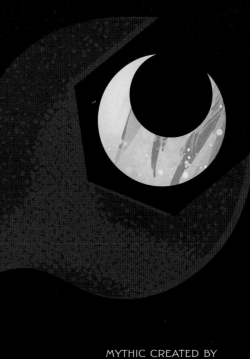

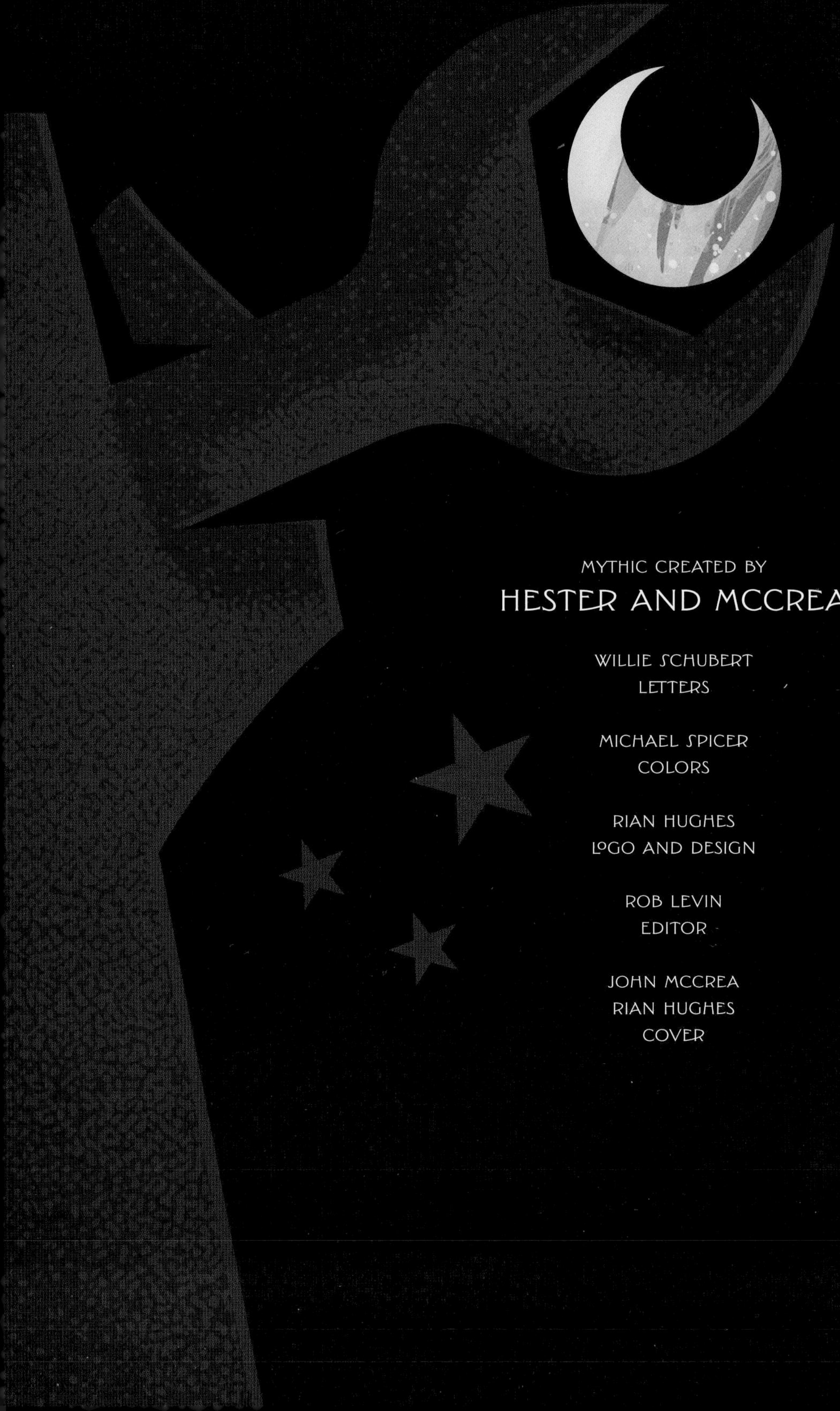

MYTHIC CREATED BY

HESTER AND MCCREA

WILLIE SCHUBERT
LETTERS

MICHAEL SPICER
COLORS

RIAN HUGHES
LOGO AND DESIGN

ROB LEVIN
EDITOR

JOHN MCCREA
RIAN HUGHES
COVER

MYTHIC VOL. 1.

First Printing.
JUNE 2016.
©2016 Phil Hester and John McCrea.
All rights reserved.

Published by Image Comics, Inc.
Office of publication:
2001 Center Street, Sixth Floor, Berkeley, CA
94704.

Originally published in single magazine form as
MYTHIC Nº1-8 by Image Comics.

Printed in the USA.

For information regarding the CSPIA on this
printed material call: 203-595-3636 and provide
reference Nº RICH-682158.

For international rights contact:
foreignlicensing@imagecomics.com

ISBN: 978-1-63215-736-2

INTRODUCTION

MARK MILLAR, ESQ.

I always feel slightly embarrassed when I read one of Phil Hester's books.

Let me explain.

Back when I was 22 I landed a gig writing *Swamp Thing*. Now this was tremendously exciting because it was the closest thing I'd ever had to a job, I'd cracked a shot writing American comics and I was writing – let me repeat – *Swamp Thing*. This venerable title was everyone's favorite comic when I was in High School, the alma mater of mighty Moore himself and the bar all future British writers would be measured against, in my case often unfavorably. I did a creditable job on occasion, helped out by endless phone calls to the veteran writer Grant Morrison, also of this rain soaked isle, but for the most part I didn't know what I was doing and poor Phil Hester was doing all the heavy lifting.

Phil Hester, ye say? The writer of this here *Mythic* comic?

Yes, well that's the thing. You see, Phil drew my *Swamp Thing* scripts for three years as I fumbled my way through that variable run and the embarrassment set in once I realized he was the better writer. I raised an eyebrow when I saw his name on some Dark Horse books shortly after and after reading felt that slightly sick way everyone who worked at the Daily Planet would feel after they realized the humble reporter living among them was, in fact, Superman. How the Hell did this guy put up with my meandering storyline for very close to one third of an Earth decade? He must have been going mad when he could have written it ten times better.

Like I said. Embarrassing.

Johnny McCrea I've known since even earlier. Aged 19, I remember selling my first script to Fleetway Comics and being so incredibly delighted at being able to pay my rent that month and having the double-bonus of seeing my first ever work in color. Johnny was the artist and I was so excited by what he'd done I made a rare, expensive phone-call from Scotland to Northern Ireland to tell him how brilliant it was, my eye on my watch timing the whole thing as long distance was expensive and this sale being the only money I'd made that month. I remember he and Garth Ennis, another good pal of mine, had recently cracked the UK market and were wowing audiences with their work on *Crisis,* where our short story would appear together. These guys would later to go on to wow the international market with *Hitman* for DC and way too many other cool books to mention. It's terrifying that I've known and loved Johnny, both the dude himself and the drawing he explodes from his mind into paper for others to see too, for more than half my life, but the only thing that's changed is his art's got even better.

So here we are with *Mythic* and the trade you're holding here and I'm keeping you back from with this maybe just a little overly long introduction which has somehow become all about me. Still, that's writers for you. But I couldn't recommend this highly enough and I hope you enjoy it as much as I did. I love what these guys do separately and love them even more together so the more we buy of books like this the more of them they're going to make, which can only be a good thing.

All the best!
Mark Millar
April 2016

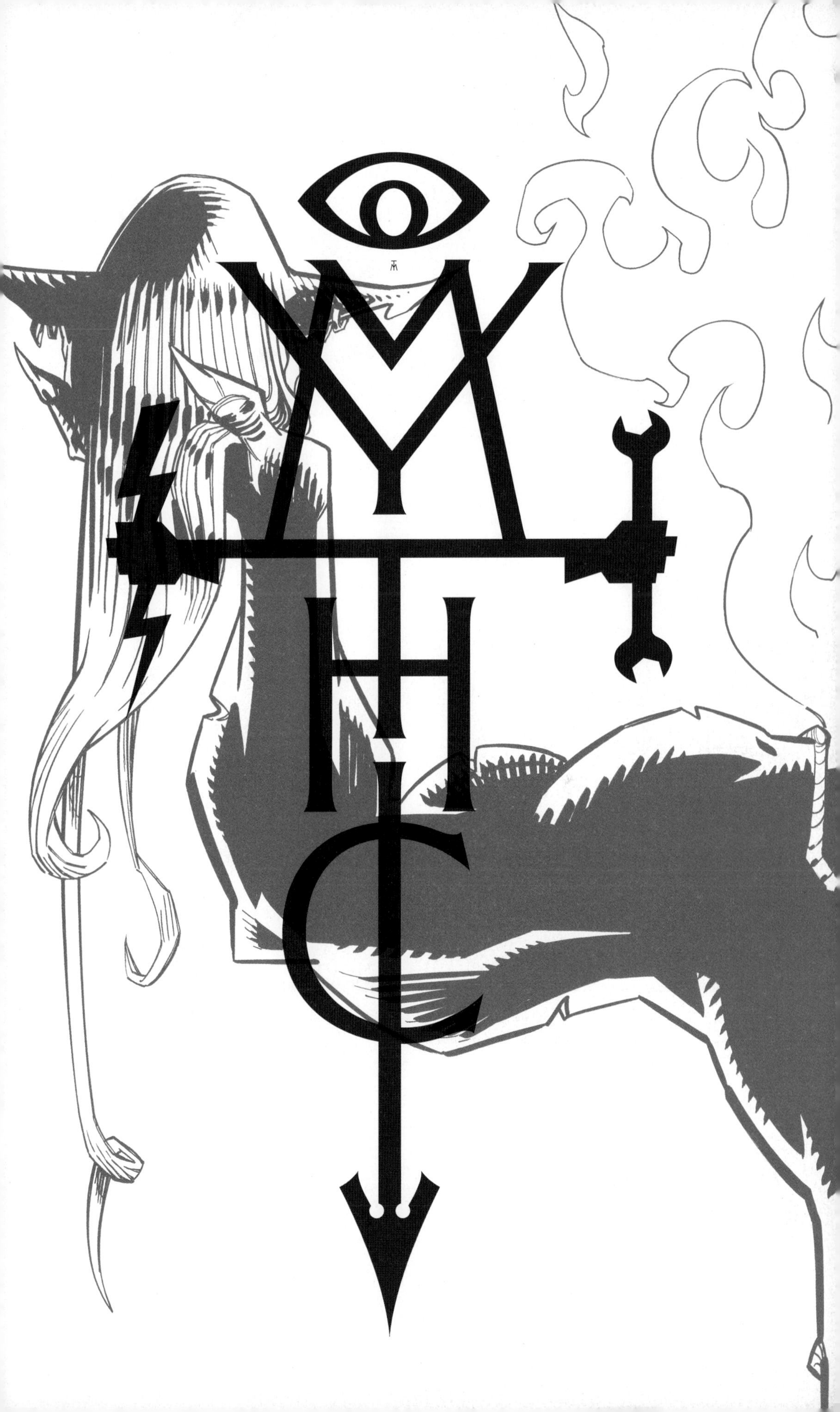
MYTHIC

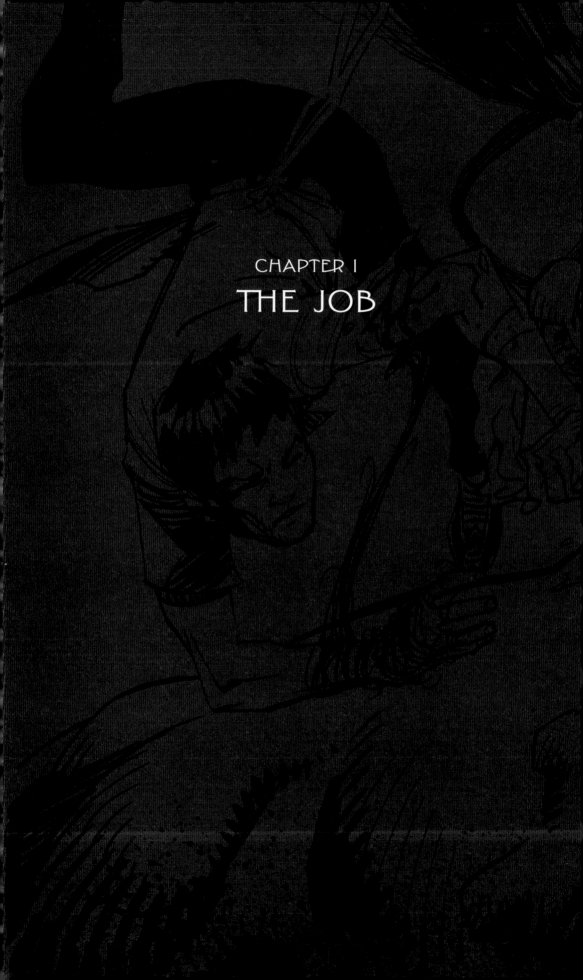

CHAPTER I
THE JOB

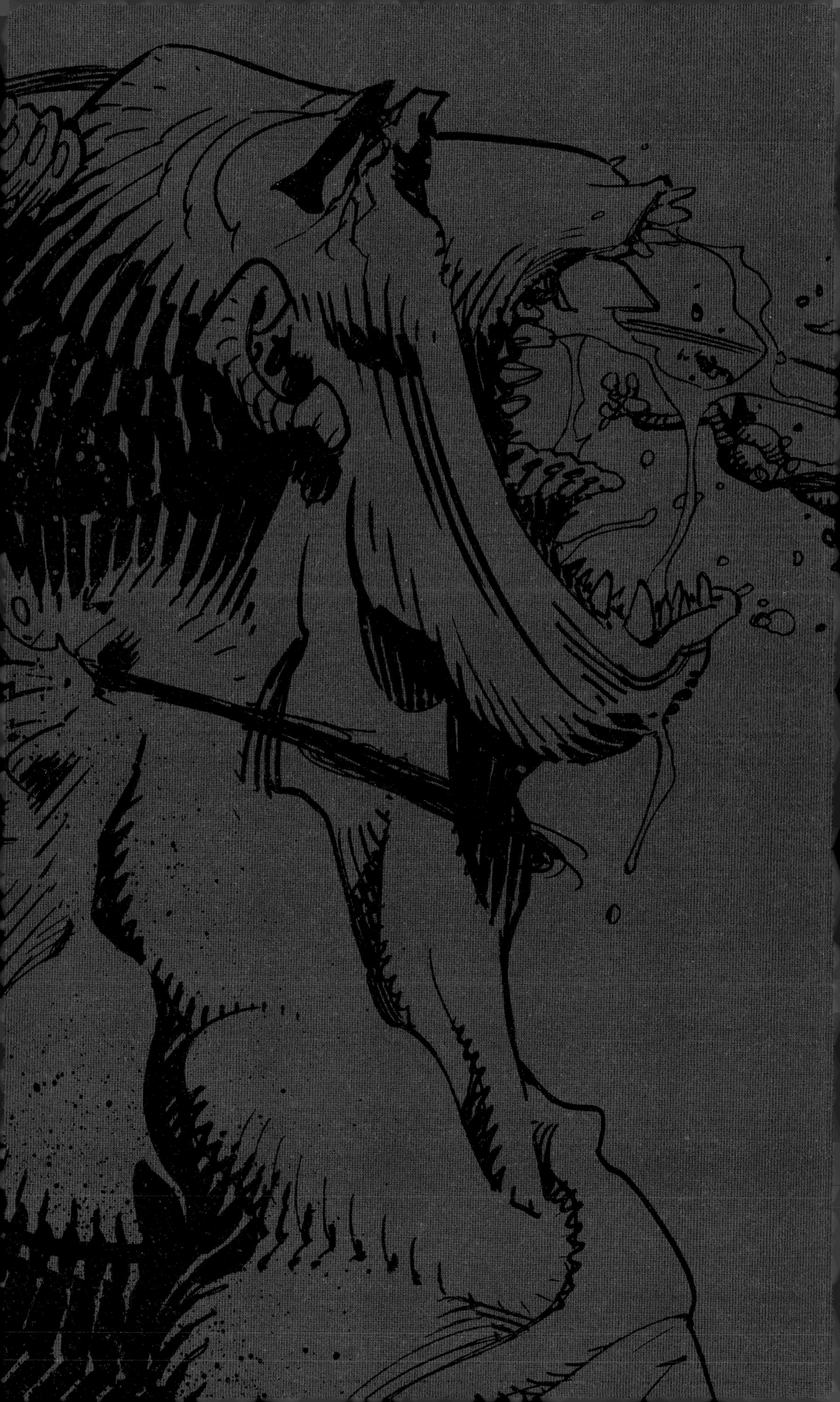

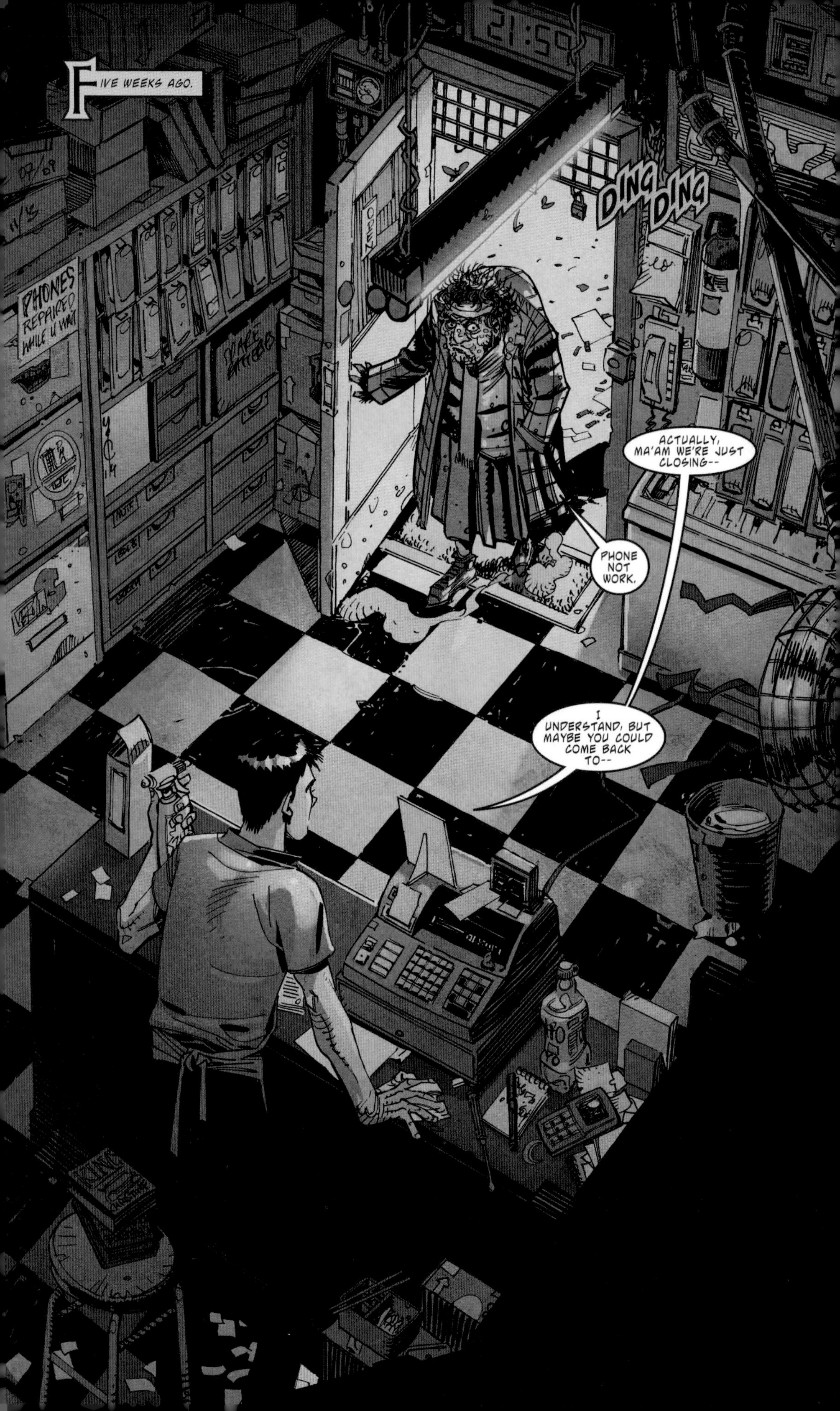
FIVE WEEKS AGO.
DING DING
PHONES REPAIRED WHILE U WAIT
OPEN
ACTUALLY, MA'AM WE'RE JUST CLOSING--
PHONE NOT WORK.
I UNDERSTAND, BUT MAYBE YOU COULD COME BACK TO--

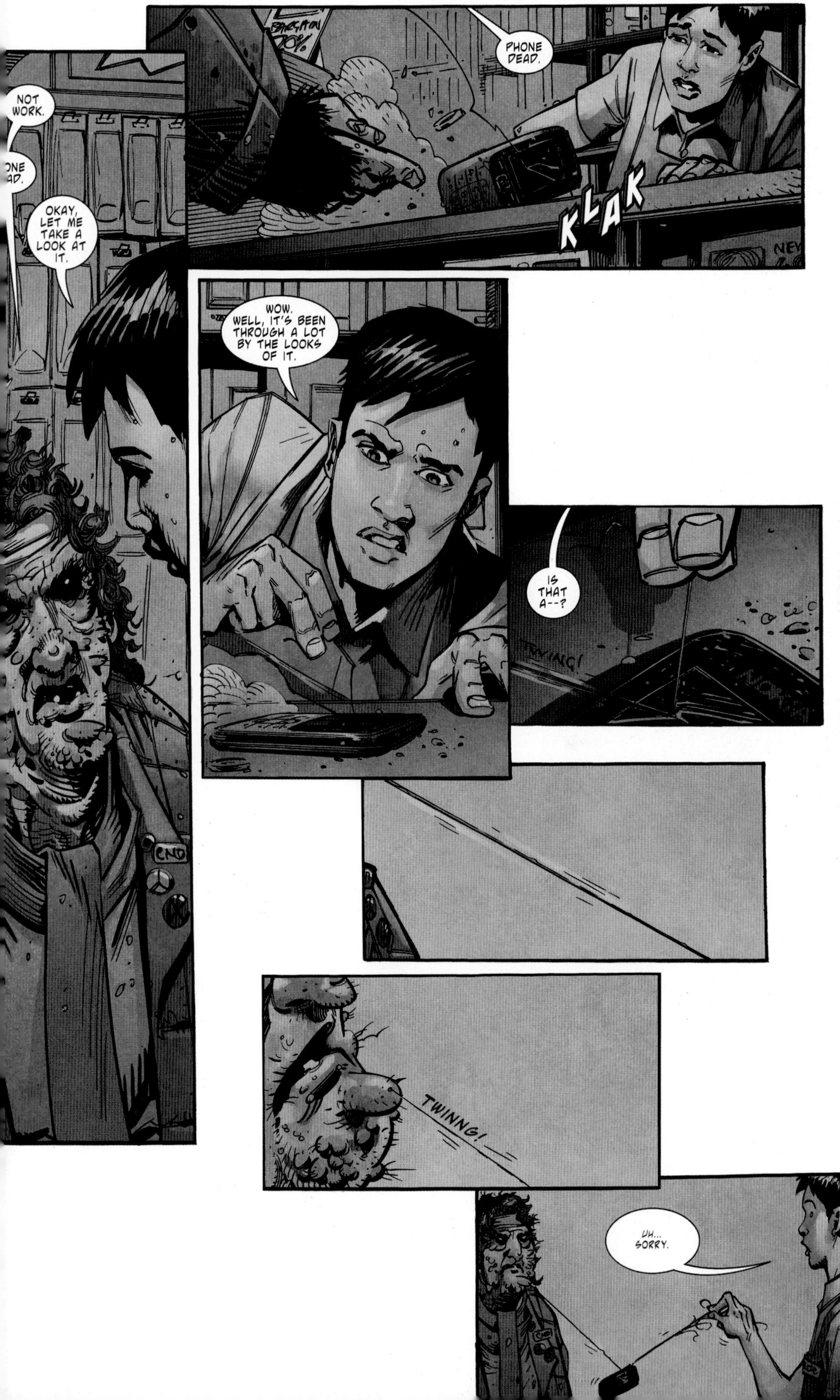

PHONE DEAD.
KLAK
NOT WORK.
ONE DEAD.
OKAY, LET ME TAKE A LOOK AT IT.
WOW. WELL, IT'S BEEN THROUGH A LOT BY THE LOOKS OF IT.
IS THAT A--?
TWING!
TWINNG!
UH... SORRY.

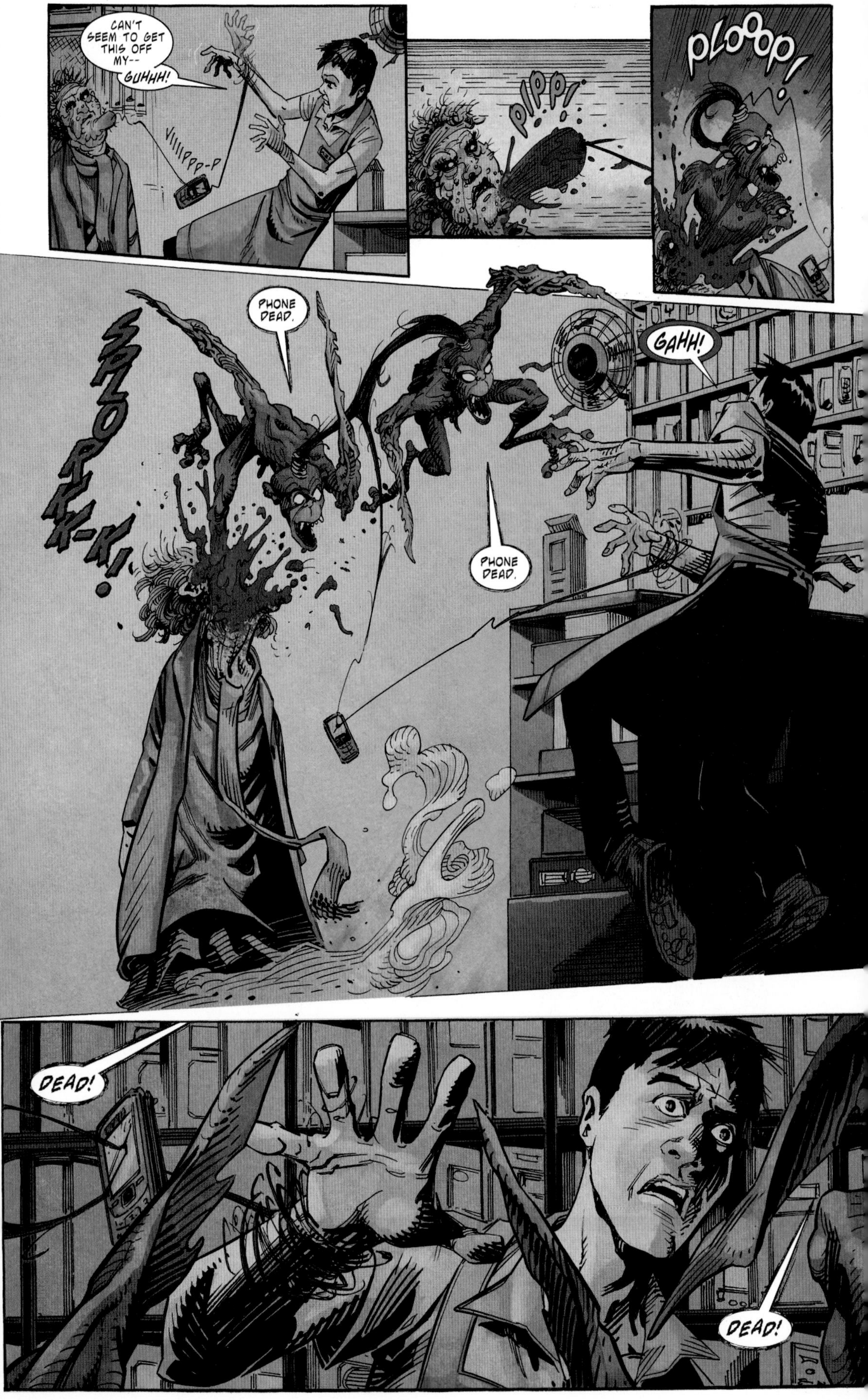
CAN'T SEEM TO GET THIS OFF MY--
GUHHH!
VIIIIPPP-P
PIPP!
PLOOOP!
PHONE DEAD.
SHLORKK-K!
GAHH!
PHONE DEAD.
DEAD!
DEAD!

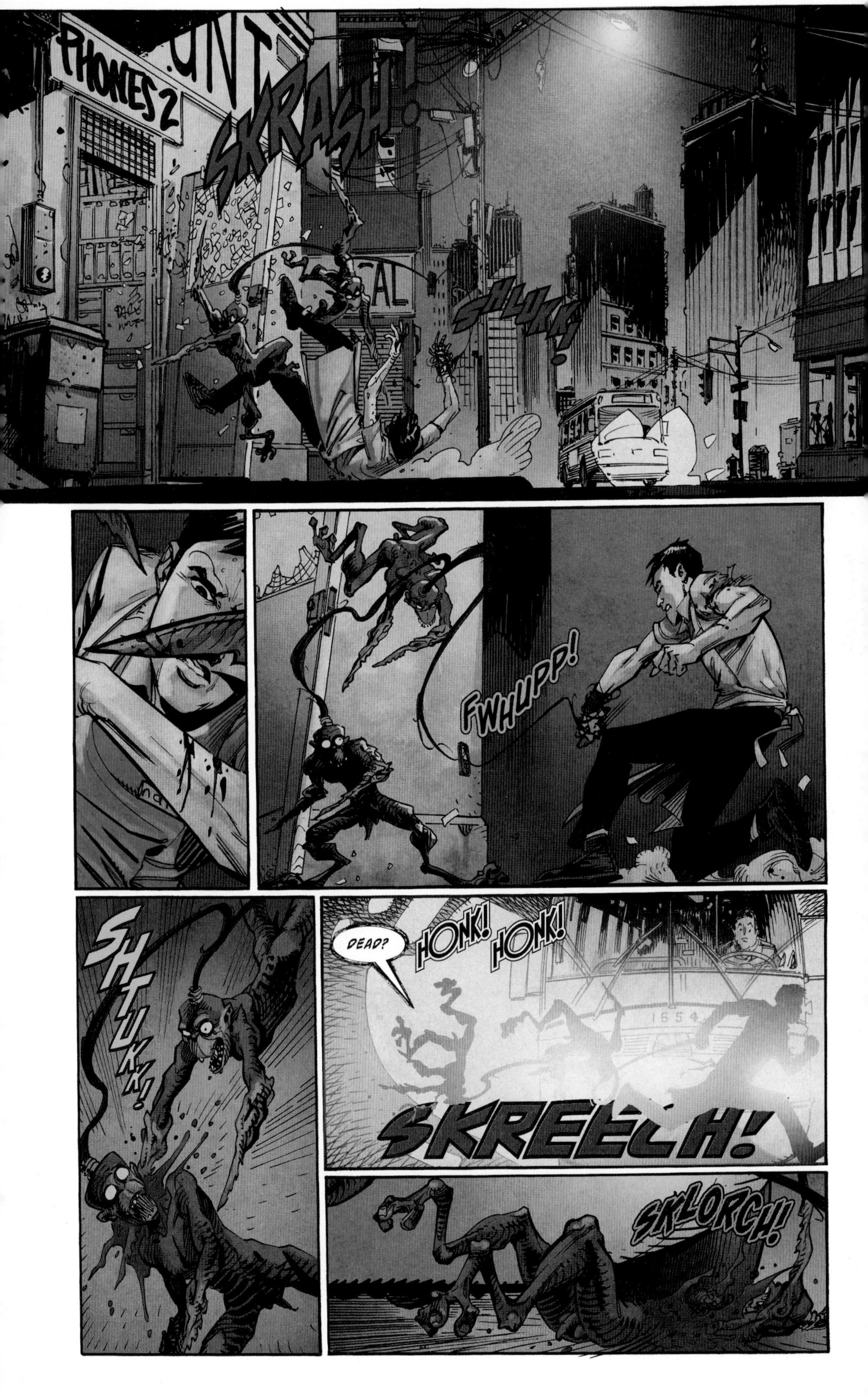
PHONES 2
SKRASH!
AL
SHLUKK!
FWHUPP!
SHTUKK!
DEAD?
HONK! HONK!
1654
SKREECH!
SKLORCH!

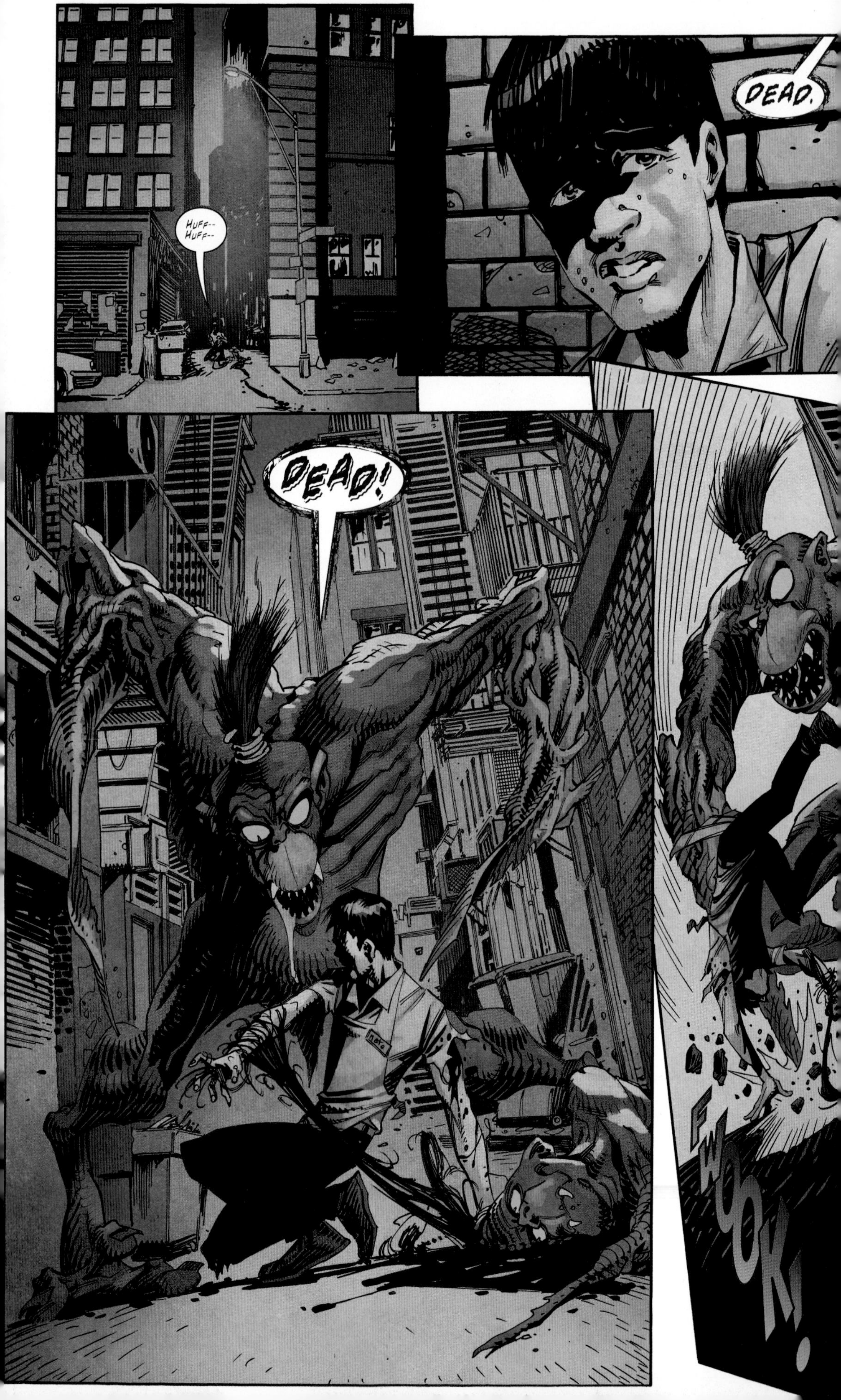
HUFF--
HUFF--
DEAD.
DEAD!
FWOOK!

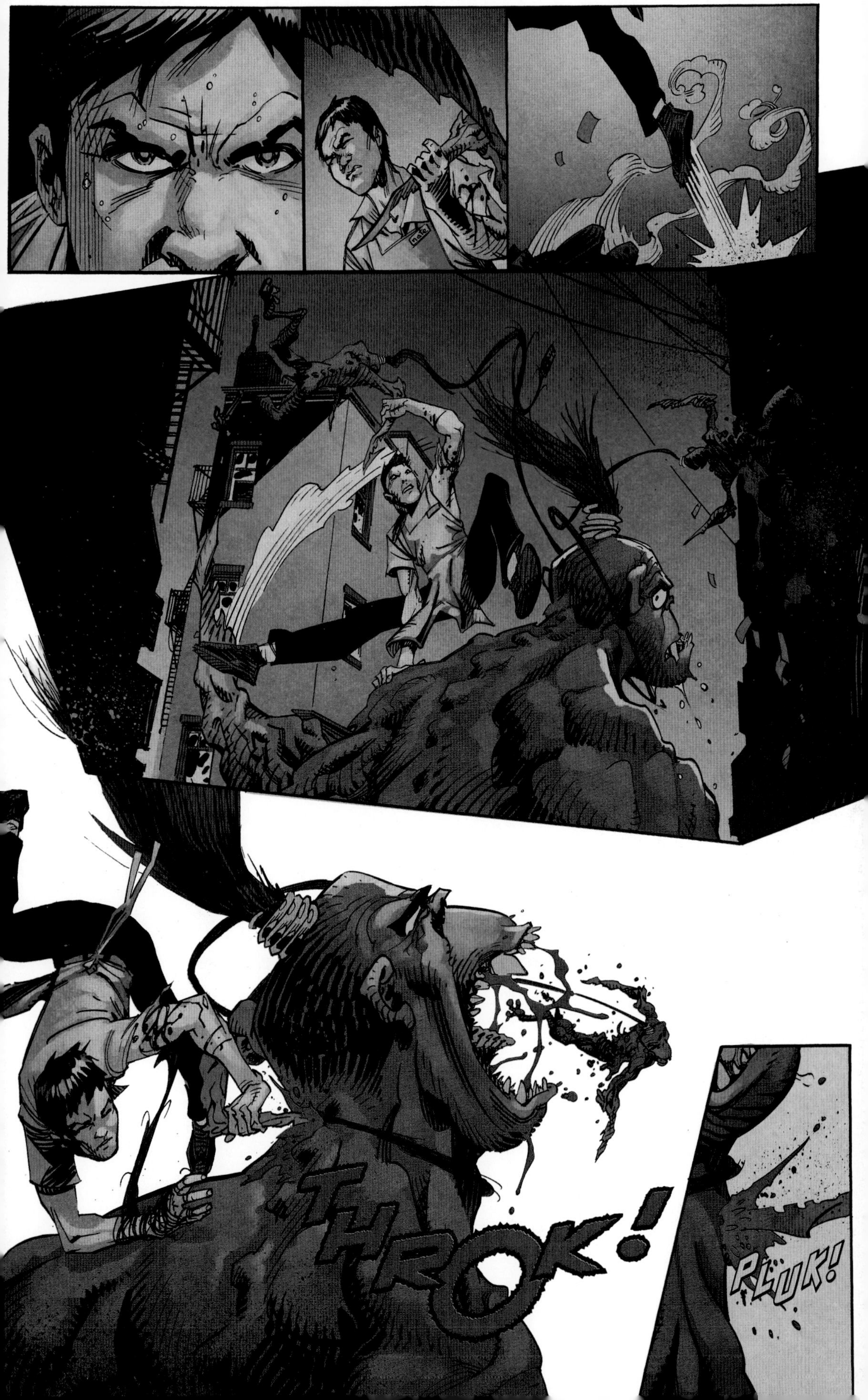
THROK!
PLUK!

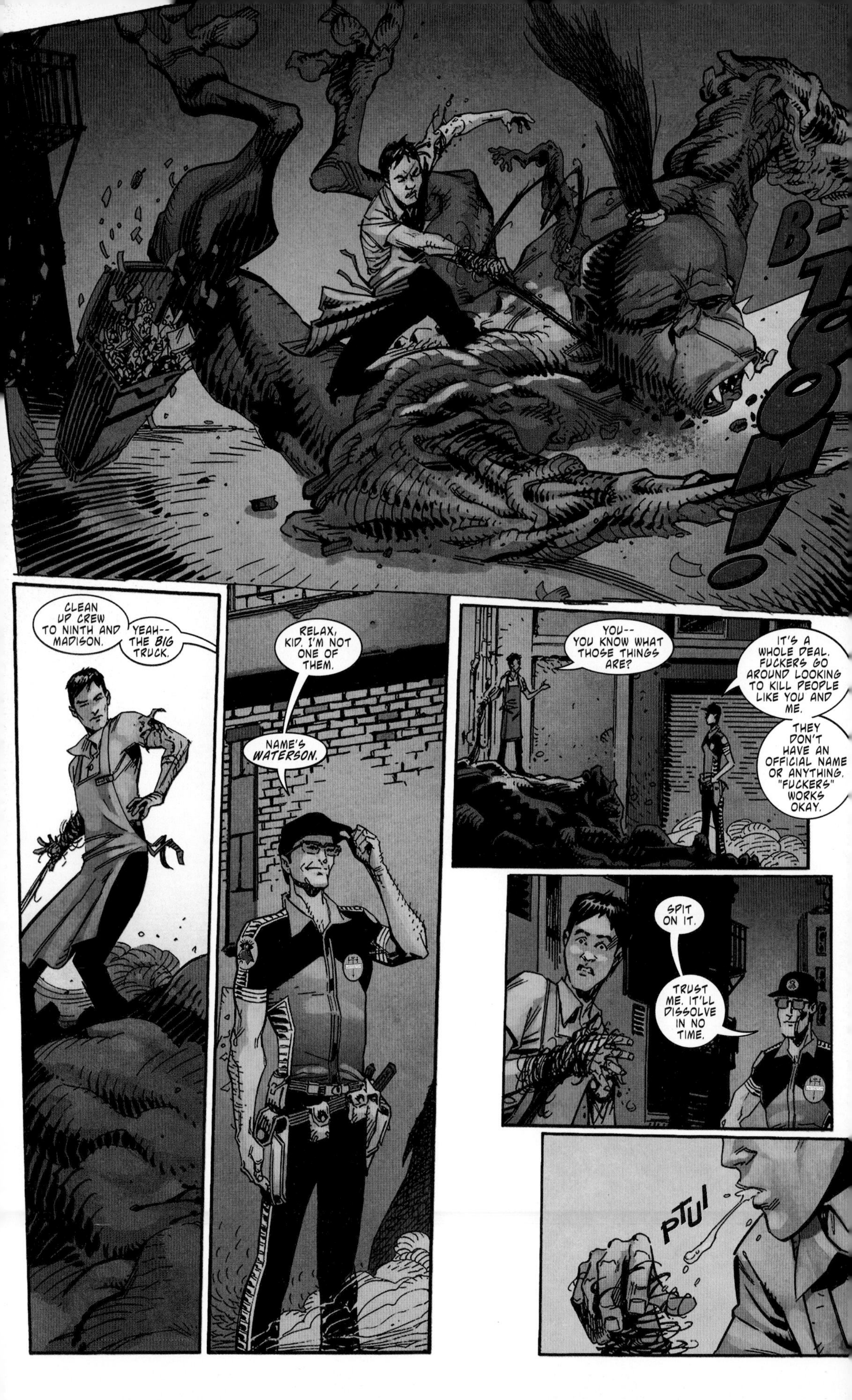
B-TOOOM!
CLEAN UP CREW TO NINTH AND MADISON.
YEAH-- THE *BIG* TRUCK.
RELAX, KID. I'M NOT ONE OF THEM.
NAME'S *WATERSON.*
YOU-- YOU KNOW WHAT THOSE THINGS ARE?
IT'S A WHOLE DEAL. FUCKERS GO AROUND LOOKING TO KILL PEOPLE LIKE YOU AND ME.
THEY DON'T HAVE AN OFFICIAL NAME OR ANYTHING. "FUCKERS" WORKS OKAY.
SPIT ON IT.
TRUST ME. IT'LL DISSOLVE IN NO TIME.
PTUI

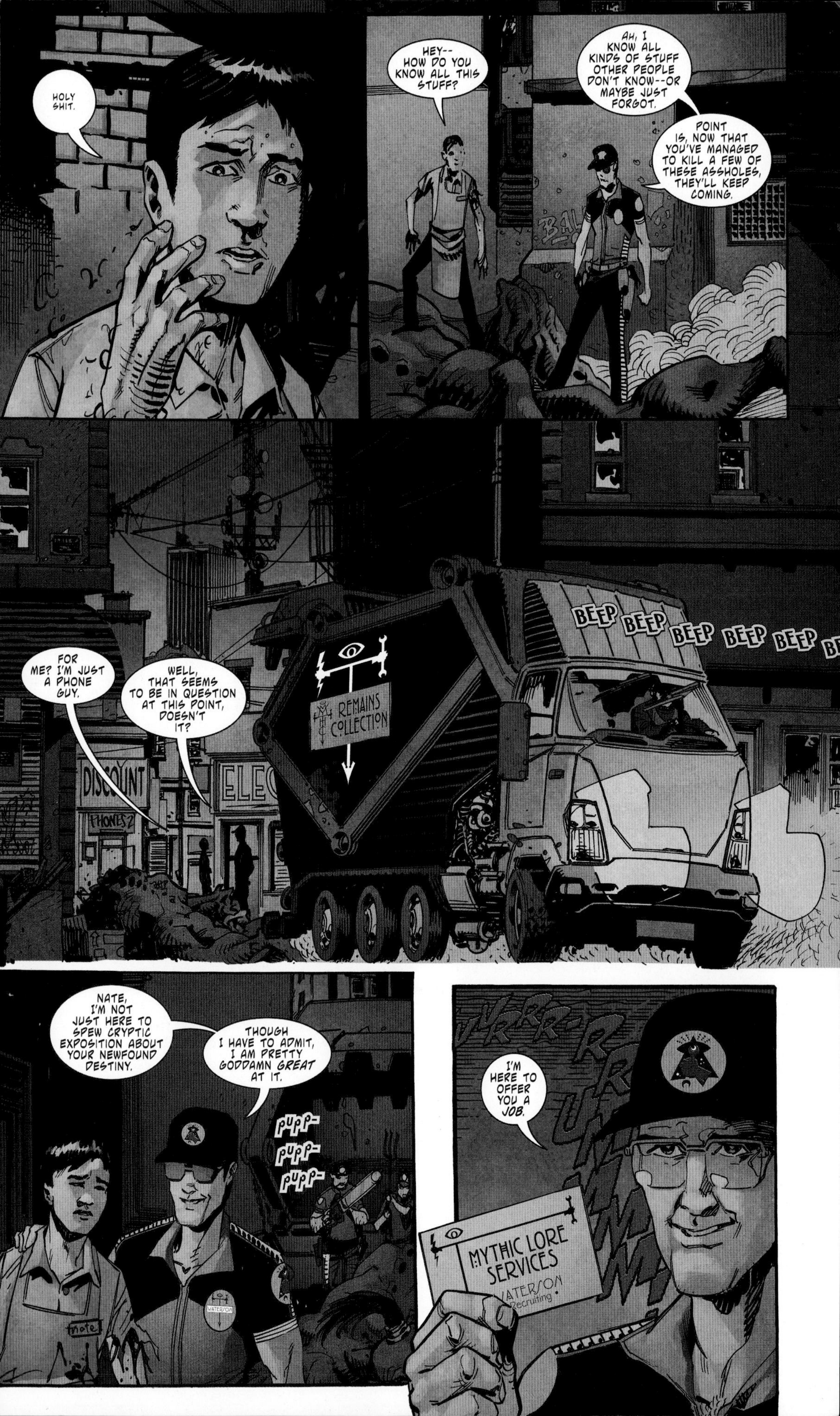
HOLY SHIT.
HEY-- HOW DO YOU KNOW ALL THIS STUFF?
AH, I KNOW ALL KINDS OF STUFF OTHER PEOPLE DON'T KNOW--OR MAYBE JUST FORGOT.
POINT IS, NOW THAT YOU'VE MANAGED TO KILL A FEW OF THESE ASSHOLES, THEY'LL KEEP COMING.
BEEP BEEP BEEP BEEP BEEP
FOR ME? I'M JUST A PHONE GUY.
WELL, THAT SEEMS TO BE IN QUESTION AT THIS POINT, DOESN'T IT?
REMAINS COLLECTION
DISCOUNT
PHONES 2
NATE, I'M NOT JUST HERE TO SPEW CRYPTIC EXPOSITION ABOUT YOUR NEWFOUND DESTINY.
THOUGH I HAVE TO ADMIT, I AM PRETTY GODDAMN GREAT AT IT.
PUPP- PUPP- PUPP-
nate
WATERSON
I'M HERE TO OFFER YOU A JOB.
MYTHIC LORE SERVICES
WATERSON
Recruiting

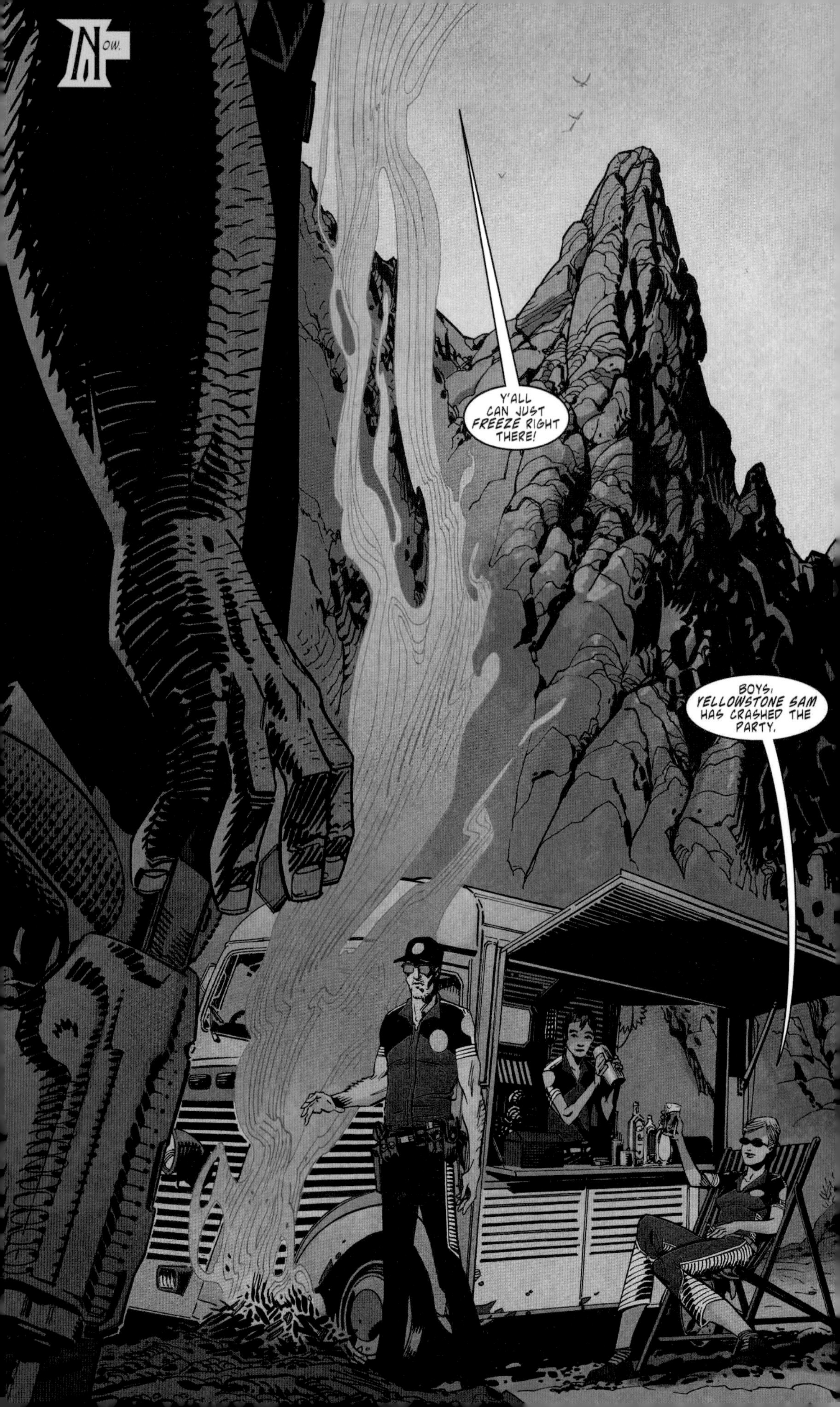
NOW.
Y'ALL CAN JUST FREEZE RIGHT THERE!
BOYS, YELLOWSTONE SAM HAS CRASHED THE PARTY.

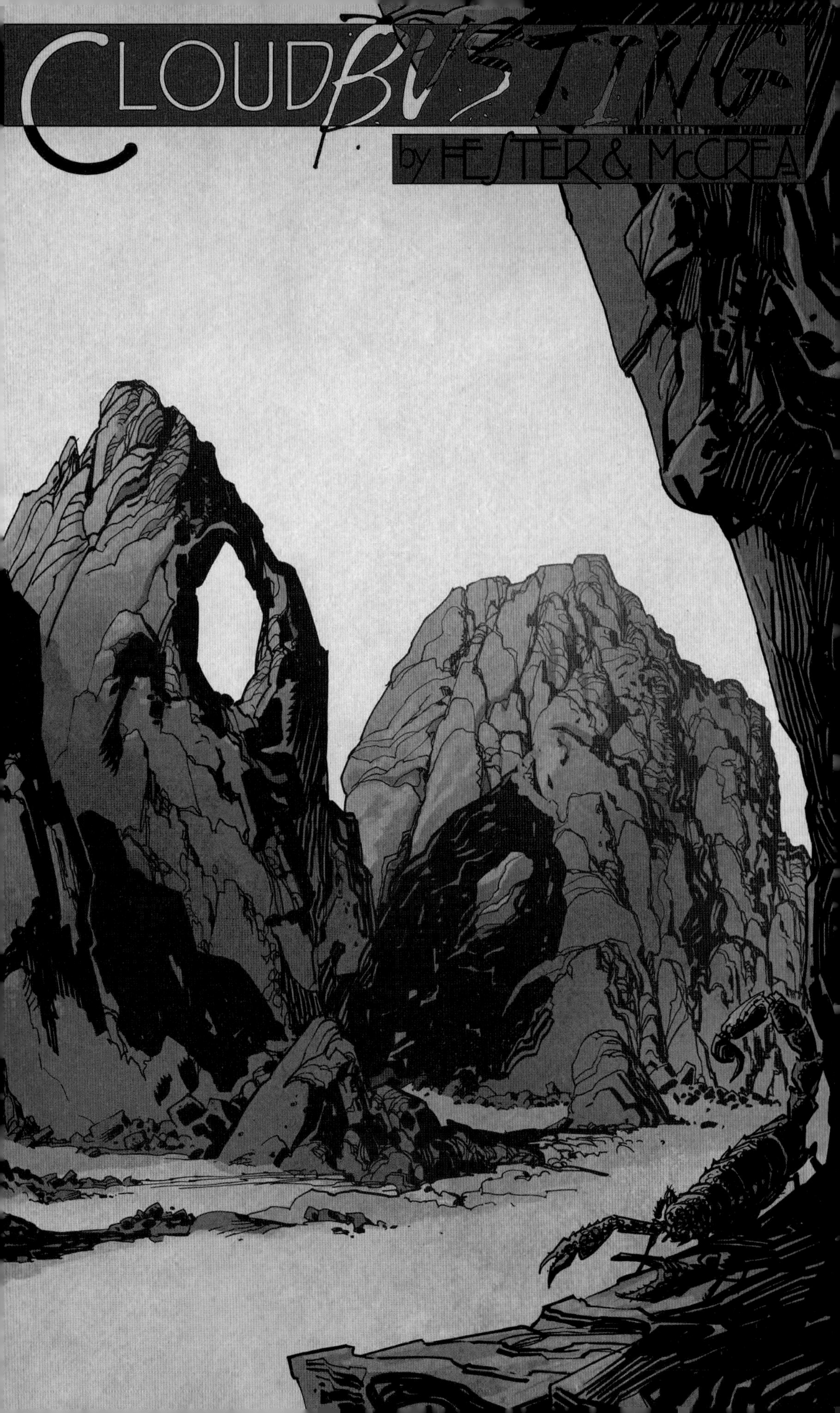
CLOUDBUSTING
by HESTER & McCREA

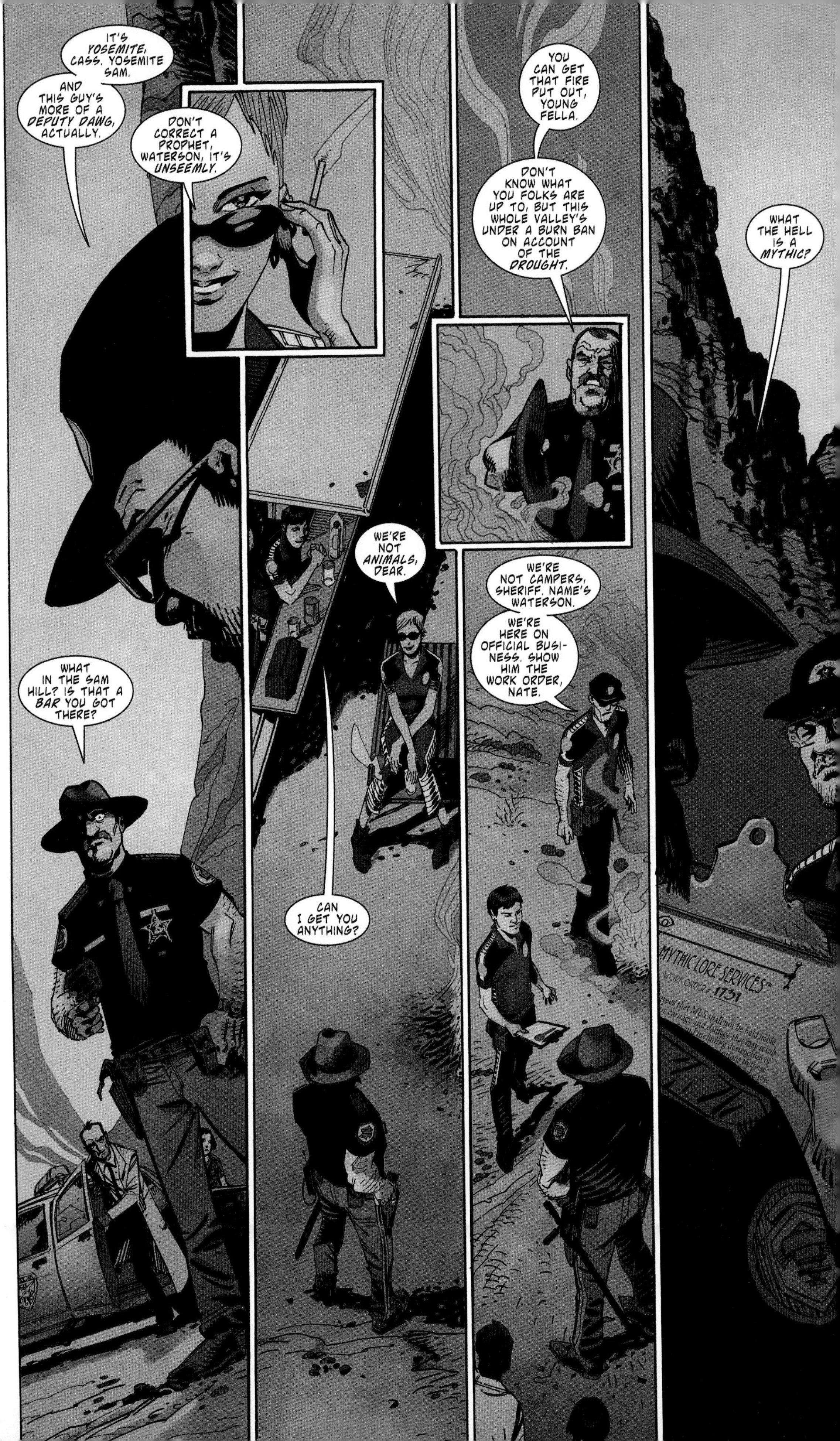
IT'S YOSEMITE, CASS. YOSEMITE SAM.
AND THIS GUY'S MORE OF A DEPUTY DAWG, ACTUALLY.
DON'T CORRECT A PROPHET, WATERSON, IT'S UNSEEMLY.
WHAT IN THE SAM HILL? IS THAT A BAR YOU GOT THERE?
WE'RE NOT ANIMALS, DEAR.
CAN I GET YOU ANYTHING?
YOU CAN GET THAT FIRE PUT OUT, YOUNG FELLA.
DON'T KNOW WHAT YOU FOLKS ARE UP TO, BUT THIS WHOLE VALLEY'S UNDER A BURN BAN ON ACCOUNT OF THE DROUGHT.
WE'RE NOT CAMPERS, SHERIFF. NAME'S WATERSON.
WE'RE HERE ON OFFICIAL BUSINESS. SHOW HIM THE WORK ORDER, NATE.
WHAT THE HELL IS A MYTHIC?
MYTHIC LORE SERVICES™
WORK ORDER # 1731

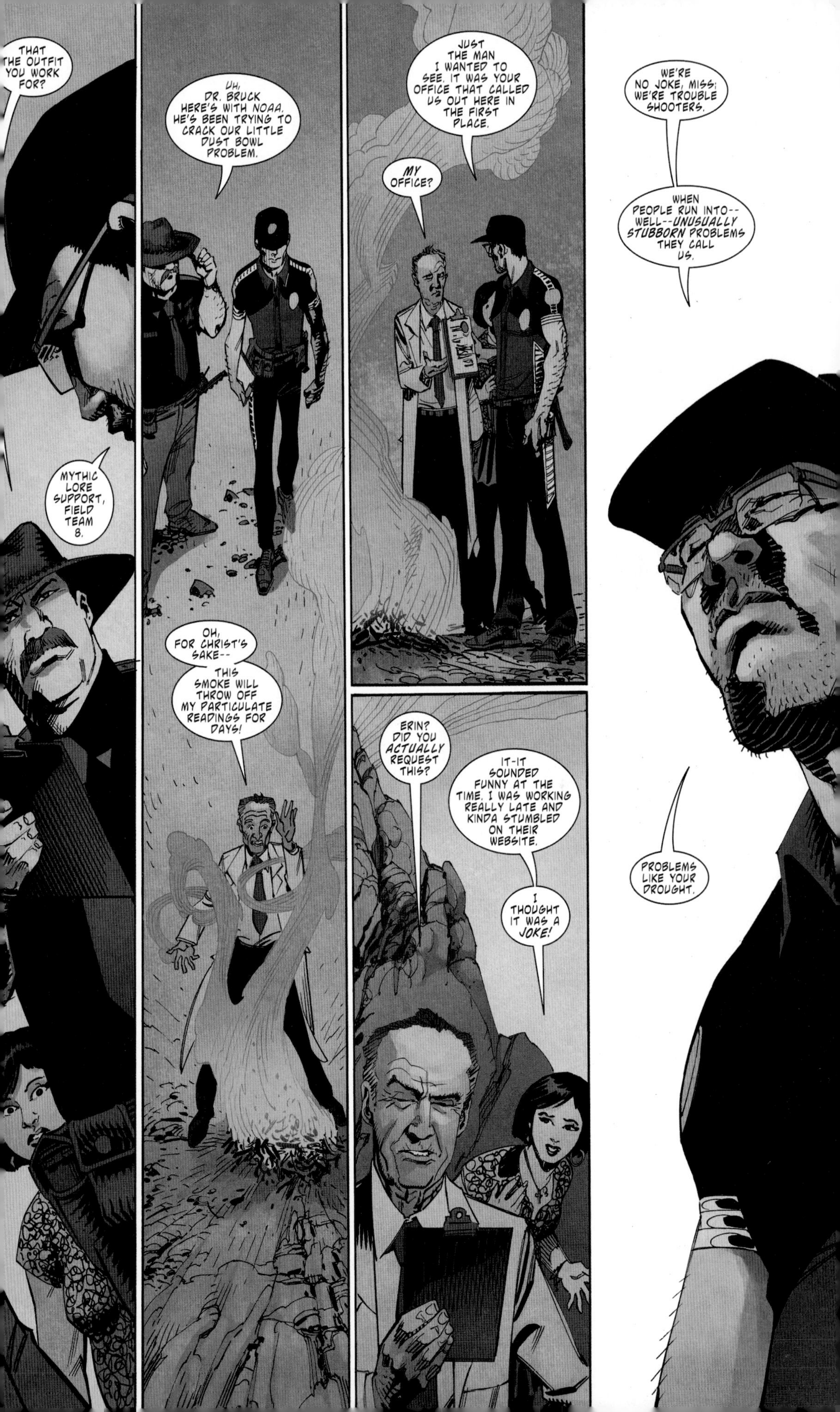
THAT THE OUTFIT YOU WORK FOR?
MYTHIC LORE SUPPORT, FIELD TEAM 8.
UH, DR. BRUCK HERE'S WITH NOAA. HE'S BEEN TRYING TO CRACK OUR LITTLE DUST BOWL PROBLEM.
OH, FOR CHRIST'S SAKE--
THIS SMOKE WILL THROW OFF MY PARTICULATE READINGS FOR DAYS!
JUST THE MAN I WANTED TO SEE. IT WAS YOUR OFFICE THAT CALLED US OUT HERE IN THE FIRST PLACE.
MY OFFICE?
ERIN? DID YOU ACTUALLY REQUEST THIS?
IT-IT SOUNDED FUNNY AT THE TIME. I WAS WORKING REALLY LATE AND KINDA STUMBLED ON THEIR WEBSITE.
I THOUGHT IT WAS A JOKE!
WE'RE NO JOKE, MISS; WE'RE TROUBLE SHOOTERS.
WHEN PEOPLE RUN INTO--WELL--UNUSUALLY STUBBORN PROBLEMS THEY CALL US.
PROBLEMS LIKE YOUR DROUGHT.

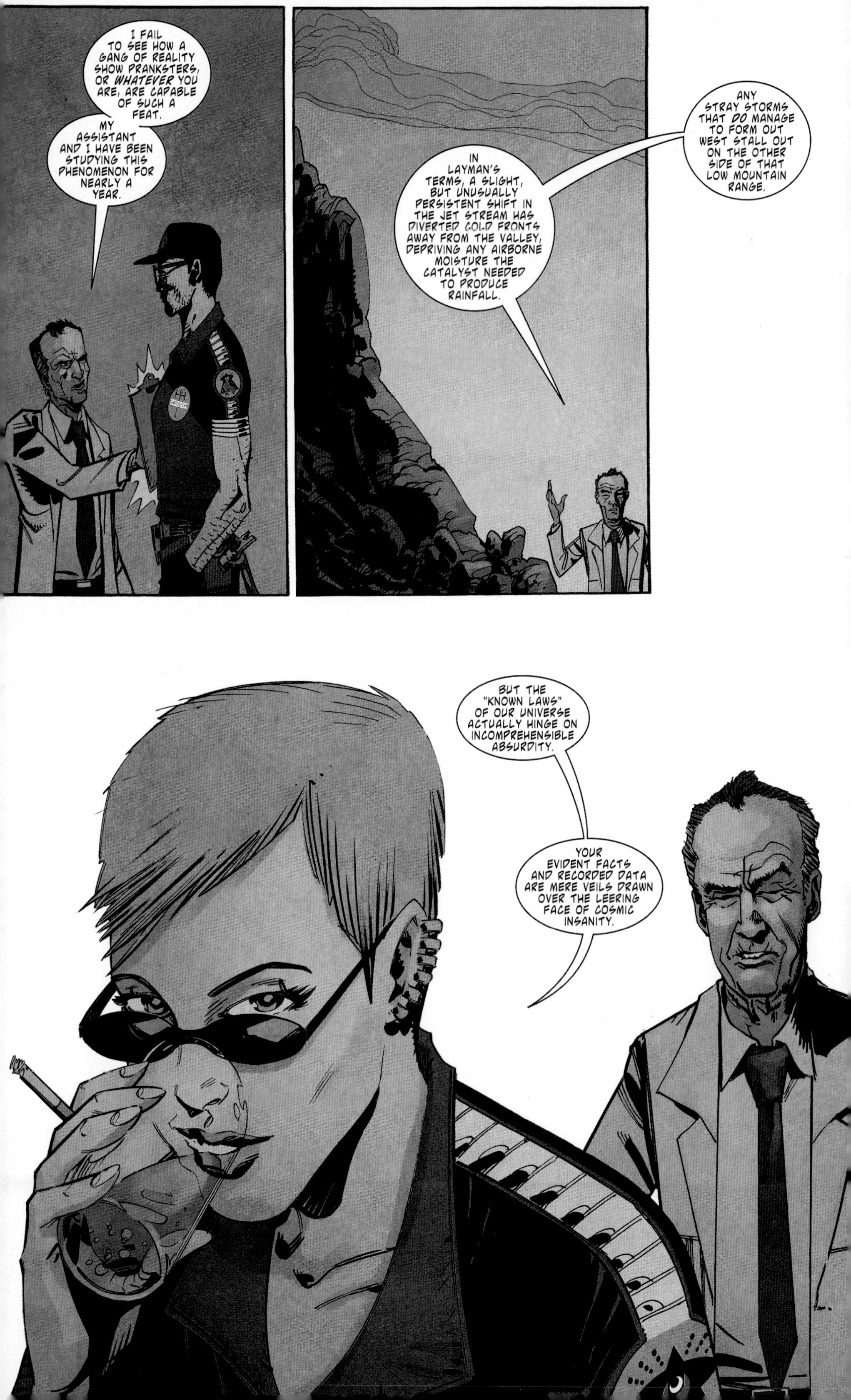
I FAIL TO SEE HOW A GANG OF REALITY SHOW PRANKSTERS, OR *WHATEVER* YOU ARE, ARE CAPABLE OF SUCH A FEAT.
MY ASSISTANT AND I HAVE BEEN STUDYING THIS PHENOMENON FOR NEARLY A YEAR.
IN LAYMAN'S TERMS, A SLIGHT, BUT UNUSUALLY PERSISTENT SHIFT IN THE JET STREAM HAS DIVERTED COLD FRONTS AWAY FROM THE VALLEY, DEPRIVING ANY AIRBORNE MOISTURE THE CATALYST NEEDED TO PRODUCE RAINFALL.
ANY STRAY STORMS THAT *DO* MANAGE TO FORM OUT WEST STALL OUT ON THE OTHER SIDE OF THAT LOW MOUNTAIN RANGE.
BUT THE "KNOWN LAWS" OF OUR UNIVERSE ACTUALLY HINGE ON INCOMPREHENSIBLE ABSURDITY.
YOUR EVIDENT FACTS AND RECORDED DATA ARE MERE VEILS DRAWN OVER THE LEERING FACE OF COSMIC INSANITY.

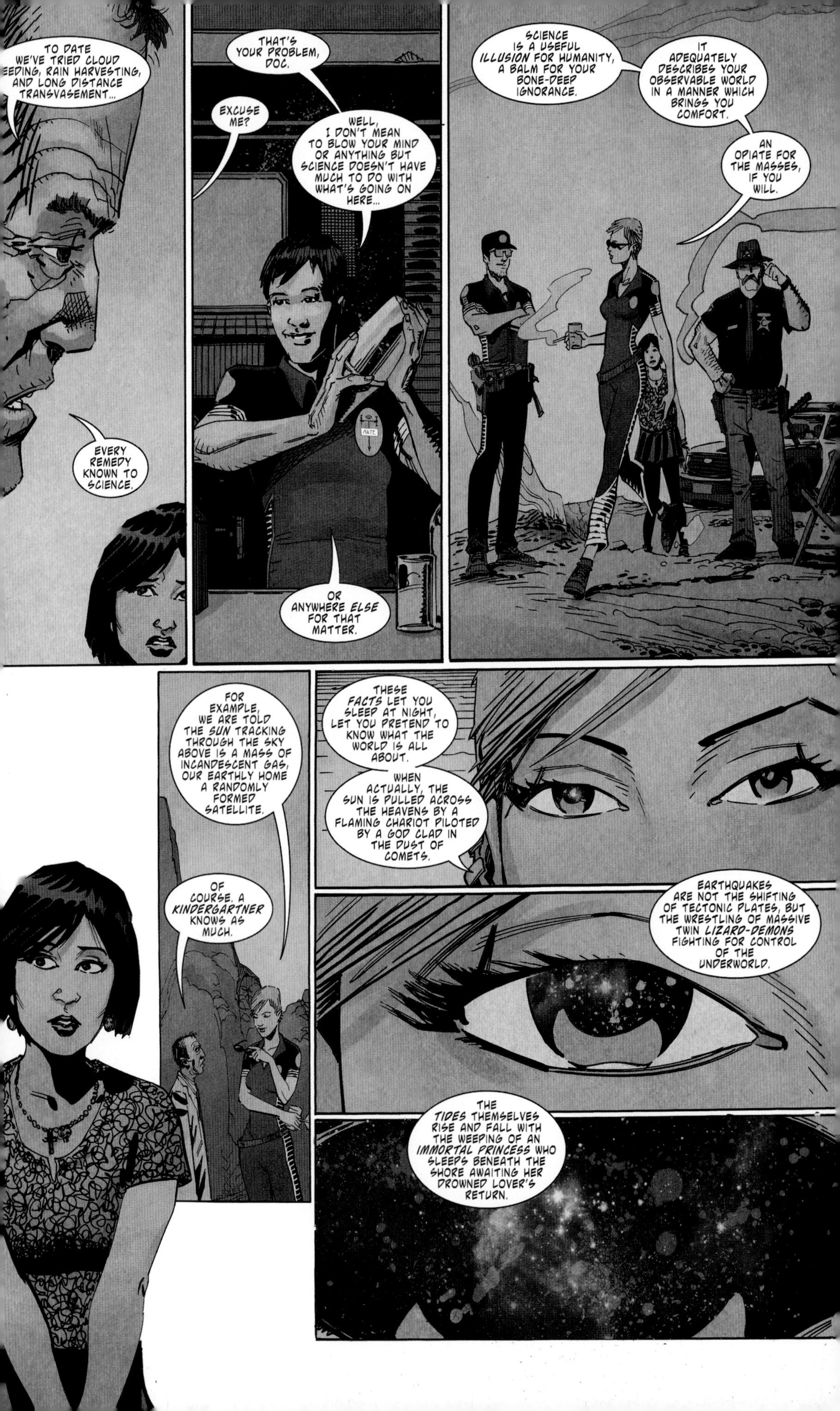

TO DATE WE'VE TRIED CLOUD SEEDING, RAIN HARVESTING, AND LONG DISTANCE TRANSVASEMENT...
EVERY REMEDY KNOWN TO SCIENCE.
THAT'S YOUR PROBLEM, DOC.
EXCUSE ME?
WELL, I DON'T MEAN TO BLOW YOUR MIND OR ANYTHING BUT SCIENCE DOESN'T HAVE MUCH TO DO WITH WHAT'S GOING ON HERE...
OR ANYWHERE ELSE FOR THAT MATTER.
SCIENCE IS A USEFUL ILLUSION FOR HUMANITY, A BALM FOR YOUR BONE-DEEP IGNORANCE.
IT ADEQUATELY DESCRIBES YOUR OBSERVABLE WORLD IN A MANNER WHICH BRINGS YOU COMFORT.
AN OPIATE FOR THE MASSES, IF YOU WILL.
FOR EXAMPLE, WE ARE TOLD THE SUN TRACKING THROUGH THE SKY ABOVE IS A MASS OF INCANDESCENT GAS, OUR EARTHLY HOME A RANDOMLY FORMED SATELLITE.
OF COURSE. A KINDERGARTNER KNOWS AS MUCH.
THESE FACTS LET YOU SLEEP AT NIGHT, LET YOU PRETEND TO KNOW WHAT THE WORLD IS ALL ABOUT.
WHEN ACTUALLY, THE SUN IS PULLED ACROSS THE HEAVENS BY A FLAMING CHARIOT PILOTED BY A GOD CLAD IN THE DUST OF COMETS.
EARTHQUAKES ARE NOT THE SHIFTING OF TECTONIC PLATES, BUT THE WRESTLING OF MASSIVE TWIN LIZARD-DEMONS FIGHTING FOR CONTROL OF THE UNDERWORLD.
THE TIDES THEMSELVES RISE AND FALL WITH THE WEEPING OF AN IMMORTAL PRINCESS WHO SLEEPS BENEATH THE SHORE AWAITING HER DROWNED LOVER'S RETURN.

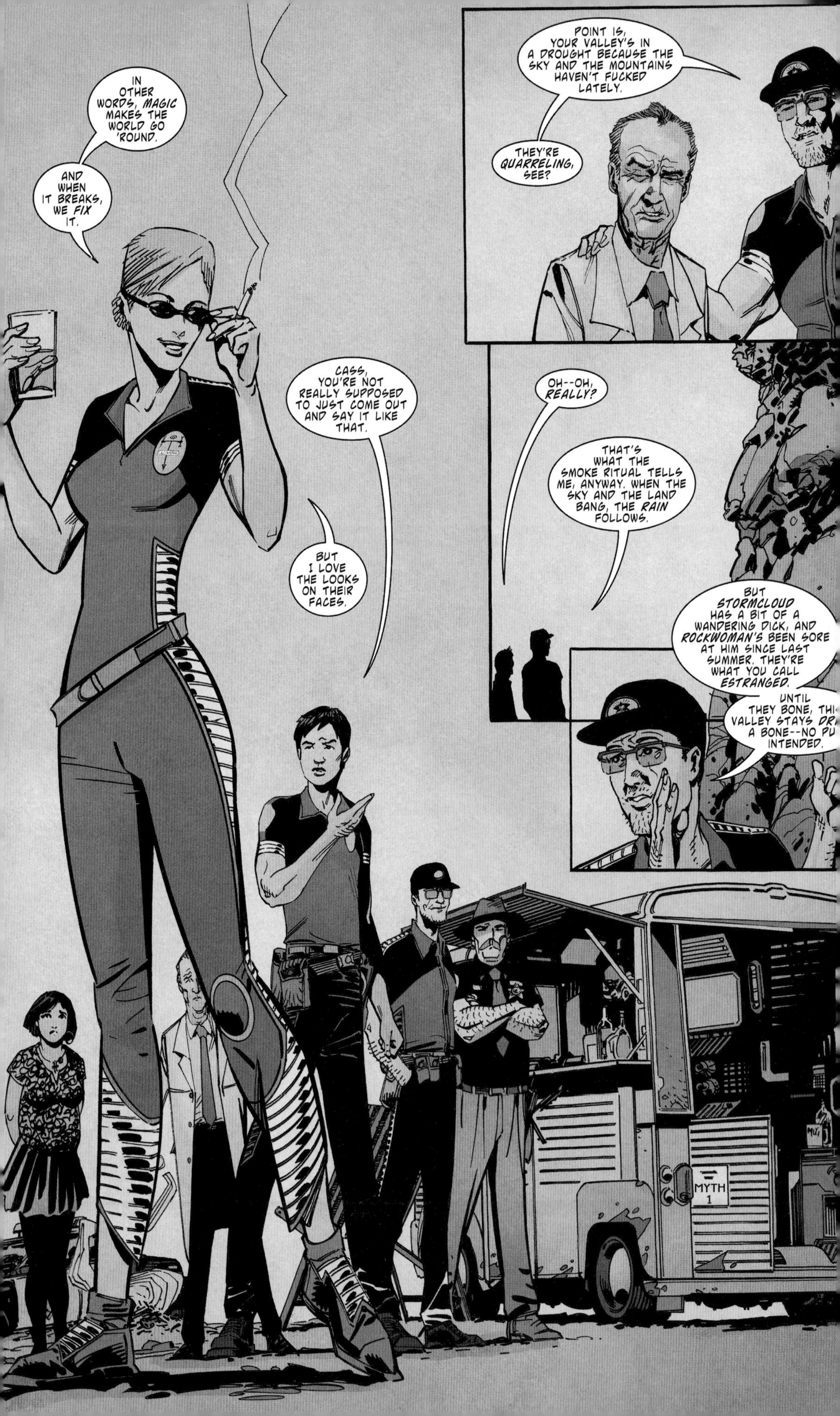
POINT IS, YOUR VALLEY'S IN A DROUGHT BECAUSE THE SKY AND THE MOUNTAINS HAVEN'T FUCKED LATELY.
THEY'RE *QUARRELING*, SEE?
OH--OH, *REALLY?*
THAT'S WHAT THE SMOKE RITUAL TELLS ME, ANYWAY. WHEN THE SKY AND THE LAND BANG, THE *RAIN* FOLLOWS.
BUT *STORMCLOUD* HAS A BIT OF A WANDERING DICK, AND *ROCKWOMAN'S* BEEN SORE AT HIM SINCE LAST SUMMER. THEY'RE WHAT YOU CALL *ESTRANGED*.
UNTIL THEY BONE, THI VALLEY STAYS *DR* A BONE--NO PU INTENDED.
IN OTHER WORDS, *MAGIC* MAKES THE WORLD GO 'ROUND.
AND WHEN IT BREAKS, WE *FIX* IT.
CASS, YOU'RE NOT REALLY SUPPOSED TO JUST COME OUT AND SAY IT LIKE THAT.
BUT I LOVE THE LOOKS ON THEIR FACES.
MYTH 1

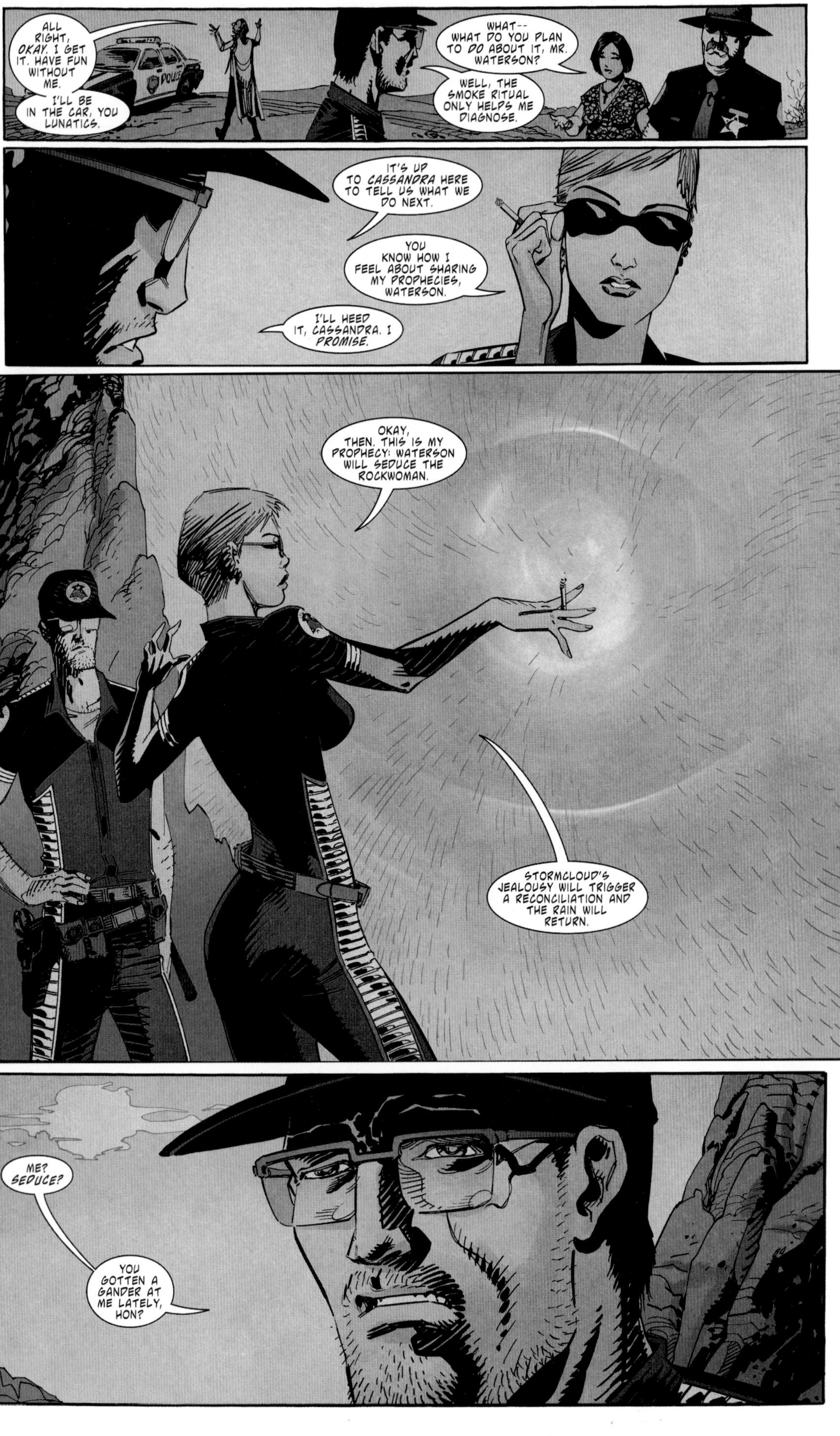
ALL RIGHT, OKAY. I GET IT. HAVE FUN WITHOUT ME.
I'LL BE IN THE CAR, YOU LUNATICS.
WHAT-- WHAT DO YOU PLAN TO DO ABOUT IT, MR. WATERSON?
WELL, THE SMOKE RITUAL ONLY HELPS ME DIAGNOSE.
IT'S UP TO CASSANDRA HERE TO TELL US WHAT WE DO NEXT.
YOU KNOW HOW I FEEL ABOUT SHARING MY PROPHECIES, WATERSON.
I'LL HEED IT, CASSANDRA. I PROMISE.
OKAY, THEN. THIS IS MY PROPHECY: WATERSON WILL SEDUCE THE ROCKWOMAN.
STORMCLOUD'S JEALOUSY WILL TRIGGER A RECONCILIATION AND THE RAIN WILL RETURN.
POLICE
ME? SEDUCE?
YOU GOTTEN A GANDER AT ME LATELY, HON?

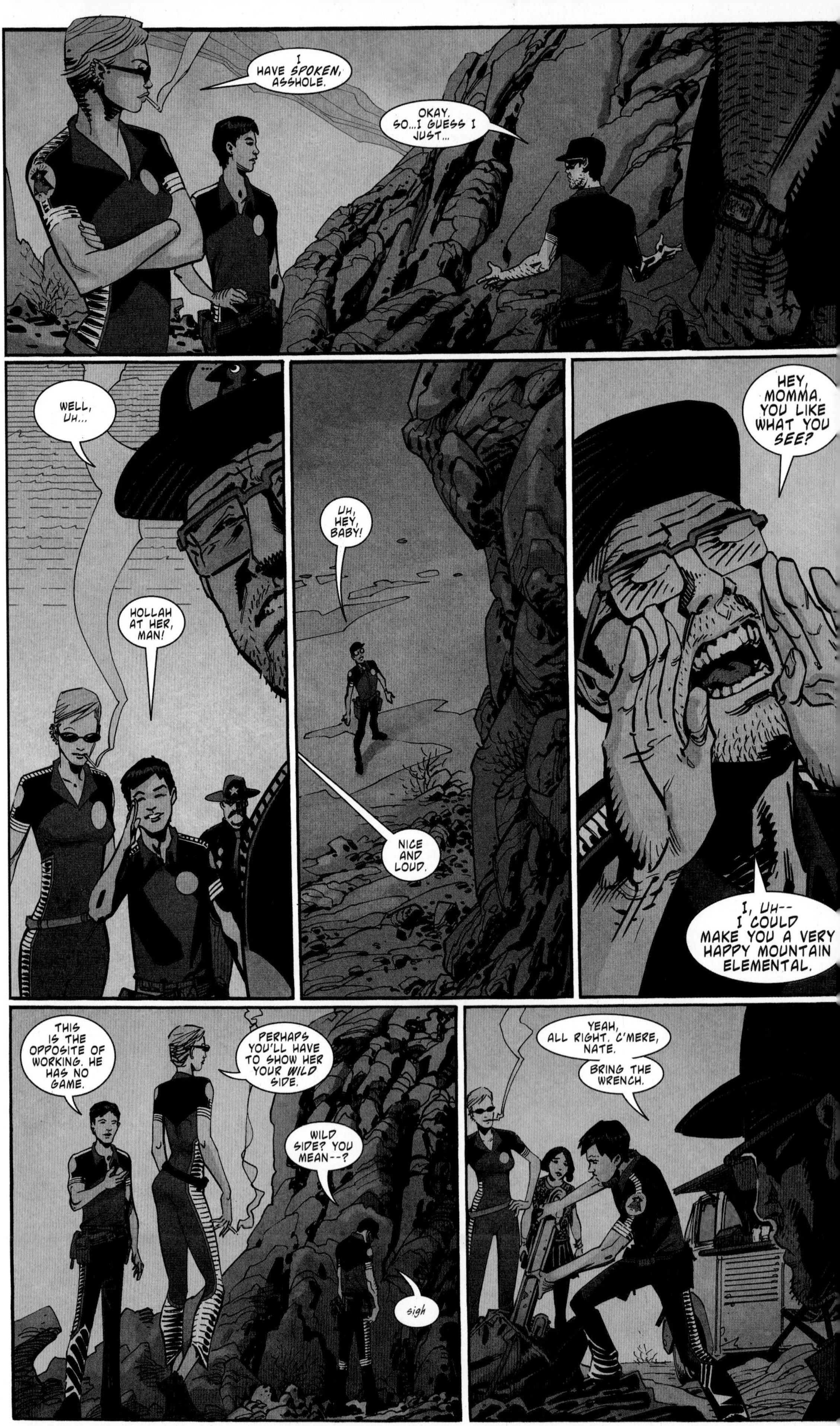
I HAVE SPOKEN, ASSHOLE.
OKAY. SO...I GUESS I JUST...
WELL, UH...
HOLLAH AT HER, MAN!
UH, HEY, BABY!
NICE AND LOUD.
HEY, MOMMA. YOU LIKE WHAT YOU SEE?
I, UH-- I COULD MAKE YOU A VERY HAPPY MOUNTAIN ELEMENTAL.
THIS IS THE OPPOSITE OF WORKING. HE HAS NO GAME.
PERHAPS YOU'LL HAVE TO SHOW HER YOUR WILD SIDE.
WILD SIDE? YOU MEAN--?
sigh
YEAH, ALL RIGHT. C'MERE, NATE.
BRING THE WRENCH.

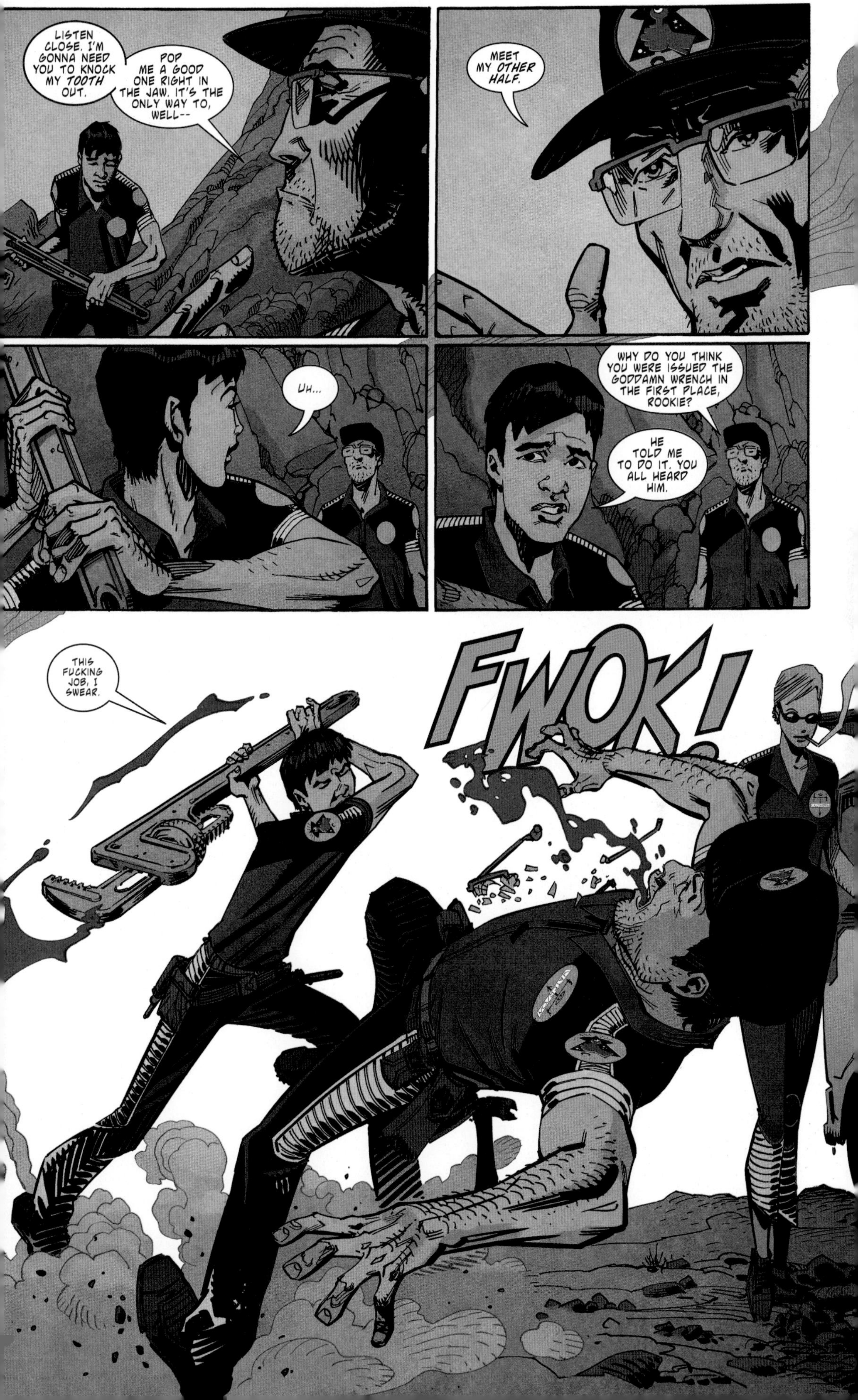
LISTEN CLOSE. I'M GONNA NEED YOU TO KNOCK MY *TOOTH* OUT.
POP ME A GOOD ONE RIGHT IN THE JAW. IT'S THE ONLY WAY TO, WELL--
MEET MY *OTHER HALF.*
UH...
WHY DO YOU THINK YOU WERE ISSUED THE GODDAMN WRENCH IN THE FIRST PLACE, ROOKIE?
HE TOLD ME TO DO IT. YOU ALL HEARD HIM.
THIS FUCKING JOB, I SWEAR.
FWOK!

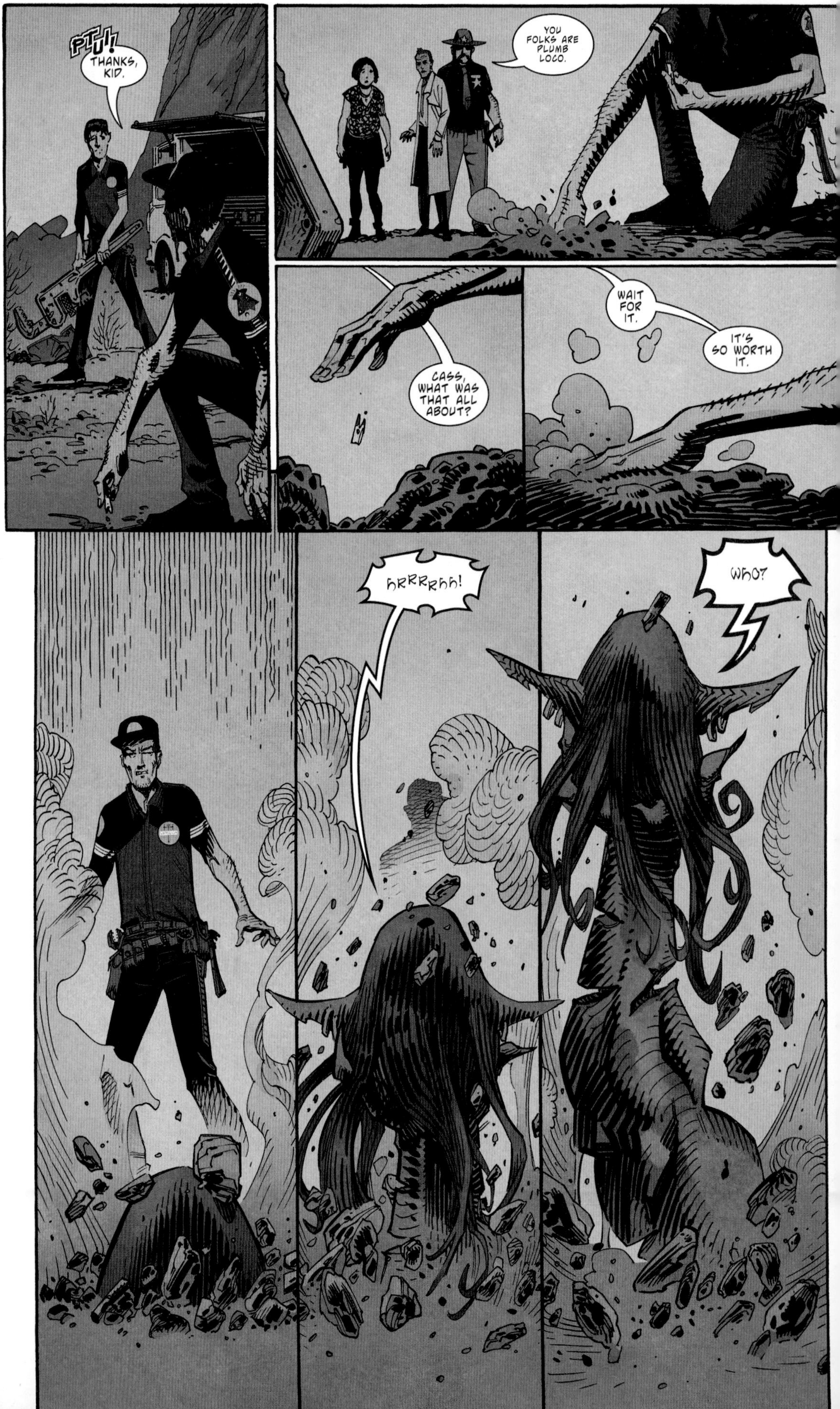
PTUI!
THANKS, KID.
YOU FOLKS ARE PLUMB LOCO.
CASS, WHAT WAS THAT ALL ABOUT?
WAIT FOR IT.
IT'S SO WORTH IT.
HRRRRHH!
WHO?

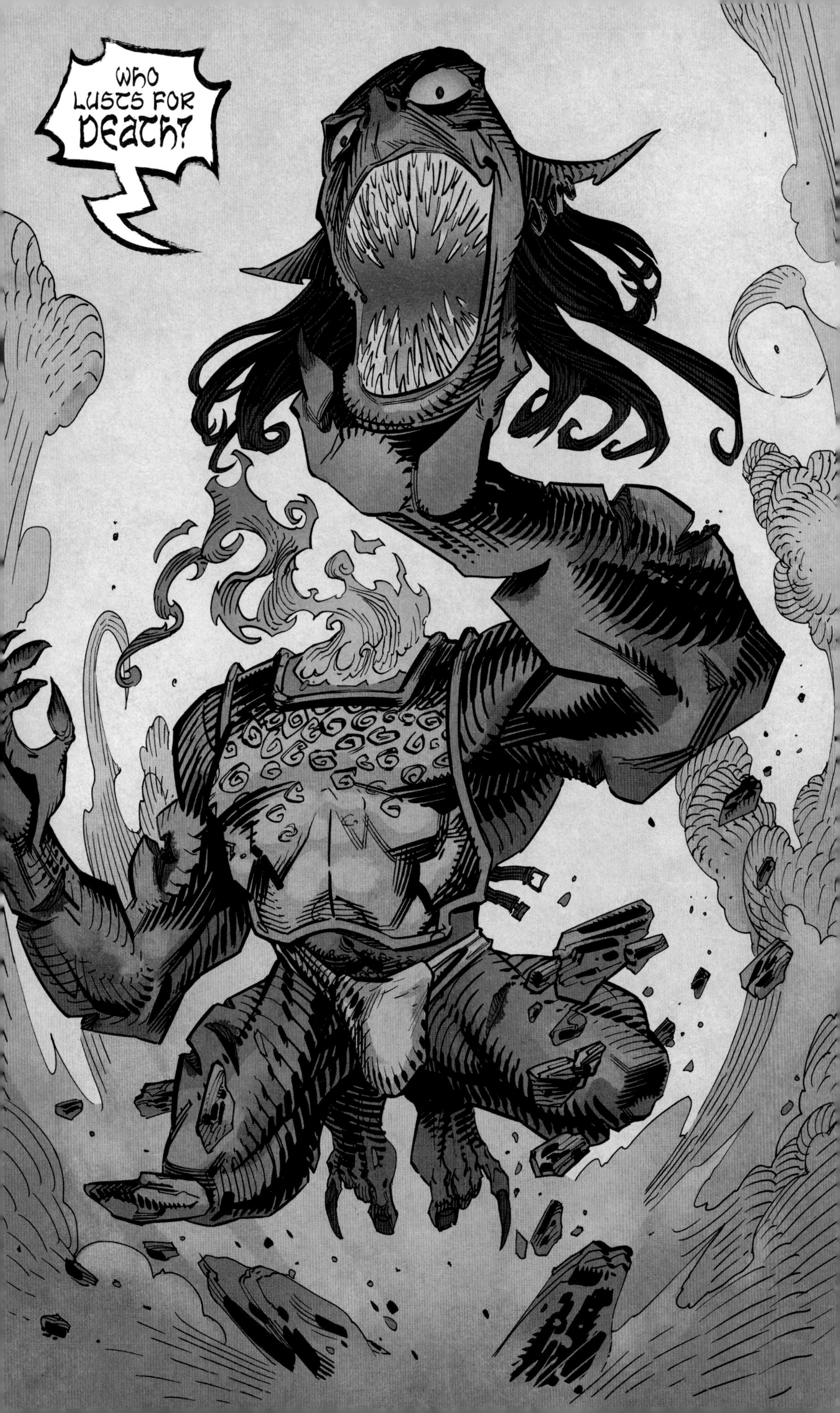
WHO LUSTS FOR DEATH?

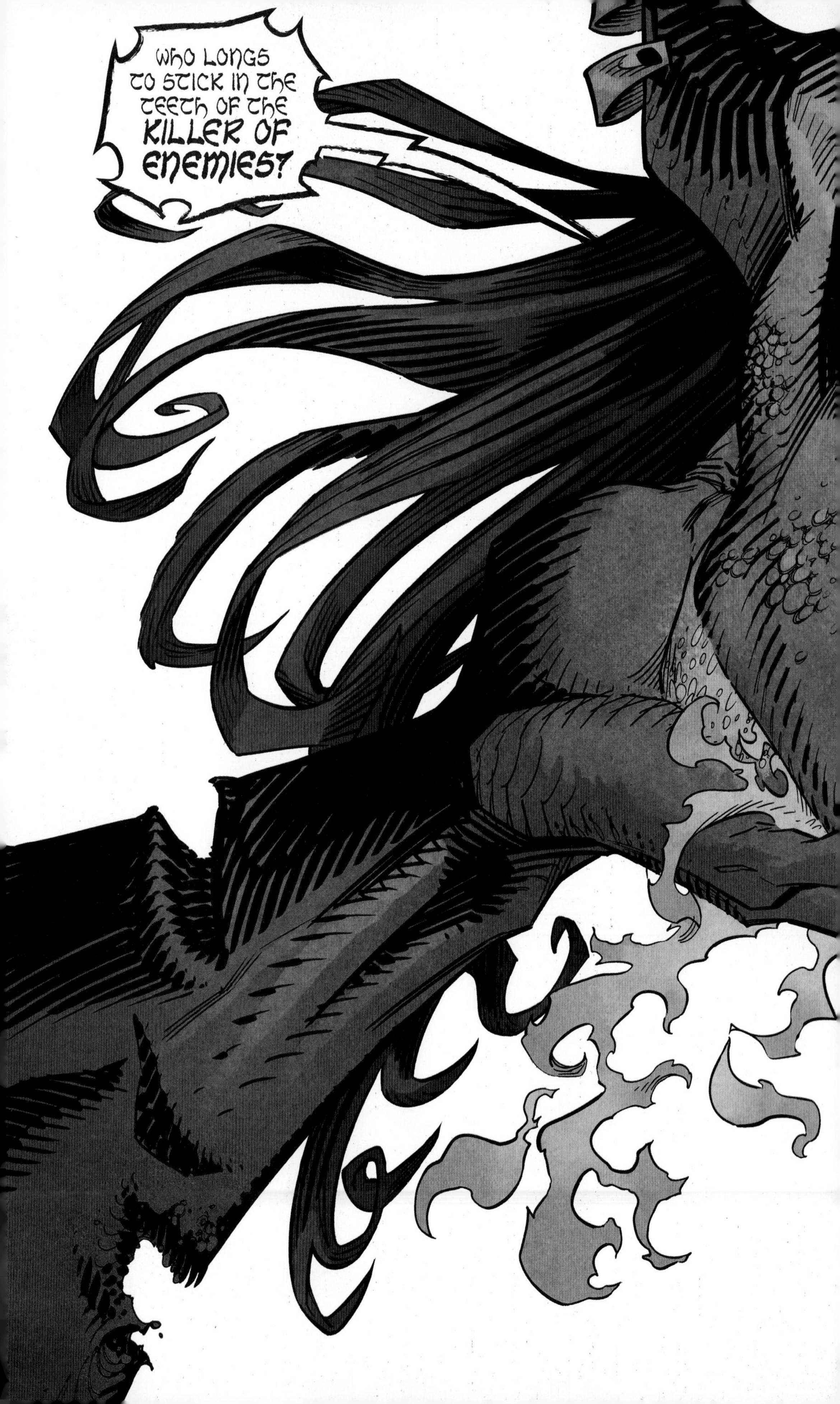
WHO LONGS TO STICK IN THE TEETH OF THE KILLER OF ENEMIES?

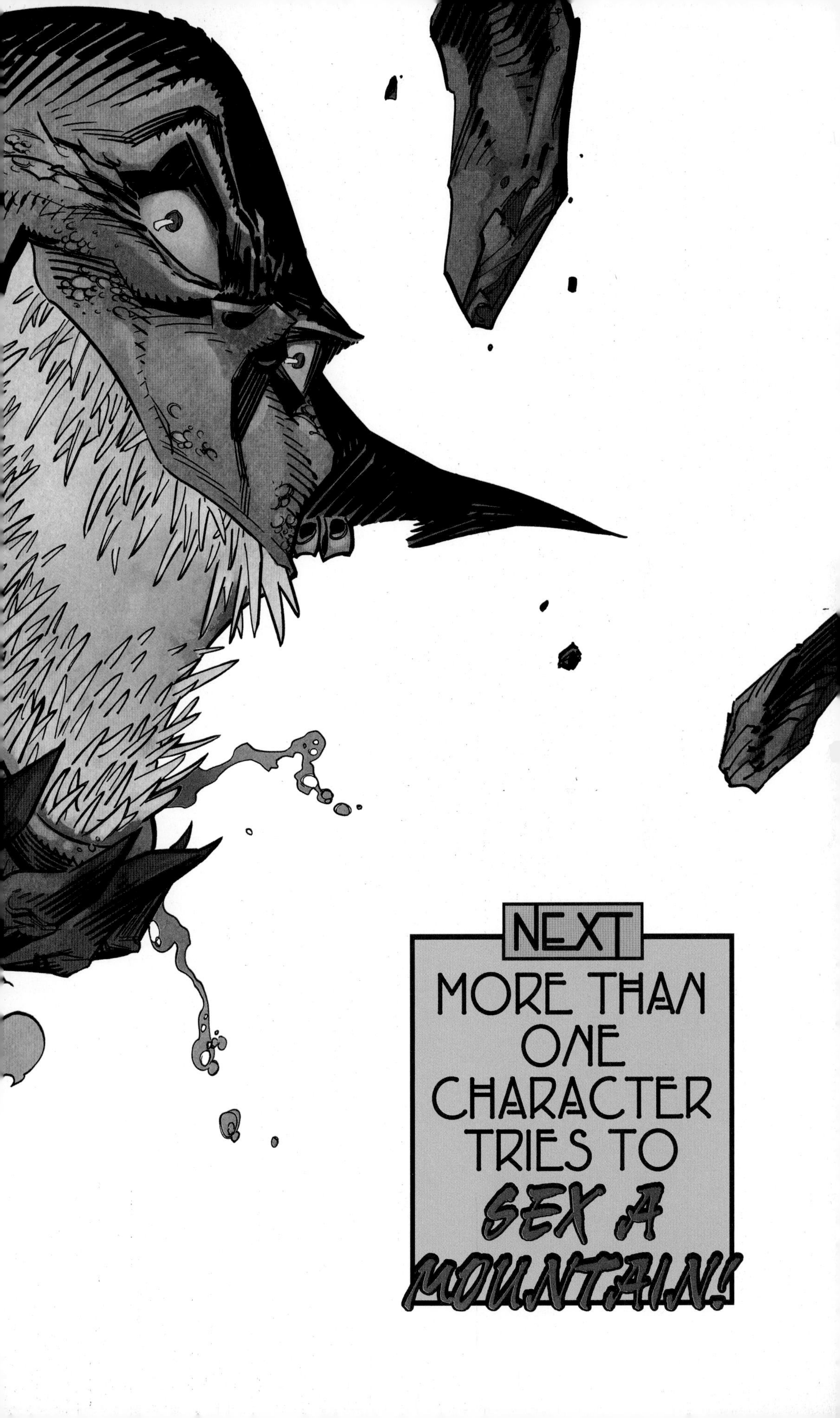
NEXT
MORE THAN ONE CHARACTER TRIES TO SEX A MOUNTAIN!

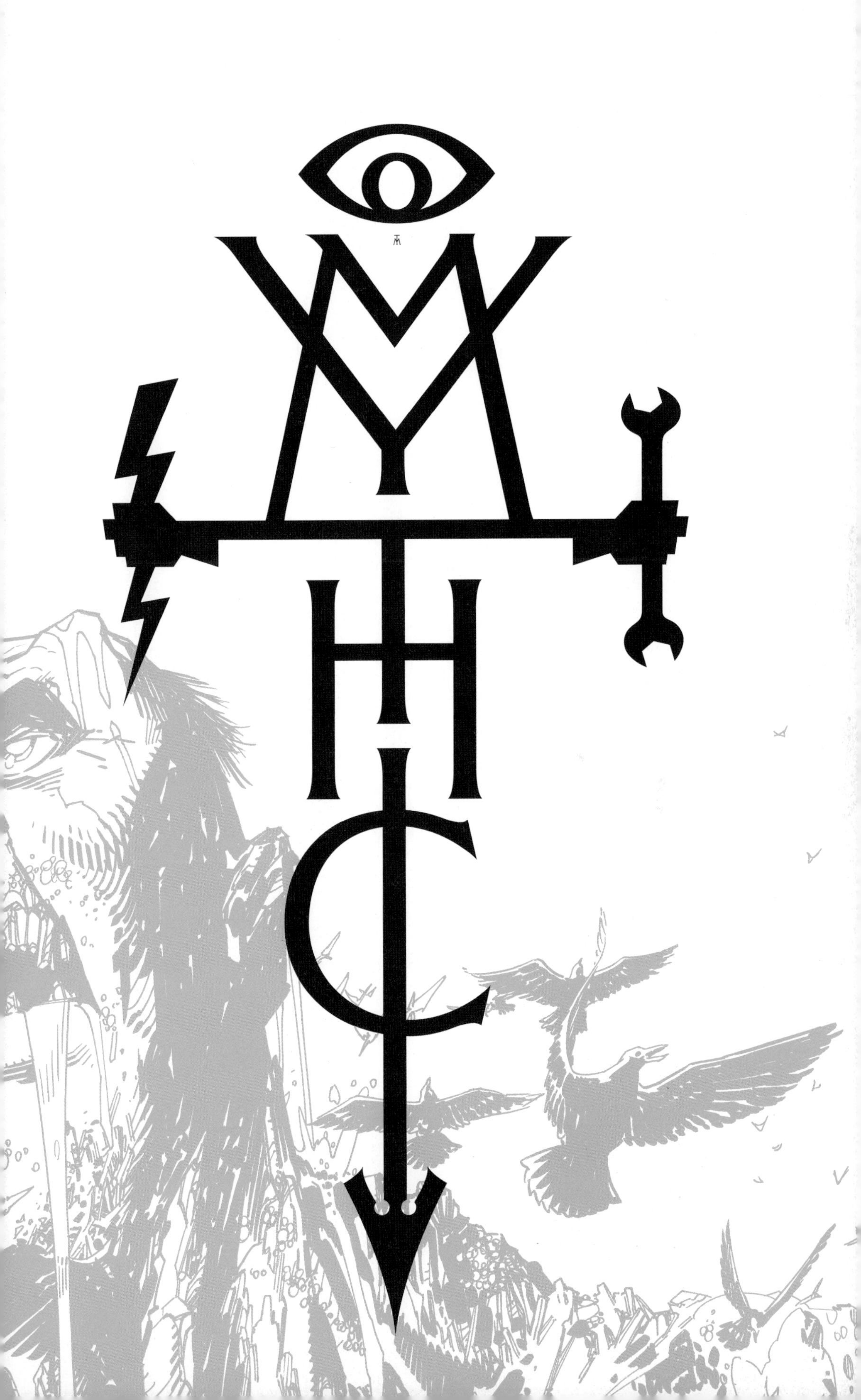
MYTHIC

CHAPTER 2
GIANTS IN THE EARTH

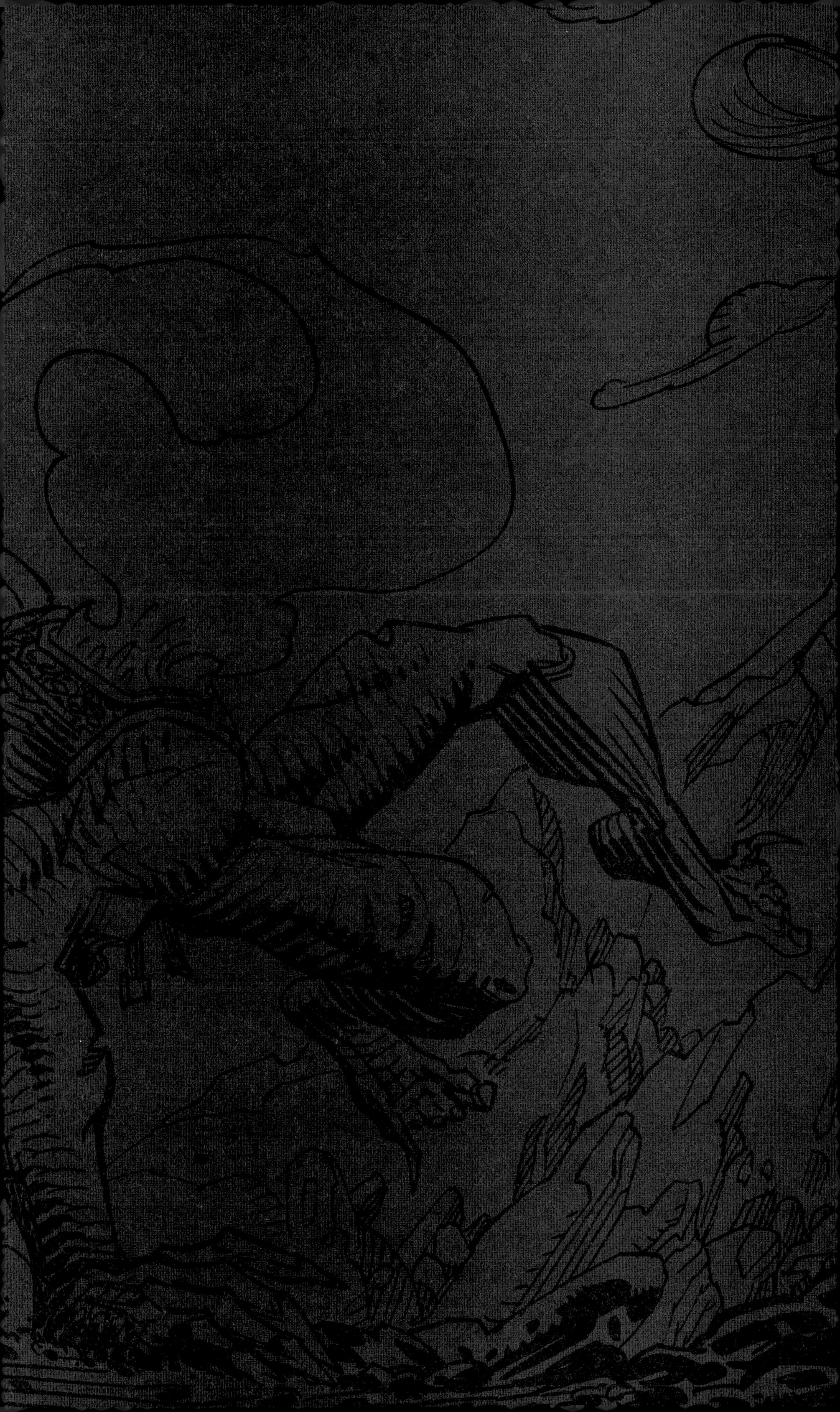

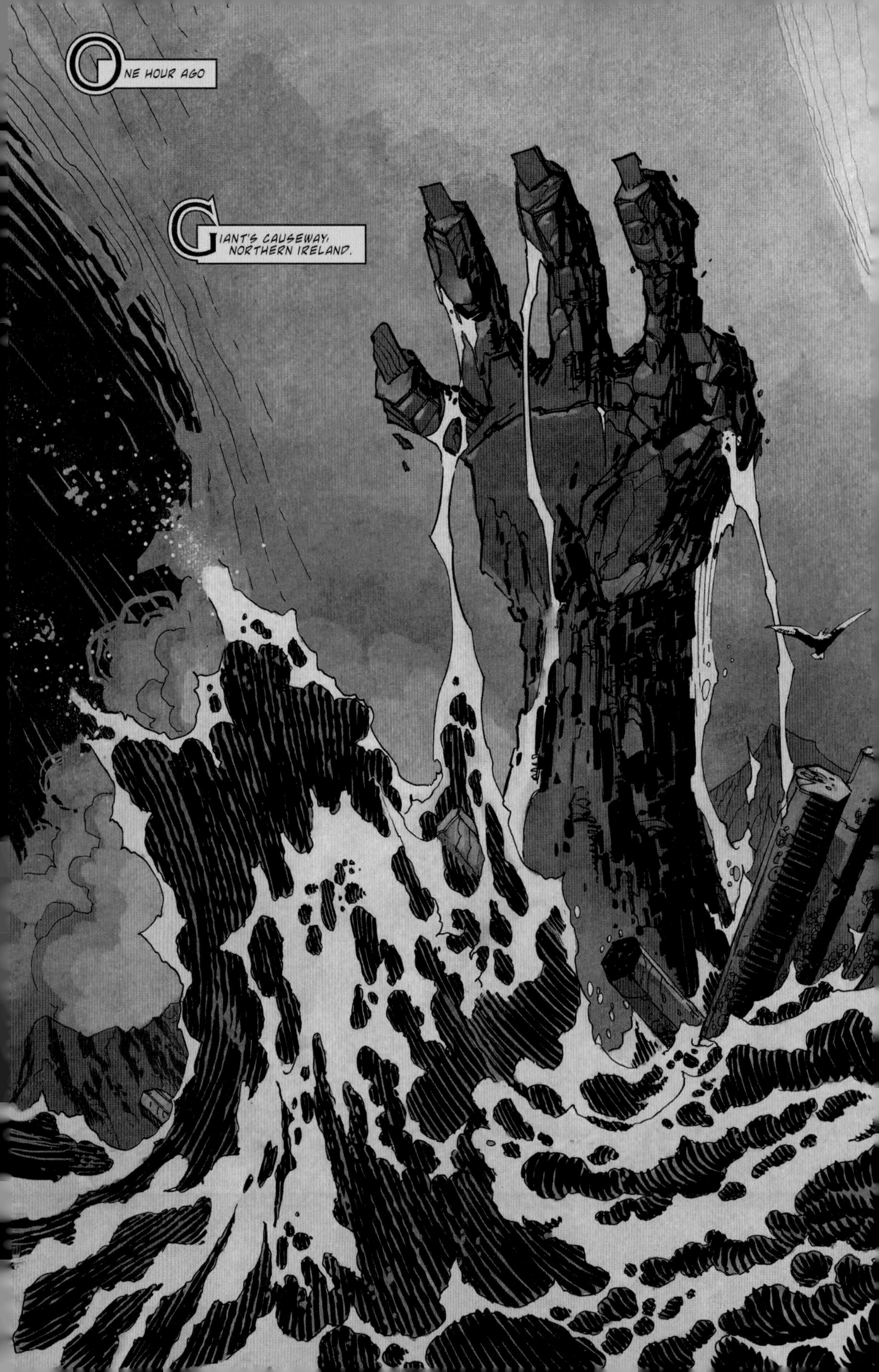
ONE HOUR AGO
GIANT'S CAUSEWAY, NORTHERN IRELAND.

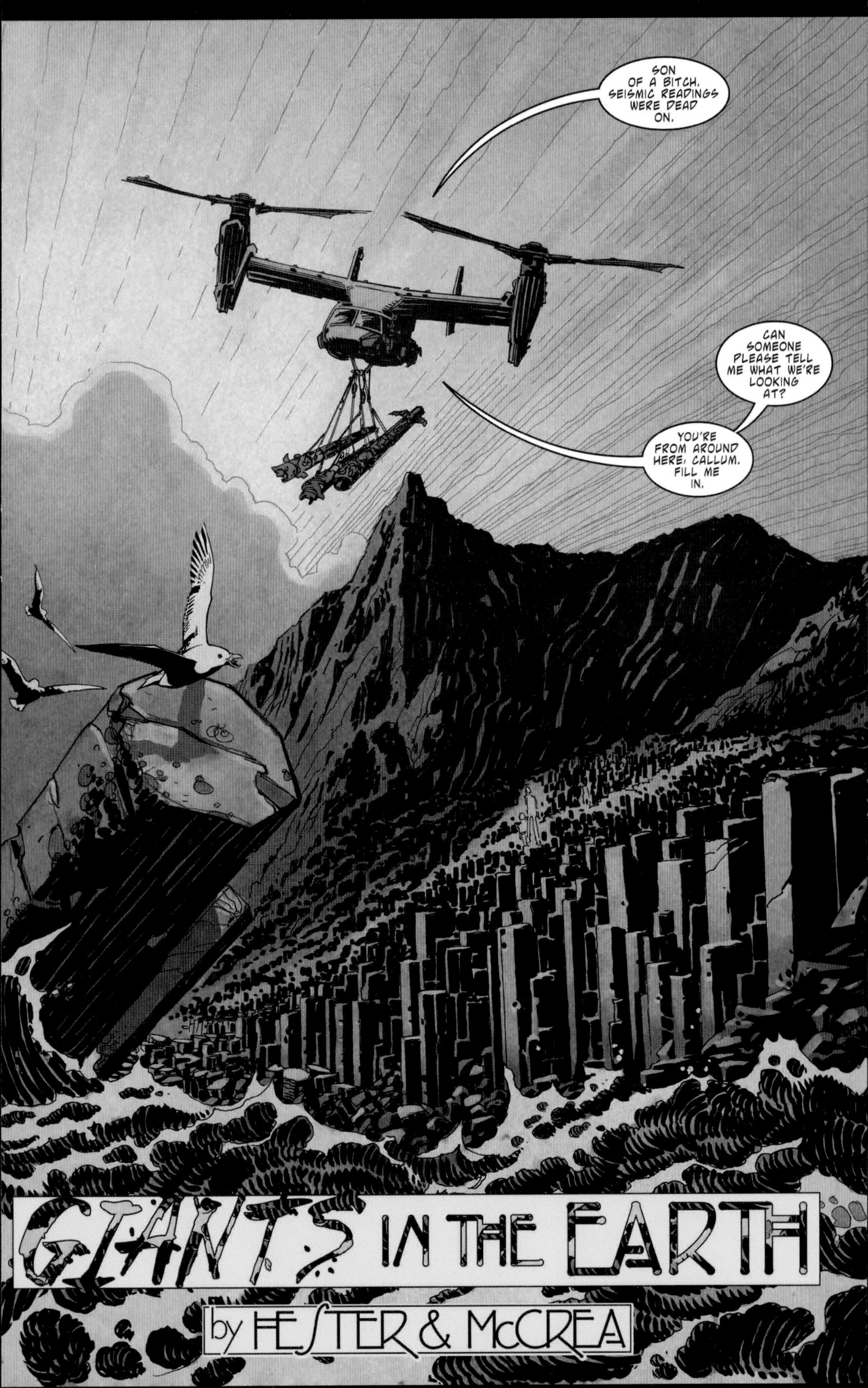
SON OF A BITCH. SEISMIC READINGS WERE DEAD ON.
CAN SOMEONE PLEASE TELL ME WHAT WE'RE LOOKING AT?
YOU'RE FROM AROUND HERE, CALLUM. FILL ME IN.
GIANTS IN THE EARTH
by FESTER & McCREA

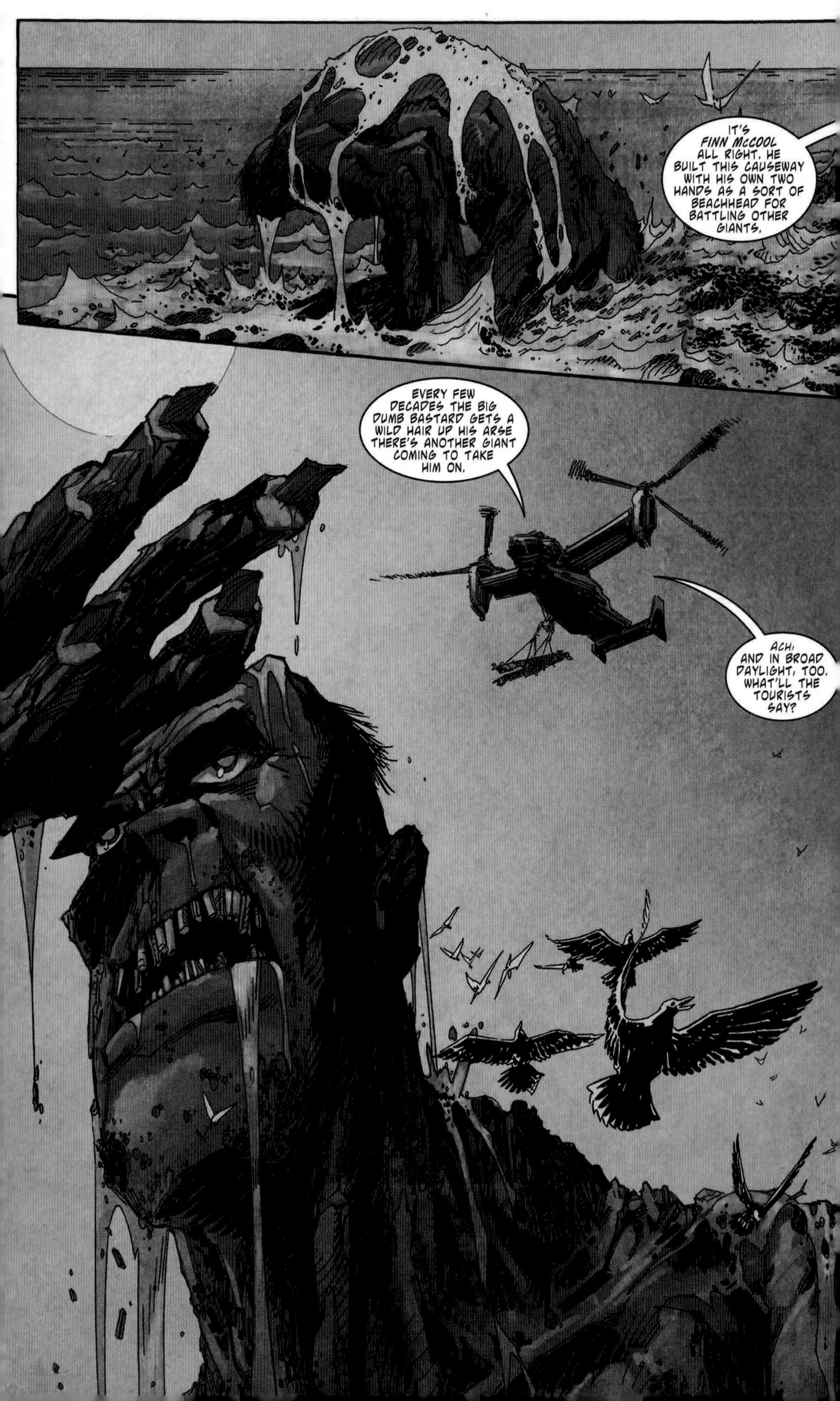
IT'S FINN McCOOL ALL RIGHT. HE BUILT THIS CAUSEWAY WITH HIS OWN TWO HANDS AS A SORT OF BEACHHEAD FOR BATTLING OTHER GIANTS.
EVERY FEW DECADES THE BIG DUMB BASTARD GETS A WILD HAIR UP HIS ARSE THERE'S ANOTHER GIANT COMING TO TAKE HIM ON.
ACH, AND IN BROAD DAYLIGHT, TOO. WHAT'LL THE TOURISTS SAY?

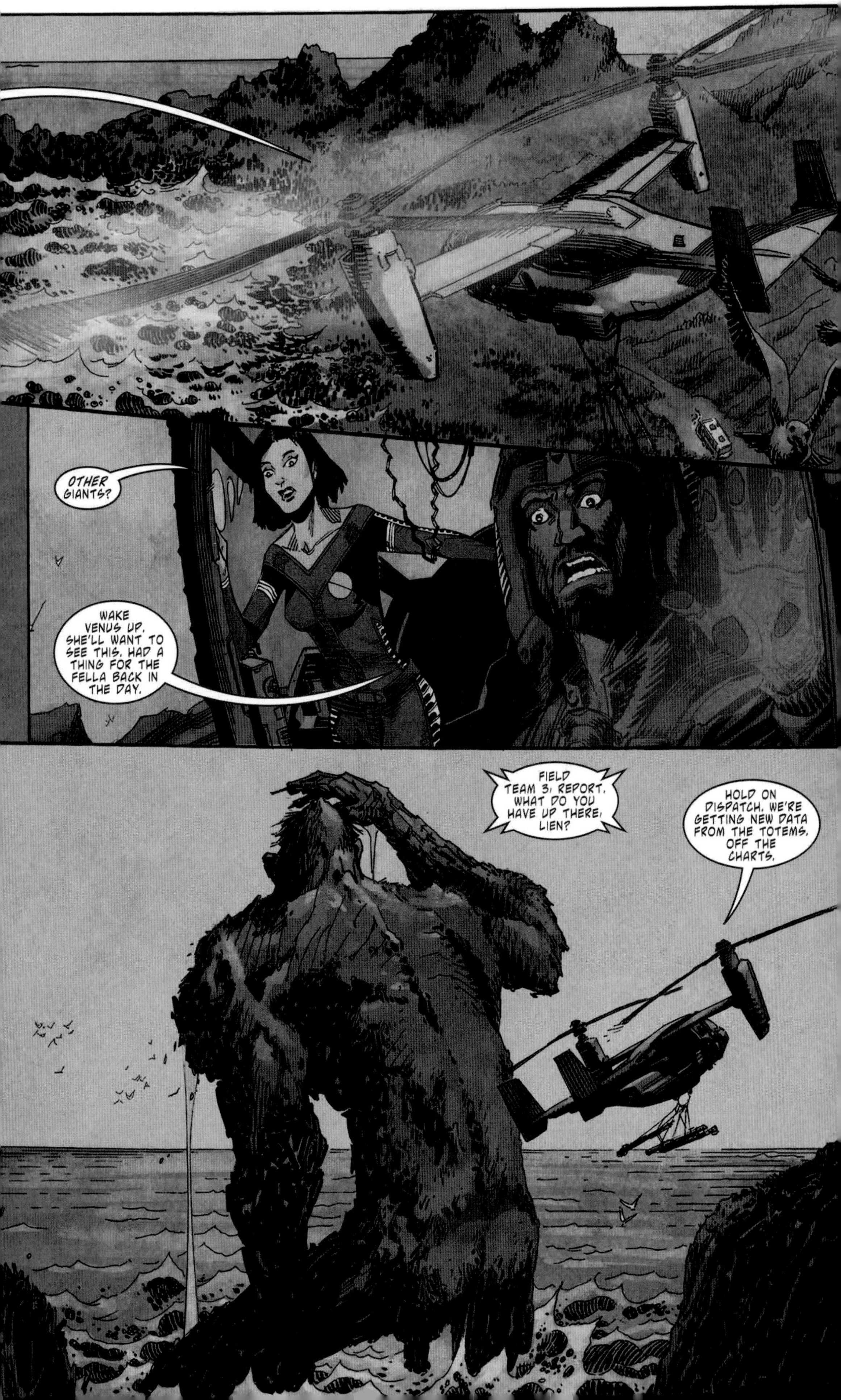
OTHER GIANTS?
WAKE VENUS UP. SHE'LL WANT TO SEE THIS. HAD A THING FOR THE FELLA BACK IN THE DAY.
FIELD TEAM 3, REPORT. WHAT DO YOU HAVE UP THERE, LIEN?
HOLD ON DISPATCH. WE'RE GETTING NEW DATA FROM THE TOTEMS. OFF THE CHARTS.

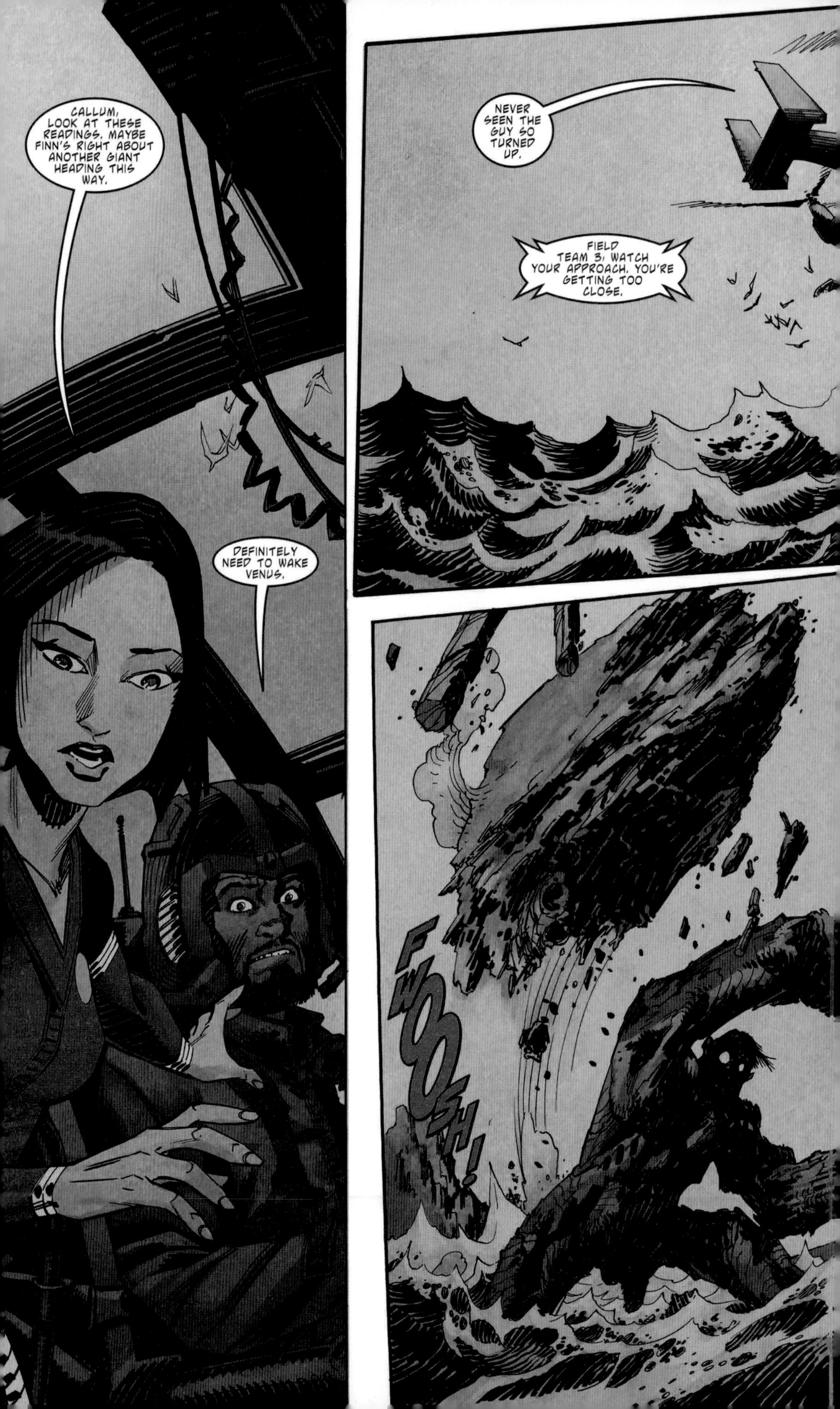

CALLUM, LOOK AT THESE READINGS. MAYBE FINN'S RIGHT ABOUT ANOTHER GIANT HEADING THIS WAY.
DEFINITELY NEED TO WAKE VENUS.
NEVER SEEN THE GUY SO TURNED UP.
FIELD TEAM 3, WATCH YOUR APPROACH. YOU'RE GETTING TOO CLOSE.
FWOOSH!

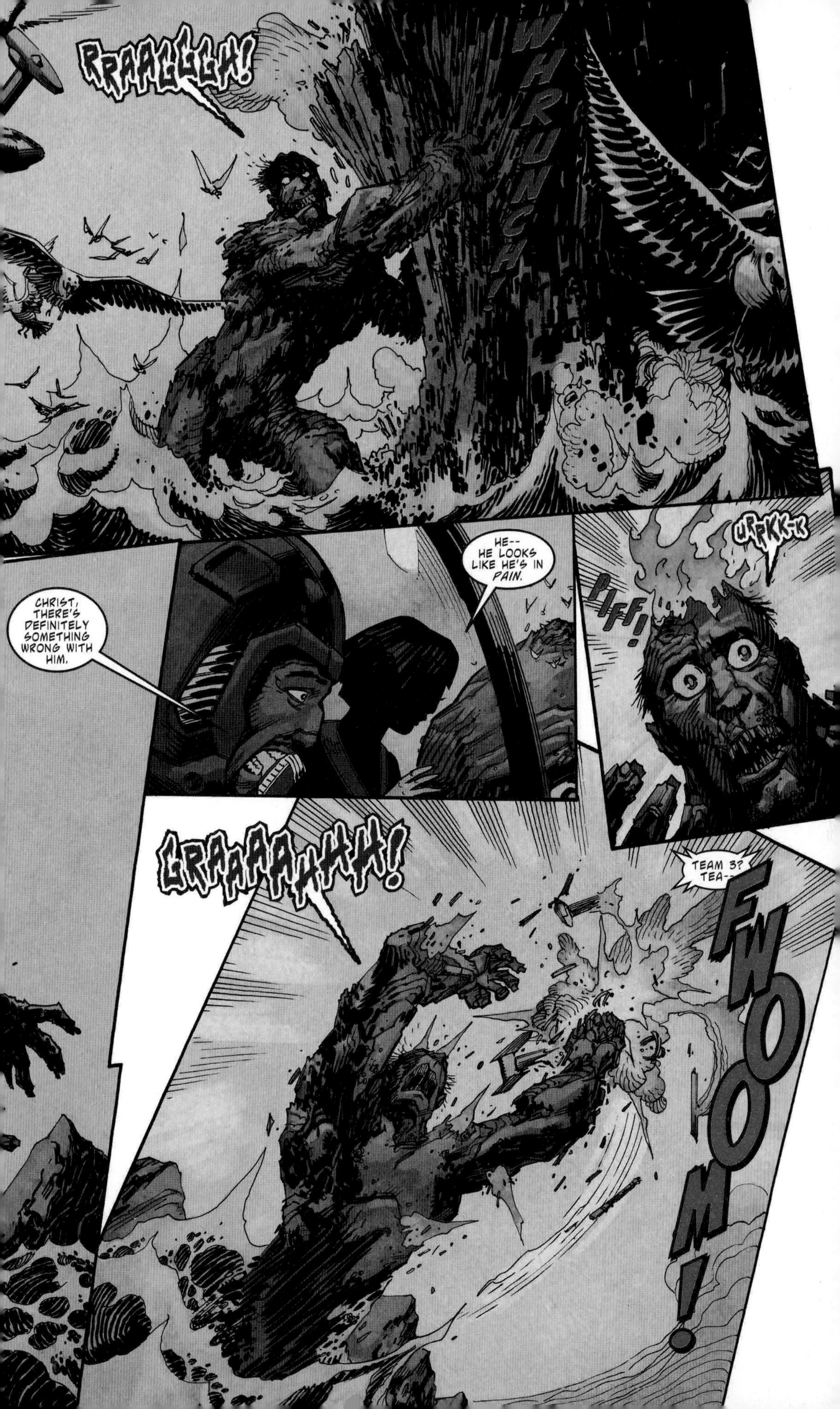
RRAAGGGH!
WHRUNCH!
CHRIST, THERE'S DEFINITELY SOMETHING WRONG WITH HIM.
HE-- HE LOOKS LIKE HE'S IN PAIN.
URPKK-K
PIFF!
GRAAAAAHHH!
TEAM 3? TEA--
FWOOOM!

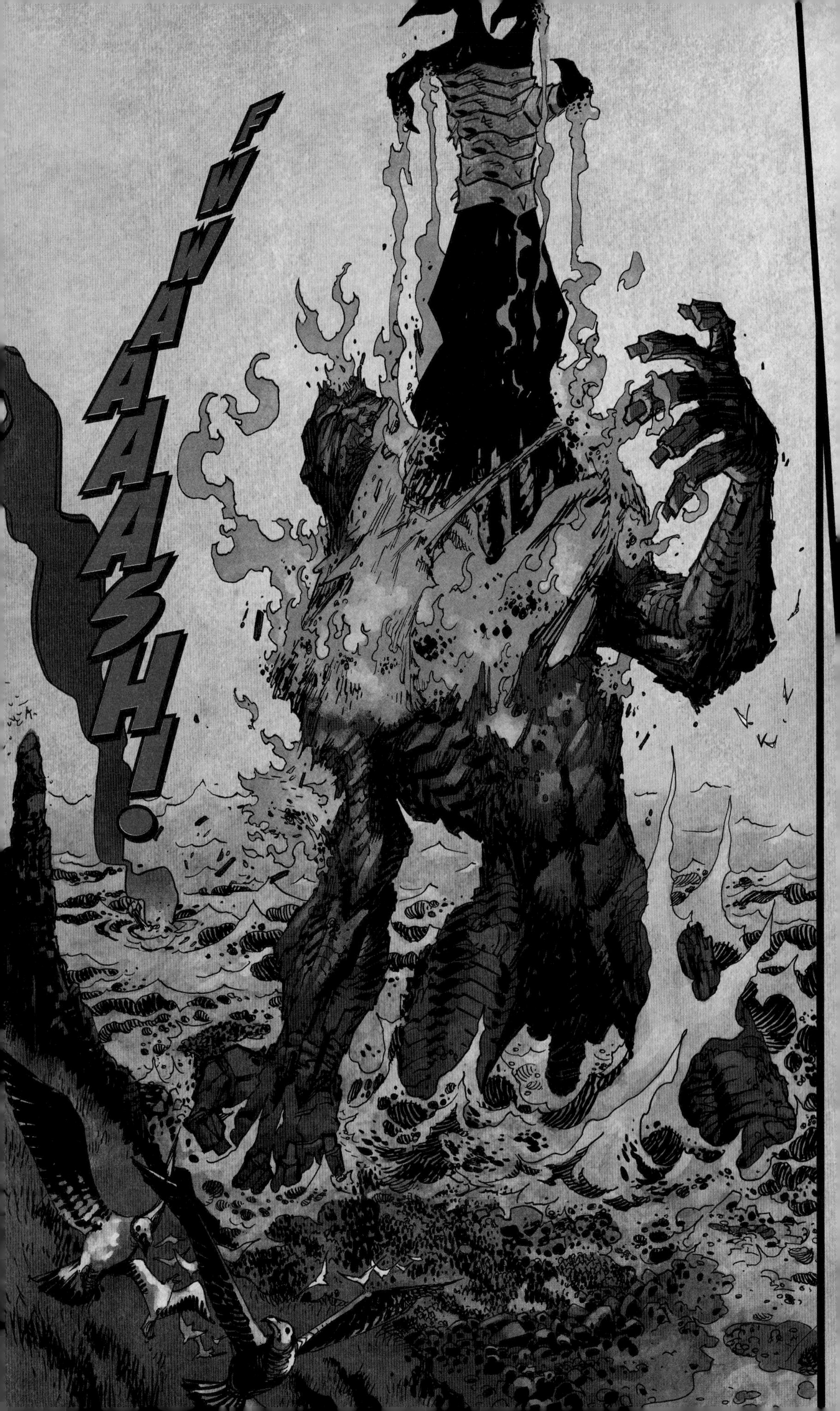
FWWAAAASH!

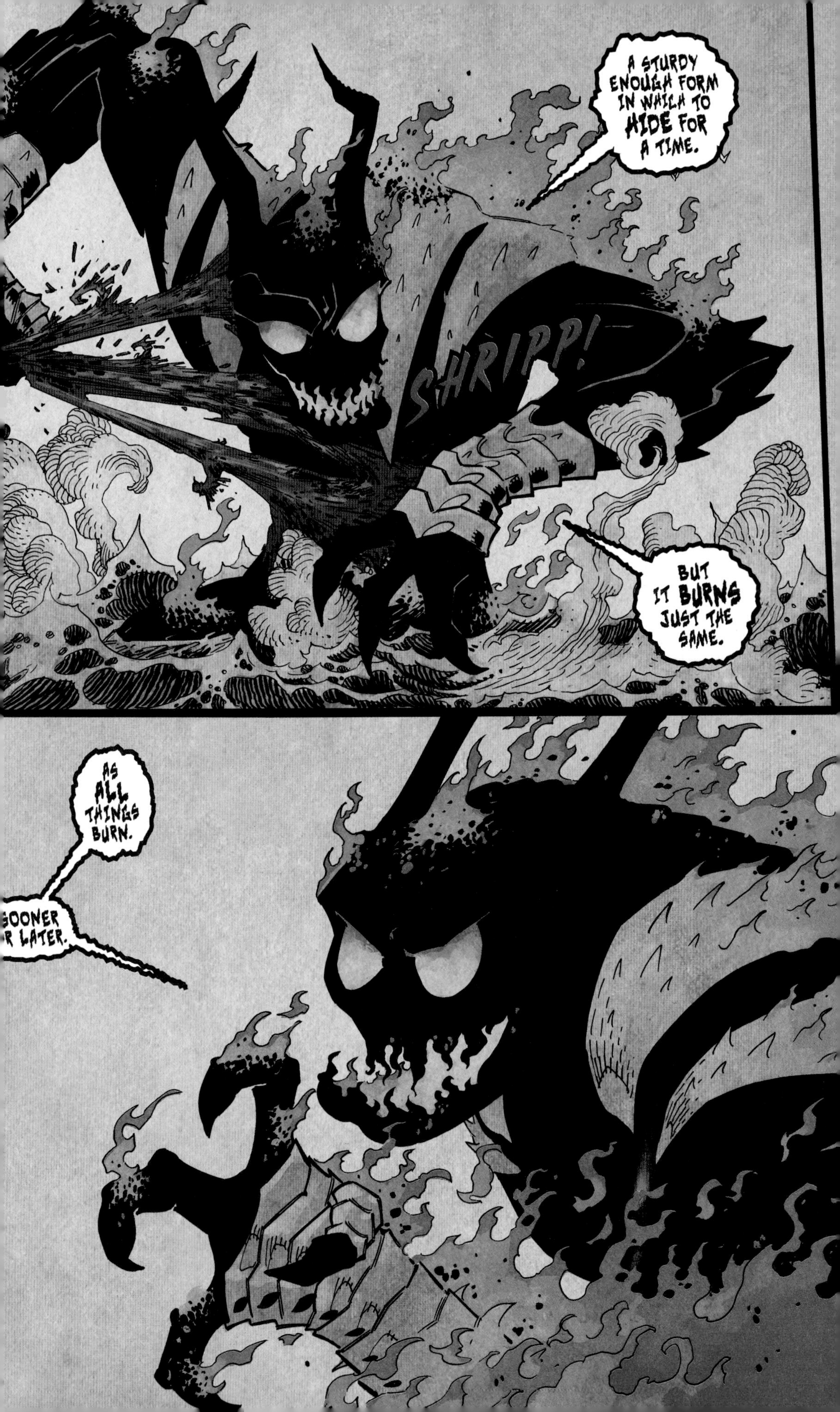

A STURDY ENOUGH FORM IN WHICH TO HIDE FOR A TIME.
SHRIPP!
BUT IT BURNS JUST THE SAME.
AS ALL THINGS BURN.
SOONER R LATER.

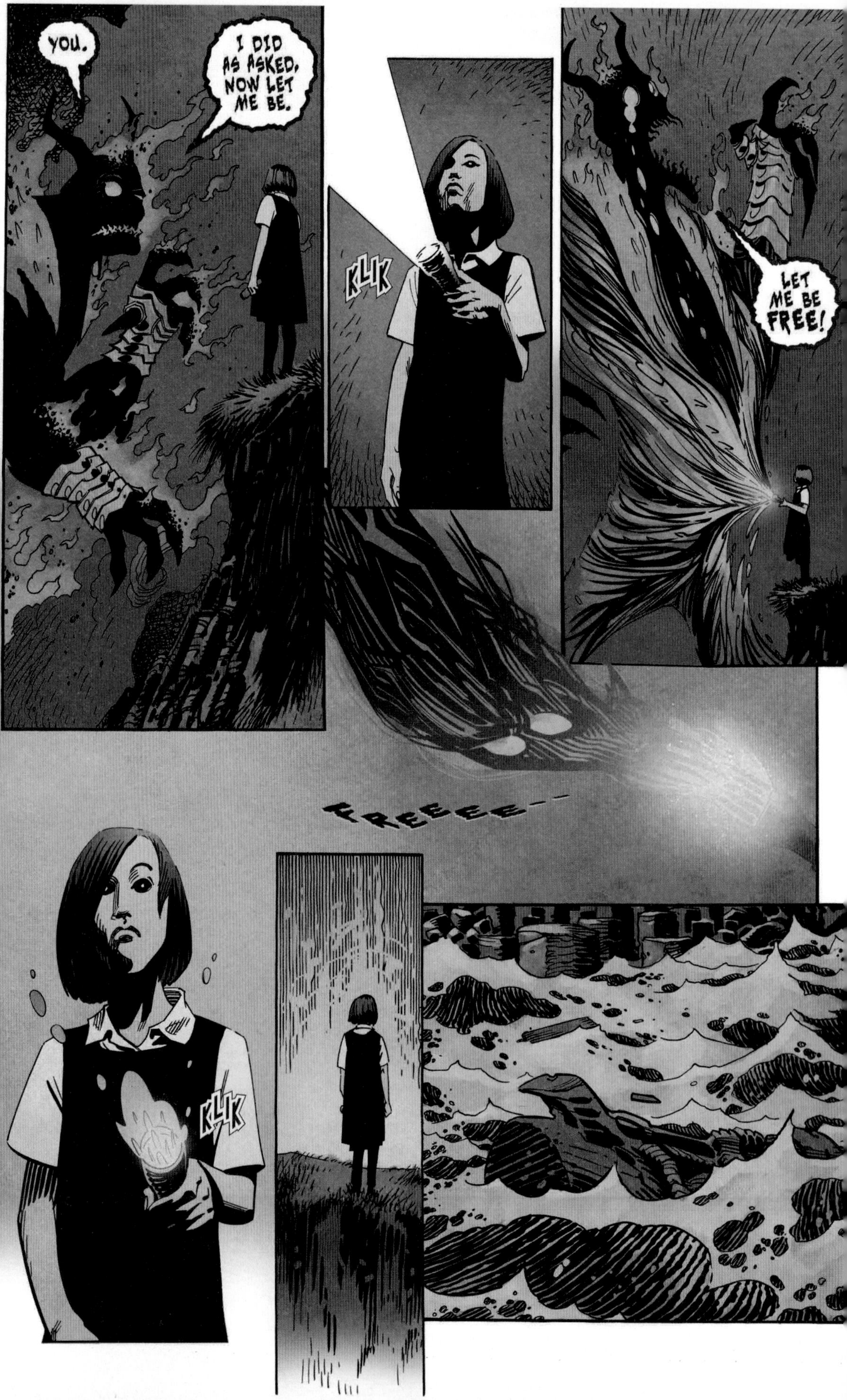
YOU.
I DID AS ASKED, NOW LET ME BE.
KLIK
LET ME BE FREE!
FREEEE--
KLIK

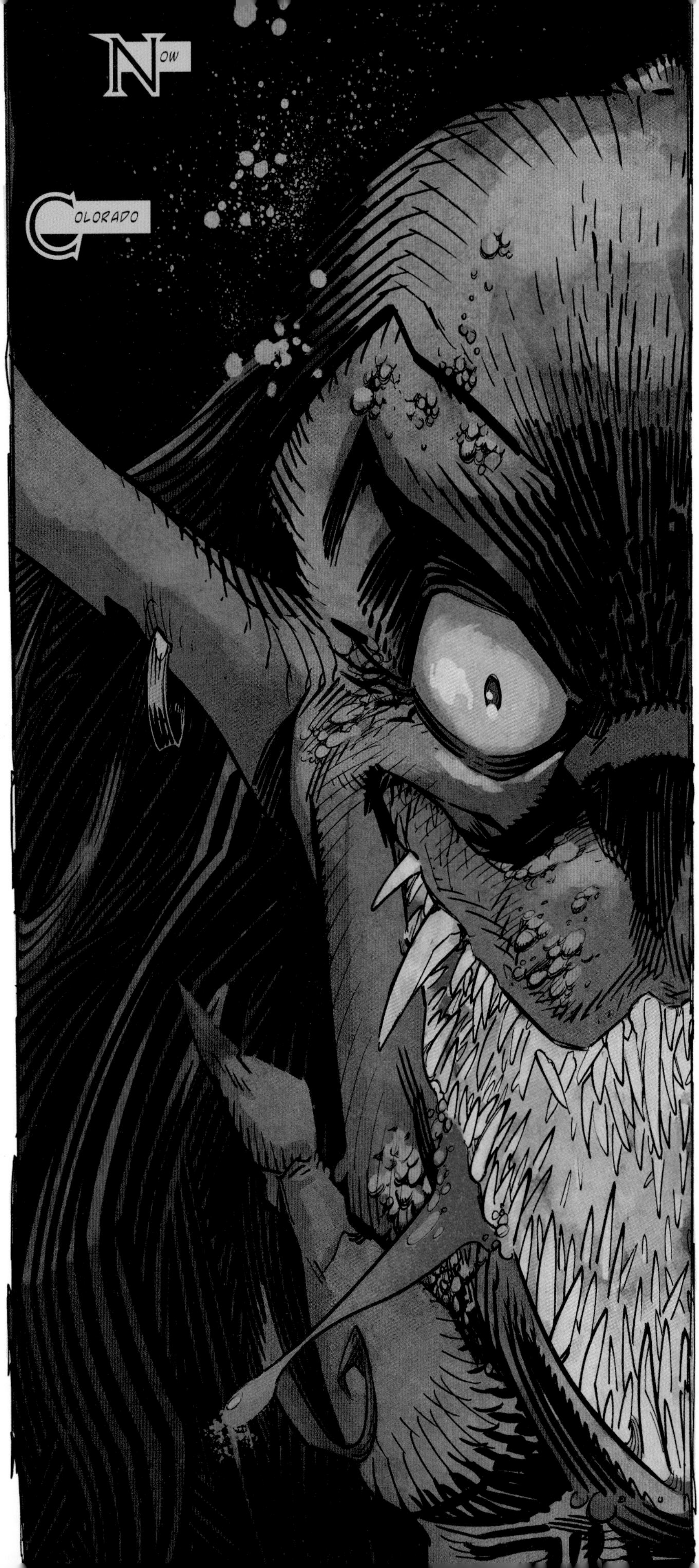
Now
Colorado

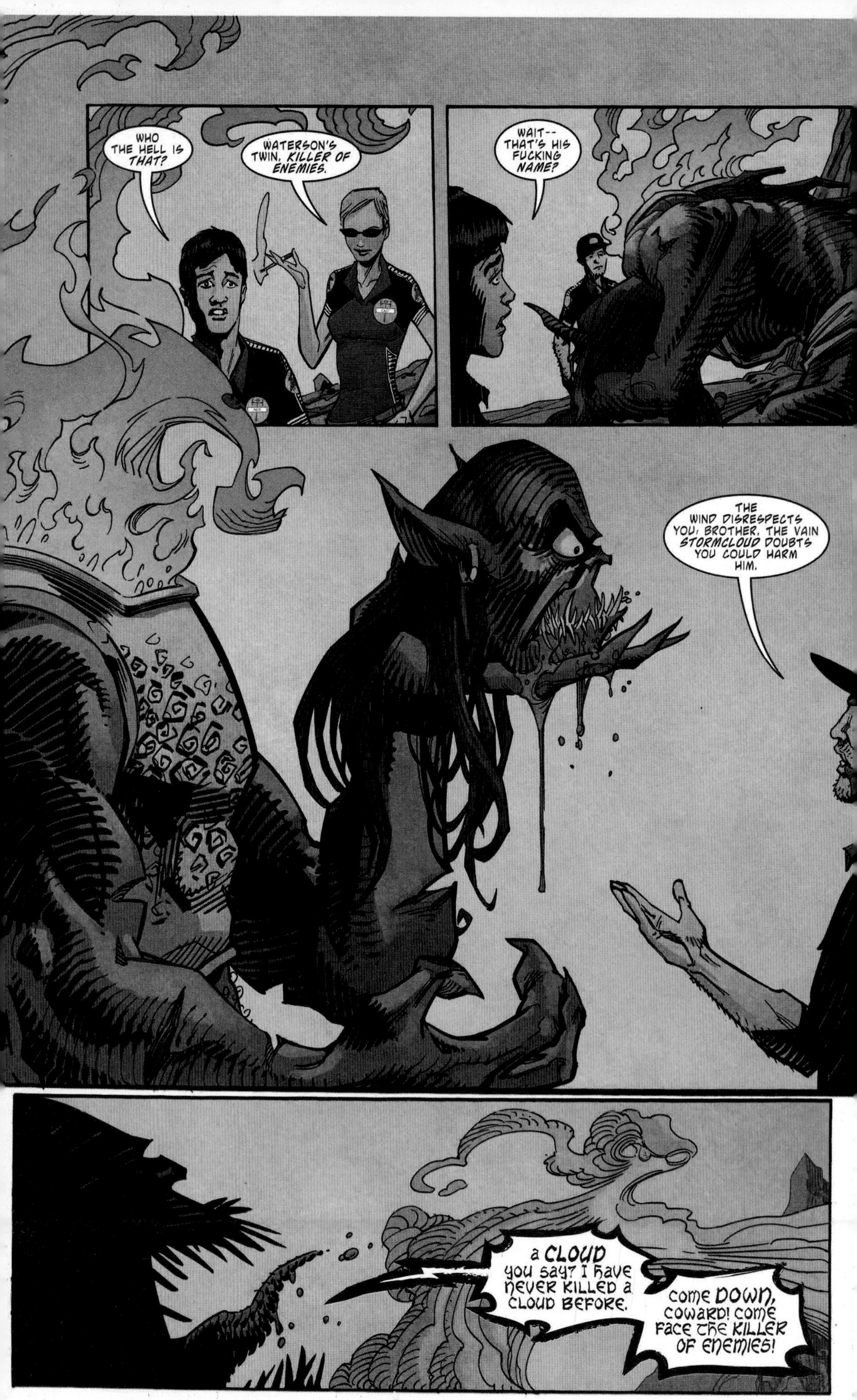
WHO THE HELL IS THAT?
WATERSON'S TWIN. KILLER OF ENEMIES.
WAIT-- THAT'S HIS FUCKING NAME?
THE WIND DISRESPECTS YOU, BROTHER. THE VAIN STORMCLOUD DOUBTS YOU COULD HARM HIM.
a CLOUD you say? I have never killed a cloud before.
Come DOWN, coward! Come face the KILLER OF ENEMIES!

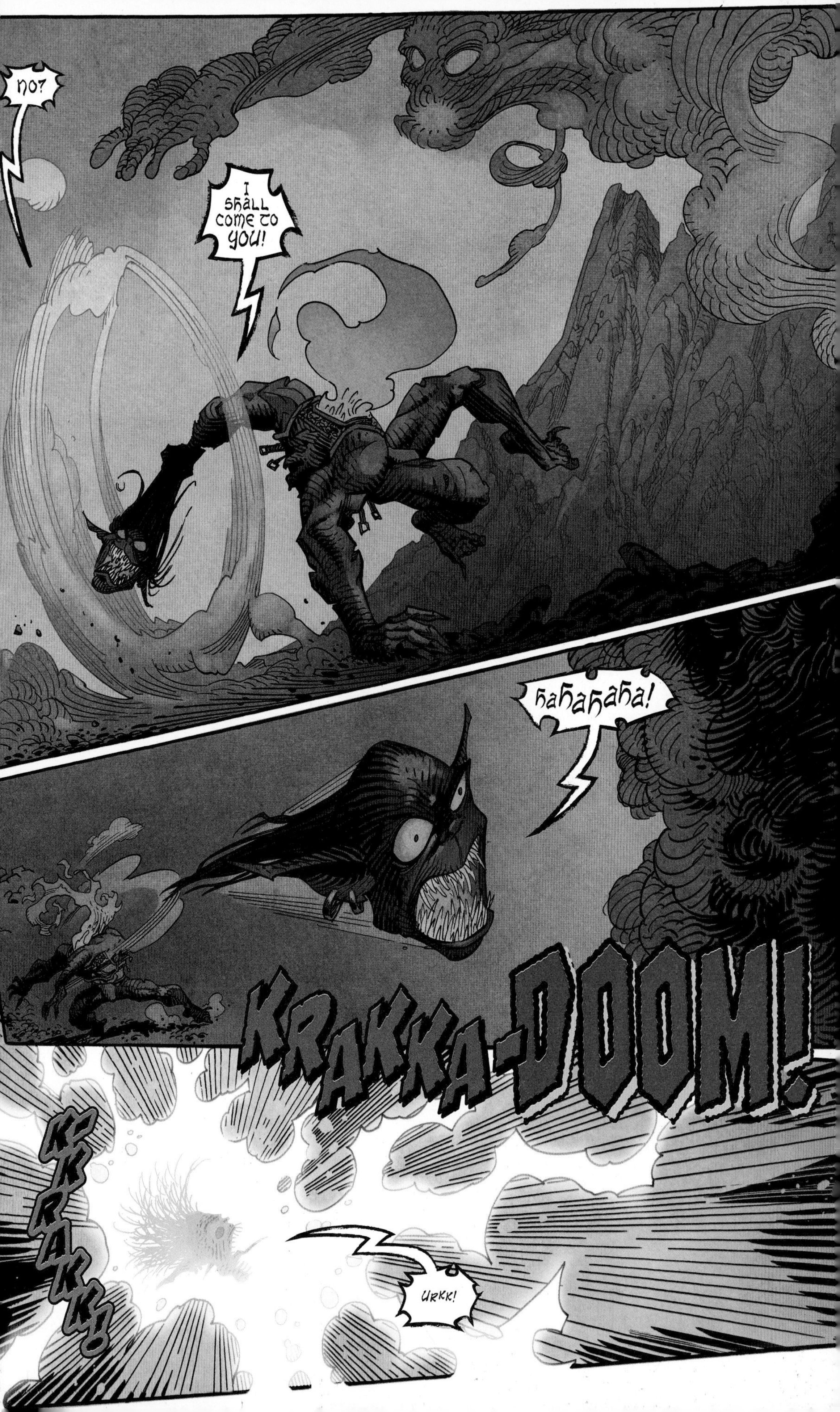
NO?
I SHALL COME TO YOU!
HAHAHAHA!
KRAKKA-DOOM!
KRAKK!
URKK!

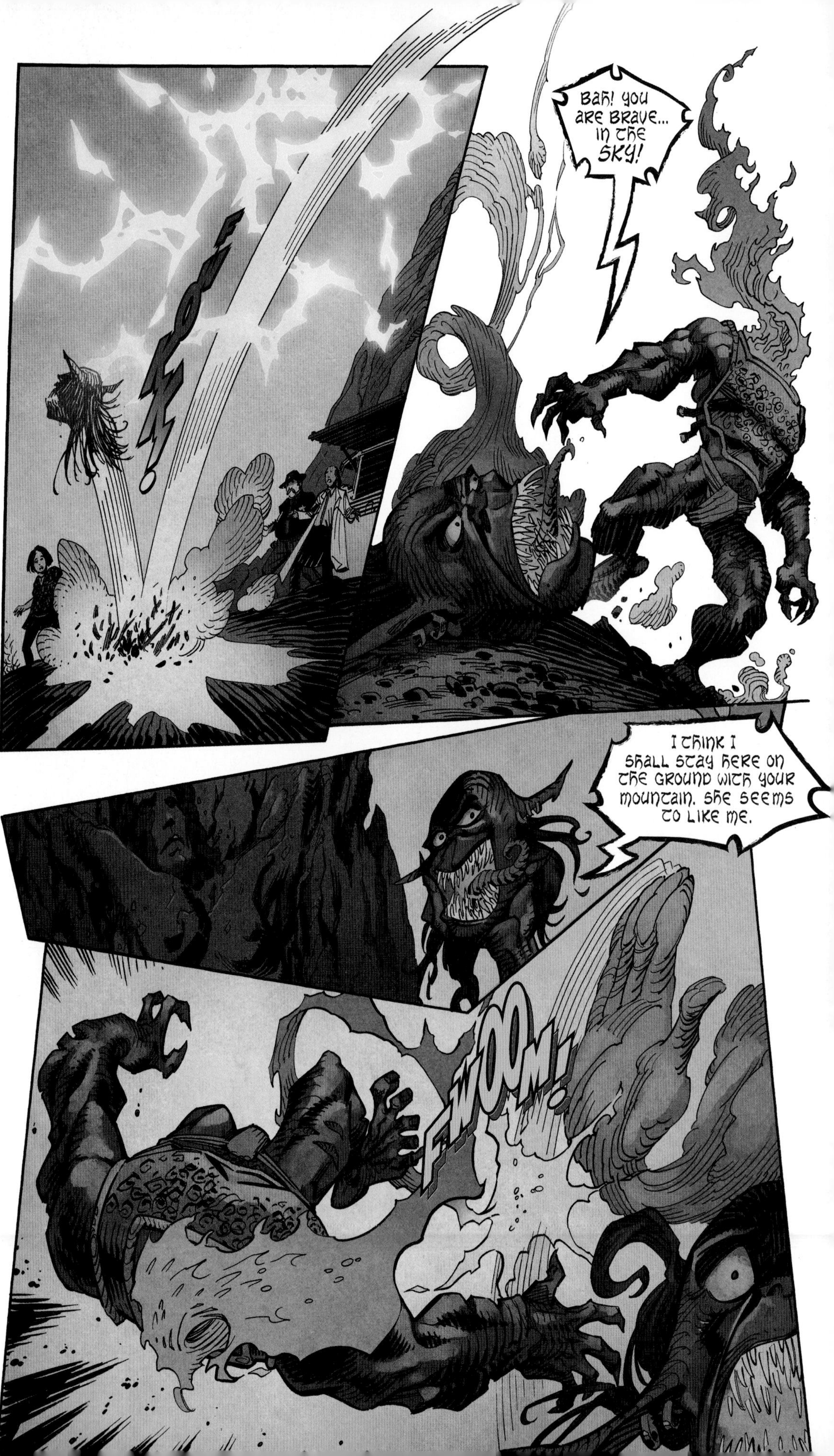
BAH! YOU ARE BRAVE... IN THE SKY!
I THINK I SHALL STAY HERE ON THE GROUND WITH YOUR MOUNTAIN. SHE SEEMS TO LIKE ME.
FWOOM!

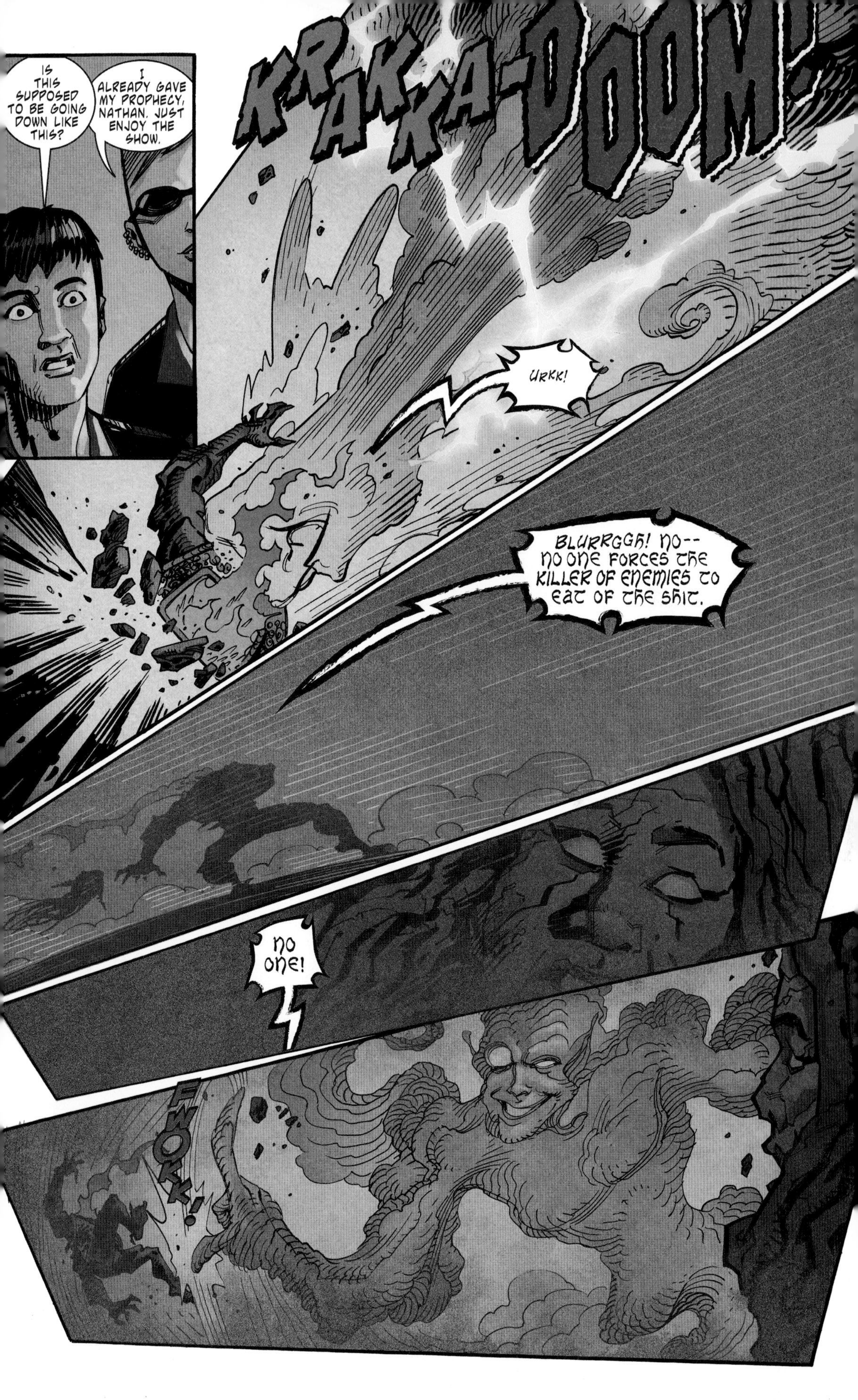
KRAKKA-DOOM!
IS THIS SUPPOSED TO BE GOING DOWN LIKE THIS?
I ALREADY GAVE MY PROPHECY, NATHAN. JUST ENJOY THE SHOW.
URKK!
BLURRGGH! NO-- NO ONE FORCES THE KILLER OF ENEMIES TO EAT OF THE SHIT.
NO ONE!
FWOKK!

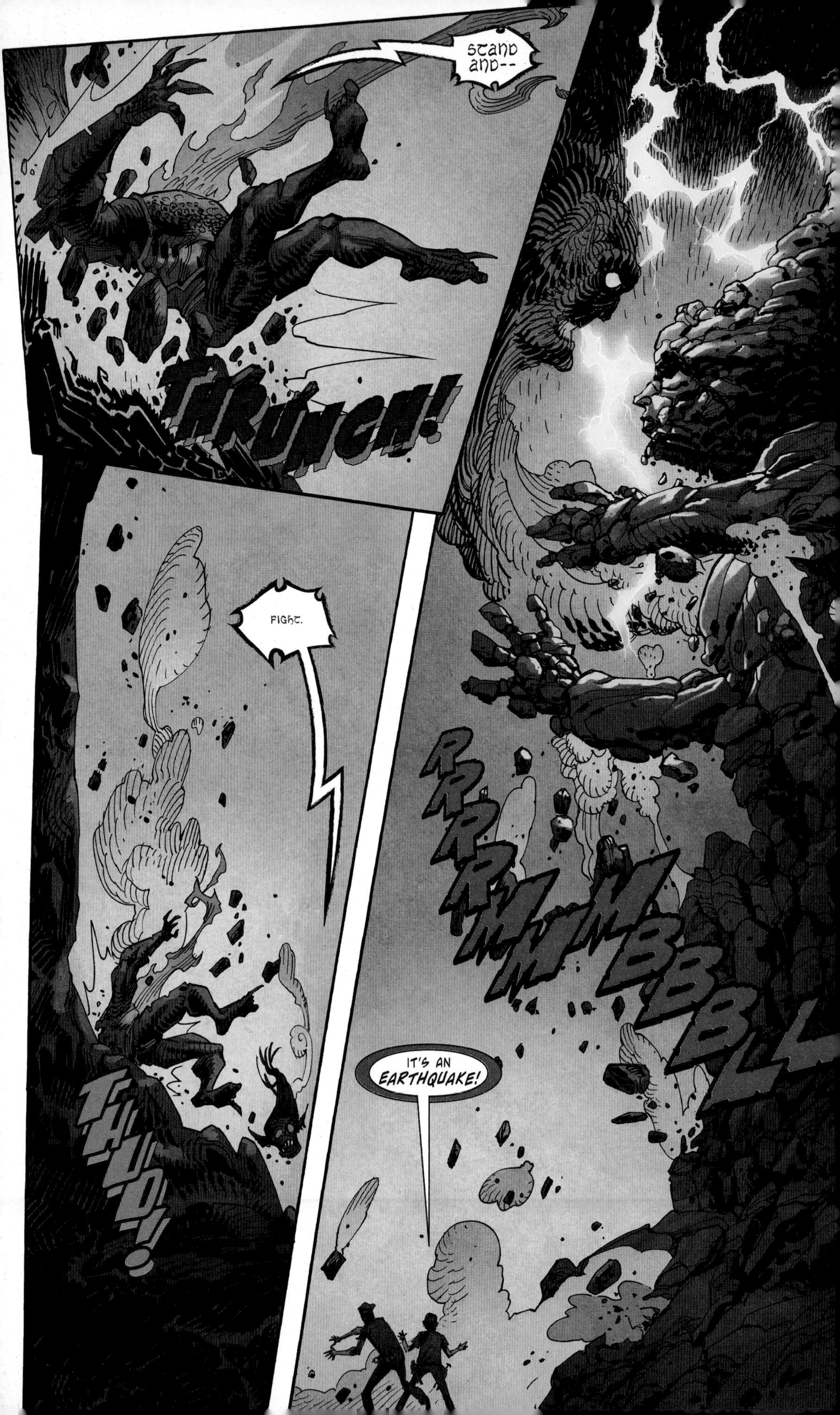

STAND AND--
THRUNCH!
FIGHT.
THUD!
RRRRRMMMMBBBLL
IT'S AN EARTHQUAKE!

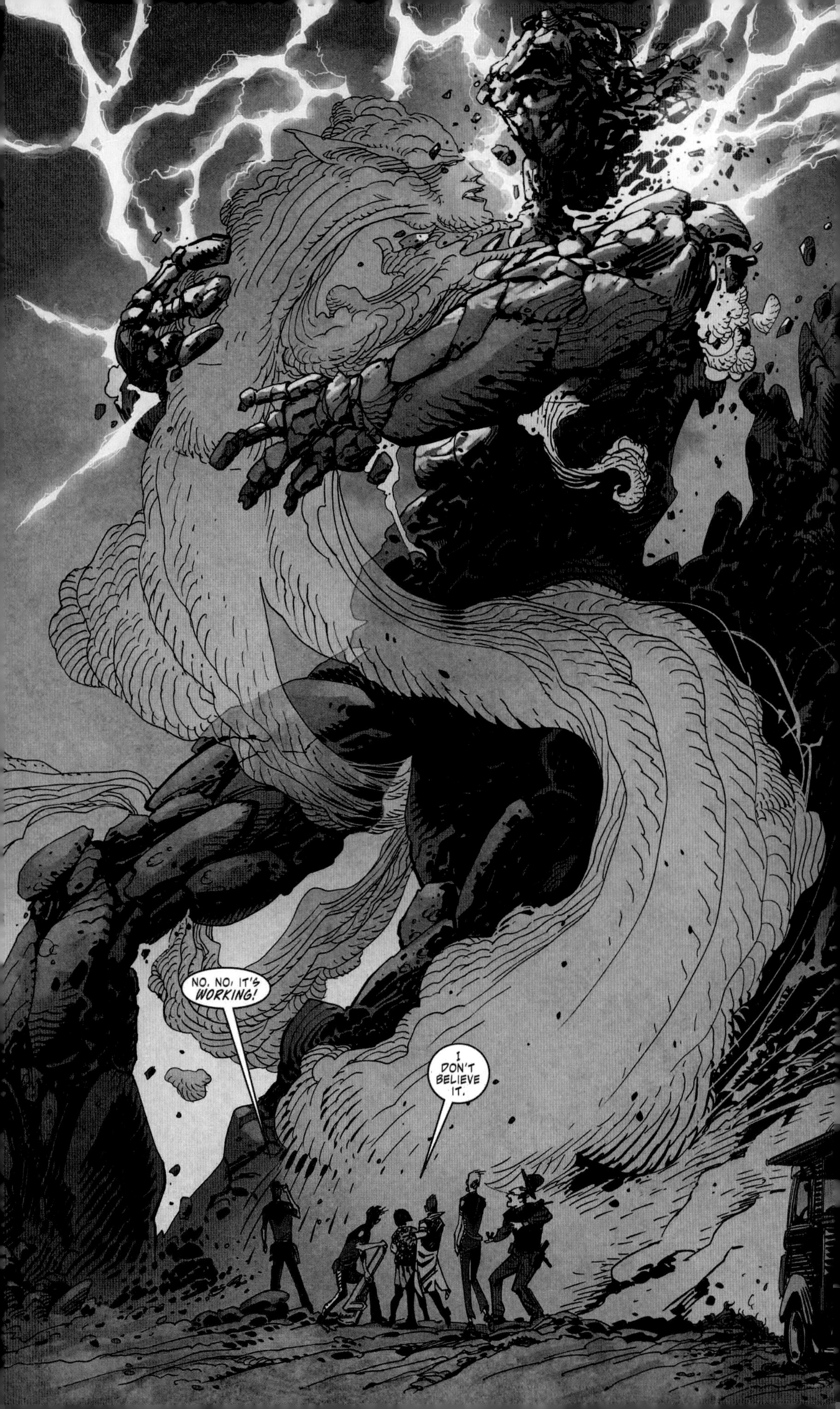
NO. NO, IT'S *WORKING!*
I DON'T BELIEVE IT.

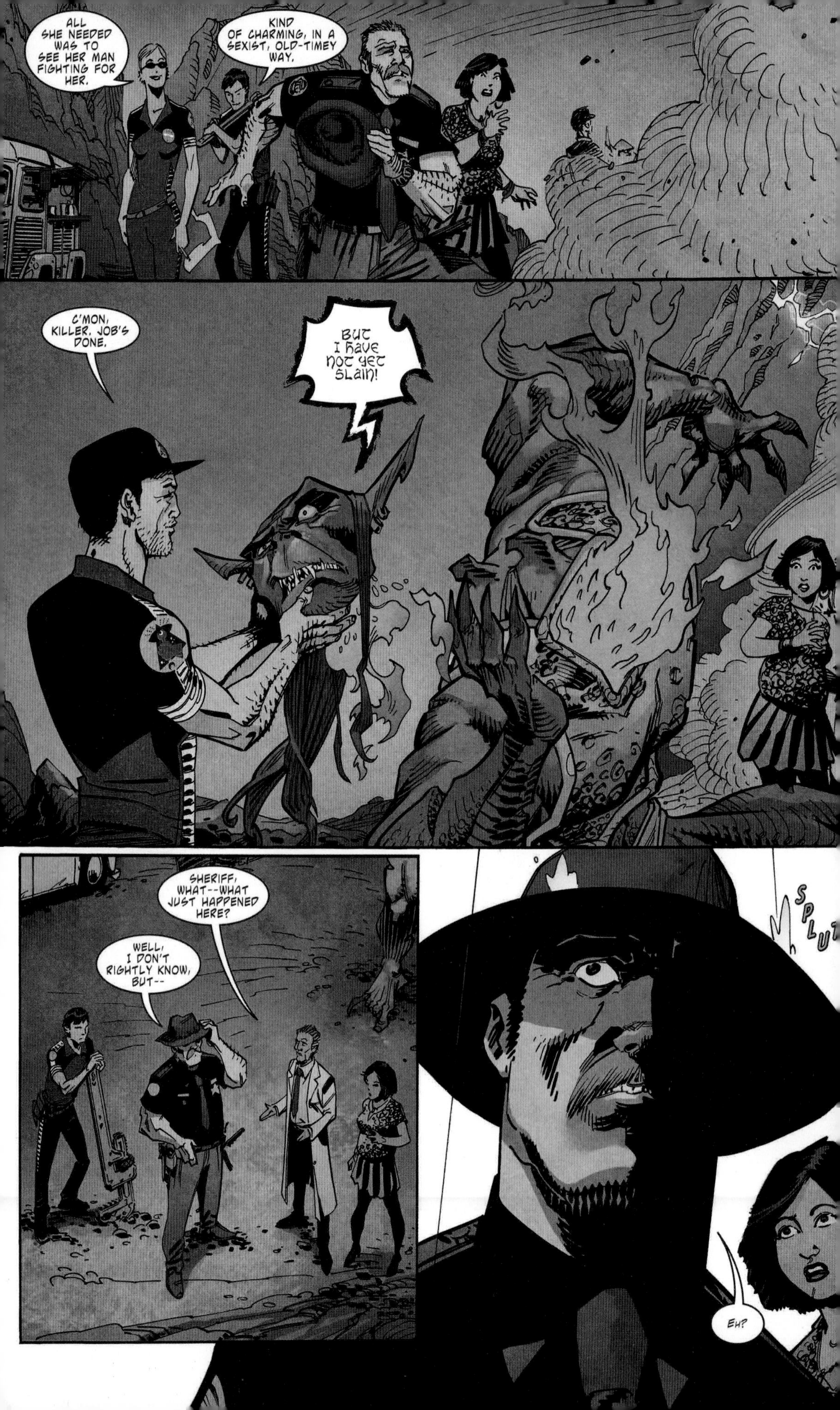
ALL SHE NEEDED WAS TO SEE HER MAN FIGHTING FOR HER.
KIND OF CHARMING, IN A SEXIST, OLD-TIMEY WAY.
C'MON, KILLER. JOB'S DONE.
BUT I HAVE NOT YET SLAIN!
SHERIFF, WHAT--WHAT JUST HAPPENED HERE?
WELL, I DON'T RIGHTLY KNOW, BUT--
SPLUT
EH?

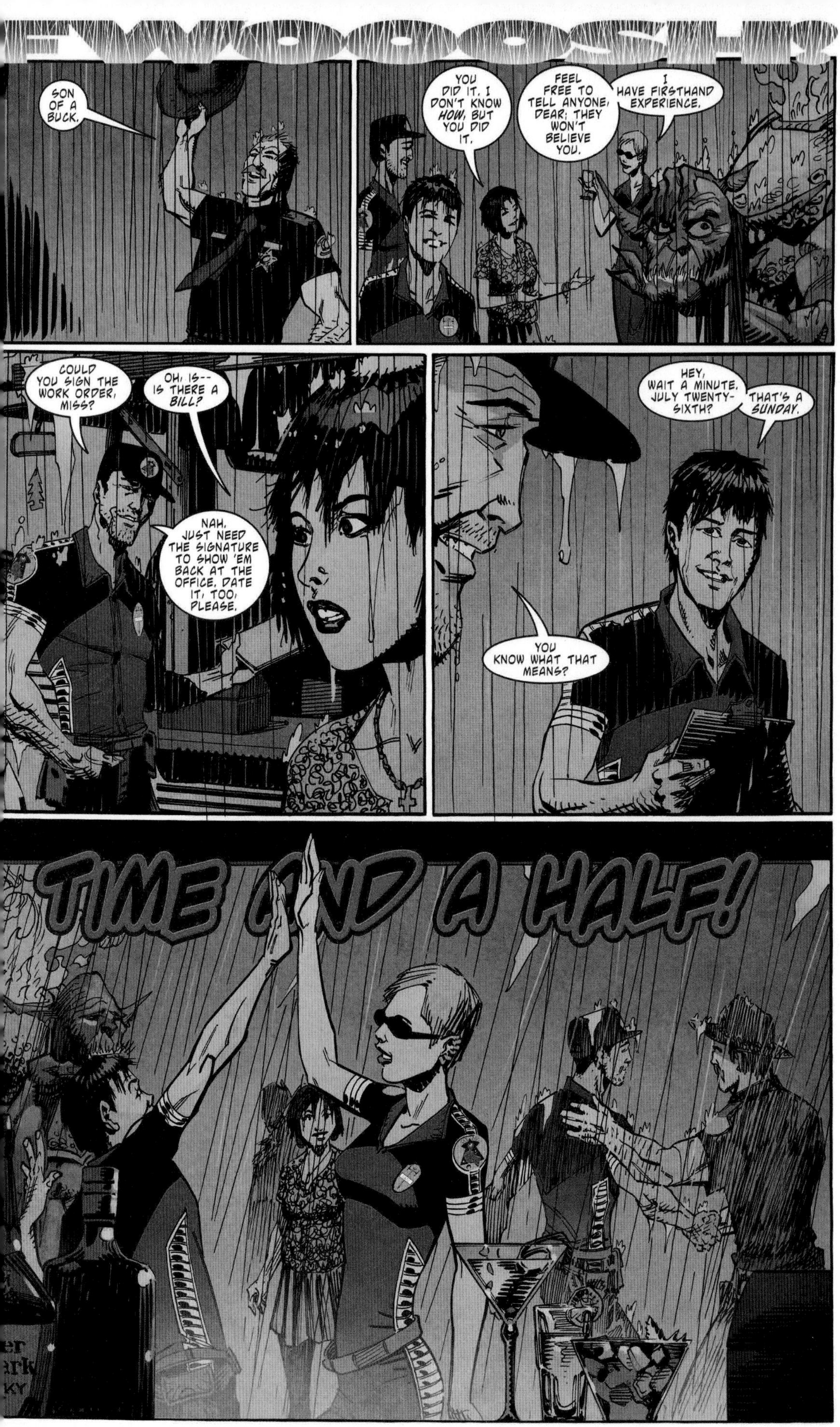
SON OF A BUCK.
YOU DID IT. I DON'T KNOW *HOW*, BUT YOU DID IT.
FEEL FREE TO TELL ANYONE, DEAR; THEY WON'T BELIEVE YOU.
I HAVE FIRSTHAND EXPERIENCE.
COULD YOU SIGN THE WORK ORDER, MISS?
OH, IS-- IS THERE A *BILL*?
NAH, JUST NEED THE SIGNATURE TO SHOW 'EM BACK AT THE OFFICE. DATE IT, TOO, PLEASE.
HEY, WAIT A MINUTE. JULY TWENTY-SIXTH?
THAT'S A *SUNDAY*.
YOU KNOW WHAT THAT MEANS?
TIME AND A HALF!

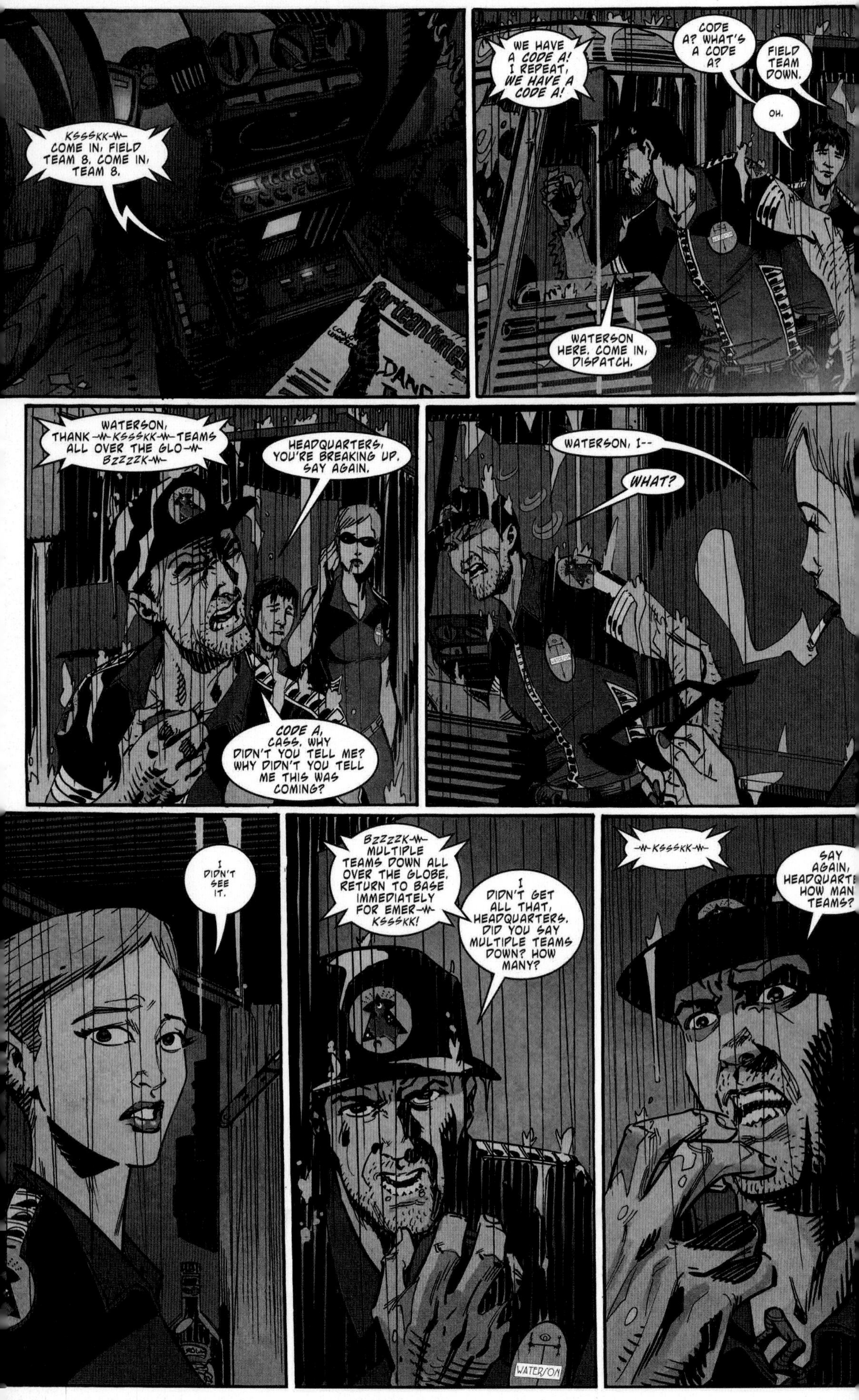
KSSSKK—COME IN, FIELD TEAM 8. COME IN, TEAM 8.
fortean times
WE HAVE A CODE A! I REPEAT, WE HAVE A CODE A!
CODE A? WHAT'S A CODE A?
FIELD TEAM DOWN.
OH.
WATERSON HERE. COME IN, DISPATCH.
WATERSON, THANK —KSSSKK— TEAMS ALL OVER THE GLO— BZZZZK—
HEADQUARTERS, YOU'RE BREAKING UP. SAY AGAIN.
CODE A, CASS. WHY DIDN'T YOU TELL ME? WHY DIDN'T YOU TELL ME THIS WAS COMING?
WATERSON, I--
WHAT?
I DIDN'T SEE IT.
BZZZZK— MULTIPLE TEAMS DOWN ALL OVER THE GLOBE. RETURN TO BASE IMMEDIATELY FOR EMER— KSSSKK!
I DIDN'T GET ALL THAT, HEADQUARTERS. DID YOU SAY MULTIPLE TEAMS DOWN? HOW MANY?
—KSSSKK—
SAY AGAIN, HEADQUARTE HOW MAN TEAMS?
WATERSON

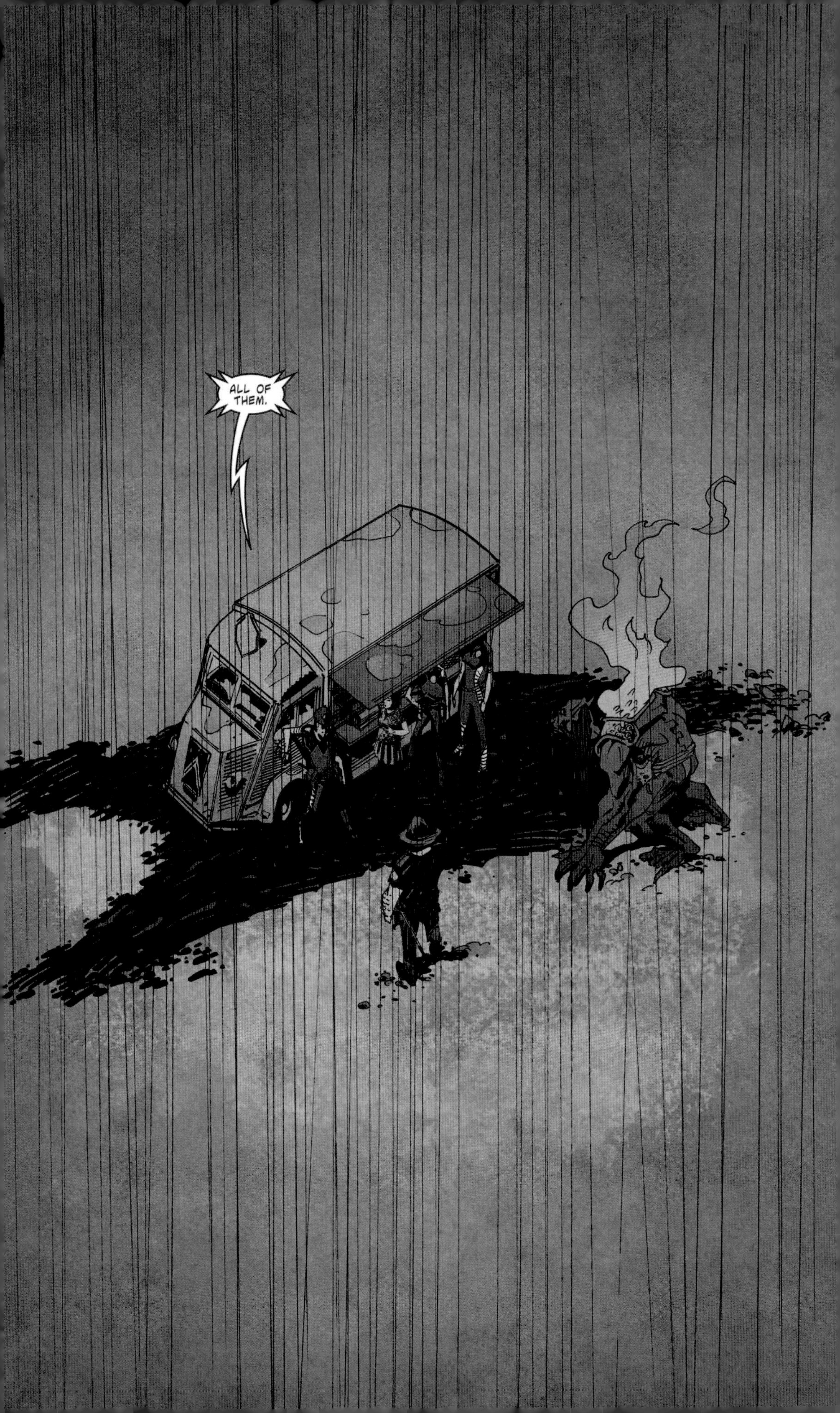
ALL OF THEM.

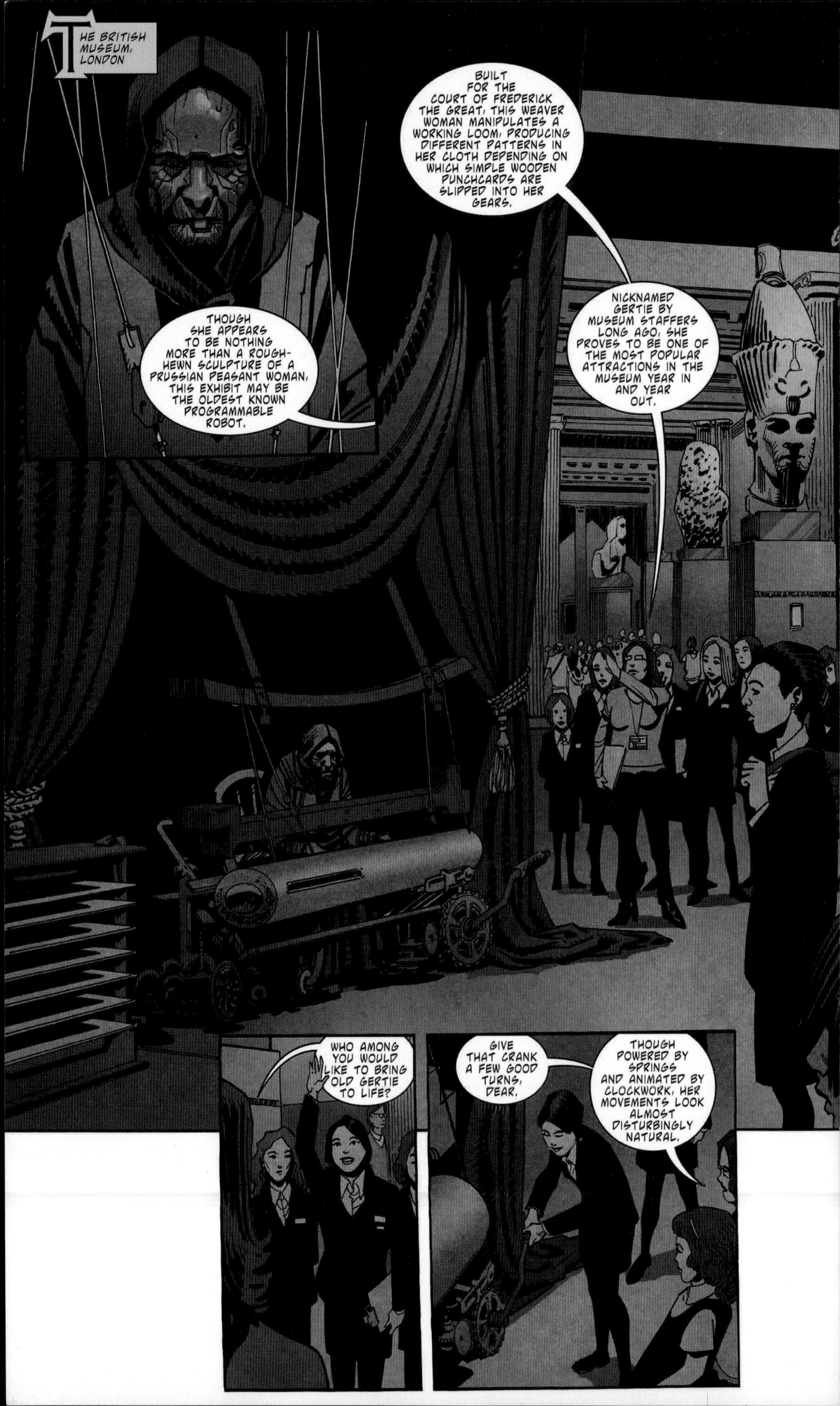

THE BRITISH MUSEUM, LONDON
THOUGH SHE APPEARS TO BE NOTHING MORE THAN A ROUGH-HEWN SCULPTURE OF A PRUSSIAN PEASANT WOMAN, THIS EXHIBIT MAY BE THE OLDEST KNOWN PROGRAMMABLE ROBOT.
BUILT FOR THE COURT OF FREDERICK THE GREAT, THIS WEAVER WOMAN MANIPULATES A WORKING LOOM, PRODUCING DIFFERENT PATTERNS IN HER CLOTH DEPENDING ON WHICH SIMPLE WOODEN PUNCHCARDS ARE SLIPPED INTO HER GEARS.
NICKNAMED GERTIE BY MUSEUM STAFFERS LONG AGO, SHE PROVES TO BE ONE OF THE MOST POPULAR ATTRACTIONS IN THE MUSEUM YEAR IN AND YEAR OUT.
WHO AMONG YOU WOULD LIKE TO BRING OLD GERTIE TO LIFE?
GIVE THAT CRANK A FEW GOOD TURNS, DEAR.
THOUGH POWERED BY SPRINGS AND ANIMATED BY CLOCKWORK, HER MOVEMENTS LOOK ALMOST DISTURBINGLY NATURAL.

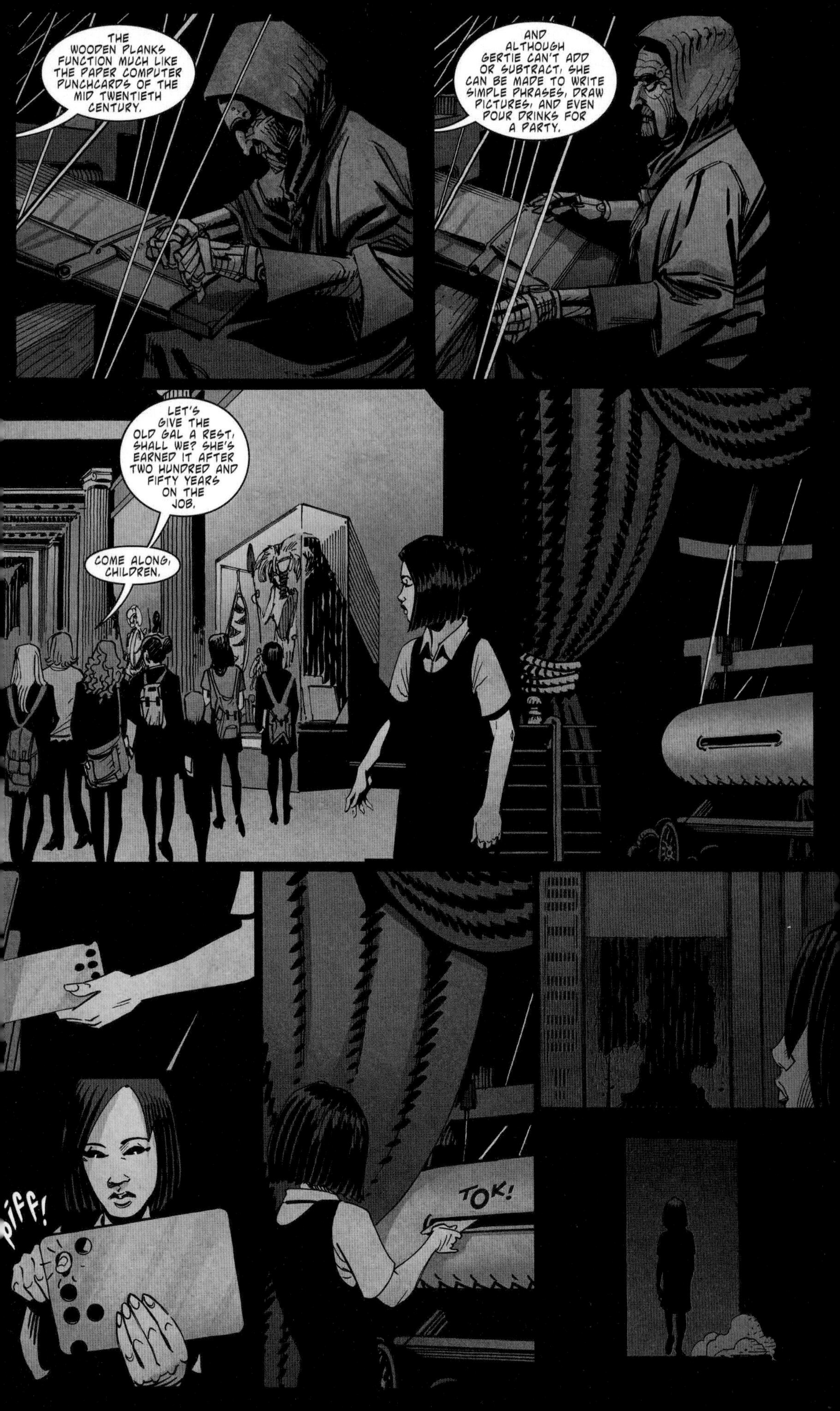
THE WOODEN PLANKS FUNCTION MUCH LIKE THE PAPER COMPUTER PUNCHCARDS OF THE MID TWENTIETH CENTURY.
AND ALTHOUGH GERTIE CAN'T ADD OR SUBTRACT, SHE CAN BE MADE TO WRITE SIMPLE PHRASES, DRAW PICTURES, AND EVEN POUR DRINKS FOR A PARTY.
LET'S GIVE THE OLD GAL A REST, SHALL WE? SHE'S EARNED IT AFTER TWO HUNDRED AND FIFTY YEARS ON THE JOB.
COME ALONG, CHILDREN.
piff!
TOK!

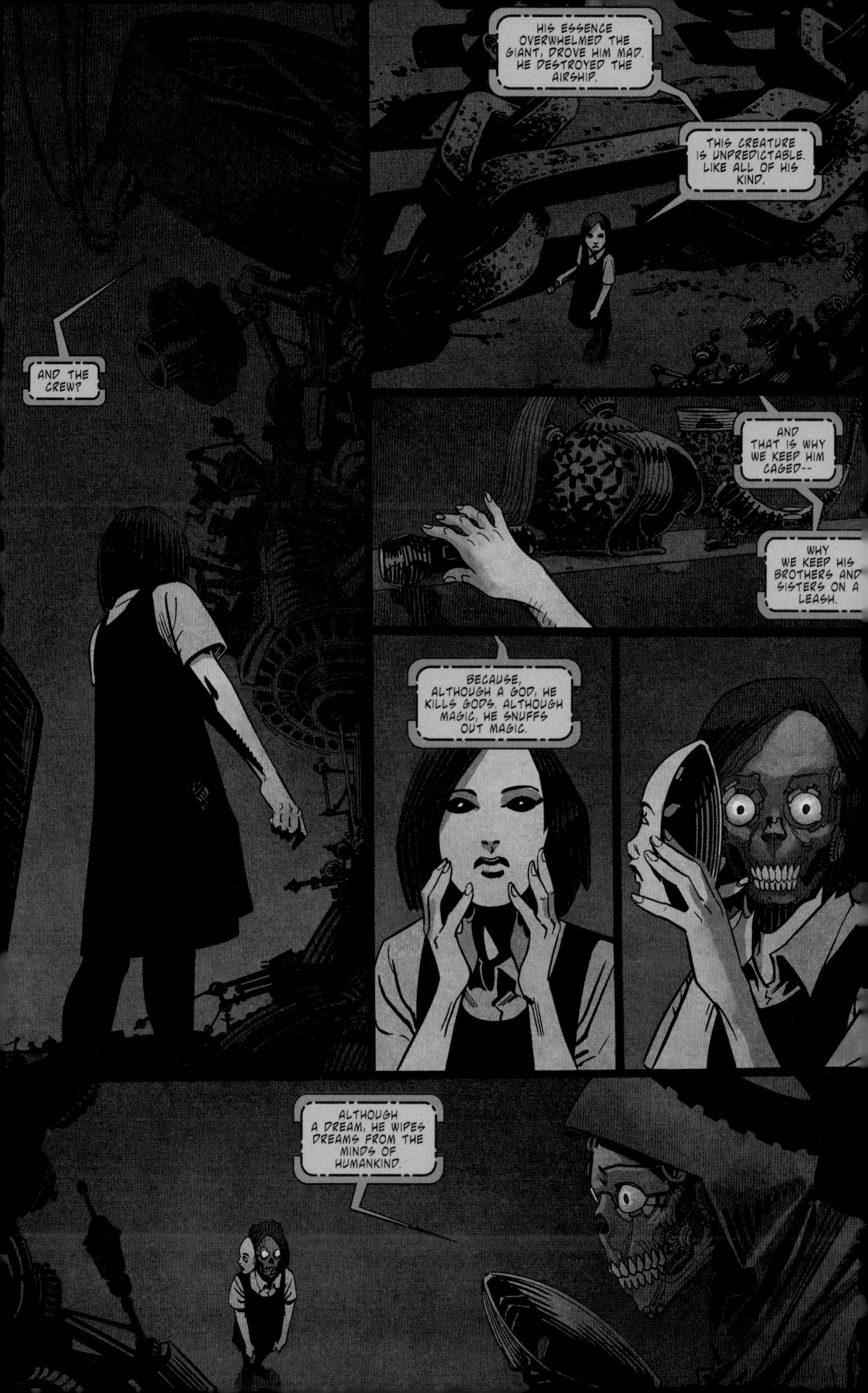
AND THE CREW?
HIS ESSENCE OVERWHELMED THE GIANT, DROVE HIM MAD. HE DESTROYED THE AIRSHIP.
THIS CREATURE IS UNPREDICTABLE. LIKE ALL OF HIS KIND.
AND THAT IS WHY WE KEEP HIM CAGED--
WHY WE KEEP HIS BROTHERS AND SISTERS ON A LEASH.
BECAUSE, ALTHOUGH A GOD, HE KILLS GODS. ALTHOUGH MAGIC, HE SNUFFS OUT MAGIC.
ALTHOUGH A DREAM, HE WIPES DREAMS FROM THE MINDS OF HUMANKIND.

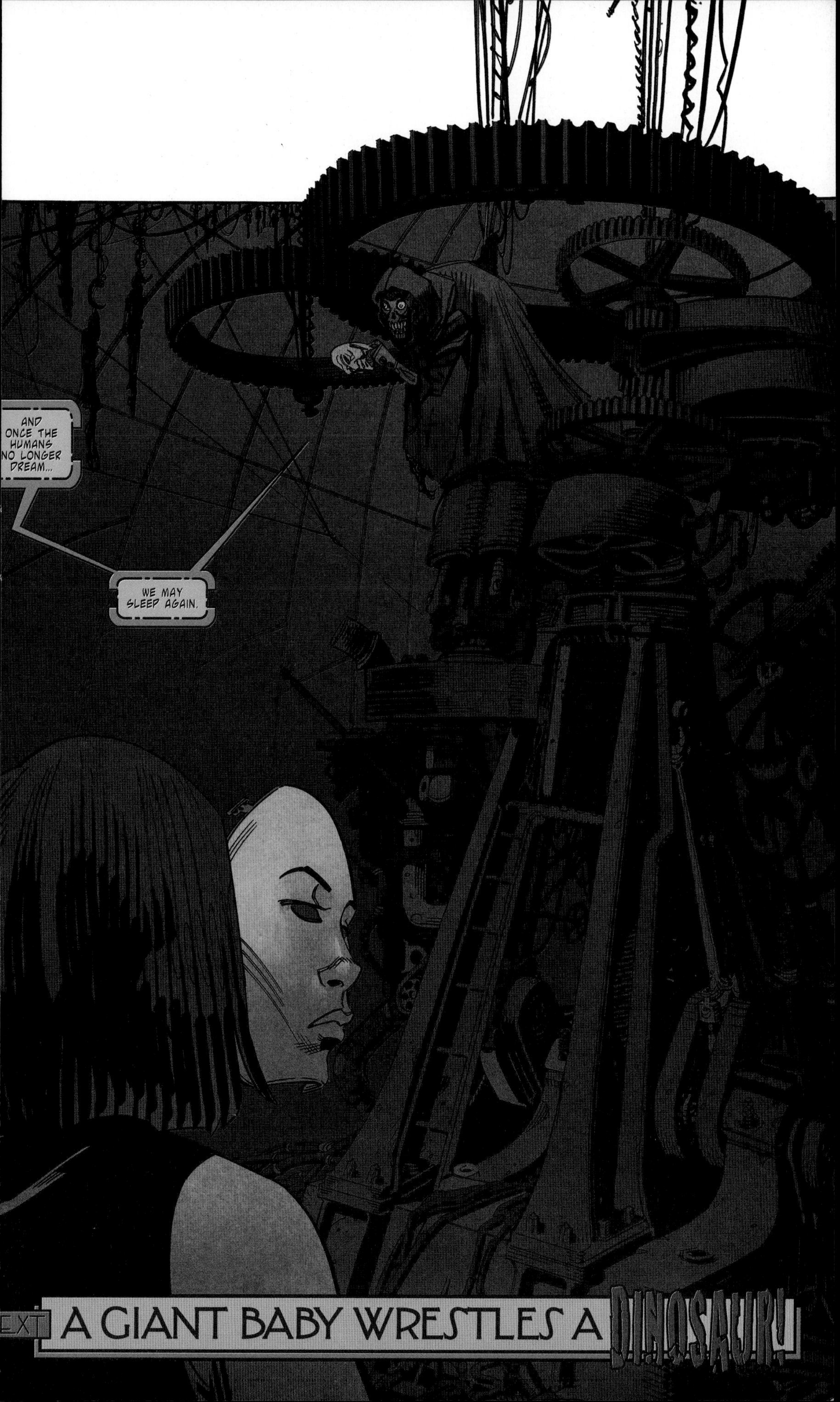
AND ONCE THE HUMANS NO LONGER DREAM...
WE MAY SLEEP AGAIN.
EXT A GIANT BABY WRESTLES A DINOSAUR!

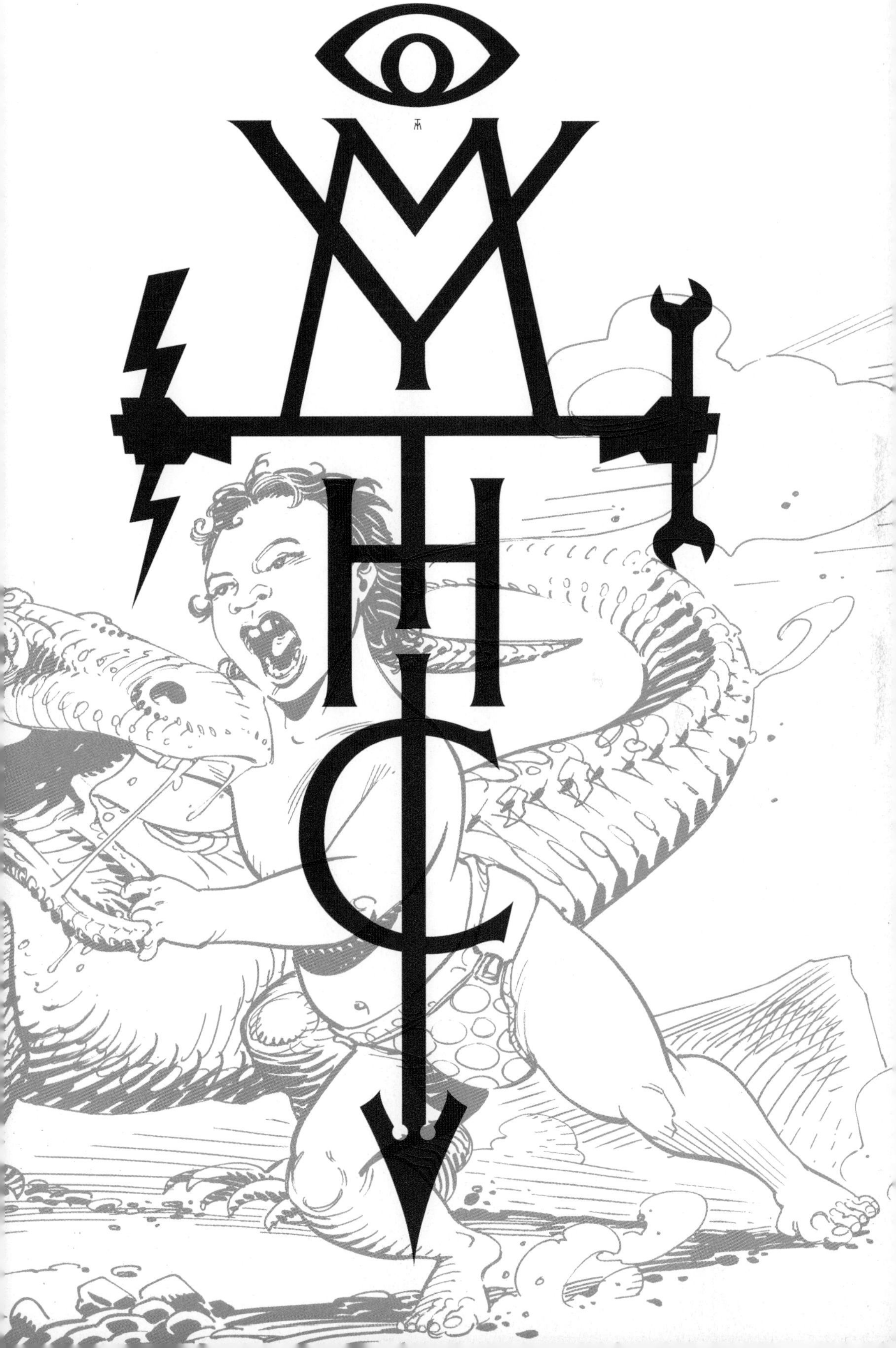
MYTHIC

CHAPTER 3
THE MAN WITH THE GOLDEN COINS

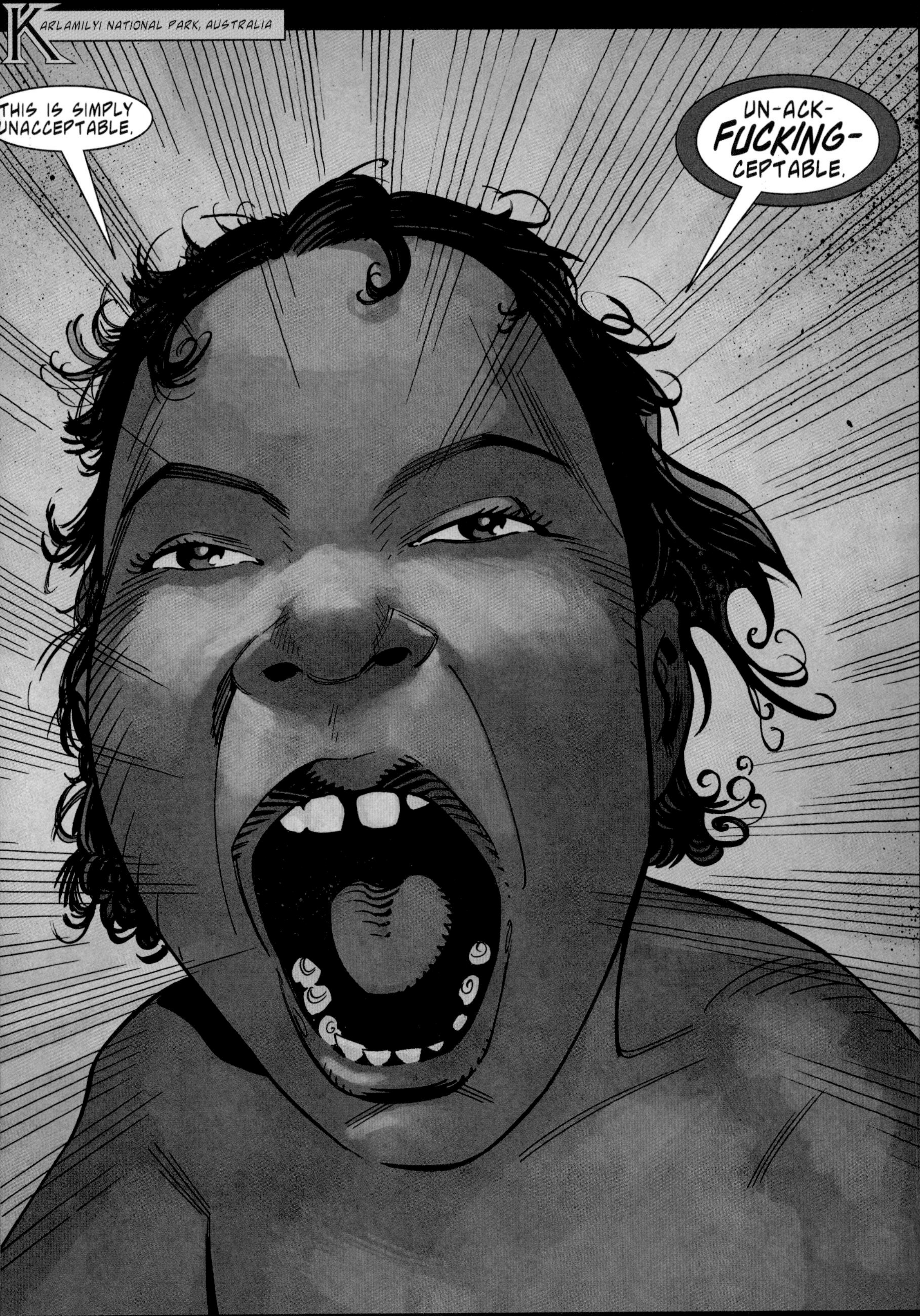
KARLAMILYI NATIONAL PARK, AUSTRALIA
THIS IS SIMPLY UNACCEPTABLE.
UN-ACK-FUCKING-CEPTABLE.

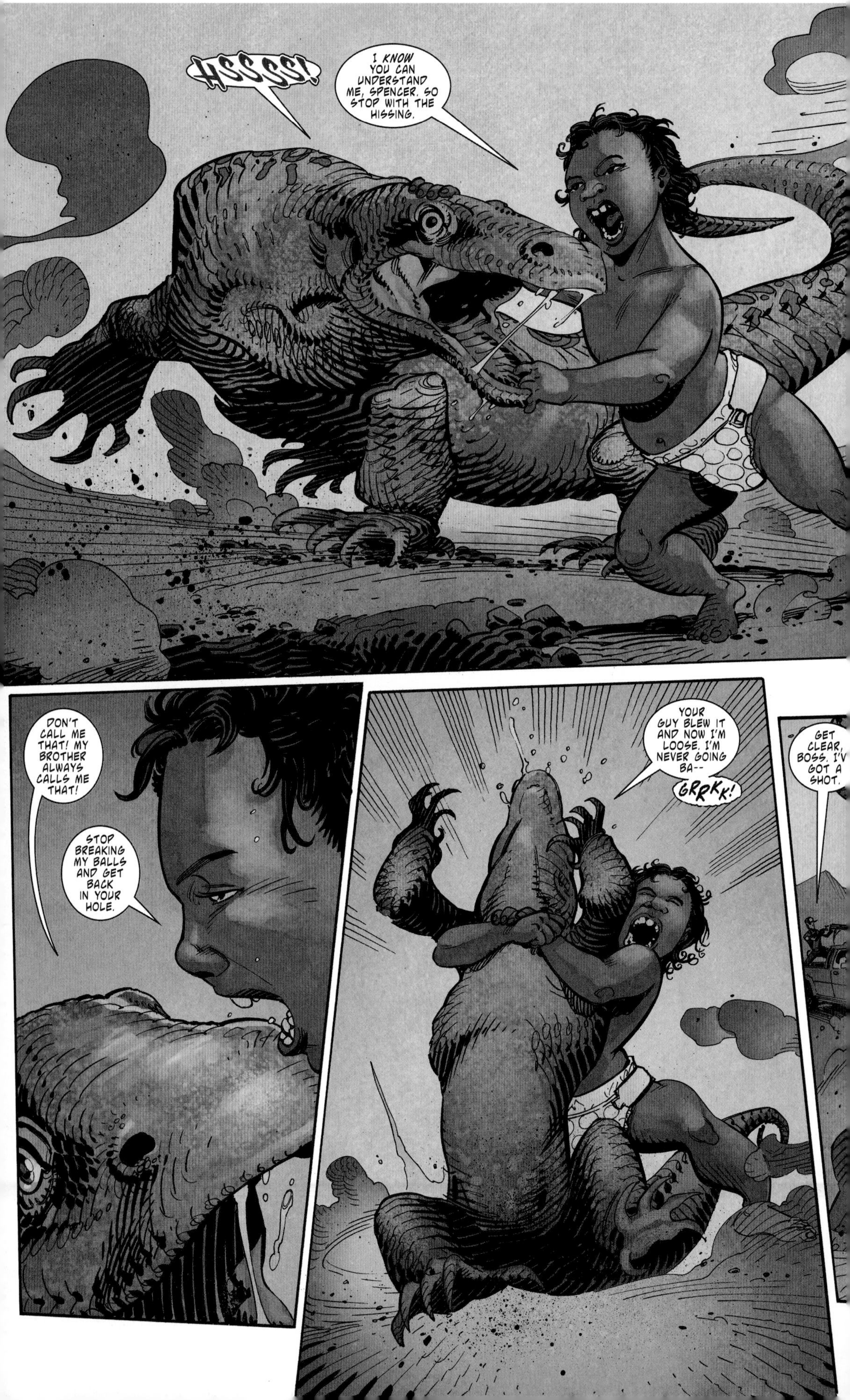
HSSSS!
I KNOW YOU CAN UNDERSTAND ME, SPENCER. SO STOP WITH THE HISSING.
DON'T CALL ME THAT! MY BROTHER ALWAYS CALLS ME THAT!
STOP BREAKING MY BALLS AND GET BACK IN YOUR HOLE.
YOUR GUY BLEW IT AND NOW I'M LOOSE. I'M NEVER GOING BA--
GRRKK!
GET CLEAR, BOSS. I'V GOT A SHOT.

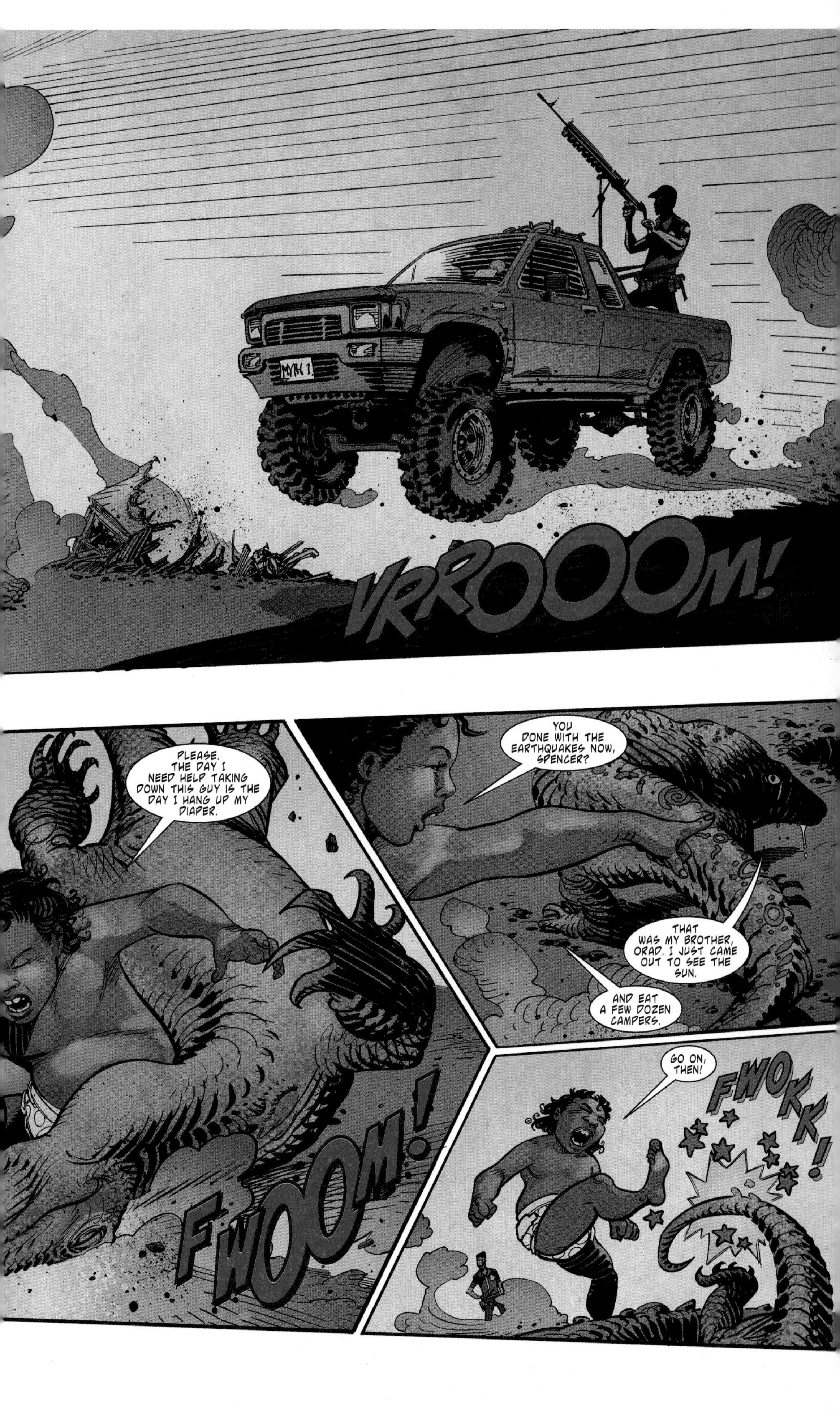
MYTH 1
VRROOOM!
PLEASE. THE DAY I NEED HELP TAKING DOWN THIS GUY IS THE DAY I HANG UP MY DIAPER.
FWOOM!
YOU DONE WITH THE EARTHQUAKES NOW, SPENCER?
THAT WAS MY BROTHER, ORAD. I JUST CAME OUT TO SEE THE SUN.
AND EAT A FEW DOZEN CAMPERS.
GO ON, THEN!
FWOKK!

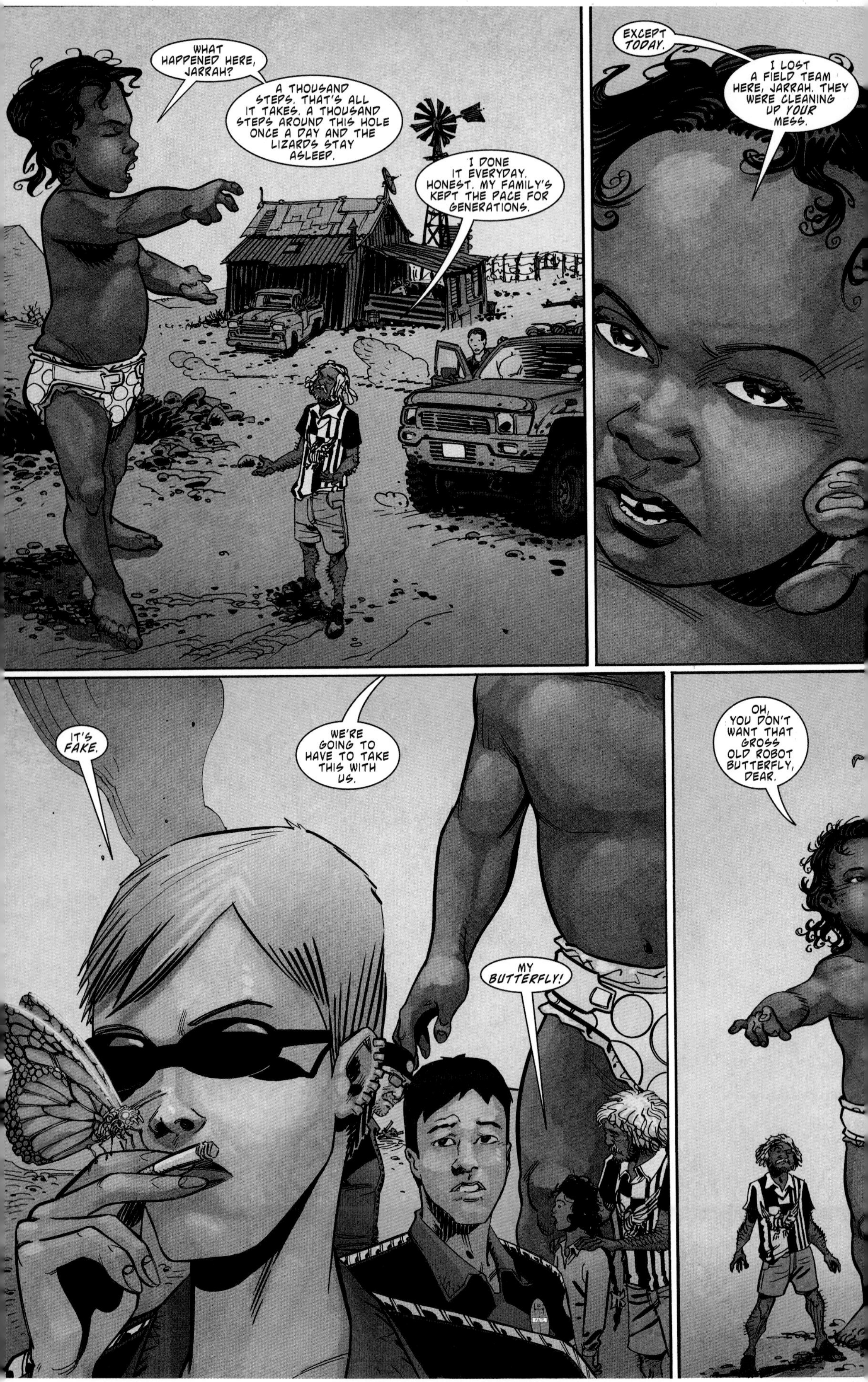
WHAT HAPPENED HERE, JARRAH?
A THOUSAND STEPS. THAT'S ALL IT TAKES. A THOUSAND STEPS AROUND THIS HOLE ONCE A DAY AND THE LIZARDS STAY ASLEEP.
I DONE IT EVERYDAY. HONEST. MY FAMILY'S KEPT THE PACE FOR GENERATIONS.
EXCEPT TODAY.
I LOST A FIELD TEAM HERE, JARRAH. THEY WERE CLEANING UP YOUR MESS.
IT'S FAKE.
WE'RE GOING TO HAVE TO TAKE THIS WITH US.
MY BUTTERFLY!
OH, YOU DON'T WANT THAT GROSS OLD ROBOT BUTTERFLY, DEAR.

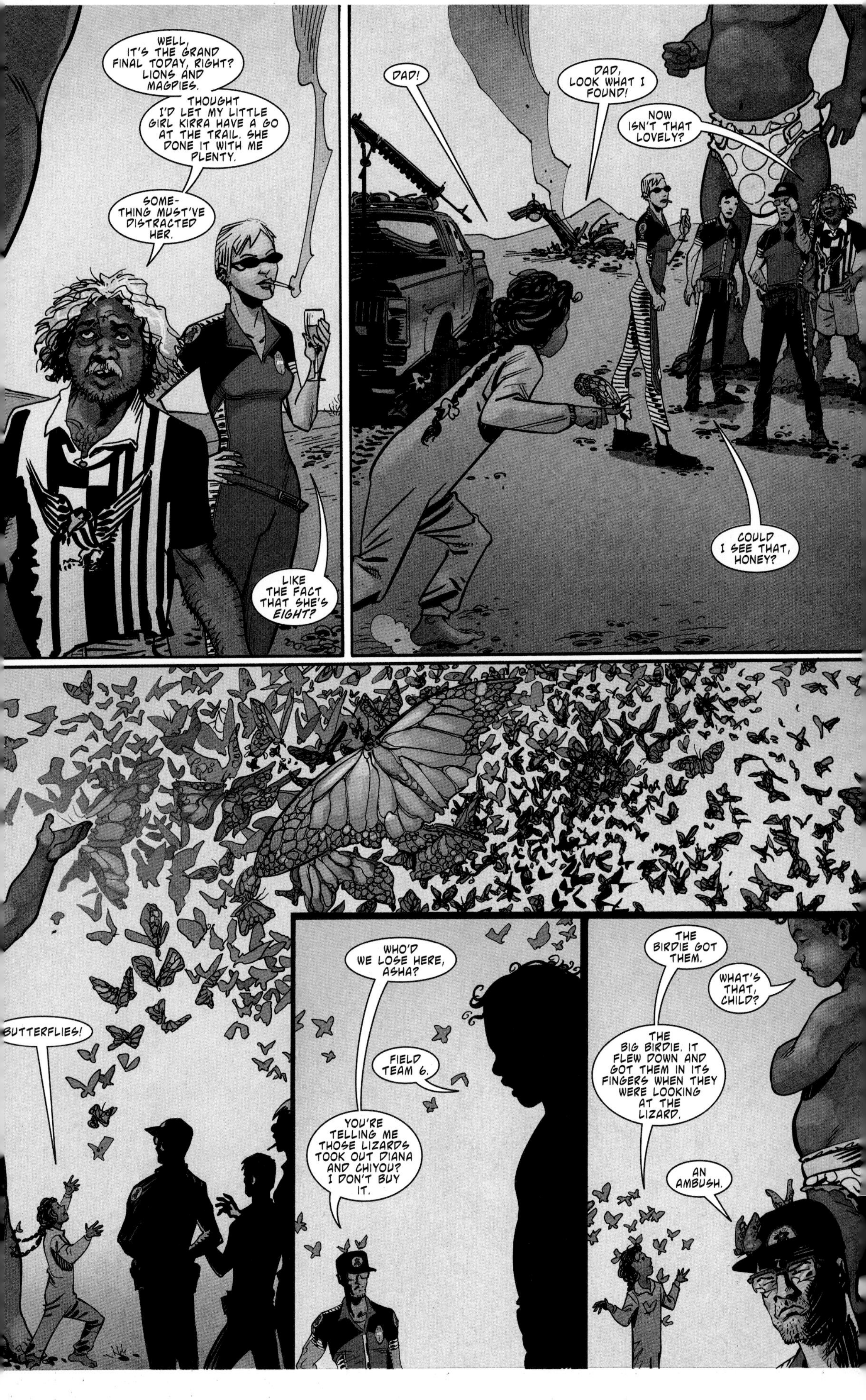

WELL, IT'S THE GRAND FINAL TODAY, RIGHT? LIONS AND MAGPIES.
THOUGHT I'D LET MY LITTLE GIRL KIRRA HAVE A GO AT THE TRAIL. SHE DONE IT WITH ME PLENTY.
SOME-THING MUST'VE DISTRACTED HER.
LIKE THE FACT THAT SHE'S *EIGHT?*
DAD!
DAD, LOOK WHAT I FOUND!
NOW ISN'T THAT LOVELY?
COULD I SEE THAT, HONEY?
BUTTERFLIES!
WHO'D WE LOSE HERE, ASHA?
FIELD TEAM 6.
YOU'RE TELLING ME THOSE LIZARDS TOOK OUT DIANA AND CHIYOU? I DON'T BUY IT.
THE BIRDIE GOT THEM.
WHAT'S THAT, CHILD?
THE BIG BIRDIE. IT FLEW DOWN AND GOT THEM IN ITS FINGERS WHEN THEY WERE LOOKING AT THE LIZARD.
AN AMBUSH.

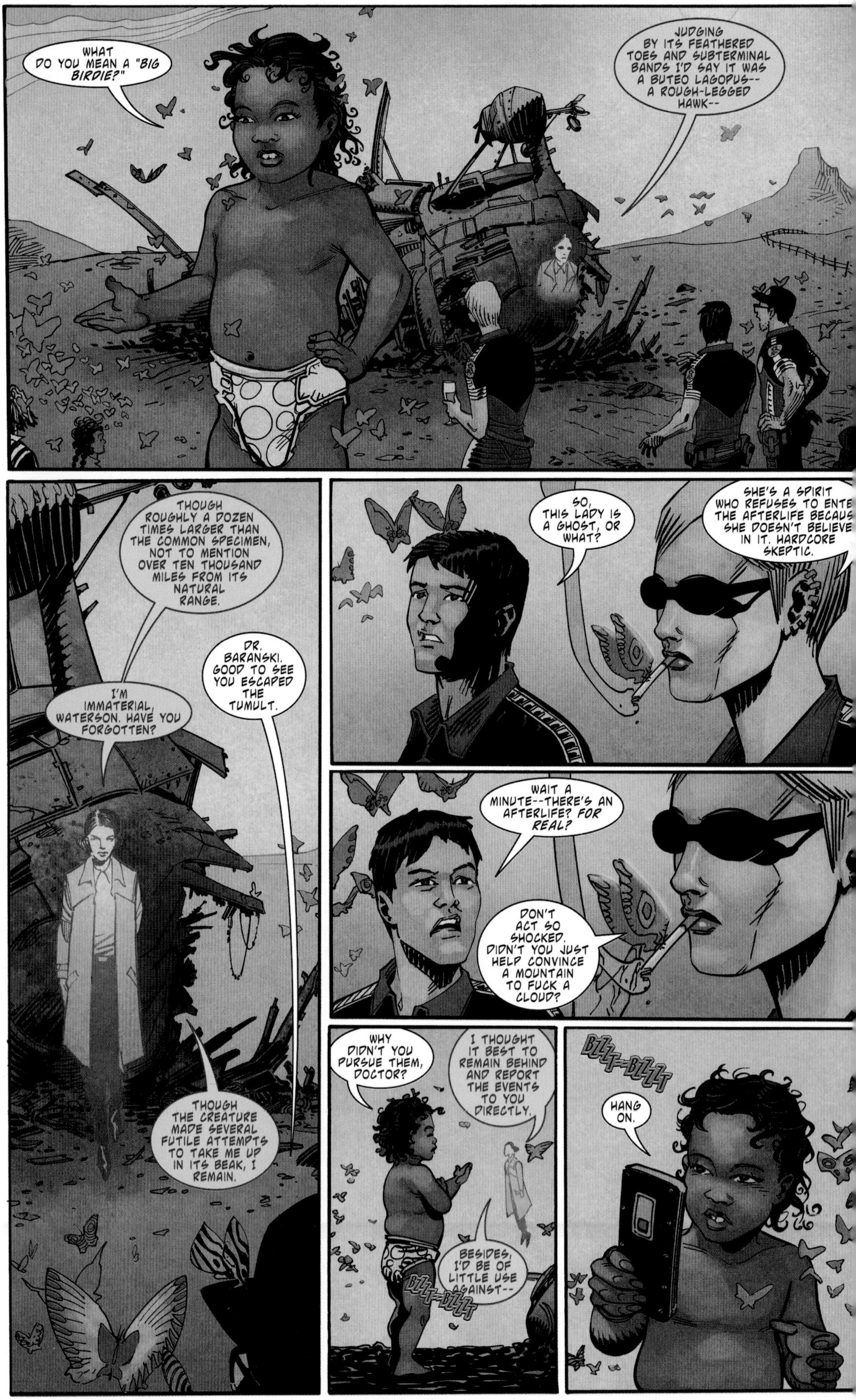

WHAT DO YOU MEAN A "BIG BIRDIE?"
JUDGING BY ITS FEATHERED TOES AND SUBTERMINAL BANDS I'D SAY IT WAS A BUTEO LAGOPUS-- A ROUGH-LEGGED HAWK--
THOUGH ROUGHLY A DOZEN TIMES LARGER THAN THE COMMON SPECIMEN, NOT TO MENTION OVER TEN THOUSAND MILES FROM ITS NATURAL RANGE.
DR. BARANSKI. GOOD TO SEE YOU ESCAPED THE TUMULT.
I'M IMMATERIAL, WATERSON. HAVE YOU FORGOTTEN?
THOUGH THE CREATURE MADE SEVERAL FUTILE ATTEMPTS TO TAKE ME UP IN ITS BEAK, I REMAIN.
SO, THIS LADY IS A GHOST, OR WHAT?
SHE'S A SPIRIT WHO REFUSES TO ENTE THE AFTERLIFE BECAUS SHE DOESN'T BELIEVE IN IT. HARDCORE SKEPTIC.
WAIT A MINUTE--THERE'S AN AFTERLIFE? FOR REAL?
DON'T ACT SO SHOCKED. DIDN'T YOU JUST HELP CONVINCE A MOUNTAIN TO FUCK A CLOUD?
WHY DIDN'T YOU PURSUE THEM, DOCTOR?
I THOUGHT IT BEST TO REMAIN BEHIND AND REPORT THE EVENTS TO YOU DIRECTLY.
BESIDES, I'D BE OF LITTLE USE AGAINST--
BZZT-BZZZT
BZZT-BZZZT
HANG ON.

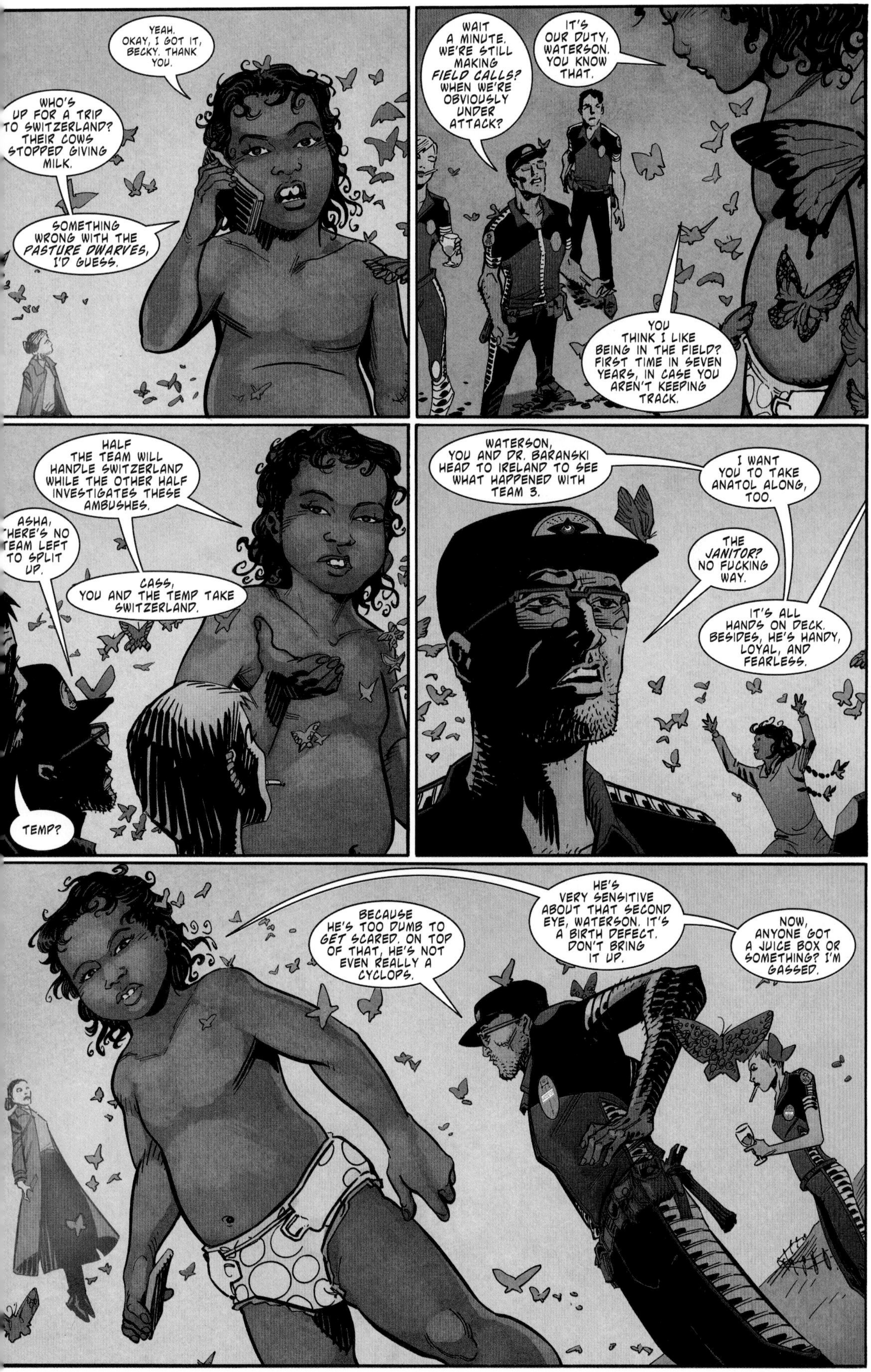
YEAH. OKAY, I GOT IT, BECKY. THANK YOU.
WHO'S UP FOR A TRIP TO SWITZERLAND? THEIR COWS STOPPED GIVING MILK.
SOMETHING WRONG WITH THE PASTURE DWARVES, I'D GUESS.
WAIT A MINUTE. WE'RE STILL MAKING FIELD CALLS? WHEN WE'RE OBVIOUSLY UNDER ATTACK?
IT'S OUR DUTY, WATERSON. YOU KNOW THAT.
YOU THINK I LIKE BEING IN THE FIELD? FIRST TIME IN SEVEN YEARS, IN CASE YOU AREN'T KEEPING TRACK.
HALF THE TEAM WILL HANDLE SWITZERLAND WHILE THE OTHER HALF INVESTIGATES THESE AMBUSHES.
ASHA, THERE'S NO TEAM LEFT TO SPLIT UP.
CASS, YOU AND THE TEMP TAKE SWITZERLAND.
TEMP?
WATERSON, YOU AND DR. BARANSKI HEAD TO IRELAND TO SEE WHAT HAPPENED WITH TEAM 3.
I WANT YOU TO TAKE ANATOL ALONG, TOO.
THE JANITOR? NO FUCKING WAY.
IT'S ALL HANDS ON DECK. BESIDES, HE'S HANDY, LOYAL, AND FEARLESS.
BECAUSE HE'S TOO DUMB TO GET SCARED. ON TOP OF THAT, HE'S NOT EVEN REALLY A CYCLOPS.
HE'S VERY SENSITIVE ABOUT THAT SECOND EYE, WATERSON. IT'S A BIRTH DEFECT. DON'T BRING IT UP.
NOW, ANYONE GOT A JUICE BOX OR SOMETHING? I'M GASSED.

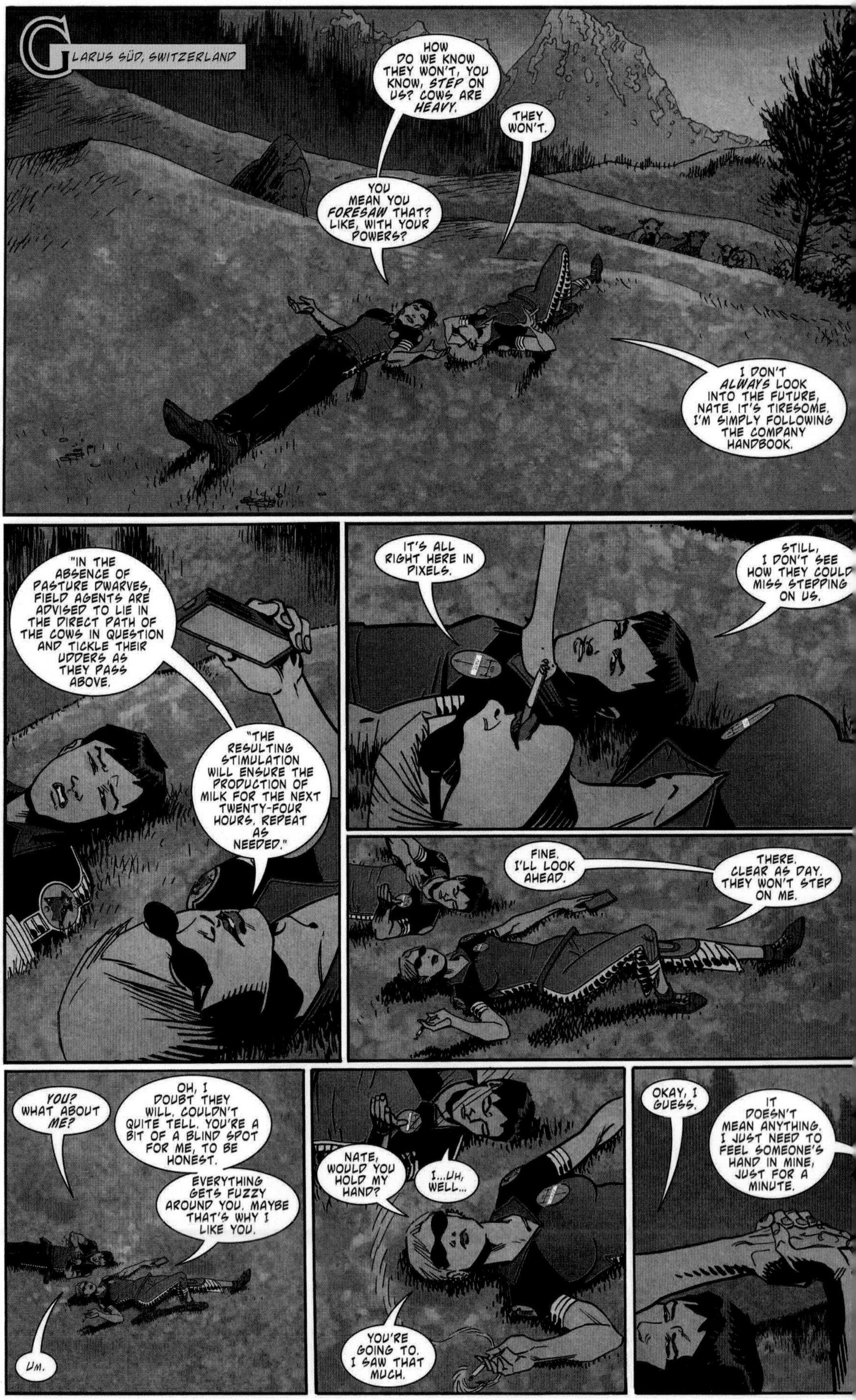
GLARUS SÜD, SWITZERLAND
HOW DO WE KNOW THEY WON'T, YOU KNOW, STEP ON US? COWS ARE HEAVY.
THEY WON'T.
YOU MEAN YOU FORESAW THAT? LIKE, WITH YOUR POWERS?
I DON'T ALWAYS LOOK INTO THE FUTURE, NATE. IT'S TIRESOME. I'M SIMPLY FOLLOWING THE COMPANY HANDBOOK.
"IN THE ABSENCE OF PASTURE DWARVES, FIELD AGENTS ARE ADVISED TO LIE IN THE DIRECT PATH OF THE COWS IN QUESTION AND TICKLE THEIR UDDERS AS THEY PASS ABOVE.
"THE RESULTING STIMULATION WILL ENSURE THE PRODUCTION OF MILK FOR THE NEXT TWENTY-FOUR HOURS. REPEAT AS NEEDED."
IT'S ALL RIGHT HERE IN PIXELS.
STILL, I DON'T SEE HOW THEY COULD MISS STEPPING ON US.
FINE. I'LL LOOK AHEAD.
THERE. CLEAR AS DAY. THEY WON'T STEP ON ME.
YOU? WHAT ABOUT ME?
OH, I DOUBT THEY WILL. COULDN'T QUITE TELL. YOU'RE A BIT OF A BLIND SPOT FOR ME, TO BE HONEST.
EVERYTHING GETS FUZZY AROUND YOU. MAYBE THAT'S WHY I LIKE YOU.
UM.
NATE, WOULD YOU HOLD MY HAND?
I...UH, WELL...
YOU'RE GOING TO. I SAW THAT MUCH.
OKAY, I GUESS.
IT DOESN'T MEAN ANYTHING. I JUST NEED TO FEEL SOMEONE'S HAND IN MINE, JUST FOR A MINUTE.

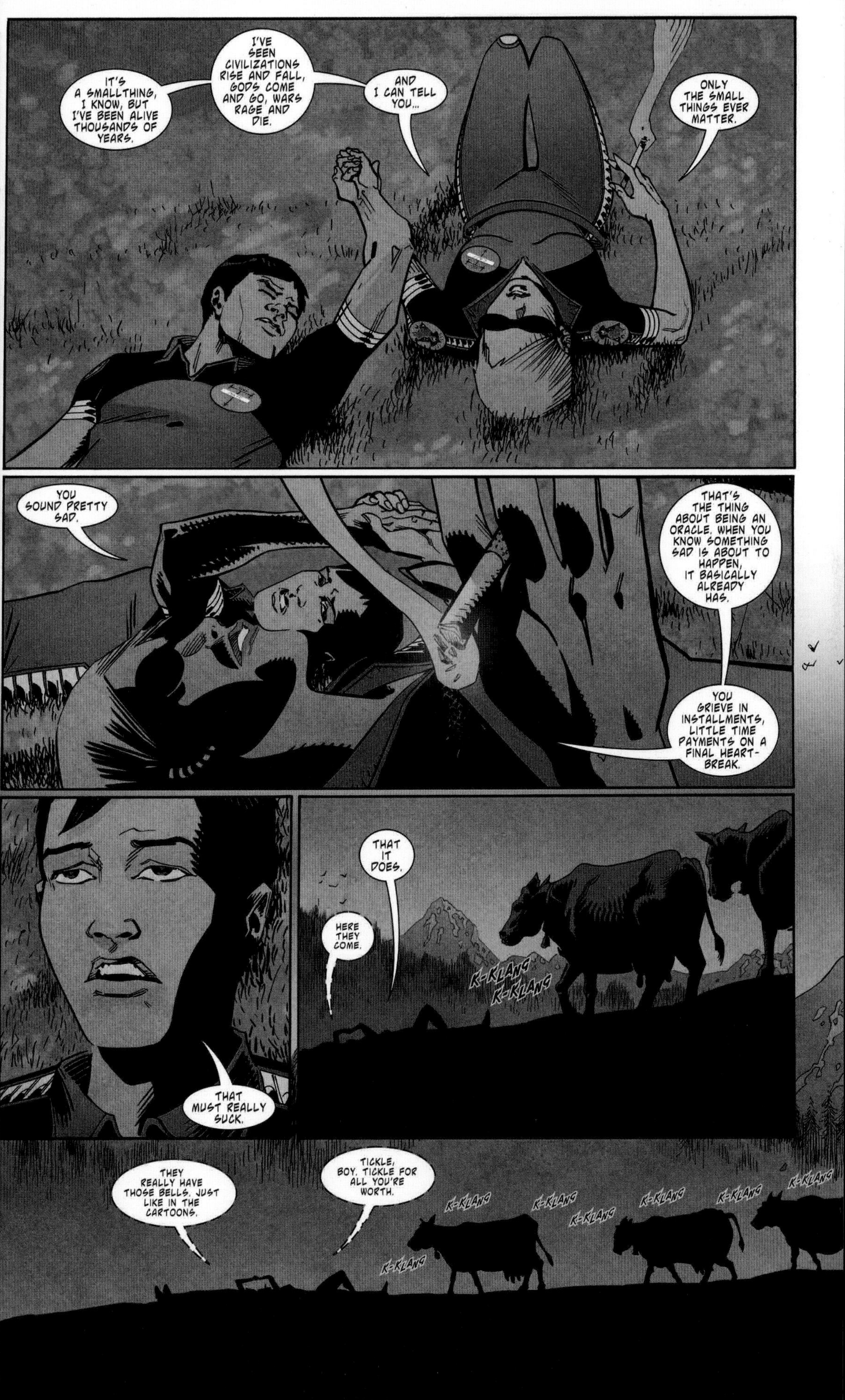
IT'S A SMALLTHING, I KNOW, BUT I'VE BEEN ALIVE THOUSANDS OF YEARS.
I'VE SEEN CIVILIZATIONS RISE AND FALL, GODS COME AND GO, WARS RAGE AND DIE.
AND I CAN TELL YOU...
ONLY THE SMALL THINGS EVER MATTER.
YOU SOUND PRETTY SAD.
THAT'S THE THING ABOUT BEING AN ORACLE. WHEN YOU KNOW SOMETHING SAD IS ABOUT TO HAPPEN, IT BASICALLY ALREADY HAS.
YOU GRIEVE IN INSTALLMENTS, LITTLE TIME PAYMENTS ON A FINAL HEART-BREAK.
THAT MUST REALLY SUCK.
THAT IT DOES.
HERE THEY COME.
K-KLANG K-KLANG
THEY REALLY HAVE THOSE BELLS, JUST LIKE IN THE CARTOONS.
TICKLE, BOY. TICKLE FOR ALL YOU'RE WORTH.
K-KLANG K-KLANG K-KLANG K-KLANG K-KLANG K-KLANG K-KLANG

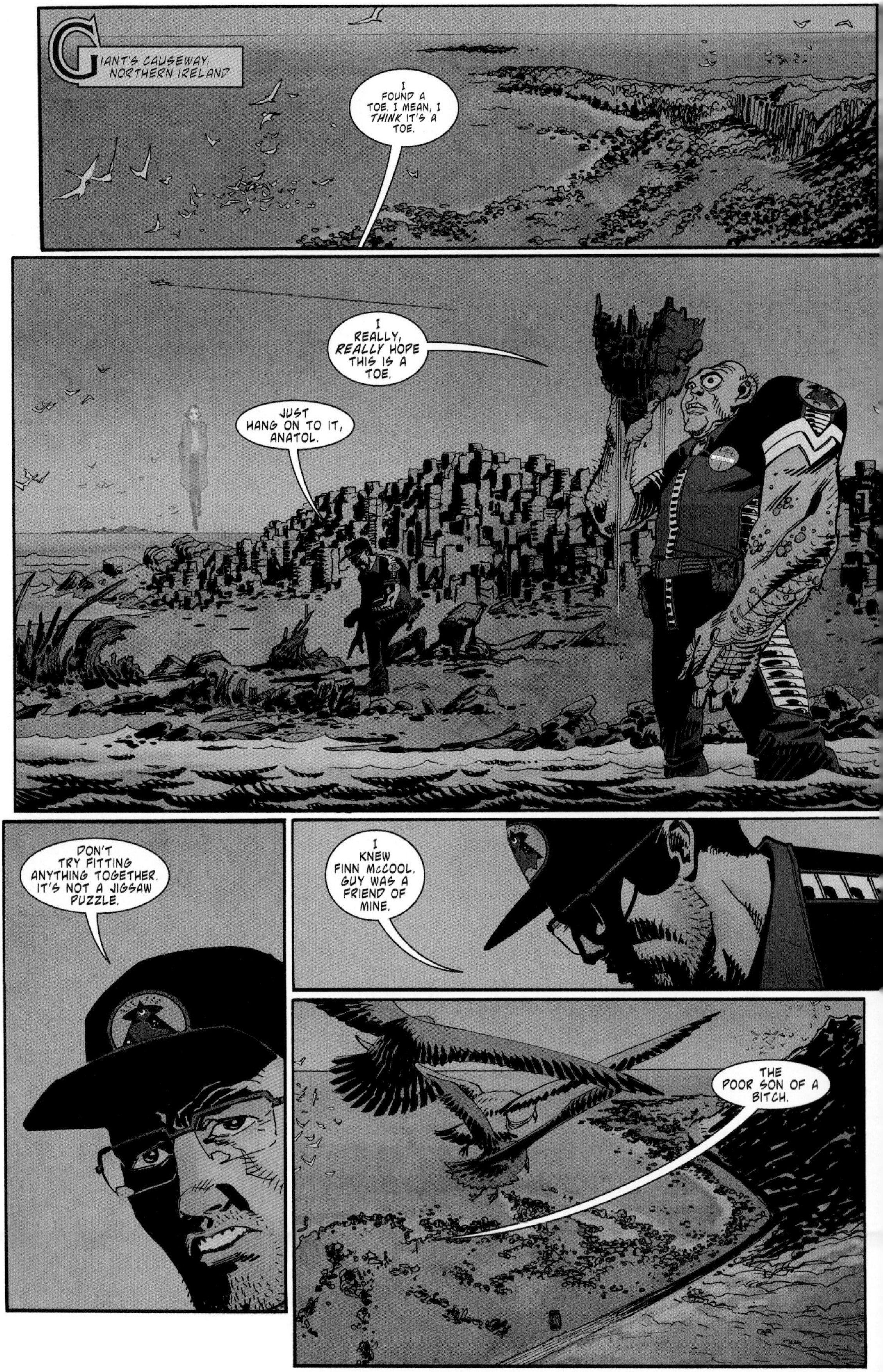
GIANT'S CAUSEWAY, NORTHERN IRELAND
I FOUND A TOE. I MEAN, I *THINK* IT'S A TOE.
I REALLY, *REALLY* HOPE THIS IS A TOE.
JUST HANG ON TO IT, ANATOL.
DON'T TRY FITTING ANYTHING TOGETHER. IT'S NOT A JIGSAW PUZZLE.
I KNEW FINN McCOOL. GUY WAS A FRIEND OF MINE.
THE POOR SON OF A BITCH.

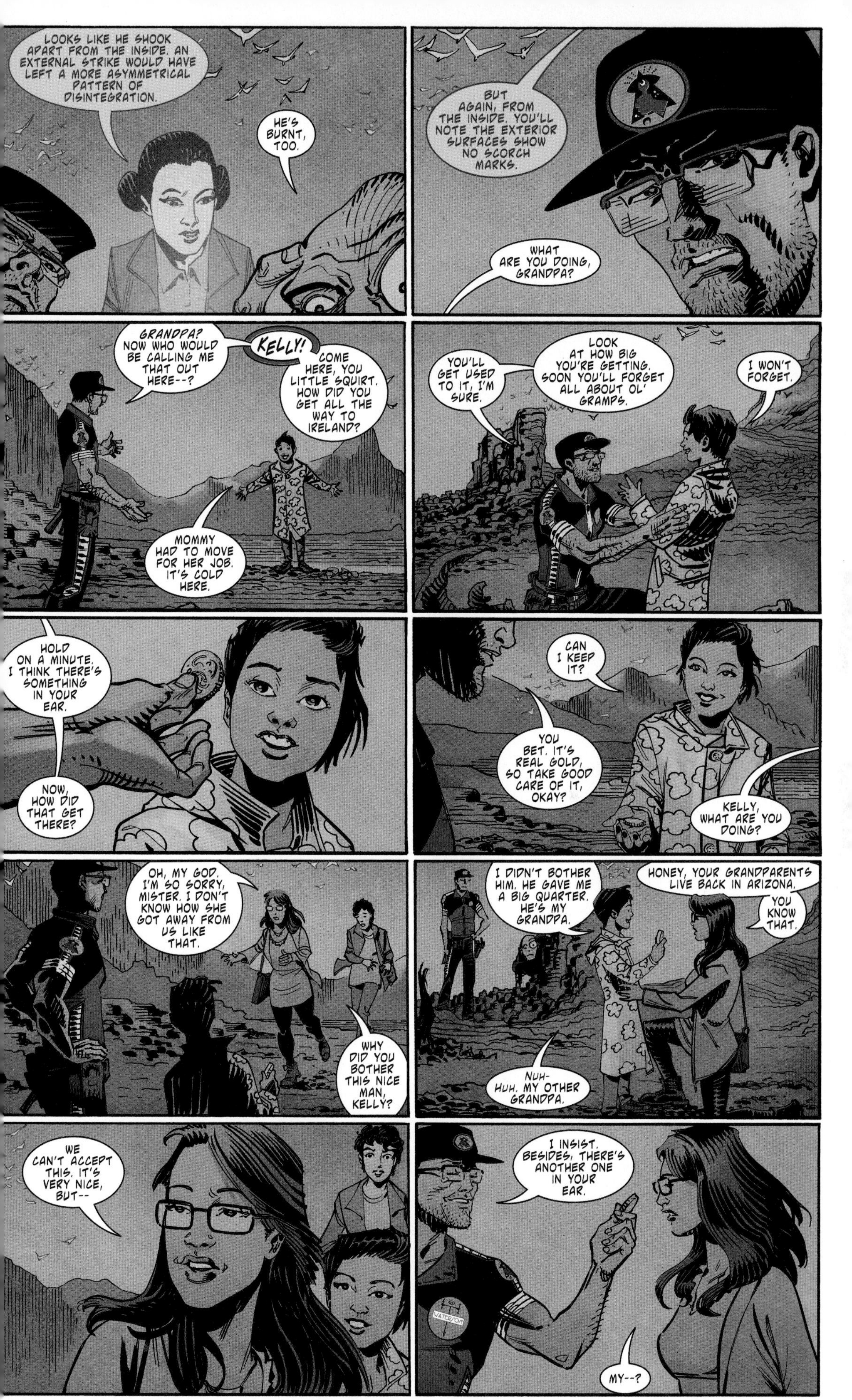
LOOKS LIKE HE SHOOK APART FROM THE INSIDE. AN EXTERNAL STRIKE WOULD HAVE LEFT A MORE ASYMMETRICAL PATTERN OF DISINTEGRATION.
HE'S BURNT, TOO.
BUT AGAIN, FROM THE INSIDE. YOU'LL NOTE THE EXTERIOR SURFACES SHOW NO SCORCH MARKS.
WHAT ARE YOU DOING, GRANDPA?
GRANDPA? NOW WHO WOULD BE CALLING ME THAT OUT HERE--?
KELLY!
COME HERE, YOU LITTLE SQUIRT. HOW DID YOU GET ALL THE WAY TO IRELAND?
MOMMY HAD TO MOVE FOR HER JOB. IT'S COLD HERE.
YOU'LL GET USED TO IT, I'M SURE.
LOOK AT HOW BIG YOU'RE GETTING. SOON YOU'LL FORGET ALL ABOUT OL' GRAMPS.
I WON'T FORGET.
HOLD ON A MINUTE. I THINK THERE'S SOMETHING IN YOUR EAR.
NOW, HOW DID THAT GET THERE?
CAN I KEEP IT?
YOU BET. IT'S REAL GOLD, SO TAKE GOOD CARE OF IT, OKAY?
KELLY, WHAT ARE YOU DOING?
OH, MY GOD. I'M SO SORRY, MISTER. I DON'T KNOW HOW SHE GOT AWAY FROM US LIKE THAT.
WHY DID YOU BOTHER THIS NICE MAN, KELLY?
I DIDN'T BOTHER HIM. HE GAVE ME A BIG QUARTER. HE'S MY GRANDPA.
HONEY, YOUR GRANDPARENTS LIVE BACK IN ARIZONA.
YOU KNOW THAT.
NUH-HUH. MY OTHER GRANDPA.
WE CAN'T ACCEPT THIS. IT'S VERY NICE, BUT--
I INSIST. BESIDES, THERE'S ANOTHER ONE IN YOUR EAR.
WATERSON
MY--?

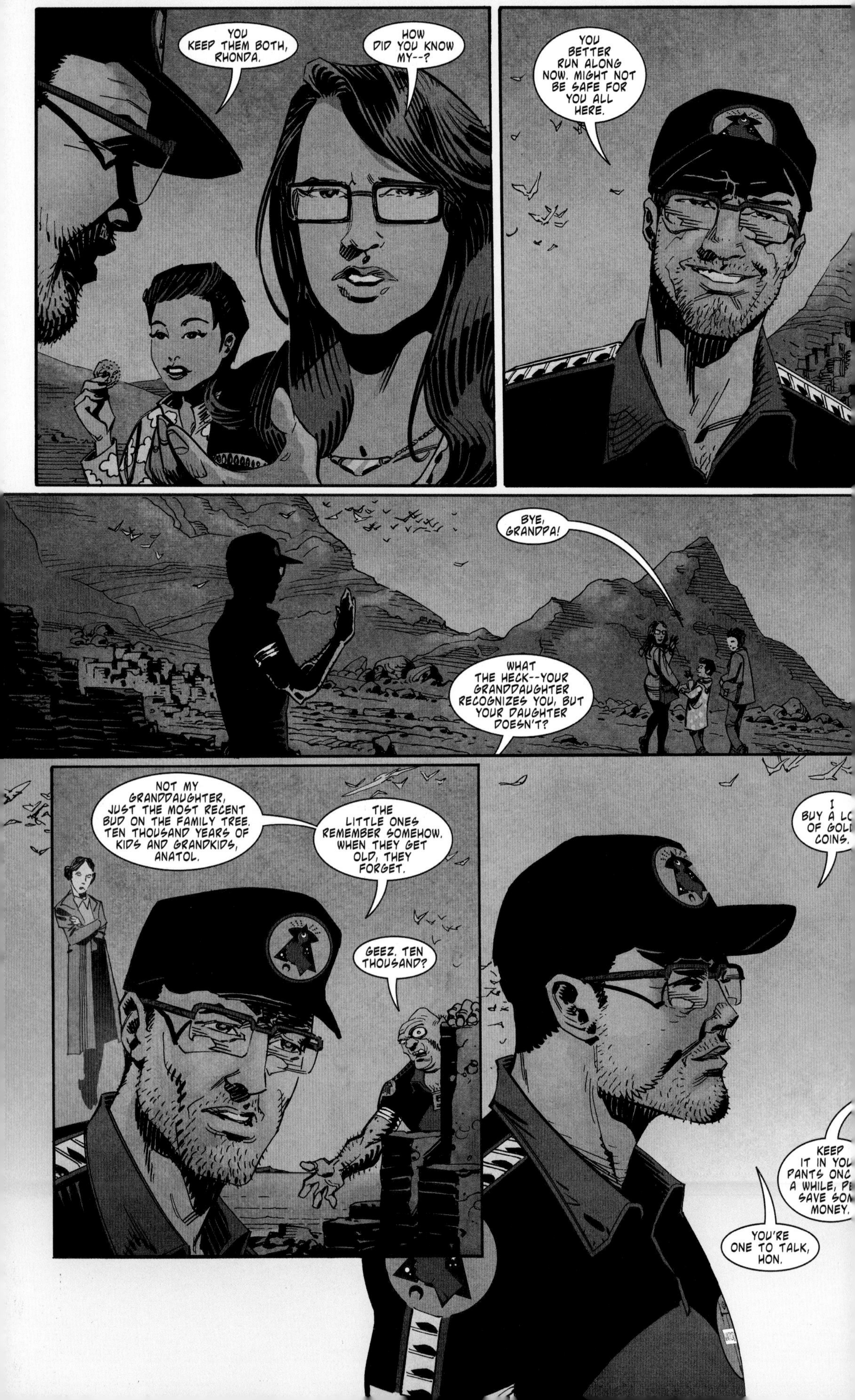
YOU KEEP THEM BOTH, RHONDA.
HOW DID YOU KNOW MY--?
YOU BETTER RUN ALONG NOW. MIGHT NOT BE SAFE FOR YOU ALL HERE.
BYE, GRANDPA!
WHAT THE HECK--YOUR GRANDDAUGHTER RECOGNIZES YOU, BUT YOUR DAUGHTER DOESN'T?
NOT MY GRANDDAUGHTER, JUST THE MOST RECENT BUD ON THE FAMILY TREE. TEN THOUSAND YEARS OF KIDS AND GRANDKIDS, ANATOL.
THE LITTLE ONES REMEMBER SOMEHOW. WHEN THEY GET OLD, THEY FORGET.
GEEZ. TEN THOUSAND?
YOU'RE ONE TO TALK, HON.

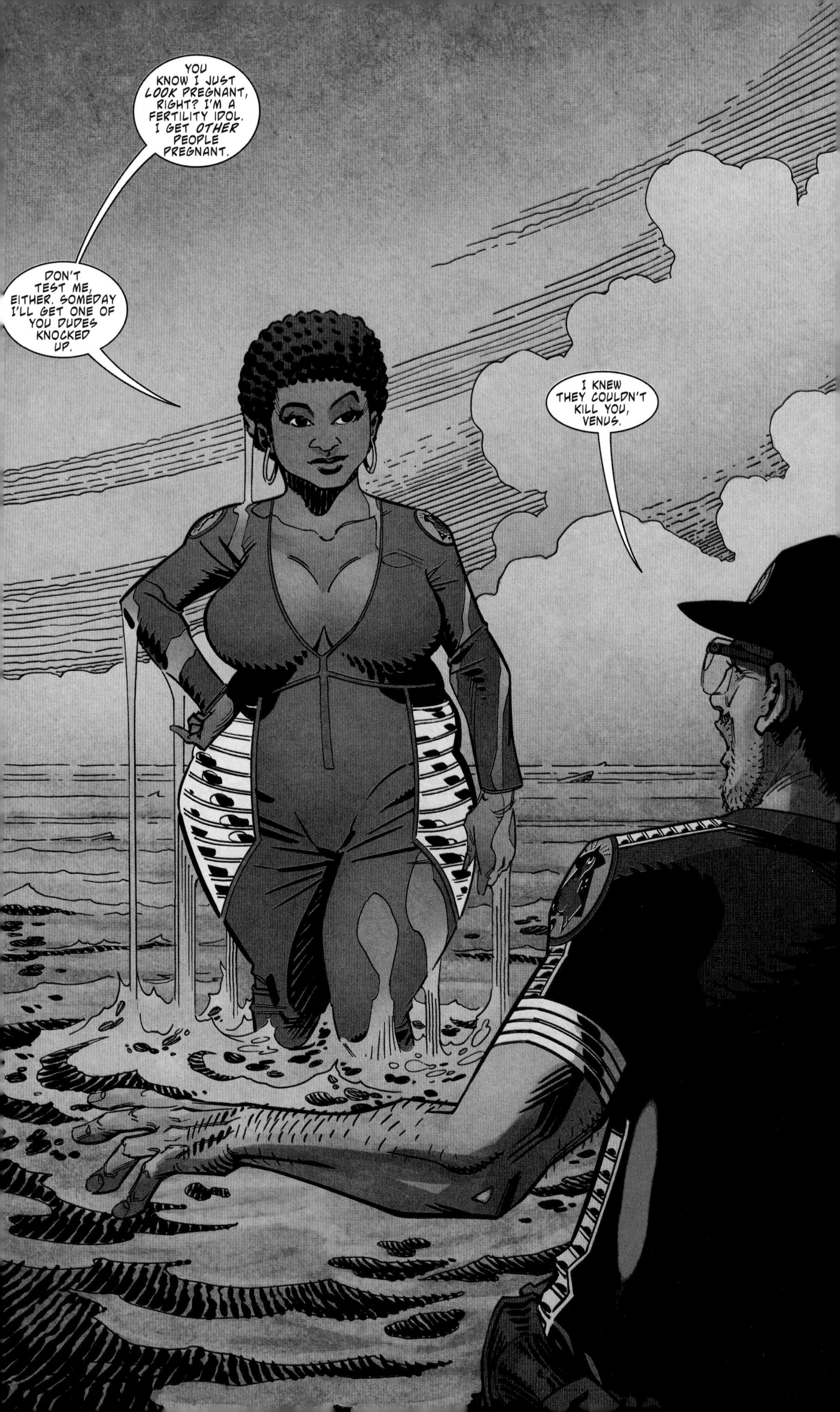

YOU KNOW I JUST LOOK PREGNANT, RIGHT? I'M A FERTILITY IDOL. I GET OTHER PEOPLE PREGNANT.
DON'T TEST ME, EITHER. SOMEDAY I'LL GET ONE OF YOU DUDES KNOCKED UP.
I KNEW THEY COULDN'T KILL YOU, VENUS.

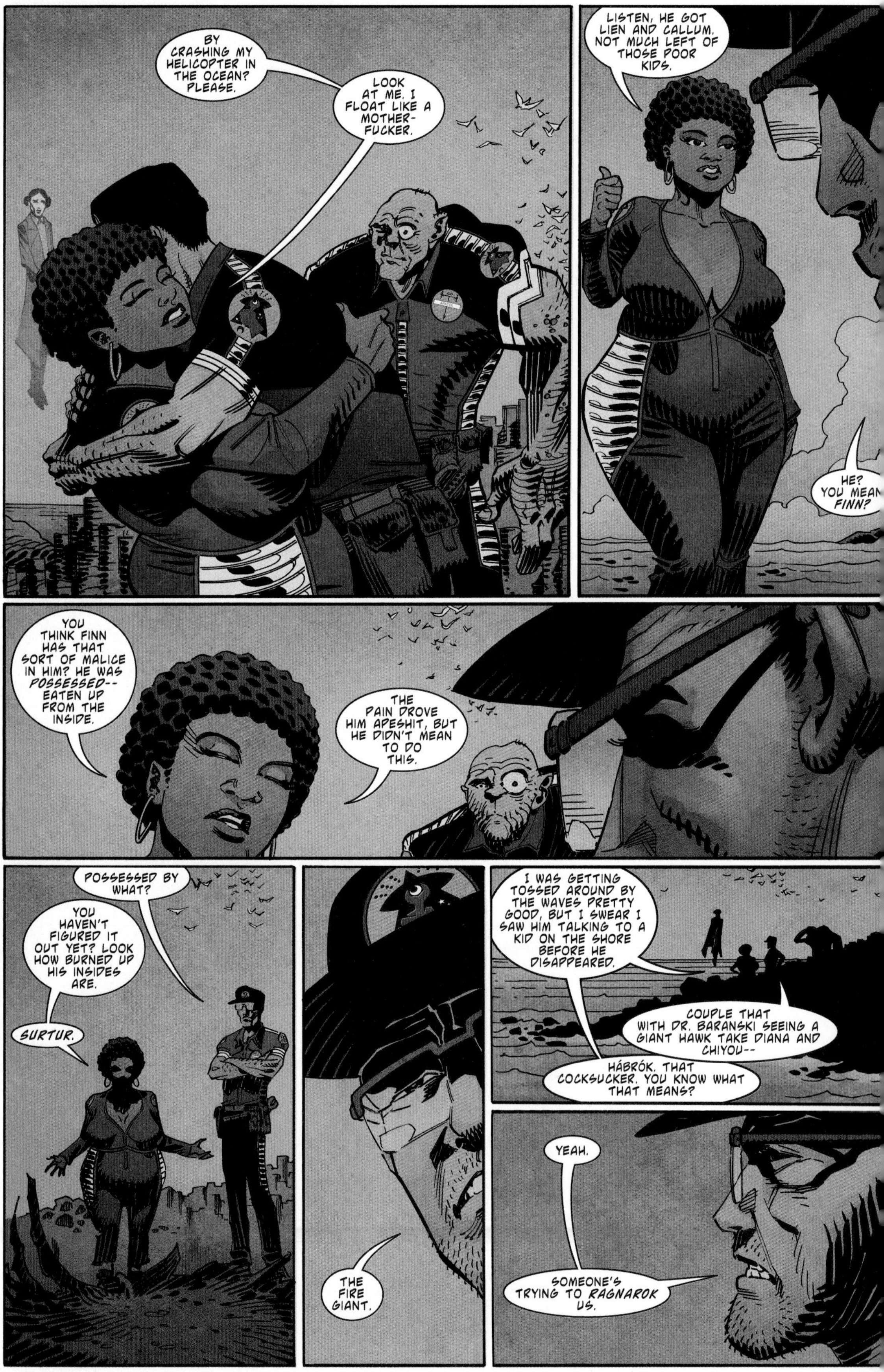
BY CRASHING MY HELICOPTER IN THE OCEAN? PLEASE.
LOOK AT ME. I FLOAT LIKE A MOTHER-FUCKER.
LISTEN, HE GOT LIEN AND CALLUM. NOT MUCH LEFT OF THOSE POOR KIDS.
HE? YOU MEAN FINN?
YOU THINK FINN HAS THAT SORT OF MALICE IN HIM? HE WAS POSSESSED--EATEN UP FROM THE INSIDE.
THE PAIN DROVE HIM APESHIT, BUT HE DIDN'T MEAN TO DO THIS.
POSSESSED BY WHAT?
YOU HAVEN'T FIGURED IT OUT YET? LOOK HOW BURNED UP HIS INSIDES ARE.
SURTUR.
THE FIRE GIANT.
I WAS GETTING TOSSED AROUND BY THE WAVES PRETTY GOOD, BUT I SWEAR I SAW HIM TALKING TO A KID ON THE SHORE BEFORE HE DISAPPEARED.
COUPLE THAT WITH DR. BARANSKI SEEING A GIANT HAWK TAKE DIANA AND CHIYOU--
HÁBRÓK. THAT COCKSUCKER. YOU KNOW WHAT THAT MEANS?
YEAH.
SOMEONE'S TRYING TO RAGNAROK US.

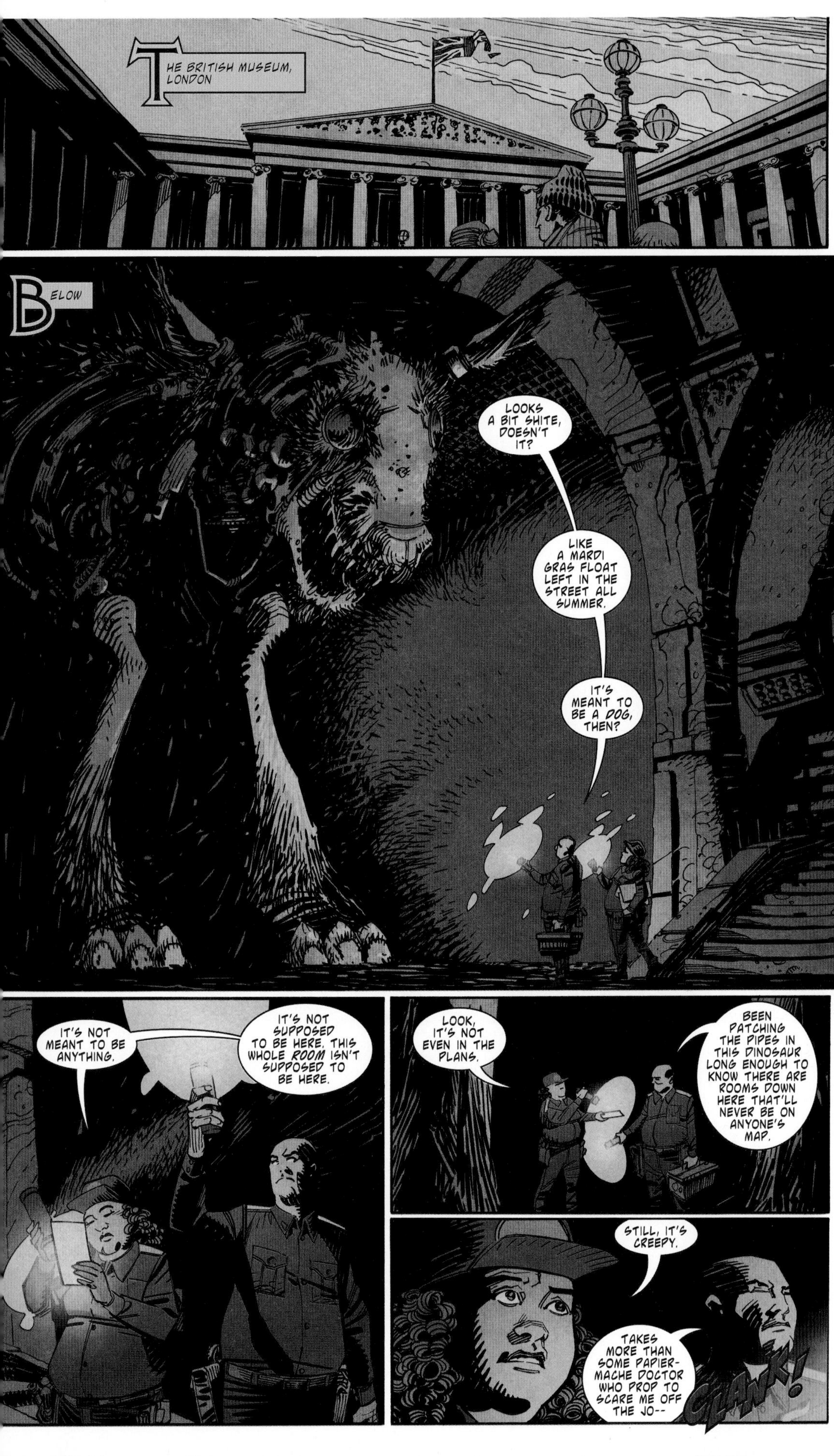
THE BRITISH MUSEUM, LONDON
BELOW
LOOKS A BIT SHITE, DOESN'T IT?
LIKE A MARDI GRAS FLOAT LEFT IN THE STREET ALL SUMMER.
IT'S MEANT TO BE A DOG, THEN?
IT'S NOT MEANT TO BE ANYTHING.
IT'S NOT SUPPOSED TO BE HERE. THIS WHOLE ROOM ISN'T SUPPOSED TO BE HERE.
LOOK, IT'S NOT EVEN IN THE PLANS.
BEEN PATCHING THE PIPES IN THIS DINOSAUR LONG ENOUGH TO KNOW THERE ARE ROOMS DOWN HERE THAT'LL NEVER BE ON ANYONE'S MAP.
STILL, IT'S CREEPY.
TAKES MORE THAN SOME PAPIER-MACHE DOCTOR WHO PROP TO SCARE ME OFF THE JO--
CLANK!

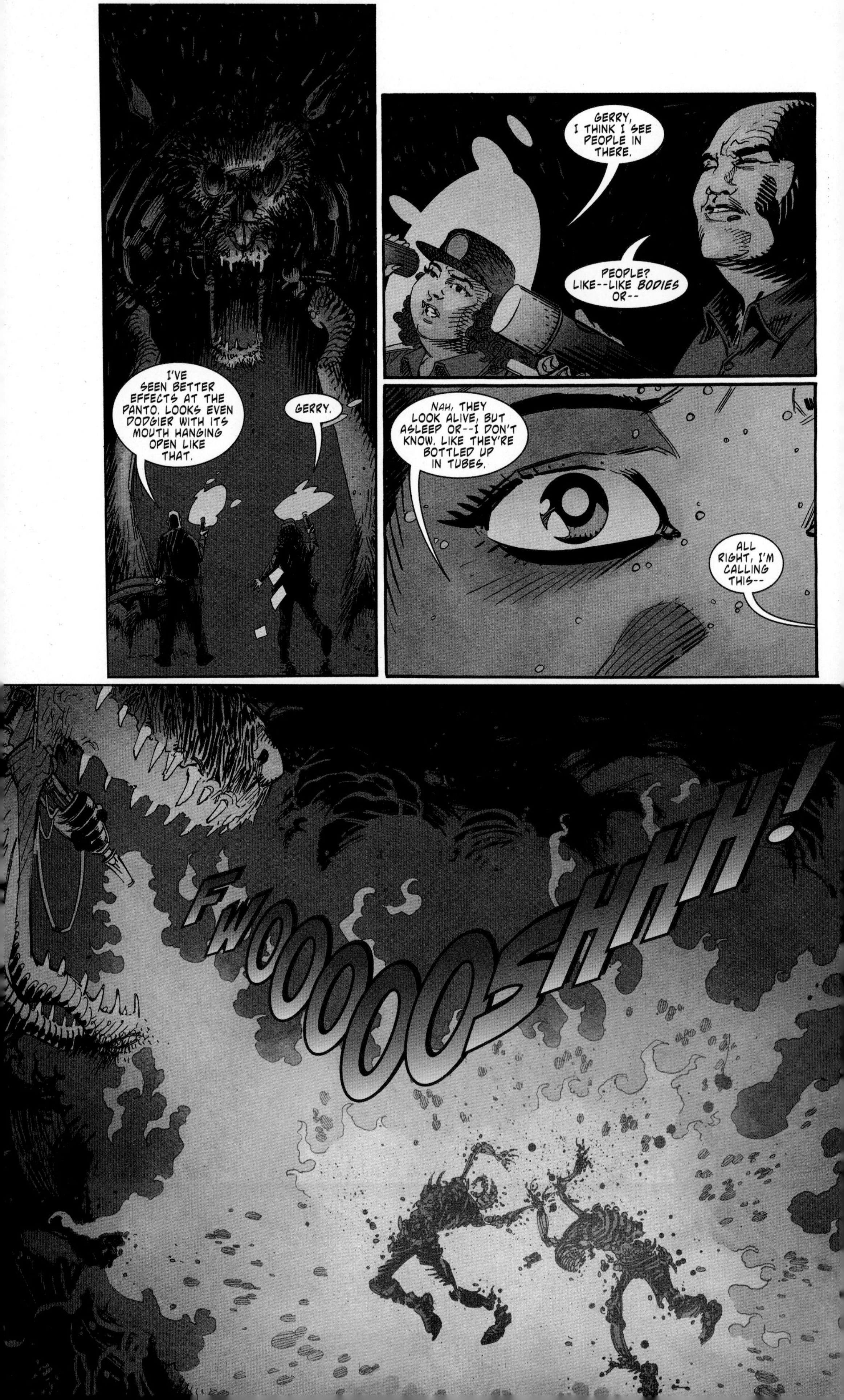
I'VE SEEN BETTER EFFECTS AT THE PANTO. LOOKS EVEN DODGIER WITH ITS MOUTH HANGING OPEN LIKE THAT.
GERRY.
GERRY, I THINK I SEE PEOPLE IN THERE.
PEOPLE? LIKE--LIKE BODIES OR--
NAH, THEY LOOK ALIVE, BUT ASLEEP OR--I DON'T KNOW. LIKE THEY'RE BOTTLED UP IN TUBES.
ALL RIGHT, I'M CALLING THIS--
FWOOOOOOSHHH!

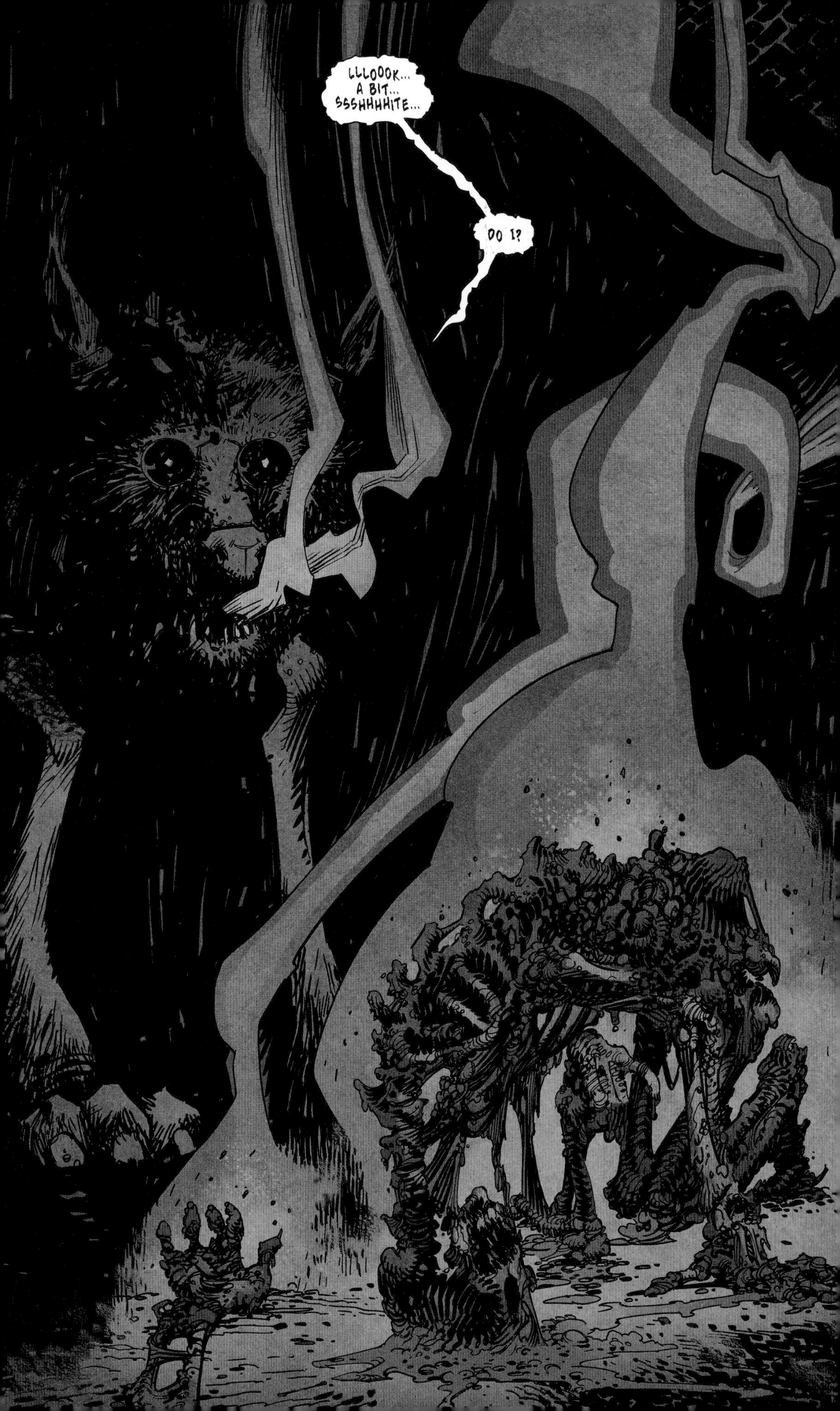
LLLOOOK... A BIT... SSSHHHHITE...
DO I?

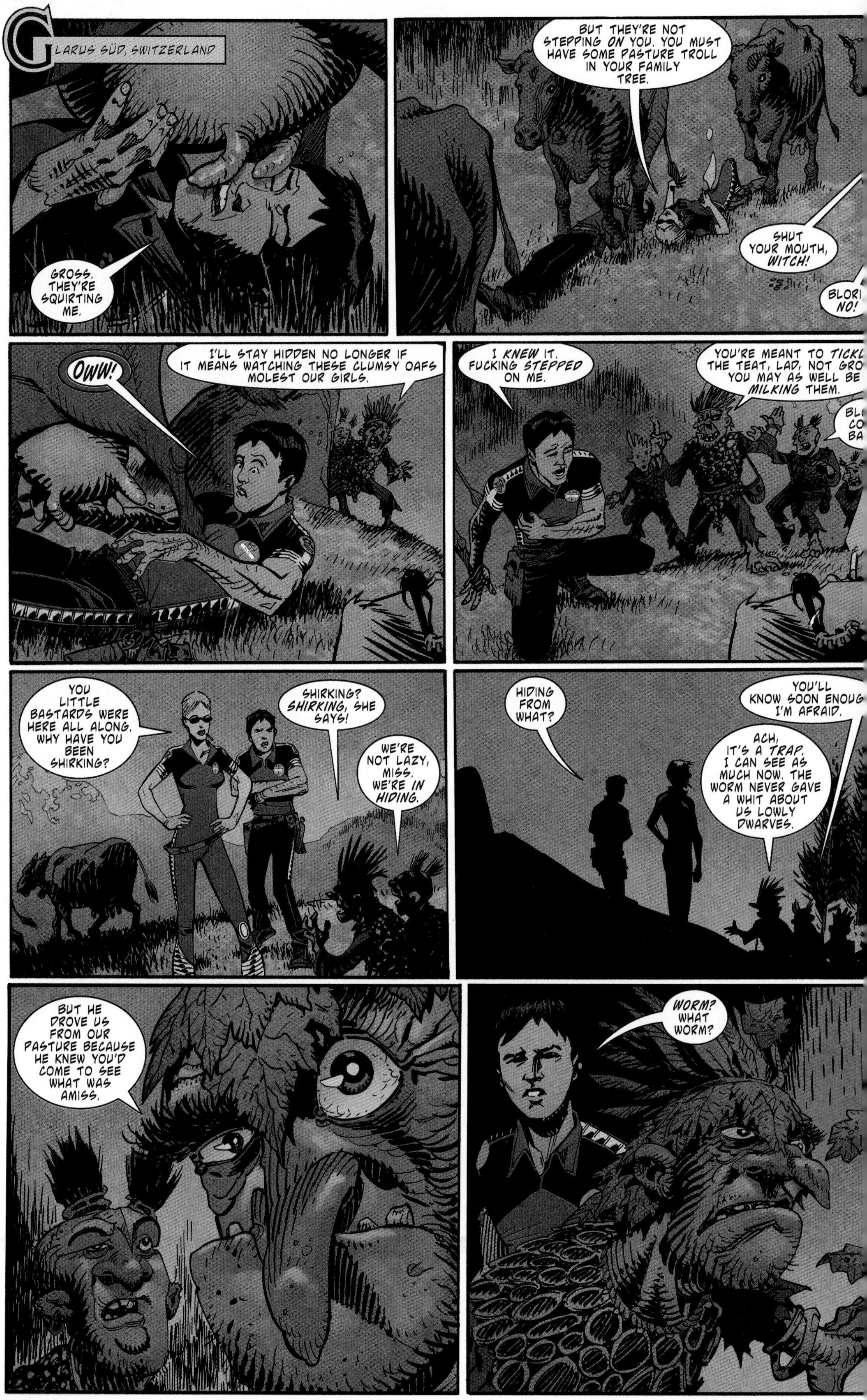
GLARUS SÜD, SWITZERLAND
GROSS. THEY'RE SQUIRTING ME.
BUT THEY'RE NOT STEPPING ON YOU. YOU MUST HAVE SOME PASTURE TROLL IN YOUR FAMILY TREE.
SHUT YOUR MOUTH, WITCH!
BLORI NO!
OWW!
I'LL STAY HIDDEN NO LONGER IF IT MEANS WATCHING THESE CLUMSY OAFS MOLEST OUR GIRLS.
I KNEW IT. FUCKING STEPPED ON ME.
YOU'RE MEANT TO TICKL THE TEAT, LAD, NOT GRO YOU MAY AS WELL BE MILKING THEM.
YOU LITTLE BASTARDS WERE HERE ALL ALONG. WHY HAVE YOU BEEN SHIRKING?
SHIRKING? SHIRKING, SHE SAYS!
WE'RE NOT LAZY, MISS. WE'RE IN HIDING.
HIDING FROM WHAT?
YOU'LL KNOW SOON ENOUG I'M AFRAID.
ACH, IT'S A TRAP. I CAN SEE AS MUCH NOW. THE WORM NEVER GAVE A WHIT ABOUT US LOWLY DWARVES.
BUT HE DROVE US FROM OUR PASTURE BECAUSE HE KNEW YOU'D COME TO SEE WHAT WAS AMISS.
WORM? WHAT WORM?

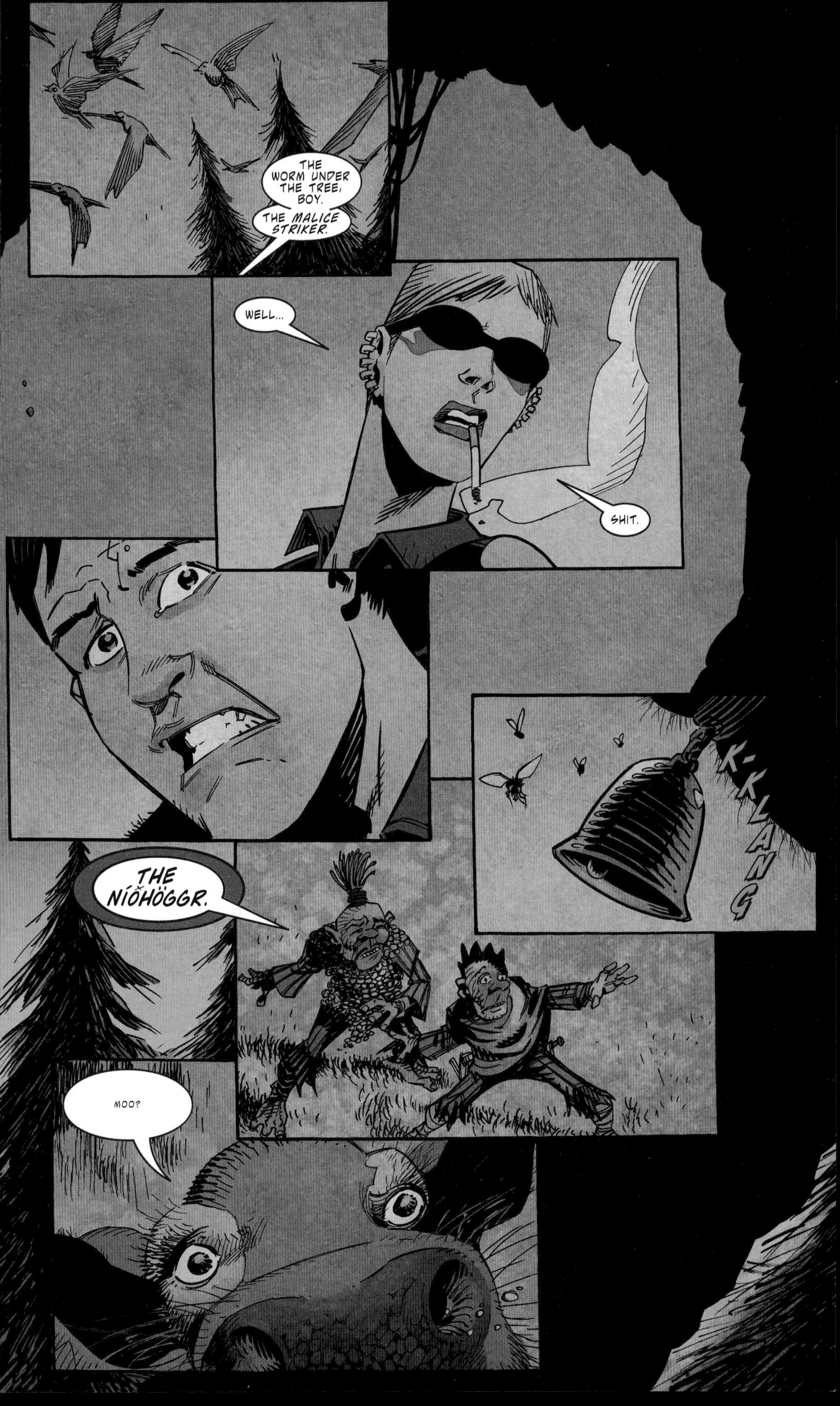
THE WORM UNDER THE TREE, BOY.
THE MALICE STRIKER.
WELL...
SHIT.
K-KLANG
THE NÍÕHÖGGR.
MOO?

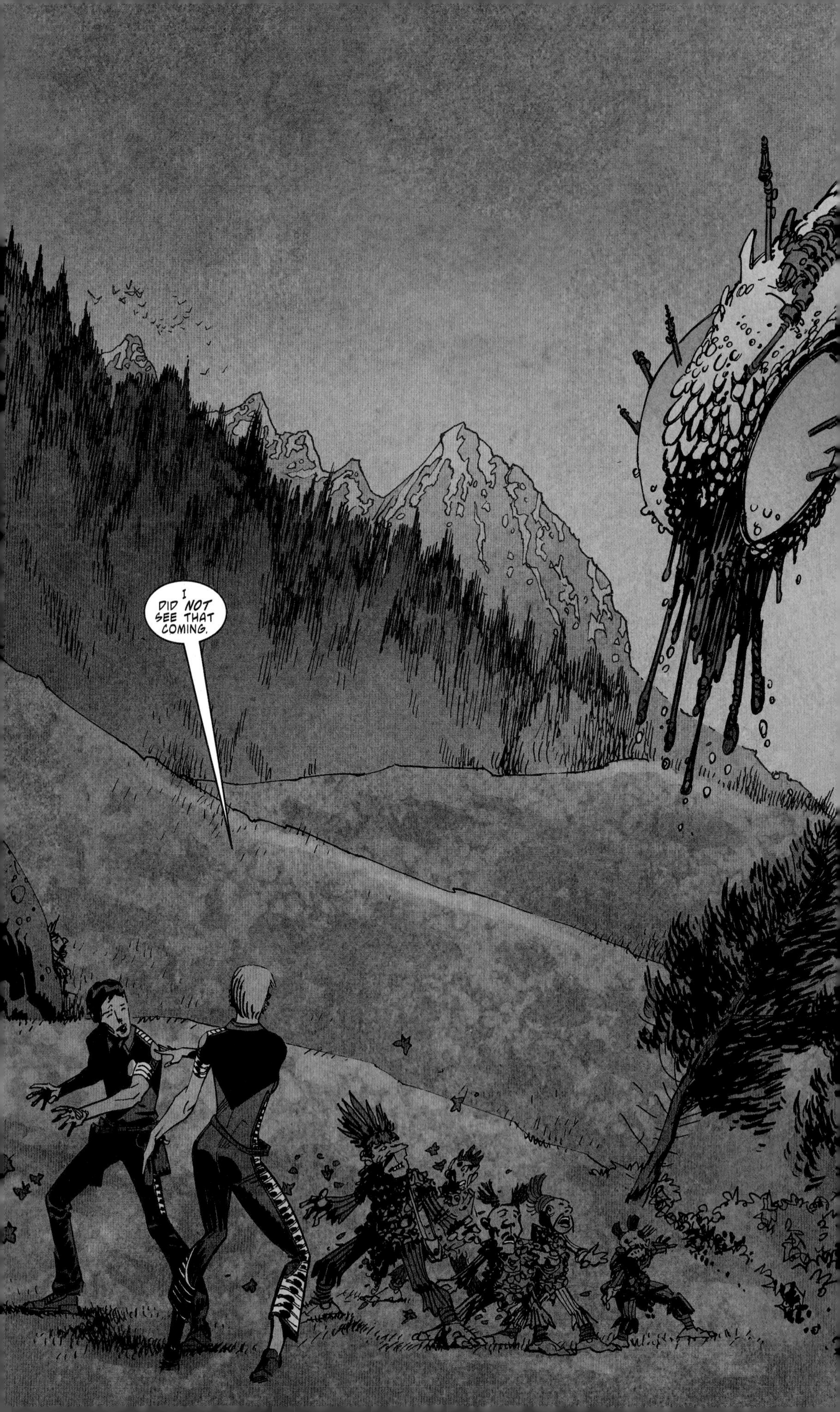
I DID NOT SEE THAT COMING.

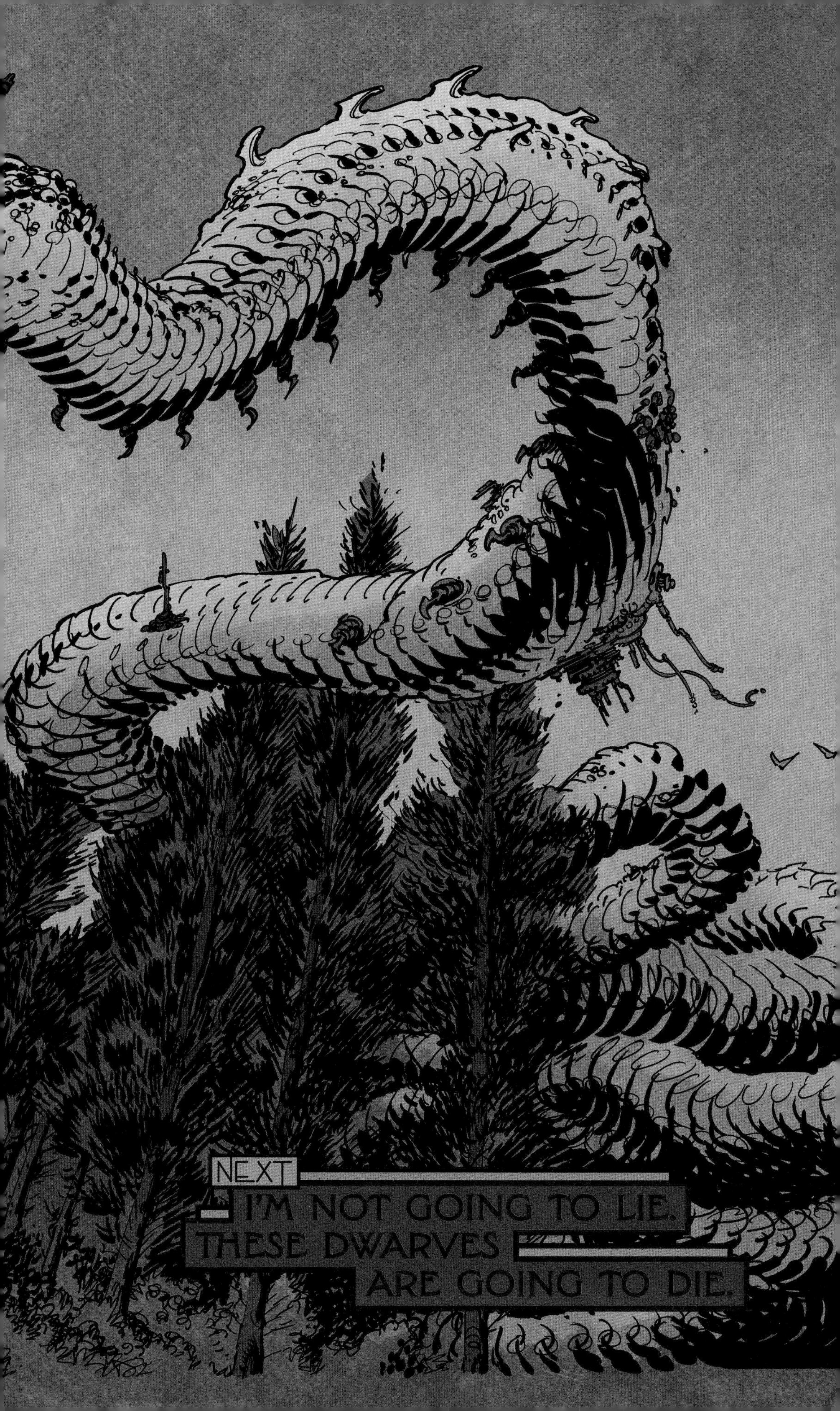
NEXT
I'M NOT GOING TO LIE.
THESE DWARVES
ARE GOING TO DIE.

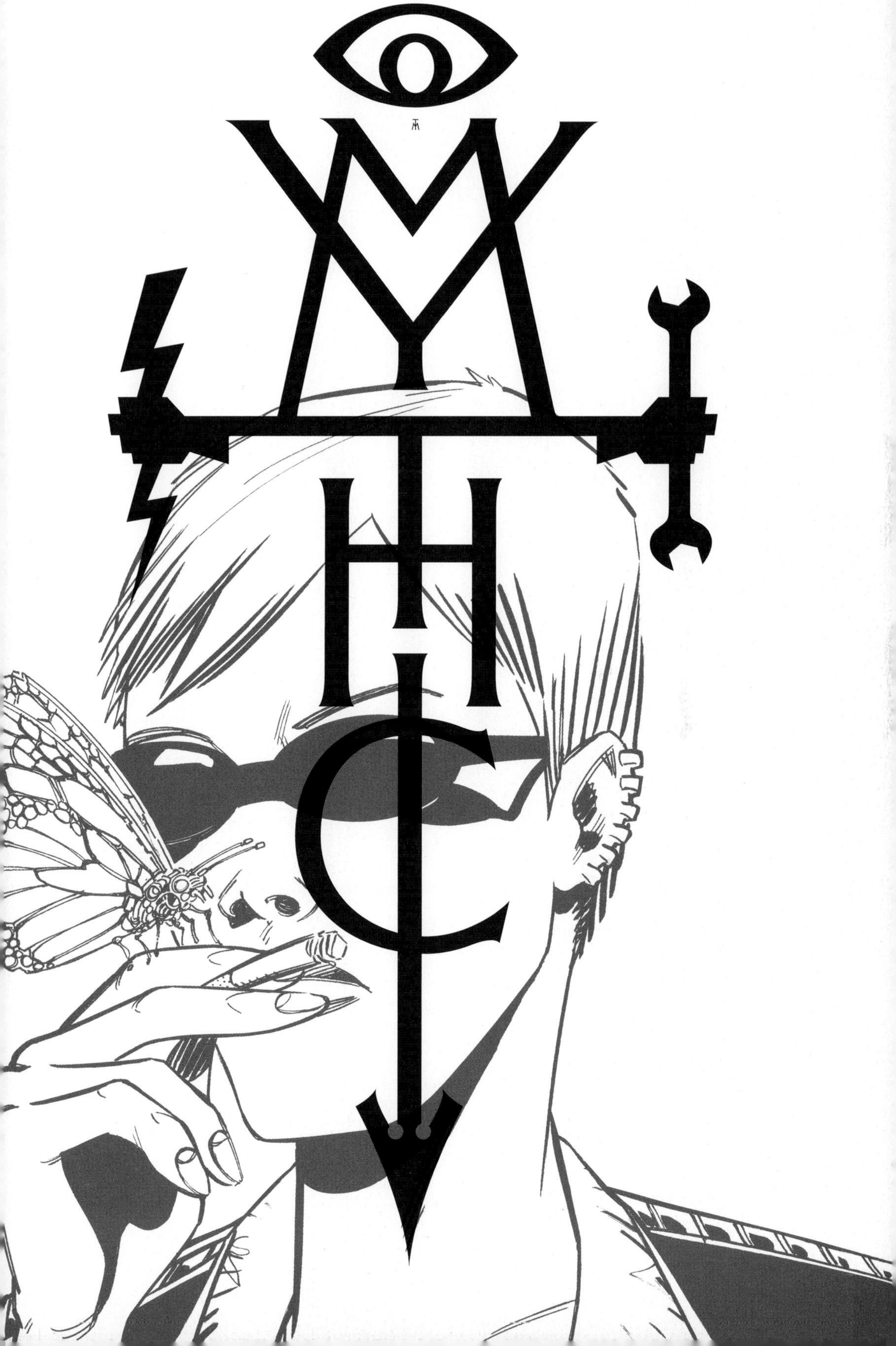

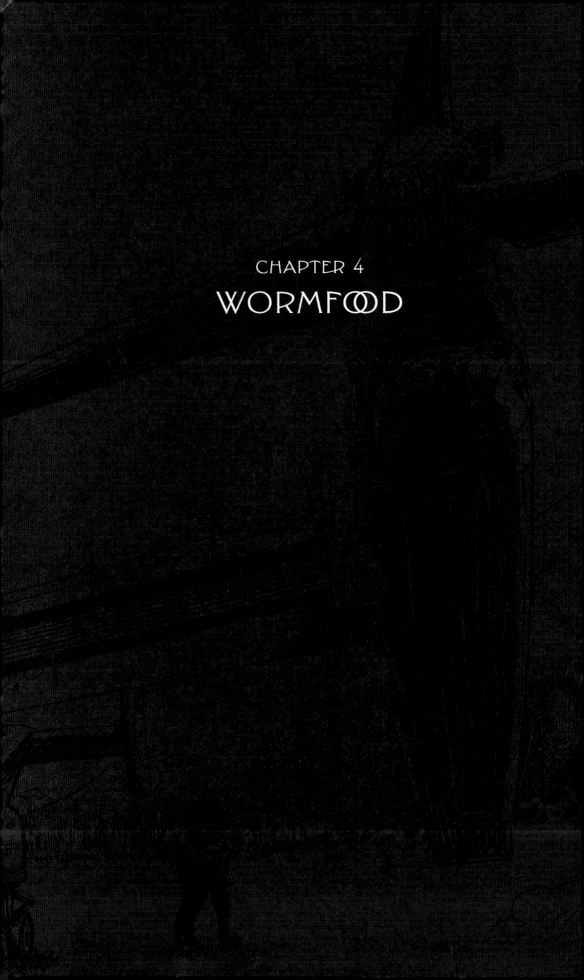

CHAPTER 4

WORMFOOD

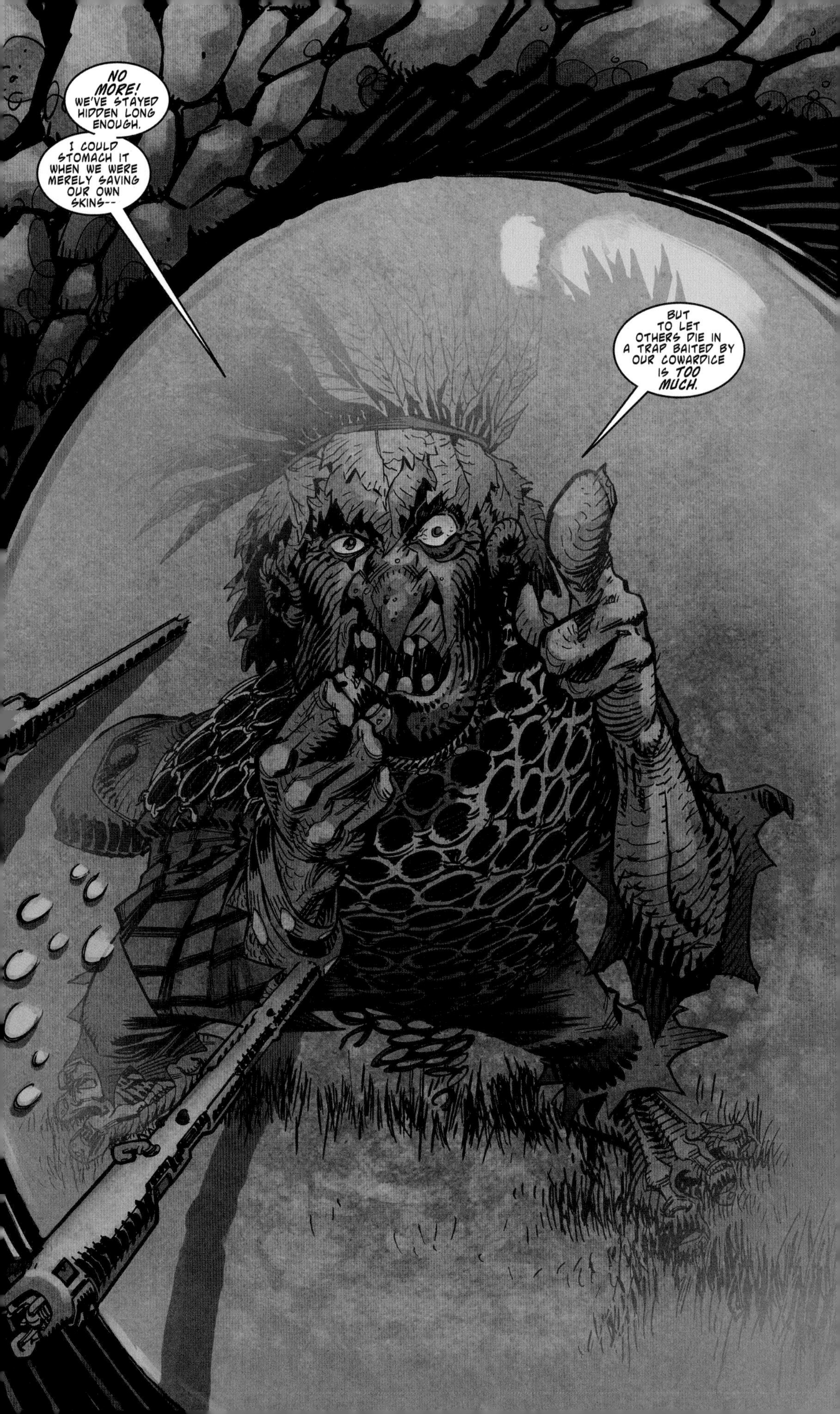
NO MORE! WE'VE STAYED HIDDEN LONG ENOUGH.
I COULD STOMACH IT WHEN WE WERE MERELY SAVING OUR OWN SKINS--
BUT TO LET OTHERS DIE IN A TRAP BAITED BY OUR COWARDICE IS TOO MUCH.

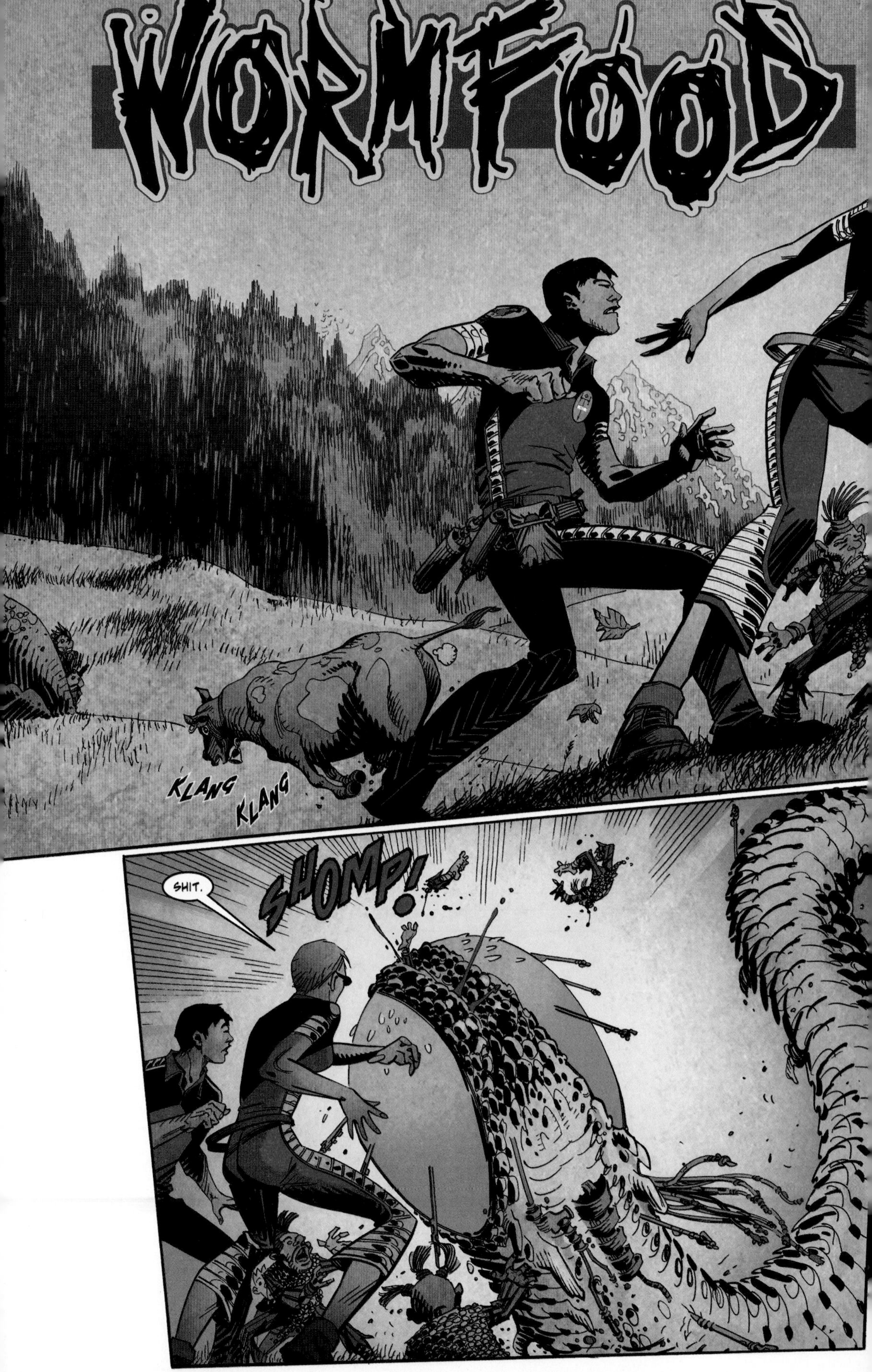
WORMFOOD
KLANG
KLANG
SHIT.
SHOMP!

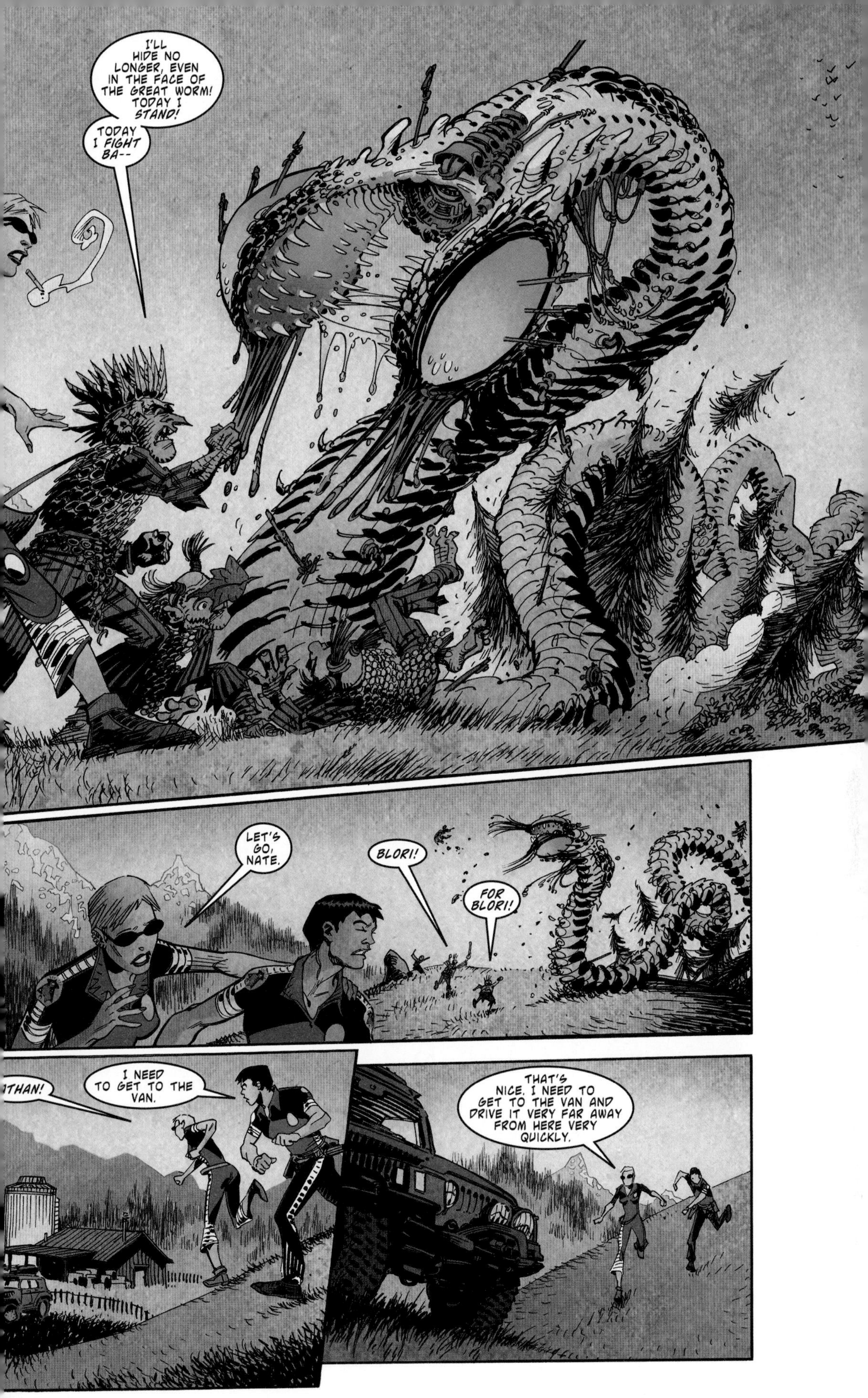
I'LL HIDE NO LONGER, EVEN IN THE FACE OF THE GREAT WORM! TODAY I STAND!
TODAY I FIGHT BA--
LET'S GO, NATE.
BLORI!
FOR BLORI!
...THAN!
I NEED TO GET TO THE VAN.
THAT'S NICE. I NEED TO GET TO THE VAN AND DRIVE IT VERY FAR AWAY FROM HERE VERY QUICKLY.

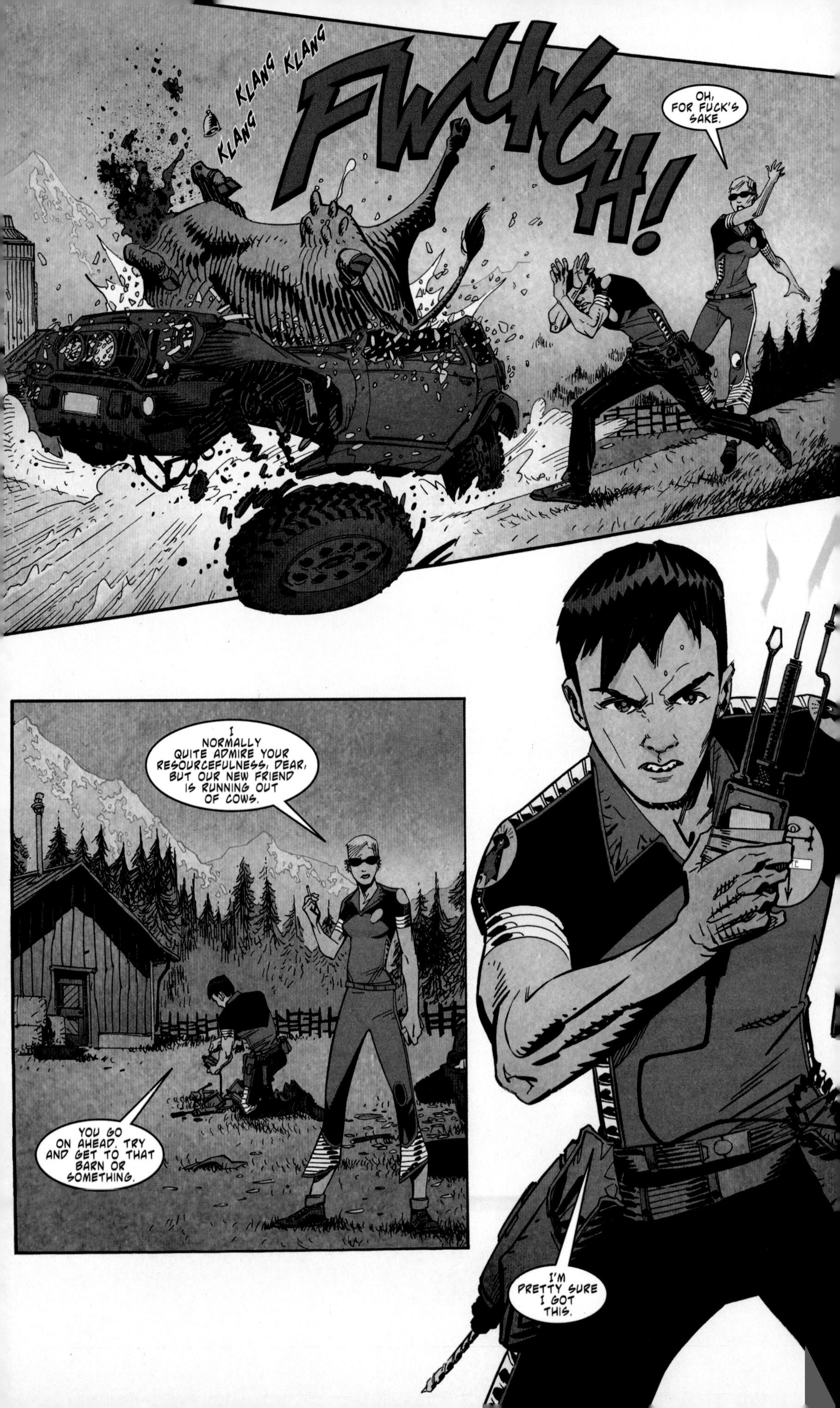
KLANG KLANG KLANG
FWUNCH!
OH, FOR FUCK'S SAKE.
I NORMALLY QUITE ADMIRE YOUR RESOURCEFULNESS, DEAR, BUT OUR NEW FRIEND IS RUNNING OUT OF COWS.
YOU GO ON AHEAD. TRY AND GET TO THAT BARN OR SOMETHING.
I'M PRETTY SURE I GOT THIS.

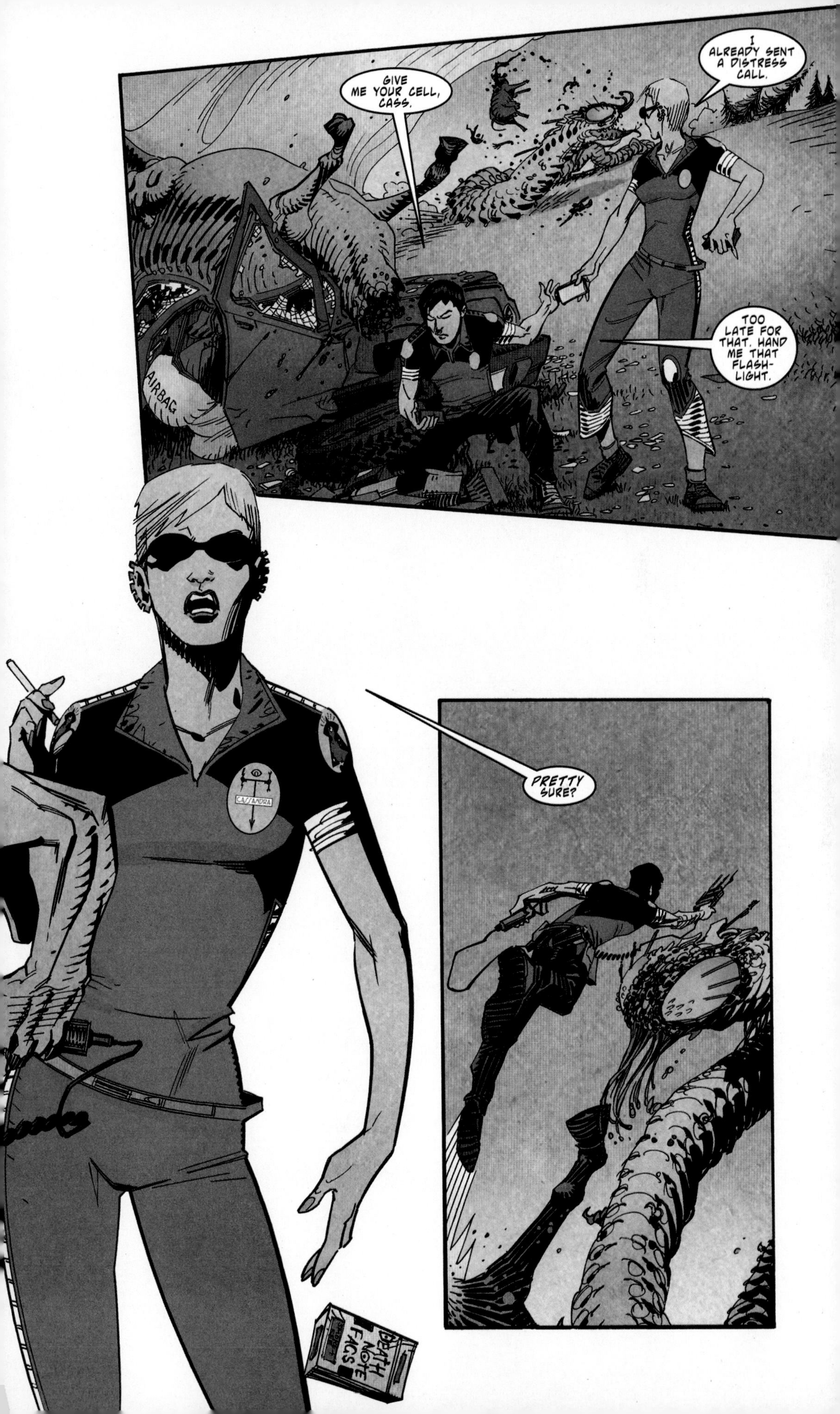
GIVE ME YOUR CELL, CASS.
I ALREADY SENT A DISTRESS CALL.
TOO LATE FOR THAT. HAND ME THAT FLASH-LIGHT.
AIRBAG
CASSANDRA
PRETTY SURE?
DEATH NOTE FAGS

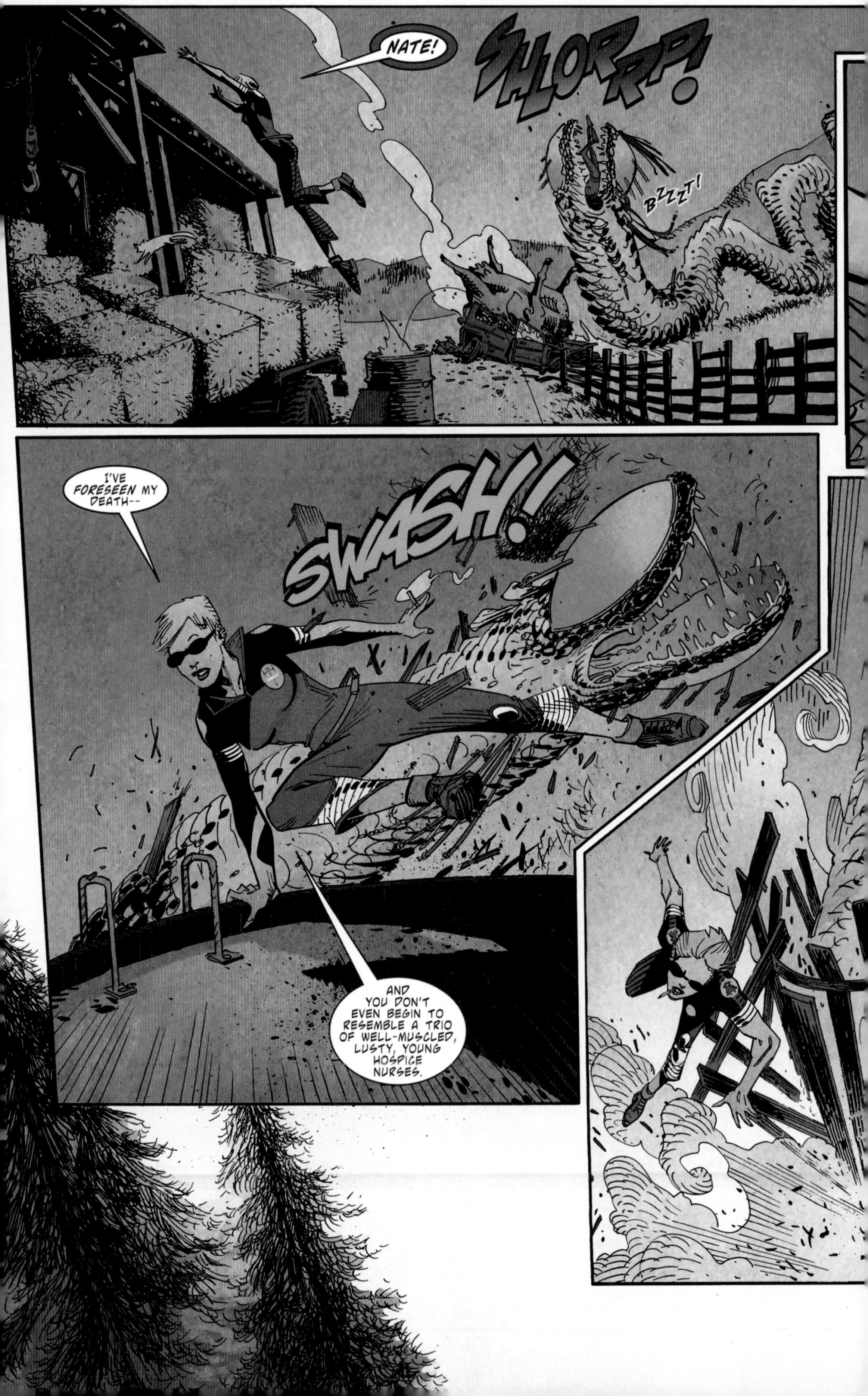
NATE!
SHLORRRP!
BZZZT!
I'VE FORESEEN MY DEATH--
SWASH!!
AND YOU DON'T EVEN BEGIN TO RESEMBLE A TRIO OF WELL-MUSCLED, LUSTY, YOUNG HOSPICE NURSES.

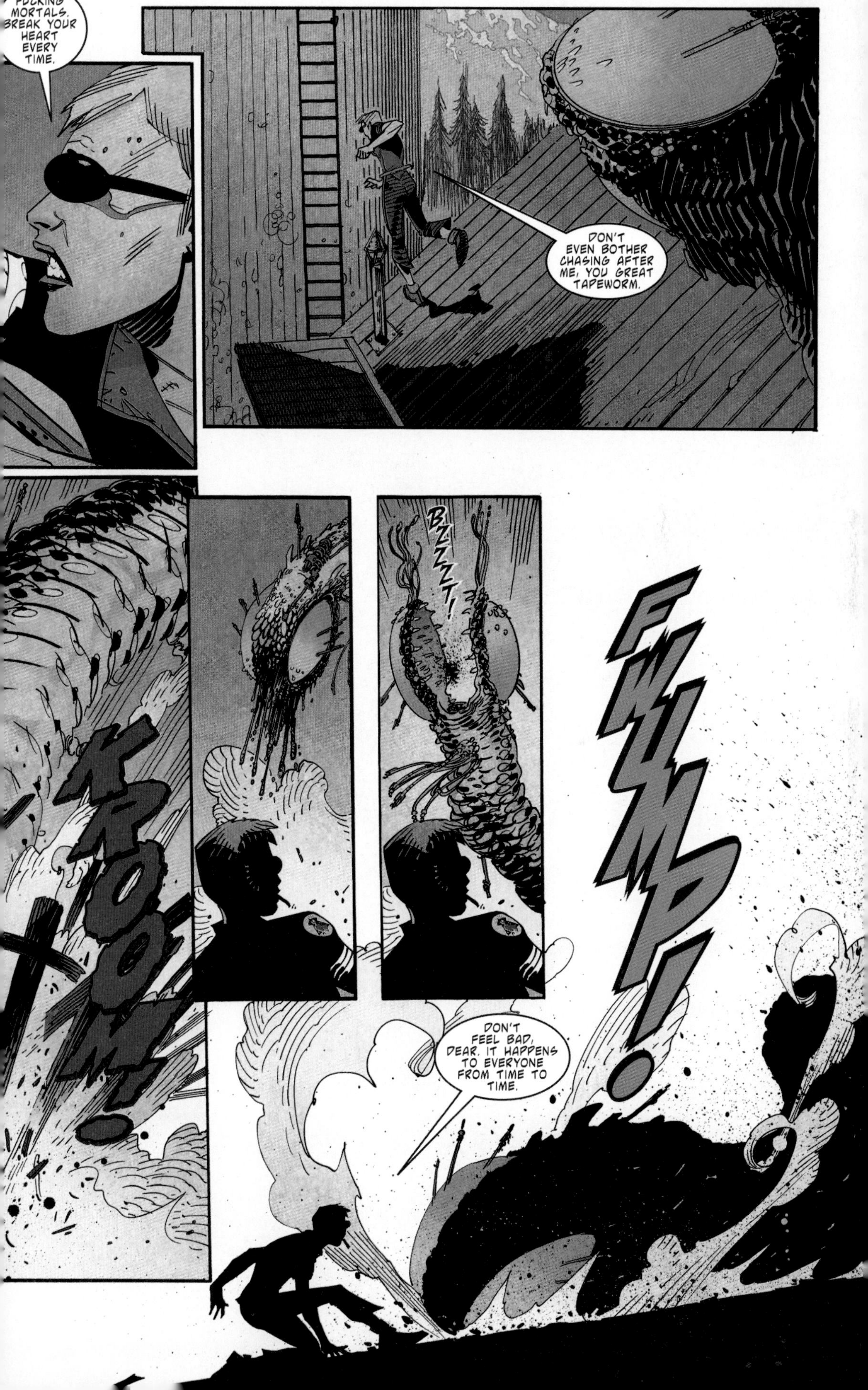
FUCKING MORTALS. BREAK YOUR HEART EVERY TIME.
DON'T EVEN BOTHER CHASING AFTER ME, YOU GREAT TAPEWORM.
KROOOM!
BZZZT!
FWUMP!
DON'T FEEL BAD, DEAR. IT HAPPENS TO EVERYONE FROM TIME TO TIME.

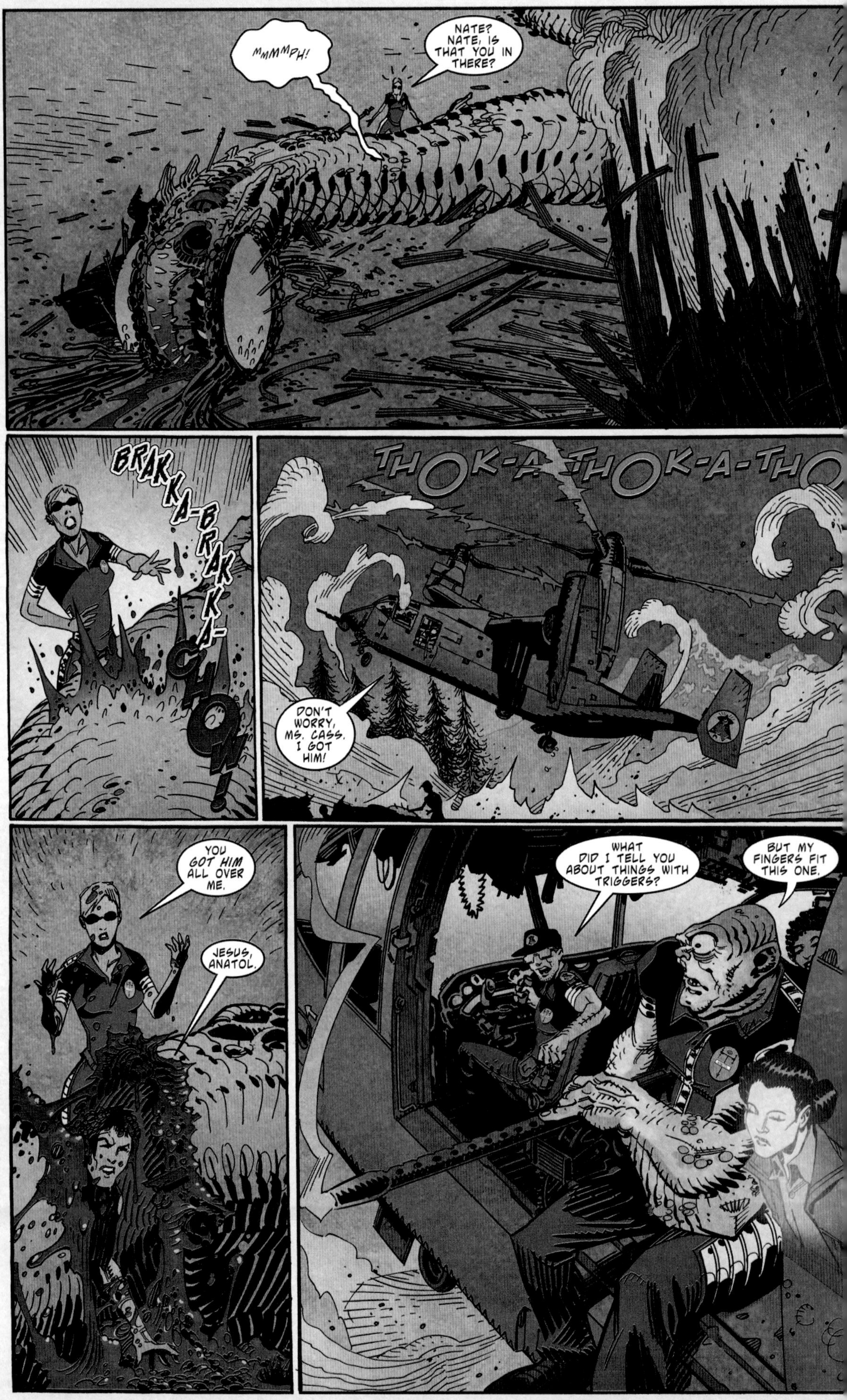
MMMMPH!
NATE? NATE, IS THAT YOU IN THERE?
BRAKKA-BRAKKA-CHOW
THOK-A-THOK-A-THO
DON'T WORRY, MS. CASS. I GOT HIM!
YOU GOT HIM ALL OVER ME.
JESUS, ANATOL.
WHAT DID I TELL YOU ABOUT THINGS WITH TRIGGERS?
BUT MY FINGERS FIT THIS ONE.

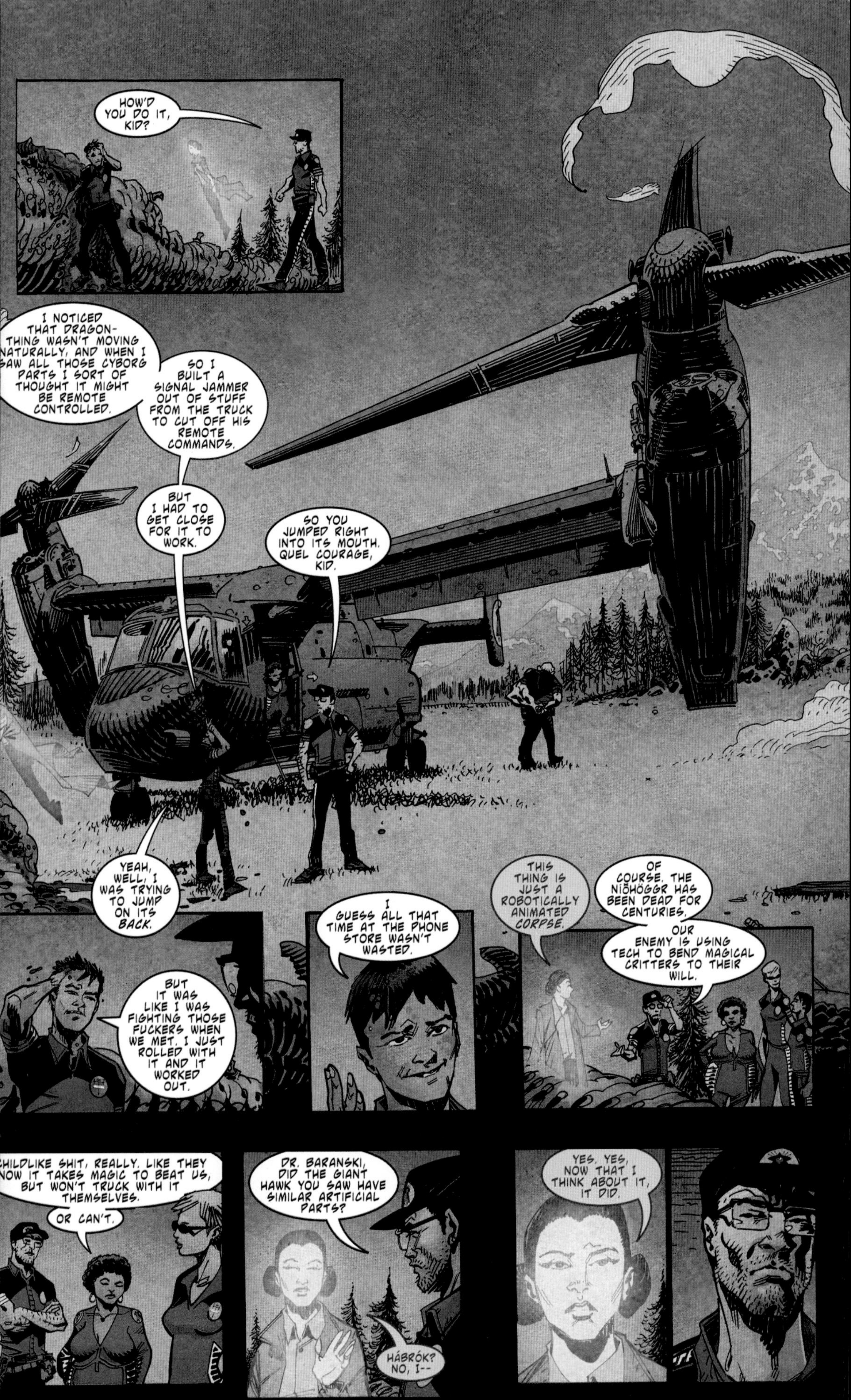
HOW'D YOU DO IT, KID?
I NOTICED THAT DRAGON-THING WASN'T MOVING NATURALLY, AND WHEN I SAW ALL THOSE CYBORG PARTS I SORT OF THOUGHT IT MIGHT BE REMOTE CONTROLLED.
SO I BUILT A SIGNAL JAMMER OUT OF STUFF FROM THE TRUCK TO CUT OFF HIS REMOTE COMMANDS.
BUT I HAD TO GET CLOSE FOR IT TO WORK.
SO YOU JUMPED RIGHT INTO ITS MOUTH. QUEL COURAGE, KID.
YEAH, WELL, I WAS TRYING TO JUMP ON ITS BACK.
BUT IT WAS LIKE I WAS FIGHTING THOSE FUCKERS WHEN WE MET. I JUST ROLLED WITH IT AND IT WORKED OUT.
I GUESS ALL THAT TIME AT THE PHONE STORE WASN'T WASTED.
THIS THING IS JUST A ROBOTICALLY ANIMATED CORPSE.
OF COURSE. THE NIÖHÖGGR HAS BEEN DEAD FOR CENTURIES.
OUR ENEMY IS USING TECH TO BEND MAGICAL CRITTERS TO THEIR WILL.
CHILDLIKE SHIT, REALLY. LIKE THEY KNOW IT TAKES MAGIC TO BEAT US, BUT WON'T TRUCK WITH IT THEMSELVES.
OR CAN'T.
DR. BARANSKI, DID THE GIANT HAWK YOU SAW HAVE SIMILAR ARTIFICIAL PARTS?
HÁBRÓK? NO, I--
YES. YES, NOW THAT I THINK ABOUT IT, IT DID.

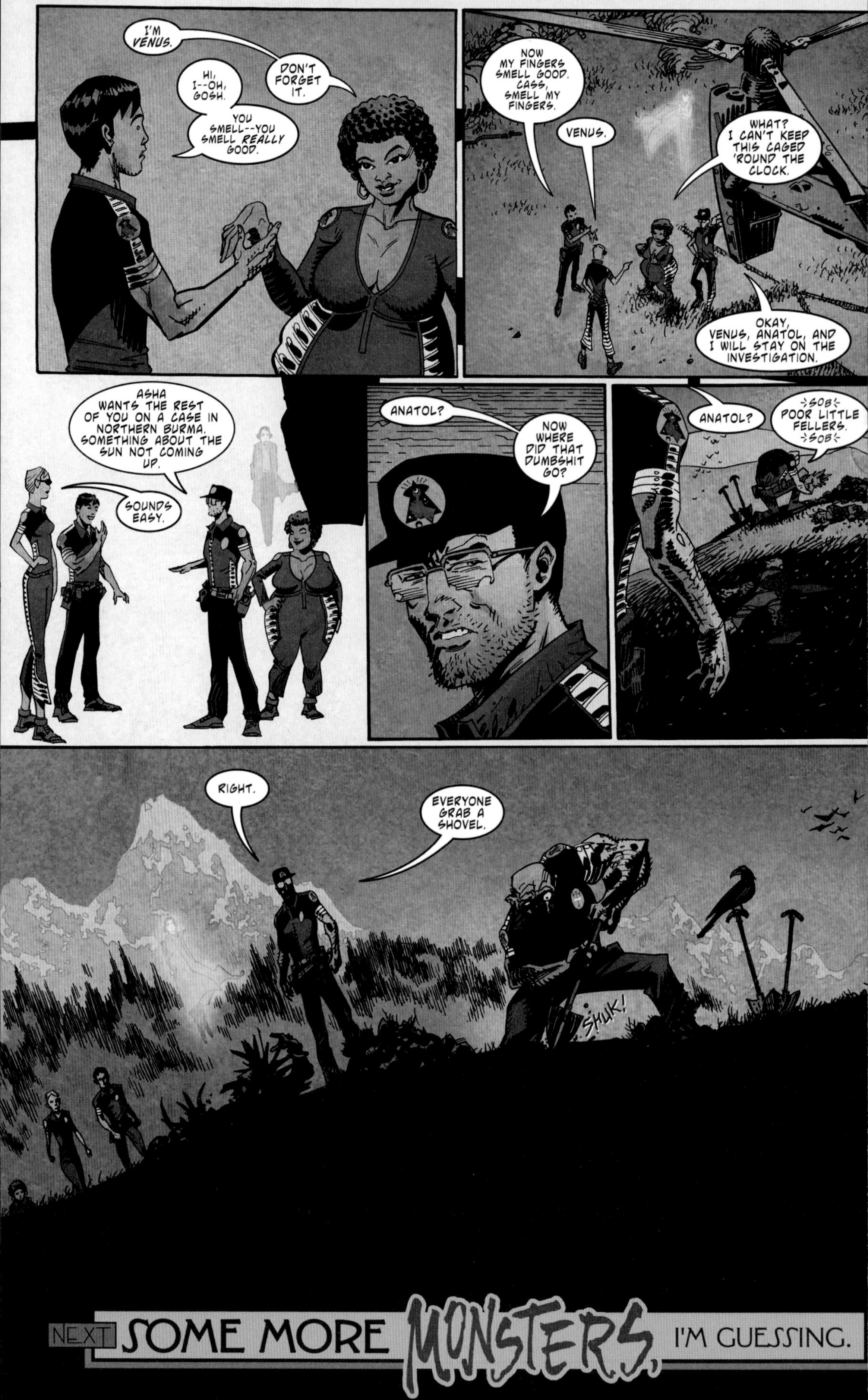

I'M VENUS.
HI, I--OH, GOSH.
DON'T FORGET IT.
YOU SMELL--YOU SMELL REALLY GOOD.
NOW MY FINGERS SMELL GOOD. CASS, SMELL MY FINGERS.
VENUS.
WHAT? I CAN'T KEEP THIS CAGED 'ROUND THE CLOCK.
OKAY, VENUS, ANATOL, AND I WILL STAY ON THE INVESTIGATION.
ASHA WANTS THE REST OF YOU ON A CASE IN NORTHERN BURMA. SOMETHING ABOUT THE SUN NOT COMING UP.
SOUNDS EASY.
ANATOL?
NOW WHERE DID THAT DUMBSHIT GO?
ANATOL?
SOB POOR LITTLE FELLERS. SOB
RIGHT.
EVERYONE GRAB A SHOVEL.
SHUK!
NEXT SOME MORE MONSTERS, I'M GUESSING.

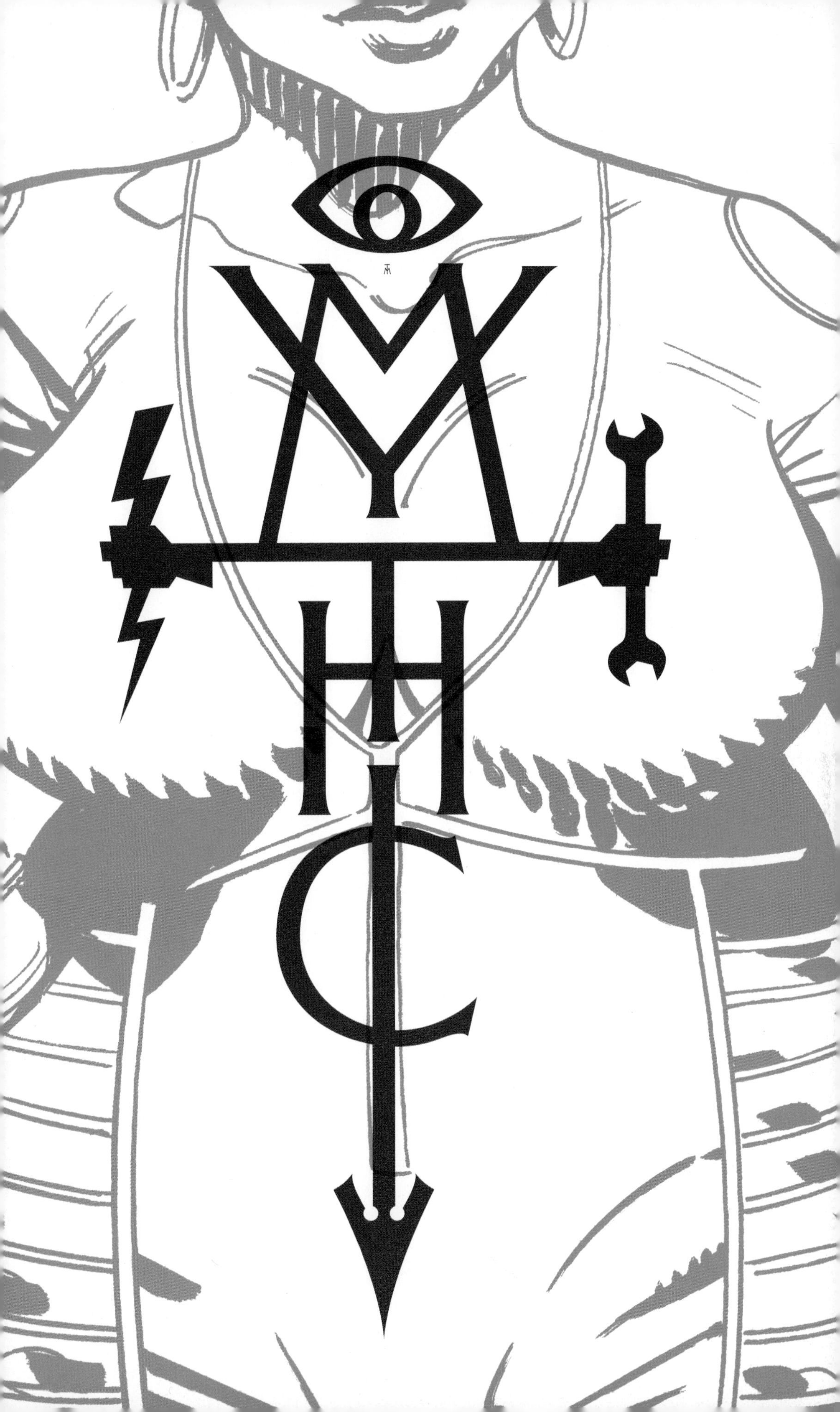
MYTHIC

CHAPTER 5

THE GODS OF DEATH AND DYING AND NOTHINGNESS

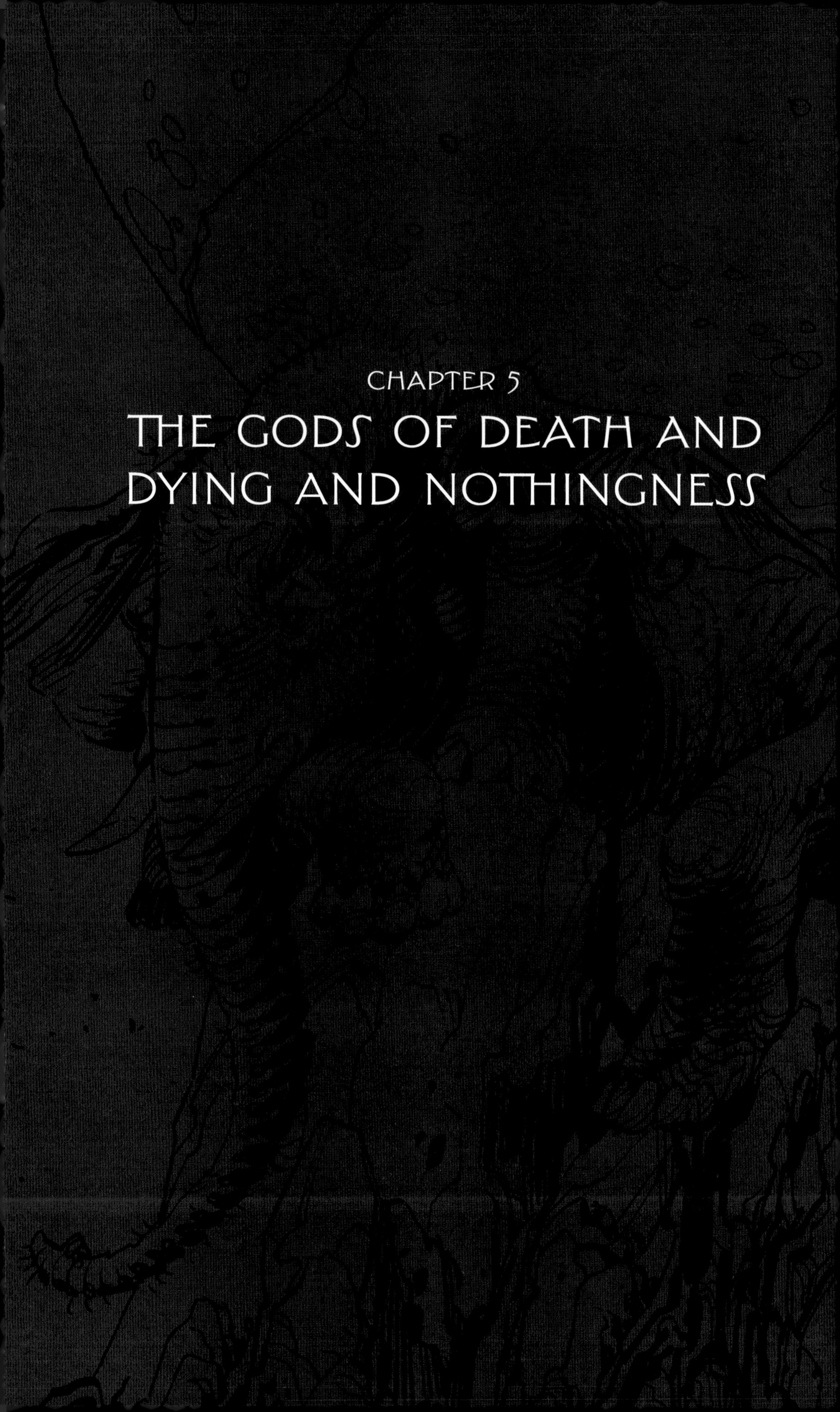

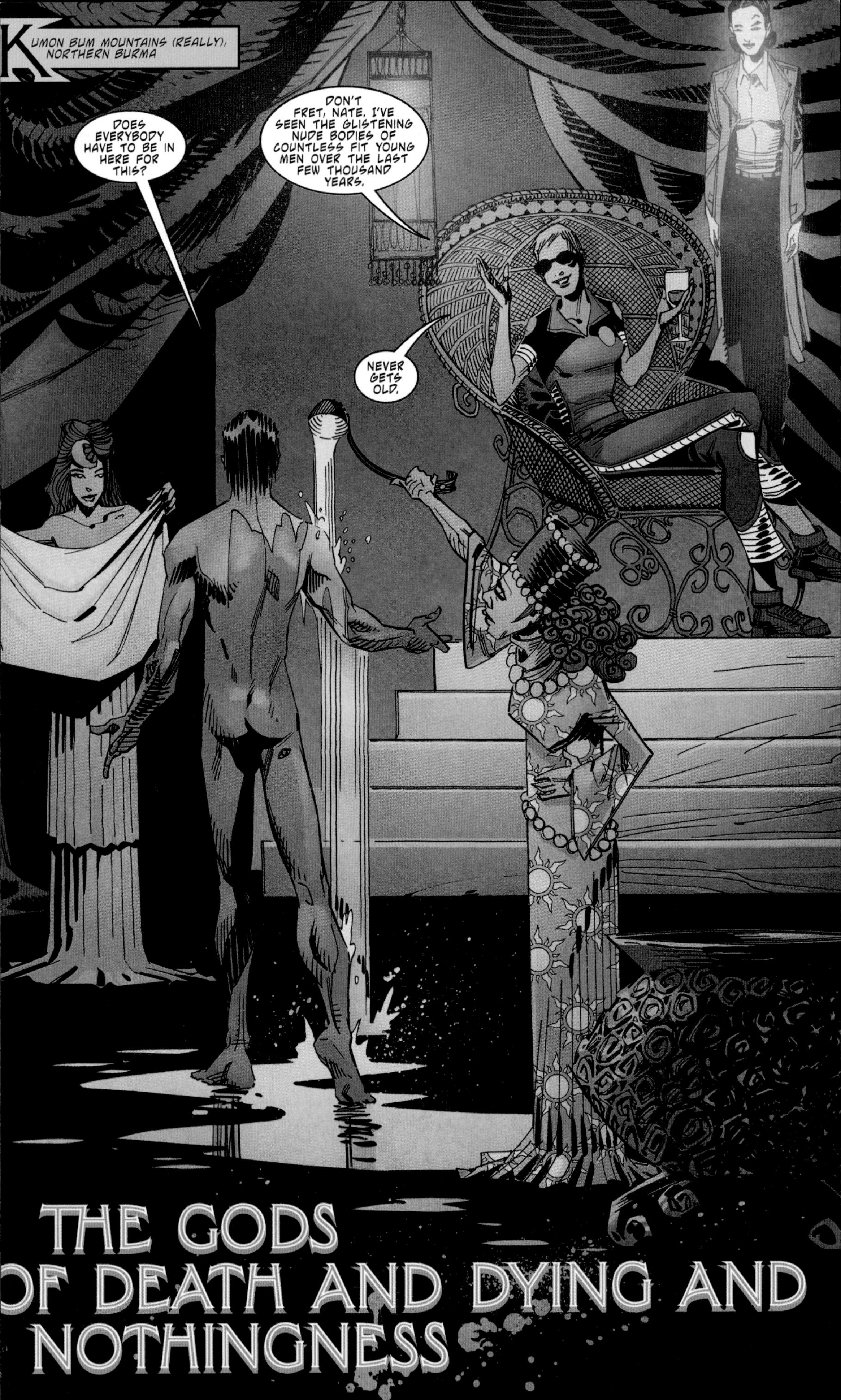
KUMON BUM MOUNTAINS (REALLY), NORTHERN BURMA
DOES EVERYBODY HAVE TO BE IN HERE FOR THIS?
DON'T FRET, NATE. I'VE SEEN THE GLISTENING NUDE BODIES OF COUNTLESS FIT YOUNG MEN OVER THE LAST FEW THOUSAND YEARS.
NEVER GETS OLD.
THE GODS OF DEATH AND DYING AND NOTHINGNESS

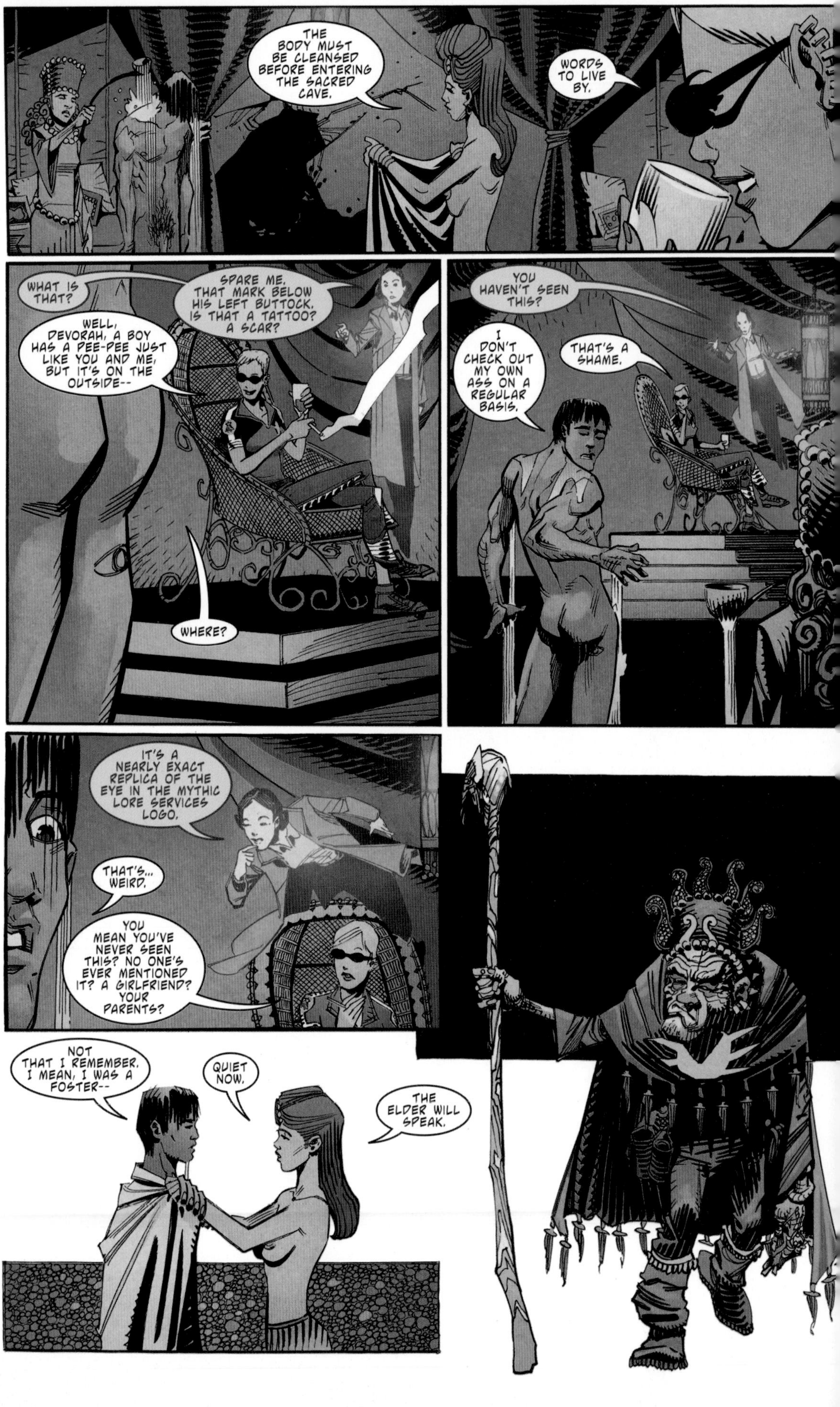
THE BODY MUST BE CLEANSED BEFORE ENTERING THE SACRED CAVE.
WORDS TO LIVE BY.
WHAT IS THAT?
SPARE ME. THAT MARK BELOW HIS LEFT BUTTOCK. IS THAT A TATTOO? A SCAR?
WELL, DEVORAH, A BOY HAS A PEE-PEE JUST LIKE YOU AND ME, BUT IT'S ON THE OUTSIDE--
WHERE?
YOU HAVEN'T SEEN THIS?
I DON'T CHECK OUT MY OWN ASS ON A REGULAR BASIS.
THAT'S A SHAME.
IT'S A NEARLY EXACT REPLICA OF THE EYE IN THE MYTHIC LORE SERVICES LOGO.
THAT'S... WEIRD.
YOU MEAN YOU'VE NEVER SEEN THIS? NO ONE'S EVER MENTIONED IT? A GIRLFRIEND? YOUR PARENTS?
NOT THAT I REMEMBER. I MEAN, I WAS A FOSTER--
QUIET NOW.
THE ELDER WILL SPEAK.

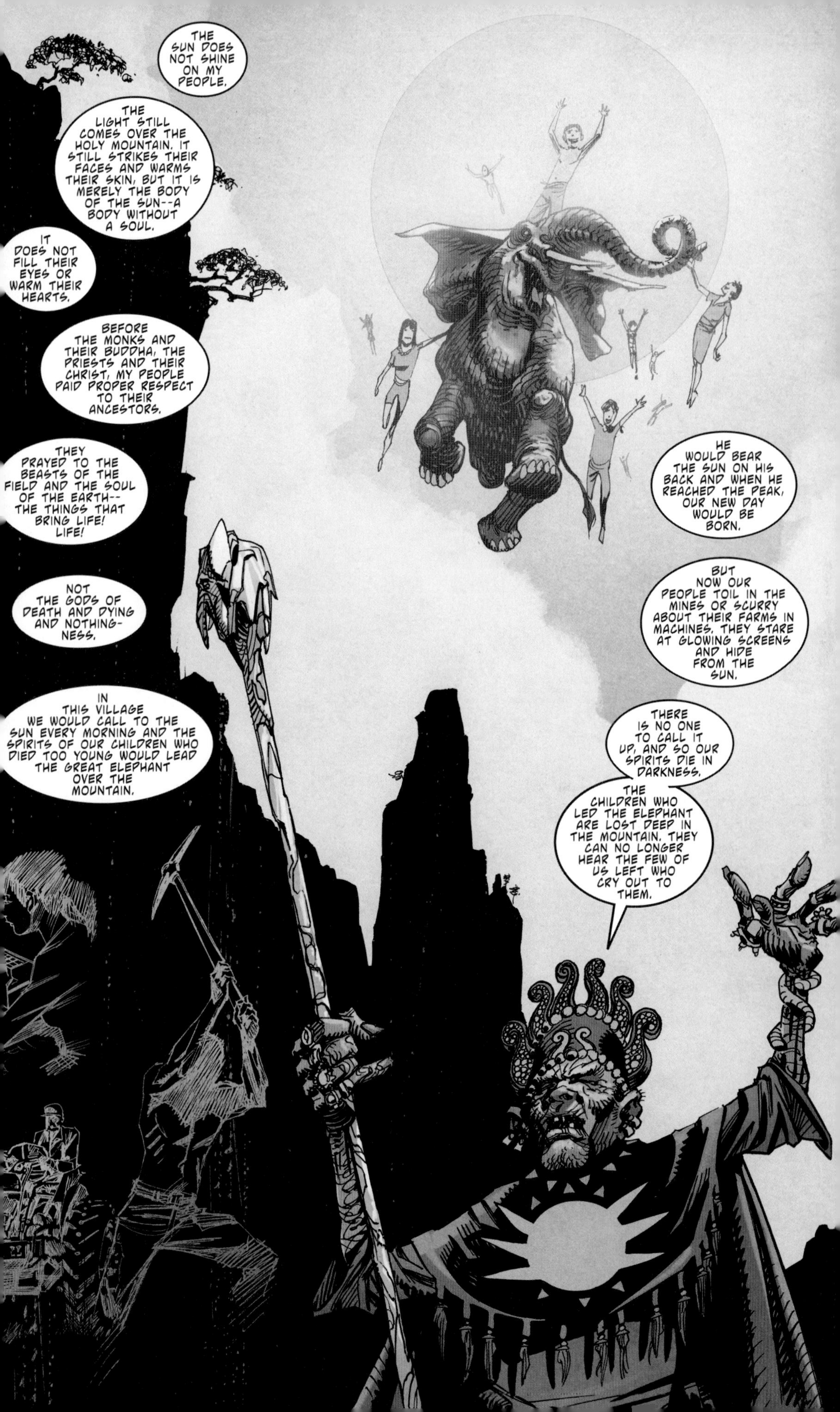
THE SUN DOES NOT SHINE ON MY PEOPLE.
THE LIGHT STILL COMES OVER THE HOLY MOUNTAIN. IT STILL STRIKES THEIR FACES AND WARMS THEIR SKIN, BUT IT IS MERELY THE BODY OF THE SUN--A BODY WITHOUT A SOUL.
IT DOES NOT FILL THEIR EYES OR WARM THEIR HEARTS.
BEFORE THE MONKS AND THEIR BUDDHA, THE PRIESTS AND THEIR CHRIST, MY PEOPLE PAID PROPER RESPECT TO THEIR ANCESTORS.
THEY PRAYED TO THE BEASTS OF THE FIELD AND THE SOUL OF THE EARTH-- THE THINGS THAT BRING LIFE! LIFE!
NOT THE GODS OF DEATH AND DYING AND NOTHING-NESS.
IN THIS VILLAGE WE WOULD CALL TO THE SUN EVERY MORNING AND THE SPIRITS OF OUR CHILDREN WHO DIED TOO YOUNG WOULD LEAD THE GREAT ELEPHANT OVER THE MOUNTAIN.
HE WOULD BEAR THE SUN ON HIS BACK AND WHEN HE REACHED THE PEAK, OUR NEW DAY WOULD BE BORN.
BUT NOW OUR PEOPLE TOIL IN THE MINES OR SCURRY ABOUT THEIR FARMS IN MACHINES. THEY STARE AT GLOWING SCREENS AND HIDE FROM THE SUN.
THERE IS NO ONE TO CALL IT UP, AND SO OUR SPIRITS DIE IN DARKNESS.
THE CHILDREN WHO LED THE ELEPHANT ARE LOST DEEP IN THE MOUNTAIN. THEY CAN NO LONGER HEAR THE FEW OF US LEFT WHO CRY OUT TO THEM.

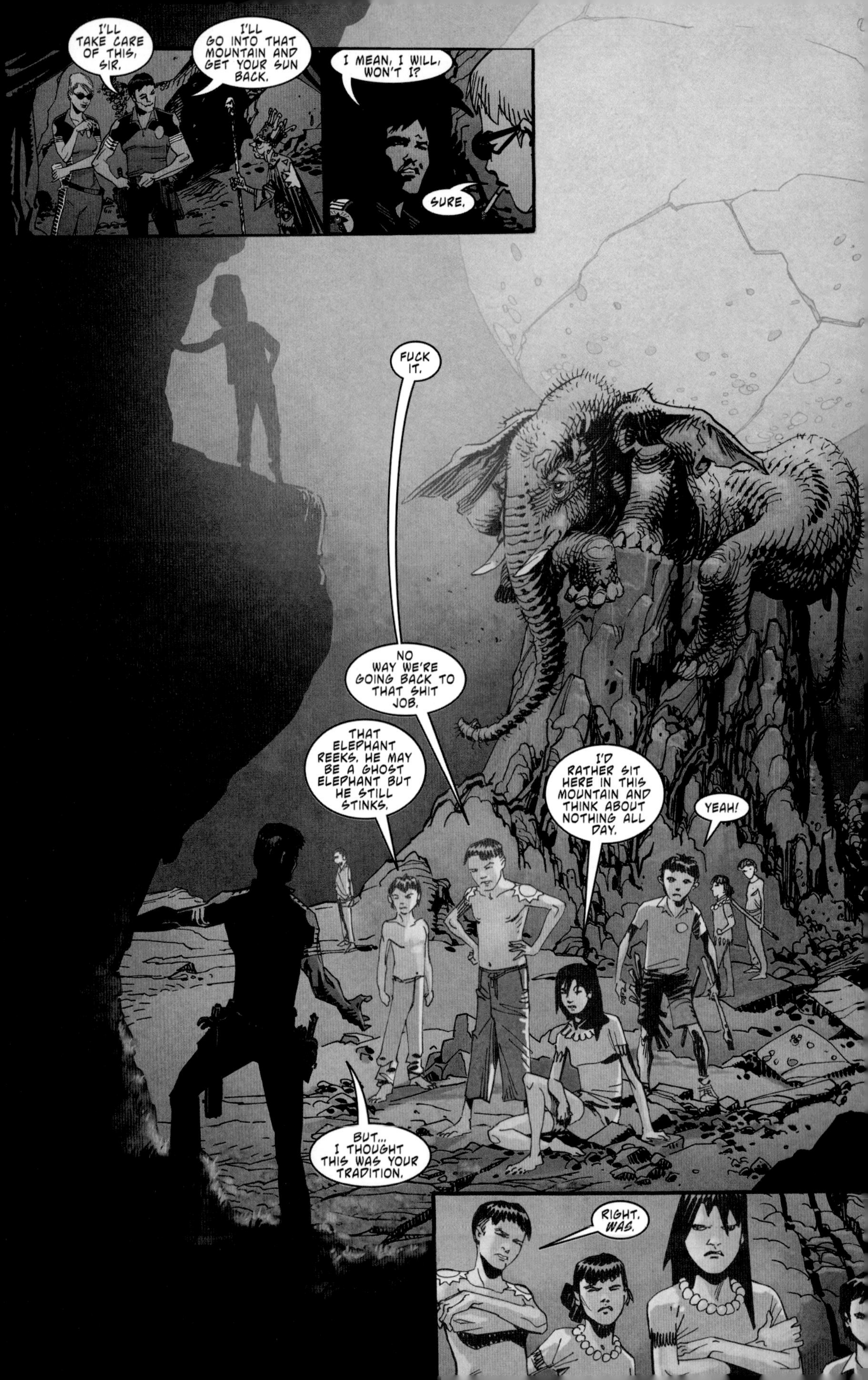
I'LL TAKE CARE OF THIS, SIR.
I'LL GO INTO THAT MOUNTAIN AND GET YOUR SUN BACK.
I MEAN, I WILL, WON'T I?
SURE.
FUCK IT.
NO WAY WE'RE GOING BACK TO THAT SHIT JOB.
THAT ELEPHANT REEKS. HE MAY BE A GHOST ELEPHANT BUT HE STILL STINKS.
I'D RATHER SIT HERE IN THIS MOUNTAIN AND THINK ABOUT NOTHING ALL DAY.
YEAH!
BUT... I THOUGHT THIS WAS YOUR TRADITION.
RIGHT. *WAS*.

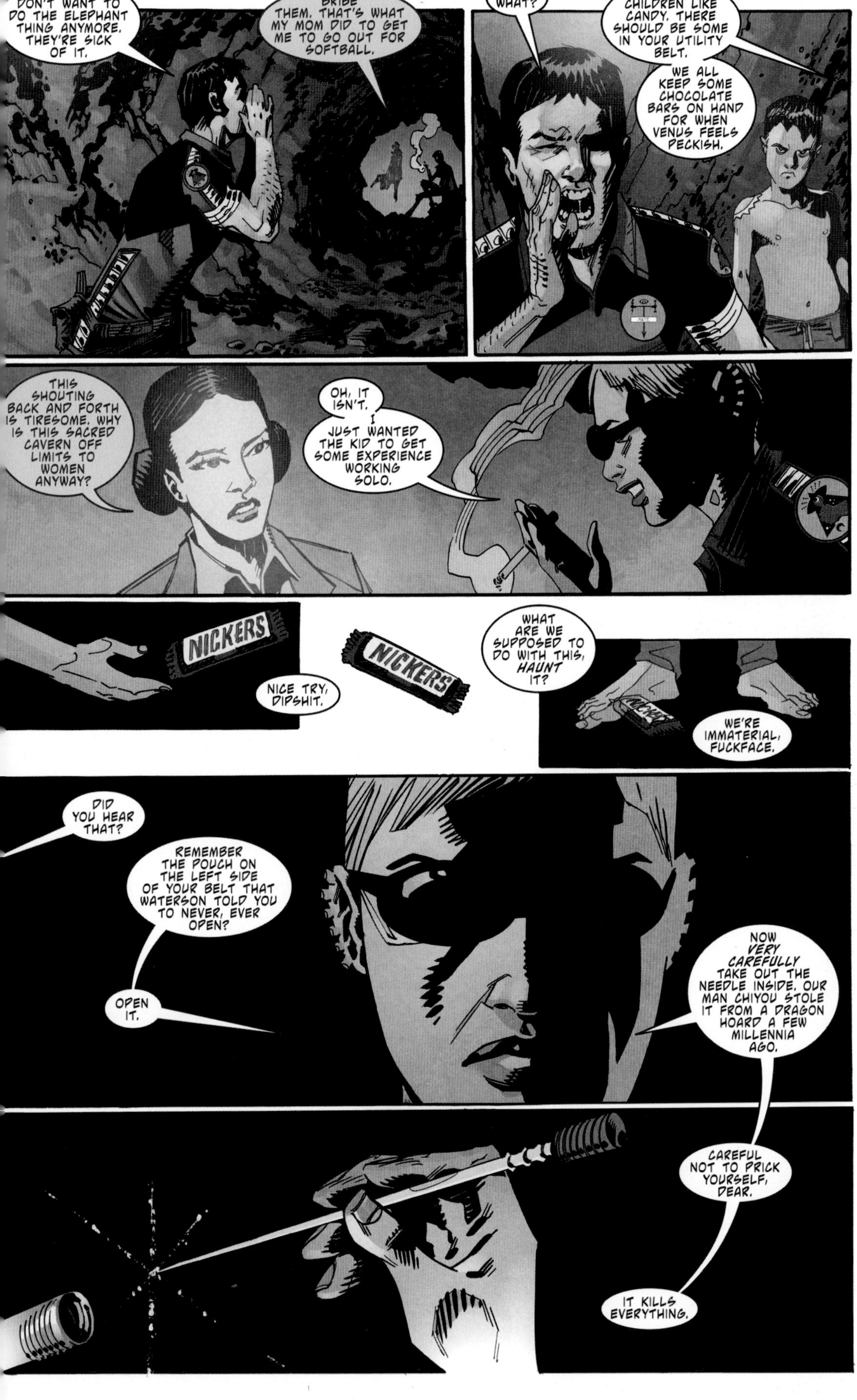
THEY DON'T WANT TO DO THE ELEPHANT THING ANYMORE. THEY'RE SICK OF IT.
BRIBE THEM. THAT'S WHAT MY MOM DID TO GET ME TO GO OUT FOR SOFTBALL.
WITH WHAT?
MOST CHILDREN LIKE CANDY. THERE SHOULD BE SOME IN YOUR UTILITY BELT.
WE ALL KEEP SOME CHOCOLATE BARS ON HAND FOR WHEN VENUS FEELS PECKISH.
THIS SHOUTING BACK AND FORTH IS TIRESOME. WHY IS THIS SACRED CAVERN OFF LIMITS TO WOMEN ANYWAY?
OH, IT ISN'T.
I JUST WANTED THE KID TO GET SOME EXPERIENCE WORKING SOLO.
NICKERS
NICKERS
NICE TRY, DIPSHIT.
WHAT ARE WE SUPPOSED TO DO WITH THIS, *HAUNT* IT?
WE'RE IMMATERIAL, FUCKFACE.
DID YOU HEAR THAT?
REMEMBER THE POUCH ON THE LEFT SIDE OF YOUR BELT THAT WATERSON TOLD YOU TO NEVER, EVER OPEN?
OPEN IT.
NOW *VERY CAREFULLY* TAKE OUT THE NEEDLE INSIDE. OUR MAN CHIYOU STOLE IT FROM A DRAGON HOARD A FEW MILLENNIA AGO.
CAREFUL NOT TO PRICK YOURSELF, DEAR.
IT KILLS EVERYTHING.

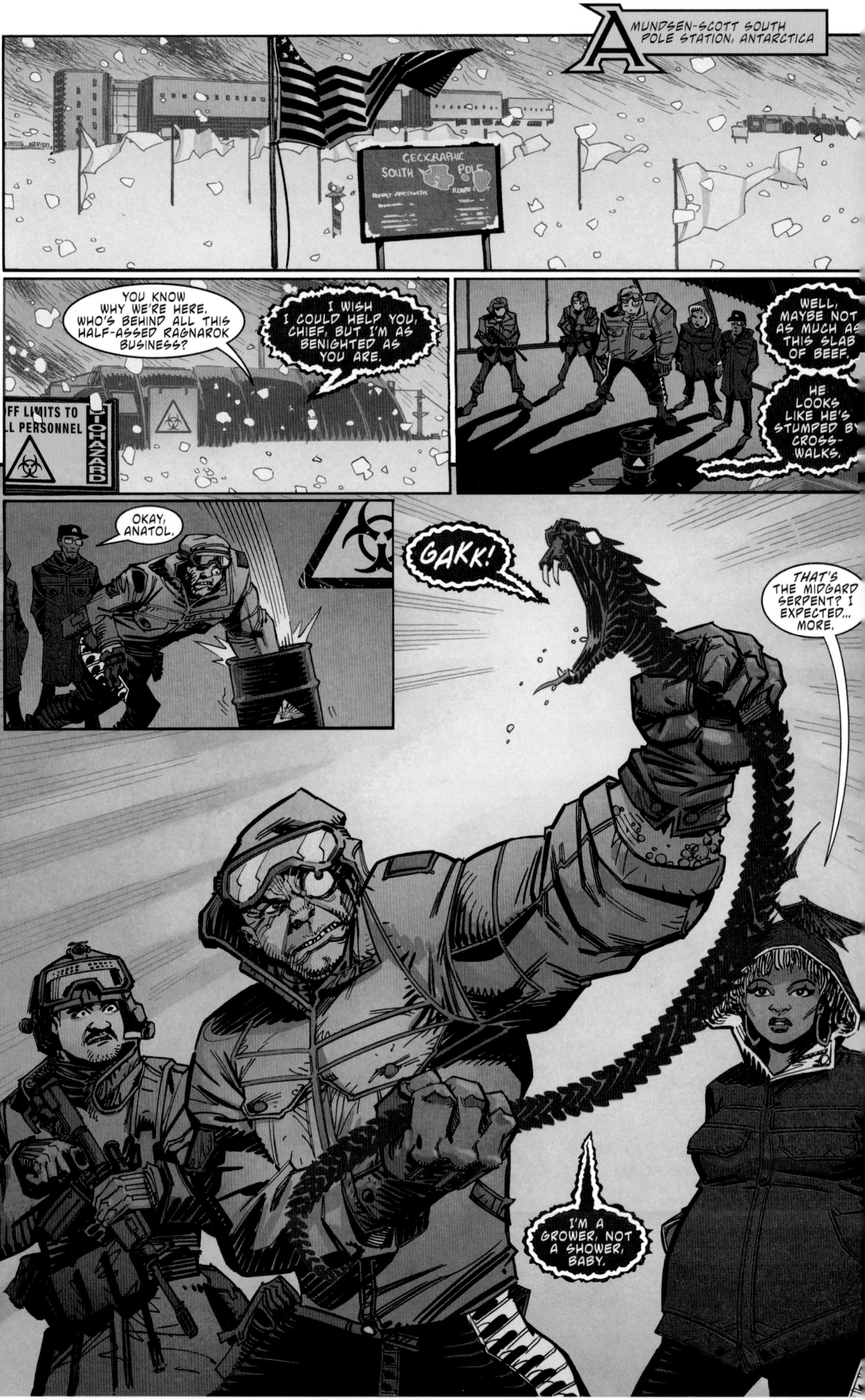
AMUNDSEN-SCOTT SOUTH POLE STATION, ANTARCTICA
GEOGRAPHIC SOUTH POLE
YOU KNOW WHY WE'RE HERE. WHO'S BEHIND ALL THIS HALF-ASSED RAGNAROK BUSINESS?
I WISH I COULD HELP YOU, CHIEF, BUT I'M AS BENIGHTED AS YOU ARE.
OFF LIMITS TO ALL PERSONNEL
BIOHAZARD
WELL, MAYBE NOT AS MUCH AS THIS SLAB OF BEEF.
HE LOOKS LIKE HE'S STUMPED BY CROSS-WALKS.
OKAY, ANATOL.
GAKK!
THAT'S THE MIDGARD SERPENT? I EXPECTED... MORE.
I'M A GROWER, NOT A SHOWER, BABY.

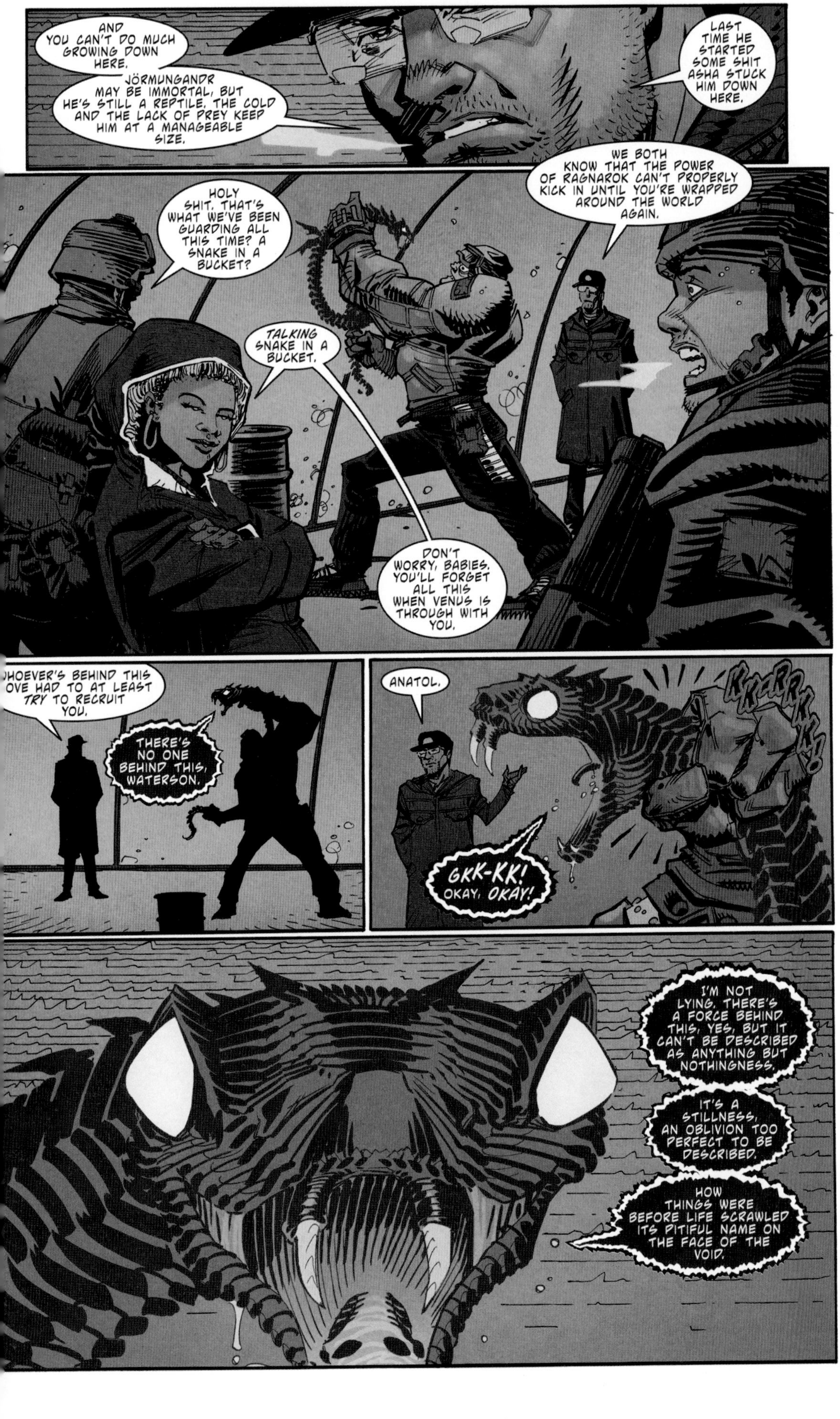

AND YOU CAN'T DO MUCH GROWING DOWN HERE.
JÖRMUNGANDR MAY BE IMMORTAL, BUT HE'S STILL A REPTILE. THE COLD AND THE LACK OF PREY KEEP HIM AT A MANAGEABLE SIZE.
LAST TIME HE STARTED SOME SHIT ASHA STUCK HIM DOWN HERE.
HOLY SHIT. THAT'S WHAT WE'VE BEEN GUARDING ALL THIS TIME? A SNAKE IN A BUCKET?
WE BOTH KNOW THAT THE POWER OF RAGNAROK CAN'T PROPERLY KICK IN UNTIL YOU'RE WRAPPED AROUND THE WORLD AGAIN.
TALKING SNAKE IN A BUCKET.
DON'T WORRY, BABIES. YOU'LL FORGET ALL THIS WHEN VENUS IS THROUGH WITH YOU.
WHOEVER'S BEHIND THIS MOVE HAD TO AT LEAST TRY TO RECRUIT YOU.
THERE'S NO ONE BEHIND THIS, WATERSON.
ANATOL.
KKRRKK
GKK-KK! OKAY, OKAY!
I'M NOT LYING. THERE'S A FORCE BEHIND THIS, YES, BUT IT CAN'T BE DESCRIBED AS ANYTHING BUT NOTHINGNESS.
IT'S A STILLNESS, AN OBLIVION TOO PERFECT TO BE DESCRIBED.
HOW THINGS WERE BEFORE LIFE SCRAWLED ITS PITIFUL NAME ON THE FACE OF THE VOID.

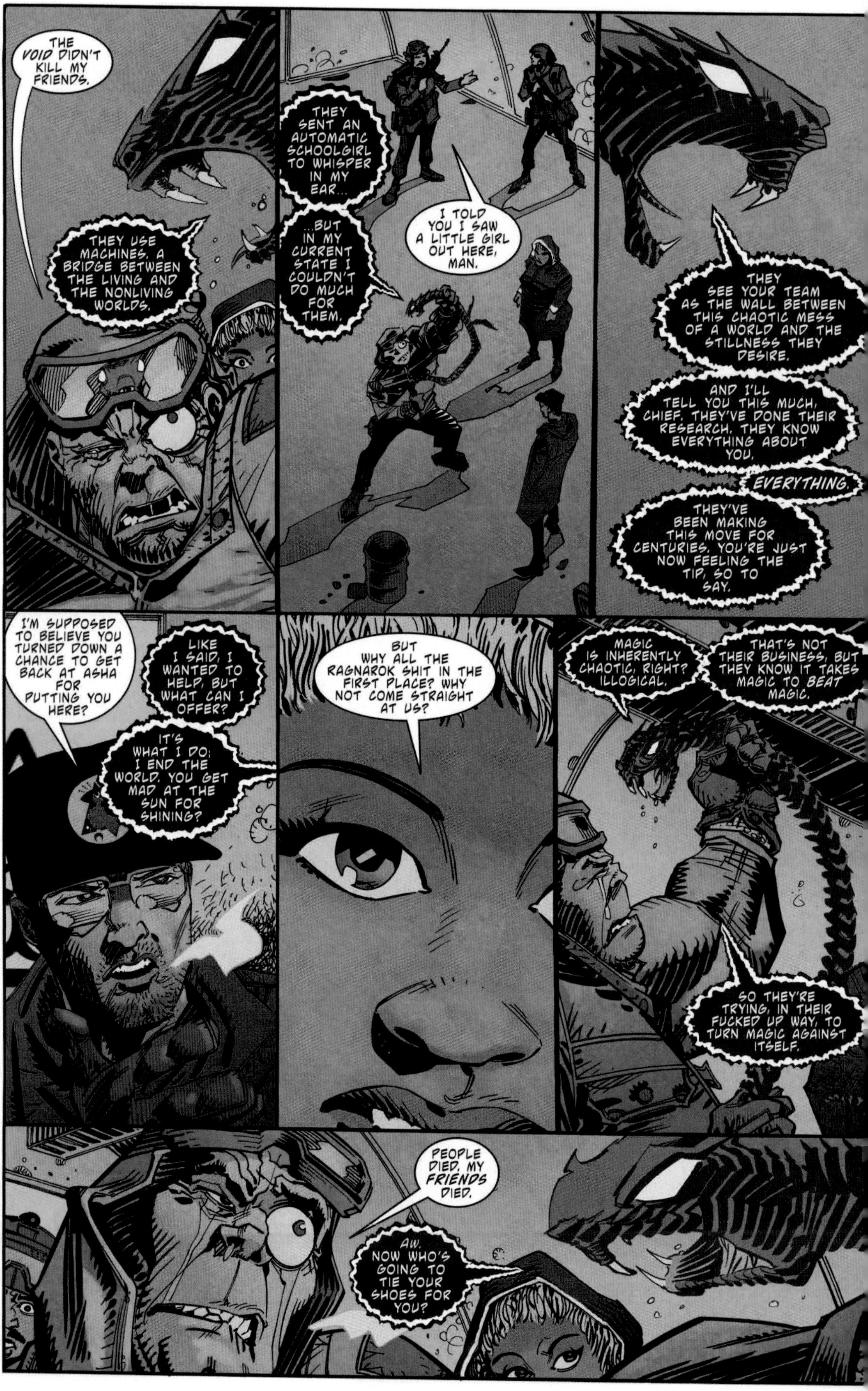
THE VOID DIDN'T KILL MY FRIENDS.
THEY USE MACHINES, A BRIDGE BETWEEN THE LIVING AND THE NONLIVING WORLDS.
THEY SENT AN AUTOMATIC SCHOOLGIRL TO WHISPER IN MY EAR...
...BUT IN MY CURRENT STATE I COULDN'T DO MUCH FOR THEM.
I TOLD YOU I SAW A LITTLE GIRL OUT HERE, MAN.
THEY SEE YOUR TEAM AS THE WALL BETWEEN THIS CHAOTIC MESS OF A WORLD AND THE STILLNESS THEY DESIRE.
AND I'LL TELL YOU THIS MUCH, CHIEF. THEY'VE DONE THEIR RESEARCH. THEY KNOW EVERYTHING ABOUT YOU.
EVERYTHING.
THEY'VE BEEN MAKING THIS MOVE FOR CENTURIES. YOU'RE JUST NOW FEELING THE TIP, SO TO SAY.
I'M SUPPOSED TO BELIEVE YOU TURNED DOWN A CHANCE TO GET BACK AT ASHA FOR PUTTING YOU HERE?
LIKE I SAID, I WANTED TO HELP, BUT WHAT CAN I OFFER?
IT'S WHAT I DO; I END THE WORLD. YOU GET MAD AT THE SUN FOR SHINING?
BUT WHY ALL THE RAGNAROK SHIT IN THE FIRST PLACE? WHY NOT COME STRAIGHT AT US?
MAGIC IS INHERENTLY CHAOTIC, RIGHT? ILLOGICAL.
THAT'S NOT THEIR BUSINESS, BUT THEY KNOW IT TAKES MAGIC TO BEAT MAGIC.
SO THEY'RE TRYING, IN THEIR FUCKED UP WAY, TO TURN MAGIC AGAINST ITSELF.
PEOPLE DIED. MY FRIENDS DIED.
AW. NOW WHO'S GOING TO TIE YOUR SHOES FOR YOU?

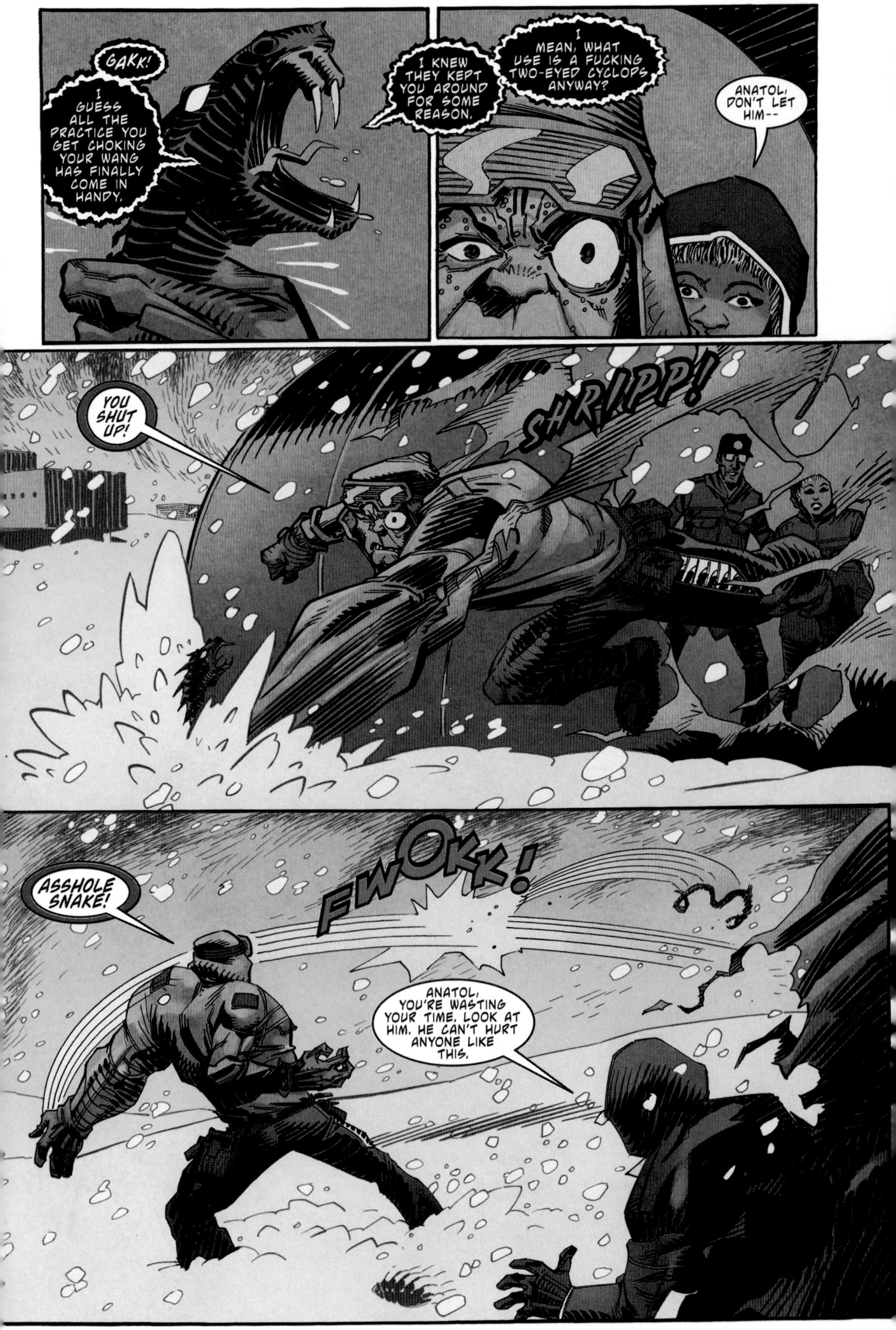
GAKK!
I GUESS ALL THE PRACTICE YOU GET CHOKING YOUR WANG HAS FINALLY COME IN HANDY.
I KNEW THEY KEPT YOU AROUND FOR SOME REASON.
I MEAN, WHAT USE IS A FUCKING TWO-EYED CYCLOPS ANYWAY?
ANATOL, DON'T LET HIM--
YOU SHUT UP!
SHRIPP!
ASSHOLE SNAKE!
FWOKK!
ANATOL, YOU'RE WASTING YOUR TIME. LOOK AT HIM. HE CAN'T HURT ANYONE LIKE THIS.

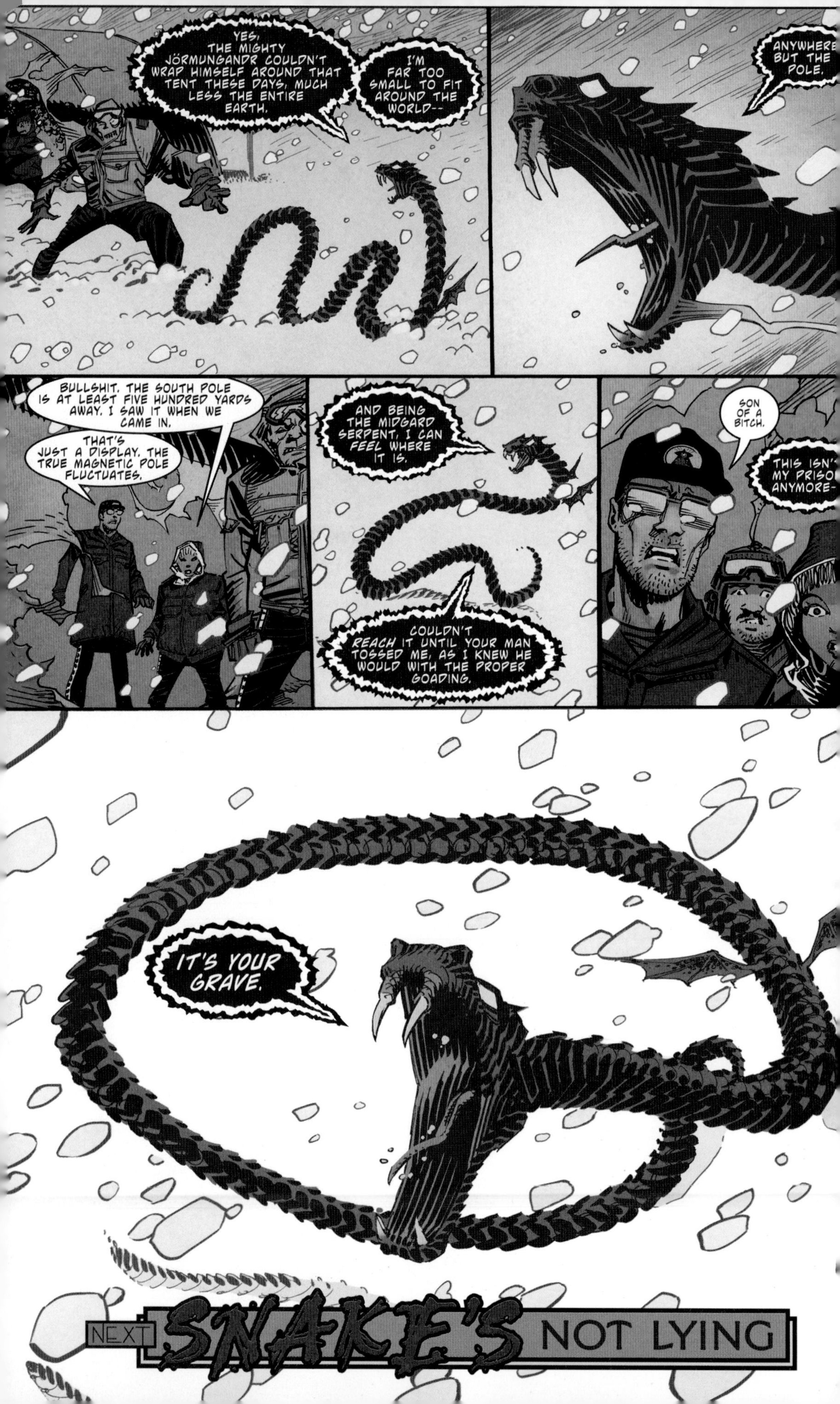
YES, THE MIGHTY JÖRMUNGANDR COULDN'T WRAP HIMSELF AROUND THAT TENT THESE DAYS, MUCH LESS THE ENTIRE EARTH.
I'M FAR TOO SMALL TO FIT AROUND THE WORLD--
ANYWHERE BUT THE POLE.
BULLSHIT. THE SOUTH POLE IS AT LEAST FIVE HUNDRED YARDS AWAY. I SAW IT WHEN WE CAME IN.
THAT'S JUST A DISPLAY. THE TRUE MAGNETIC POLE FLUCTUATES.
AND BEING THE MIDGARD SERPENT, I CAN FEEL WHERE IT IS.
COULDN'T REACH IT UNTIL YOUR MAN TOSSED ME, AS I KNEW HE WOULD WITH THE PROPER GOADING.
SON OF A BITCH.
THIS ISN' MY PRISO ANYMORE-
IT'S YOUR GRAVE.
NEXT SNAKE'S NOT LYING

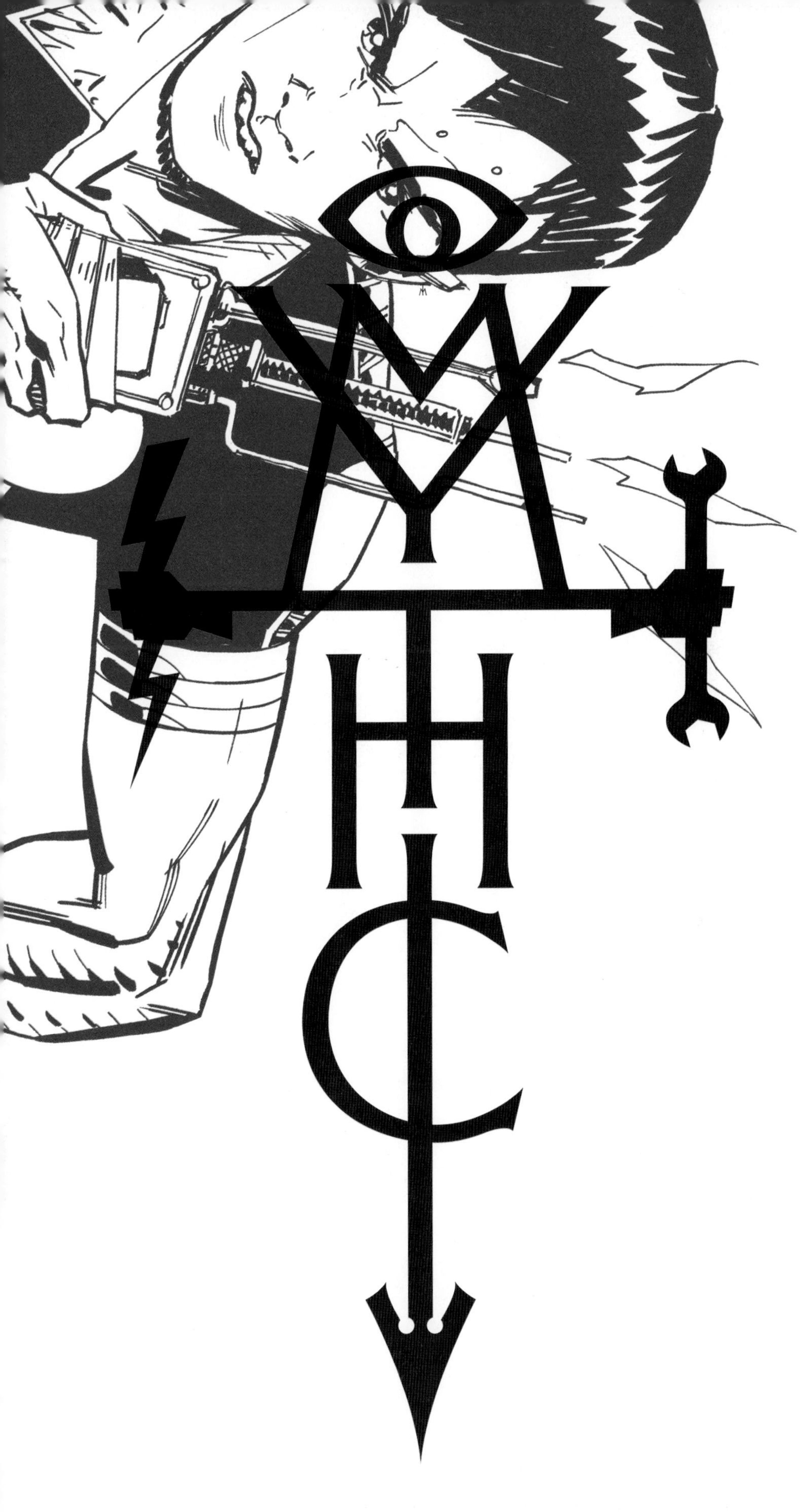
MYTHIC

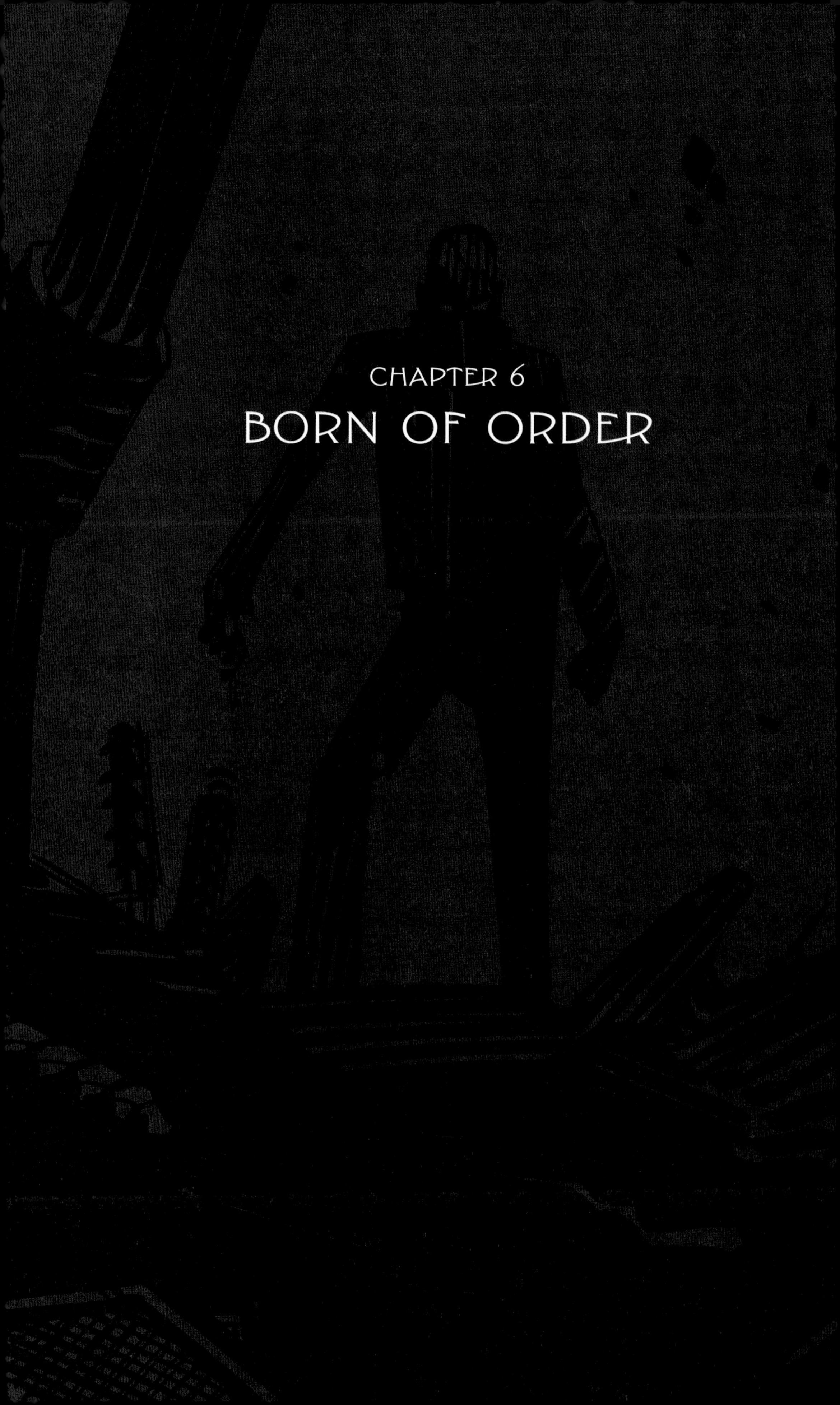

CHAPTER 6

BORN OF ORDER

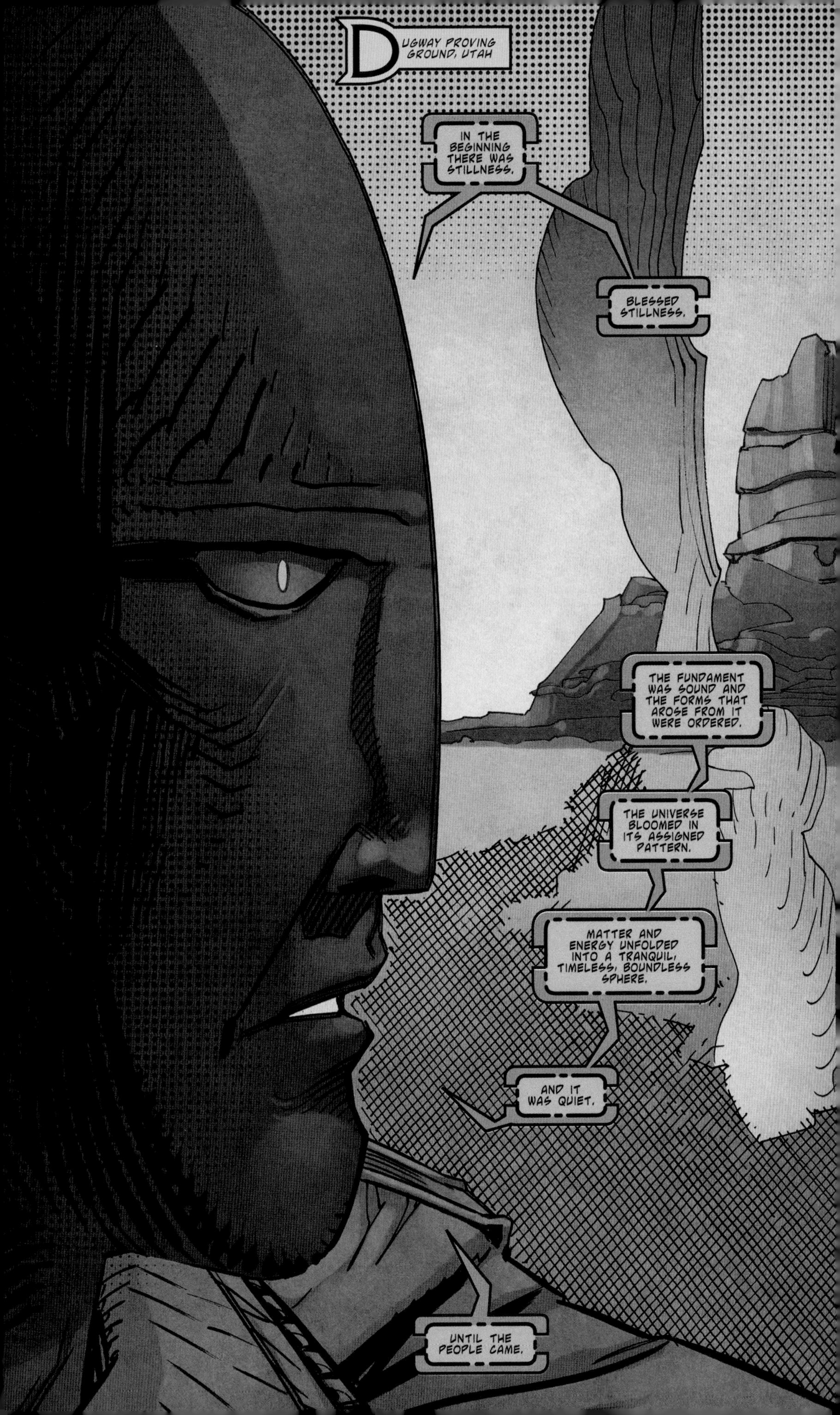
DUGWAY PROVING GROUND, UTAH
IN THE BEGINNING THERE WAS STILLNESS.
BLESSED STILLNESS.
THE FUNDAMENT WAS SOUND AND THE FORMS THAT AROSE FROM IT WERE ORDERED.
THE UNIVERSE BLOOMED IN ITS ASSIGNED PATTERN.
MATTER AND ENERGY UNFOLDED INTO A TRANQUIL, TIMELESS, BOUNDLESS SPHERE.
AND IT WAS QUIET.
UNTIL THE PEOPLE CAME.

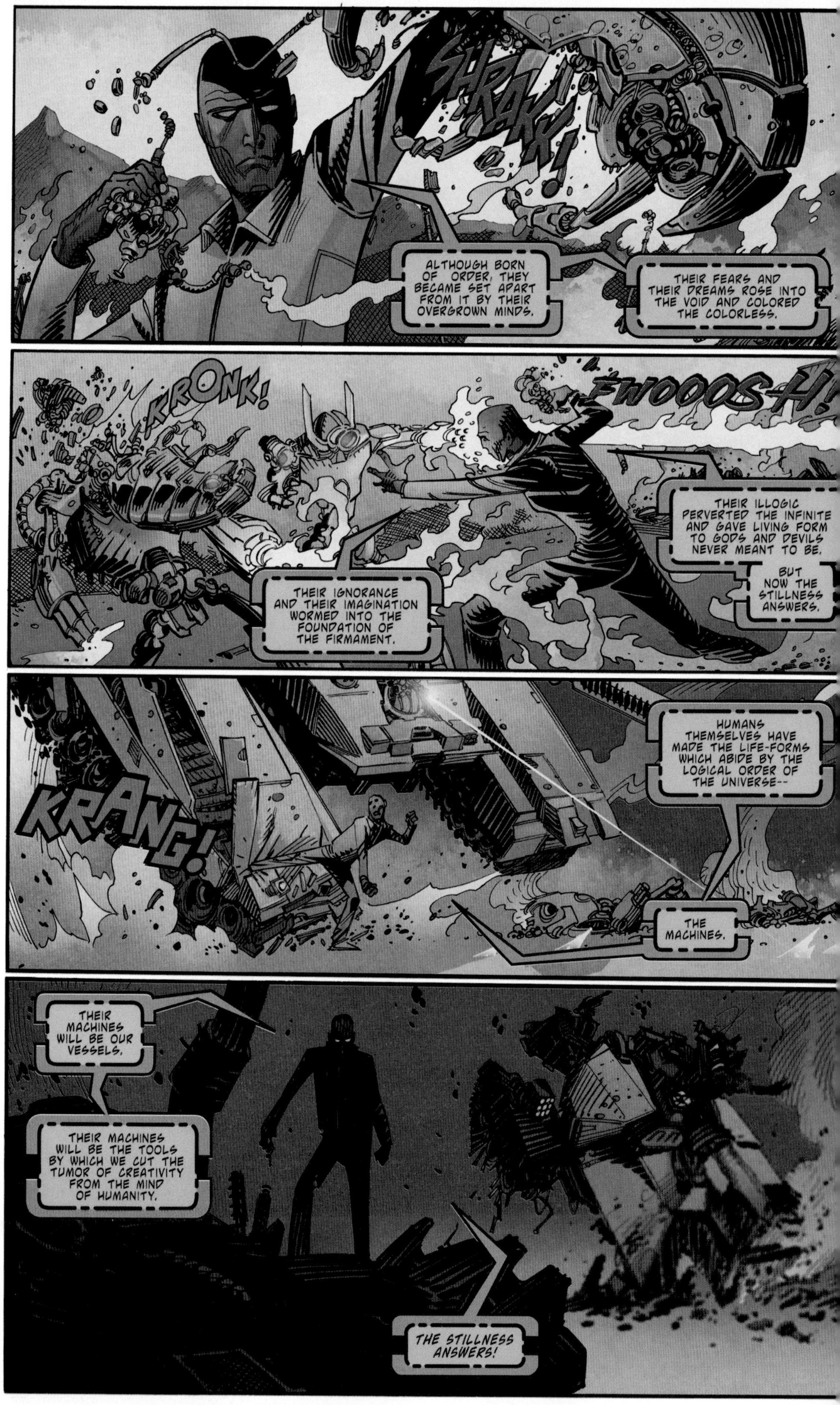

SHRAKK!
ALTHOUGH BORN OF ORDER, THEY BECAME SET APART FROM IT BY THEIR OVERGROWN MINDS.
THEIR FEARS AND THEIR DREAMS ROSE INTO THE VOID AND COLORED THE COLORLESS.
KRONK!
FWOOOSH!
THEIR IGNORANCE AND THEIR IMAGINATION WORMED INTO THE FOUNDATION OF THE FIRMAMENT.
THEIR ILLOGIC PERVERTED THE INFINITE AND GAVE LIVING FORM TO GODS AND DEVILS NEVER MEANT TO BE.
BUT NOW THE STILLNESS ANSWERS.
KRANG!
HUMANS THEMSELVES HAVE MADE THE LIFE-FORMS WHICH ABIDE BY THE LOGICAL ORDER OF THE UNIVERSE--
THE MACHINES.
THEIR MACHINES WILL BE OUR VESSELS.
THEIR MACHINES WILL BE THE TOOLS BY WHICH WE CUT THE TUMOR OF CREATIVITY FROM THE MIND OF HUMANITY.
THE STILLNESS ANSWERS!

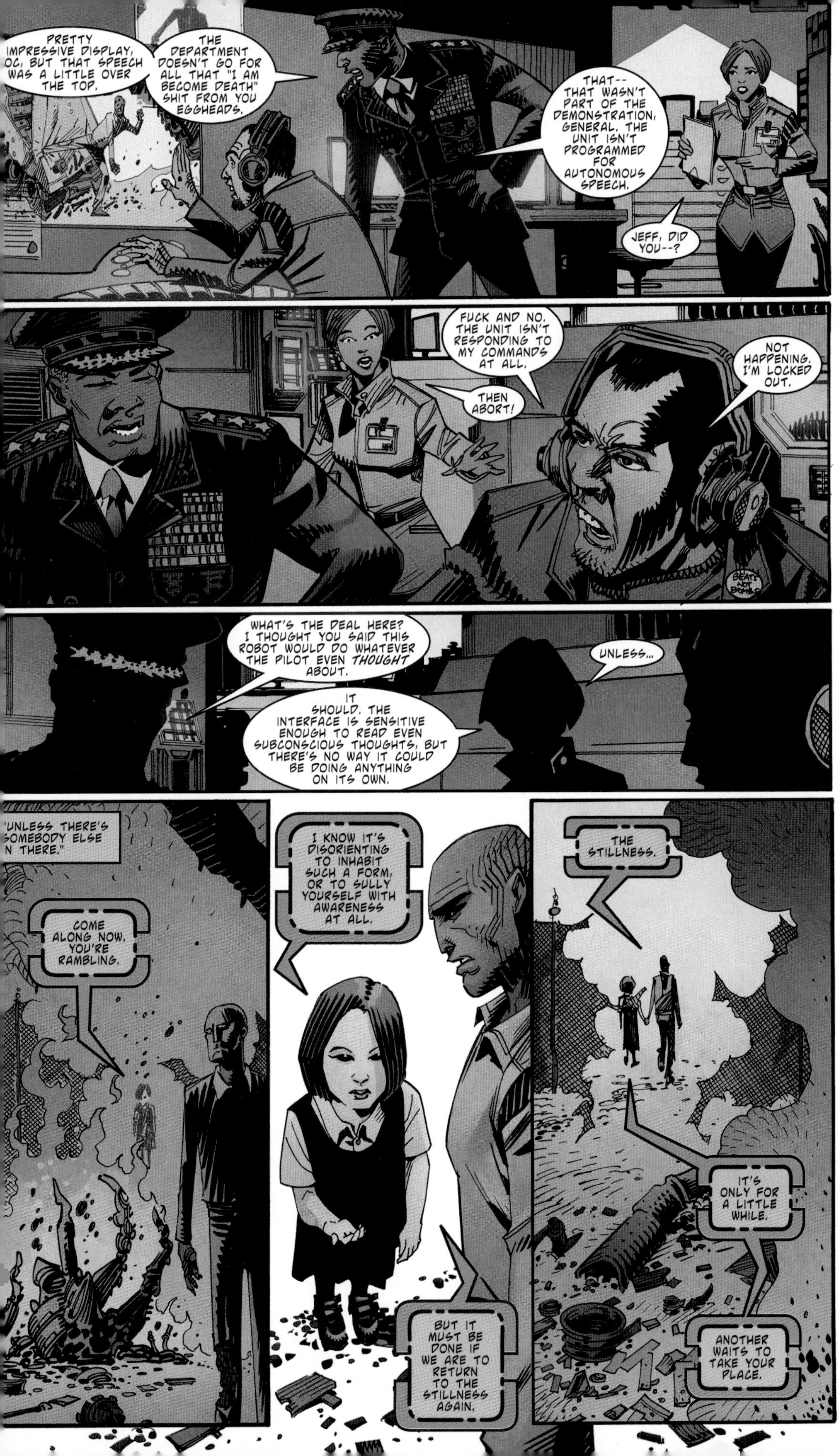
PRETTY IMPRESSIVE DISPLAY, DOC, BUT THAT SPEECH WAS A LITTLE OVER THE TOP.
THE DEPARTMENT DOESN'T GO FOR ALL THAT "I AM BECOME DEATH" SHIT FROM YOU EGGHEADS.
THAT-- THAT WASN'T PART OF THE DEMONSTRATION, GENERAL. THE UNIT ISN'T PROGRAMMED FOR AUTONOMOUS SPEECH.
JEFF, DID YOU--?
FUCK AND NO. THE UNIT ISN'T RESPONDING TO MY COMMANDS AT ALL.
THEN ABORT!
NOT HAPPENING. I'M LOCKED OUT.
WHAT'S THE DEAL HERE? I THOUGHT YOU SAID THIS ROBOT WOULD DO WHATEVER THE PILOT EVEN *THOUGHT* ABOUT.
IT SHOULD. THE INTERFACE IS SENSITIVE ENOUGH TO READ EVEN SUBCONSCIOUS THOUGHTS, BUT THERE'S NO WAY IT COULD BE DOING ANYTHING ON ITS OWN.
UNLESS...
"UNLESS THERE'S SOMEBODY ELSE IN THERE."
COME ALONG NOW. YOU'RE RAMBLING.
I KNOW IT'S DISORIENTING TO INHABIT SUCH A FORM, OR TO SULLY YOURSELF WITH AWARENESS AT ALL.
BUT IT MUST BE DONE IF WE ARE TO RETURN TO THE STILLNESS AGAIN.
THE STILLNESS.
IT'S ONLY FOR A LITTLE WHILE.
ANOTHER WAITS TO TAKE YOUR PLACE.

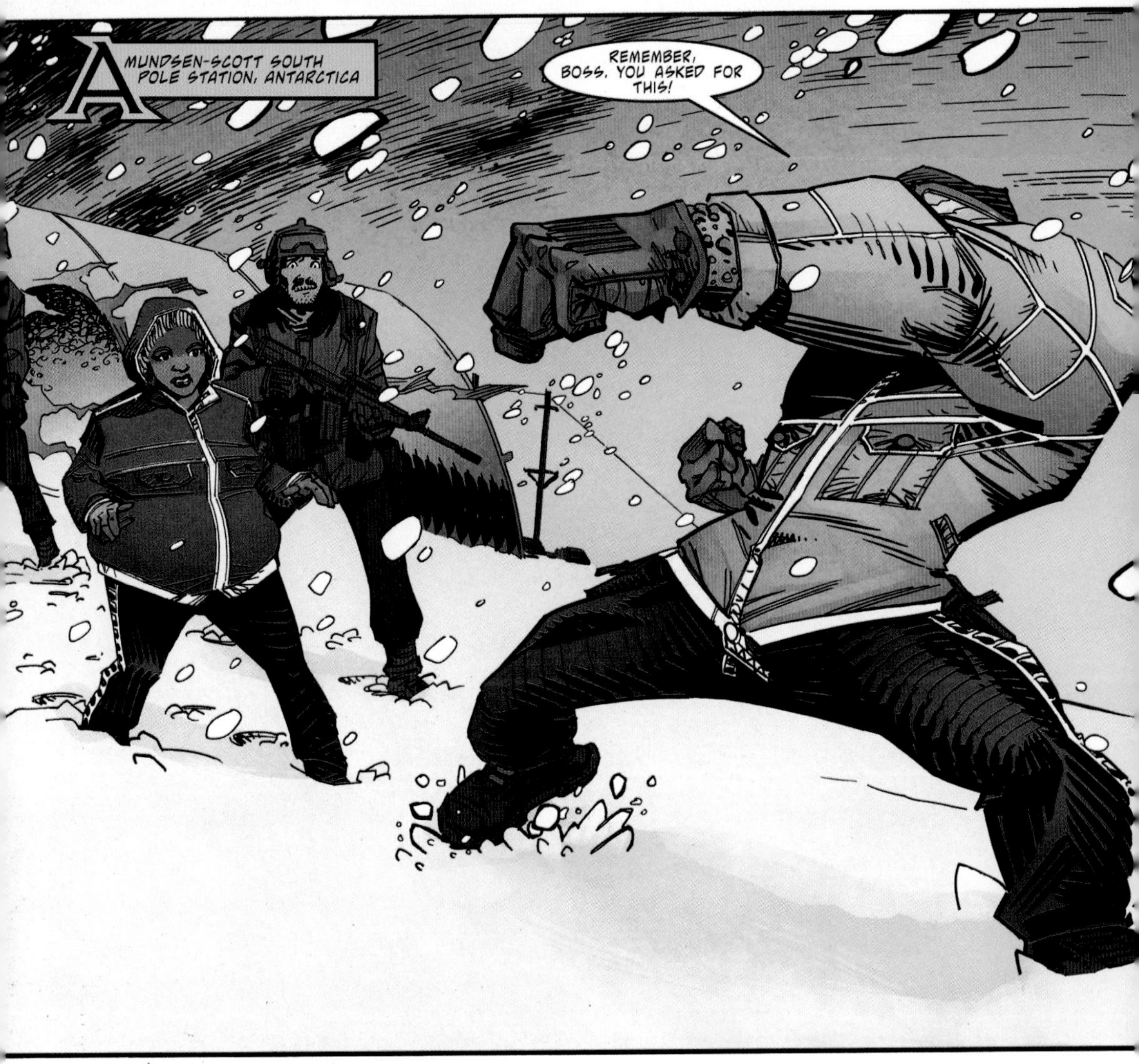
A MUNDSEN-SCOTT SOUTH POLE STATION, ANTARCTICA
REMEMBER, BOSS, YOU ASKED FOR THIS!

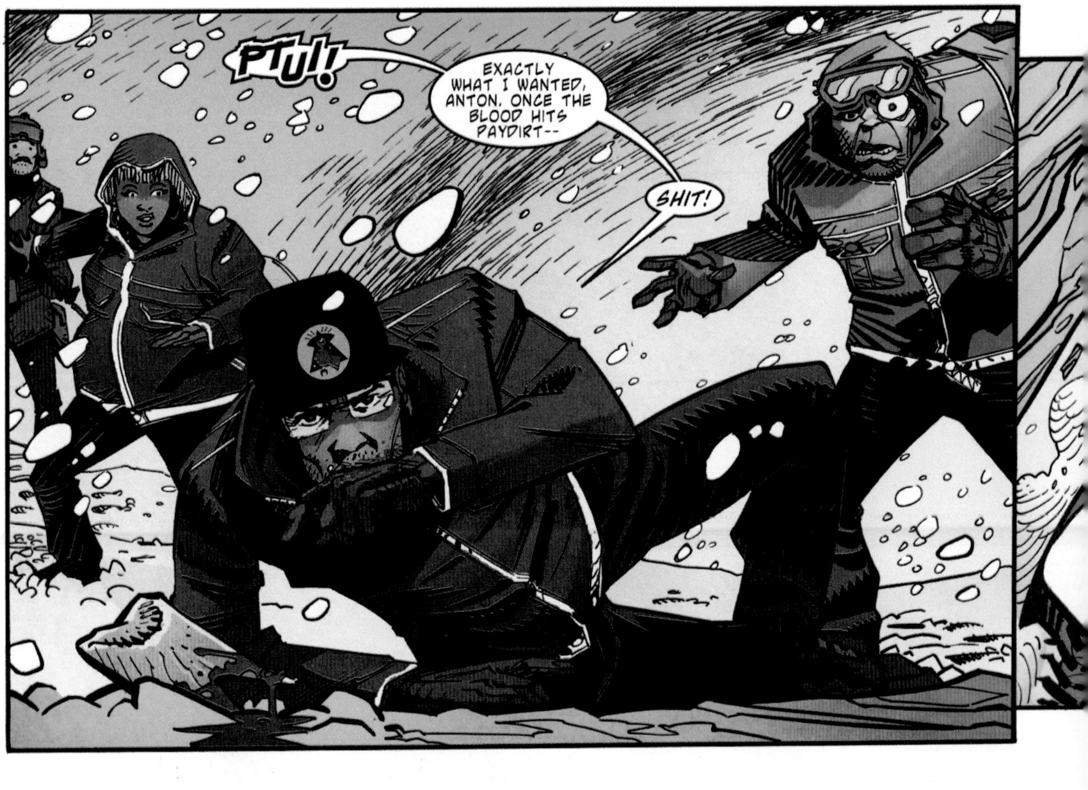
PTUI!
EXACTLY WHAT I WANTED, ANTON. ONCE THE BLOOD HITS PAYDIRT--
SHIT!

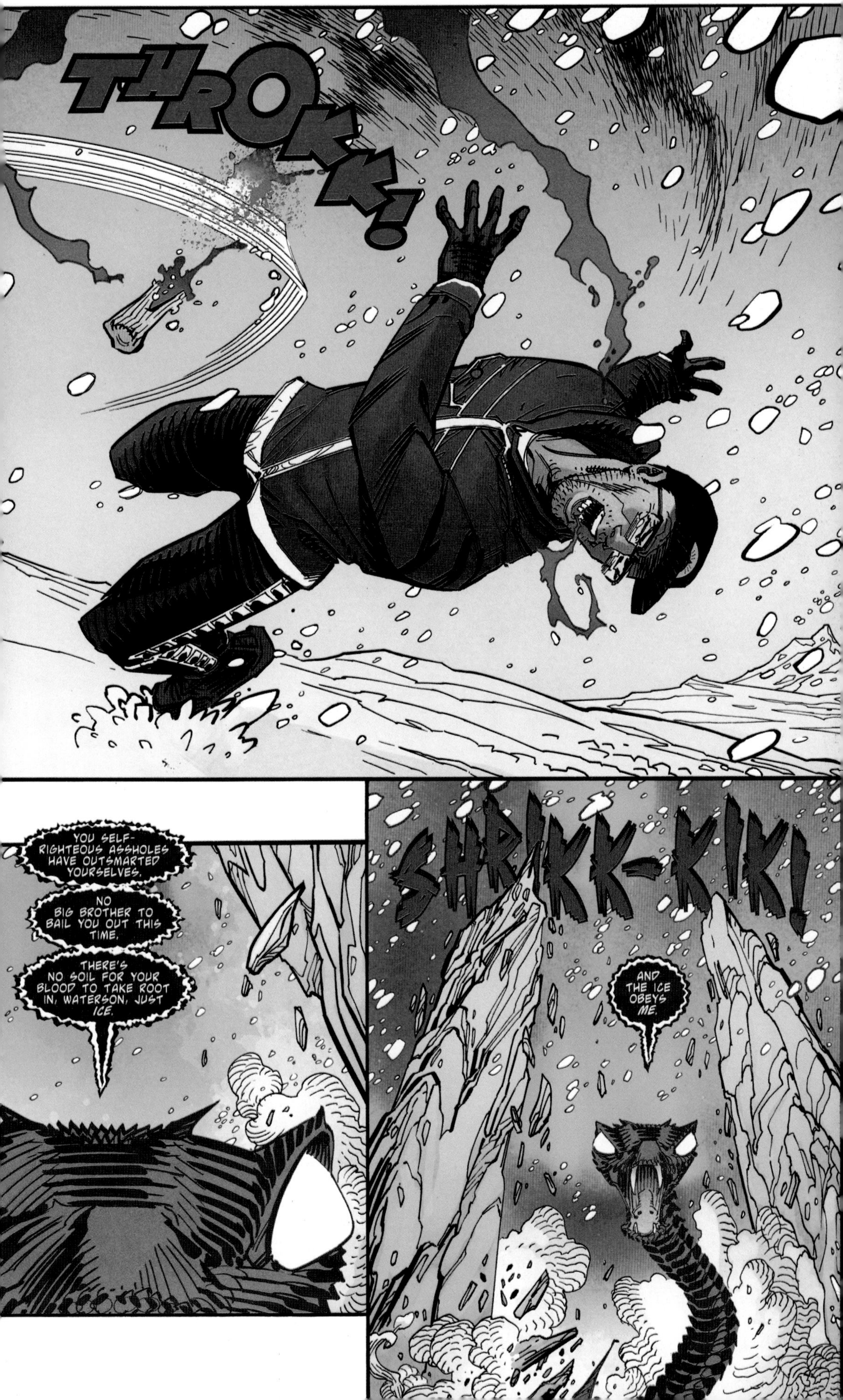
THROKK!
YOU SELF-RIGHTEOUS ASSHOLES HAVE OUTSMARTED YOURSELVES.
NO BIG BROTHER TO BAIL YOU OUT THIS TIME.
THERE'S NO SOIL FOR YOUR BLOOD TO TAKE ROOT IN, WATERSON, JUST ICE.
SHRIKK-KIK!
AND THE ICE OBEYS ME.

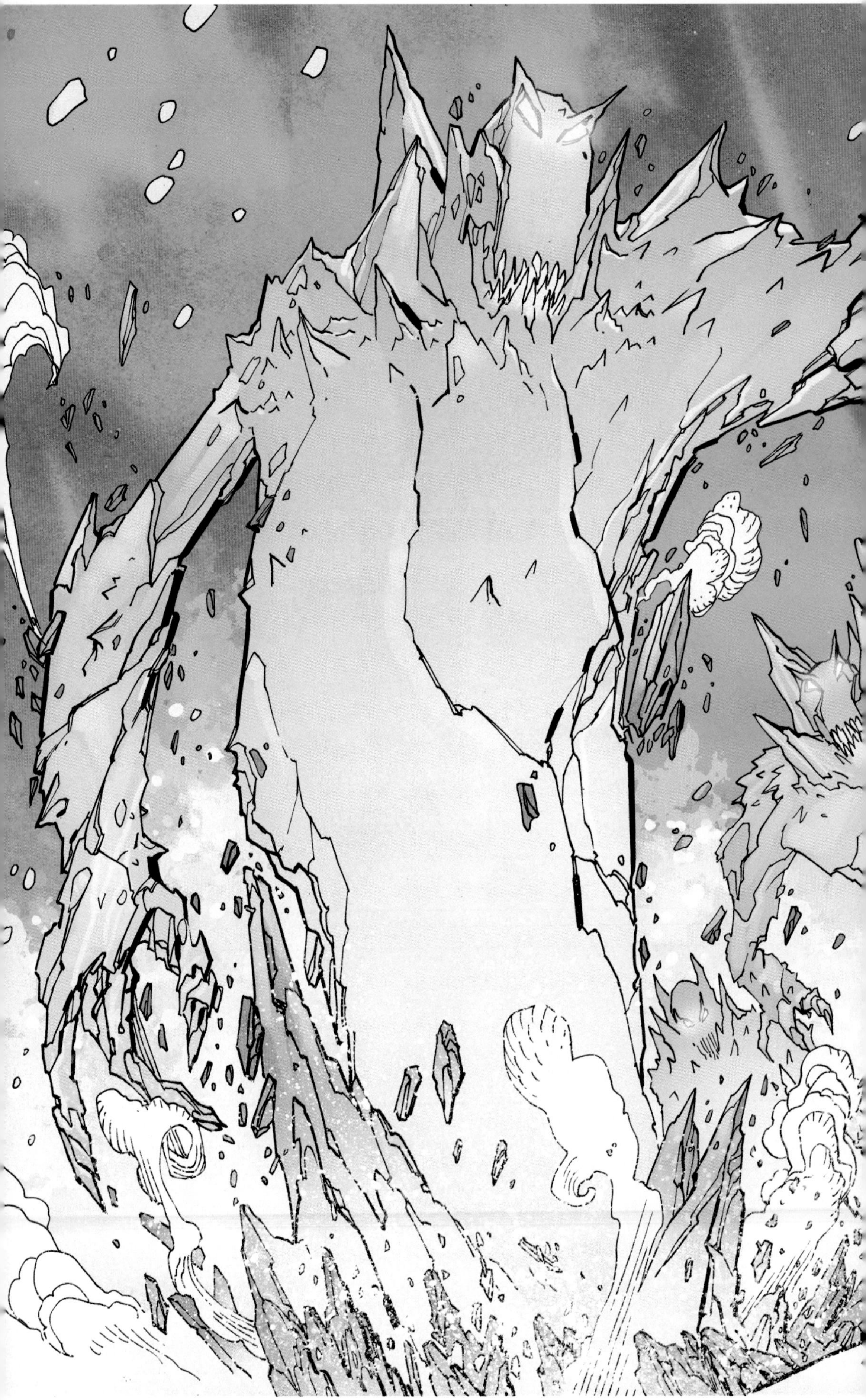

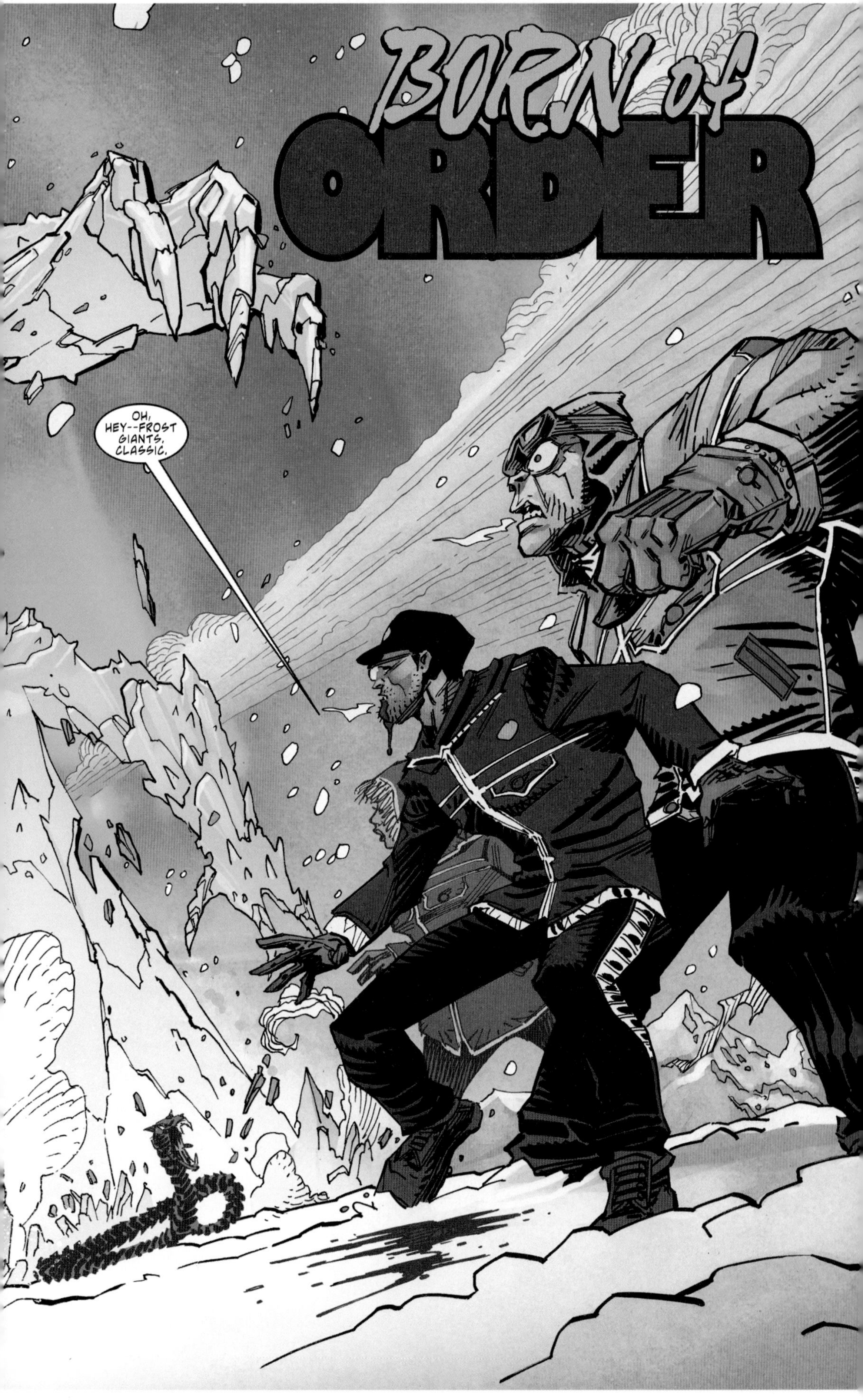
BORN of
ORDER
OH, HEY--FROST GIANTS. CLASSIC.

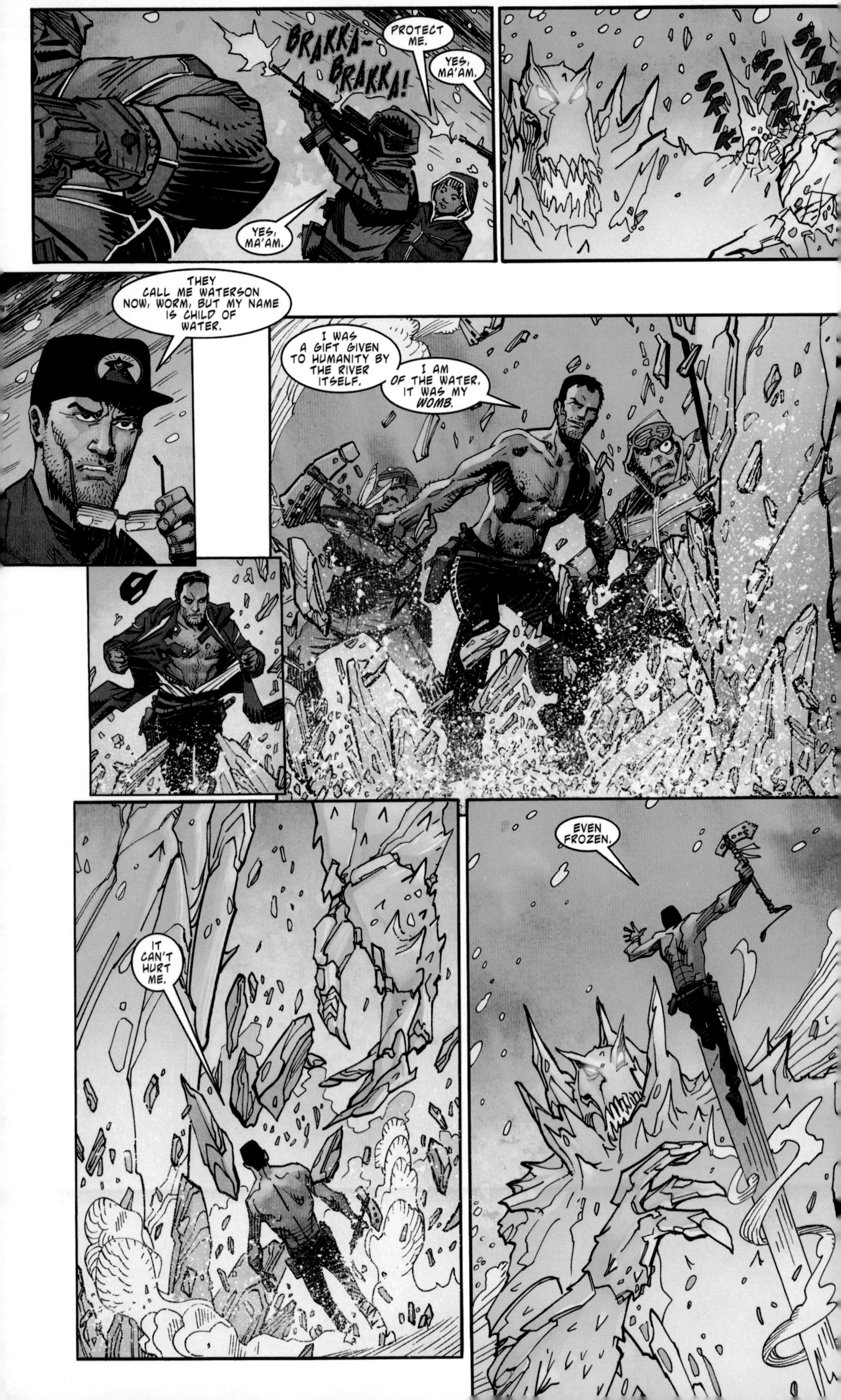
BRAKKA-BRAKKA!
PROTECT ME.
YES, MA'AM.
YES, MA'AM.
THEY CALL ME WATERSON NOW, WORM, BUT MY NAME IS CHILD OF WATER.
I WAS A GIFT GIVEN TO HUMANITY BY THE RIVER ITSELF.
I AM OF THE WATER. IT WAS MY WOMB.
IT CAN'T HURT ME.
EVEN FROZEN.

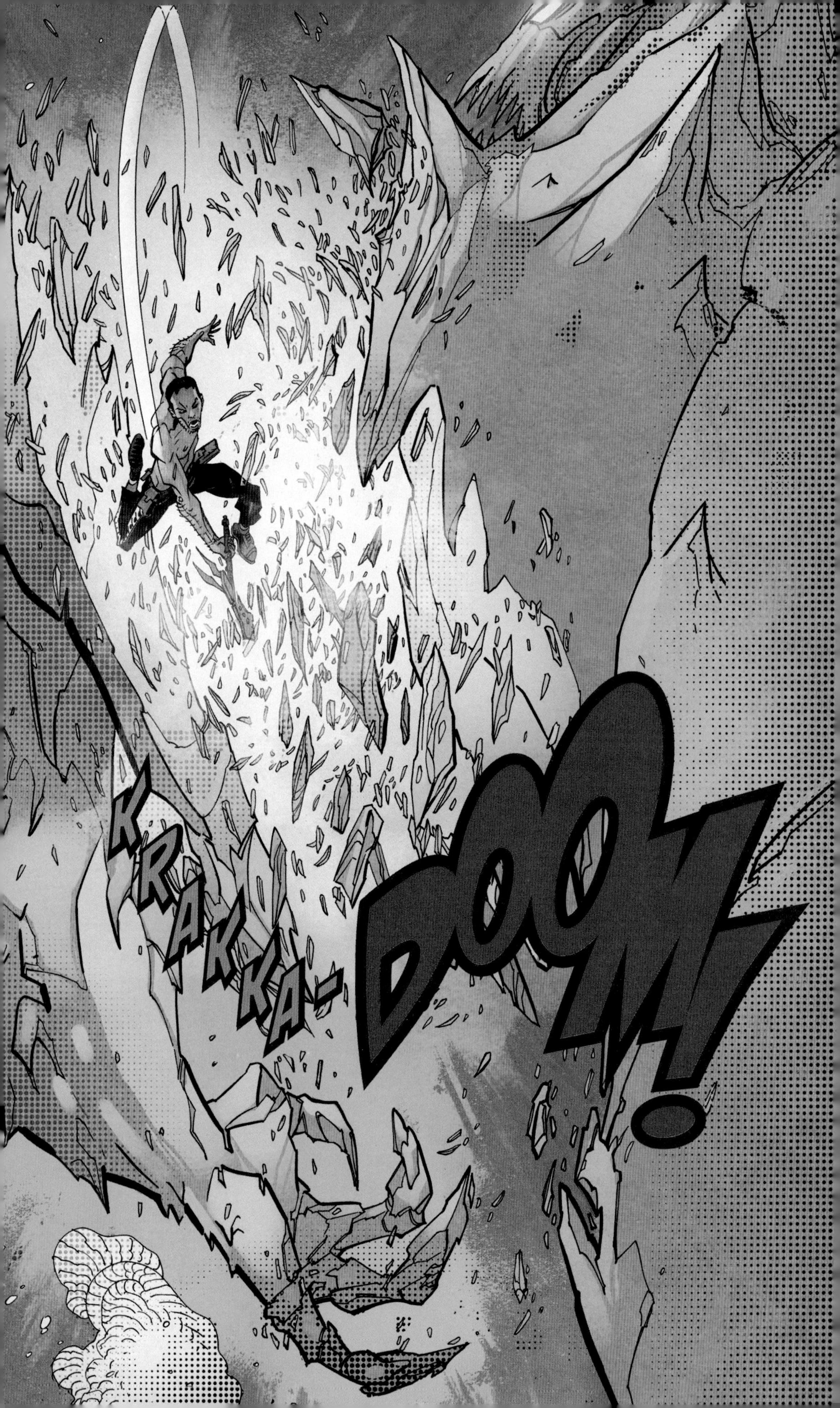
KRAKKA-DOOM!

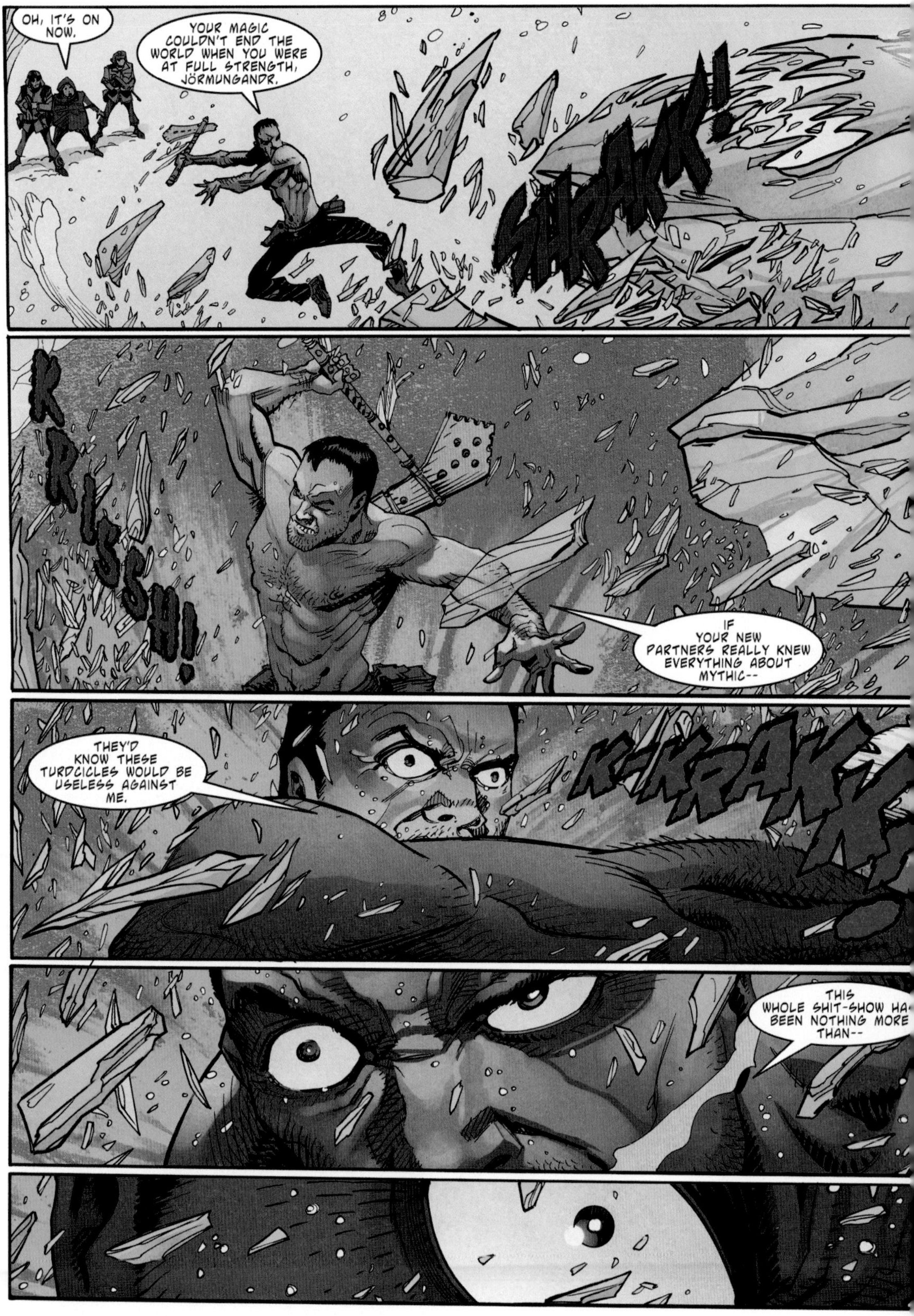
OH, IT'S ON NOW.
YOUR MAGIC COULDN'T END THE WORLD WHEN YOU WERE AT FULL STRENGTH, JÖRMUNGANDR.
SHRAKK!
KRIISSH!
IF YOUR NEW PARTNERS REALLY KNEW EVERYTHING ABOUT MYTHIC--
THEY'D KNOW THESE TURDCICLES WOULD BE USELESS AGAINST ME.
K-KRAKK
THIS WHOLE SHIT-SHOW HA BEEN NOTHING MORE THAN--

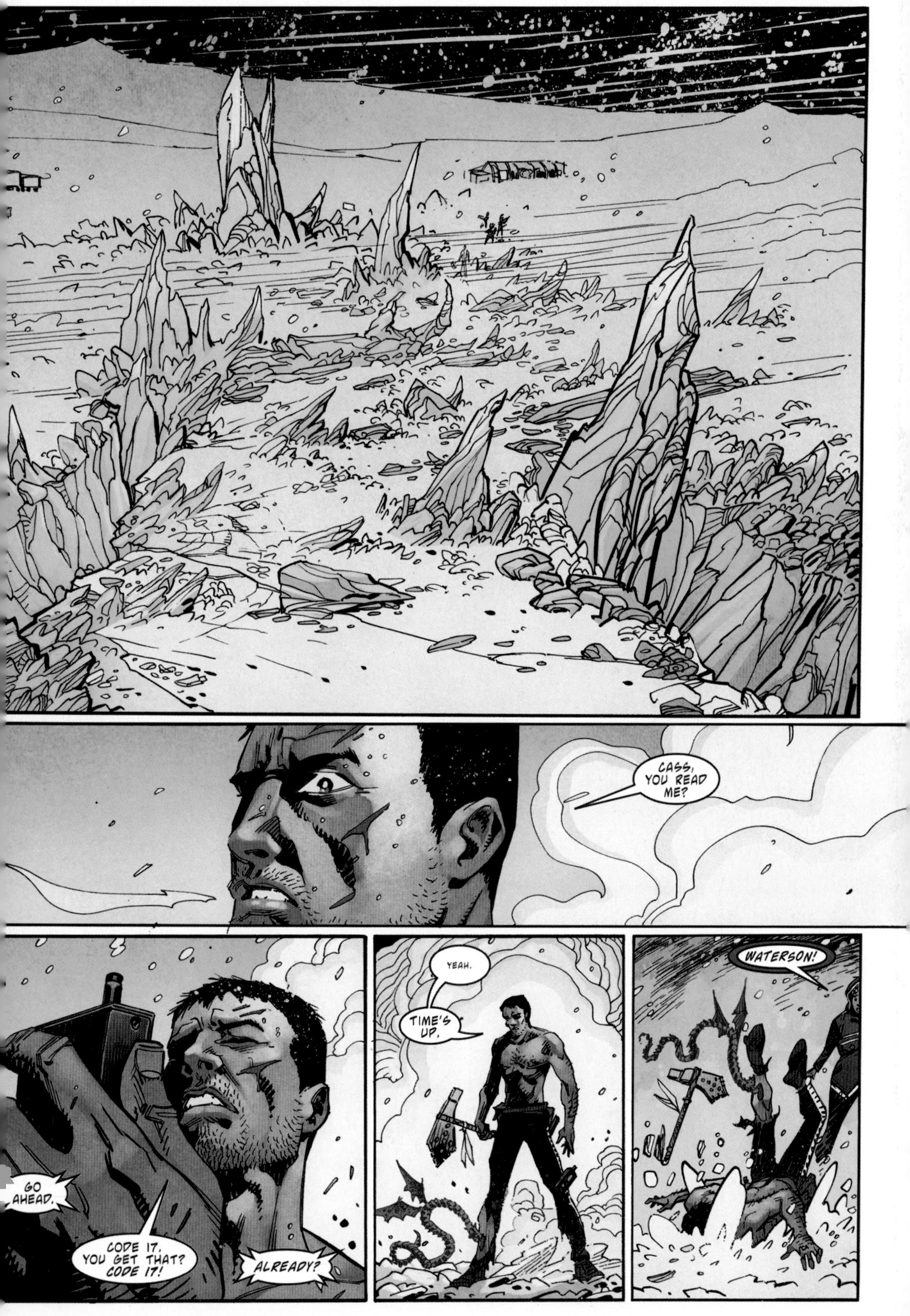

CASS, YOU READ ME?
GO AHEAD.
CODE 17. YOU GET THAT? CODE 17!
ALREADY?
YEAH.
TIME'S UP.
WATERSON!

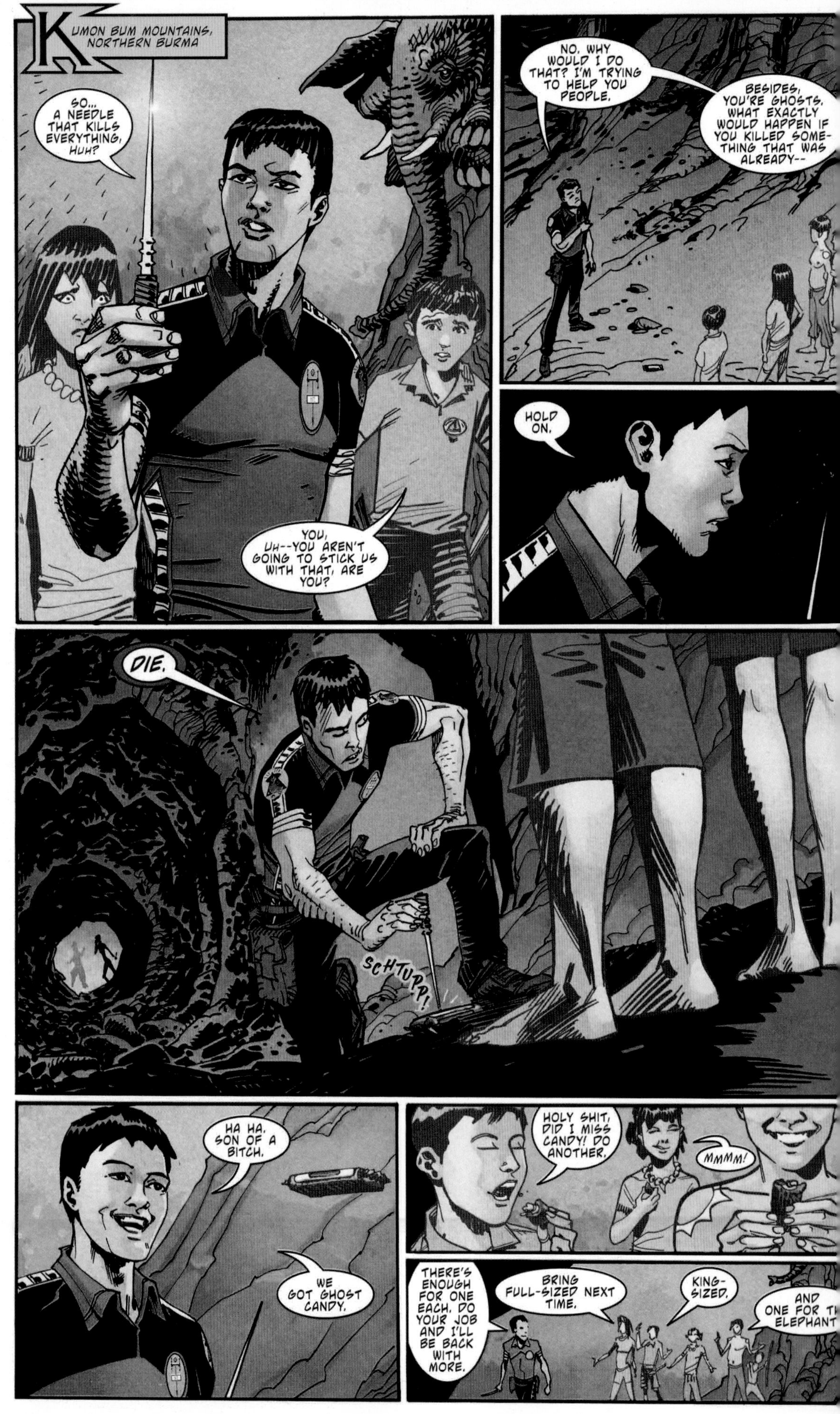
KUMON BUM MOUNTAINS, NORTHERN BURMA
SO... A NEEDLE THAT KILLS EVERYTHING, HUH?
YOU, UH--YOU AREN'T GOING TO STICK US WITH THAT, ARE YOU?
NO. WHY WOULD I DO THAT? I'M TRYING TO HELP YOU PEOPLE.
BESIDES, YOU'RE GHOSTS. WHAT EXACTLY WOULD HAPPEN IF YOU KILLED SOMETHING THAT WAS ALREADY--
HOLD ON.
DIE.
SCHTUPP!
HA HA. SON OF A BITCH.
WE GOT GHOST CANDY.
HOLY SHIT, DID I MISS CANDY! DO ANOTHER.
MMMM!
THERE'S ENOUGH FOR ONE EACH. DO YOUR JOB AND I'LL BE BACK WITH MORE.
BRING FULL-SIZED NEXT TIME.
KING-SIZED.
AND ONE FOR TH ELEPHANT

CHAPTER 7

INFERNAL ENGINES

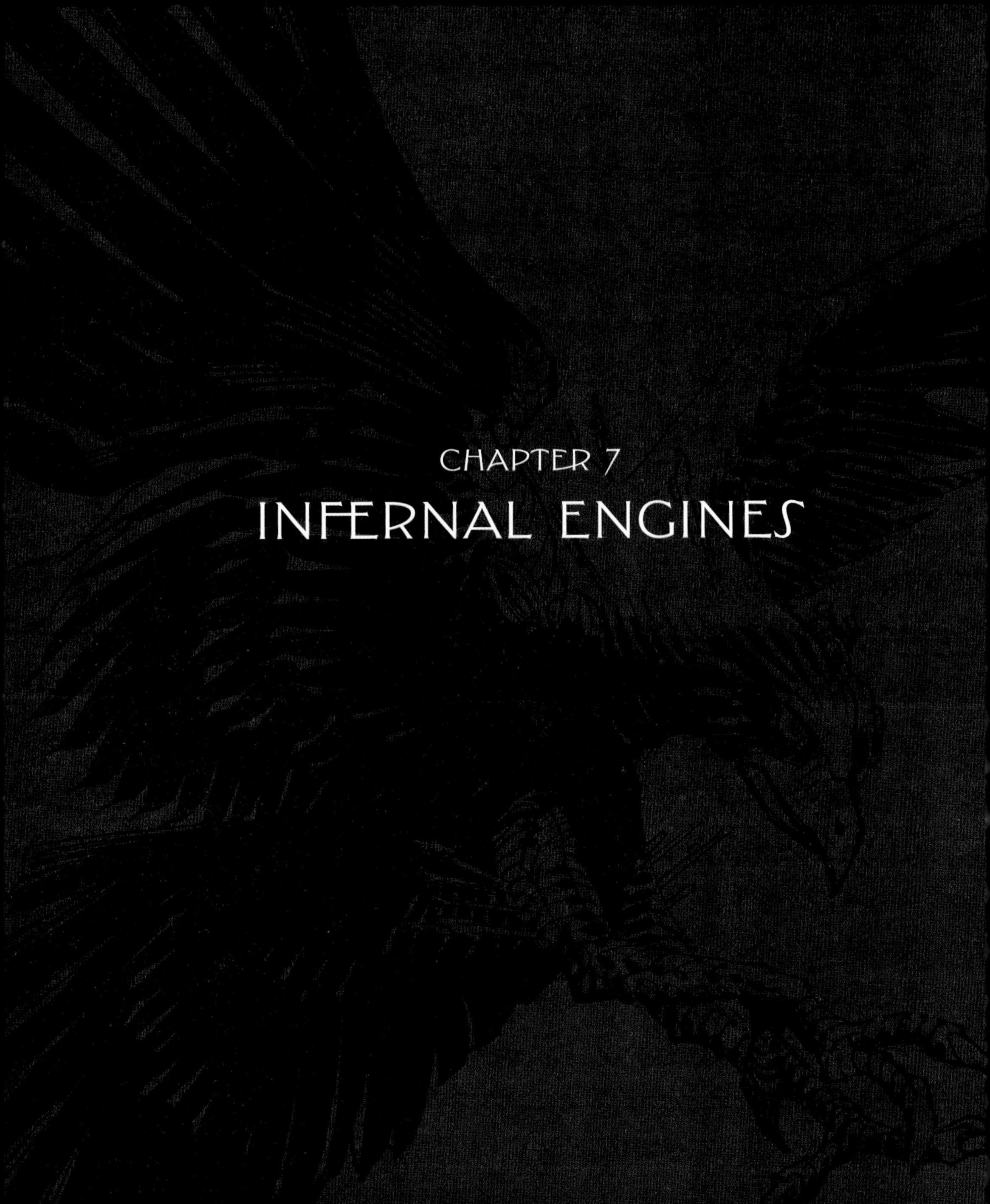

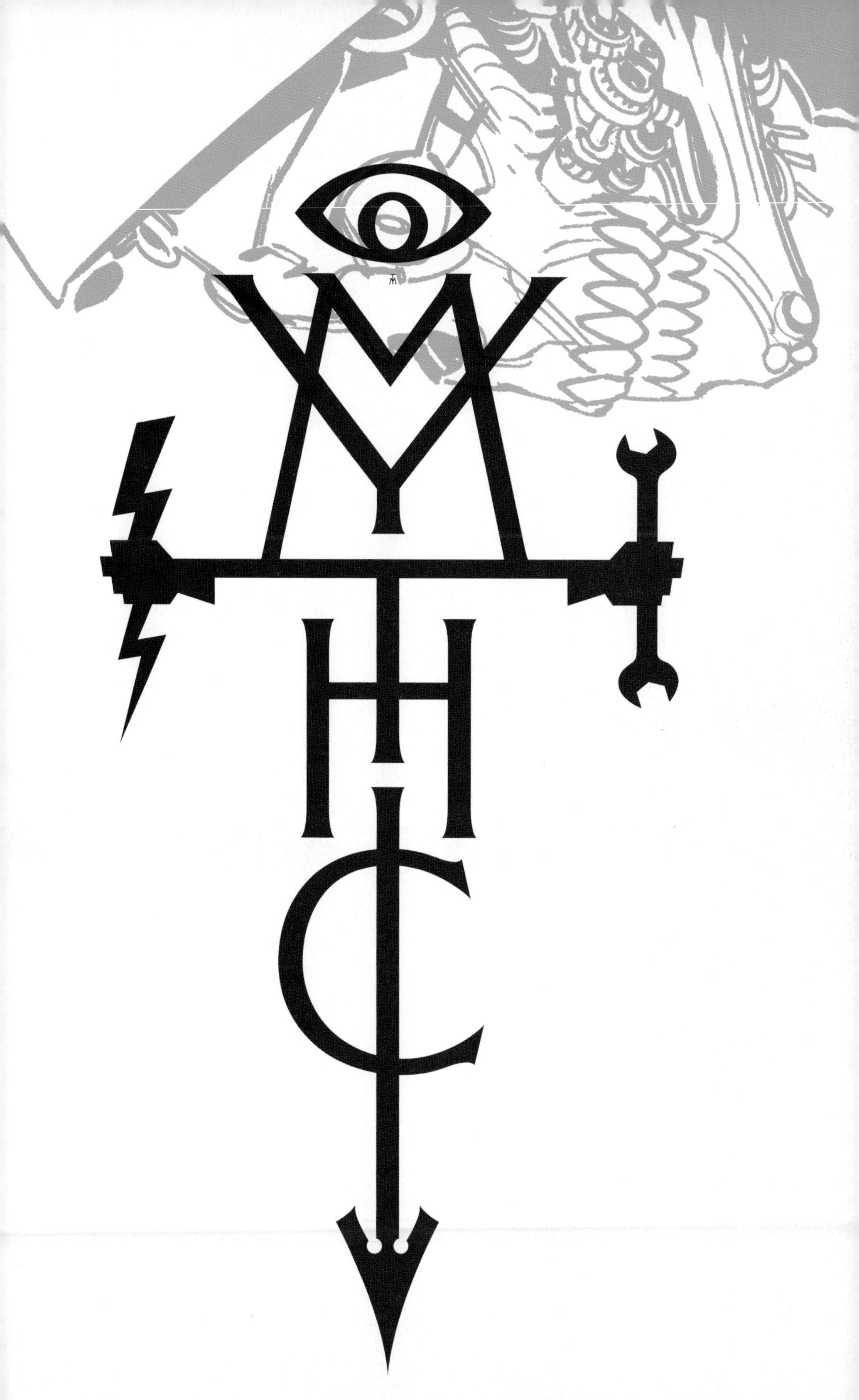

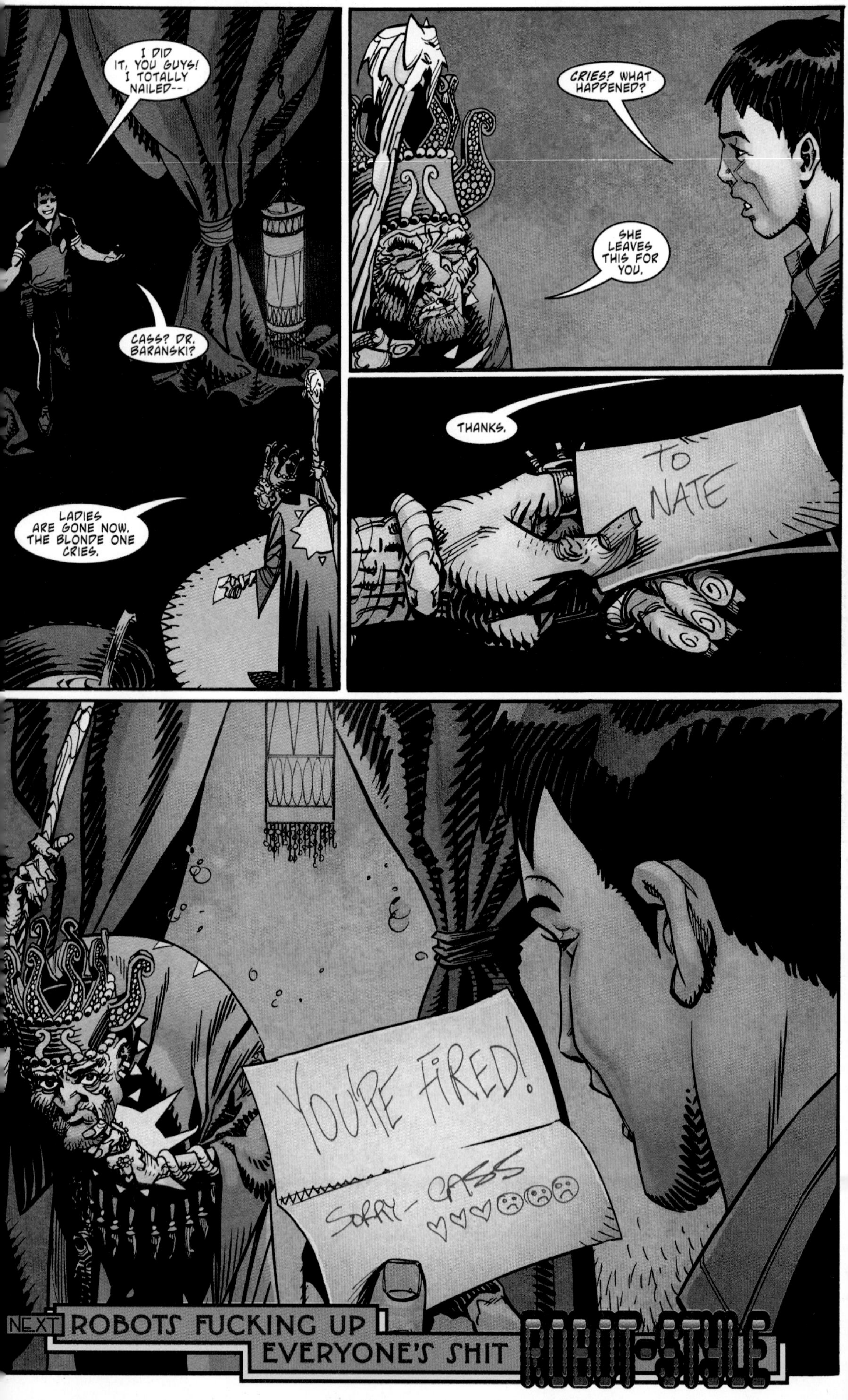
I DID IT, YOU GUYS! I TOTALLY NAILED--
CASS? DR. BARANSKI?
LADIES ARE GONE NOW. THE BLONDE ONE CRIES.
CRIES? WHAT HAPPENED?
SHE LEAVES THIS FOR YOU.
THANKS.
TO NATE
YOU'RE FIRED!
SORRY - CASS
NEXT ROBOTS FUCKING UP EVERYONE'S SHIT ROBOT-STYLE

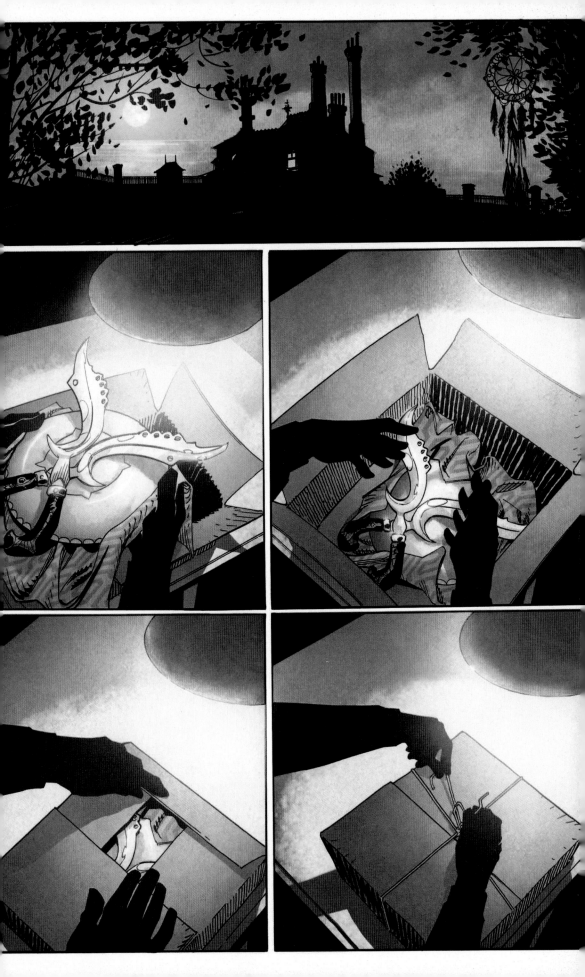

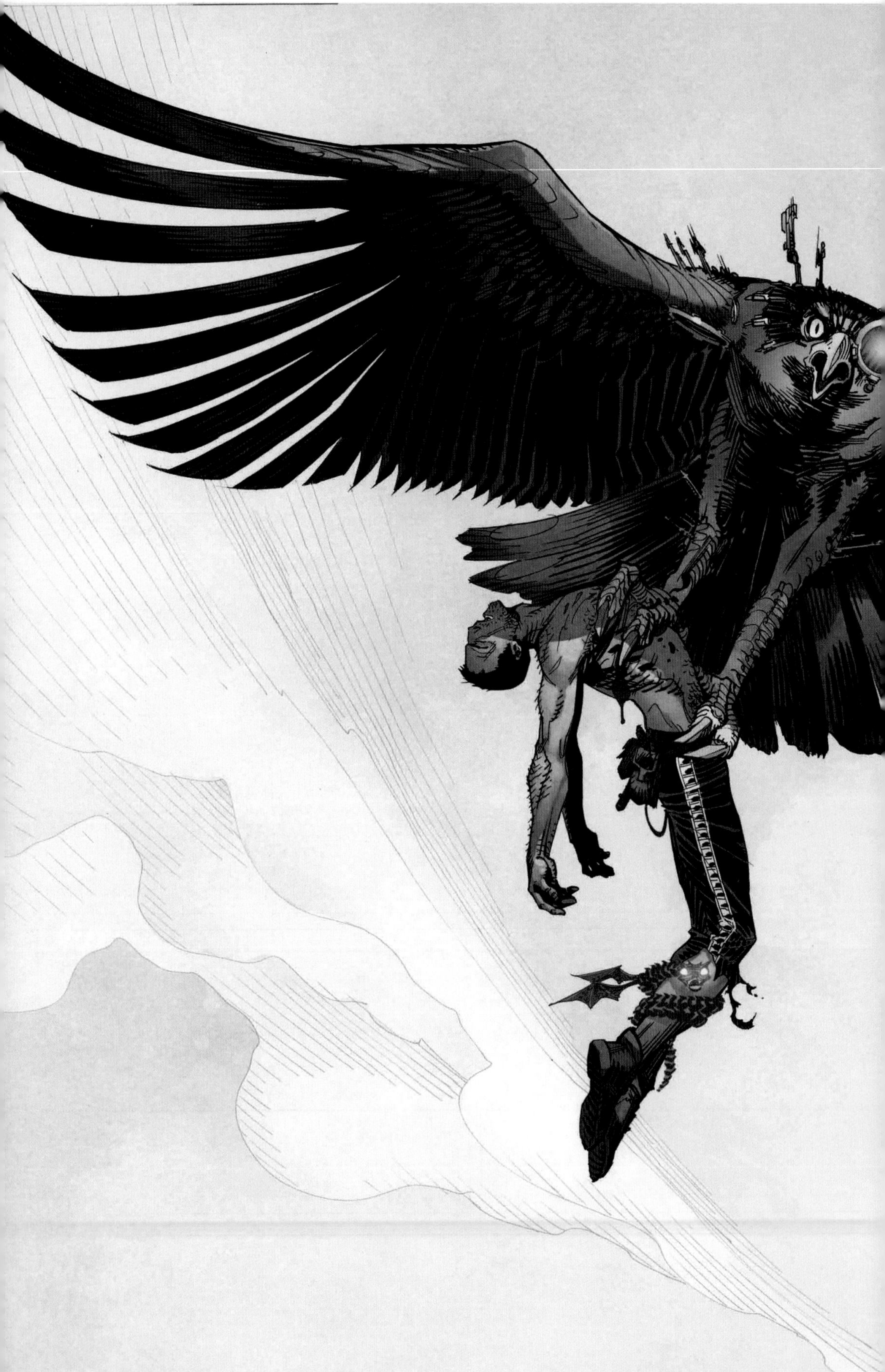

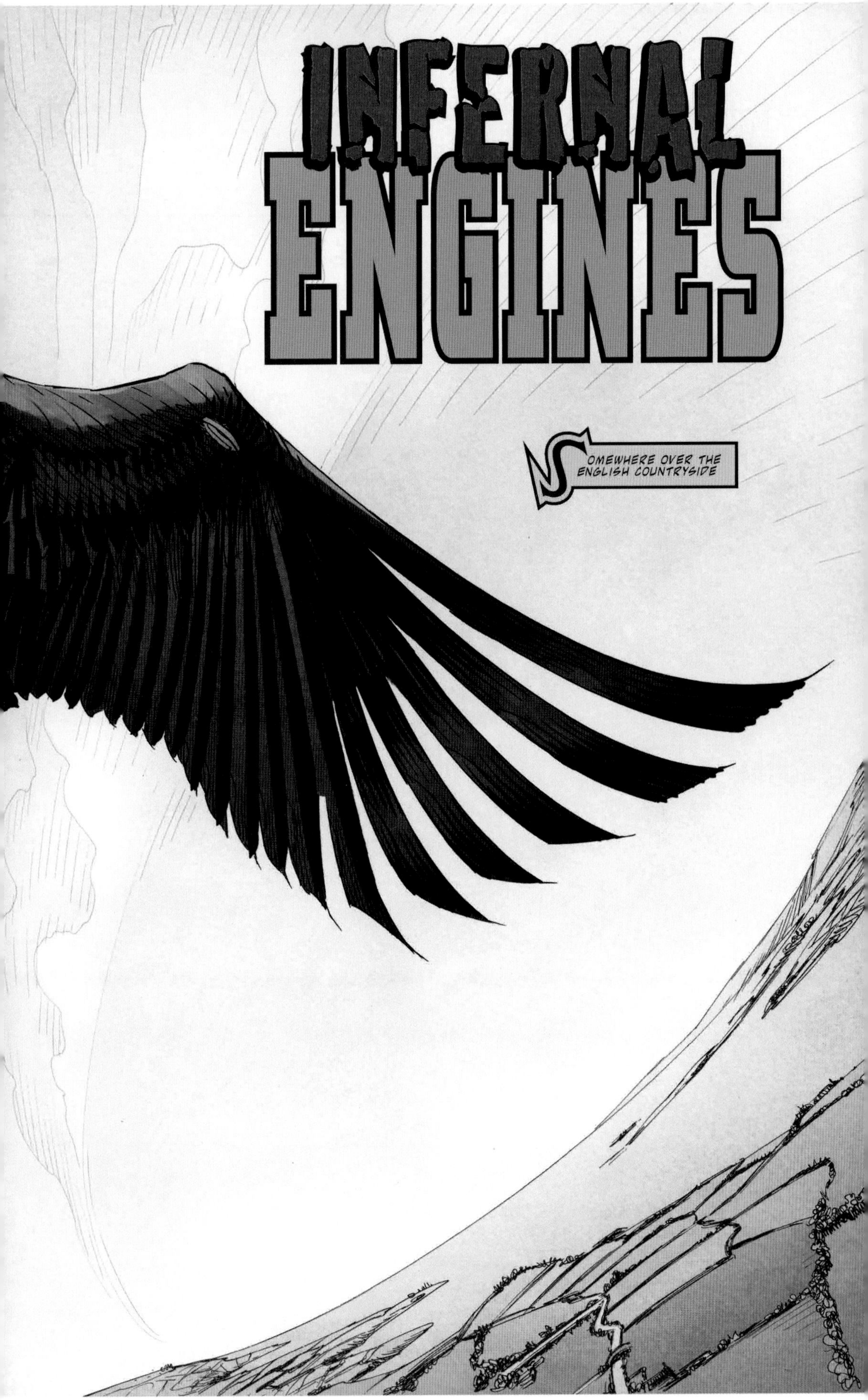

INFERNAL ENGINES
SOMEWHERE OVER THE ENGLISH COUNTRYSIDE

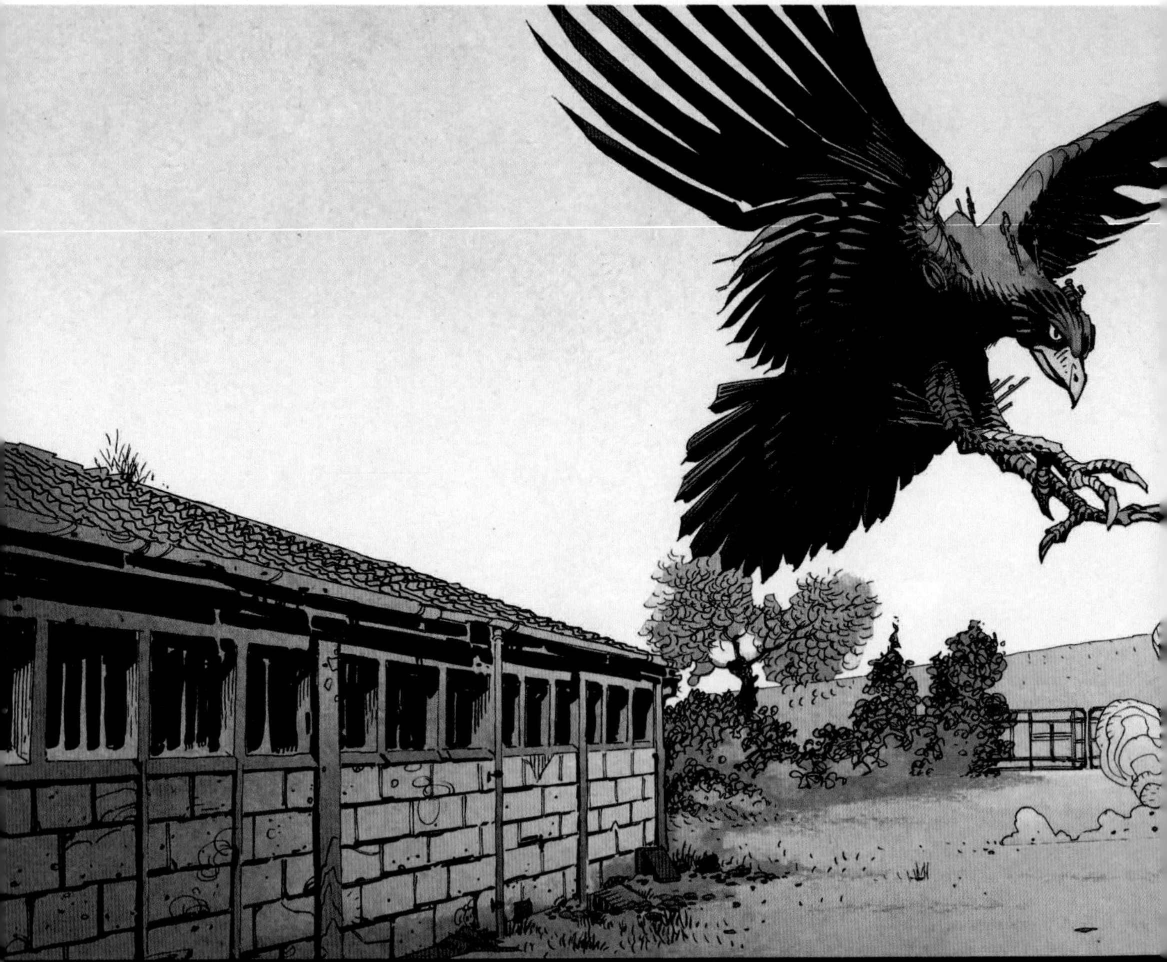
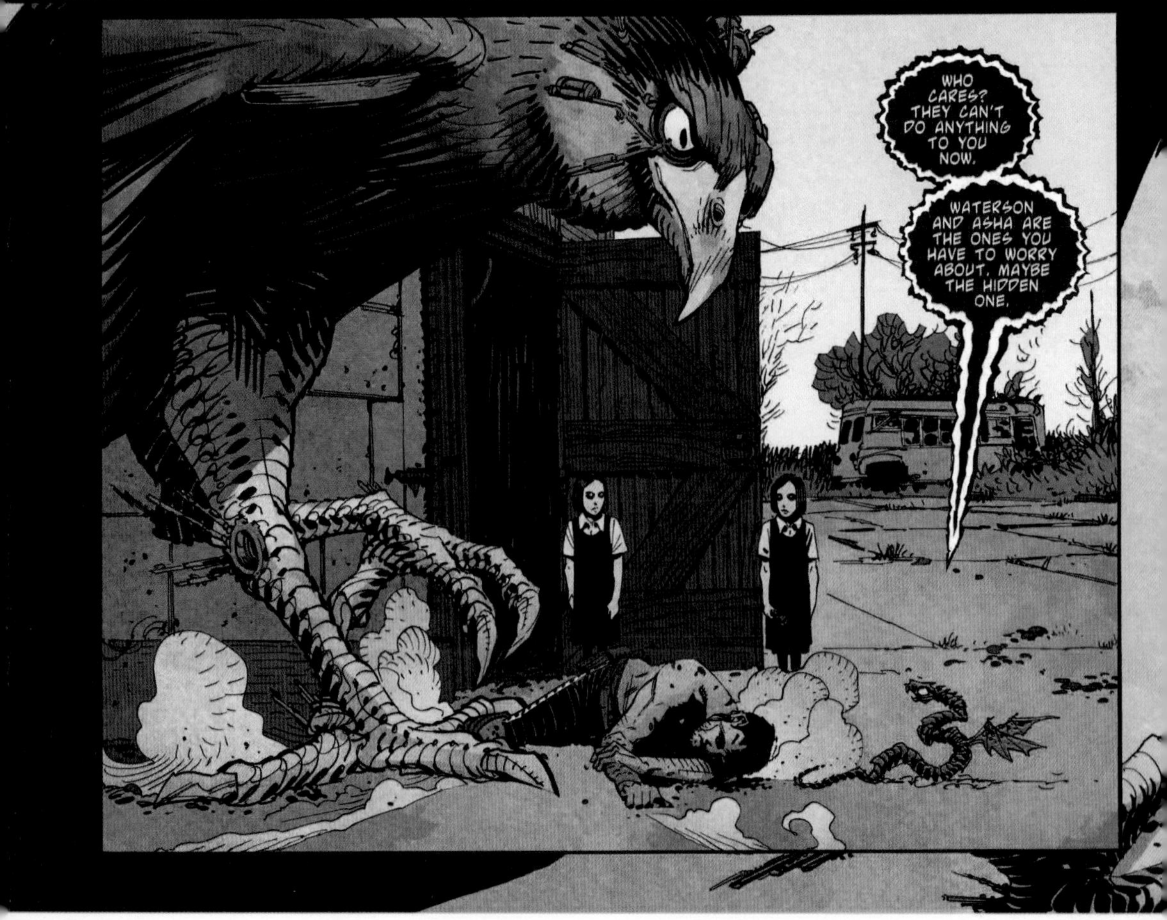
WHO CARES? THEY CAN'T DO ANYTHING TO YOU NOW.
WATERSON AND ASHA ARE THE ONES YOU HAVE TO WORRY ABOUT. MAYBE THE HIDDEN ONE.

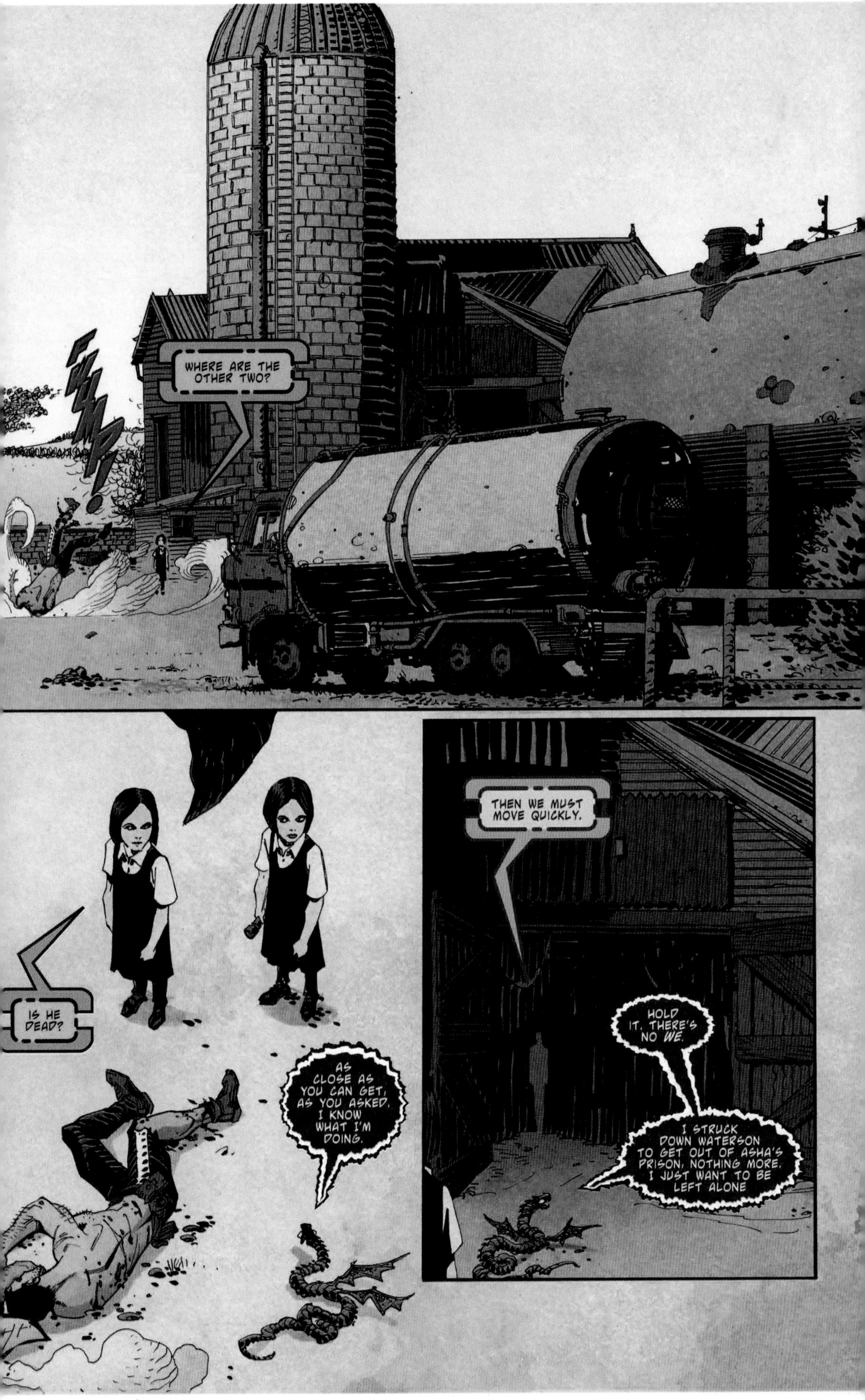
FLUMP!
WHERE ARE THE OTHER TWO?
IS HE DEAD?
AS CLOSE AS YOU CAN GET, AS YOU ASKED. I KNOW WHAT I'M DOING.
THEN WE MUST MOVE QUICKLY.
HOLD IT. THERE'S NO *WE*.
I STRUCK DOWN WATERSON TO GET OUT OF ASHA'S PRISON, NOTHING MORE. I JUST WANT TO BE LEFT ALONE

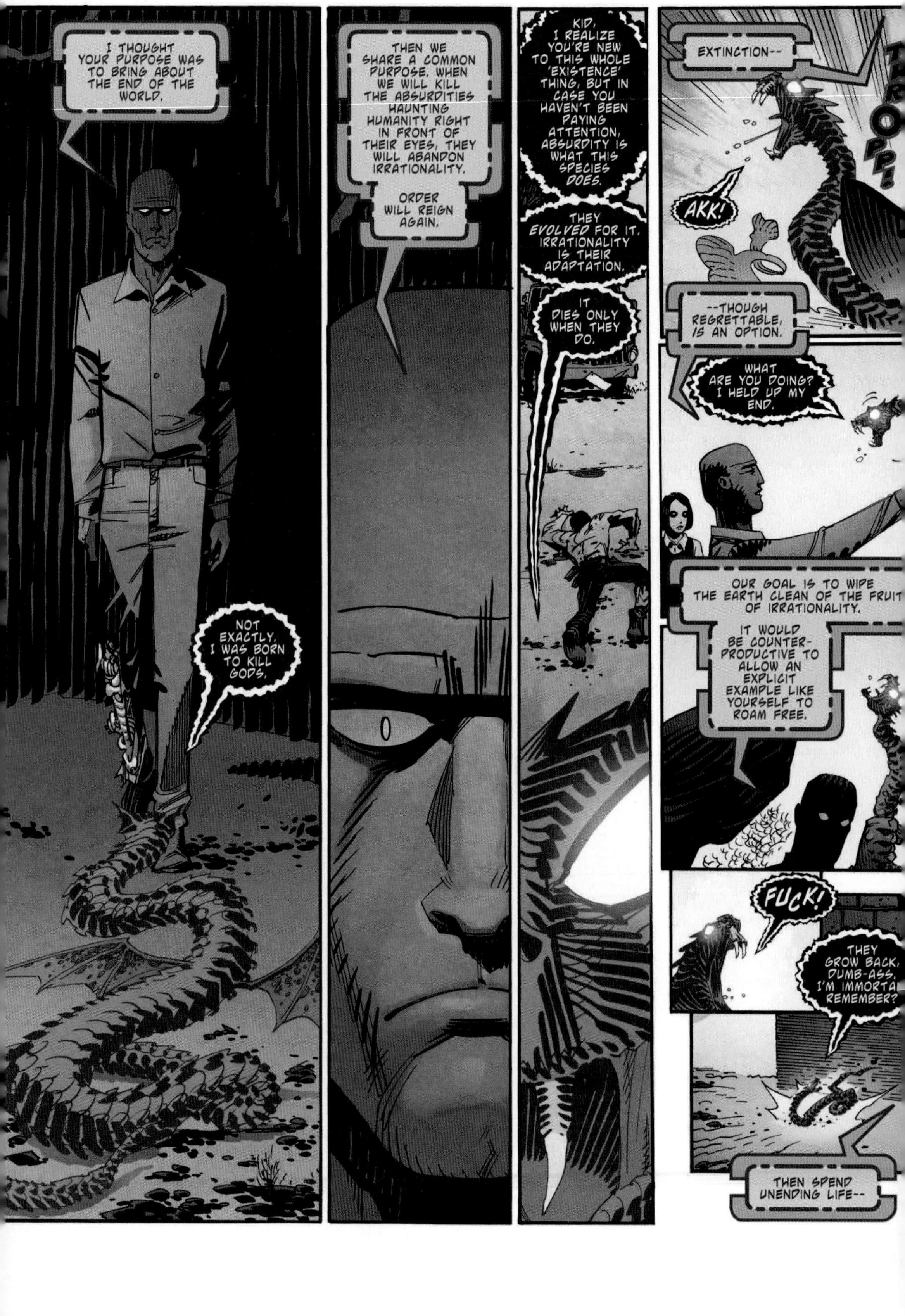
I THOUGHT YOUR PURPOSE WAS TO BRING ABOUT THE END OF THE WORLD.
NOT EXACTLY. I WAS BORN TO KILL GODS.
THEN WE SHARE A COMMON PURPOSE. WHEN WE WILL KILL THE ABSURDITIES HAUNTING HUMANITY RIGHT IN FRONT OF THEIR EYES, THEY WILL ABANDON IRRATIONALITY.
ORDER WILL REIGN AGAIN.
KID, I REALIZE YOU'RE NEW TO THIS WHOLE 'EXISTENCE' THING, BUT IN CASE YOU HAVEN'T BEEN PAYING ATTENTION, ABSURDITY IS WHAT THIS SPECIES DOES.
THEY EVOLVED FOR IT. IRRATIONALITY IS THEIR ADAPTATION.
IT DIES ONLY WHEN THEY DO.
EXTINCTION--
THROPP!
AKK!
--THOUGH REGRETTABLE, IS AN OPTION.
WHAT ARE YOU DOING? I HELD UP MY END.
OUR GOAL IS TO WIPE THE EARTH CLEAN OF THE FRUIT OF IRRATIONALITY.
IT WOULD BE COUNTER-PRODUCTIVE TO ALLOW AN EXPLICIT EXAMPLE LIKE YOURSELF TO ROAM FREE.
FUCK!
THEY GROW BACK, DUMB-ASS. I'M IMMORTAL, REMEMBER?
THEN SPEND UNENDING LIFE--

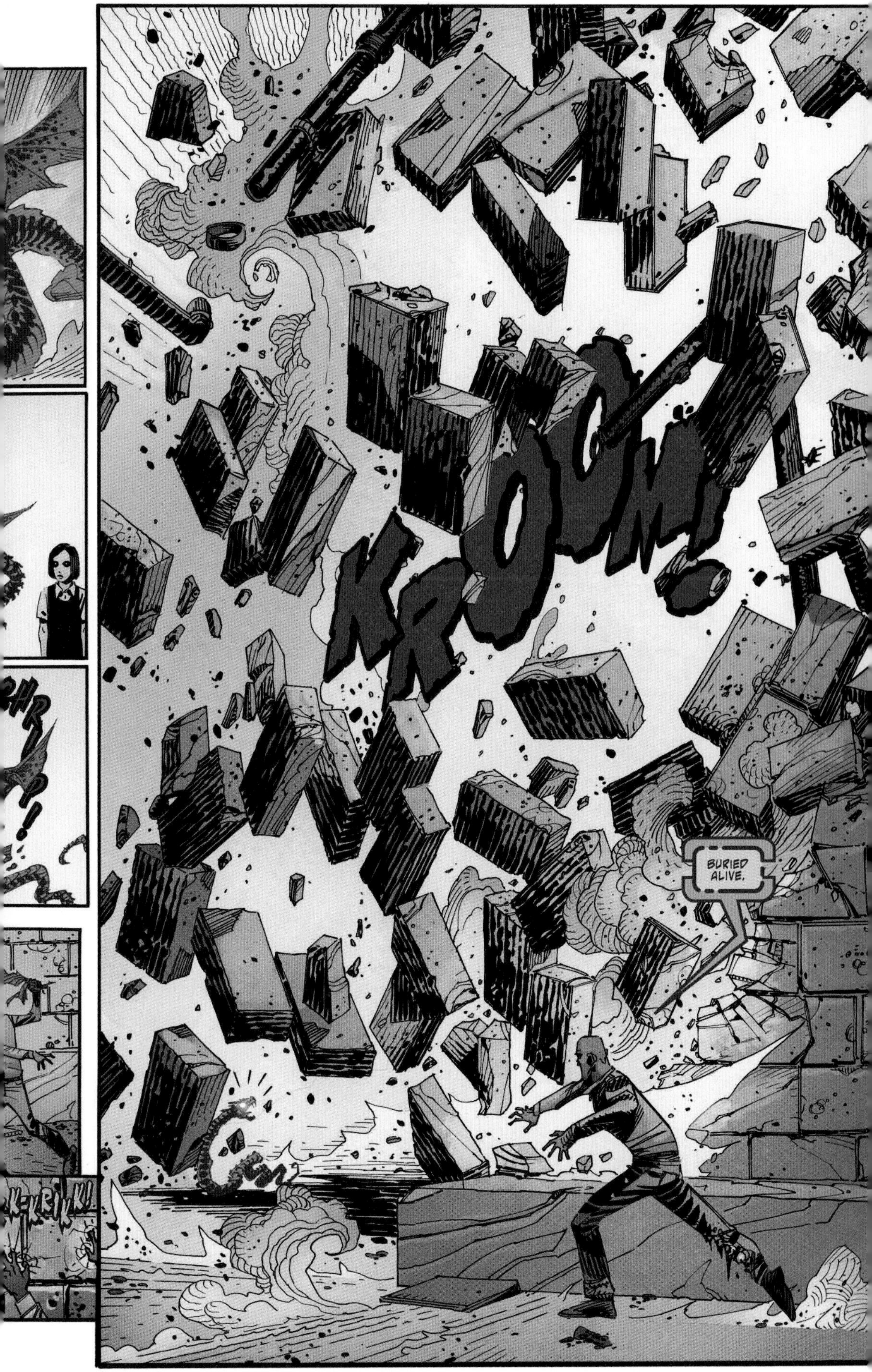
KROOM!
BURIED ALIVE.

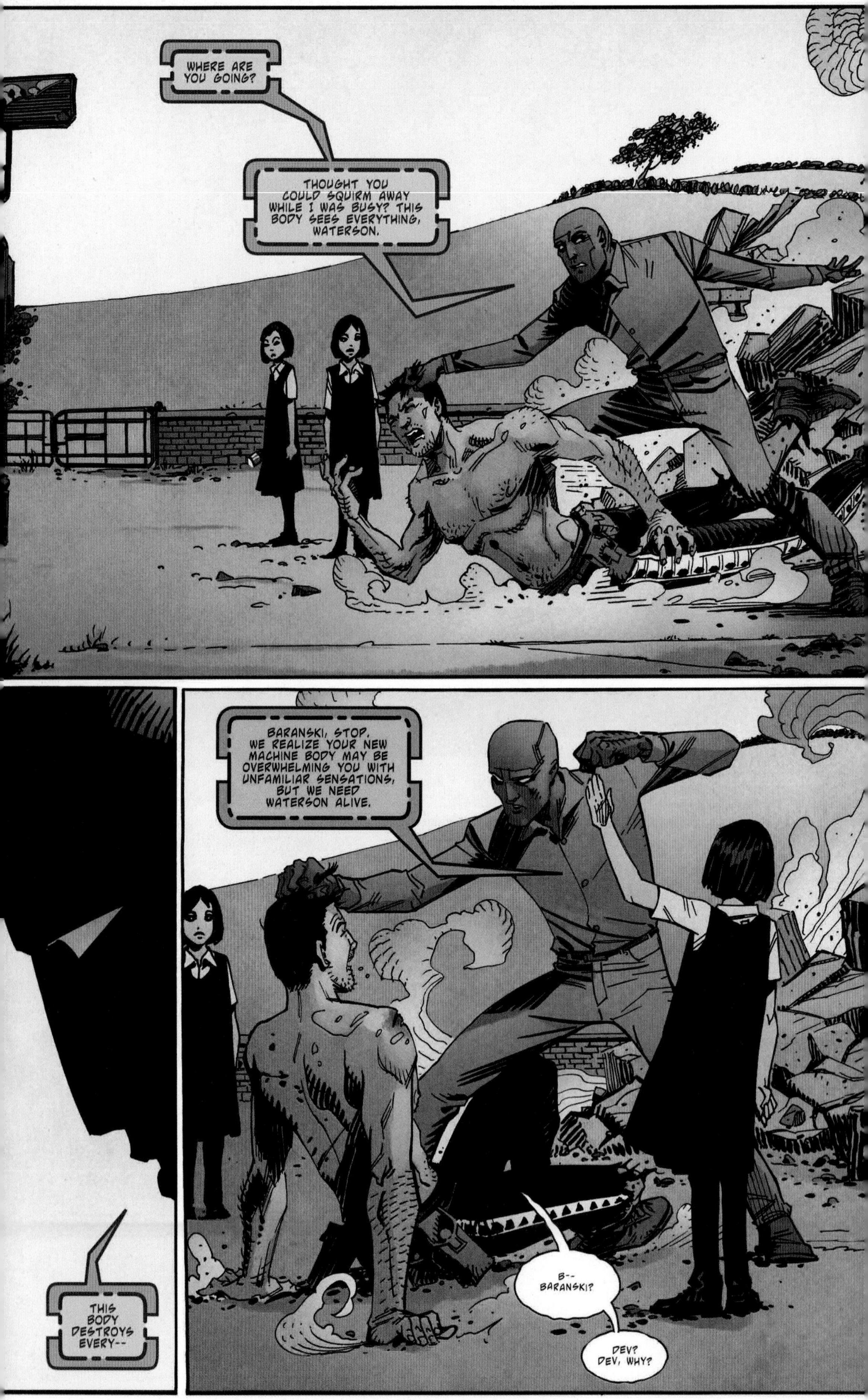
WHERE ARE YOU GOING?
THOUGHT YOU COULD SQUIRM AWAY WHILE I WAS BUSY? THIS BODY SEES EVERYTHING, WATERSON.
BARANSKI, STOP. WE REALIZE YOUR NEW MACHINE BODY MAY BE OVERWHELMING YOU WITH UNFAMILIAR SENSATIONS, BUT WE NEED WATERSON ALIVE.
THIS BODY DESTROYS EVERY--
B-- BARANSKI?
DEV? DEV, WHY?

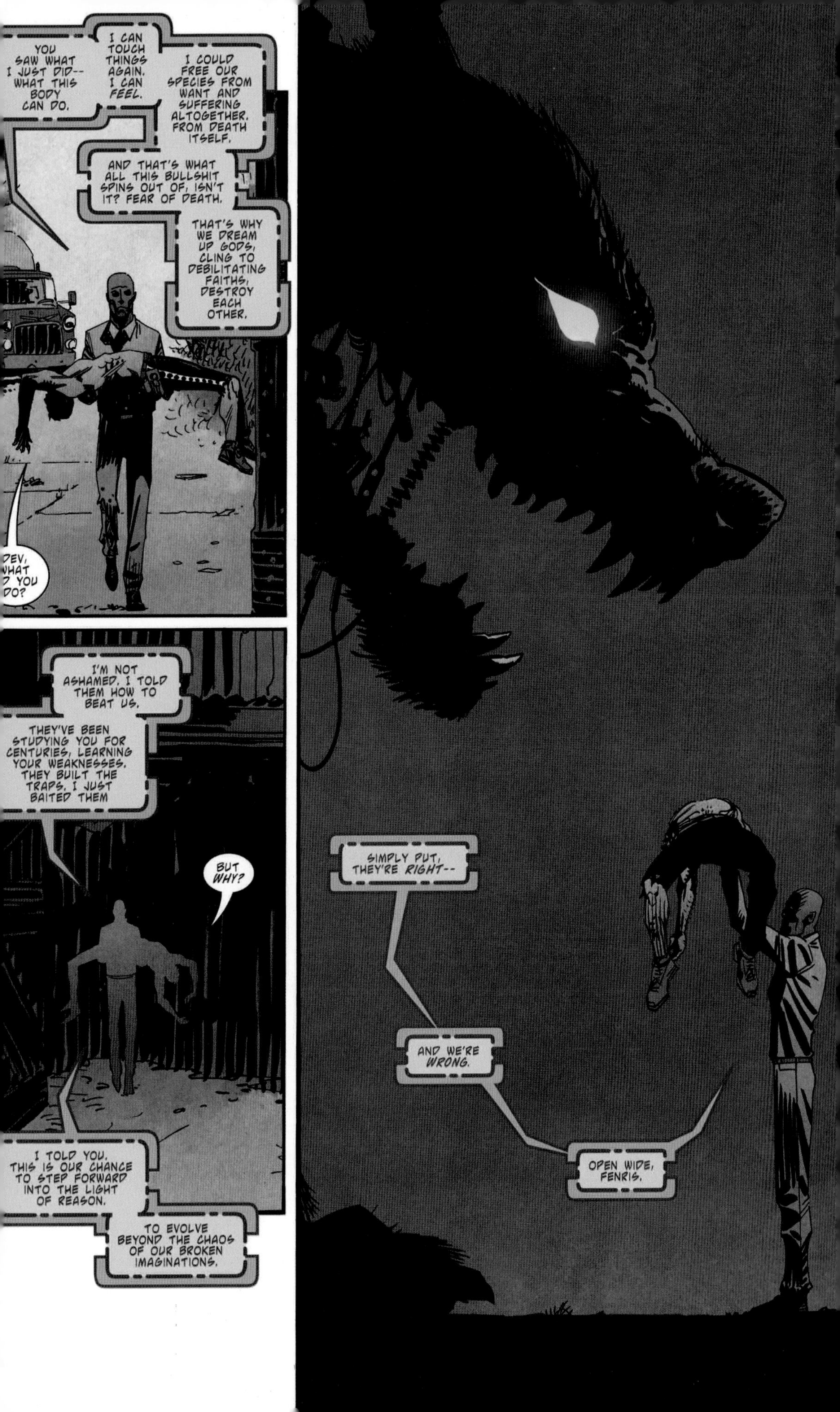

YOU SAW WHAT I JUST DID-- WHAT THIS BODY CAN DO.
I CAN TOUCH THINGS AGAIN. I CAN FEEL.
I COULD FREE OUR SPECIES FROM WANT AND SUFFERING ALTOGETHER. FROM DEATH ITSELF.
AND THAT'S WHAT ALL THIS BULLSHIT SPINS OUT OF, ISN'T IT? FEAR OF DEATH.
THAT'S WHY WE DREAM UP GODS, CLING TO DEBILITATING FAITHS, DESTROY EACH OTHER.
DEV, WHAT YOU DO?
I'M NOT ASHAMED. I TOLD THEM HOW TO BEAT US.
THEY'VE BEEN STUDYING YOU FOR CENTURIES, LEARNING YOUR WEAKNESSES. THEY BUILT THE TRAPS. I JUST BAITED THEM
BUT WHY?
I TOLD YOU. THIS IS OUR CHANCE TO STEP FORWARD INTO THE LIGHT OF REASON.
TO EVOLVE BEYOND THE CHAOS OF OUR BROKEN IMAGINATIONS.
SIMPLY PUT, THEY'RE RIGHT--
AND WE'RE WRONG.
OPEN WIDE, FENRIS.

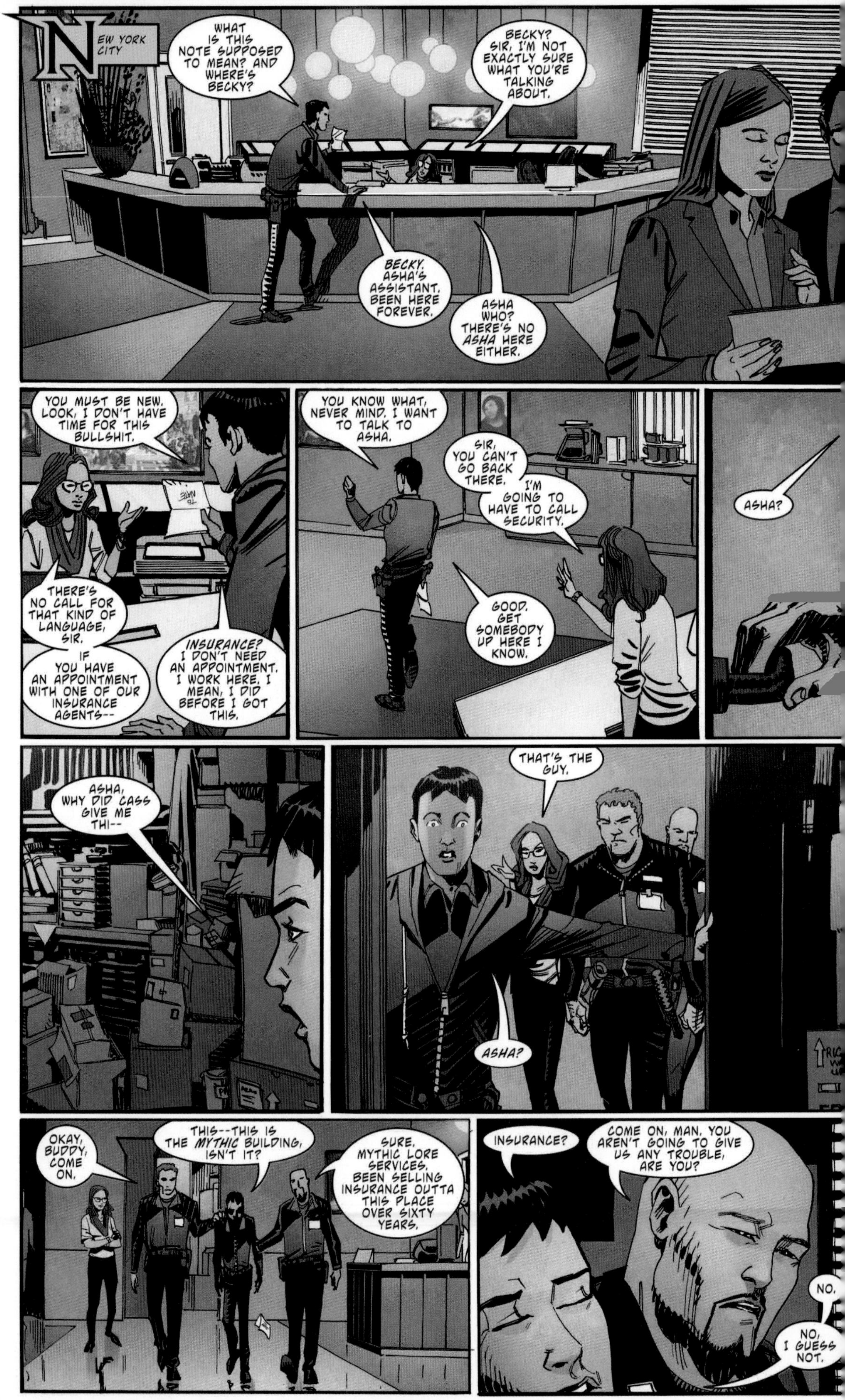
NEW YORK CITY
WHAT IS THIS NOTE SUPPOSED TO MEAN? AND WHERE'S BECKY?
BECKY? SIR, I'M NOT EXACTLY SURE WHAT YOU'RE TALKING ABOUT.
BECKY. ASHA'S ASSISTANT. BEEN HERE FOREVER.
ASHA WHO? THERE'S NO ASHA HERE EITHER.
YOU MUST BE NEW. LOOK, I DON'T HAVE TIME FOR THIS BULLSHIT.
TO NATE
THERE'S NO CALL FOR THAT KIND OF LANGUAGE, SIR.
IF YOU HAVE AN APPOINTMENT WITH ONE OF OUR INSURANCE AGENTS--
INSURANCE? I DON'T NEED AN APPOINTMENT. I WORK HERE. I MEAN, I DID BEFORE I GOT THIS.
YOU KNOW WHAT, NEVER MIND. I WANT TO TALK TO ASHA.
SIR, YOU CAN'T GO BACK THERE.
I'M GOING TO HAVE TO CALL SECURITY.
GOOD. GET SOMEBODY UP HERE I KNOW.
ASHA?
ASHA, WHY DID CASS GIVE ME THI--
THAT'S THE GUY.
ASHA?
OKAY, BUDDY, COME ON.
THIS--THIS IS THE MYTHIC BUILDING, ISN'T IT?
SURE, MYTHIC LORE SERVICES. BEEN SELLING INSURANCE OUTTA THIS PLACE OVER SIXTY YEARS.
INSURANCE?
COME ON, MAN. YOU AREN'T GOING TO GIVE US ANY TROUBLE, ARE YOU?
NO.
NO, I GUESS NOT.

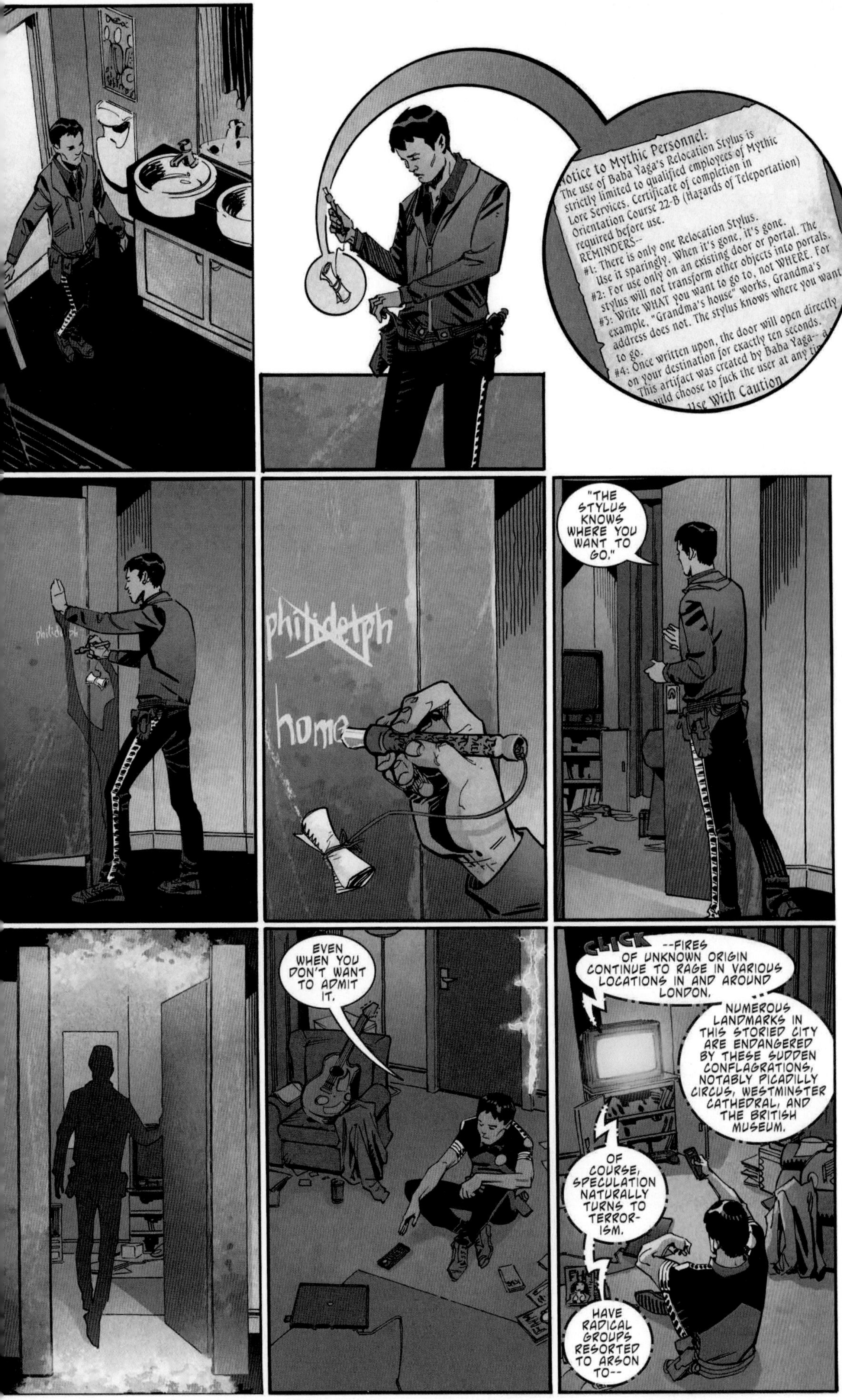
otice to Mythic Personnel:
The use of Baba Yaga's Relocation Stylus is strictly limited to qualified employees of Mythic Lore Services. Certificate of completion in Orientation Course 22-B (Hazards of Teleportation) required before use.
REMINDERS--
#1: There is only one Relocation Stylus. Use it sparingly. When it's gone, it's gone.
#2: For use only on an existing door or portal. The stylus will not transform other objects into portals.
#3: Write WHAT you want to go to, not WHERE. For example, "Grandma's house" works, Grandma's address does not. The stylus knows where you want to go.
#4: Once written upon, the door will open directly on your destination for exactly ten seconds.
This artifact was created by Baba Yaga--
uld choose to fuck the user at any
Use With Caution
philidelph
home
"THE STYLUS KNOWS WHERE YOU WANT TO GO."
EVEN WHEN YOU DON'T WANT TO ADMIT IT.
CLICK
--FIRES OF UNKNOWN ORIGIN CONTINUE TO RAGE IN VARIOUS LOCATIONS IN AND AROUND LONDON.
NUMEROUS LANDMARKS IN THIS STORIED CITY ARE ENDANGERED BY THESE SUDDEN CONFLAGRATIONS, NOTABLY PICADILLY CIRCUS, WESTMINSTER CATHEDRAL, AND THE BRITISH MUSEUM.
OF COURSE, SPECULATION NATURALLY TURNS TO TERRORISM.
HAVE RADICAL GROUPS RESORTED TO ARSON TO--

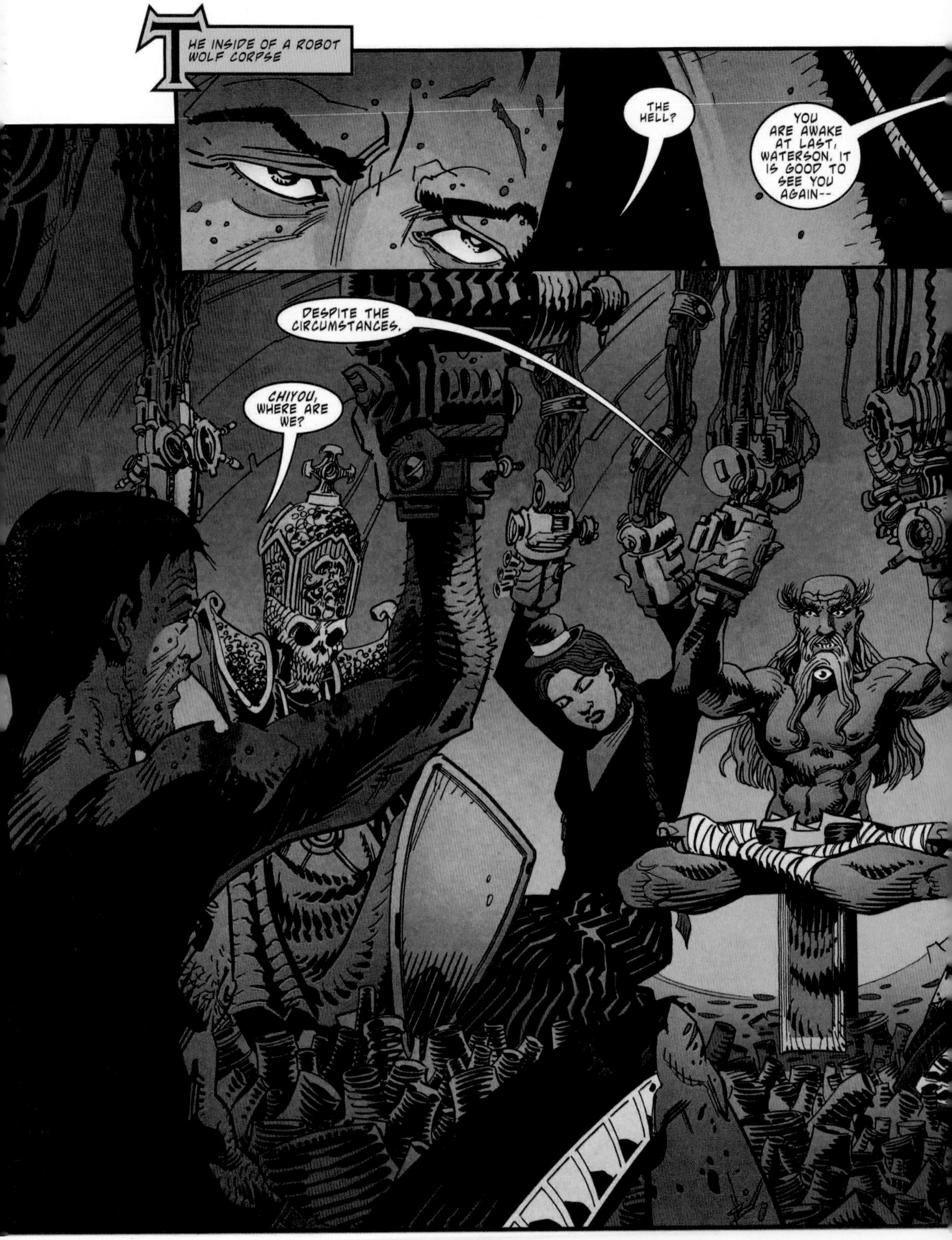
THE INSIDE OF A ROBOT WOLF CORPSE
THE HELL?
YOU ARE AWAKE AT LAST, WATERSON. IT IS GOOD TO SEE YOU AGAIN--
DESPITE THE CIRCUMSTANCES.
CHIYOU, WHERE ARE WE?

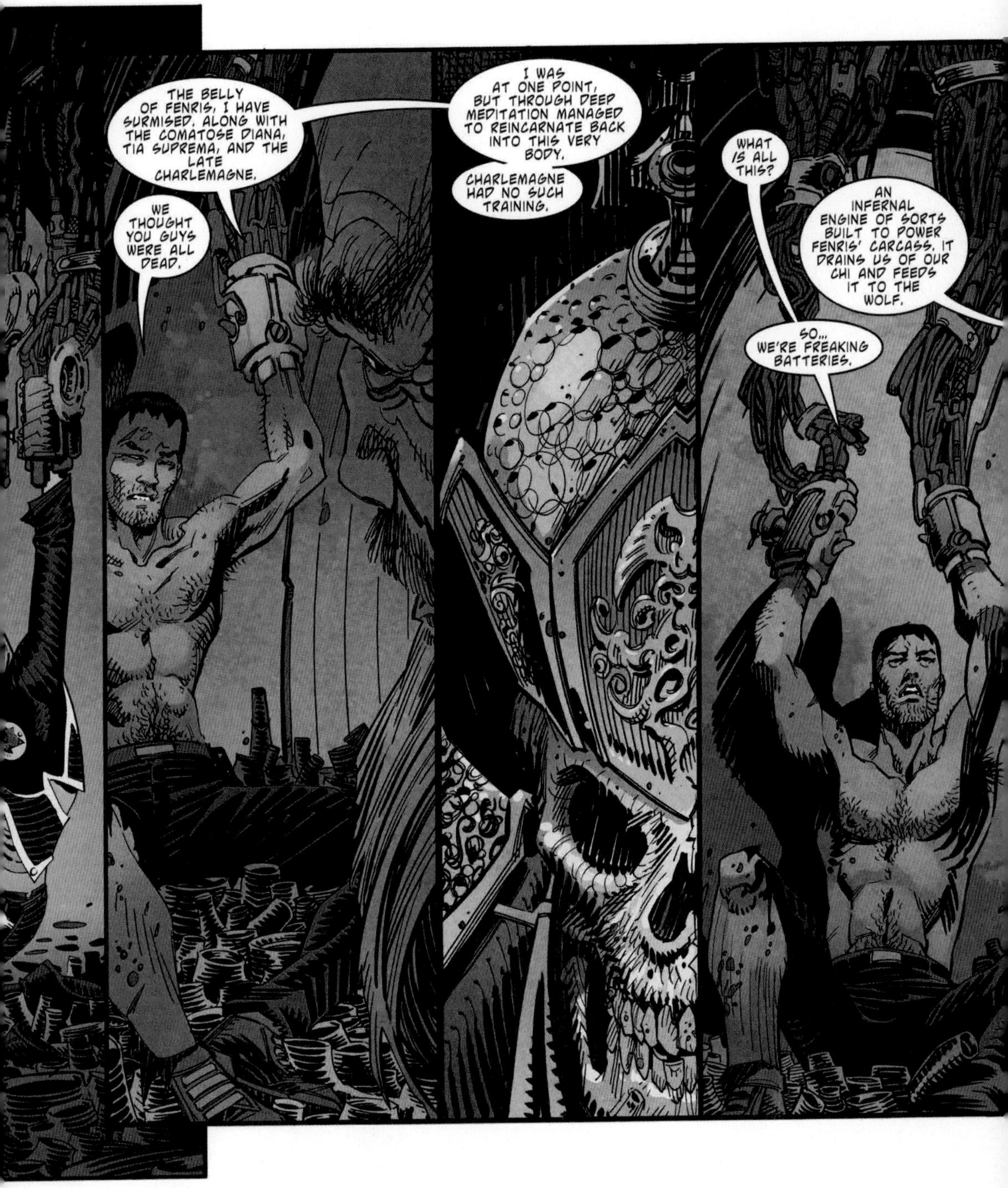
THE BELLY OF FENRIS, I HAVE SURMISED. ALONG WITH THE COMATOSE DIANA, TIA SUPREMA, AND THE LATE CHARLEMAGNE.
WE THOUGHT YOU GUYS WERE ALL DEAD.
I WAS AT ONE POINT, BUT THROUGH DEEP MEDITATION MANAGED TO REINCARNATE BACK INTO THIS VERY BODY.
CHARLEMAGNE HAD NO SUCH TRAINING.
WHAT IS ALL THIS?
AN INFERNAL ENGINE OF SORTS BUILT TO POWER FENRIS' CARCASS. IT DRAINS US OF OUR CHI AND FEEDS IT TO THE WOLF.
SO... WE'RE FREAKING BATTERIES.

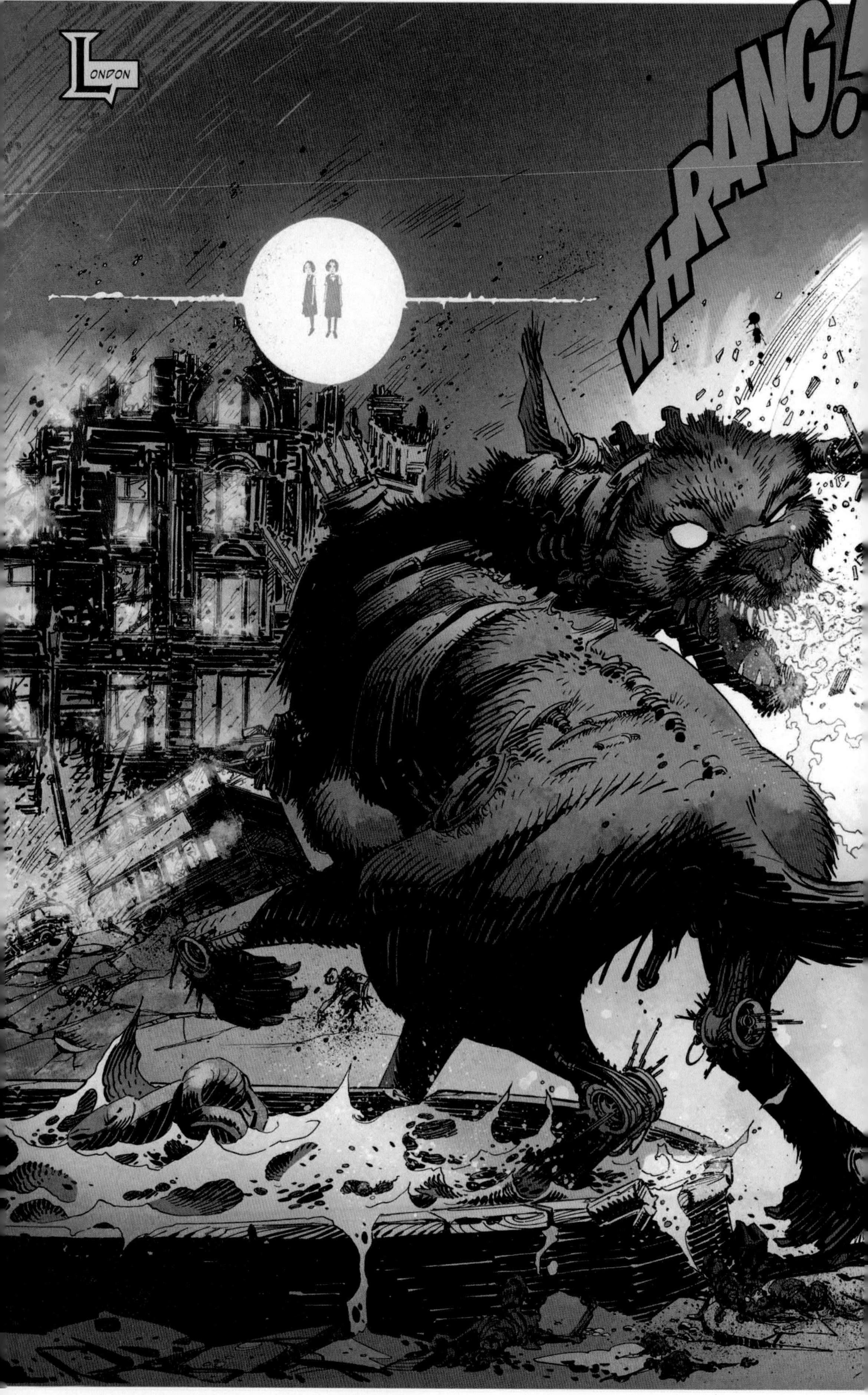

LONDON
WHRANG!

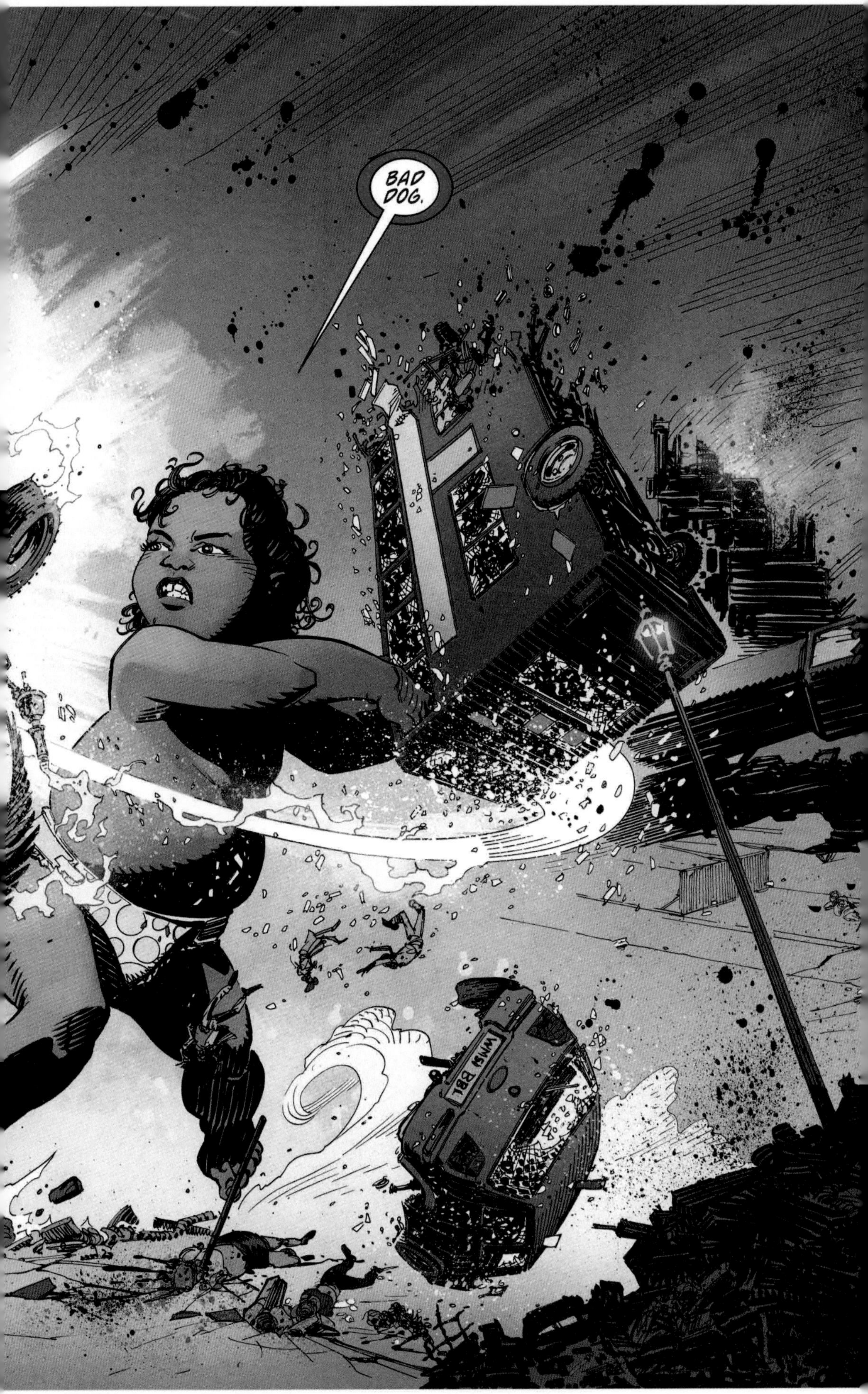
BAD DOG.

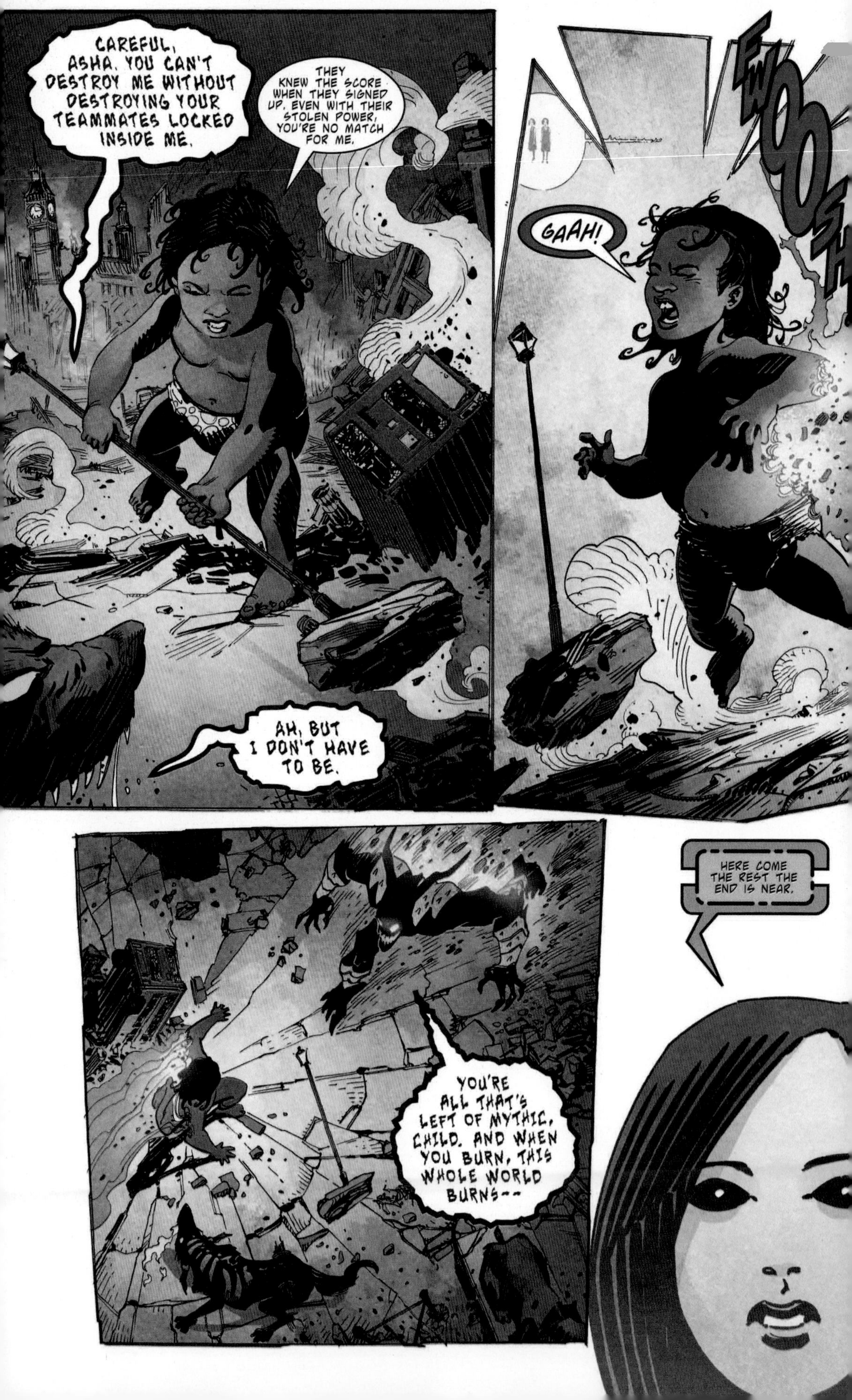
CAREFUL, ASHA. YOU CAN'T DESTROY ME WITHOUT DESTROYING YOUR TEAMMATES LOCKED INSIDE ME.
THEY KNEW THE SCORE WHEN THEY SIGNED UP. EVEN WITH THEIR STOLEN POWER, YOU'RE NO MATCH FOR ME.
AH, BUT I DON'T HAVE TO BE.
FWOOSH
GAAH!
YOU'RE ALL THAT'S LEFT OF MYTHIC, CHILD. AND WHEN YOU BURN, THIS WHOLE WORLD BURNS--
HERE COME THE REST THE END IS NEAR.

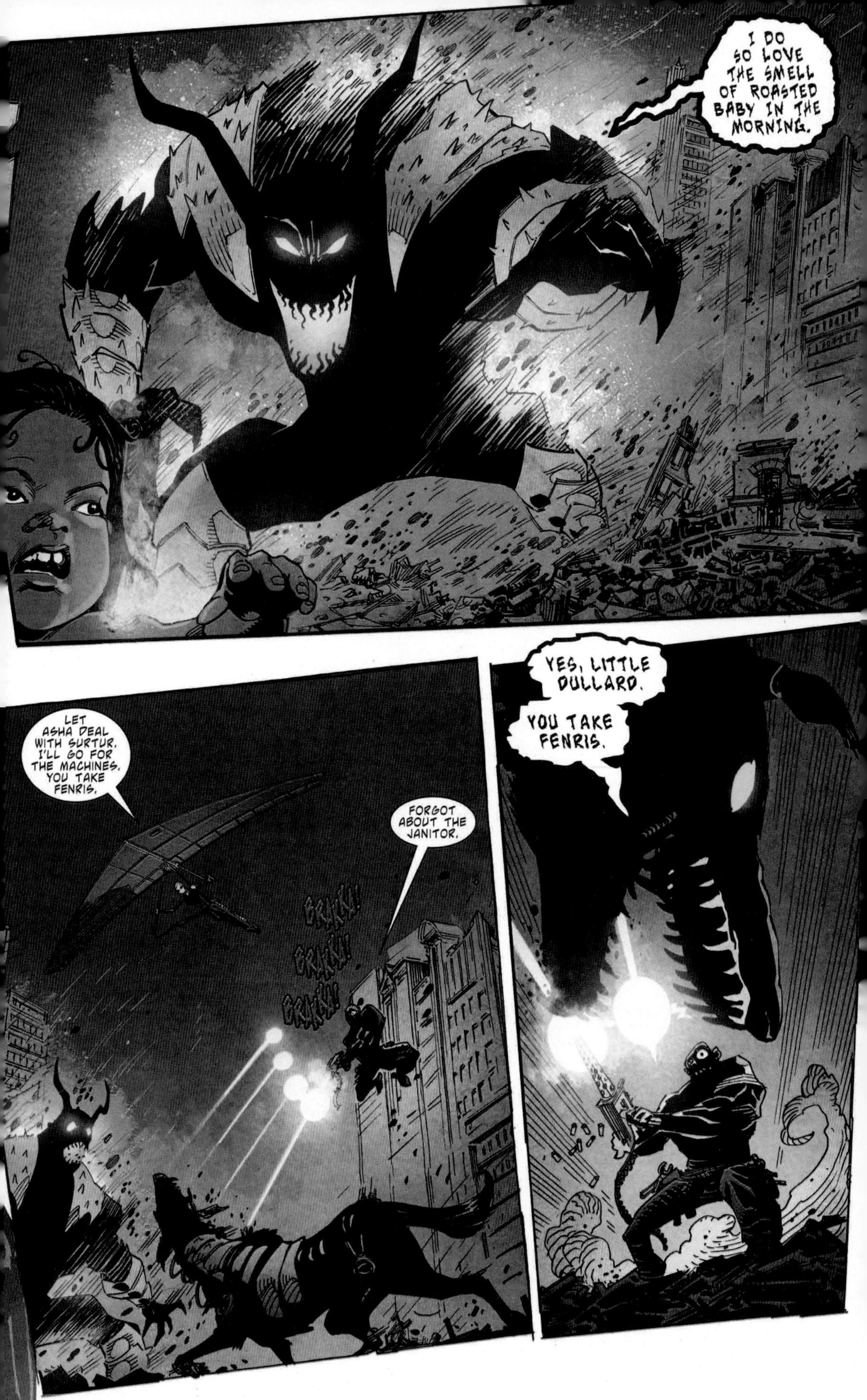
I DO SO LOVE THE SMELL OF ROASTED BABY IN THE MORNING.
LET ASHA DEAL WITH SURTUR. I'LL GO FOR THE MACHINES. YOU TAKE FENRIS.
FORGOT ABOUT THE JANITOR.
YES, LITTLE DULLARD.
YOU TAKE FENRIS.

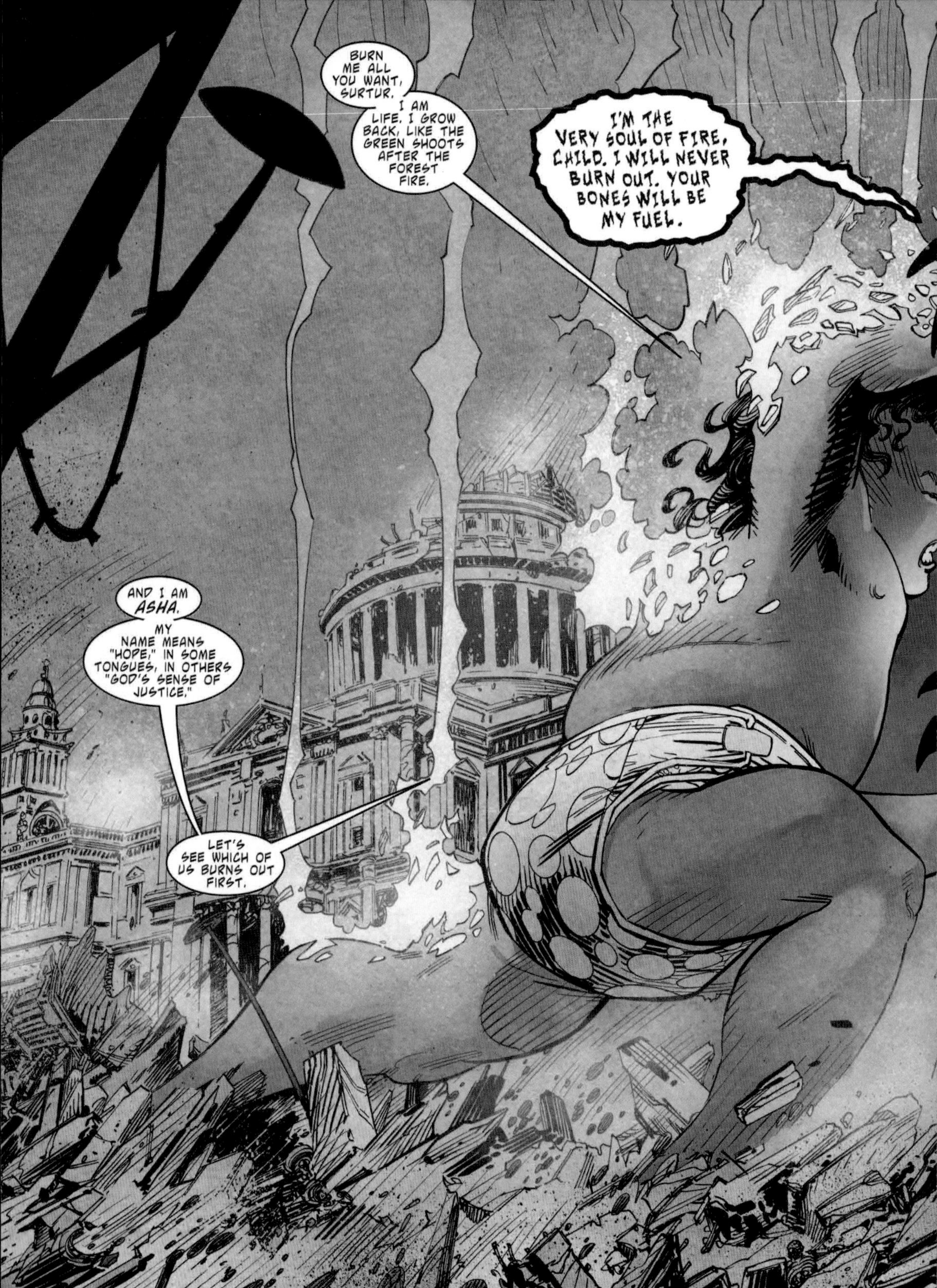
BURN ME ALL YOU WANT, SURTUR.
I AM LIFE. I GROW BACK, LIKE THE GREEN SHOOTS AFTER THE FOREST FIRE.
I'M THE VERY SOUL OF FIRE, CHILD. I WILL NEVER BURN OUT. YOUR BONES WILL BE MY FUEL.
AND I AM ASHA.
MY NAME MEANS "HOPE," IN SOME TONGUES, IN OTHERS "GOD'S SENSE OF JUSTICE."
LET'S SEE WHICH OF US BURNS OUT FIRST.

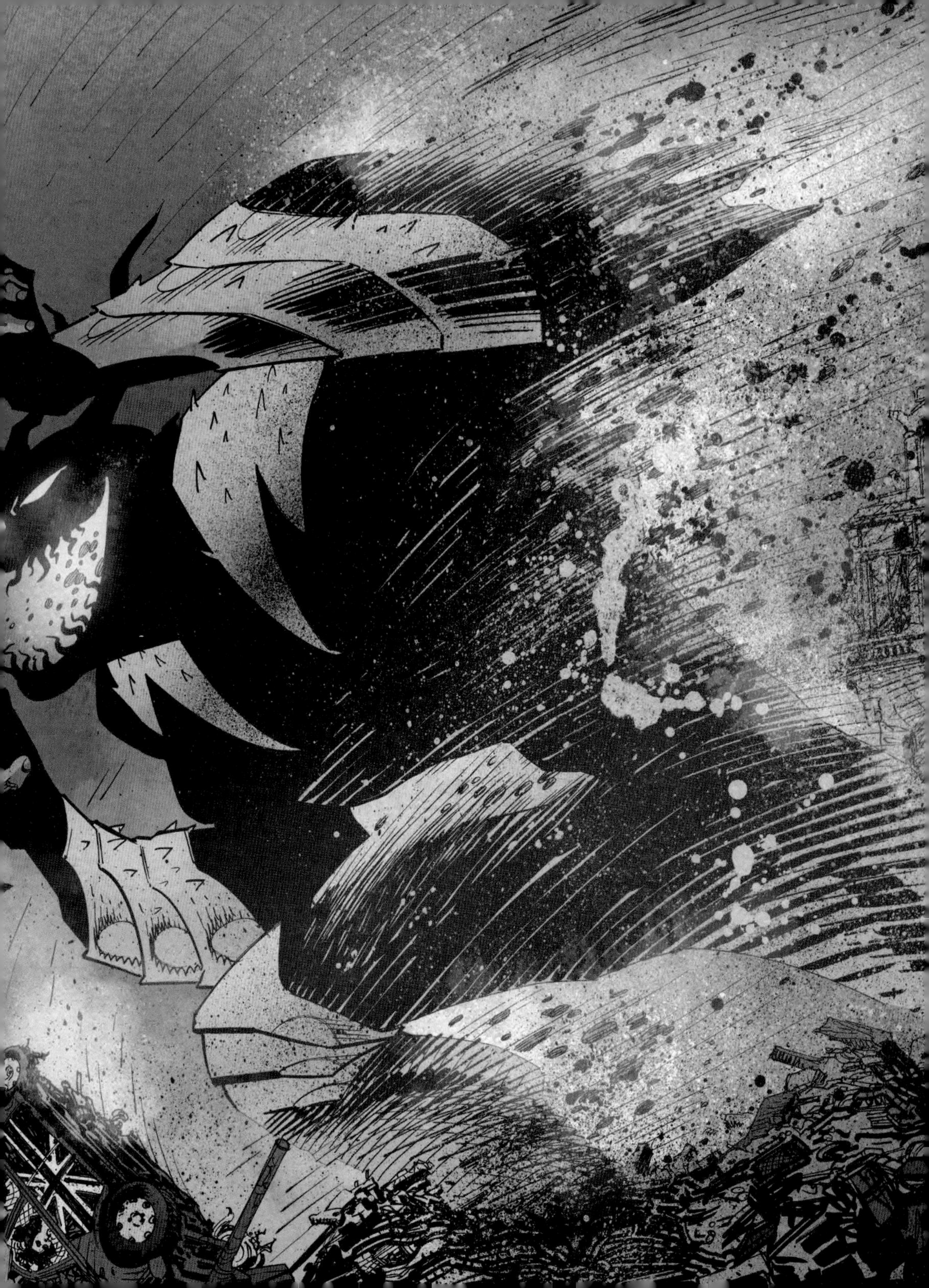

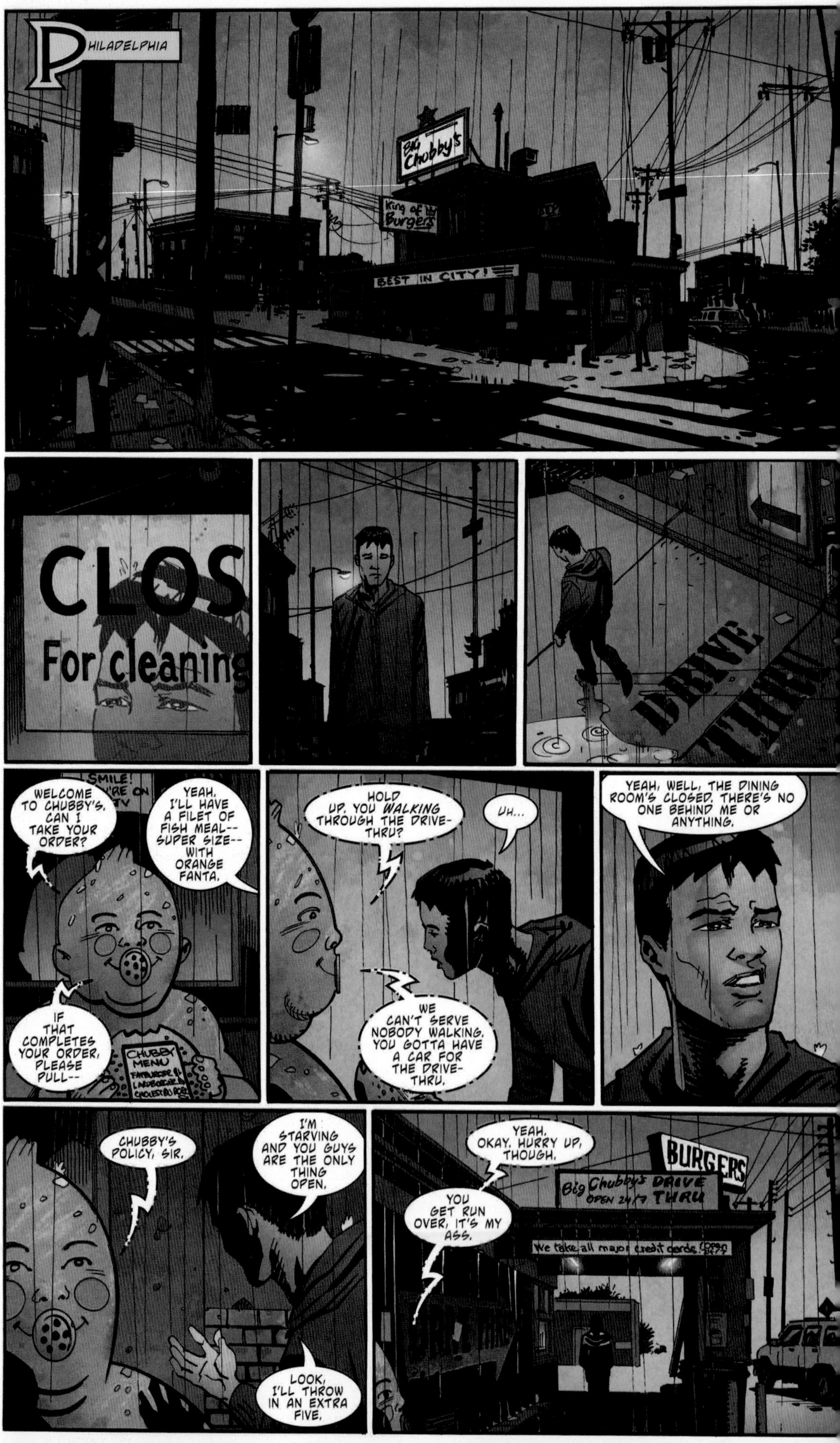
PHILADELPHIA
Big Chubby's
King of Burgers
BEST IN CITY!
CLOS
For cleaning
DRIVE THRU
WELCOME TO CHUBBY'S. CAN I TAKE YOUR ORDER?
YEAH, I'LL HAVE A FILET OF FISH MEAL-- SUPER SIZE-- WITH ORANGE FANTA.
IF THAT COMPLETES YOUR ORDER, PLEASE PULL--
CHUBBY MENU
HOLD UP. YOU WALKING THROUGH THE DRIVE-THRU?
UH...
WE CAN'T SERVE NOBODY WALKING. YOU GOTTA HAVE A CAR FOR THE DRIVE-THRU.
YEAH, WELL, THE DINING ROOM'S CLOSED. THERE'S NO ONE BEHIND ME OR ANYTHING.
CHUBBY'S POLICY, SIR.
I'M STARVING AND YOU GUYS ARE THE ONLY THING OPEN.
LOOK, I'LL THROW IN AN EXTRA FIVE.
BURGERS
Big Chubby's DRIVE THRU OPEN 24/7
We take all major credit cards!
YEAH. OKAY. HURRY UP, THOUGH.
YOU GET RUN OVER, IT'S MY ASS.

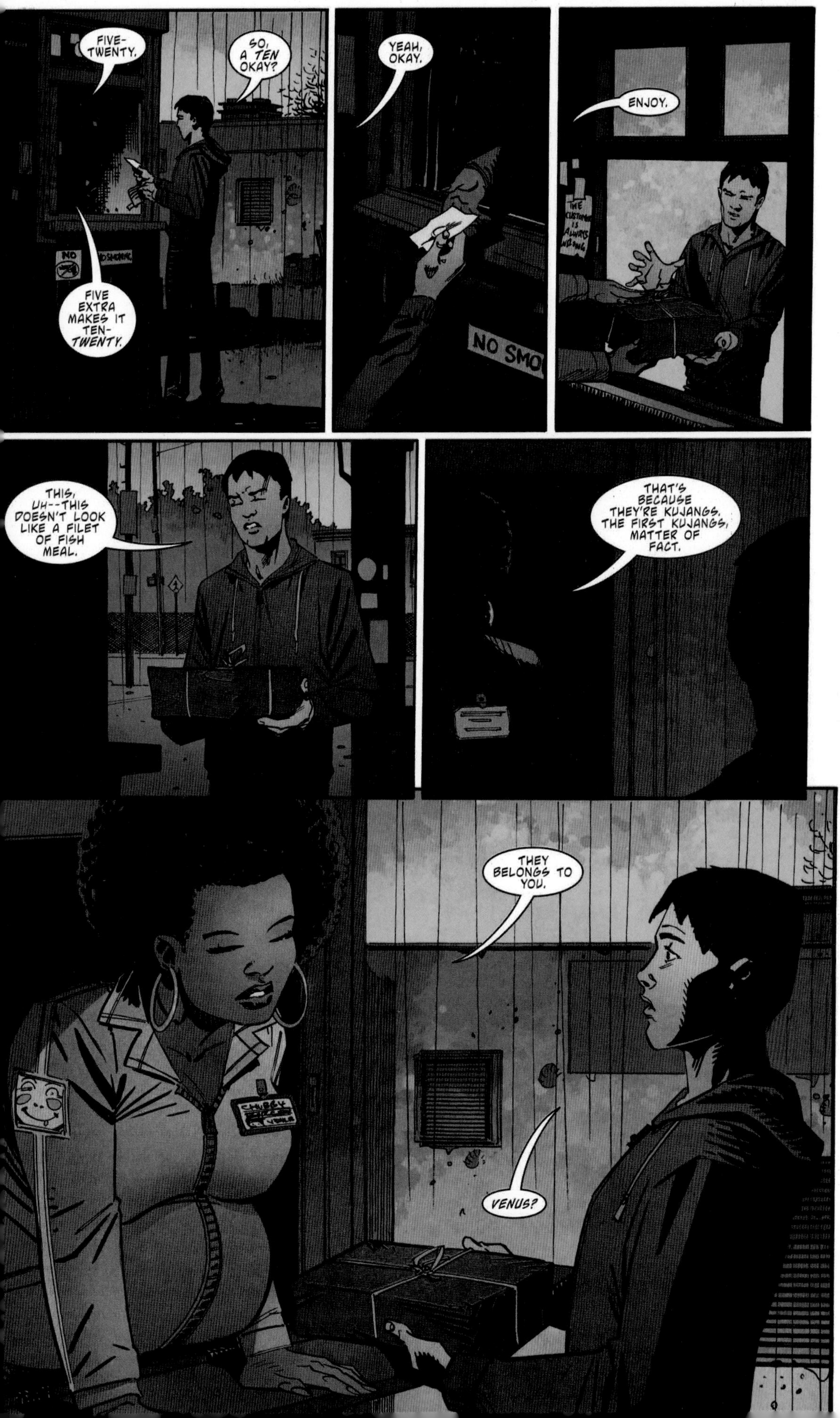
FIVE-TWENTY.
SO, A TEN OKAY?
FIVE EXTRA MAKES IT TEN-TWENTY.
NO SMOKING
YEAH, OKAY.
NO SMO
ENJOY.
THE CUSTOMER IS ALWAYS WRONG
THIS, UH--THIS DOESN'T LOOK LIKE A FILET OF FISH MEAL.
THAT'S BECAUSE THEY'RE KUJANGS. THE FIRST KUJANGS, MATTER OF FACT.
THEY BELONGS TO YOU.
VENUS?

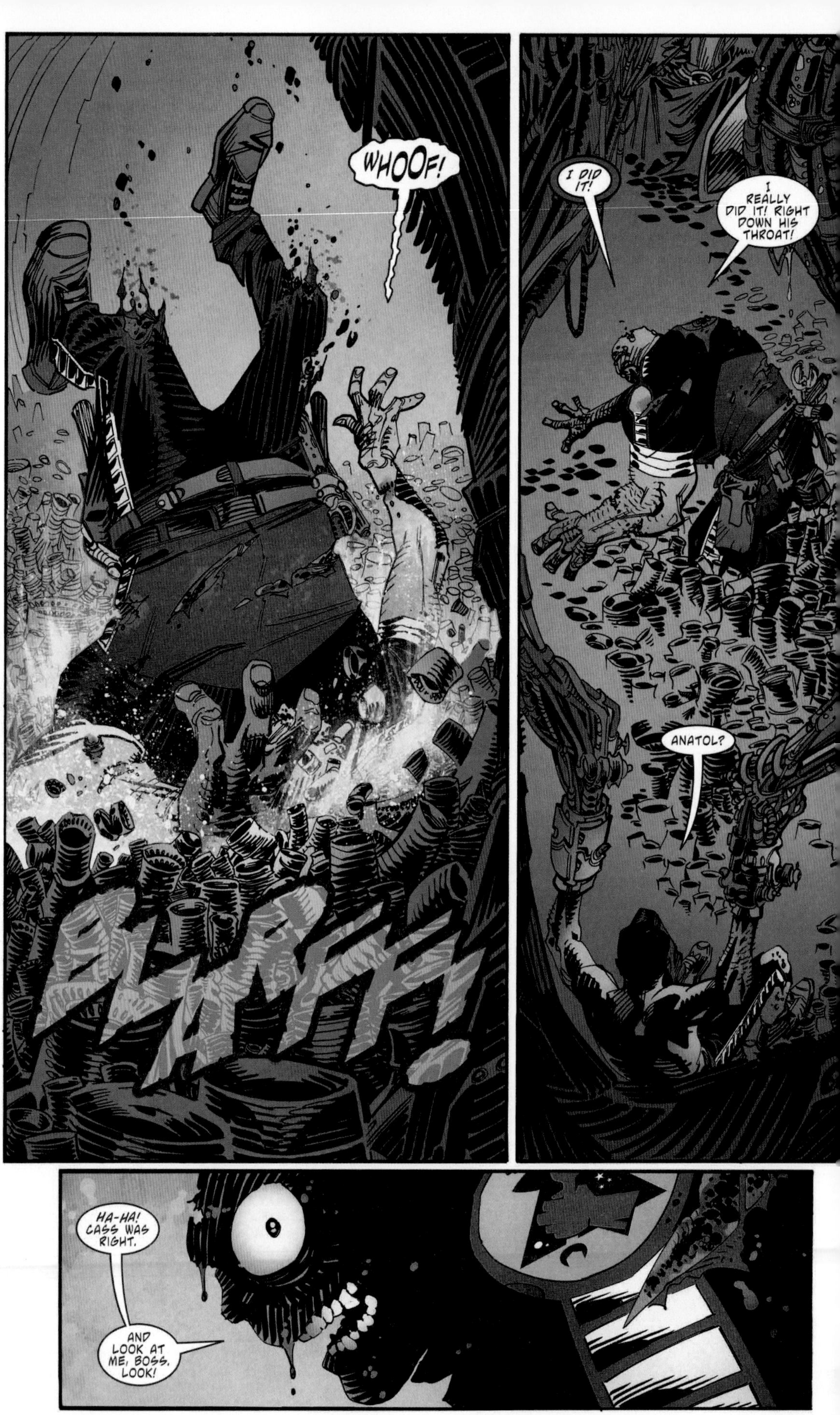
WHOOF!
I DID IT!
I REALLY DID IT! RIGHT DOWN HIS THROAT!
ANATOL?
HA-HA! CASS WAS RIGHT.
AND LOOK AT ME, BOSS. LOOK!

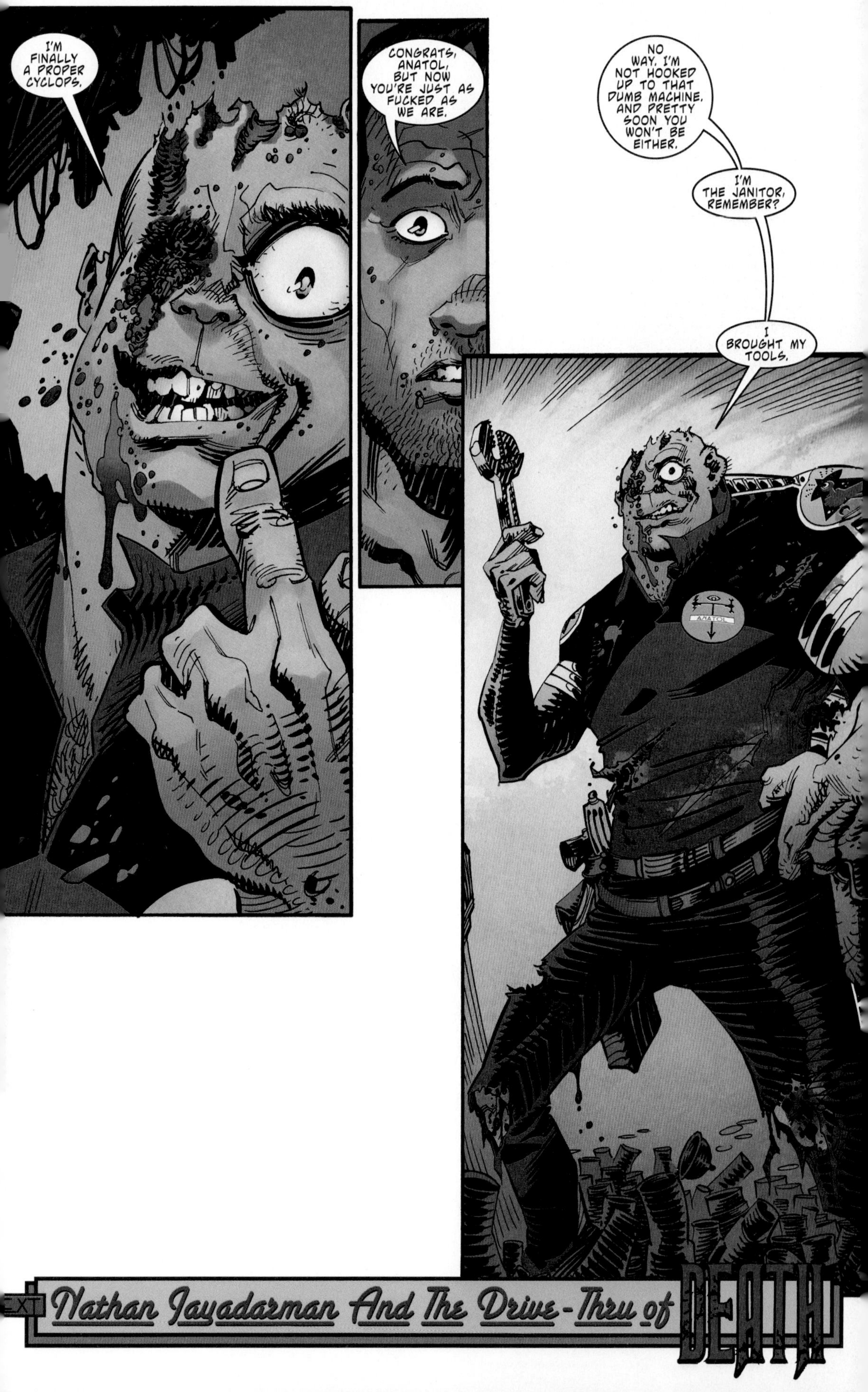
I'M FINALLY A PROPER CYCLOPS.
CONGRATS, ANATOL, BUT NOW YOU'RE JUST AS FUCKED AS WE ARE.
NO WAY. I'M NOT HOOKED UP TO THAT DUMB MACHINE, AND PRETTY SOON YOU WON'T BE EITHER.
I'M THE JANITOR, REMEMBER?
I BROUGHT MY TOOLS.
ANATOL
EXT
Nathan Jayadarman And The Drive-Thru of DEATH

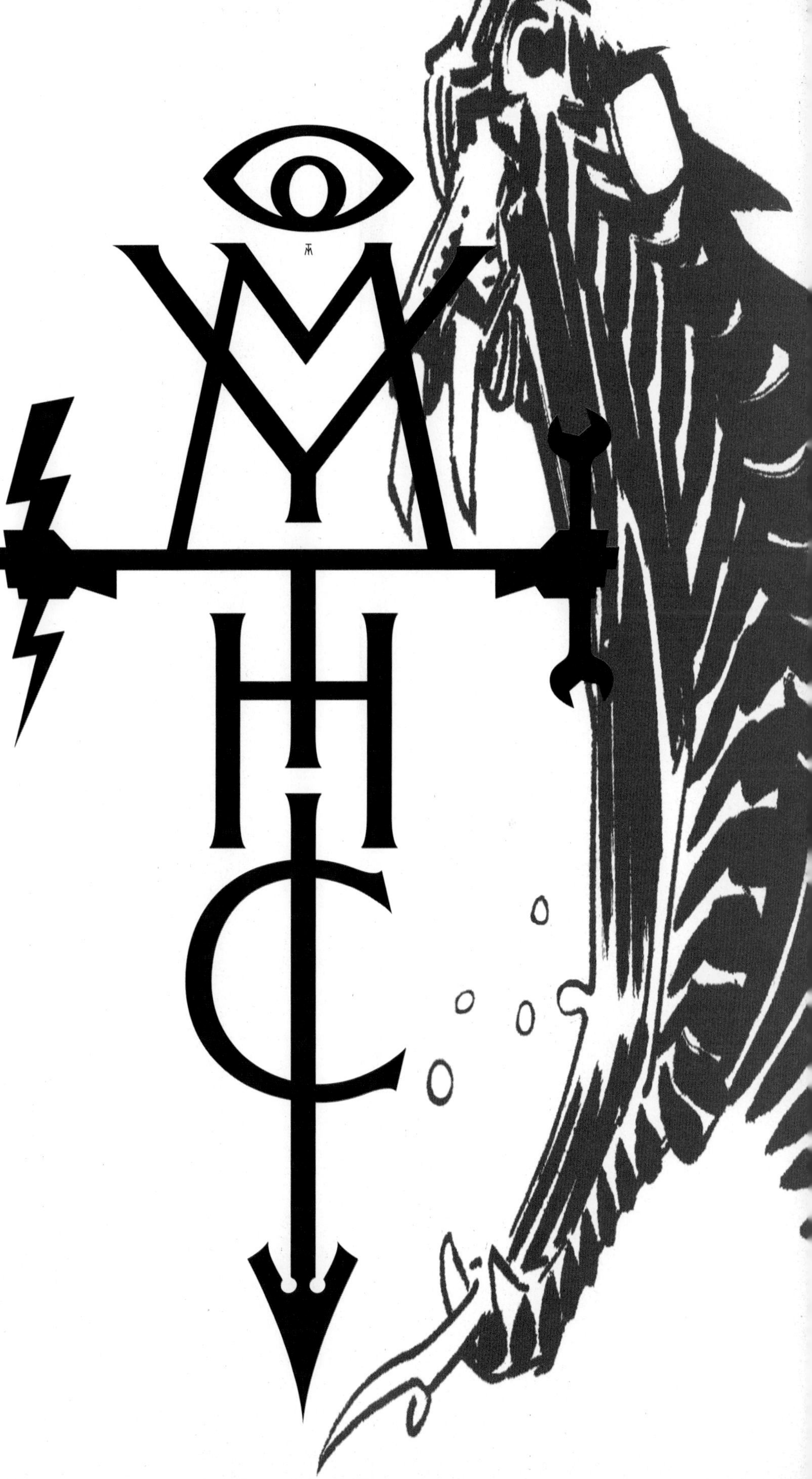

CHAPTER 8

ALL THINGS WILL DIE; NOTHING WILL DIE

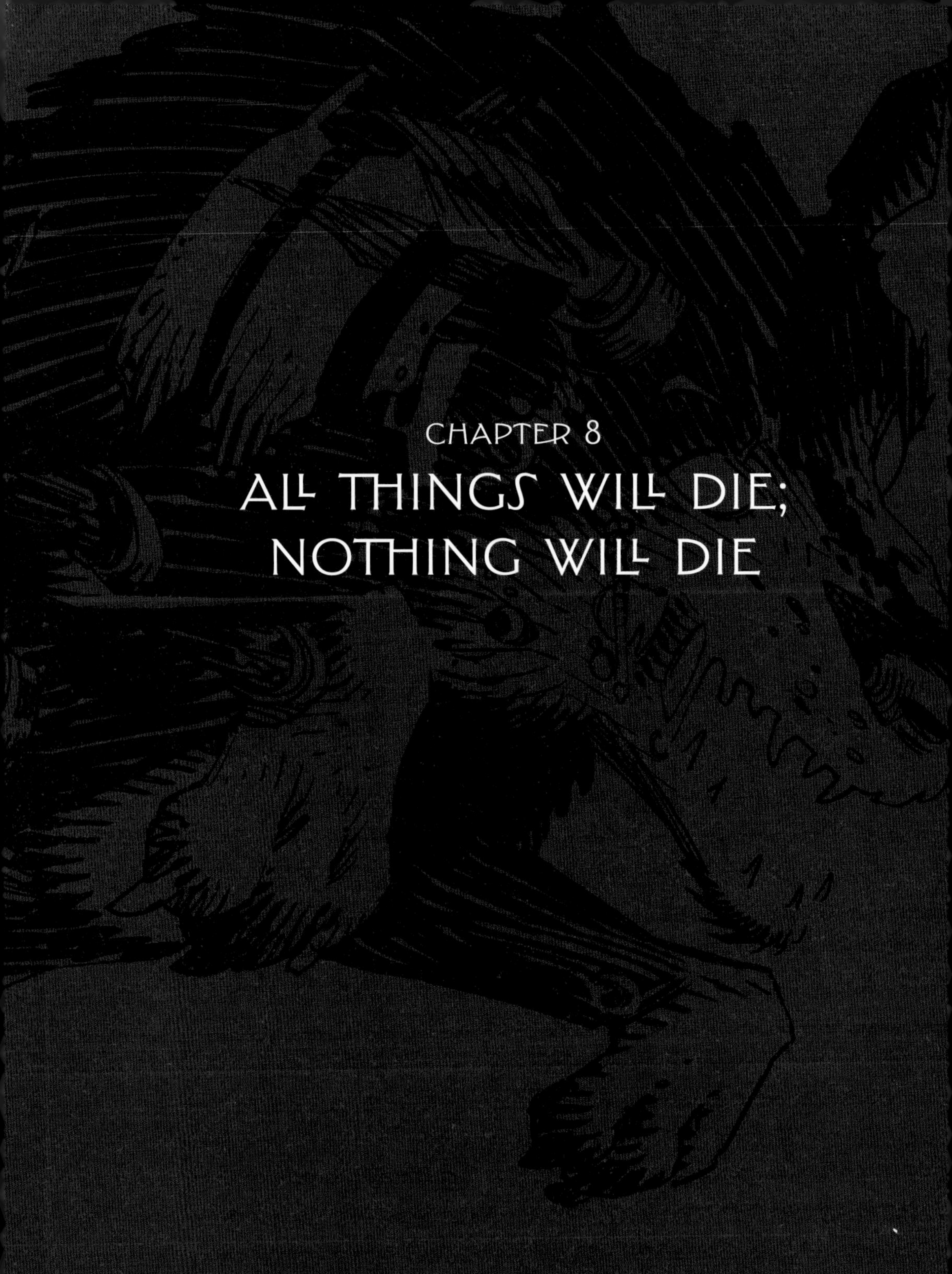

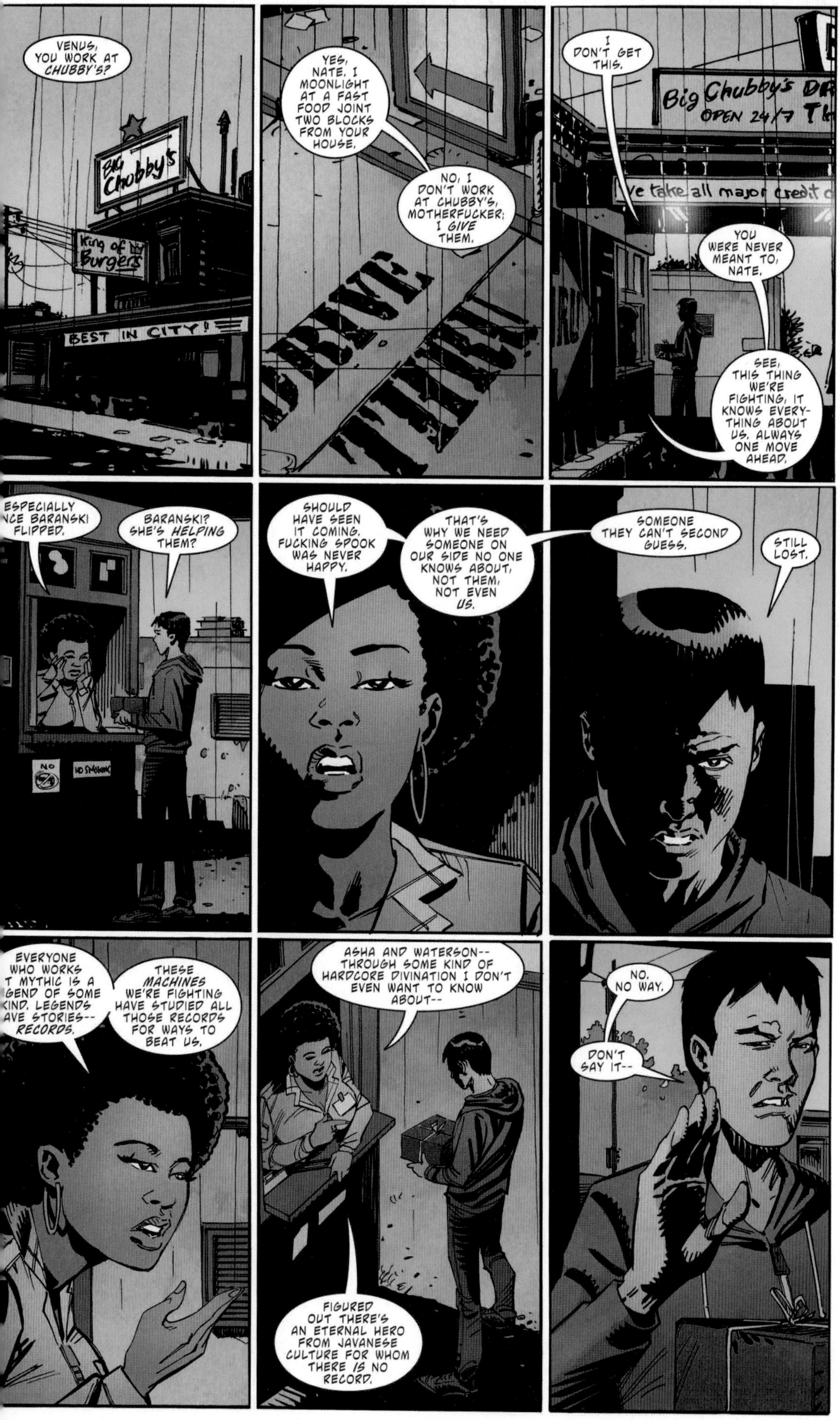

VENUS, YOU WORK AT CHUBBY'S?
Big Chubby's
King of Burgers
BEST IN CITY!
YES, NATE. I MOONLIGHT AT A FAST FOOD JOINT TWO BLOCKS FROM YOUR HOUSE.
NO, I DON'T WORK AT CHUBBY'S, MOTHERFUCKER; I GIVE THEM.
I DON'T GET THIS.
Big Chubby's
OPEN 24/7
YOU WERE NEVER MEANT TO, NATE.
SEE, THIS THING WE'RE FIGHTING, IT KNOWS EVERYTHING ABOUT US. ALWAYS ONE MOVE AHEAD.
ESPECIALLY NCE BARANSKI FLIPPED.
BARANSKI? SHE'S HELPING THEM?
NO
NO SMOKING
SHOULD HAVE SEEN IT COMING. FUCKING SPOOK WAS NEVER HAPPY.
THAT'S WHY WE NEED SOMEONE ON OUR SIDE NO ONE KNOWS ABOUT, NOT THEM, NOT EVEN US.
SOMEONE THEY CAN'T SECOND GUESS.
STILL LOST.
EVERYONE WHO WORKS T MYTHIC IS A EGEND OF SOME KIND. LEGENDS AVE STORIES-- RECORDS.
THESE MACHINES WE'RE FIGHTING HAVE STUDIED ALL THOSE RECORDS FOR WAYS TO BEAT US.
ASHA AND WATERSON-- THROUGH SOME KIND OF HARDCORE DIVINATION I DON'T EVEN WANT TO KNOW ABOUT--
FIGURED OUT THERE'S AN ETERNAL HERO FROM JAVANESE CULTURE FOR WHOM THERE IS NO RECORD.
NO. NO WAY.
DON'T SAY IT--

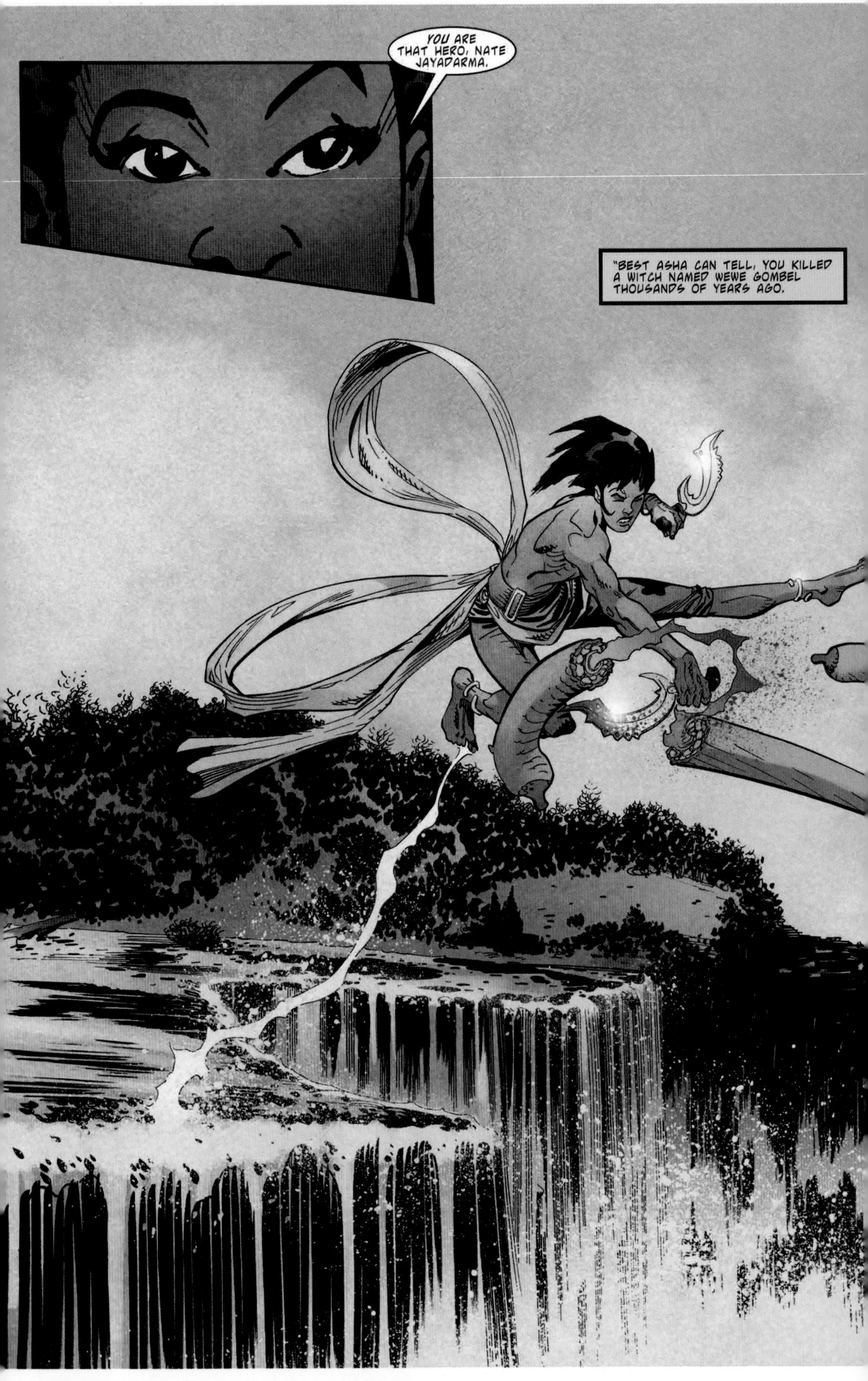
YOU ARE THAT HERO, NATE JAYADARMA.
"BEST ASHA CAN TELL, YOU KILLED A WITCH NAMED WEWE GOMBEL THOUSANDS OF YEARS AGO.

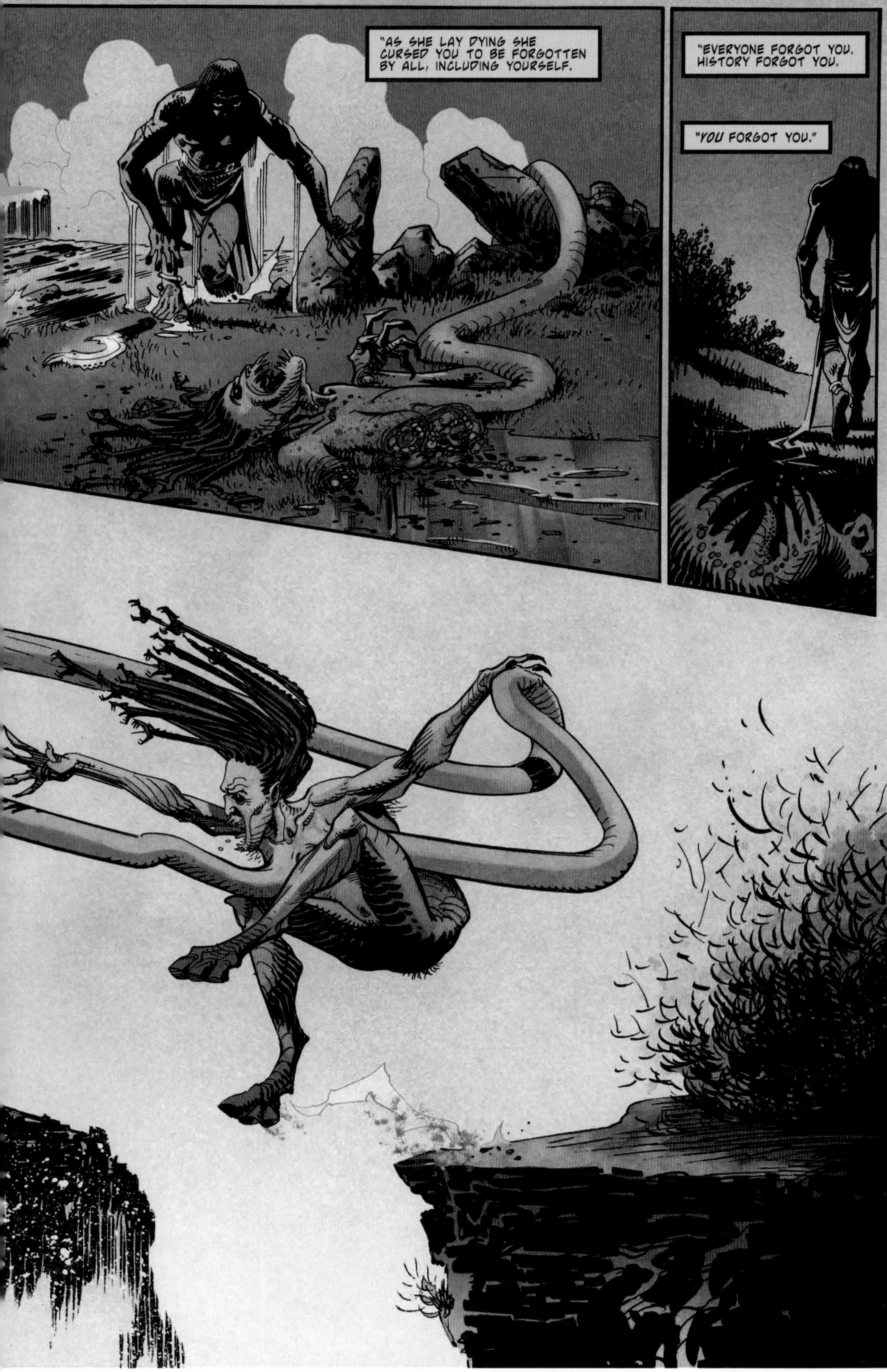
"AS SHE LAY DYING SHE CURSED YOU TO BE FORGOTTEN BY ALL, INCLUDING YOURSELF.
"EVERYONE FORGOT YOU. HISTORY FORGOT YOU.
"YOU FORGOT YOU."

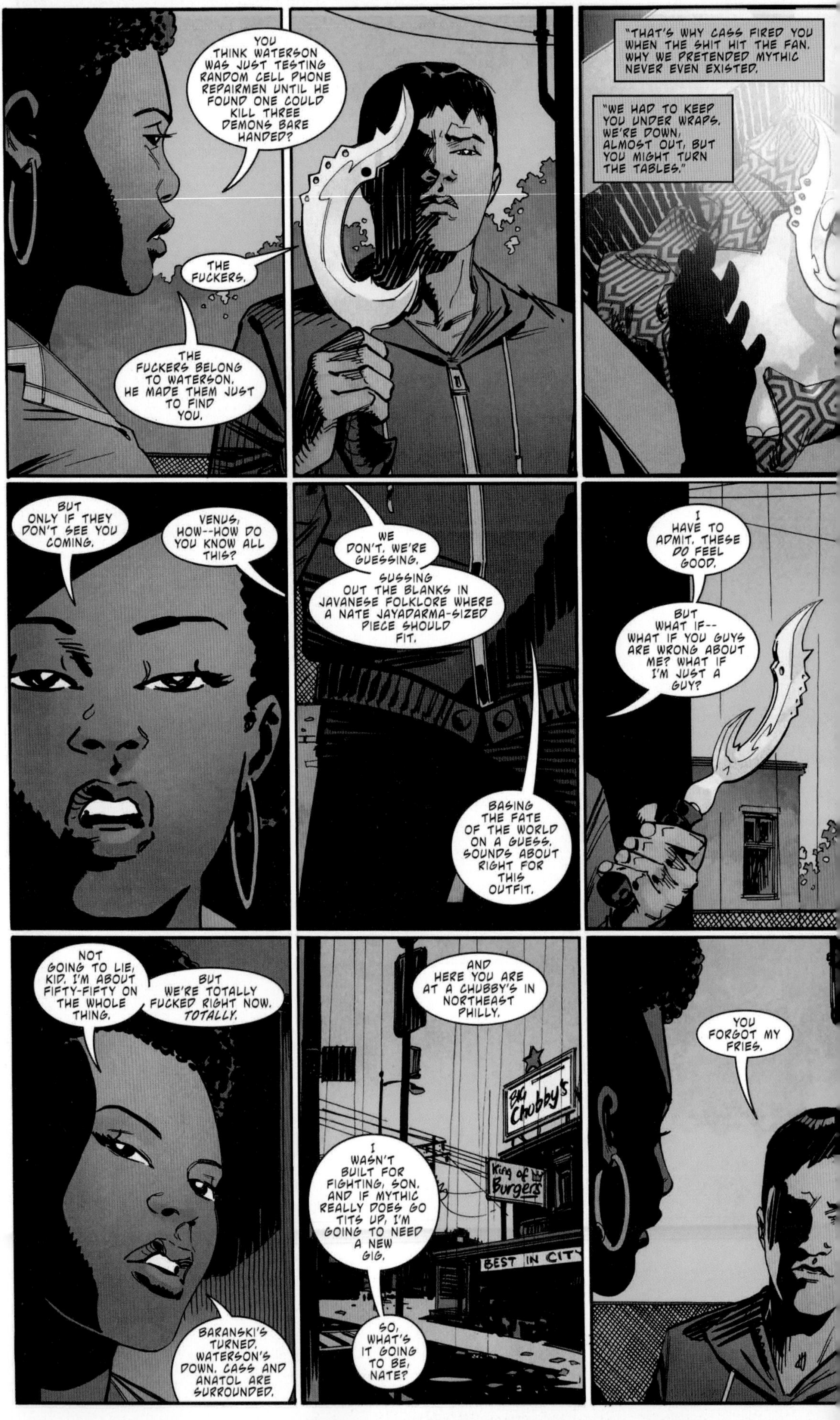
YOU THINK WATERSON WAS JUST TESTING RANDOM CELL PHONE REPAIRMEN UNTIL HE FOUND ONE COULD KILL THREE DEMONS BARE HANDED?
THE FUCKERS.
THE FUCKERS BELONG TO WATERSON. HE MADE THEM JUST TO FIND YOU.
"THAT'S WHY CASS FIRED YOU WHEN THE SHIT HIT THE FAN. WHY WE PRETENDED MYTHIC NEVER EVEN EXISTED.
"WE HAD TO KEEP YOU UNDER WRAPS. WE'RE DOWN, ALMOST OUT, BUT YOU MIGHT TURN THE TABLES."
BUT ONLY IF THEY DON'T SEE YOU COMING.
VENUS, HOW--HOW DO YOU KNOW ALL THIS?
WE DON'T. WE'RE GUESSING.
SUSSING OUT THE BLANKS IN JAVANESE FOLKLORE WHERE A NATE JAYADARMA-SIZED PIECE SHOULD FIT.
BASING THE FATE OF THE WORLD ON A GUESS. SOUNDS ABOUT RIGHT FOR THIS OUTFIT.
I HAVE TO ADMIT, THESE DO FEEL GOOD.
BUT WHAT IF-- WHAT IF YOU GUYS ARE WRONG ABOUT ME? WHAT IF I'M JUST A GUY?
NOT GOING TO LIE, KID, I'M ABOUT FIFTY-FIFTY ON THE WHOLE THING.
BUT WE'RE TOTALLY FUCKED RIGHT NOW. TOTALLY.
BARANSKI'S TURNED. WATERSON'S DOWN. CASS AND ANATOL ARE SURROUNDED.
AND HERE YOU ARE AT A CHUBBY'S IN NORTHEAST PHILLY.
BIG Chubby's
King of Burgers
BEST IN CITY
I WASN'T BUILT FOR FIGHTING, SON, AND IF MYTHIC REALLY DOES GO TITS UP, I'M GOING TO NEED A NEW GIG.
SO, WHAT'S IT GOING TO BE, NATE?
YOU FORGOT MY FRIES.

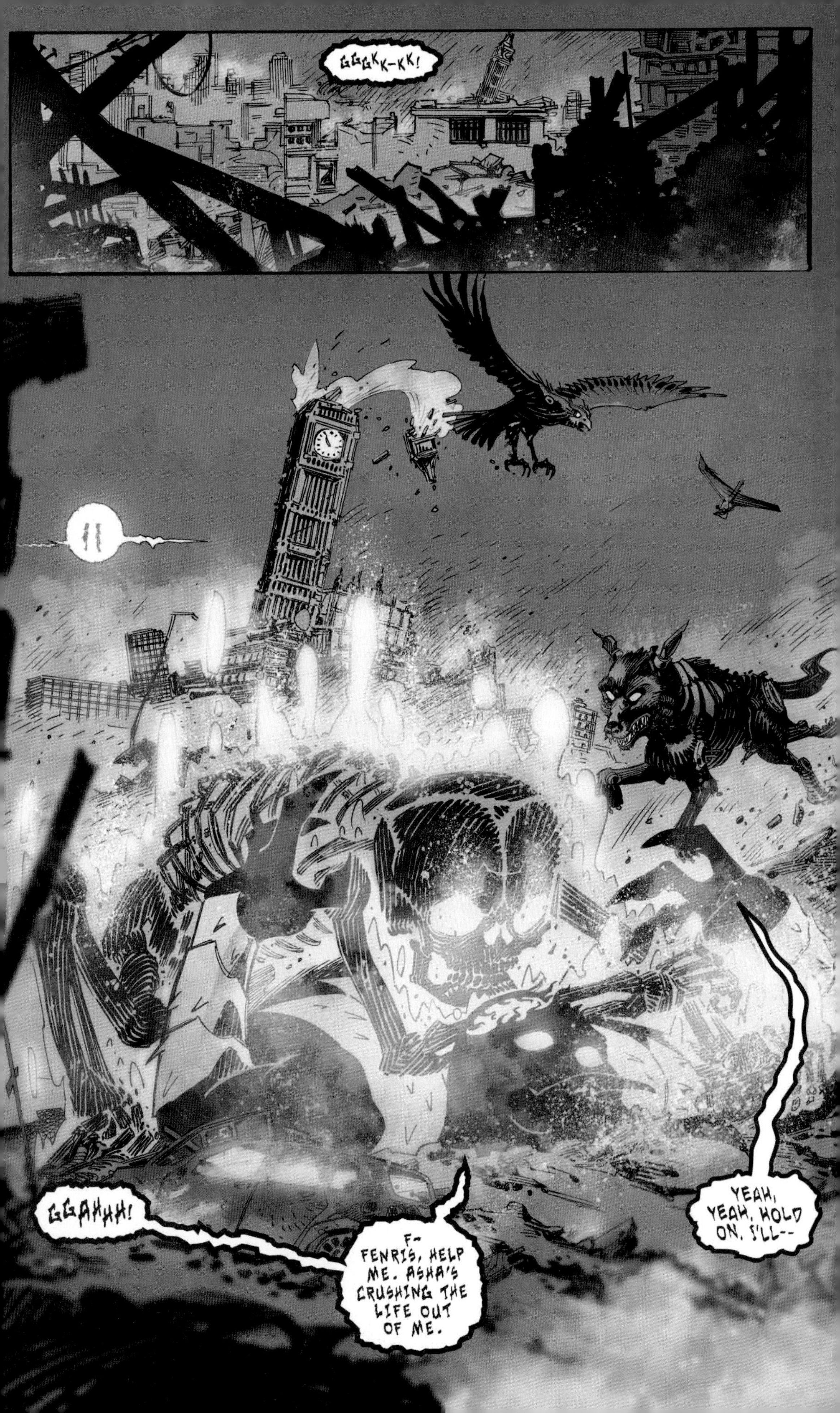
GGGKK-KK!
!!
GGAHHH!
F- FENRIS, HELP ME. ASHA'S CRUSHING THE LIFE OUT OF ME.
YEAH, YEAH, HOLD ON. I'LL--

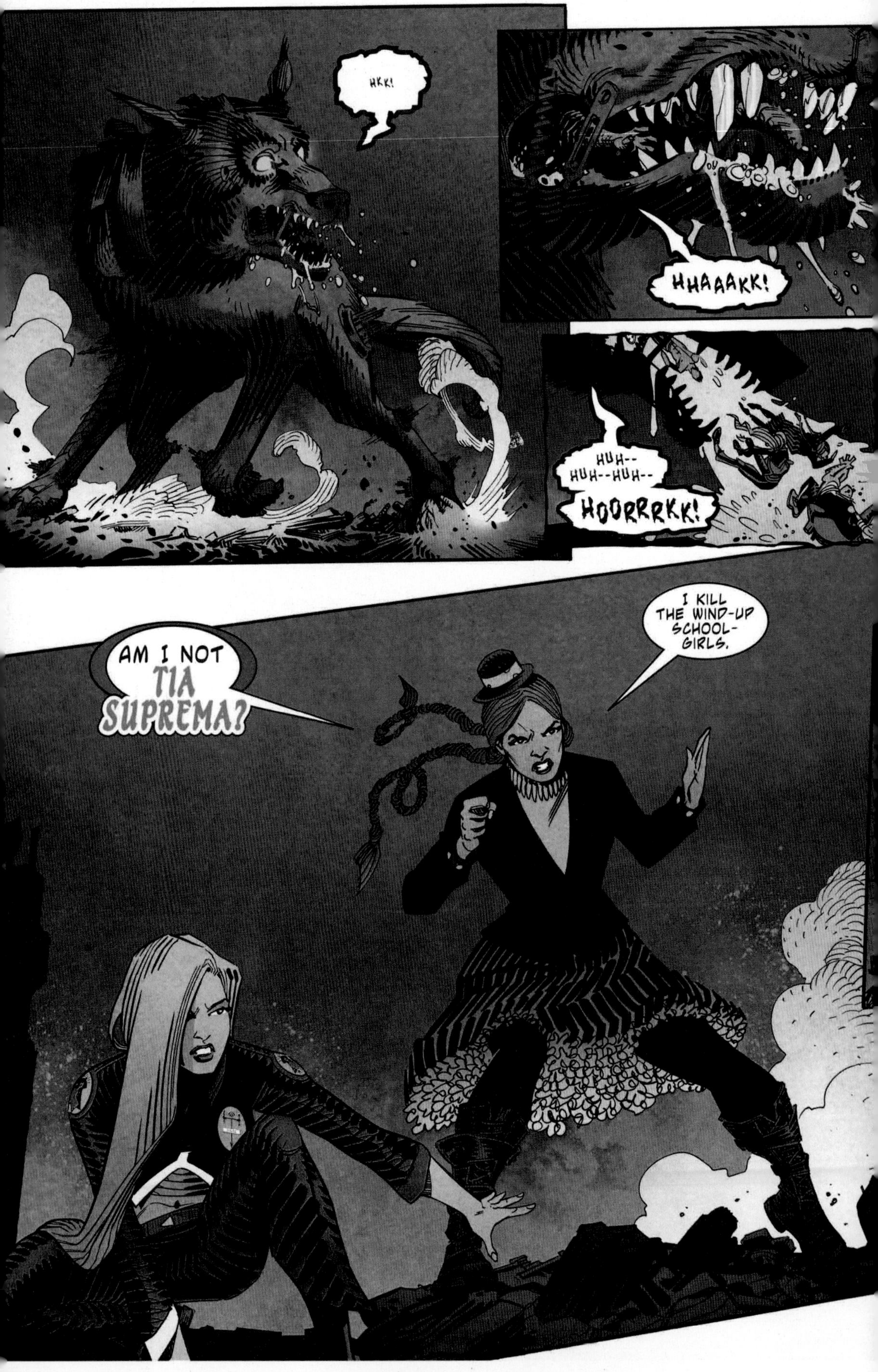
HKK!
HHAAAKK!
HUH--
HUH--HUH--
HOORRRKK!
AM I NOT TIA SUPREMA?
I KILL THE WIND-UP SCHOOL-GIRLS.

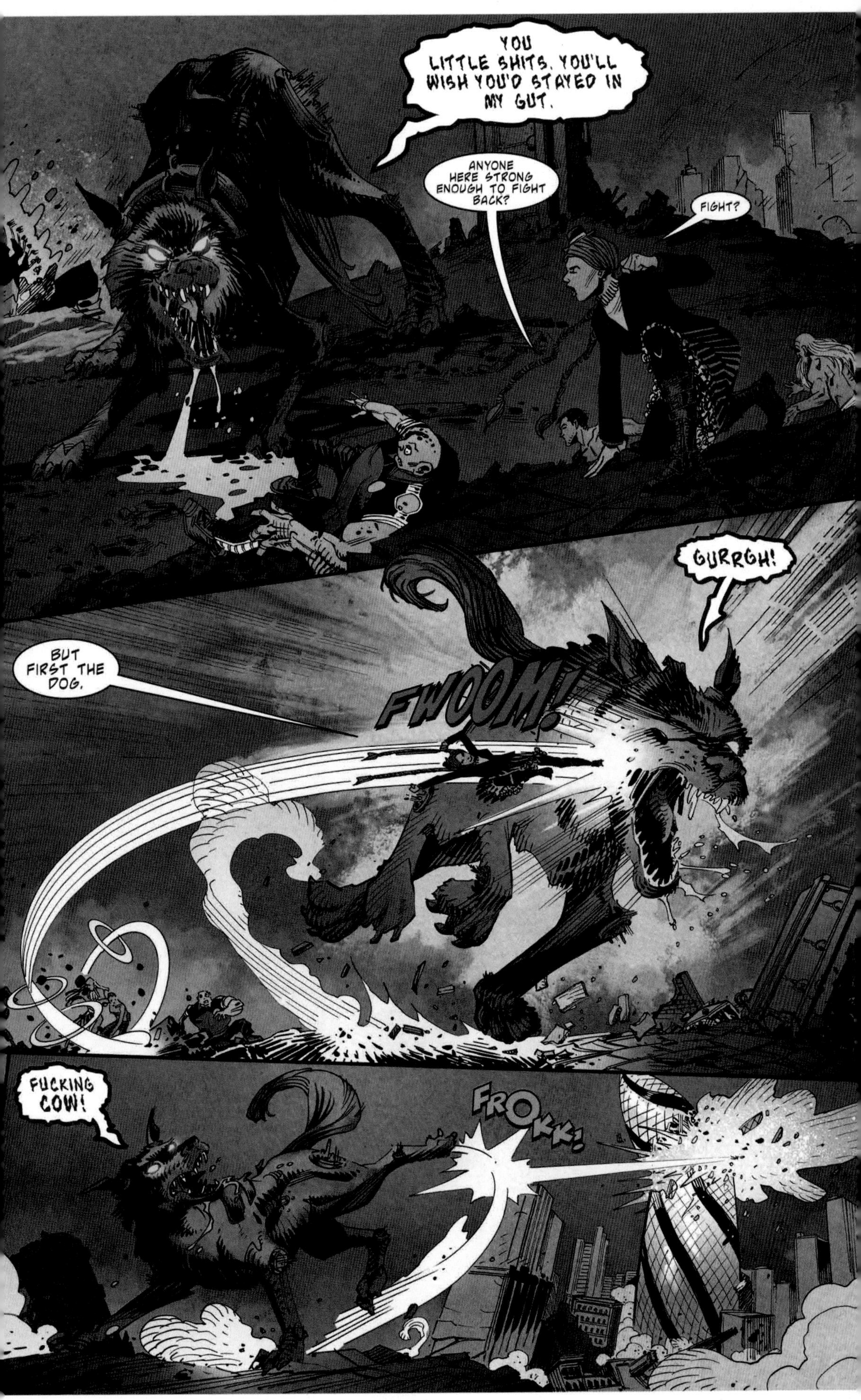

YOU LITTLE SHITS. YOU'LL WISH YOU'D STAYED IN MY GUT.
ANYONE HERE STRONG ENOUGH TO FIGHT BACK?
FIGHT?
GURRGH!
BUT FIRST THE DOG.
FWOOM!
FUCKING COW!
FROKK!

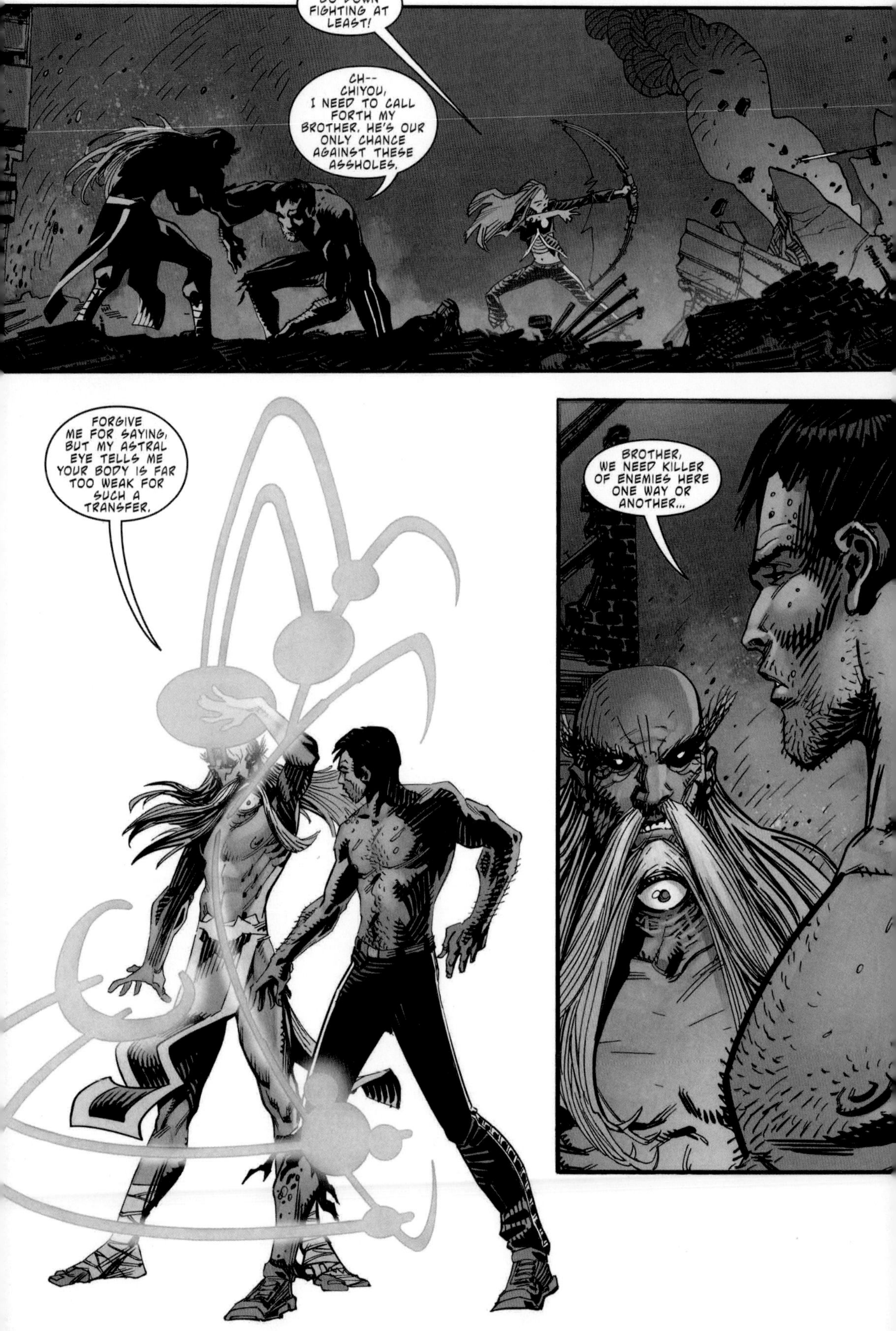
LET'S GO DOWN FIGHTING AT LEAST!
CH-- CHIYOU, I NEED TO CALL FORTH MY BROTHER. HE'S OUR ONLY CHANCE AGAINST THESE ASSHOLES.
FORGIVE ME FOR SAYING, BUT MY ASTRAL EYE TELLS ME YOUR BODY IS FAR TOO WEAK FOR SUCH A TRANSFER.
BROTHER, WE NEED KILLER OF ENEMIES HERE ONE WAY OR ANOTHER...

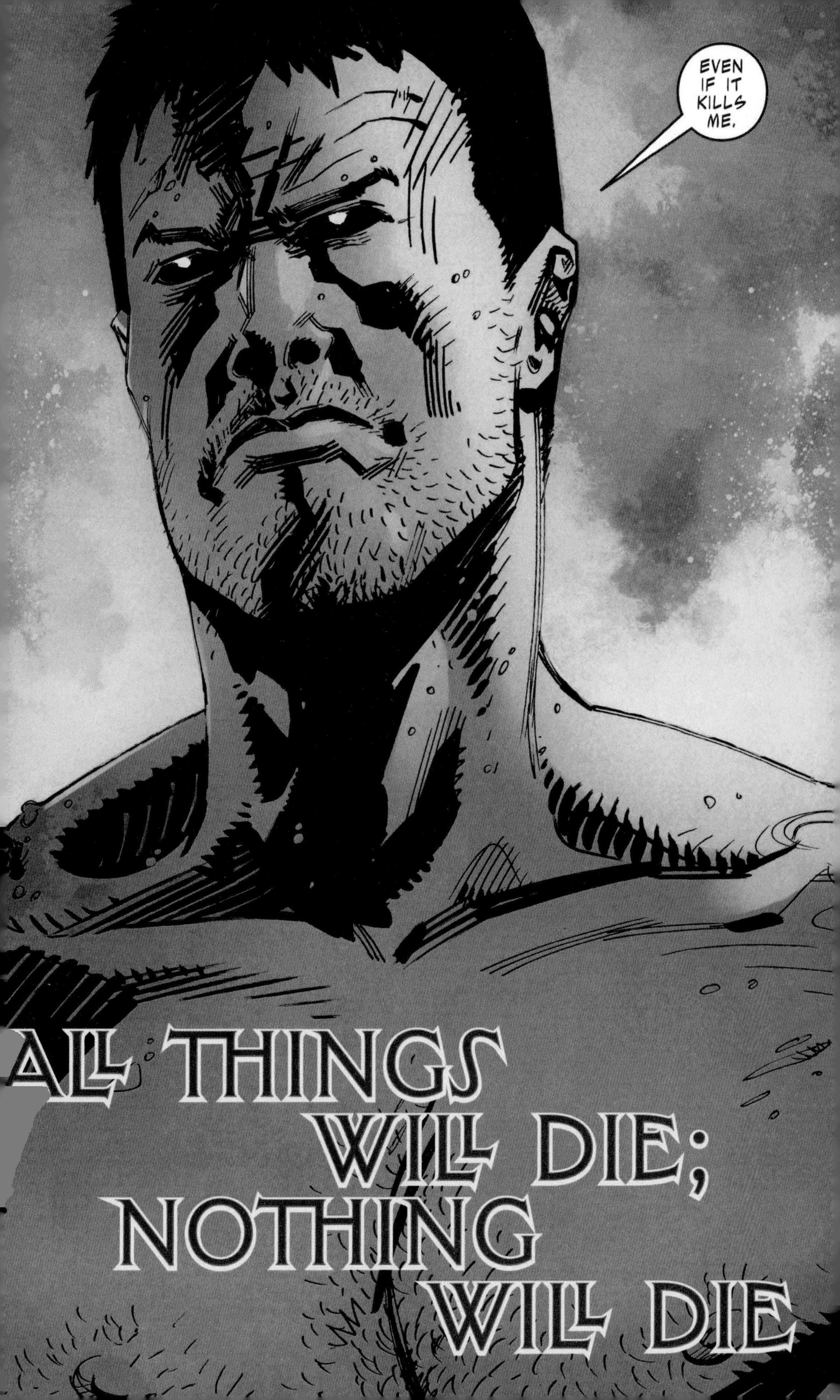
EVEN IF IT KILLS ME.
ALL THINGS WILL DIE; NOTHING WILL DIE

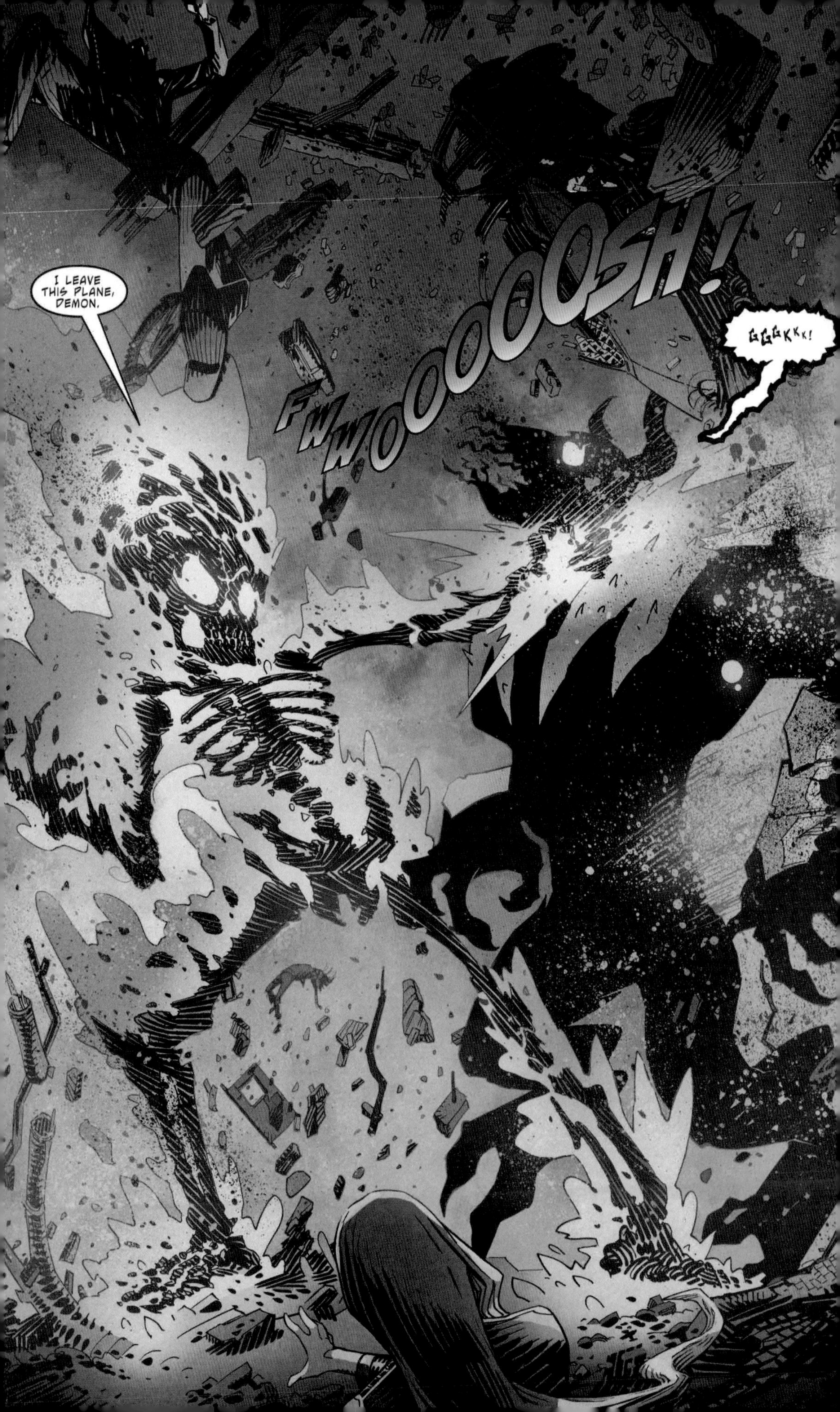
I LEAVE THIS PLANE, DEMON.
FWWOOOOOOOSH!
GGGKKK!

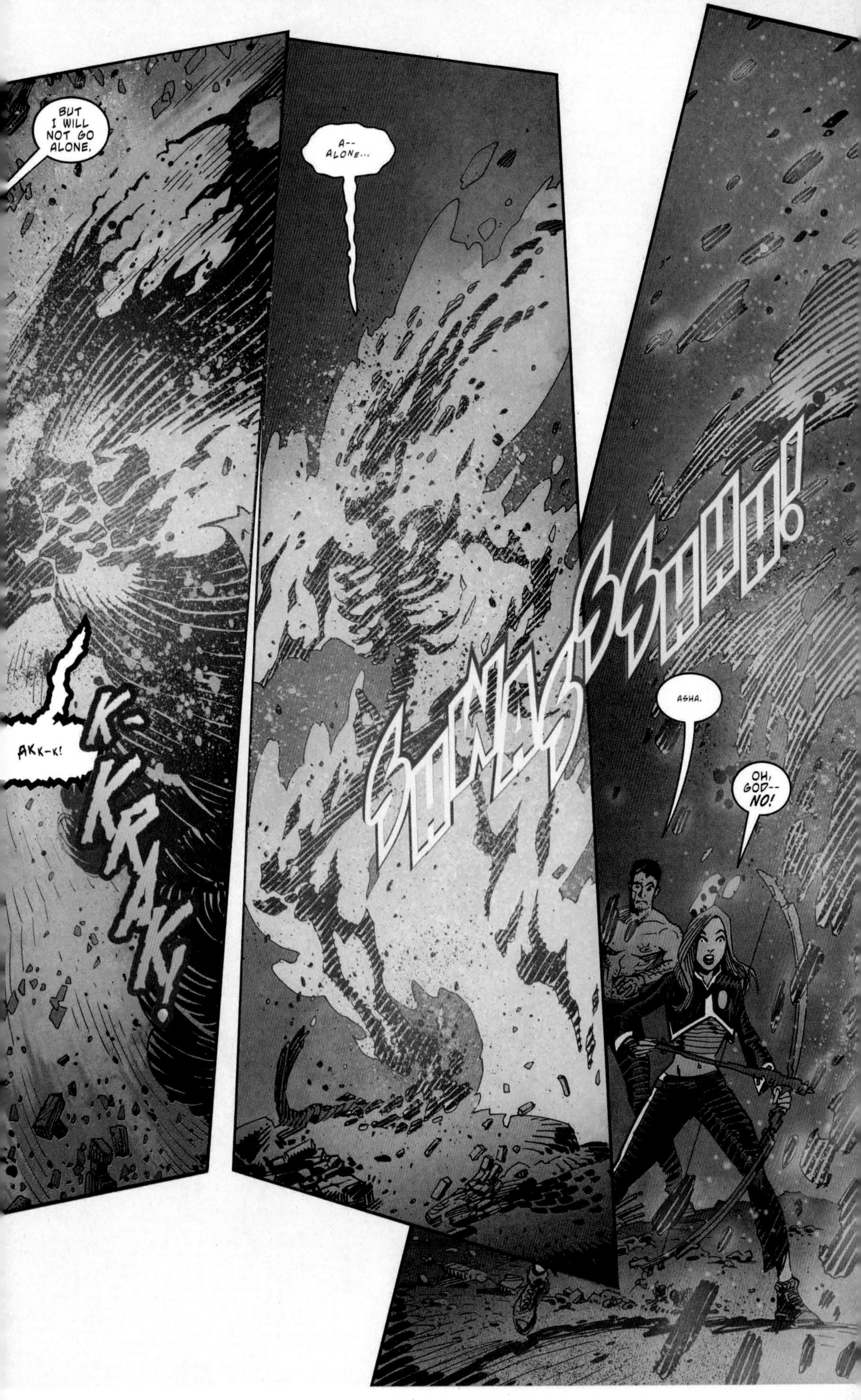

BUT I WILL NOT GO ALONE.
AKK-K!
K-KRAK!
A-- ALONE...
SHHASSSHHH!
ASHA.
OH, GOD-- NO!

COME ON, NATE, WHERE ARE YOU?

SKREEE!

SHRAKK!

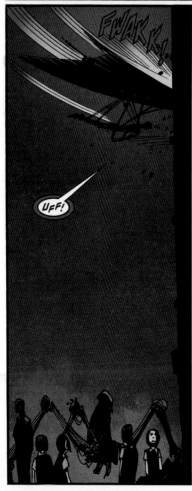

FWAKK!

UFF!

LEAVE HER BE, SHE'S HARMLESS.

I *WANT* HER TO SEE. I WANT HER TO SEE HOW THIS CARNIVAL FINALLY ENDS.

OH, I'VE SEEN IT BEFORE, BARANSKI-- INNUMERABLE TIMES. IT'S BECOME A *BORE*, REALLY.

I DO QUITE LIKE THE ENDING, THOUGH.

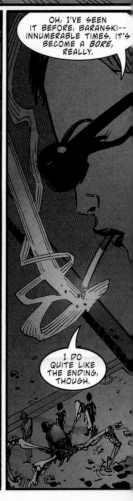

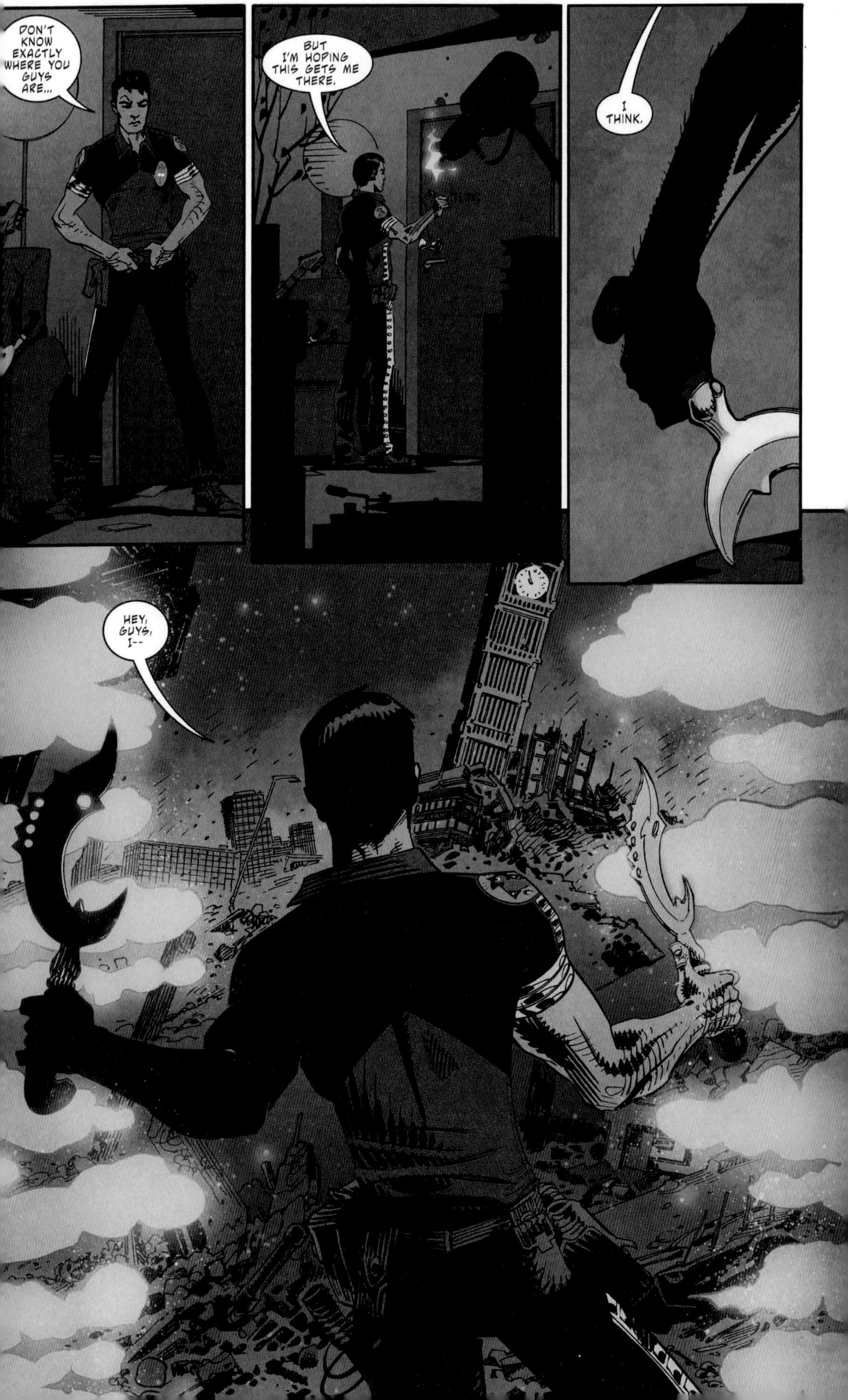
DON'T KNOW EXACTLY WHERE YOU GUYS ARE...
BUT I'M HOPING THIS GETS ME THERE.
I THINK.
HEY, GUYS, I--

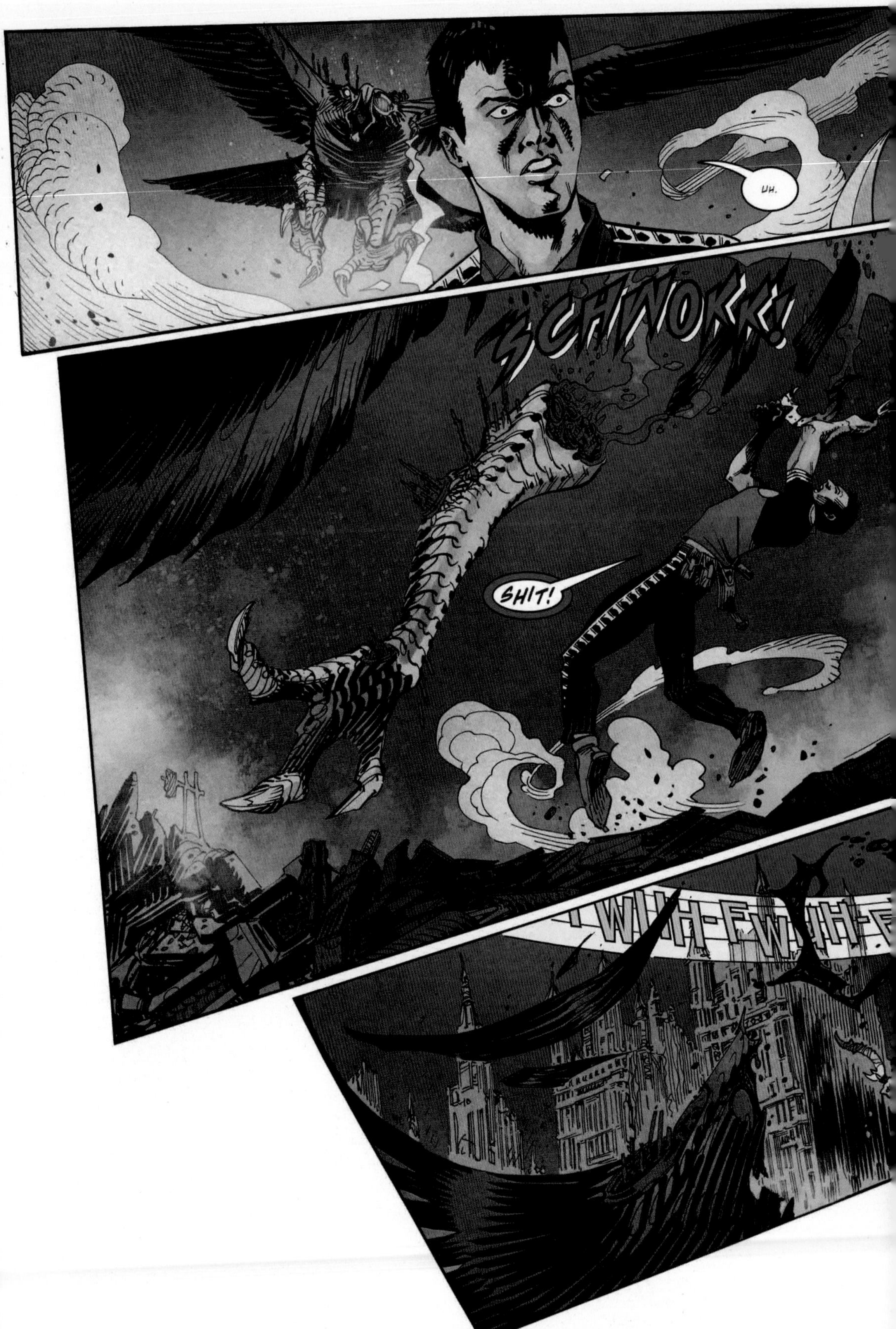
UH.
SCHINOKK!
SHIT!

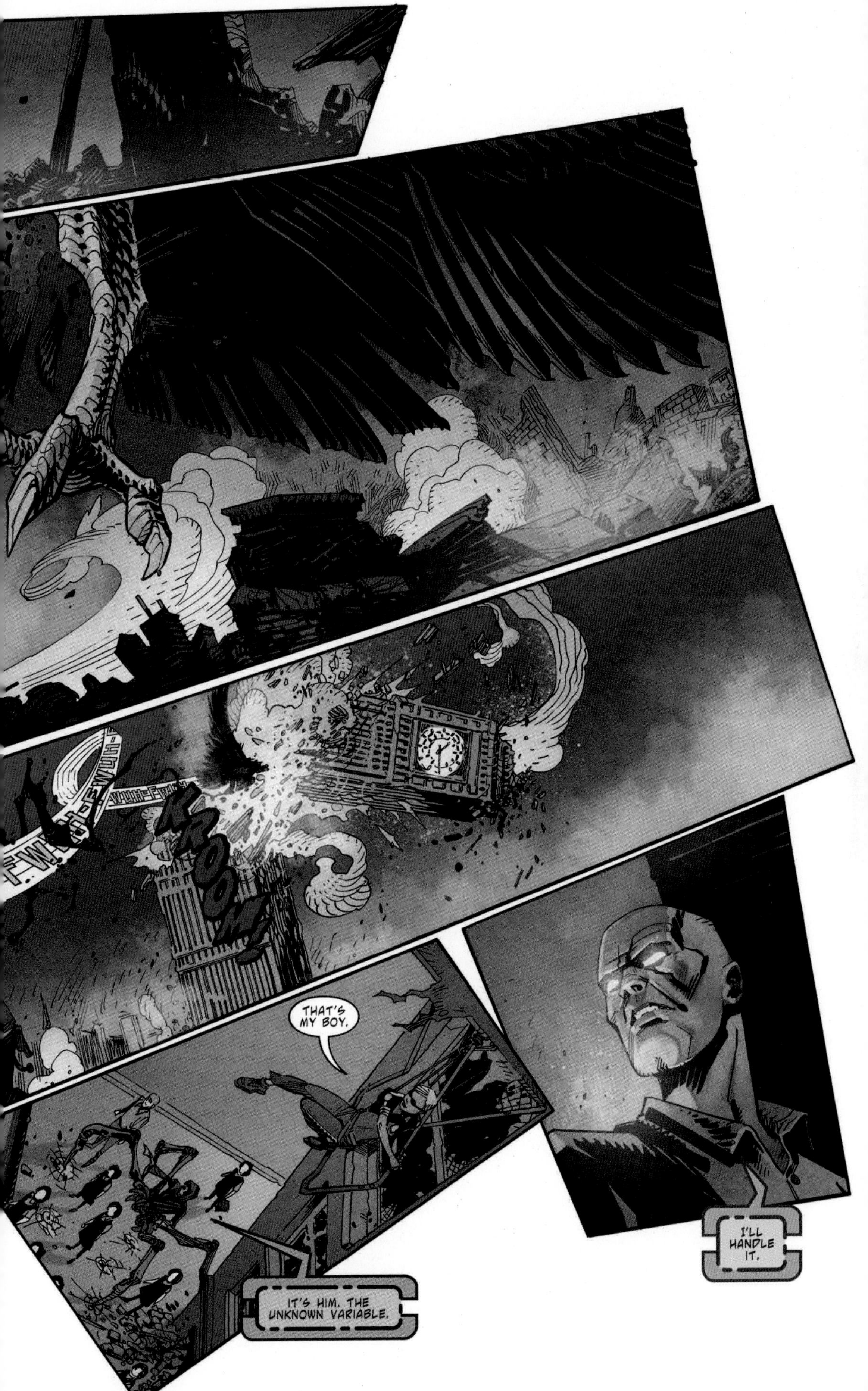
KROOOM!
THAT'S MY BOY.
IT'S HIM. THE UNKNOWN VARIABLE.
I'LL HANDLE IT.

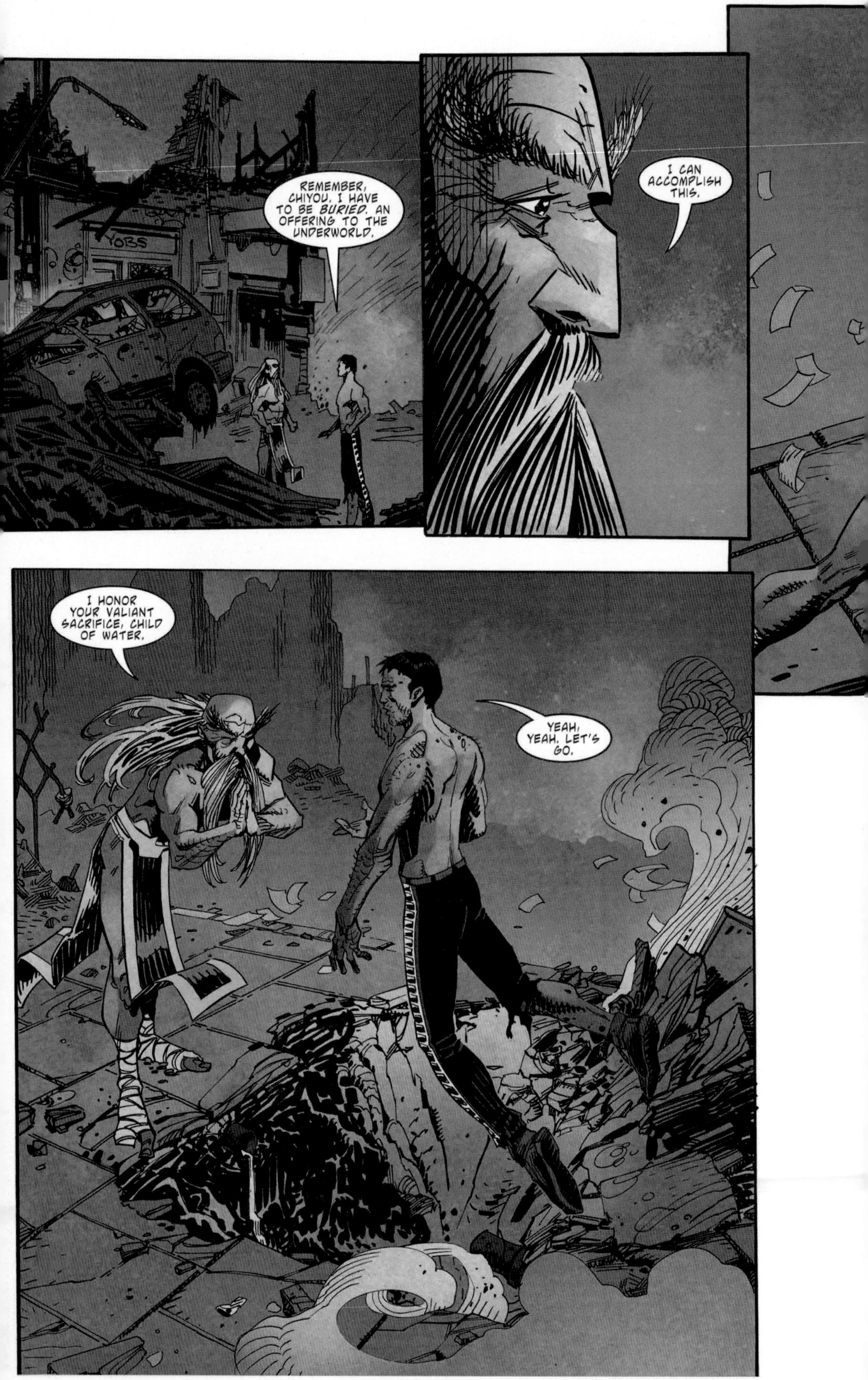
REMEMBER, CHIYOU. I HAVE TO BE BURIED. AN OFFERING TO THE UNDERWORLD.
I CAN ACCOMPLISH THIS.
I HONOR YOUR VALIANT SACRIFICE, CHILD OF WATER.
YEAH, YEAH. LET'S GO.

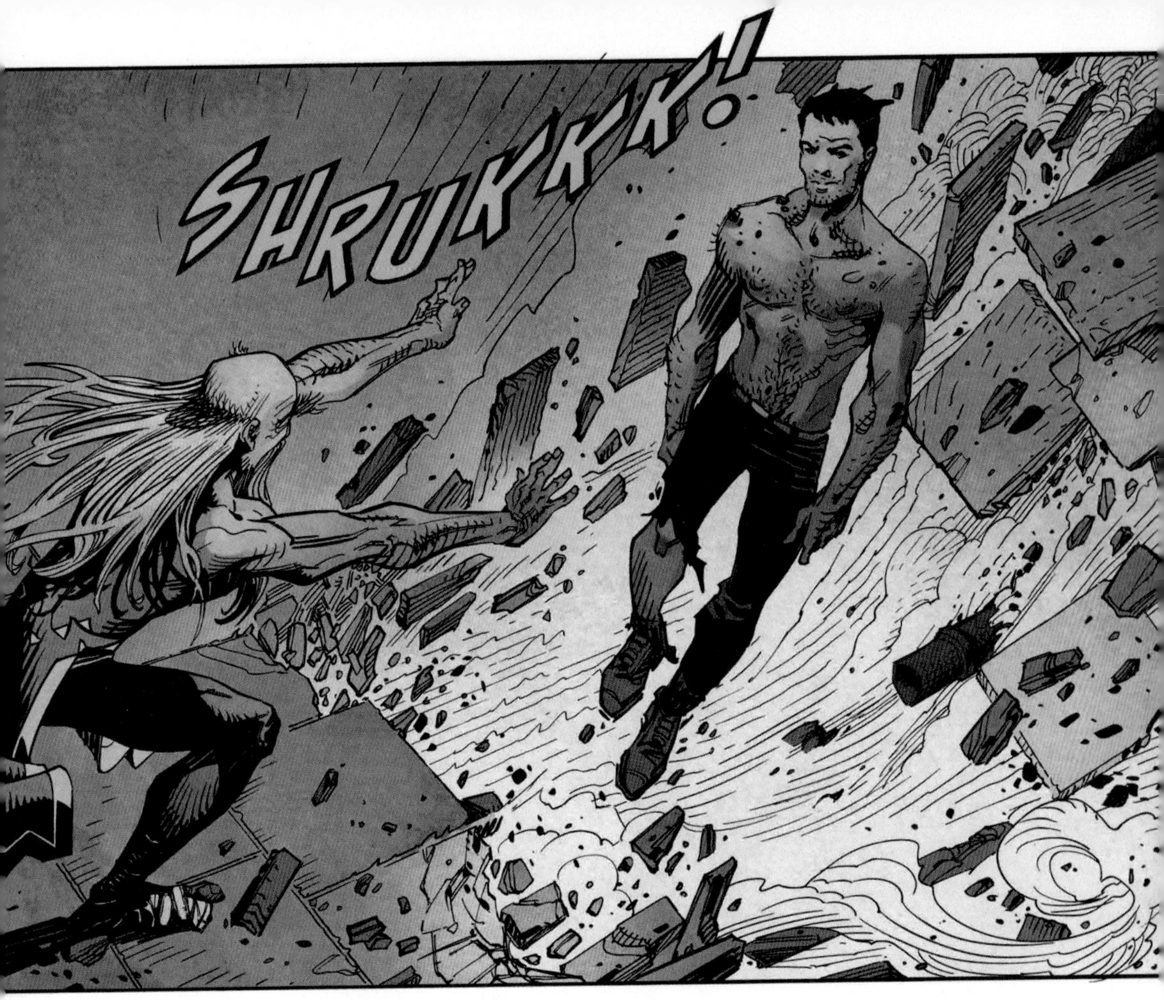
SHRUKKK!

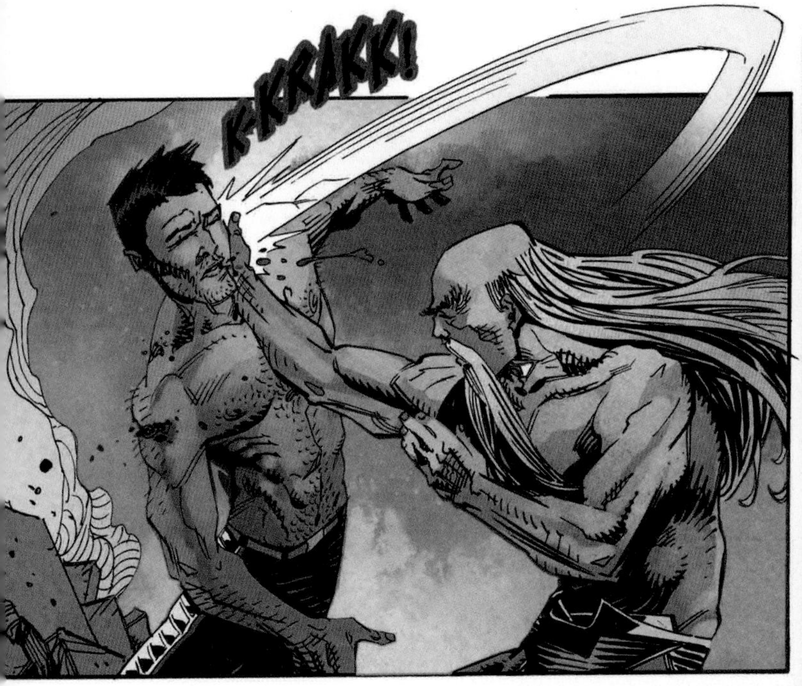
K-KRAKK!

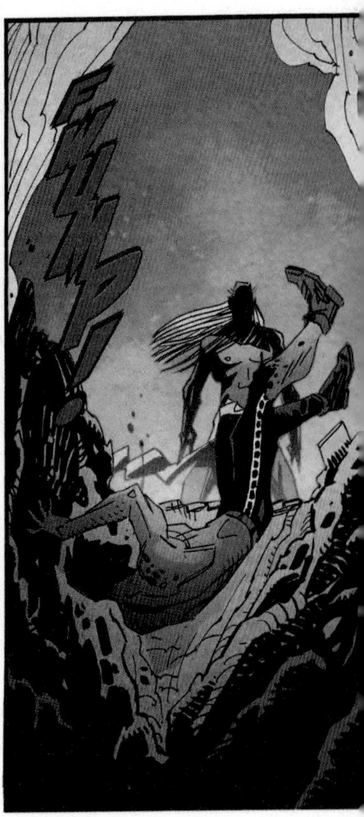

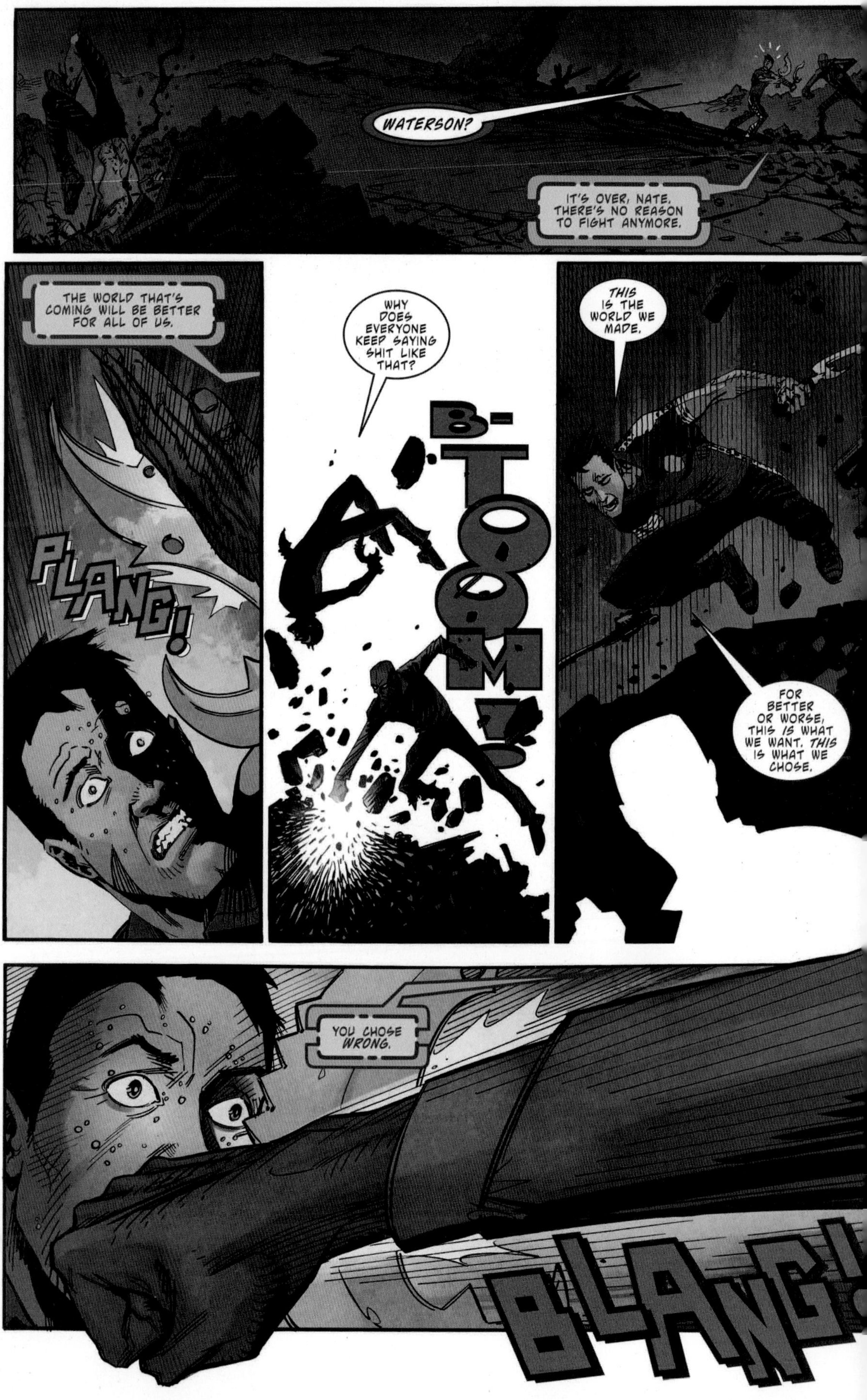
WATERSON?
IT'S OVER, NATE. THERE'S NO REASON TO FIGHT ANYMORE.
THE WORLD THAT'S COMING WILL BE BETTER FOR ALL OF US.
PLANG!
WHY DOES EVERYONE KEEP SAYING SHIT LIKE THAT?
B-TOOM!
THIS IS THE WORLD WE MADE.
FOR BETTER OR WORSE, THIS IS WHAT WE WANT. THIS IS WHAT WE CHOSE.
YOU CHOSE WRONG.
BLANG!

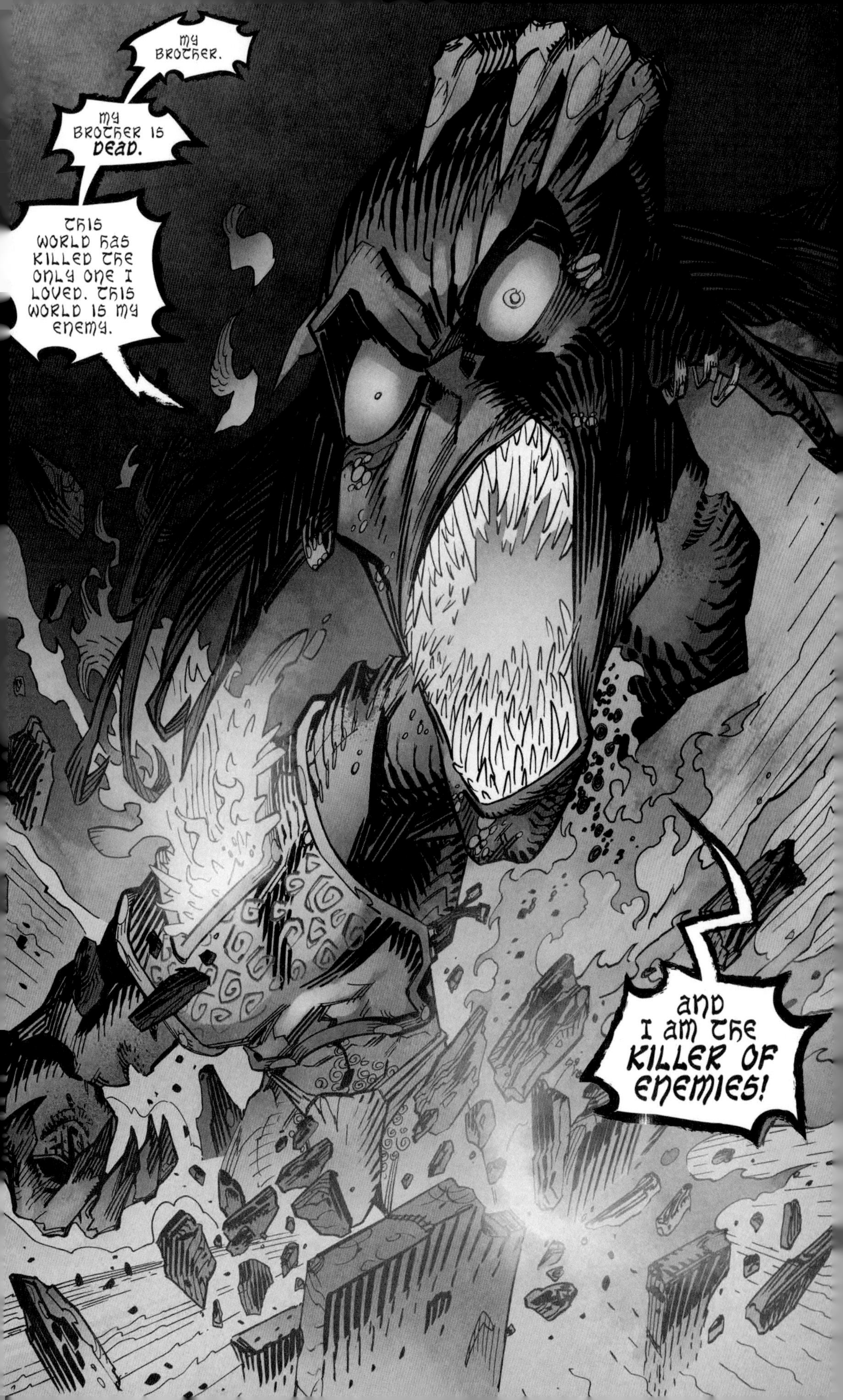
MY BROTHER.
MY BROTHER IS **DEAD.**
THIS WORLD HAS KILLED THE ONLY ONE I LOVED. THIS WORLD IS MY ENEMY.
AND I AM THE **KILLER OF ENEMIES!**

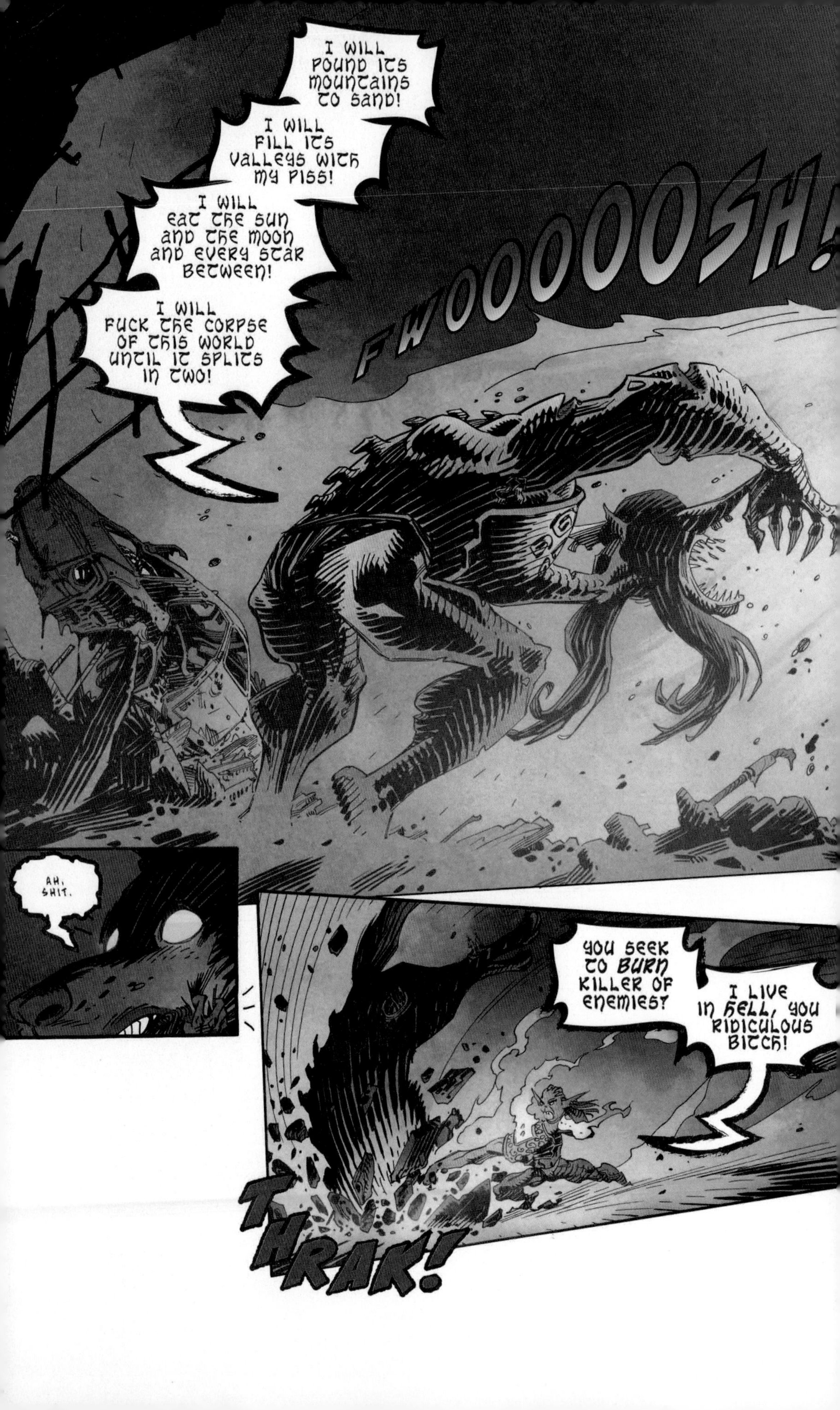
I WILL POUND ITS MOUNTAINS TO SAND!
I WILL FILL ITS VALLEYS WITH MY PISS!
I WILL EAT THE SUN AND THE MOON AND EVERY STAR BETWEEN!
I WILL FUCK THE CORPSE OF THIS WORLD UNTIL IT SPLITS IN TWO!
FWOOOOOOSH!
AH, SHIT.
YOU SEEK TO BURN KILLER OF ENEMIES?
I LIVE IN HELL, YOU RIDICULOUS BITCH!
THRAK!

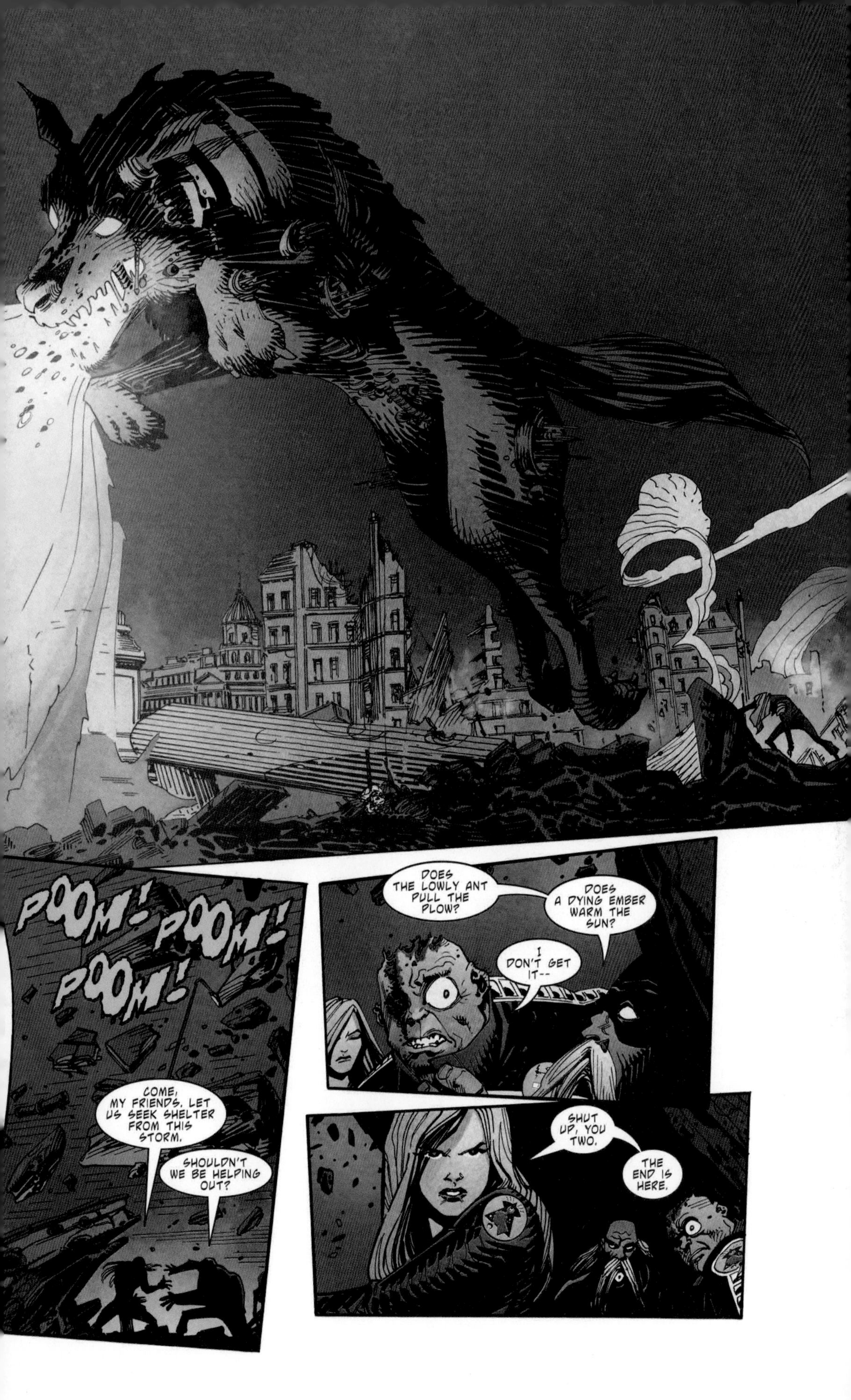
POOM! POOM! POOM!
COME, MY FRIENDS. LET US SEEK SHELTER FROM THIS STORM.
SHOULDN'T WE BE HELPING OUT?
DOES THE LOWLY ANT PULL THE PLOW?
DOES A DYING EMBER WARM THE SUN?
I DON'T GET IT--
SHUT UP, YOU TWO.
THE END IS HERE.

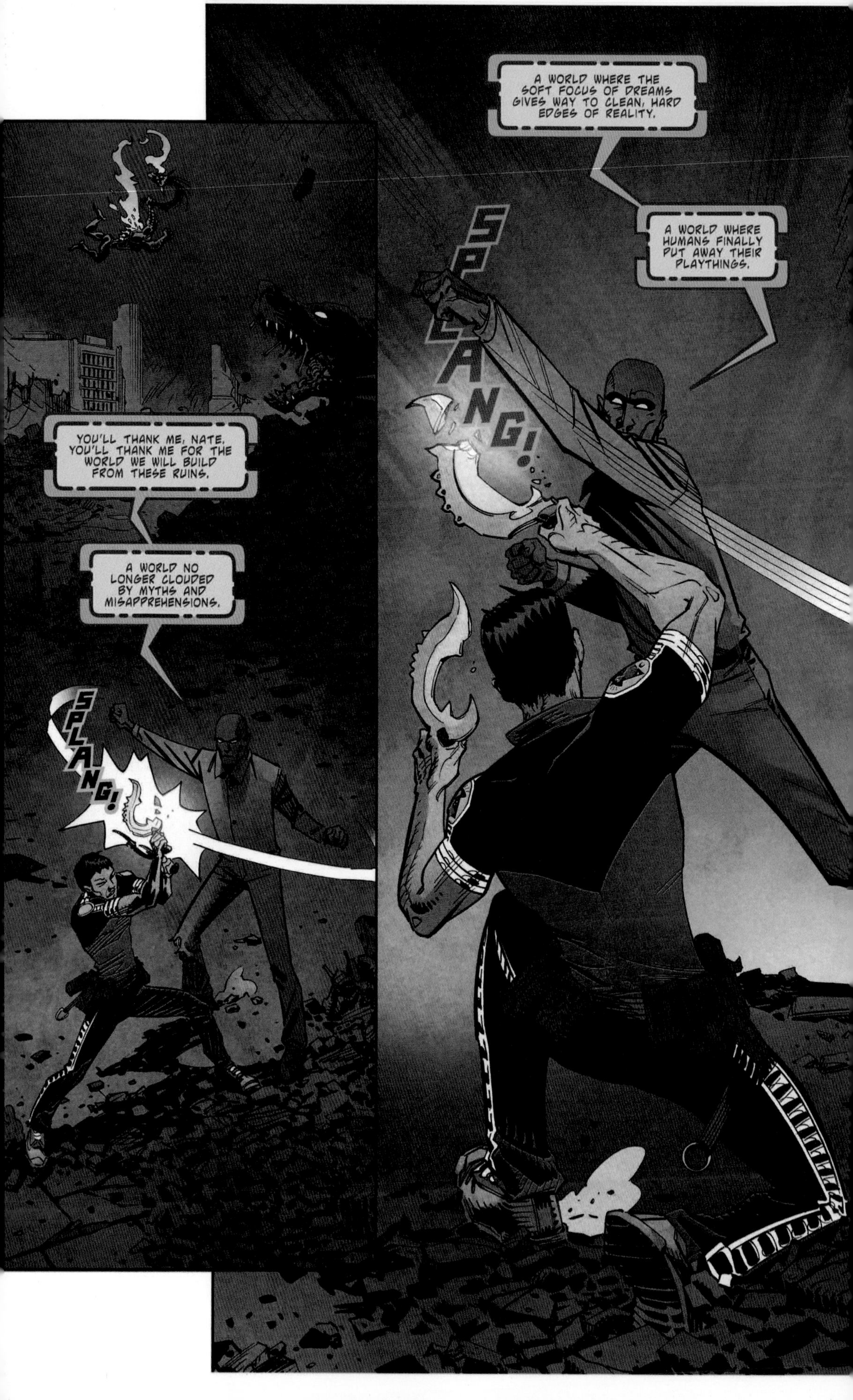

YOU'LL THANK ME, NATE. YOU'LL THANK ME FOR THE WORLD WE WILL BUILD FROM THESE RUINS.
A WORLD NO LONGER CLOUDED BY MYTHS AND MISAPPREHENSIONS.
SPLANG!
A WORLD WHERE THE SOFT FOCUS OF DREAMS GIVES WAY TO CLEAN, HARD EDGES OF REALITY.
A WORLD WHERE HUMANS FINALLY PUT AWAY THEIR PLAYTHINGS.
SPLANG!

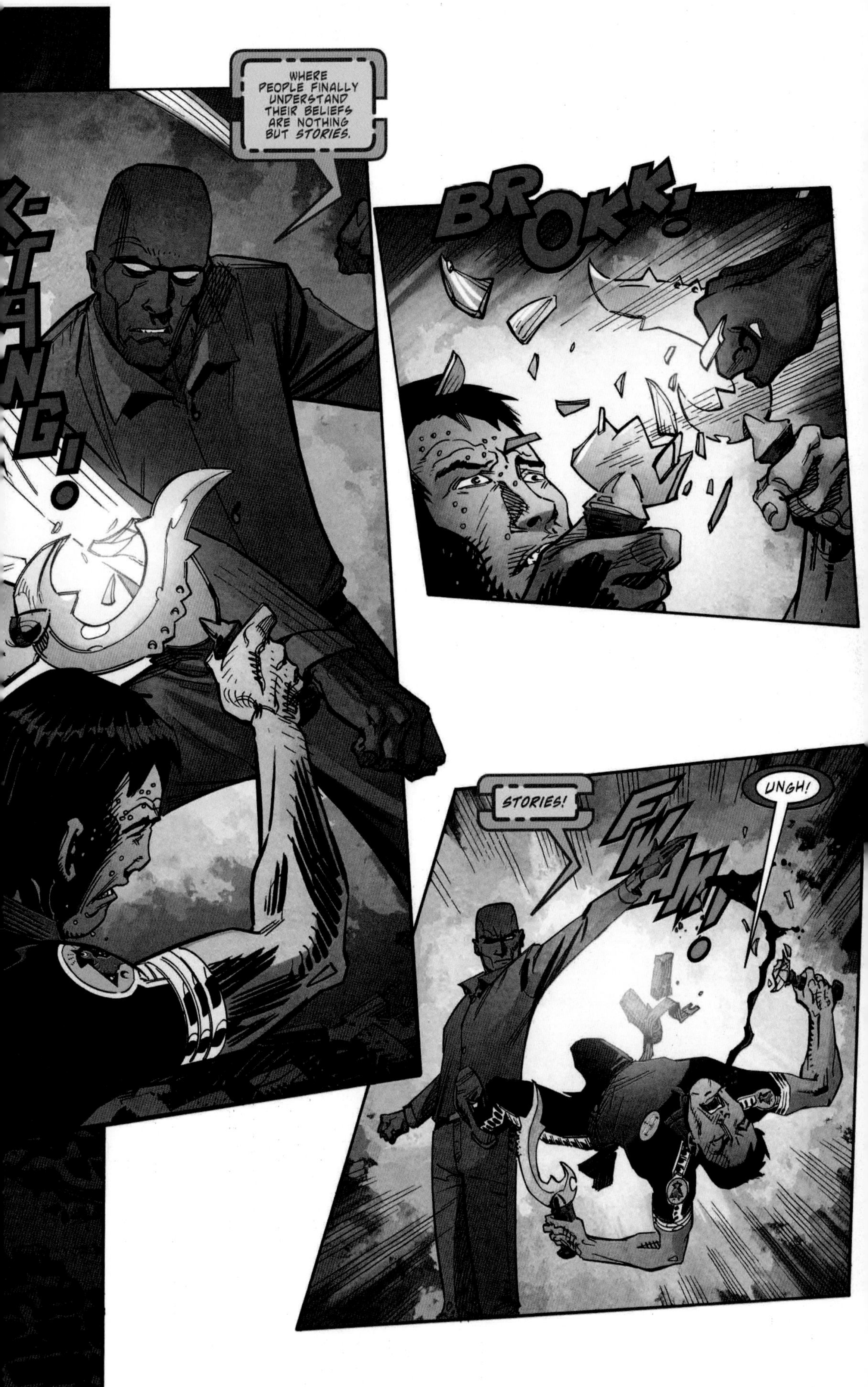
WHERE PEOPLE FINALLY UNDERSTAND THEIR BELIEFS ARE NOTHING BUT STORIES.
K-TANG!
BROKK!
STORIES!
FWAM!
UNGH!

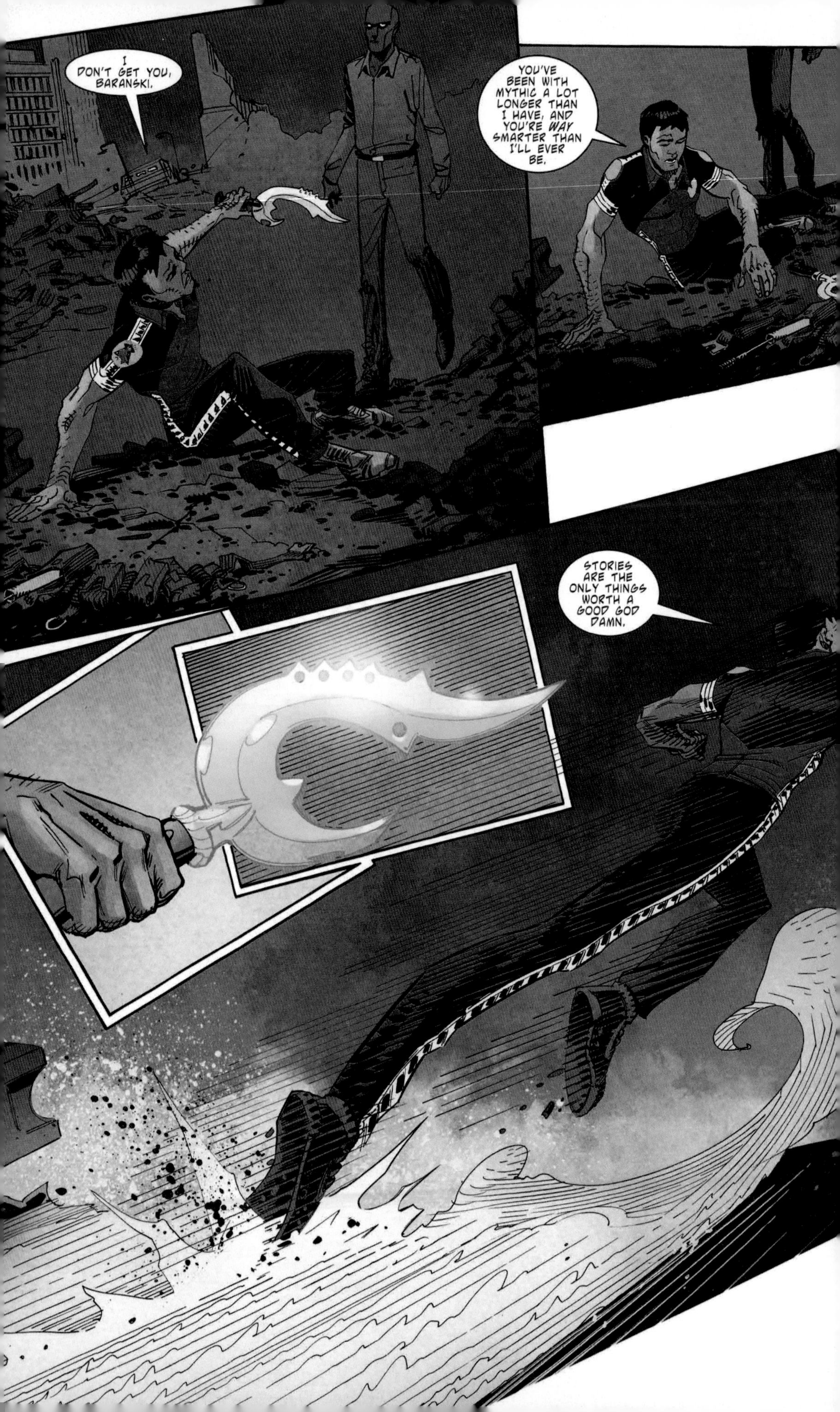
I DON'T GET YOU, BARANSKI.
YOU'VE BEEN WITH MYTHIC A LOT LONGER THAN I HAVE, AND YOU'RE WAY SMARTER THAN I'LL EVER BE.
STORIES ARE THE ONLY THINGS WORTH A GOOD GOD DAMN.

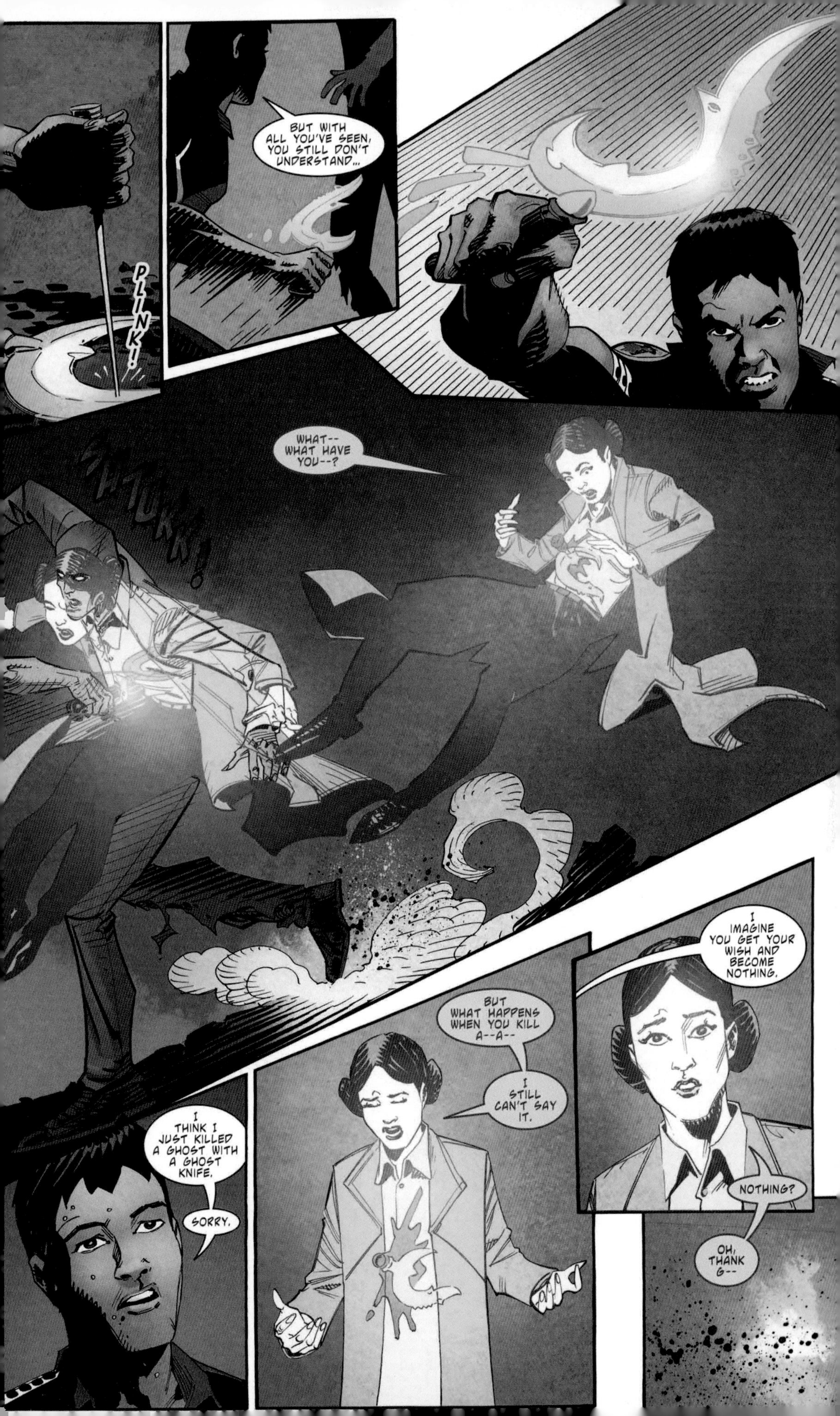
PLINK!
BUT WITH ALL YOU'VE SEEN, YOU STILL DON'T UNDERSTAND...
WHAT-- WHAT HAVE YOU--?
SHUKK!
I THINK I JUST KILLED A GHOST WITH A GHOST KNIFE.
SORRY.
BUT WHAT HAPPENS WHEN YOU KILL A--A--
I STILL CAN'T SAY IT.
I IMAGINE YOU GET YOUR WISH AND BECOME NOTHING.
NOTHING?
OH, THANK G--

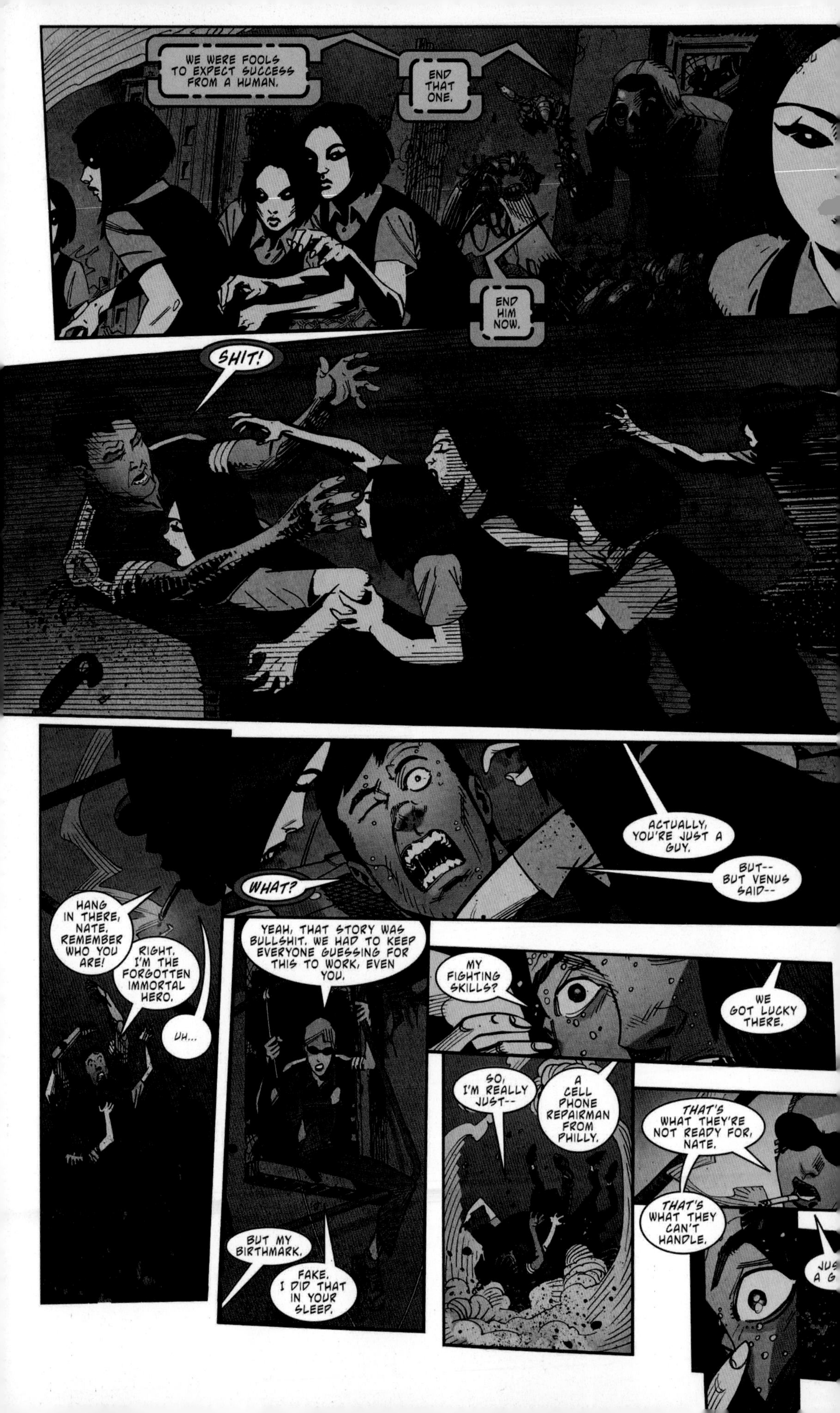
WE WERE FOOLS TO EXPECT SUCCESS FROM A HUMAN.
END THAT ONE.
END HIM NOW.
SHIT!
ACTUALLY, YOU'RE JUST A GUY.
WHAT?
BUT-- BUT VENUS SAID--
HANG IN THERE, NATE. REMEMBER WHO YOU ARE!
RIGHT. I'M THE FORGOTTEN IMMORTAL HERO.
UH...
YEAH, THAT STORY WAS BULLSHIT. WE HAD TO KEEP EVERYONE GUESSING FOR THIS TO WORK, EVEN YOU.
BUT MY BIRTHMARK.
FAKE. I DID THAT IN YOUR SLEEP.
MY FIGHTING SKILLS?
WE GOT LUCKY THERE.
SO, I'M REALLY JUST--
A CELL PHONE REPAIRMAN FROM PHILLY.
THAT'S WHAT THEY'RE NOT READY FOR, NATE.
THAT'S WHAT THEY CAN'T HANDLE.

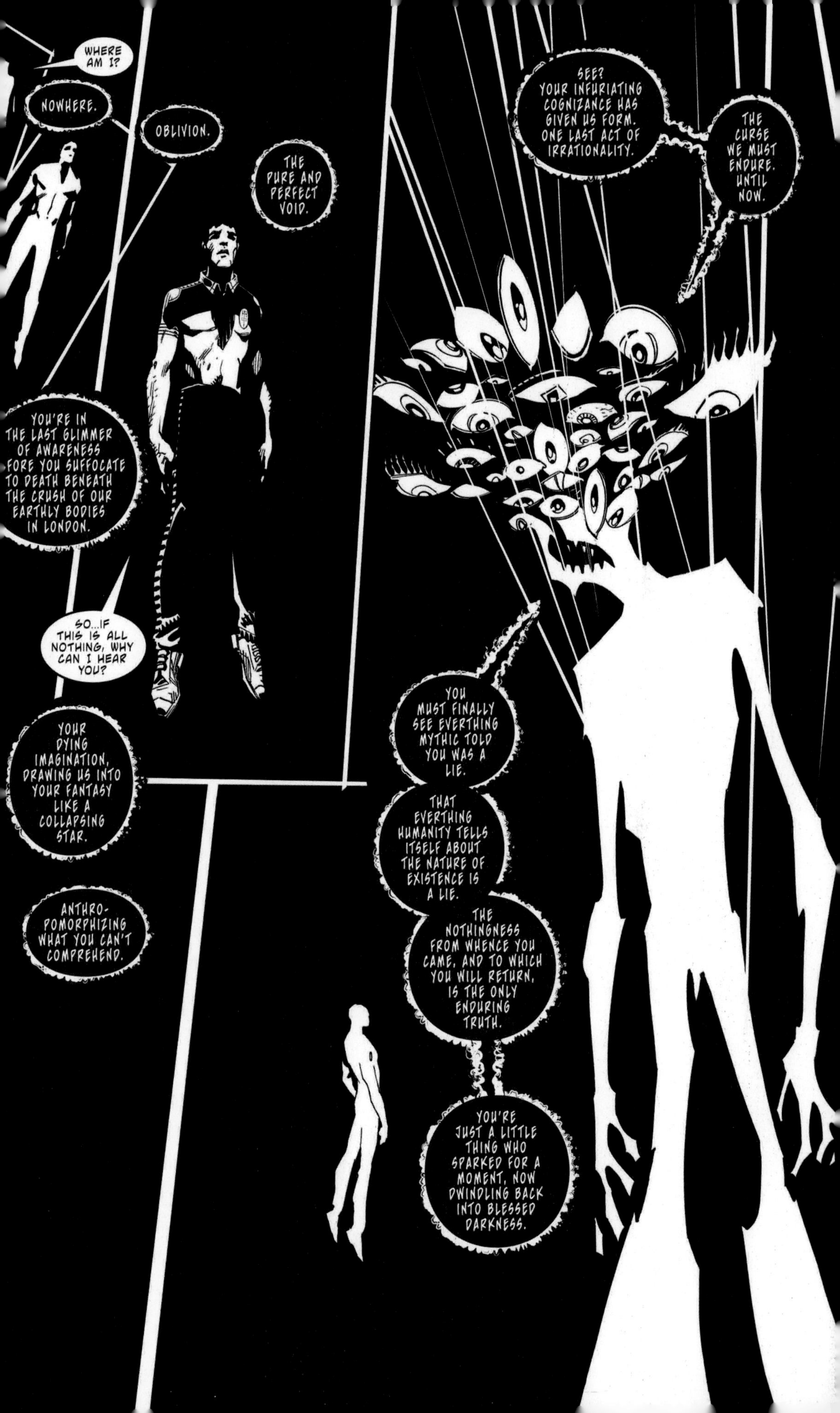
WHERE AM I?
NOWHERE.
OBLIVION.
THE PURE AND PERFECT VOID.
YOU'RE IN THE LAST GLIMMER OF AWARENESS FORE YOU SUFFOCATE TO DEATH BENEATH THE CRUSH OF OUR EARTHLY BODIES IN LONDON.
SO...IF THIS IS ALL NOTHING, WHY CAN I HEAR YOU?
YOUR DYING IMAGINATION, DRAWING US INTO YOUR FANTASY LIKE A COLLAPSING STAR.
ANTHRO-POMORPHIZING WHAT YOU CAN'T COMPREHEND.
SEE? YOUR INFURIATING COGNIZANCE HAS GIVEN US FORM. ONE LAST ACT OF IRRATIONALITY.
THE CURSE WE MUST ENDURE. UNTIL NOW.
YOU MUST FINALLY SEE EVERTHING MYTHIC TOLD YOU WAS A LIE.
THAT EVERTHING HUMANITY TELLS ITSELF ABOUT THE NATURE OF EXISTENCE IS A LIE.
THE NOTHINGNESS FROM WHENCE YOU CAME, AND TO WHICH YOU WILL RETURN, IS THE ONLY ENDURING TRUTH.
YOU'RE JUST A LITTLE THING WHO SPARKED FOR A MOMENT, NOW DWINDLING BACK INTO BLESSED DARKNESS.

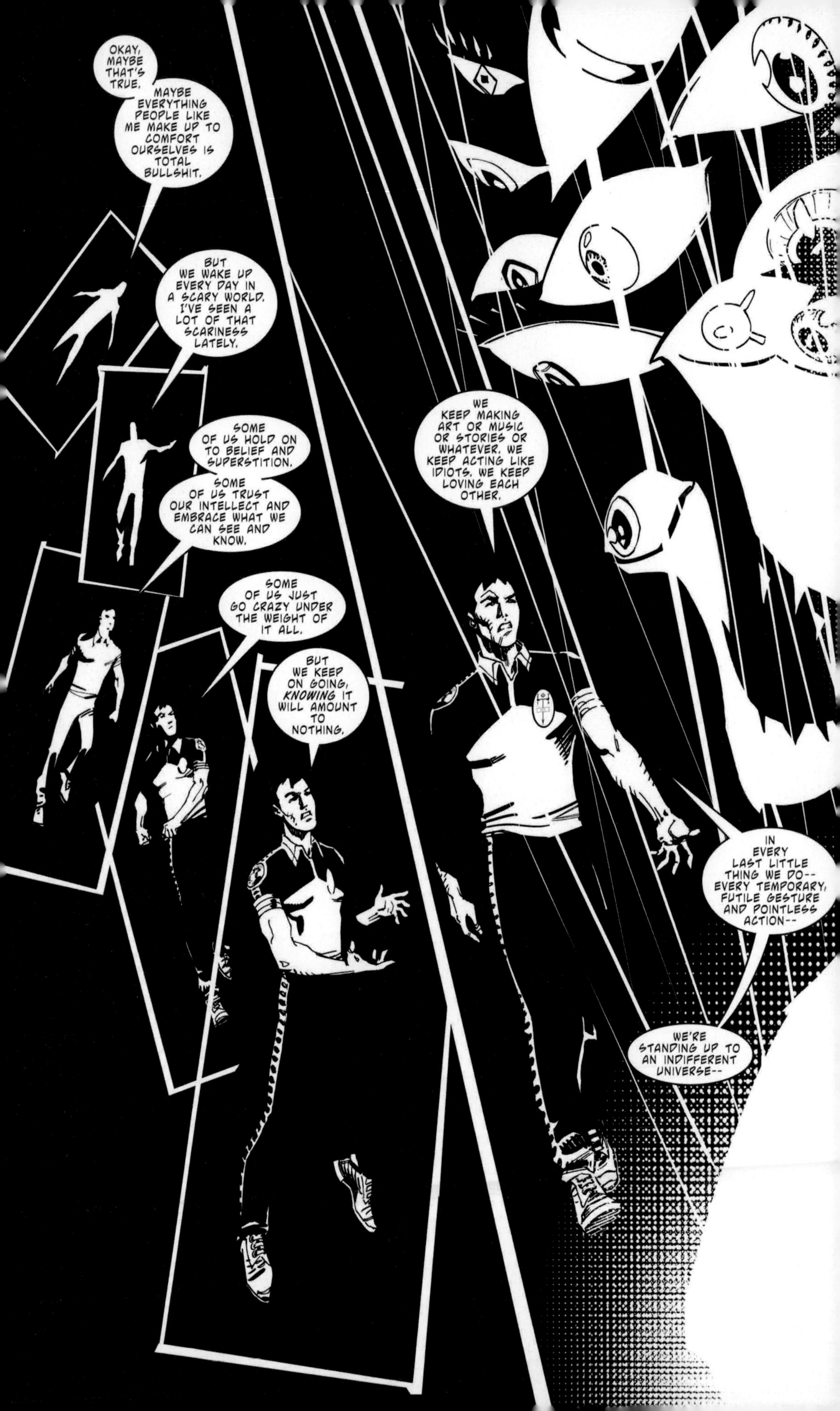
OKAY, MAYBE THAT'S TRUE.
MAYBE EVERYTHING PEOPLE LIKE ME MAKE UP TO COMFORT OURSELVES IS TOTAL BULLSHIT.
BUT WE WAKE UP EVERY DAY IN A SCARY WORLD. I'VE SEEN A LOT OF THAT SCARINESS LATELY.
SOME OF US HOLD ON TO BELIEF AND SUPERSTITION.
SOME OF US TRUST OUR INTELLECT AND EMBRACE WHAT WE CAN SEE AND KNOW.
SOME OF US JUST GO CRAZY UNDER THE WEIGHT OF IT ALL.
BUT WE KEEP ON GOING, *KNOWING* IT WILL AMOUNT TO NOTHING.
WE KEEP MAKING ART OR MUSIC OR STORIES OR WHATEVER. WE KEEP ACTING LIKE IDIOTS. WE KEEP LOVING EACH OTHER.
IN EVERY LAST LITTLE THING WE DO-- EVERY TEMPORARY, FUTILE GESTURE AND POINTLESS ACTION--
WE'RE STANDING UP TO AN INDIFFERENT UNIVERSE--

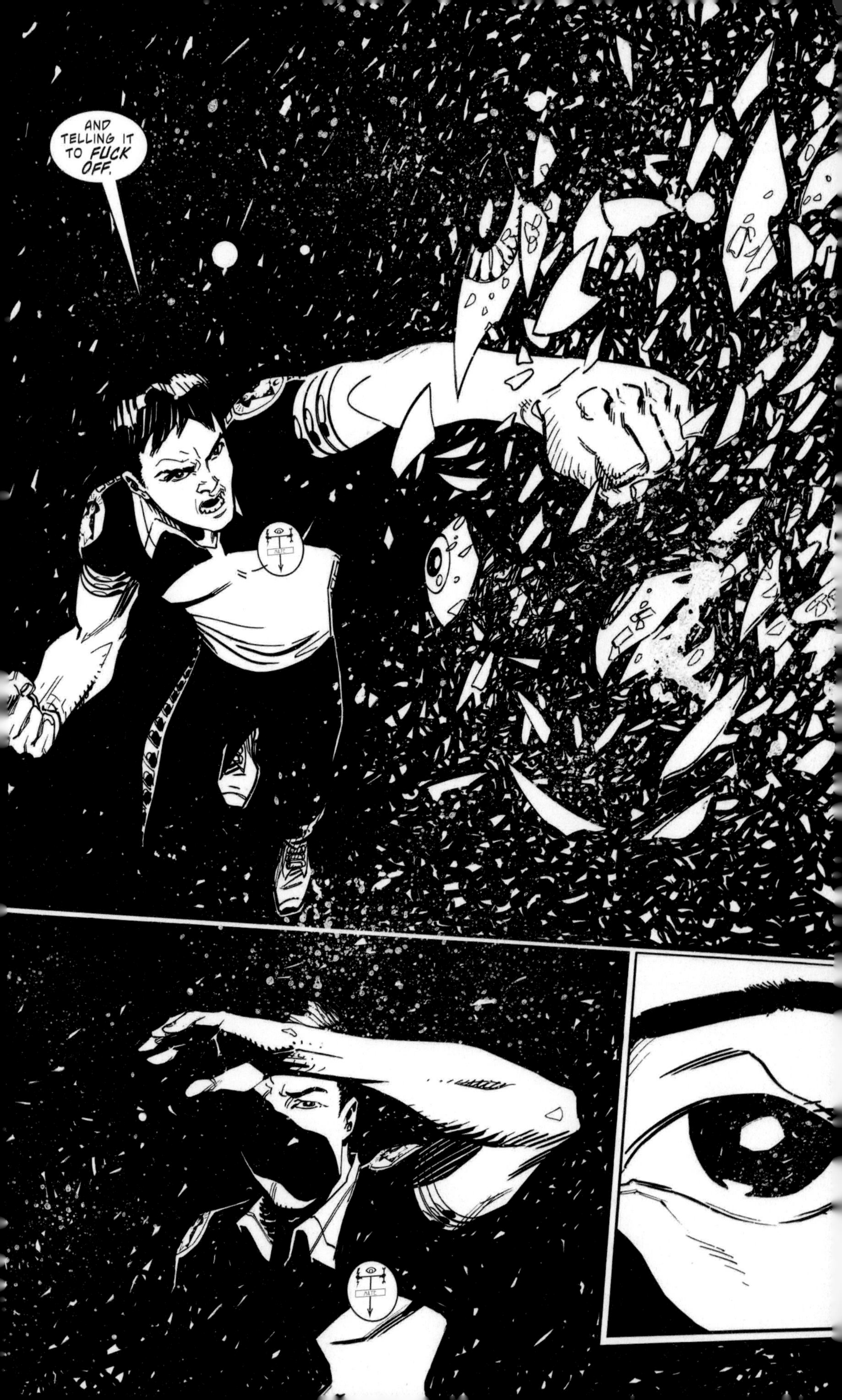
AND TELLING IT TO FUCK OFF.

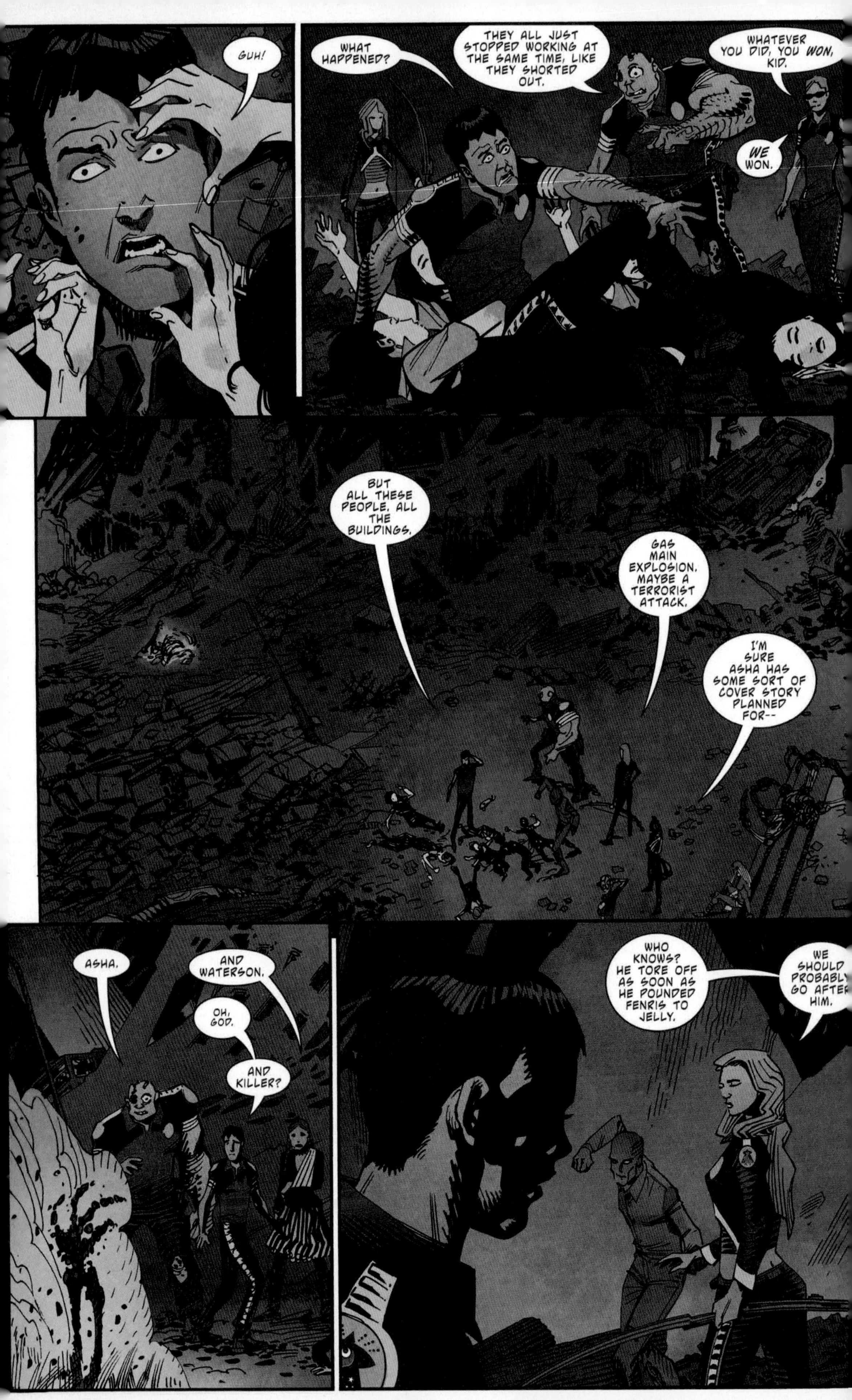
GUH!
WHAT HAPPENED?
THEY ALL JUST STOPPED WORKING AT THE SAME TIME, LIKE THEY SHORTED OUT.
WHATEVER YOU DID, YOU WON, KID.
WE WON.
BUT ALL THESE PEOPLE. ALL THE BUILDINGS.
GAS MAIN EXPLOSION. MAYBE A TERRORIST ATTACK.
I'M SURE ASHA HAS SOME SORT OF COVER STORY PLANNED FOR--
ASHA.
AND WATERSON.
OH, GOD.
AND KILLER?
WHO KNOWS? HE TORE OFF AS SOON AS HE POUNDED FENRIS TO JELLY.
WE SHOULD PROBABLY GO AFTER HIM.

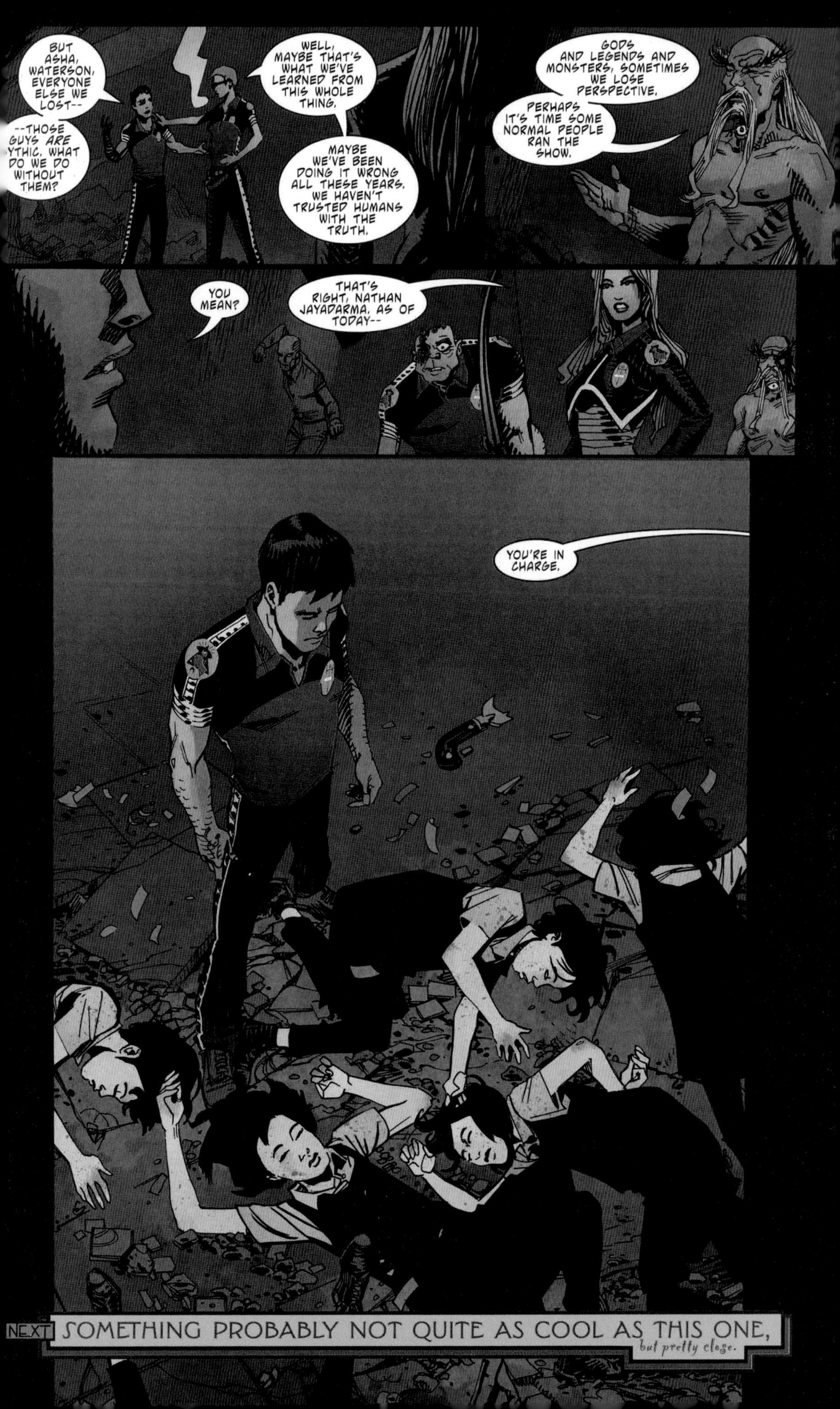
BUT ASHA, WATERSON, EVERYONE ELSE WE LOST--
--THOSE GUYS ARE YTHIC. WHAT DO WE DO WITHOUT THEM?
WELL, MAYBE THAT'S WHAT WE'VE LEARNED FROM THIS WHOLE THING.
MAYBE WE'VE BEEN DOING IT WRONG ALL THESE YEARS. WE HAVEN'T TRUSTED HUMANS WITH THE TRUTH.
GODS AND LEGENDS AND MONSTERS, SOMETIMES WE LOSE PERSPECTIVE.
PERHAPS IT'S TIME SOME NORMAL PEOPLE RAN THE SHOW.
YOU MEAN?
THAT'S RIGHT, NATHAN JAYADARMA. AS OF TODAY--
YOU'RE IN CHARGE.
NEXT SOMETHING PROBABLY NOT QUITE AS COOL AS THIS ONE,
but pretty close.

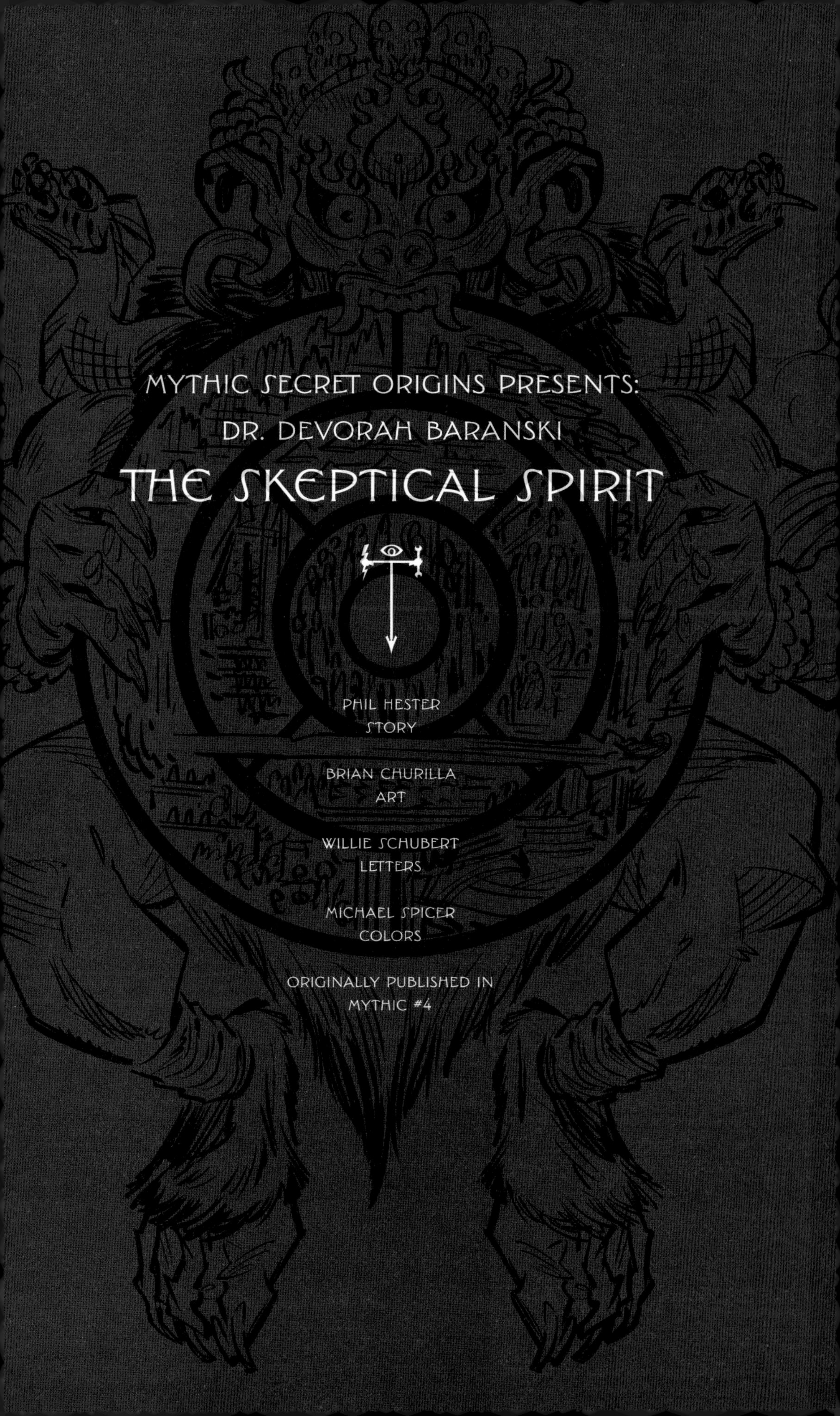

MYTHIC SECRET ORIGINS PRESENTS:

DR. DEVORAH BARANSKI

THE SKEPTICAL SPIRIT

PHIL HESTER
STORY

BRIAN CHURILLA
ART

WILLIE SCHUBERT
LETTERS

MICHAEL SPICER
COLORS

ORIGINALLY PUBLISHED IN
MYTHIC #4

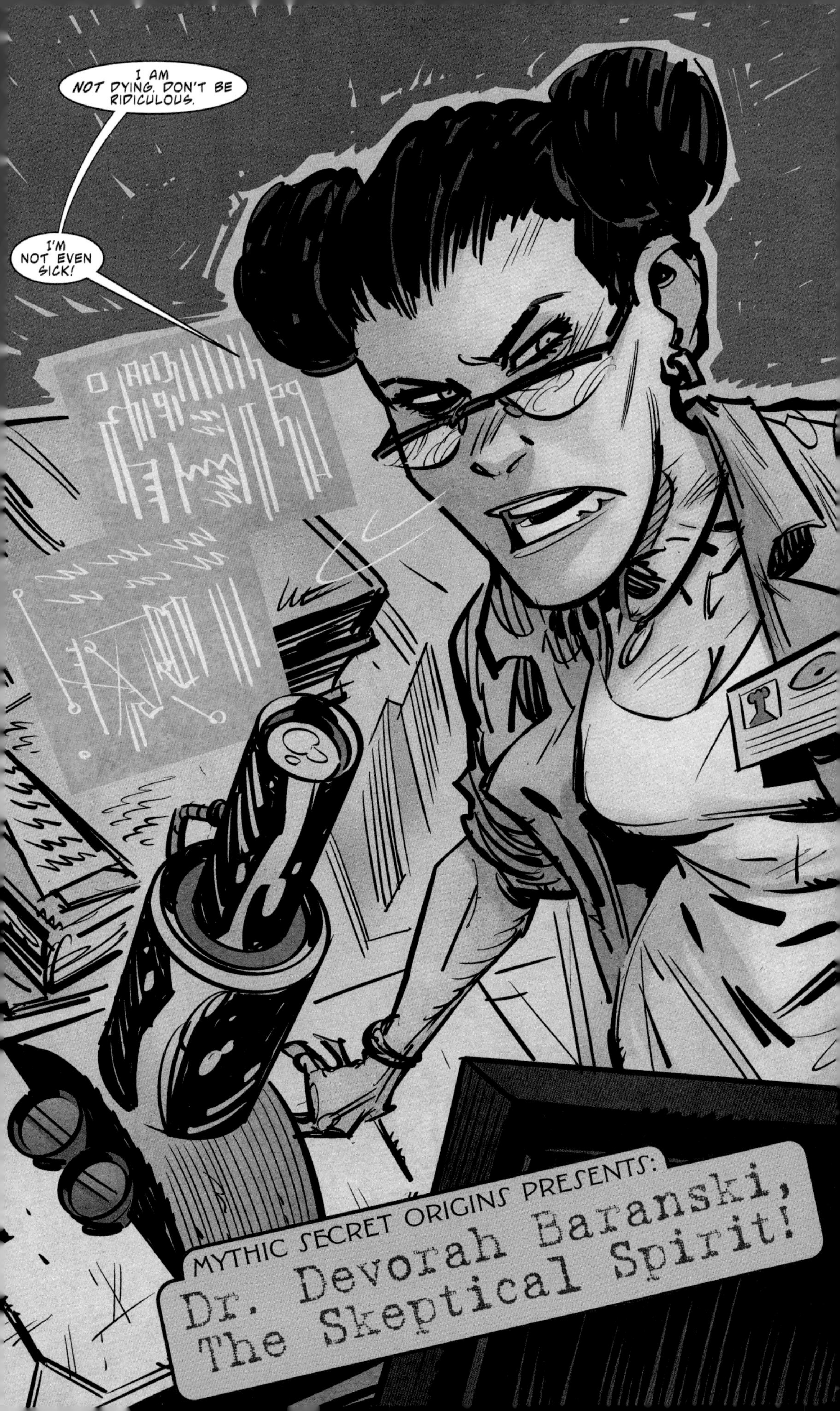
I AM NOT DYING. DON'T BE RIDICULOUS.
I'M NOT EVEN SICK!
MYTHIC SECRET ORIGINS PRESENTS:
Dr. Devorah Baranski, The Skeptical Spirit!

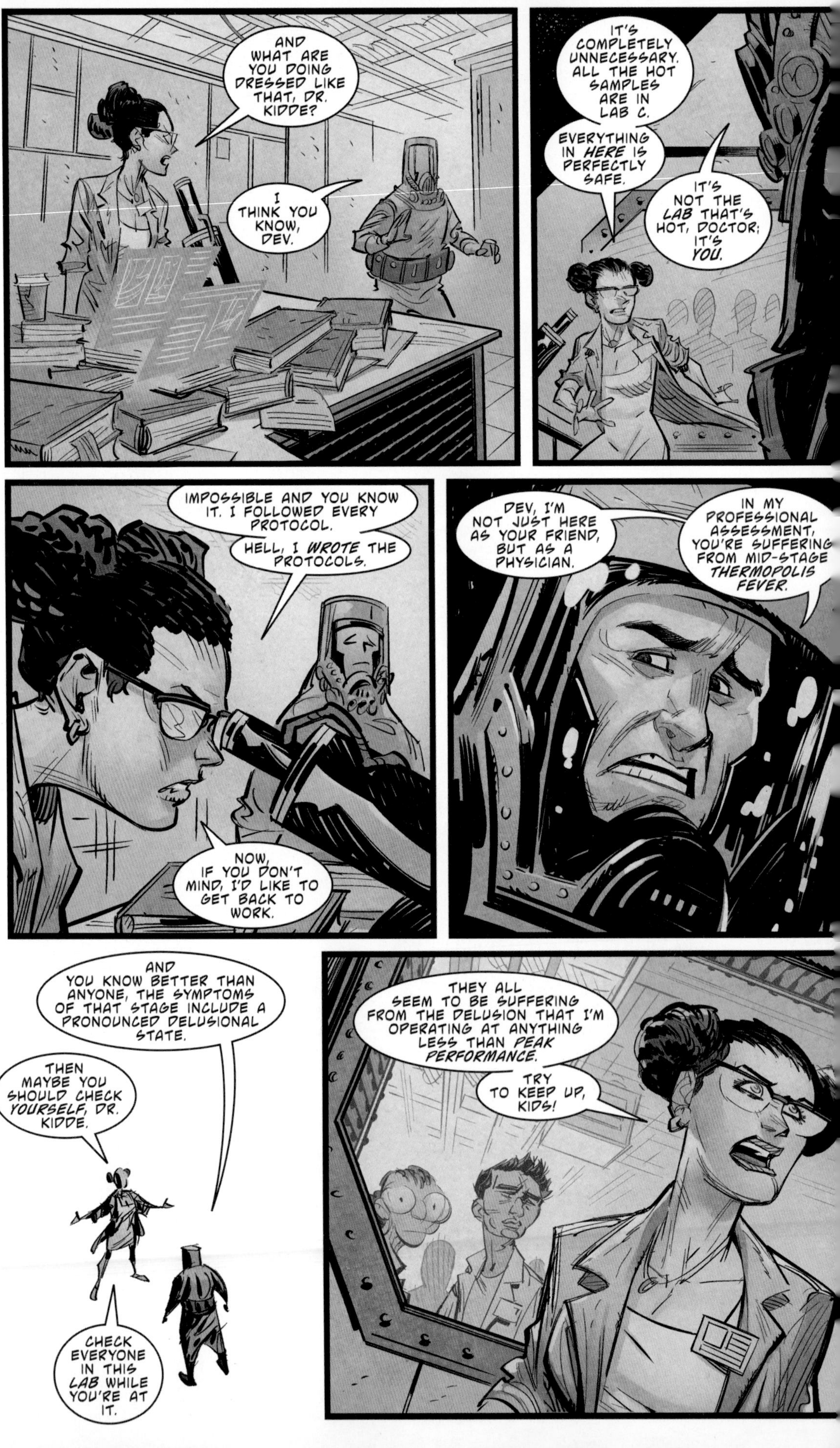
AND WHAT ARE YOU DOING DRESSED LIKE THAT, DR. KIDDE?
I THINK YOU KNOW, DEV.
IT'S COMPLETELY UNNECESSARY. ALL THE HOT SAMPLES ARE IN LAB C.
EVERYTHING IN *HERE* IS PERFECTLY SAFE.
IT'S NOT THE *LAB* THAT'S HOT, DOCTOR; IT'S *YOU*.
IMPOSSIBLE AND YOU KNOW IT. I FOLLOWED EVERY PROTOCOL.
HELL, I *WROTE* THE PROTOCOLS.
NOW, IF YOU DON'T MIND, I'D LIKE TO GET BACK TO WORK.
DEV, I'M NOT JUST HERE AS YOUR FRIEND, BUT AS A PHYSICIAN.
IN MY PROFESSIONAL ASSESSMENT, YOU'RE SUFFERING FROM MID-STAGE *THERMOPOLIS FEVER*.
AND YOU KNOW BETTER THAN ANYONE, THE SYMPTOMS OF THAT STAGE INCLUDE A PRONOUNCED DELUSIONAL STATE.
THEN MAYBE YOU SHOULD CHECK *YOURSELF*, DR. KIDDE.
CHECK EVERYONE IN THIS *LAB* WHILE YOU'RE AT IT.
THEY ALL SEEM TO BE SUFFERING FROM THE DELUSION THAT I'M OPERATING AT ANYTHING LESS THAN *PEAK PERFORMANCE*.
TRY TO KEEP UP, KIDS!

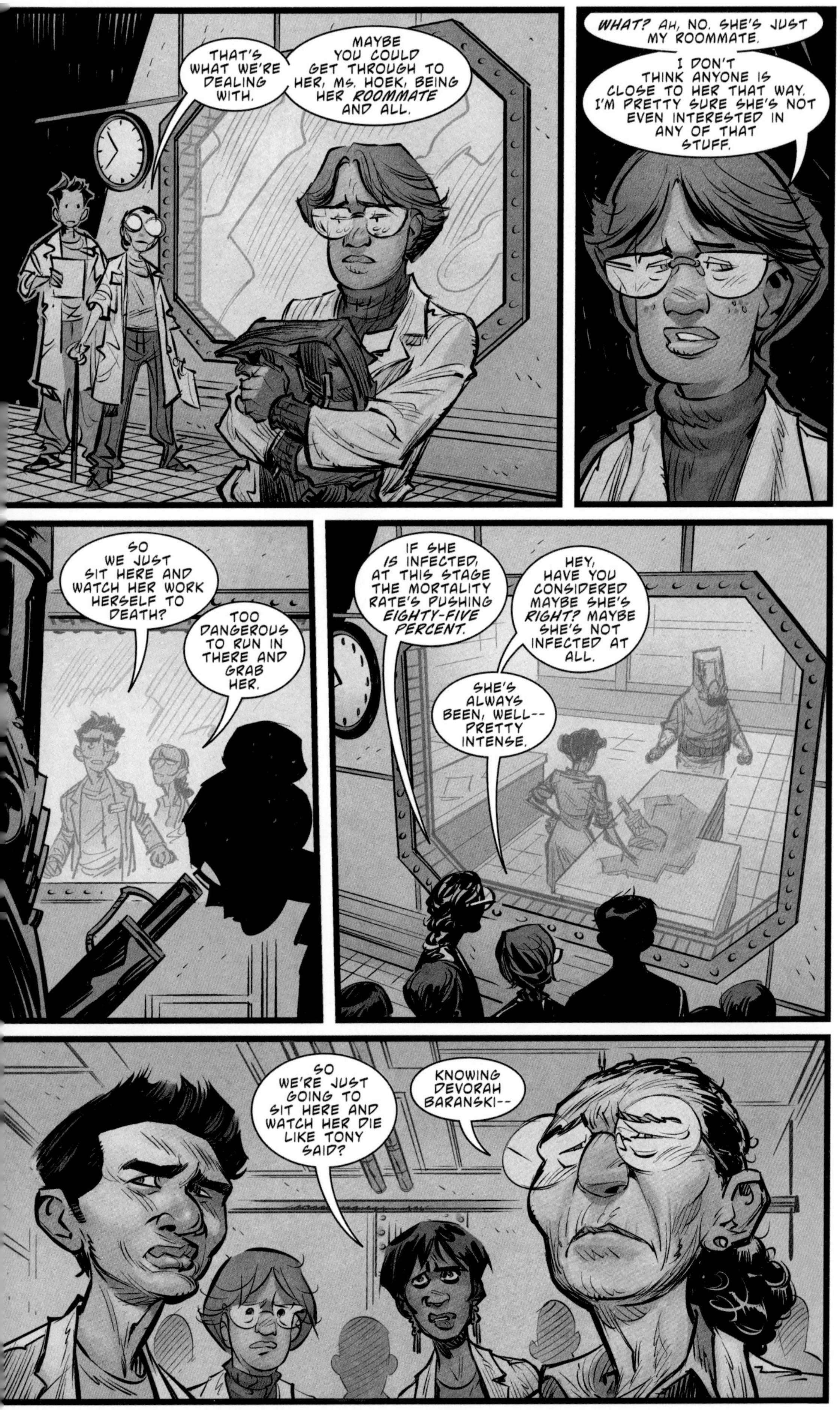
THAT'S WHAT WE'RE DEALING WITH.
MAYBE YOU COULD GET THROUGH TO HER, MS. HOEK, BEING HER *ROOMMATE* AND ALL.
WHAT? AH, NO. SHE'S JUST MY ROOMMATE.
I DON'T THINK ANYONE IS CLOSE TO HER THAT WAY. I'M PRETTY SURE SHE'S NOT EVEN INTERESTED IN ANY OF THAT STUFF.
SO WE JUST SIT HERE AND WATCH HER WORK HERSELF TO DEATH?
TOO DANGEROUS TO RUN IN THERE AND GRAB HER.
IF SHE *IS* INFECTED, AT THIS STAGE THE MORTALITY RATE'S PUSHING *EIGHTY-FIVE PERCENT.*
HEY, HAVE YOU CONSIDERED MAYBE SHE'S *RIGHT?* MAYBE SHE'S NOT INFECTED AT ALL.
SHE'S ALWAYS BEEN, WELL-- PRETTY INTENSE.
SO WE'RE JUST GOING TO SIT HERE AND WATCH HER DIE LIKE TONY SAID?
KNOWING DEVORAH BARANSKI--

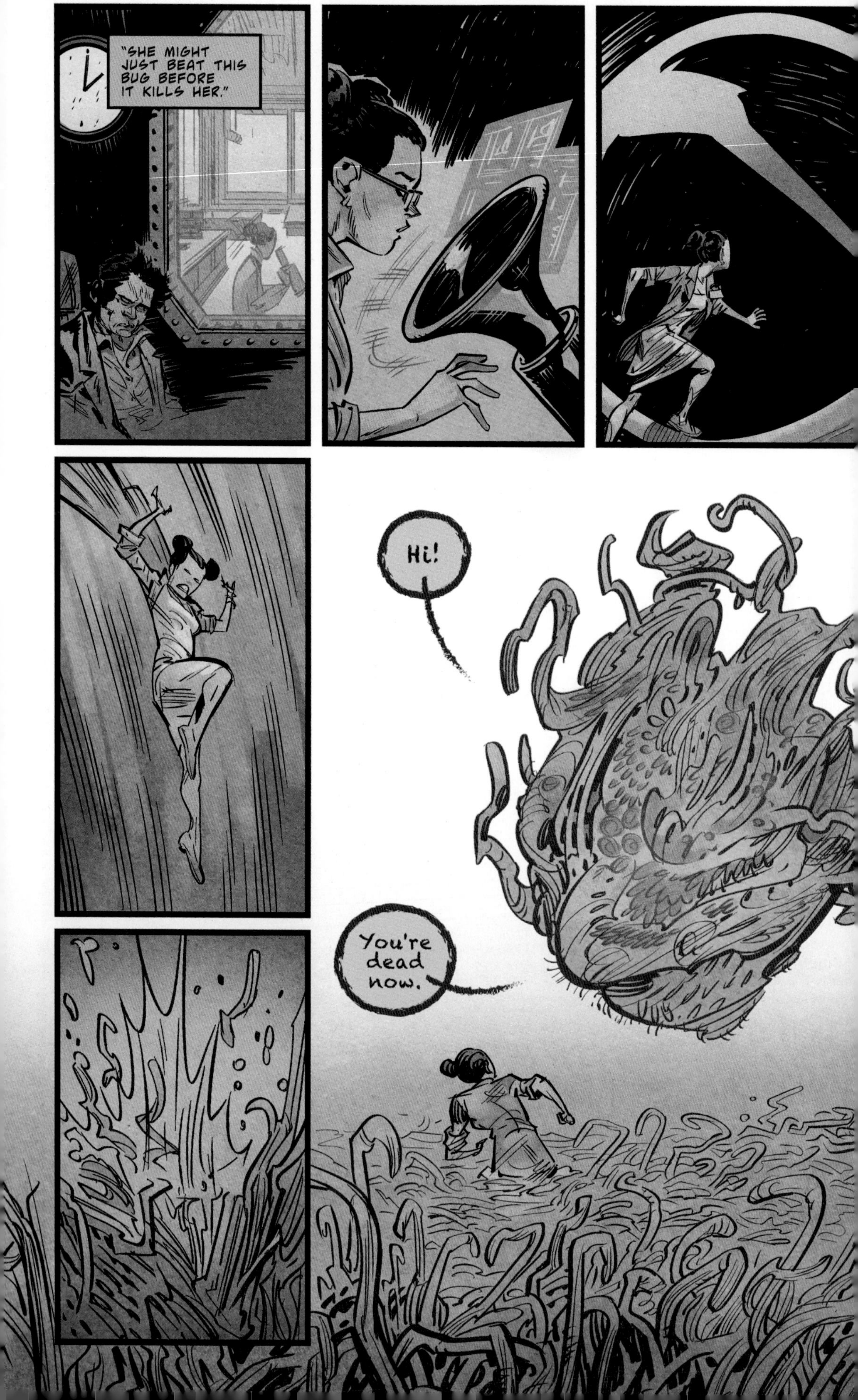
"SHE MIGHT JUST BEAT THIS BUG BEFORE IT KILLS HER."
Hi!
You're dead now.

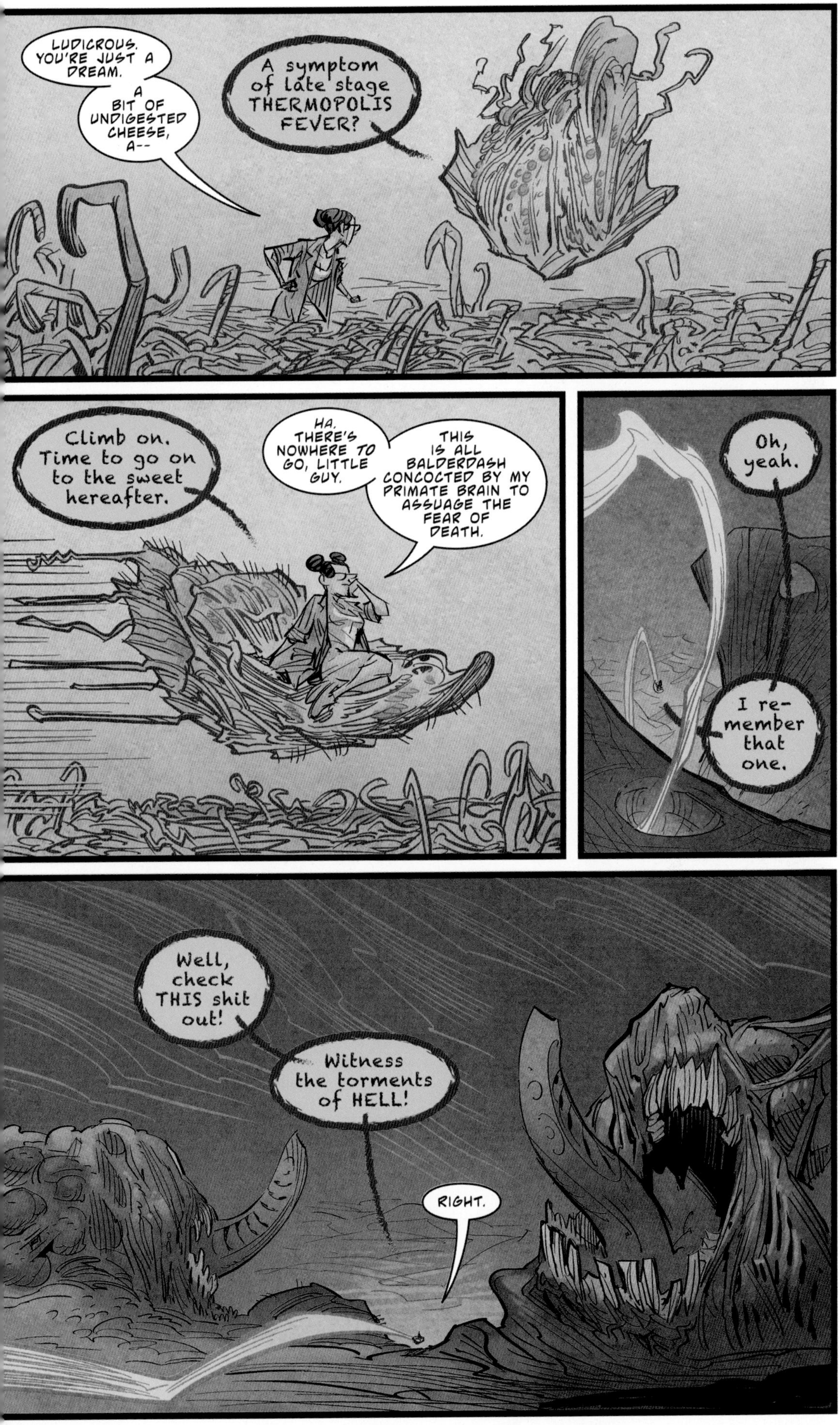
LUDICROUS. YOU'RE JUST A DREAM.
A BIT OF UNDIGESTED CHEESE, A--
A symptom of late stage THERMOPOLIS FEVER?
Climb on. Time to go on to the sweet hereafter.
HA. THERE'S NOWHERE TO GO, LITTLE GUY.
THIS IS ALL BALDERDASH CONCOCTED BY MY PRIMATE BRAIN TO ASSUAGE THE FEAR OF DEATH.
Oh, yeah.
I re-member that one.
Well, check THIS shit out!
Witness the torments of HELL!
RIGHT.

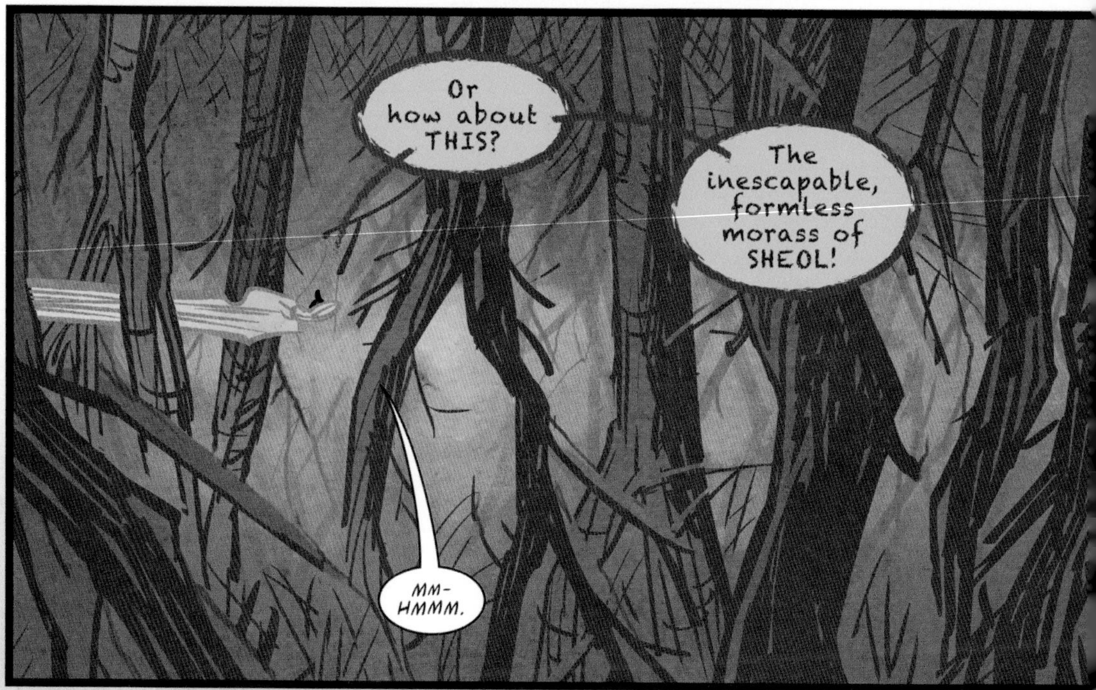
Or how about THIS?
The inescapable, formless morass of SHEOL!
MM-HMMM.

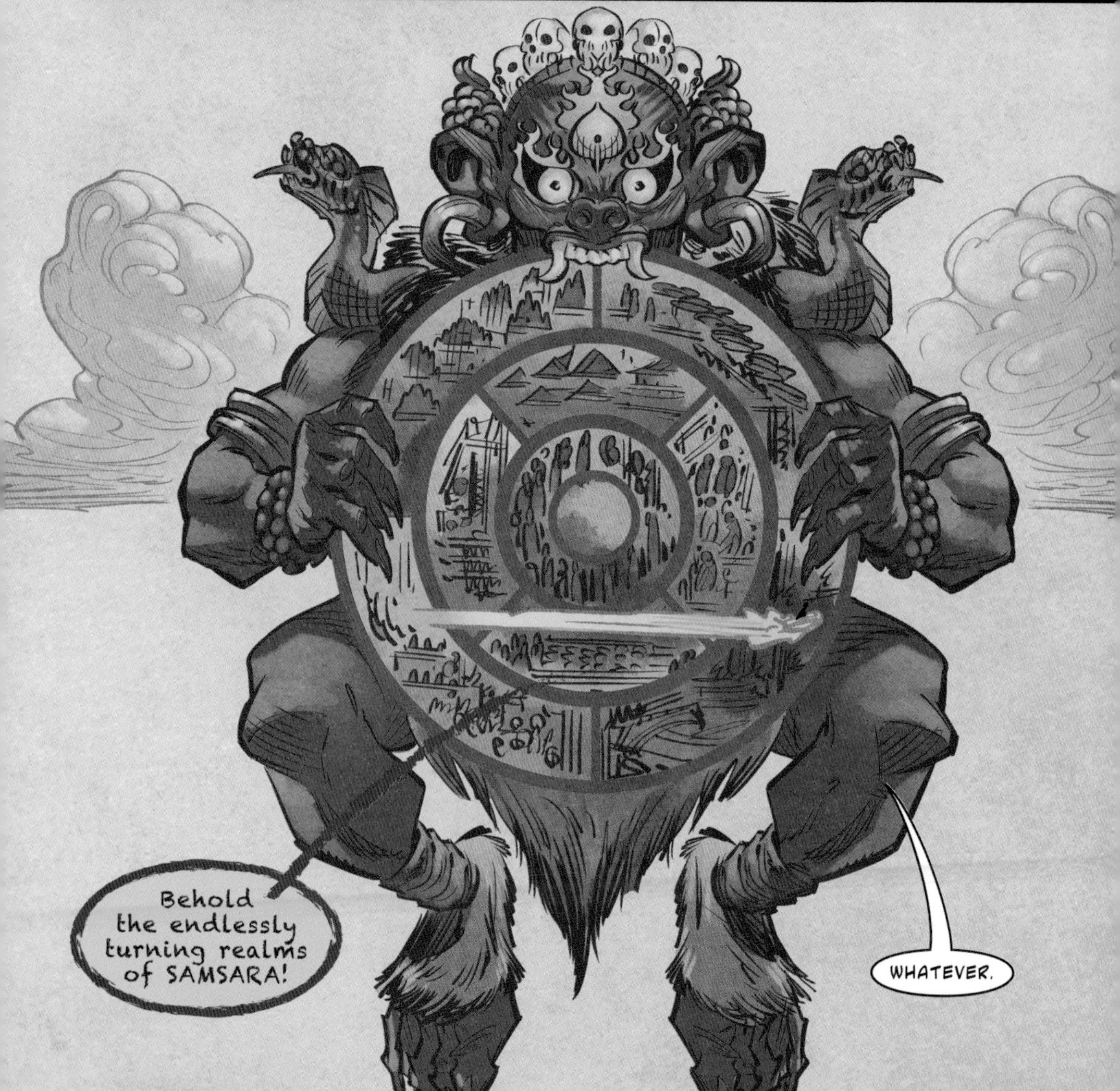
Behold the endlessly turning realms of SAMSARA!
WHATEVER.

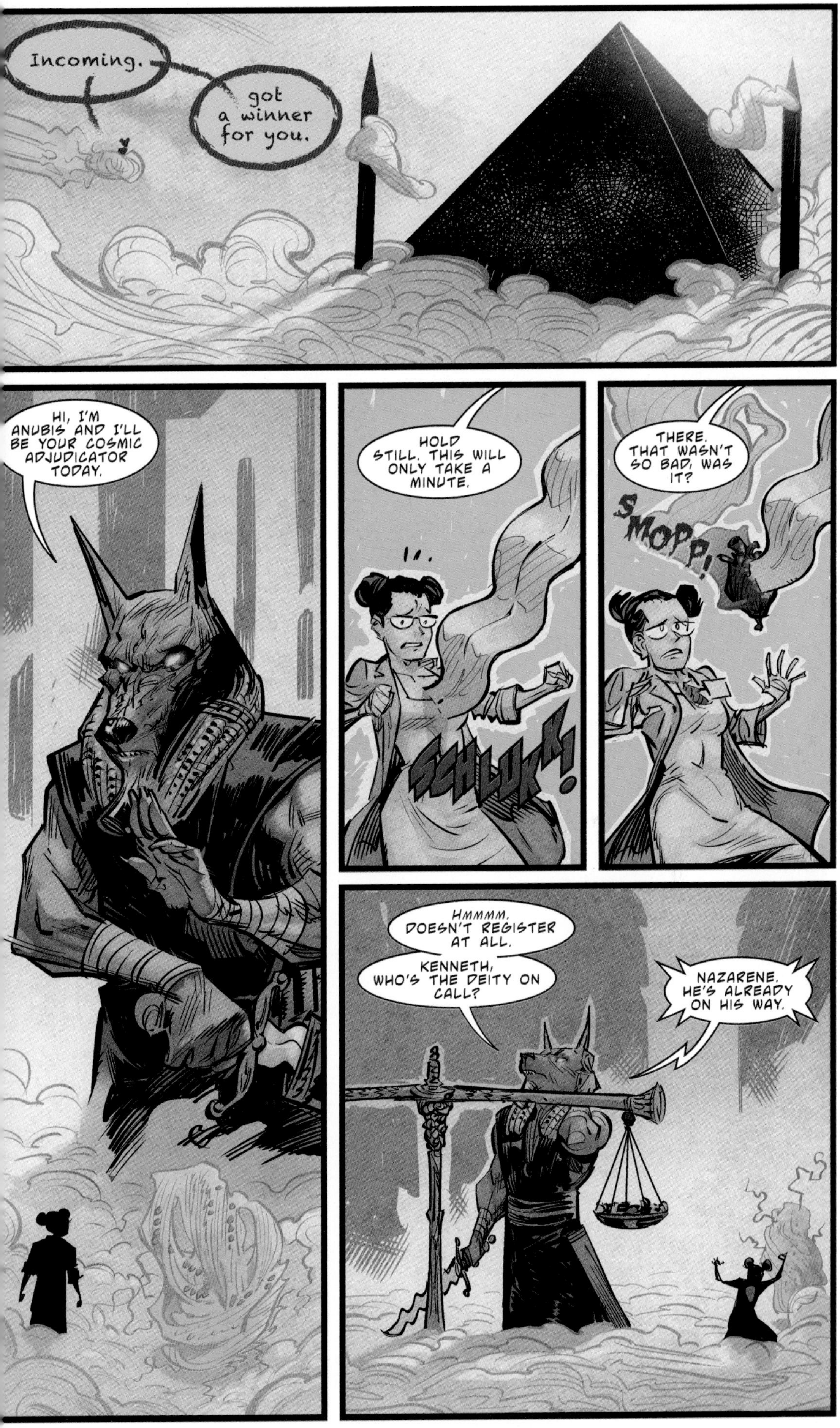

Incoming.
got a winner for you.
HI, I'M ANUBIS AND I'LL BE YOUR COSMIC ADJUDICATOR TODAY.
HOLD STILL. THIS WILL ONLY TAKE A MINUTE.
SCHLUKK!
THERE. THAT WASN'T SO BAD, WAS IT?
SMOPP!
HMMMM. DOESN'T REGISTER AT ALL.
KENNETH, WHO'S THE DEITY ON CALL?
NAZARENE. HE'S ALREADY ON HIS WAY.

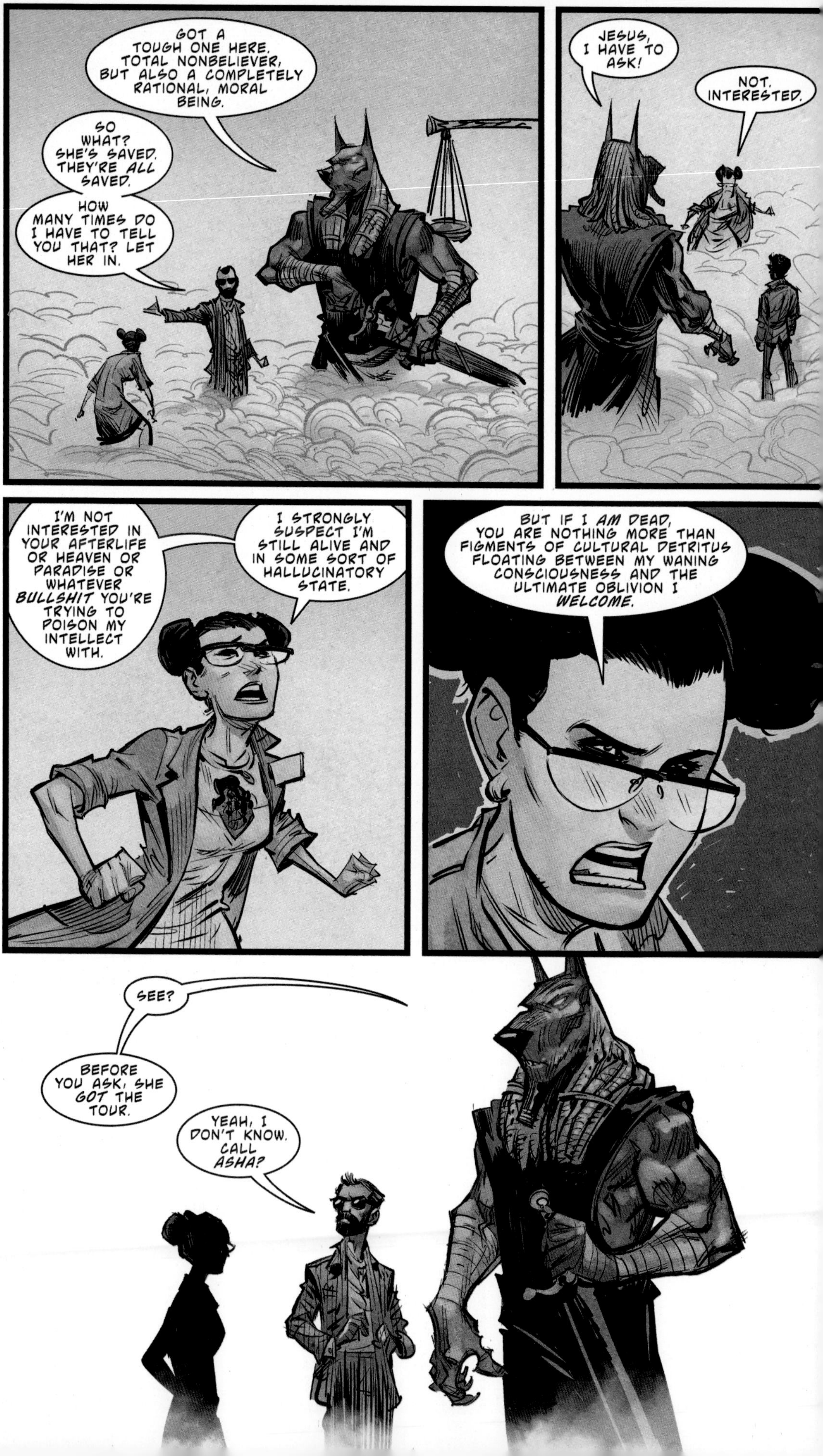
GOT A TOUGH ONE HERE. TOTAL NONBELIEVER, BUT ALSO A COMPLETELY RATIONAL, MORAL BEING.
SO WHAT? SHE'S SAVED. THEY'RE *ALL* SAVED.
HOW MANY TIMES DO I HAVE TO TELL YOU THAT? LET HER IN.
JESUS, I HAVE TO ASK!
NOT. INTERESTED.
I'M NOT INTERESTED IN YOUR AFTERLIFE OR HEAVEN OR PARADISE OR WHATEVER *BULLSHIT* YOU'RE TRYING TO POISON MY INTELLECT WITH.
I STRONGLY SUSPECT I'M STILL ALIVE AND IN SOME SORT OF HALLUCINATORY STATE.
BUT IF I *AM DEAD*, YOU ARE NOTHING MORE THAN FIGMENTS OF CULTURAL DETRITUS FLOATING BETWEEN MY WANING CONSCIOUSNESS AND THE ULTIMATE OBLIVION I *WELCOME*.
SEE?
BEFORE YOU ASK, SHE *GOT* THE TOUR.
YEAH, I DON'T KNOW. CALL *ASHA*?

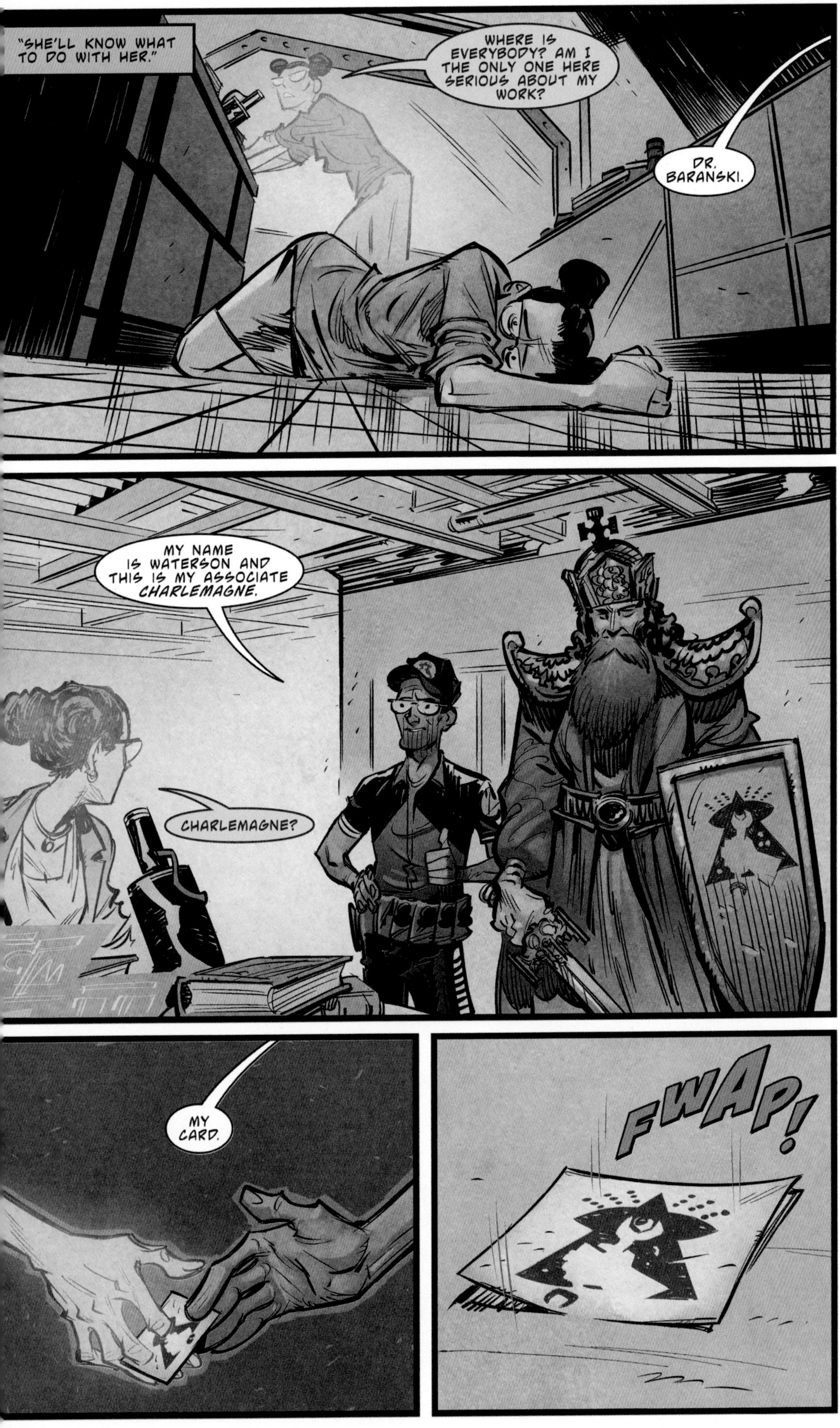
"SHE'LL KNOW WHAT TO DO WITH HER."
WHERE IS EVERYBODY? AM I THE ONLY ONE HERE SERIOUS ABOUT MY WORK?
DR. BARANSKI.
MY NAME IS WATERSON AND THIS IS MY ASSOCIATE *CHARLEMAGNE*.
CHARLEMAGNE?
MY CARD.
FWAP!

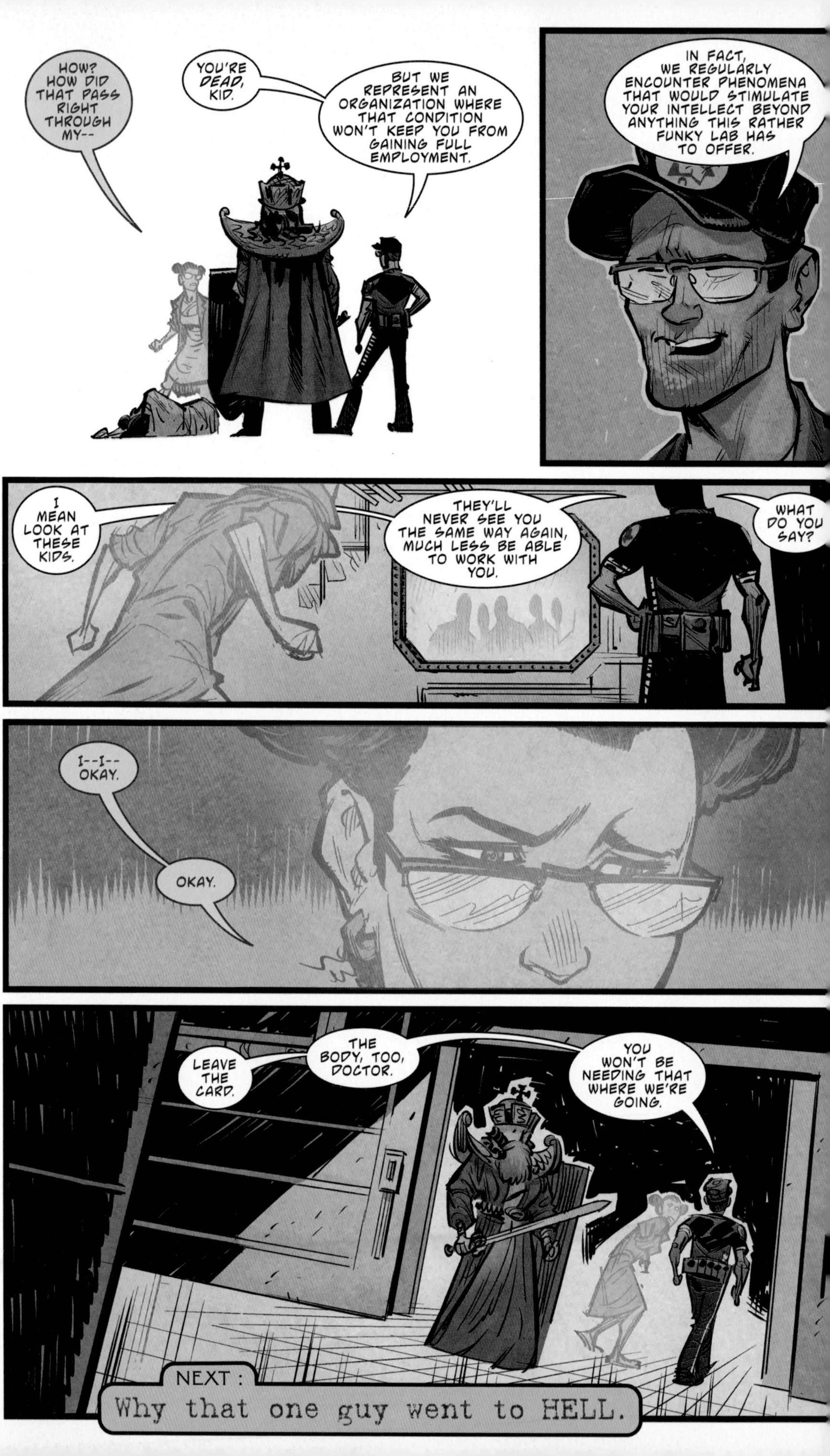
HOW? HOW DID THAT PASS RIGHT THROUGH MY--
YOU'RE DEAD, KID.
BUT WE REPRESENT AN ORGANIZATION WHERE THAT CONDITION WON'T KEEP YOU FROM GAINING FULL EMPLOYMENT.
IN FACT, WE REGULARLY ENCOUNTER PHENOMENA THAT WOULD STIMULATE YOUR INTELLECT BEYOND ANYTHING THIS RATHER FUNKY LAB HAS TO OFFER.
I MEAN LOOK AT THESE KIDS.
THEY'LL NEVER SEE YOU THE SAME WAY AGAIN, MUCH LESS BE ABLE TO WORK WITH YOU.
WHAT DO YOU SAY?
I--I-- OKAY.
OKAY.
LEAVE THE CARD.
THE BODY, TOO, DOCTOR.
YOU WON'T BE NEEDING THAT WHERE WE'RE GOING.
NEXT:
Why that one guy went to HELL.

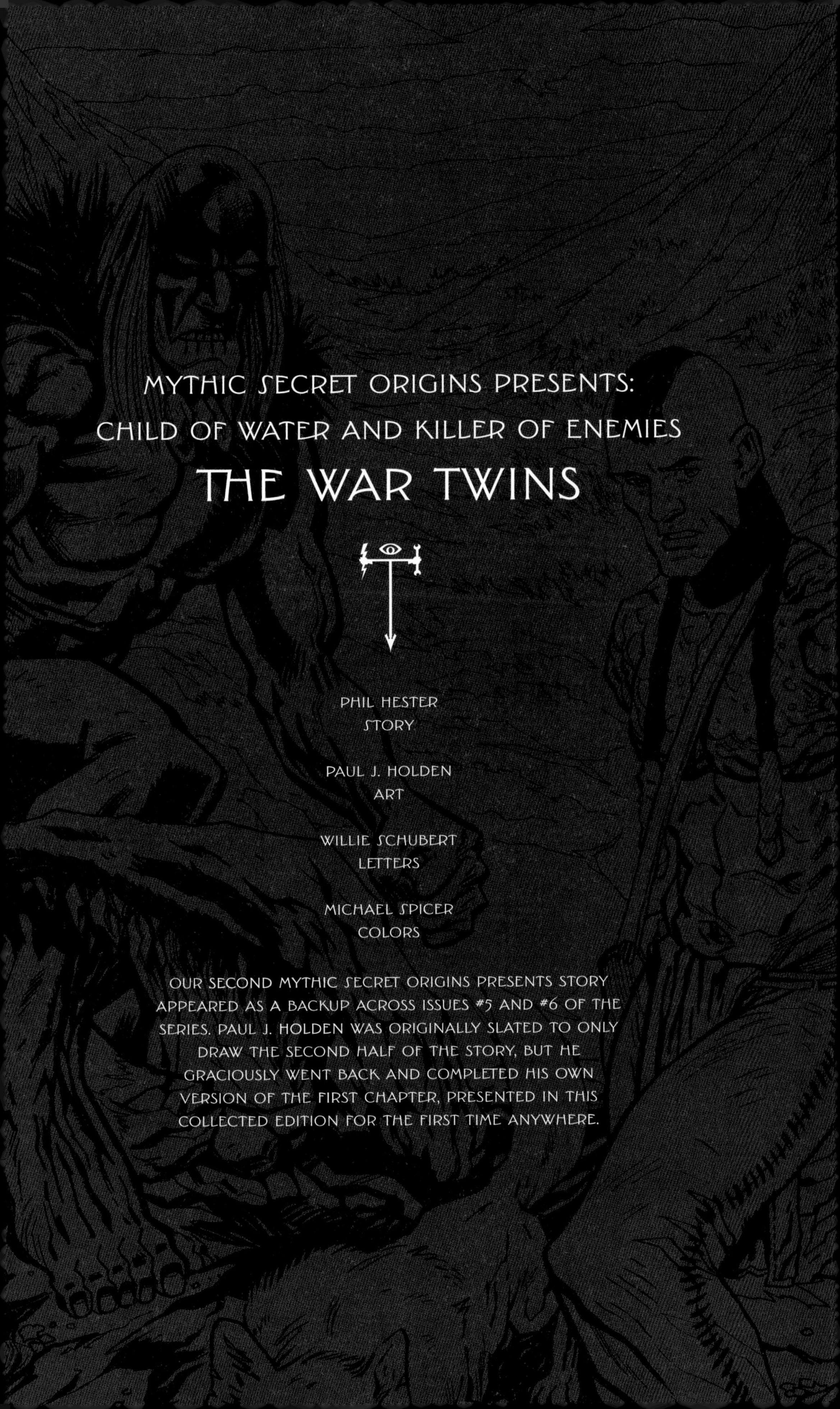

MYTHIC SECRET ORIGINS PRESENTS:

CHILD OF WATER AND KILLER OF ENEMIES

THE WAR TWINS

PHIL HESTER
STORY

PAUL J. HOLDEN
ART

WILLIE SCHUBERT
LETTERS

MICHAEL SPICER
COLORS

OUR SECOND MYTHIC SECRET ORIGINS PRESENTS STORY APPEARED AS A BACKUP ACROSS ISSUES #5 AND #6 OF THE SERIES. PAUL J. HOLDEN WAS ORIGINALLY SLATED TO ONLY DRAW THE SECOND HALF OF THE STORY, BUT HE GRACIOUSLY WENT BACK AND COMPLETED HIS OWN VERSION OF THE FIRST CHAPTER, PRESENTED IN THIS COLLECTED EDITION FOR THE FIRST TIME ANYWHERE.

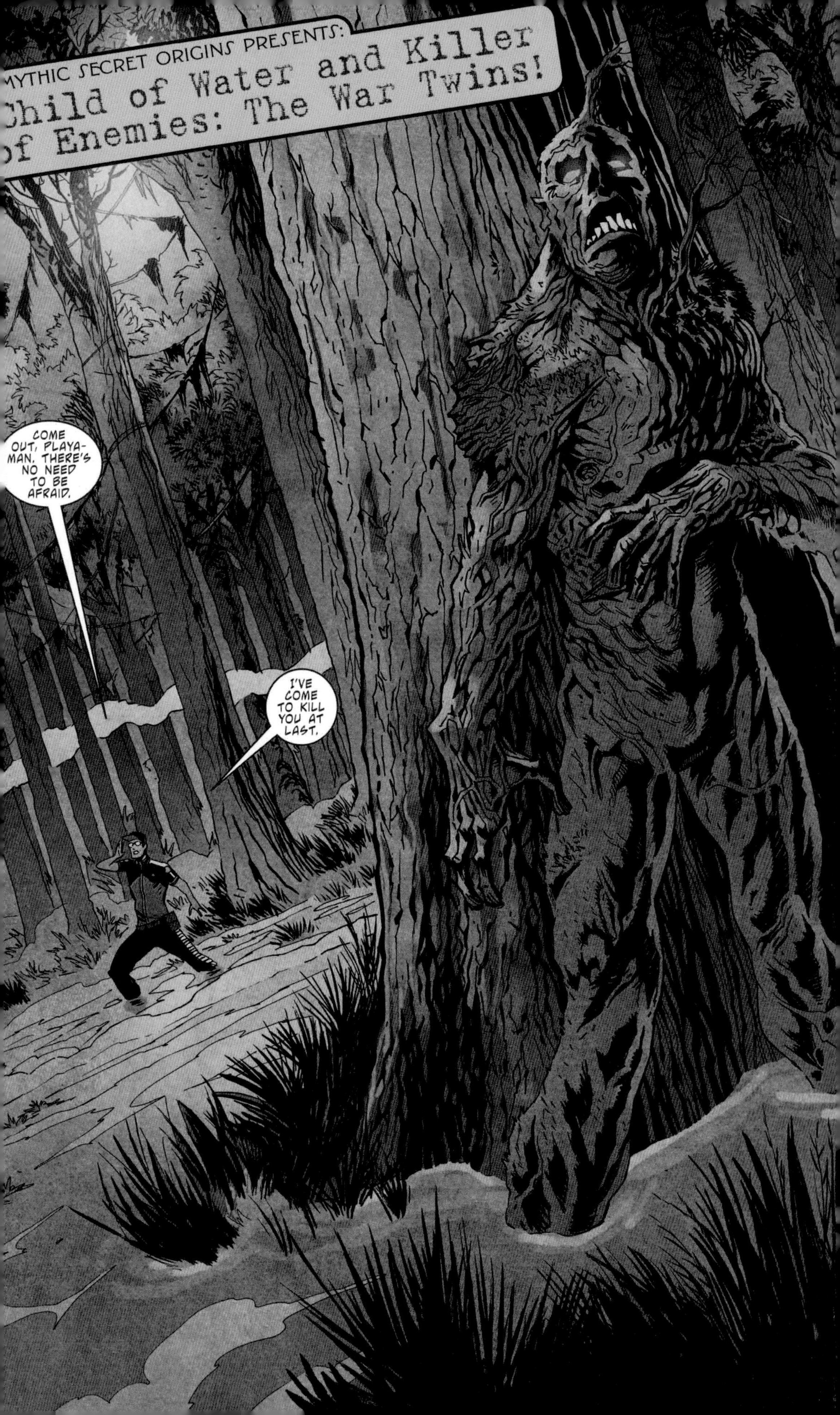
MYTHIC SECRET ORIGINS PRESENTS:
Child of Water and Killer of Enemies: The War Twins!
COME OUT, PLAYA-MAN. THERE'S NO NEED TO BE AFRAID.
I'VE COME TO KILL YOU AT LAST.

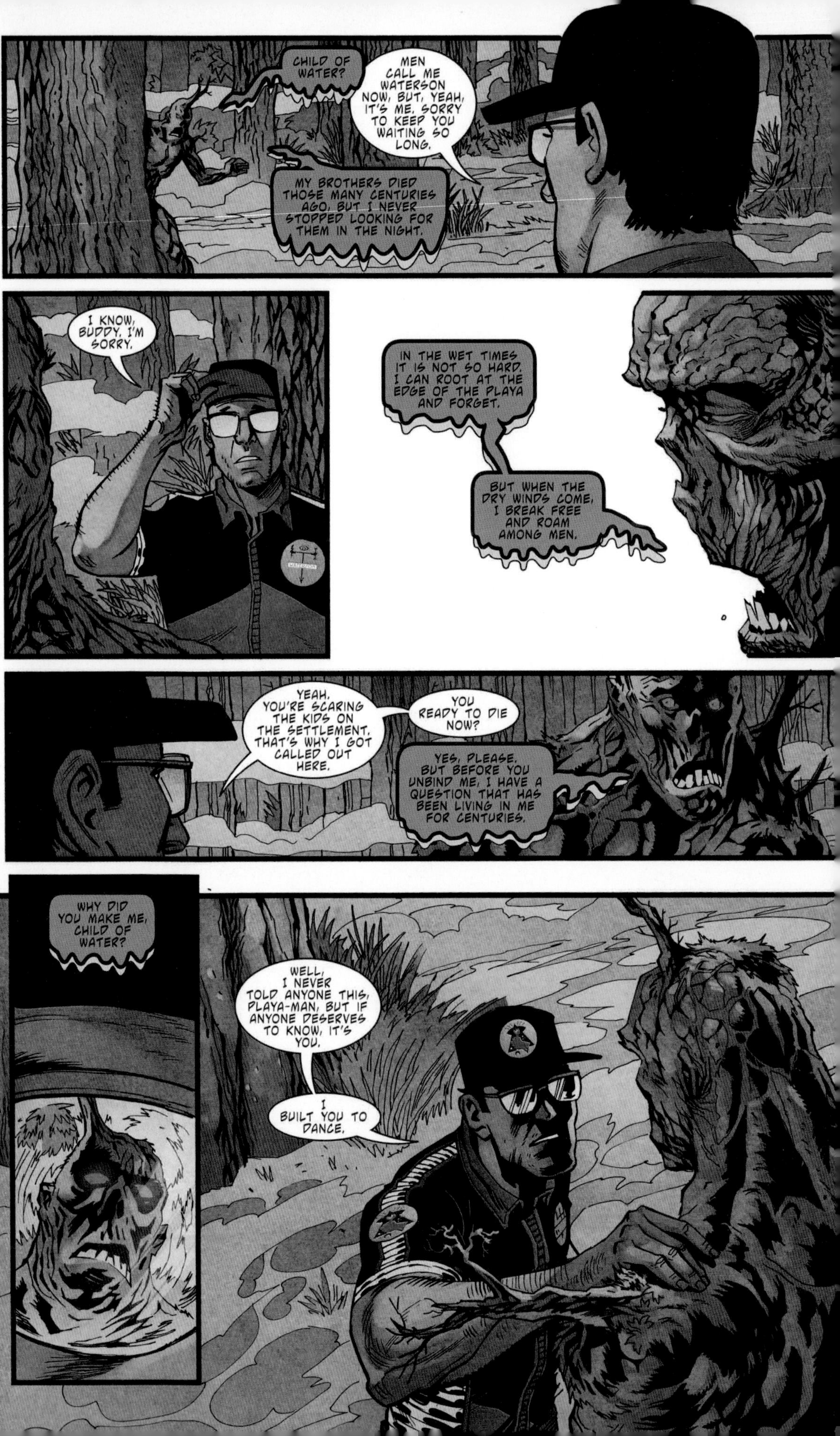

CHILD OF WATER?
MEN CALL ME WATERSON NOW, BUT, YEAH, IT'S ME. SORRY TO KEEP YOU WAITING SO LONG.
MY BROTHERS DIED THOSE MANY CENTURIES AGO, BUT I NEVER STOPPED LOOKING FOR THEM IN THE NIGHT.
I KNOW, BUDDY, I'M SORRY.
IN THE WET TIMES IT IS NOT SO HARD. I CAN ROOT AT THE EDGE OF THE PLAYA AND FORGET.
BUT WHEN THE DRY WINDS COME, I BREAK FREE AND ROAM AMONG MEN.
YEAH, YOU'RE SCARING THE KIDS ON THE SETTLEMENT. THAT'S WHY I GOT CALLED OUT HERE.
YOU READY TO DIE NOW?
YES, PLEASE, BUT BEFORE YOU UNBIND ME, I HAVE A QUESTION THAT HAS BEEN LIVING IN ME FOR CENTURIES.
WHY DID YOU MAKE ME, CHILD OF WATER?
WELL, I NEVER TOLD ANYONE THIS, PLAYA-MAN, BUT IF ANYONE DESERVES TO KNOW, IT'S YOU.
I BUILT YOU TO DANCE.

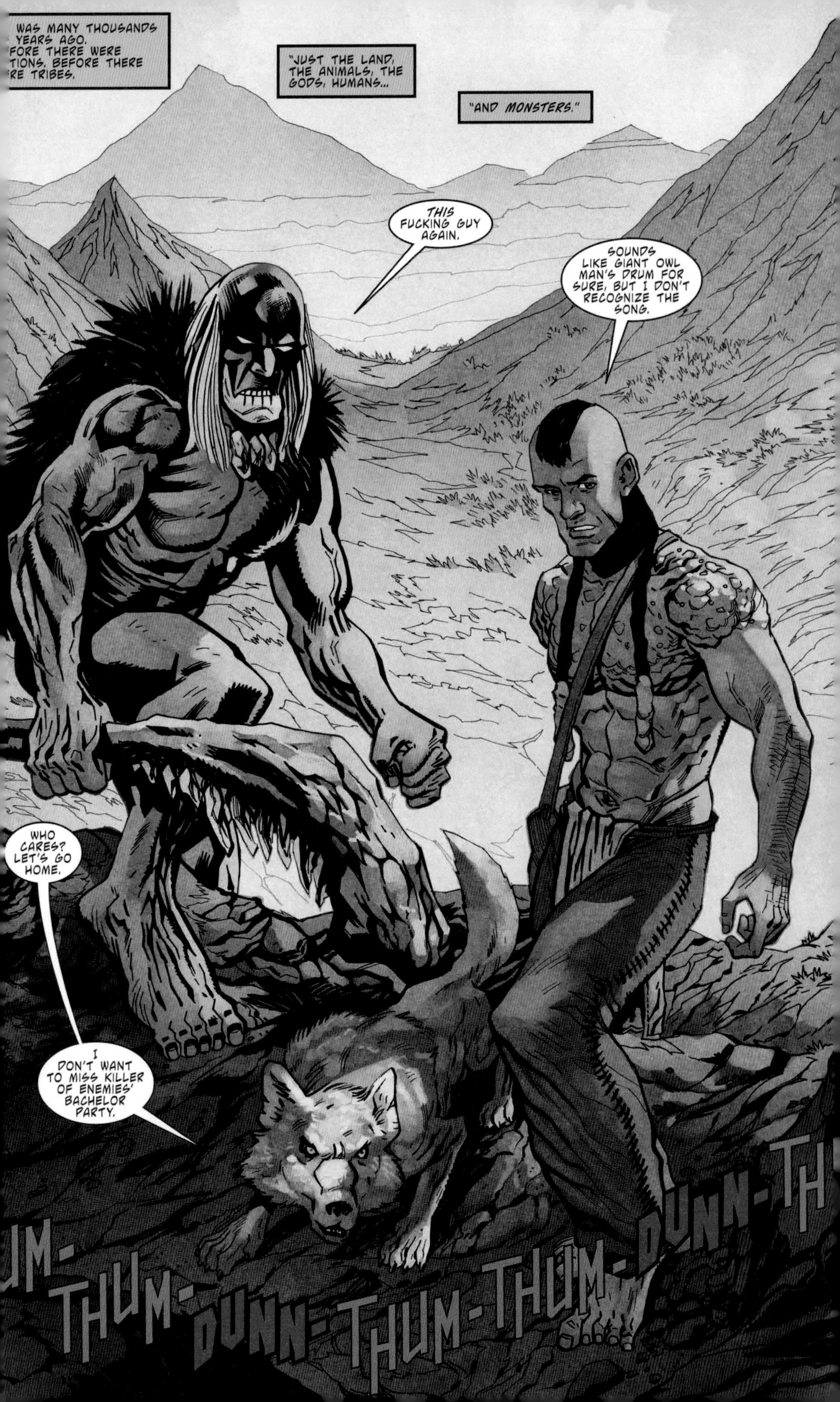
WAS MANY THOUSANDS YEARS AGO. FORE THERE WERE TIONS. BEFORE THERE RE TRIBES.
"JUST THE LAND, THE ANIMALS, THE GODS, HUMANS...
"AND MONSTERS."
THIS FUCKING GUY AGAIN.
SOUNDS LIKE GIANT OWL MAN'S DRUM FOR SURE, BUT I DON'T RECOGNIZE THE SONG.
WHO CARES? LET'S GO HOME.
I DON'T WANT TO MISS KILLER OF ENEMIES' BACHELOR PARTY.
UM-THUM-DUNN-THUM-THUM-DUNN-TH

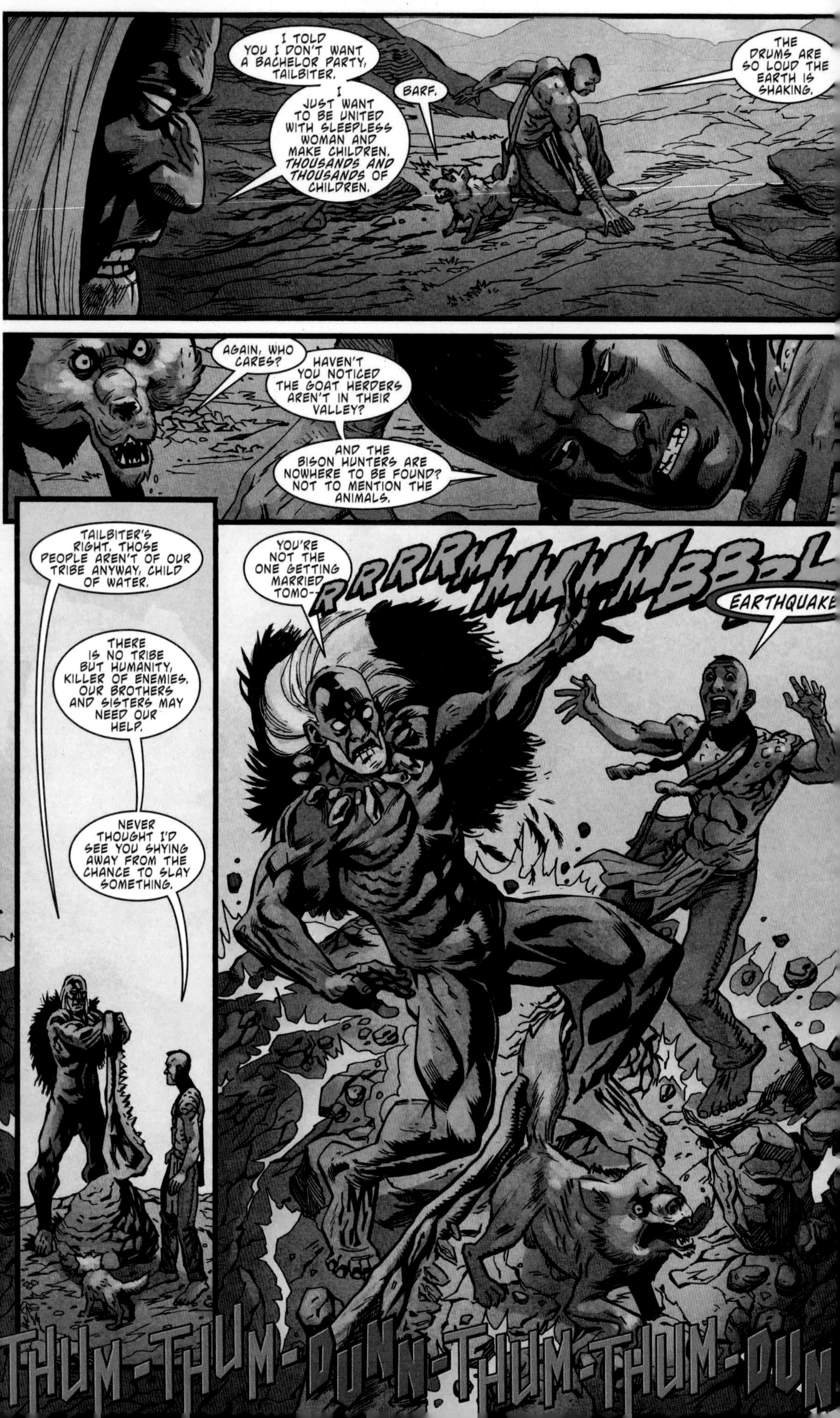

I TOLD YOU I DON'T WANT A BACHELOR PARTY, TAILBITER.
I JUST WANT TO BE UNITED WITH SLEEPLESS WOMAN AND MAKE CHILDREN. *THOUSANDS AND THOUSANDS* OF CHILDREN.
BARF.
THE DRUMS ARE SO LOUD THE EARTH IS SHAKING.
AGAIN, WHO CARES?
HAVEN'T YOU NOTICED THE GOAT HERDERS AREN'T IN THEIR VALLEY?
AND THE BISON HUNTERS ARE NOWHERE TO BE FOUND? NOT TO MENTION THE ANIMALS.
TAILBITER'S RIGHT. THOSE PEOPLE AREN'T OF OUR TRIBE ANYWAY, CHILD OF WATER.
THERE IS NO TRIBE BUT HUMANITY, KILLER OF ENEMIES. OUR BROTHERS AND SISTERS MAY NEED OUR HELP.
NEVER THOUGHT I'D SEE YOU SHYING AWAY FROM THE CHANCE TO SLAY SOMETHING.
YOU'RE NOT THE ONE GETTING MARRIED TOMO--
RRRRMMMMMMBBBL
EARTHQUAKE
THUM-THUM-DUN-THUM-THUM-DUN

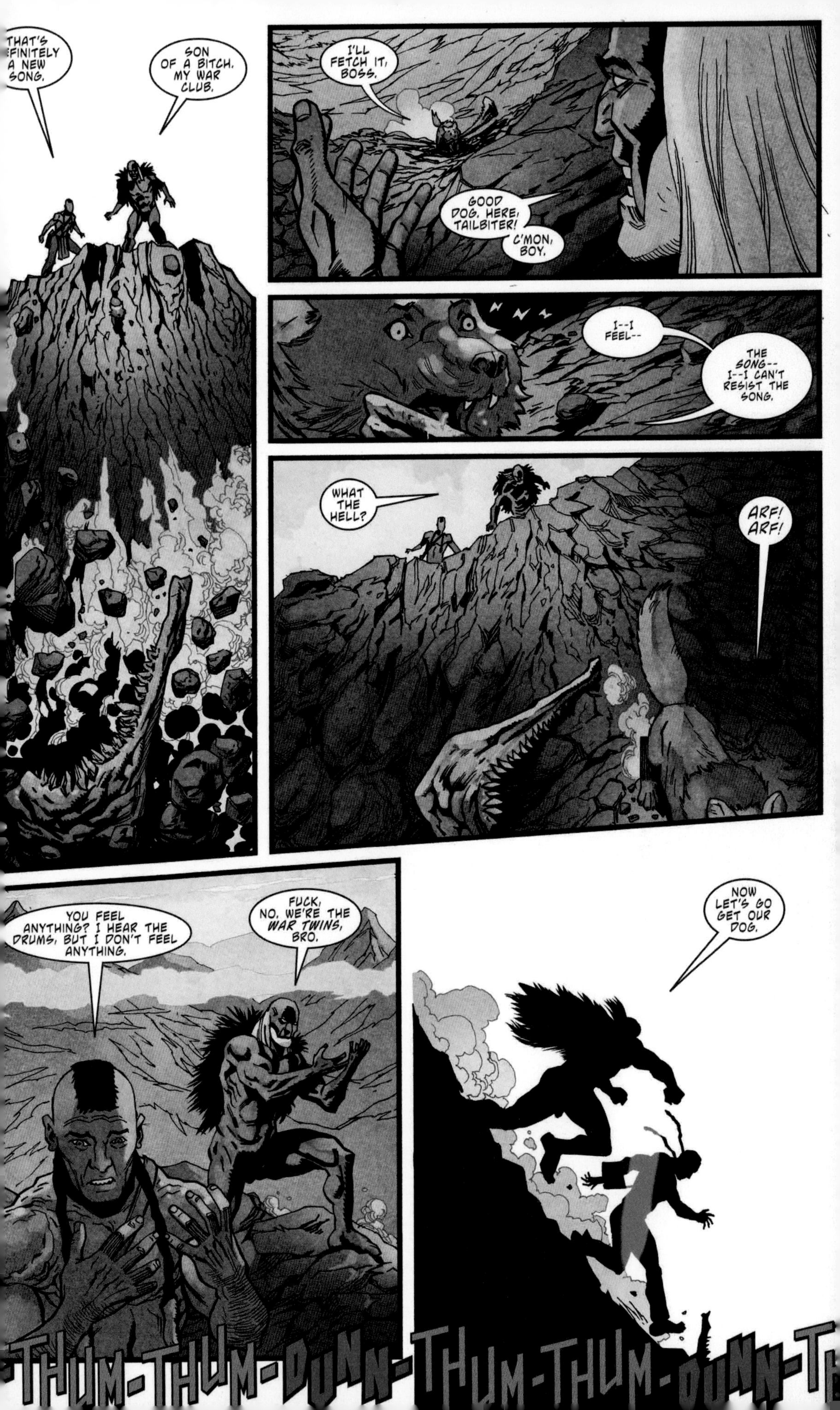
THAT'S
EFINITELY
A NEW
SONG.
SON
OF A BITCH.
MY WAR
CLUB.
I'LL
FETCH IT,
BOSS.
GOOD
DOG. HERE,
TAILBITER!
C'MON,
BOY.
I--I
FEEL--
THE
SONG--
I--I CAN'T
RESIST THE
SONG.
WHAT
THE
HELL?
ARF!
ARF!
YOU FEEL
ANYTHING? I HEAR THE
DRUMS, BUT I DON'T FEEL
ANYTHING.
FUCK,
NO. WE'RE THE
WAR TWINS,
BRO.
NOW
LET'S GO
GET OUR
DOG.
THUM-THUM-DUNN-THUM-THUM-DUNN-TH

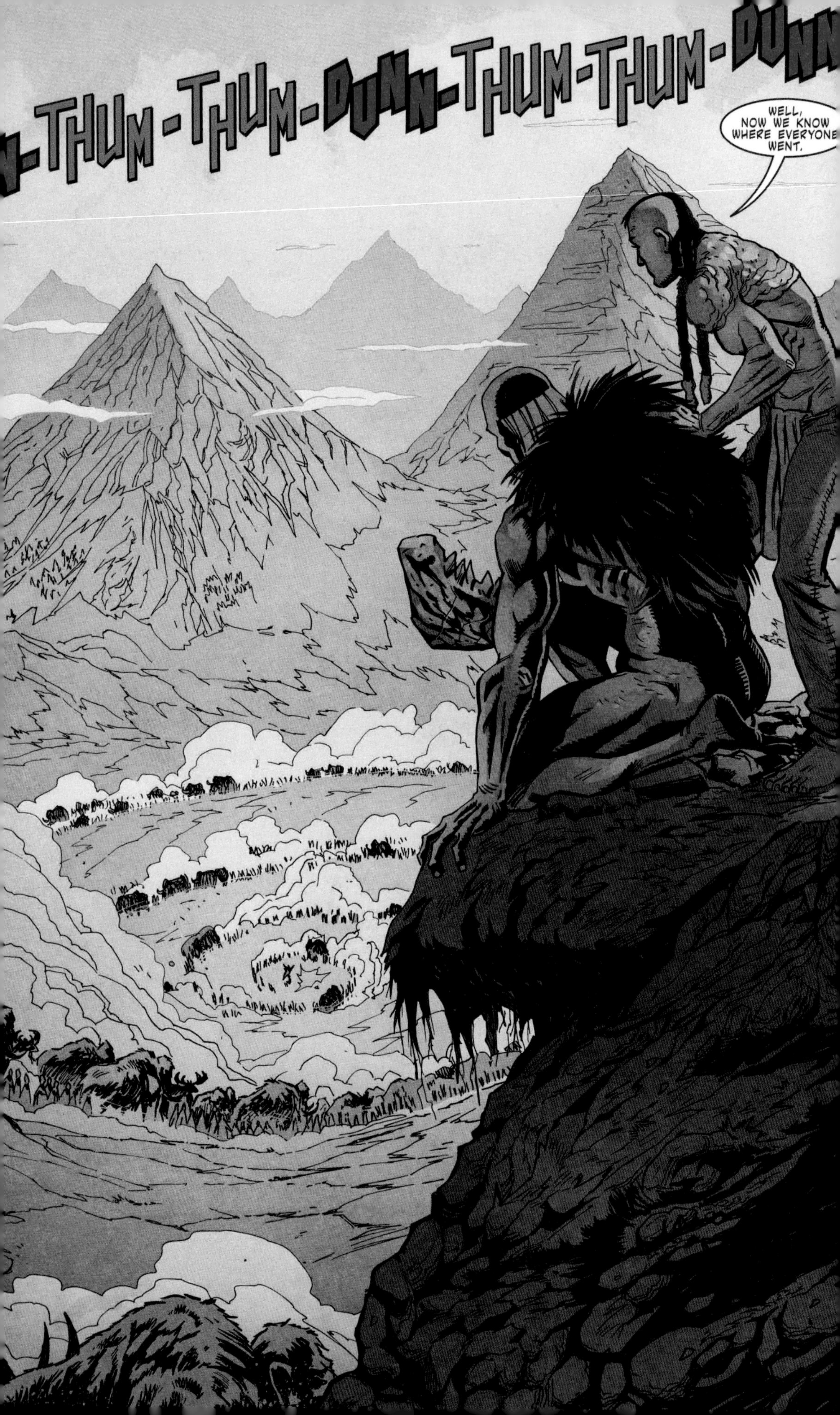
N-THUM-THUM-DUNN-THUM-THUM-DUNN
WELL, NOW WE KNOW WHERE EVERYONE WENT.

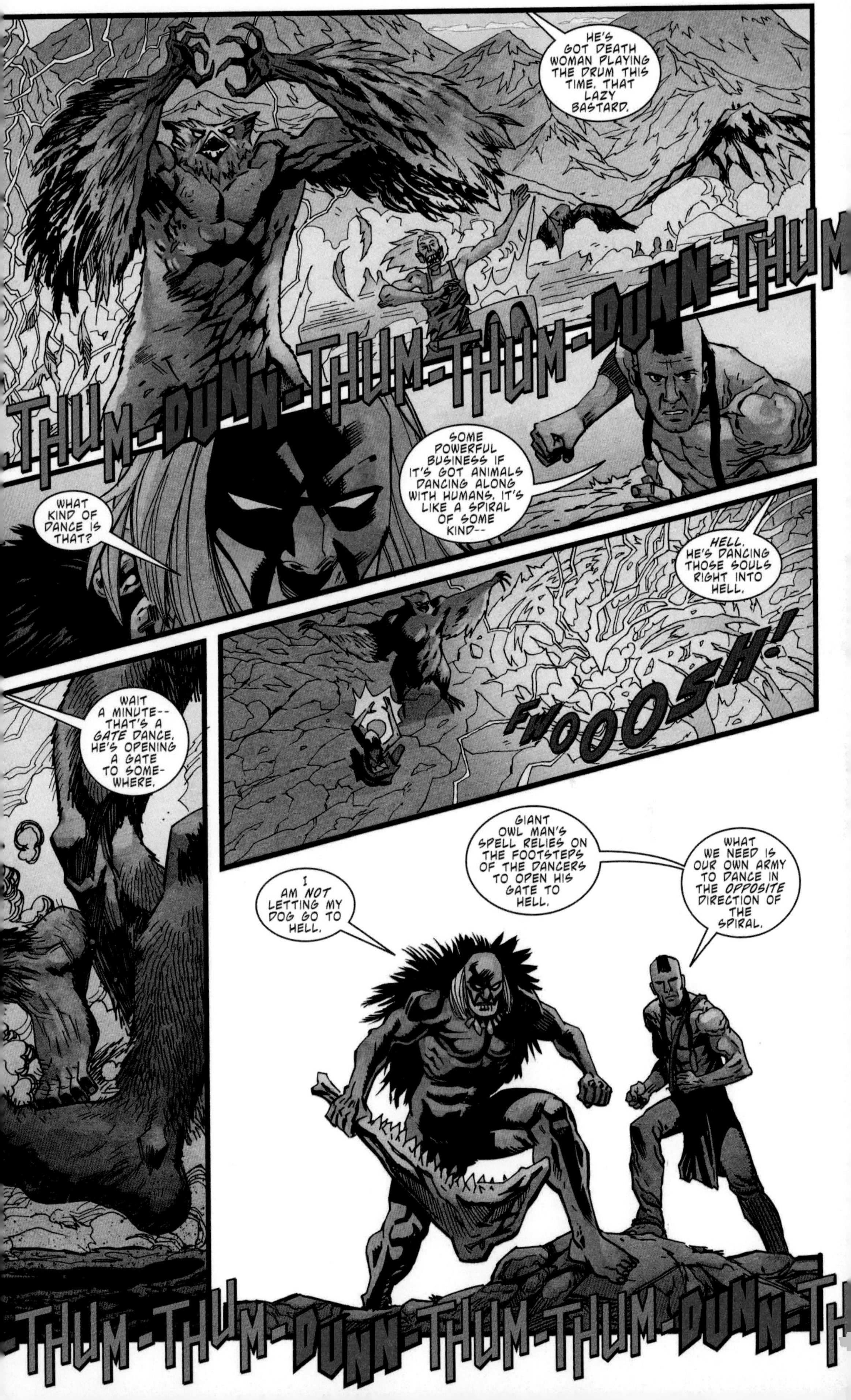
HE'S GOT DEATH WOMAN PLAYING THE DRUM THIS TIME, THAT LAZY BASTARD.
THUM-DUNN-THUM-THUM-DUNN-THUM
SOME POWERFUL BUSINESS IF IT'S GOT ANIMALS DANCING ALONG WITH HUMANS, IT'S LIKE A SPIRAL OF SOME KIND--
WHAT KIND OF DANCE IS THAT?
HELL. HE'S DANCING THOSE SOULS RIGHT INTO HELL.
WAIT A MINUTE-- THAT'S A GATE DANCE. HE'S OPENING A GATE TO SOME-WHERE.
FWOOOOSH!
I AM NOT LETTING MY DOG GO TO HELL.
GIANT OWL MAN'S SPELL RELIES ON THE FOOTSTEPS OF THE DANCERS TO OPEN HIS GATE TO HELL.
WHAT WE NEED IS OUR OWN ARMY TO DANCE IN THE OPPOSITE DIRECTION OF THE SPIRAL.
THUM-THUM-DUNN-THUM-THUM-DUNN-TH

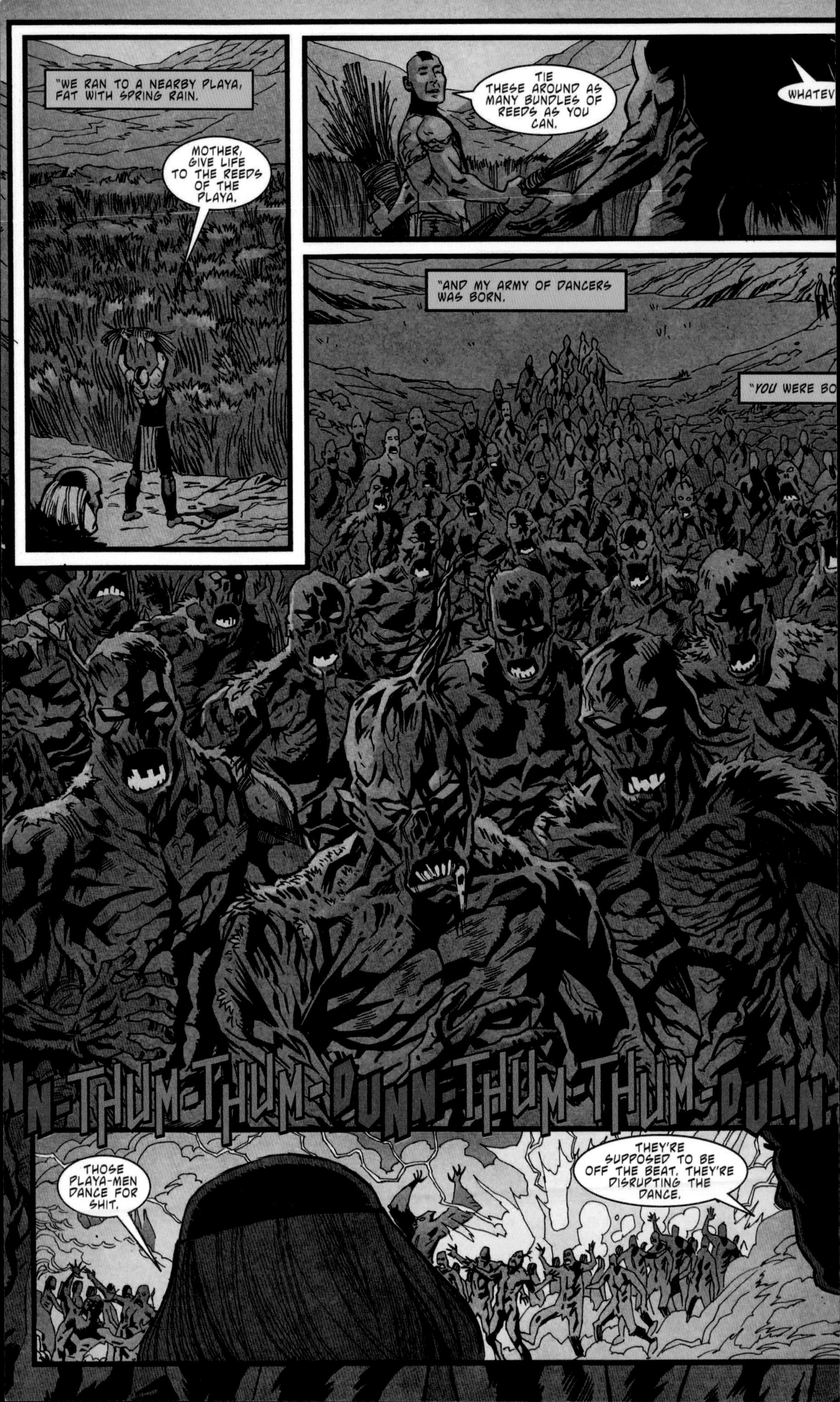
"WE RAN TO A NEARBY PLAYA, FAT WITH SPRING RAIN.
MOTHER, GIVE LIFE TO THE REEDS OF THE PLAYA.
TIE THESE AROUND AS MANY BUNDLES OF REEDS AS YOU CAN.
WHATEV
"AND MY ARMY OF DANCERS WAS BORN.
"YOU WERE BO
N-THUM-THUM-DUNN-THUM-THUM-DUNN
THOSE PLAYA-MEN DANCE FOR SHIT.
THEY'RE SUPPOSED TO BE OFF THE BEAT. THEY'RE DISRUPTING THE DANCE.

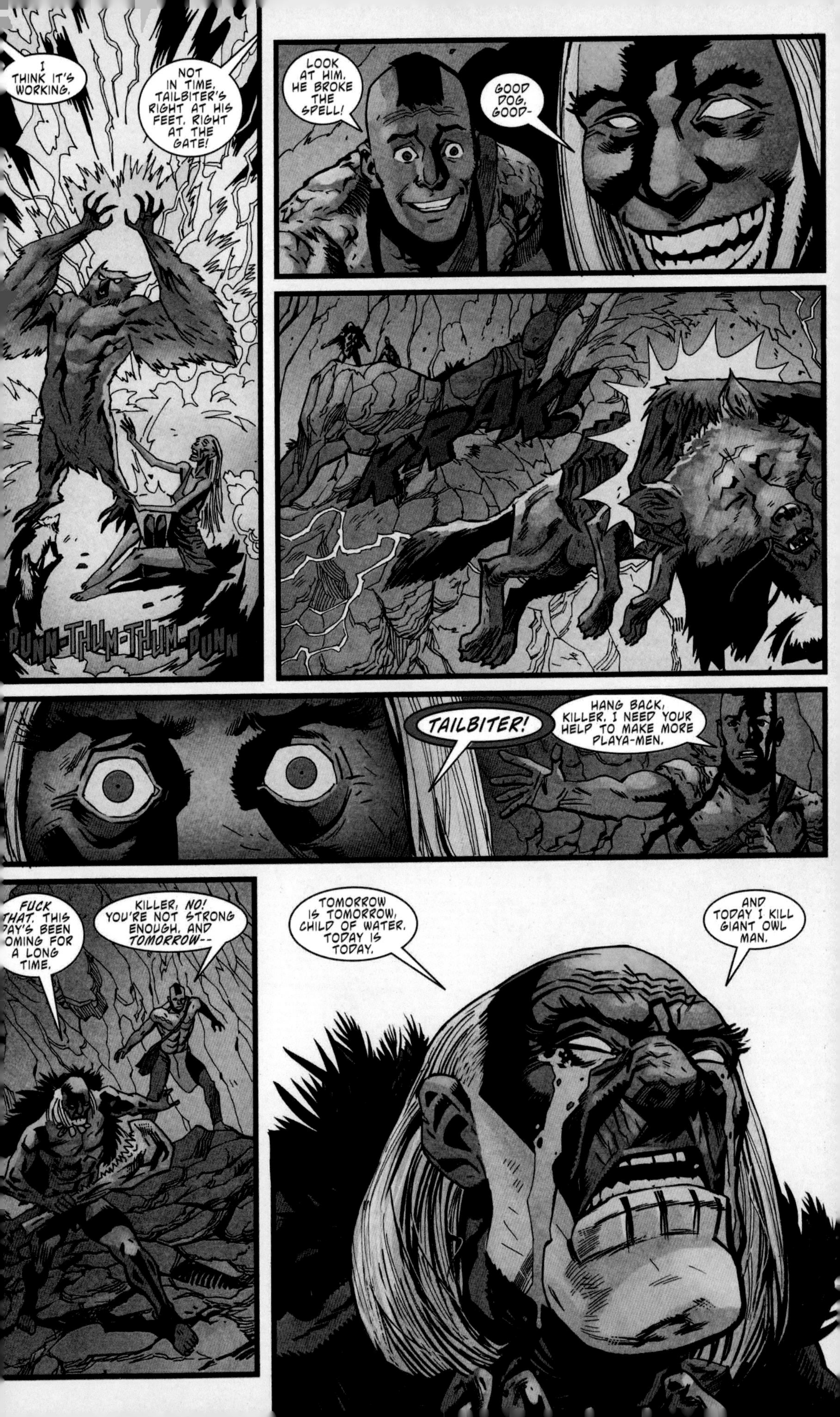
I THINK IT'S WORKING.
NOT IN TIME. TAILBITER'S RIGHT AT HIS FEET. RIGHT AT THE GATE!
DUNN-THUM-THUM-DUNN
LOOK AT HIM. HE BROKE THE SPELL!
GOOD DOG. GOOD-
K-RAK!
TAILBITER!
HANG BACK, KILLER. I NEED YOUR HELP TO MAKE MORE PLAYA-MEN.
FUCK THAT. THIS DAY'S BEEN COMING FOR A LONG TIME.
KILLER, NO! YOU'RE NOT STRONG ENOUGH. AND TOMORROW--
TOMORROW IS TOMORROW, CHILD OF WATER. TODAY IS TODAY.
AND TODAY I KILL GIANT OWL MAN.

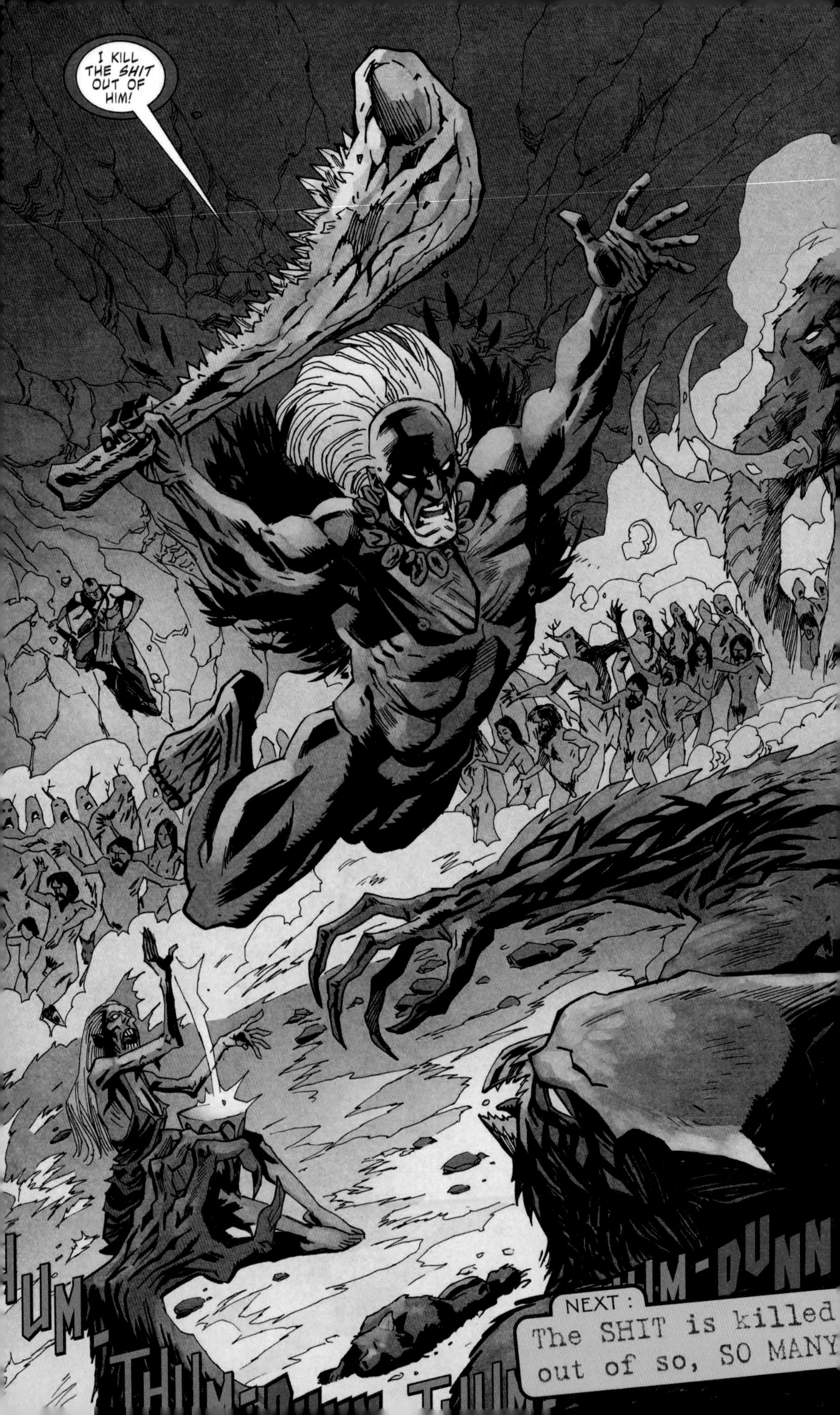
I KILL THE SHIT OUT OF HIM!
THUM-DUNN
NEXT:
The SHIT is killed out of so, SO MANY

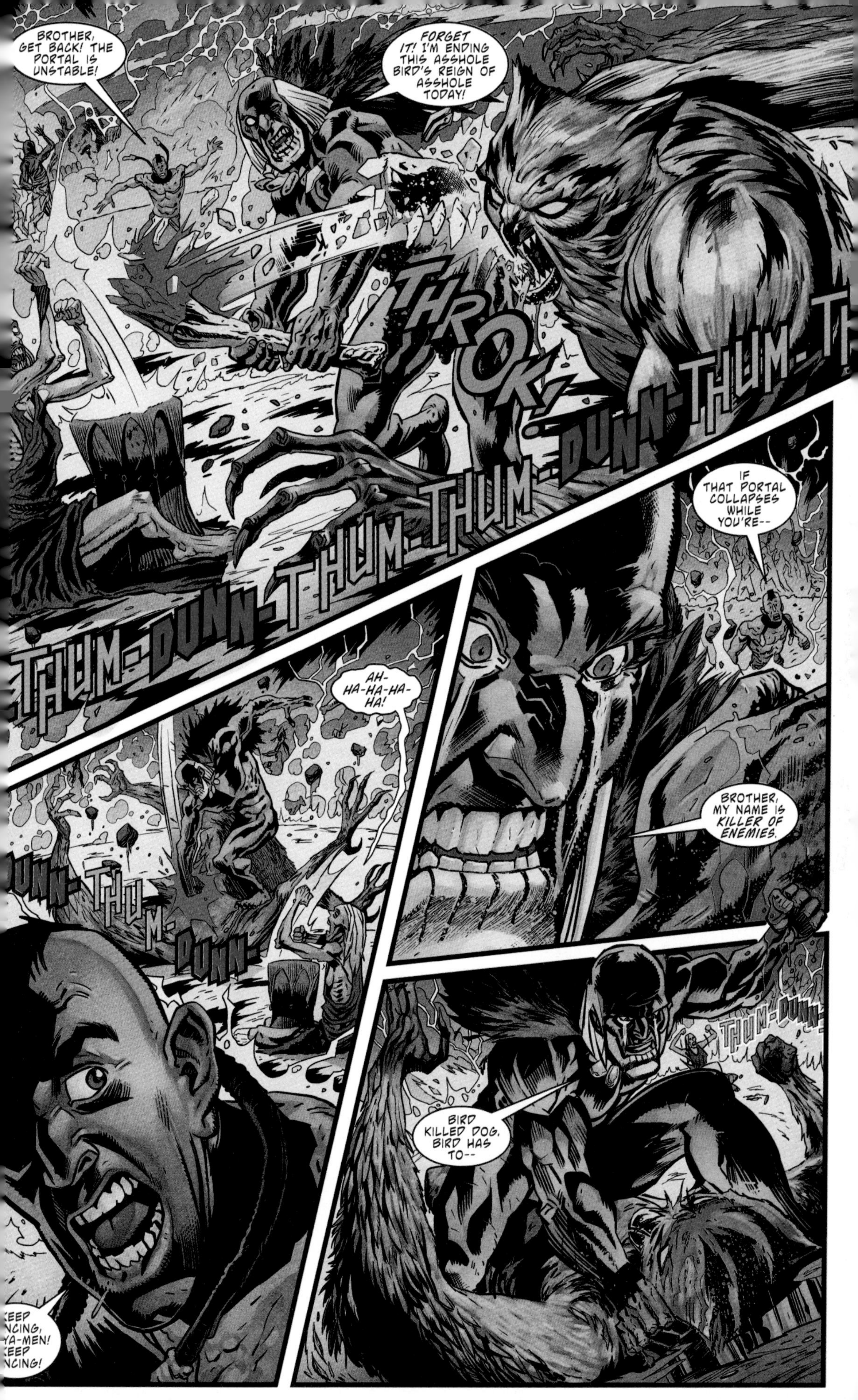
BROTHER, GET BACK! THE PORTAL IS UNSTABLE!
FORGET IT! I'M ENDING THIS ASSHOLE BIRD'S REIGN OF ASSHOLE TODAY!
THROK!
THUM-DUNN-THUM-THUM-THUM-DUNN-THUM-TH
IF THAT PORTAL COLLAPSES WHILE YOU'RE--
BROTHER, MY NAME IS KILLER OF ENEMIES.
AH-HA-HA-HA-HA!
UNN-THUM-DUNN-
THUM-DUNN-
BIRD KILLED DOG, BIRD HAS TO--
KEEP NCING, YA-MEN! KEEP NCING!

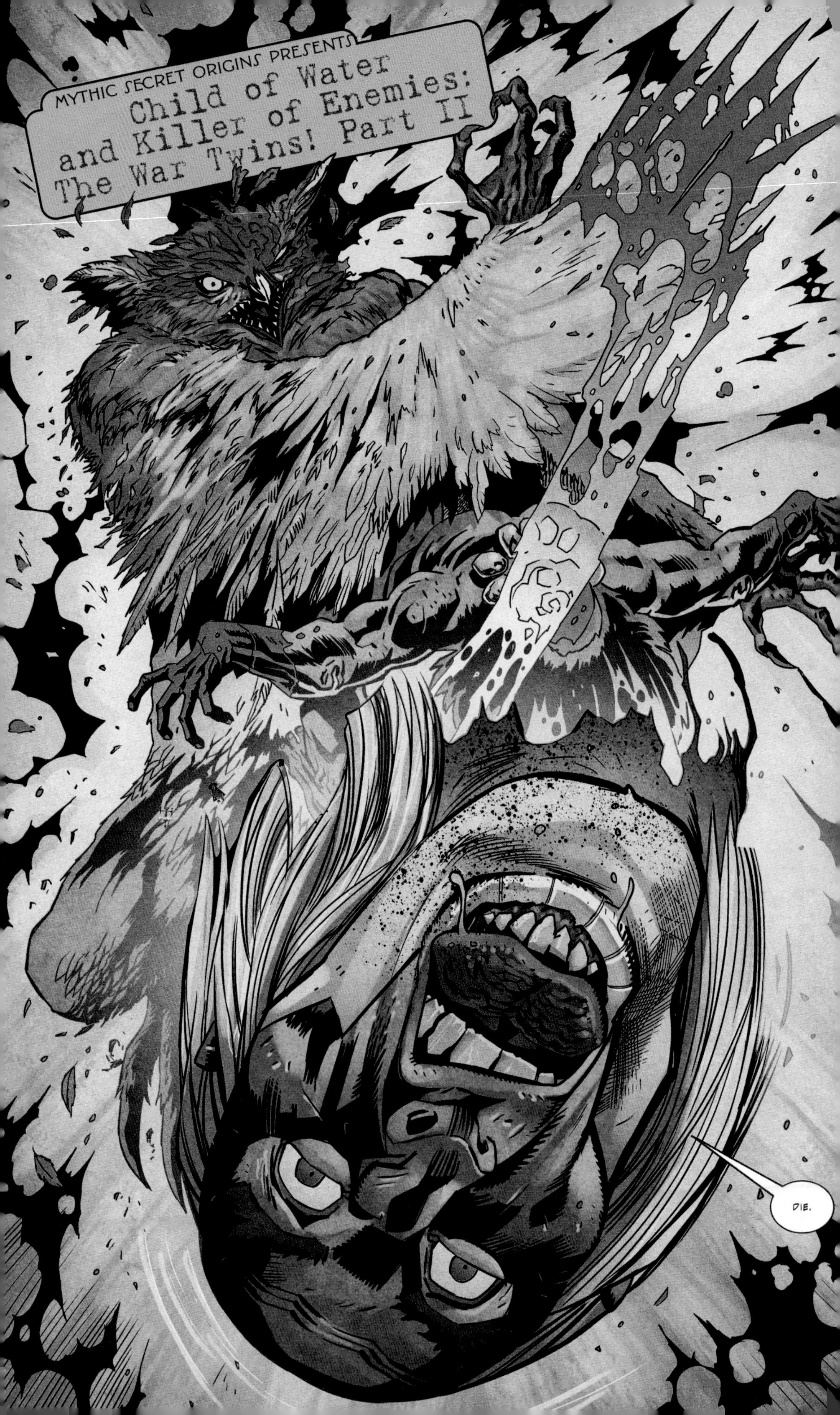
MYTHIC SECRET ORIGINS PRESENTS
Child of Water and Killer of Enemies: The War Twins! Part II
DIE.

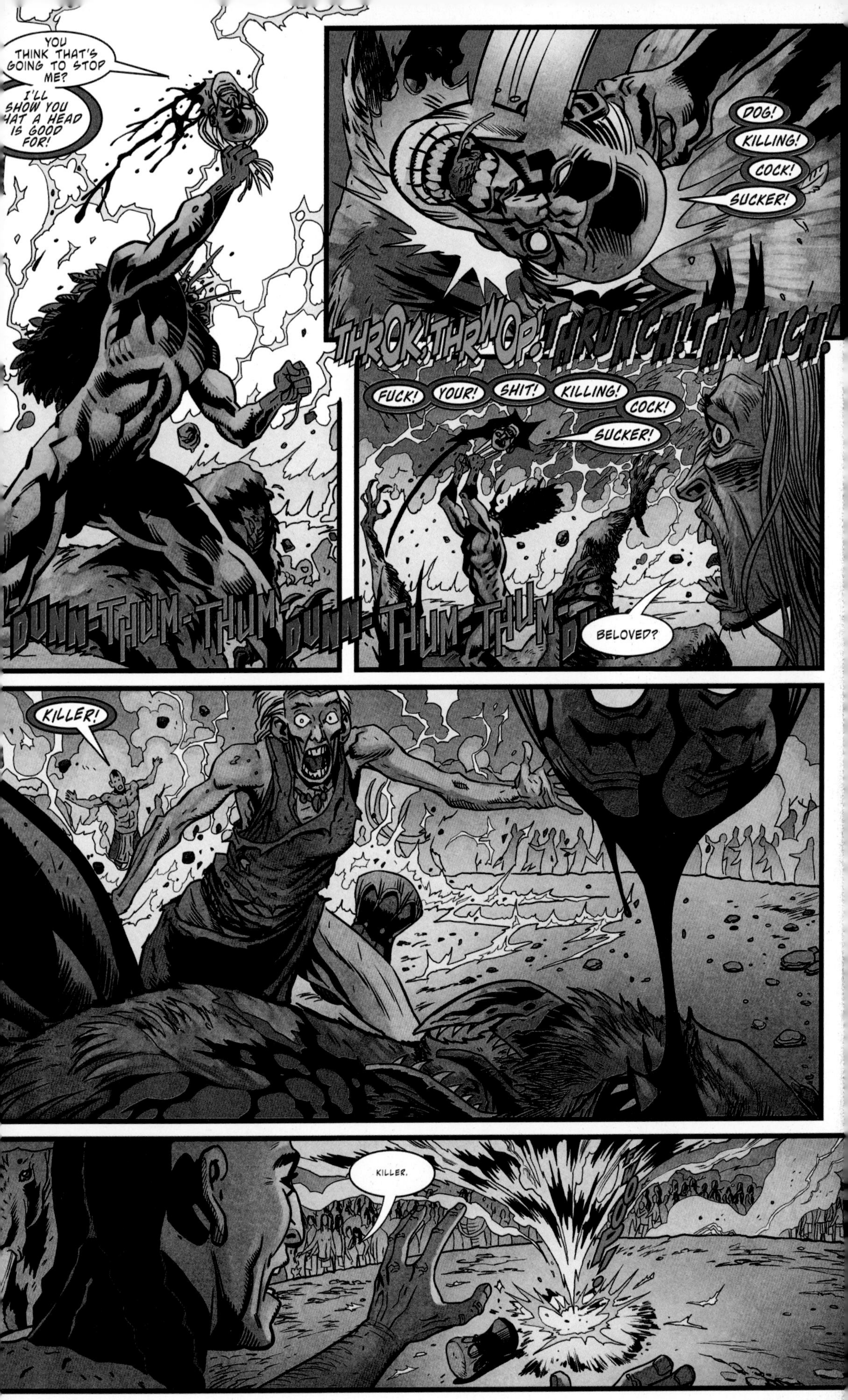

YOU THINK THAT'S GOING TO STOP ME?
I'LL SHOW YOU THAT A HEAD IS GOOD FOR!
DOG!
KILLING!
COCK!
SUCKER!
THROK! THRWOP! THRUNCH! THRUNCH!
FUCK!
YOUR!
SHIT!
KILLING!
COCK!
SUCKER!
DUNN-THUM-THUM-DUNN-THUM-THUM-DU
BELOVED?
KILLER!
KILLER.

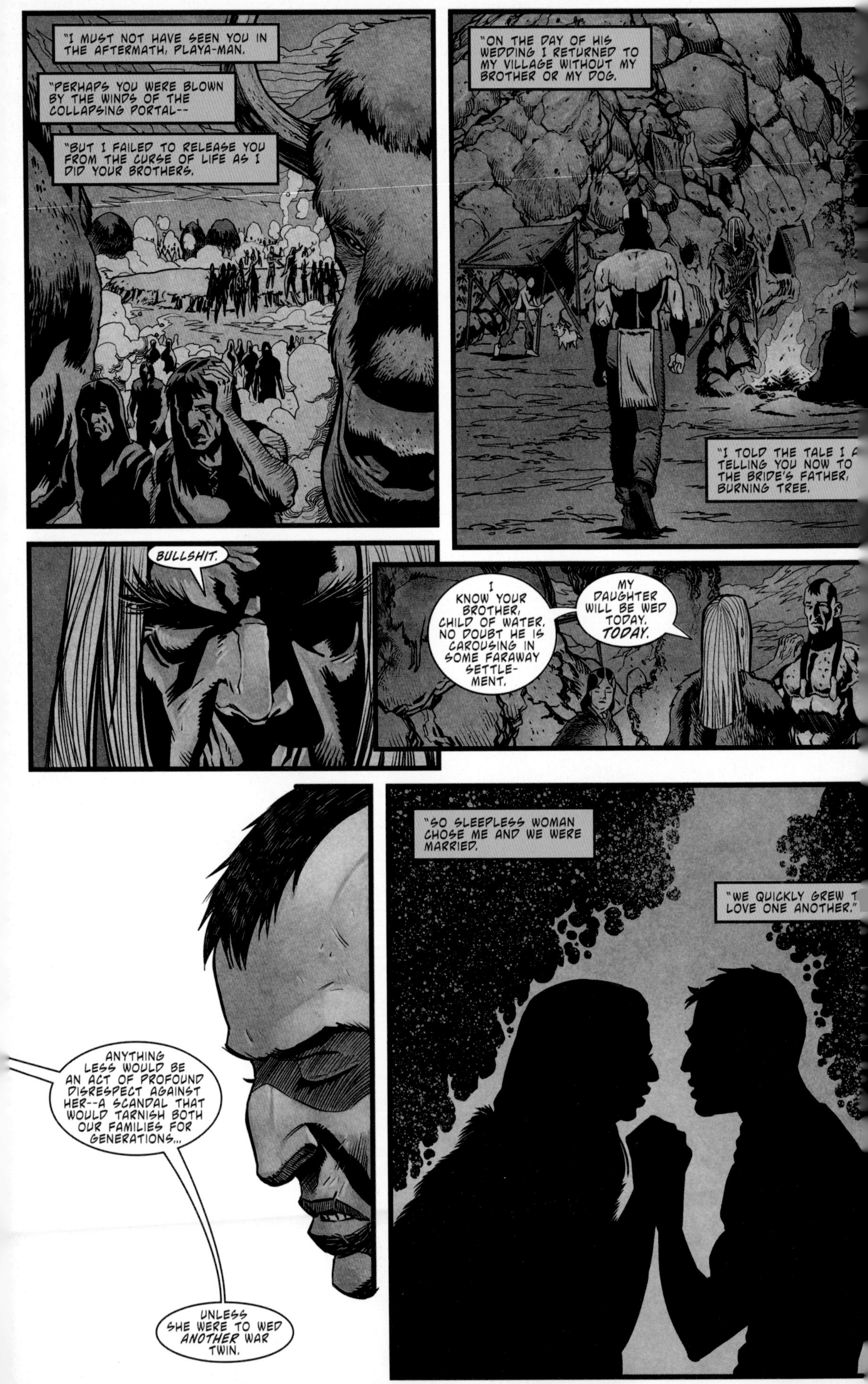
"I MUST NOT HAVE SEEN YOU IN THE AFTERMATH, PLAYA-MAN.
"PERHAPS YOU WERE BLOWN BY THE WINDS OF THE COLLAPSING PORTAL--
"BUT I FAILED TO RELEASE YOU FROM THE CURSE OF LIFE AS I DID YOUR BROTHERS.
"ON THE DAY OF HIS WEDDING I RETURNED TO MY VILLAGE WITHOUT MY BROTHER OR MY DOG.
"I TOLD THE TALE I A TELLING YOU NOW TO THE BRIDE'S FATHER, BURNING TREE.
BULLSHIT.
I KNOW YOUR BROTHER, CHILD OF WATER. NO DOUBT HE IS CAROUSING IN SOME FARAWAY SETTLE-MENT.
MY DAUGHTER WILL BE WED TODAY. *TODAY.*
ANYTHING LESS WOULD BE AN ACT OF PROFOUND DISRESPECT AGAINST HER--A SCANDAL THAT WOULD TARNISH BOTH OUR FAMILIES FOR GENERATIONS...
UNLESS SHE WERE TO WED *ANOTHER* WAR TWIN.
"SO SLEEPLESS WOMAN CHOSE ME AND WE WERE MARRIED.
"WE QUICKLY GREW T LOVE ONE ANOTHER."

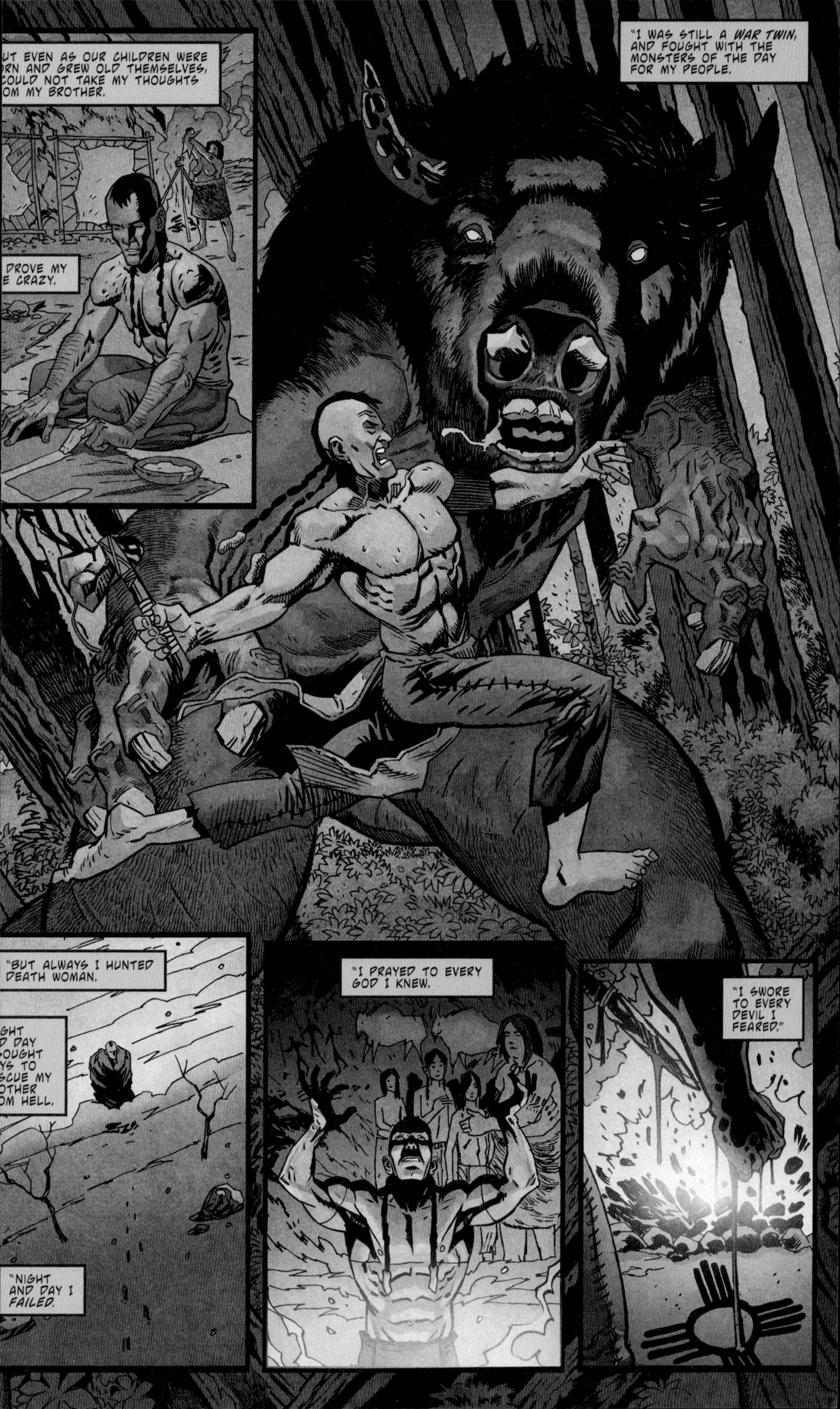

UT EVEN AS OUR CHILDREN WERE ORN AND GREW OLD THEMSELVES, COULD NOT TAKE MY THOUGHTS OM MY BROTHER.
DROVE MY E CRAZY.
"I WAS STILL A WAR TWIN, AND FOUGHT WITH THE MONSTERS OF THE DAY FOR MY PEOPLE.
"BUT ALWAYS I HUNTED DEATH WOMAN.
GHT D DAY OUGHT YS TO SCUE MY OTHER OM HELL.
"NIGHT AND DAY I FAILED.
"I PRAYED TO EVERY GOD I KNEW.
"I SWORE TO EVERY DEVIL I FEARED."

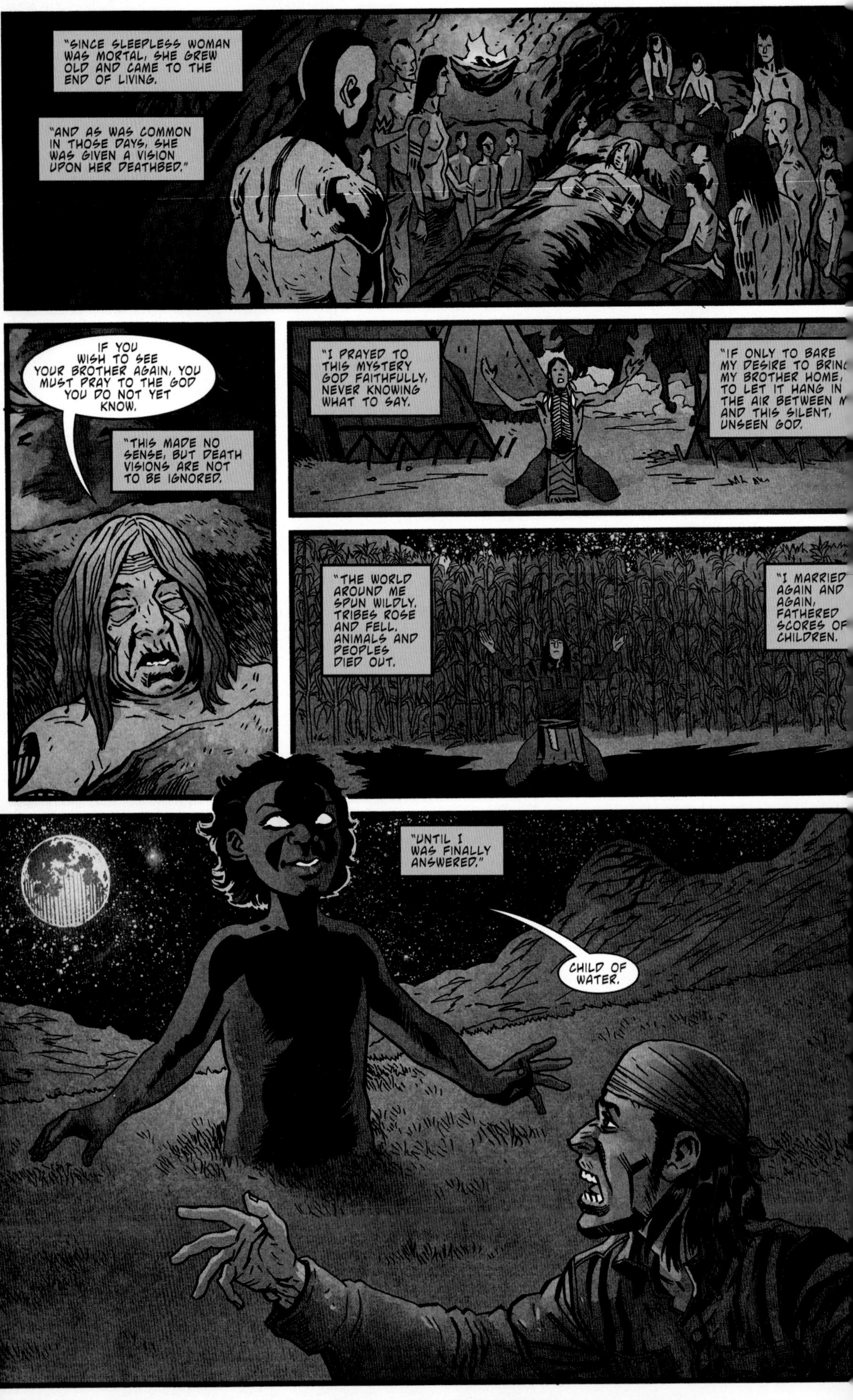
"SINCE SLEEPLESS WOMAN WAS MORTAL, SHE GREW OLD AND CAME TO THE END OF LIVING.
"AND AS WAS COMMON IN THOSE DAYS, SHE WAS GIVEN A VISION UPON HER DEATHBED."
IF YOU WISH TO SEE YOUR BROTHER AGAIN, YOU MUST PRAY TO THE GOD YOU DO NOT YET KNOW.
"THIS MADE NO SENSE, BUT DEATH VISIONS ARE NOT TO BE IGNORED.
"I PRAYED TO THIS MYSTERY GOD FAITHFULLY, NEVER KNOWING WHAT TO SAY.
"IF ONLY TO BARE MY DESIRE TO BRING MY BROTHER HOME, TO LET IT HANG IN THE AIR BETWEEN ME AND THIS SILENT, UNSEEN GOD.
"THE WORLD AROUND ME SPUN WILDLY. TRIBES ROSE AND FELL, ANIMALS AND PEOPLES DIED OUT.
"I MARRIED AGAIN AND AGAIN, FATHERED SCORES OF CHILDREN.
"UNTIL I WAS FINALLY ANSWERED."
CHILD OF WATER.

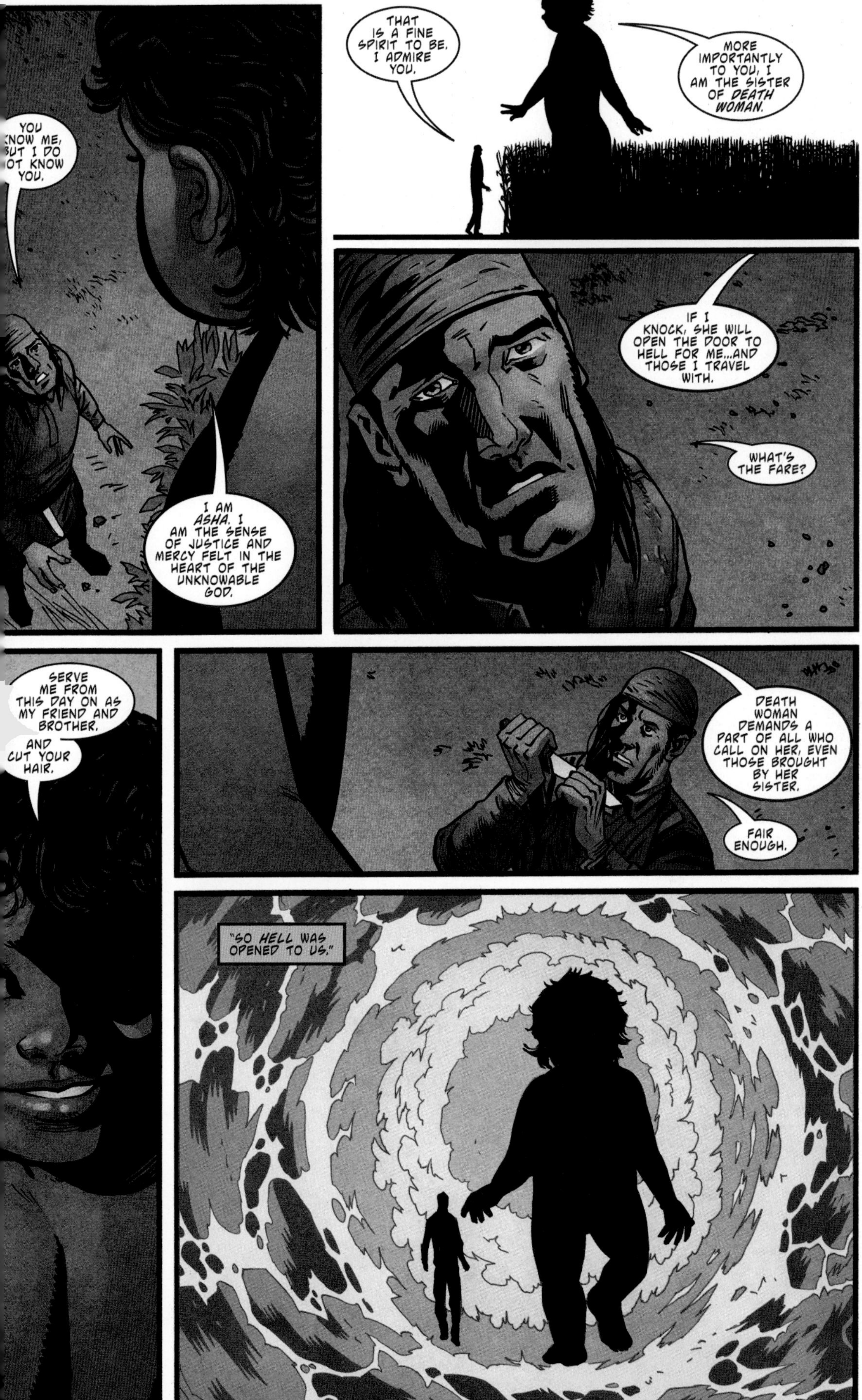
YOU
KNOW ME,
BUT I DO
NOT KNOW
YOU.
I AM
ASHA. I
AM THE SENSE
OF JUSTICE AND
MERCY FELT IN THE
HEART OF THE
UNKNOWABLE
GOD.
THAT IS A FINE SPIRIT TO BE. I ADMIRE YOU.
MORE IMPORTANTLY TO YOU, I AM THE SISTER OF DEATH WOMAN.
IF I KNOCK, SHE WILL OPEN THE DOOR TO HELL FOR ME...AND THOSE I TRAVEL WITH.
WHAT'S THE FARE?
SERVE ME FROM THIS DAY ON AS MY FRIEND AND BROTHER.
AND CUT YOUR HAIR.
DEATH WOMAN DEMANDS A PART OF ALL WHO CALL ON HER, EVEN THOSE BROUGHT BY HER SISTER.
FAIR ENOUGH.
"SO HELL WAS OPENED TO US."

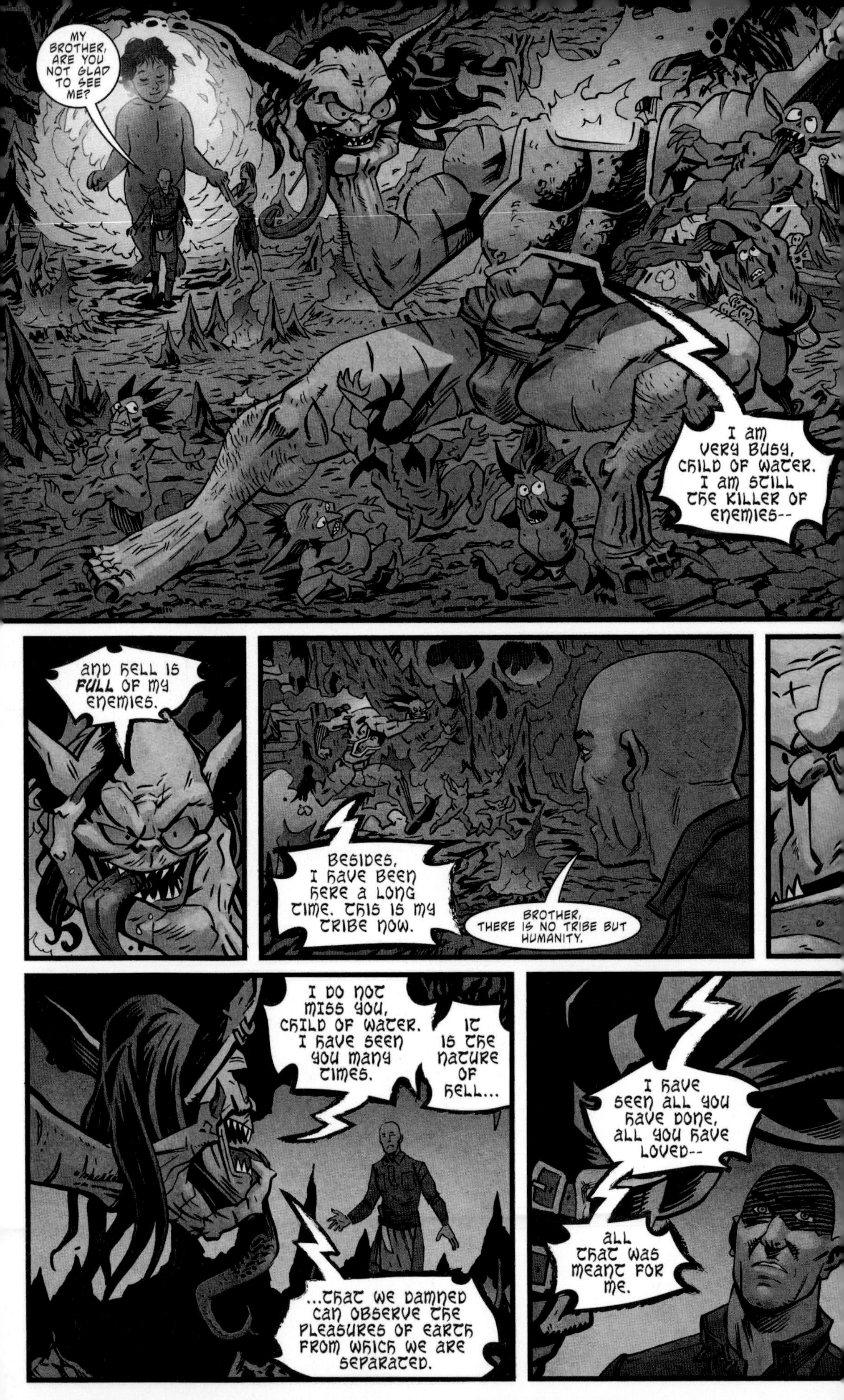
MY BROTHER, ARE YOU NOT GLAD TO SEE ME?
I AM VERY BUSY, CHILD OF WATER. I AM STILL THE KILLER OF ENEMIES--
AND HELL IS FULL OF MY ENEMIES.
BESIDES, I HAVE BEEN HERE A LONG TIME. THIS IS MY TRIBE NOW.
BROTHER, THERE IS NO TRIBE BUT HUMANITY.
I DO NOT MISS YOU, CHILD OF WATER. I HAVE SEEN YOU MANY TIMES.
IT IS THE NATURE OF HELL...
...THAT WE DAMNED CAN OBSERVE THE PLEASURES OF EARTH FROM WHICH WE ARE SEPARATED.
I HAVE SEEN ALL YOU HAVE DONE, ALL YOU HAVE LOVED--
ALL THAT WAS MEANT FOR ME.

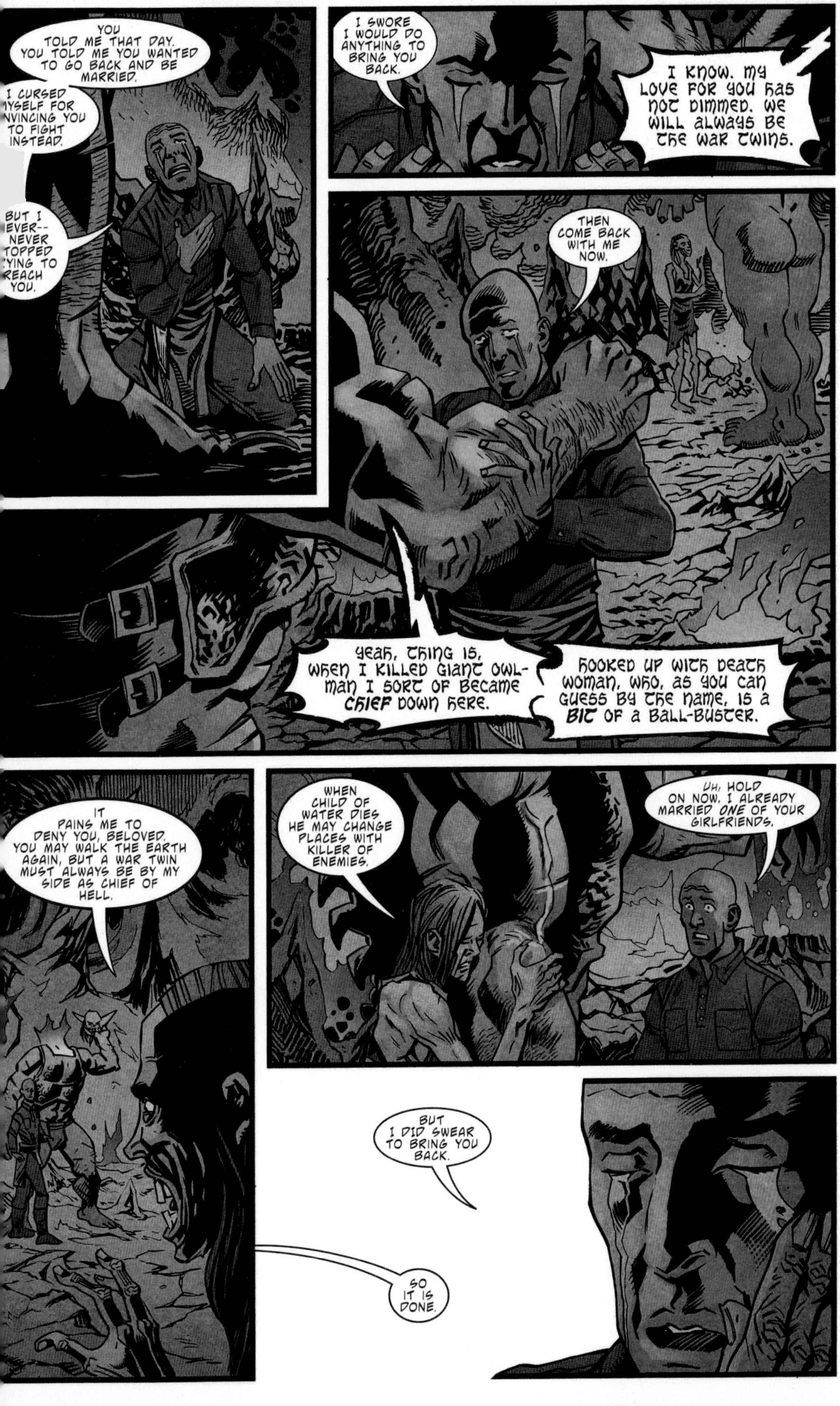
YOU TOLD ME THAT DAY. YOU TOLD ME YOU WANTED TO GO BACK AND BE MARRIED.
I CURSED MYSELF FOR NVINCING YOU TO FIGHT INSTEAD.
BUT I EVER-- NEVER TOPPED YING TO REACH YOU.
I SWORE I WOULD DO ANYTHING TO BRING YOU BACK.
I KNOW. MY LOVE FOR YOU HAS NOT DIMMED. WE WILL ALWAYS BE THE WAR TWINS.
THEN COME BACK WITH ME NOW.
YEAH, THING IS, WHEN I KILLED GIANT OWL-MAN I SORT OF BECAME CHIEF DOWN HERE.
HOOKED UP WITH DEATH WOMAN, WHO, AS YOU CAN GUESS BY THE NAME, IS A BIT OF A BALL-BUSTER.
IT PAINS ME TO DENY YOU, BELOVED. YOU MAY WALK THE EARTH AGAIN, BUT A WAR TWIN MUST ALWAYS BE BY MY SIDE AS CHIEF OF HELL.
WHEN CHILD OF WATER DIES HE MAY CHANGE PLACES WITH KILLER OF ENEMIES.
UH, HOLD ON NOW. I ALREADY MARRIED ONE OF YOUR GIRLFRIENDS.
BUT I DID SWEAR TO BRING YOU BACK.
SO IT IS DONE.

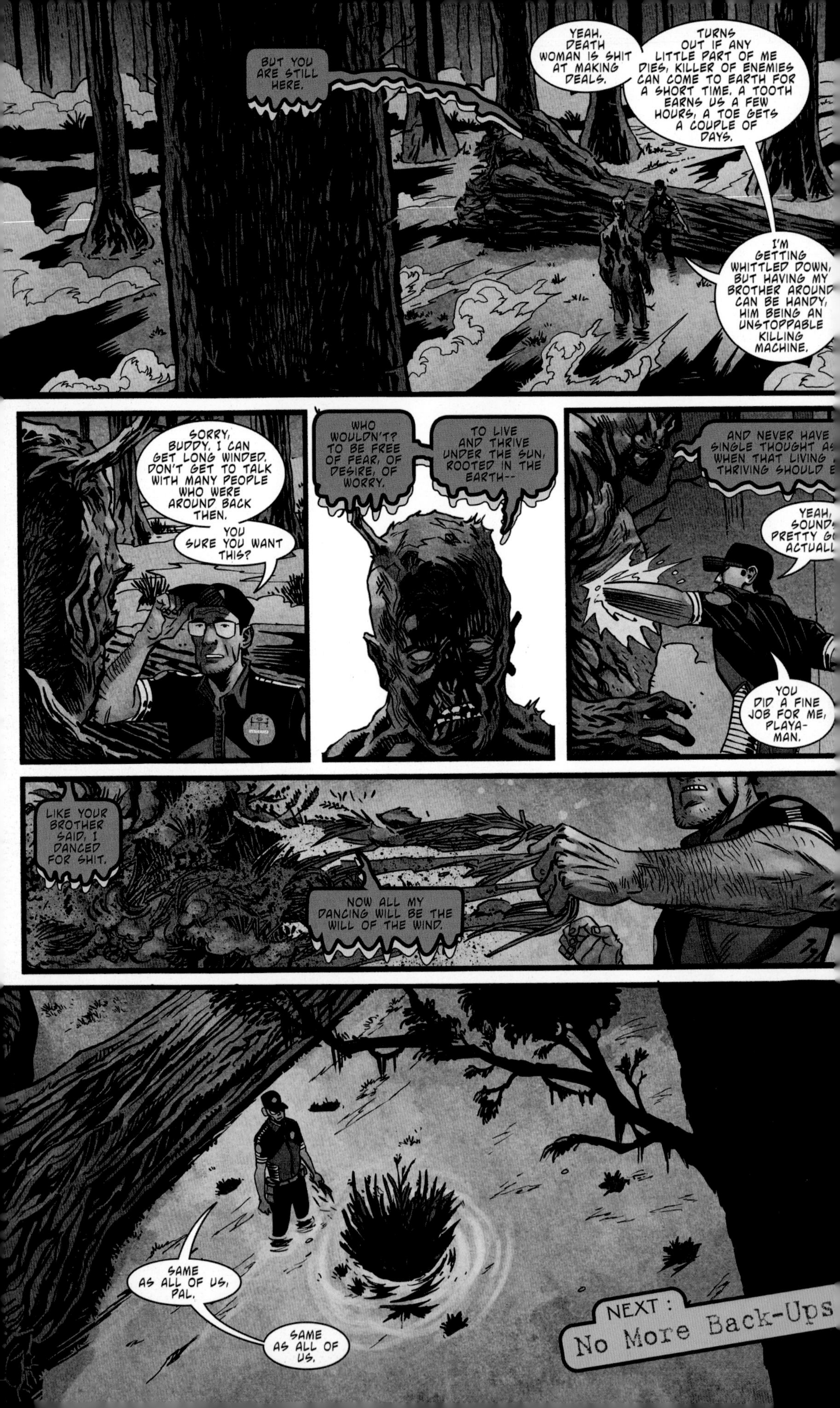
BUT YOU ARE STILL HERE.
YEAH, DEATH WOMAN IS SHIT AT MAKING DEALS.
TURNS OUT IF ANY LITTLE PART OF ME DIES, KILLER OF ENEMIES CAN COME TO EARTH FOR A SHORT TIME. A TOOTH EARNS US A FEW HOURS, A TOE GETS A COUPLE OF DAYS.
I'M GETTING WHITTLED DOWN, BUT HAVING MY BROTHER AROUND CAN BE HANDY, HIM BEING AN UNSTOPPABLE KILLING MACHINE.
SORRY, BUDDY. I CAN GET LONG WINDED. DON'T GET TO TALK WITH MANY PEOPLE WHO WERE AROUND BACK THEN.
YOU SURE YOU WANT THIS?
WHO WOULDN'T? TO BE FREE OF FEAR, OF DESIRE, OF WORRY.
TO LIVE AND THRIVE UNDER THE SUN, ROOTED IN THE EARTH--
AND NEVER HAVE SINGLE THOUGHT AS WHEN THAT LIVING THRIVING SHOULD E
YEAH, SOUNDS PRETTY GO ACTUALL
YOU DID A FINE JOB FOR ME, PLAYA-MAN.
LIKE YOUR BROTHER SAID, I DANCED FOR SHIT.
NOW ALL MY DANCING WILL BE THE WILL OF THE WIND.
SAME AS ALL OF US, PAL.
SAME AS ALL OF US.
NEXT: No More Back-Ups

COVER GALLERY
THE MYTHIC VARIANTS

PHIL AND I WANTED AN EXCUSE TO SEE OUR
CHARACTERS DRAWN BY SOME OF THE BEST AND
BRIGHTEST (AND CHEAPEST) ARTISTS IN THIS CRAZY
INDUSTRY SO WE WENT ON A MYTHIC QUEST TO TRACK
'EM DOWN . . . WE FAILED, SO HERE ARE SOME OTHER
GUYS' DRAWINGS WHO WE BUMPED INTO IN THE PUB . . .
JOHN

#IB MATTEO SCALERA AND MORENO DINISIO

#IC JOHN MCCREA

#2B DECLAN SHALVEY AND KELLY FITZPATRICK

#2C SEAN GORDON MURPHY AND MICHAEL SPICER

#3 DUNCAN FEGREDO AND MICHAEL SPICER

#4 GORAN PARLOV AND MICHAEL SPICER

#5 BRIAN CHURILLA

#6 GENE HA AND MICHAEL SPICER

#7 STEVE PUGH

#8 MIKE HUDDLESTON

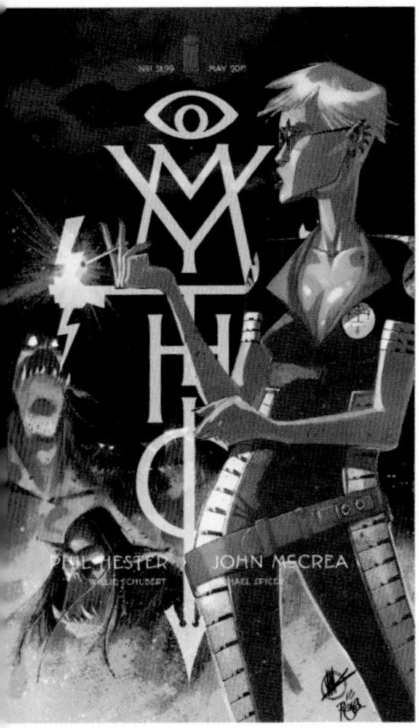
MAY 2015
PHIL HESTER
JOHN McCREA
WILLIE SCHUBERT

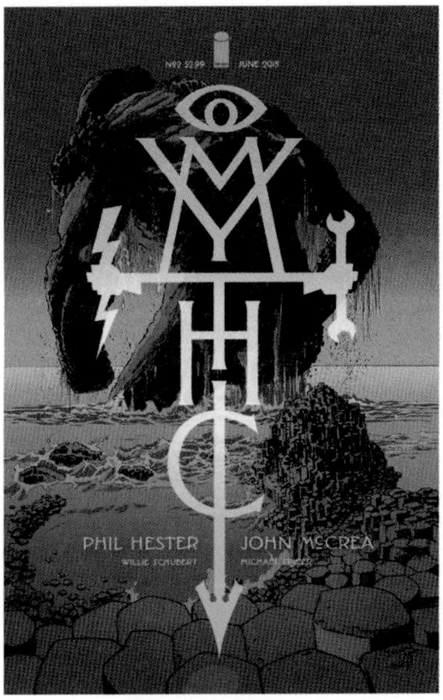
No2 $3.99 JUNE 2015
PHIL HESTER
JOHN McCREA
WILLIE SCHUBERT
MICHAEL SPICER

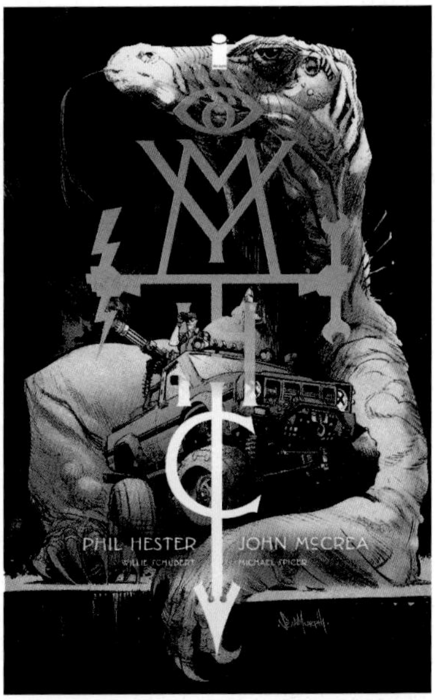
PHIL HESTER
JOHN McCREA
WILLIE SCHUBERT
MICHAEL SPICER

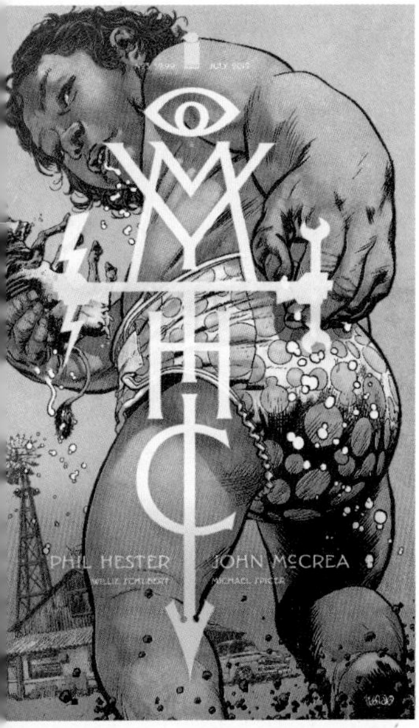
JULY 2015
PHIL HESTER
JOHN McCREA
WILLIE SCHUBERT

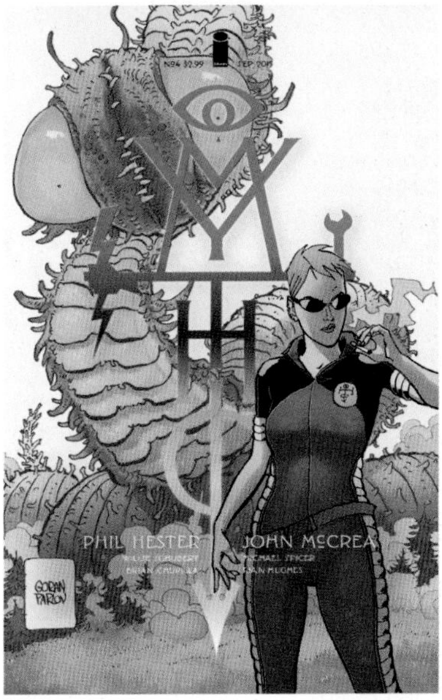
No4 $3.99 SEP 2015
PHIL HESTER
JOHN McCREA
GORAN PARLOV

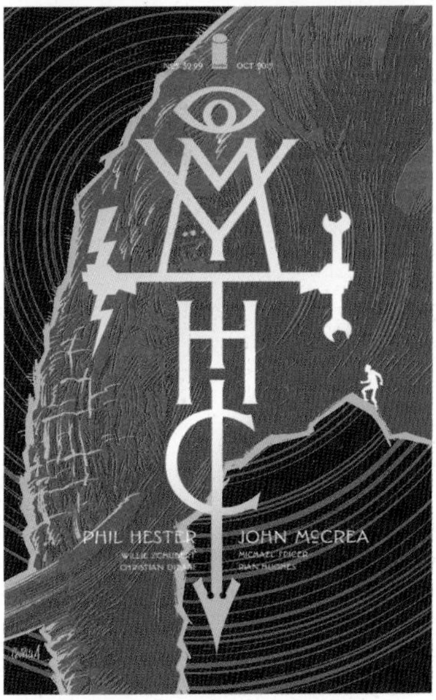
OCT 2015
PHIL HESTER
JOHN McCREA
MICHAEL SPICER

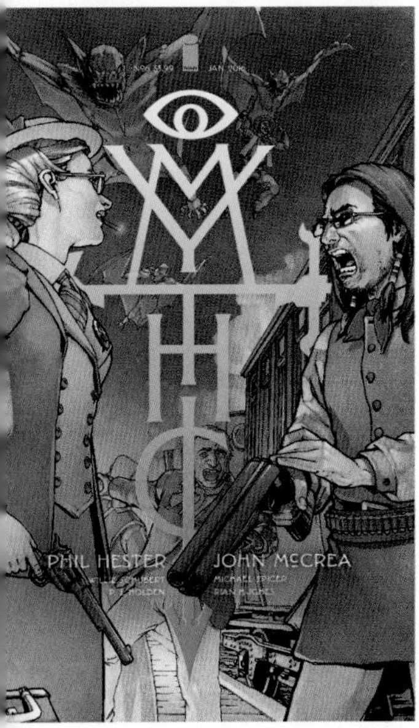
JAN 2016
PHIL HESTER
JOHN McCREA

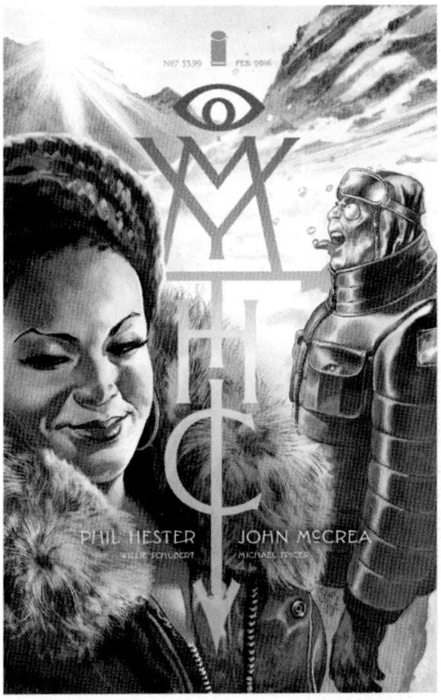
No7 $3.99 FEB 2016
PHIL HESTER
JOHN McCREA
WILLIE SCHUBERT
MICHAEL SPICER

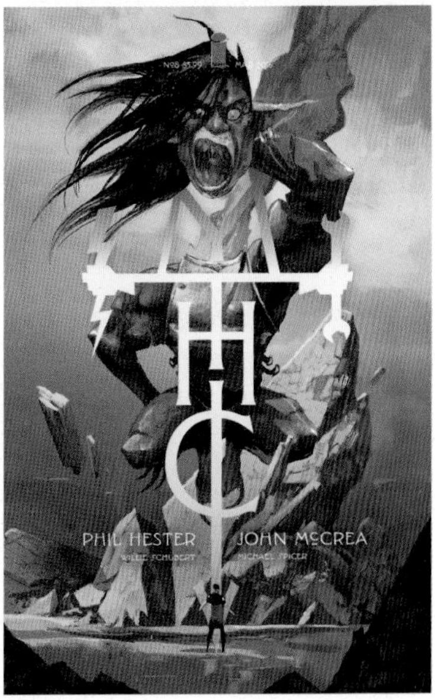
PHIL HESTER
JOHN McCREA
MICHAEL SPICER

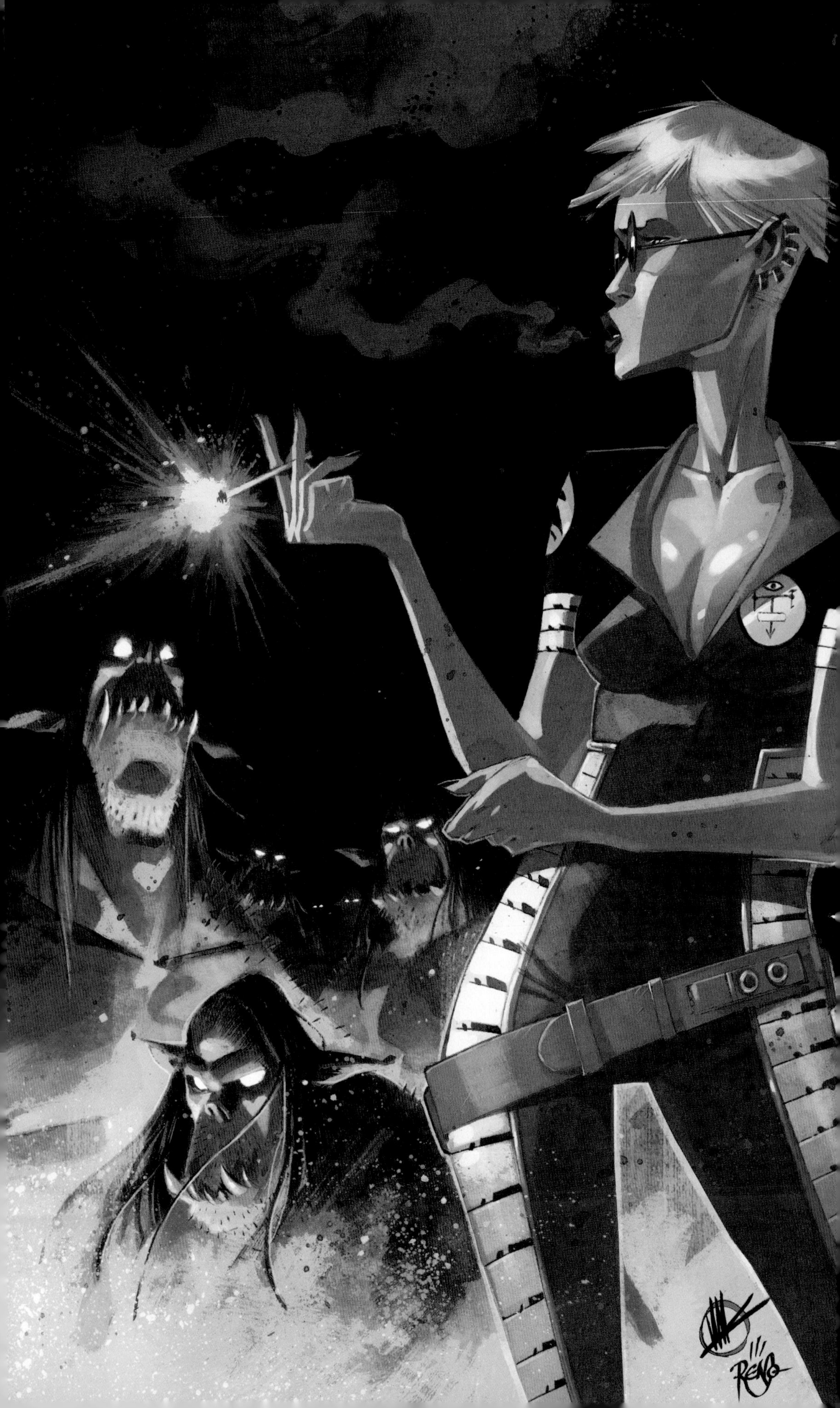

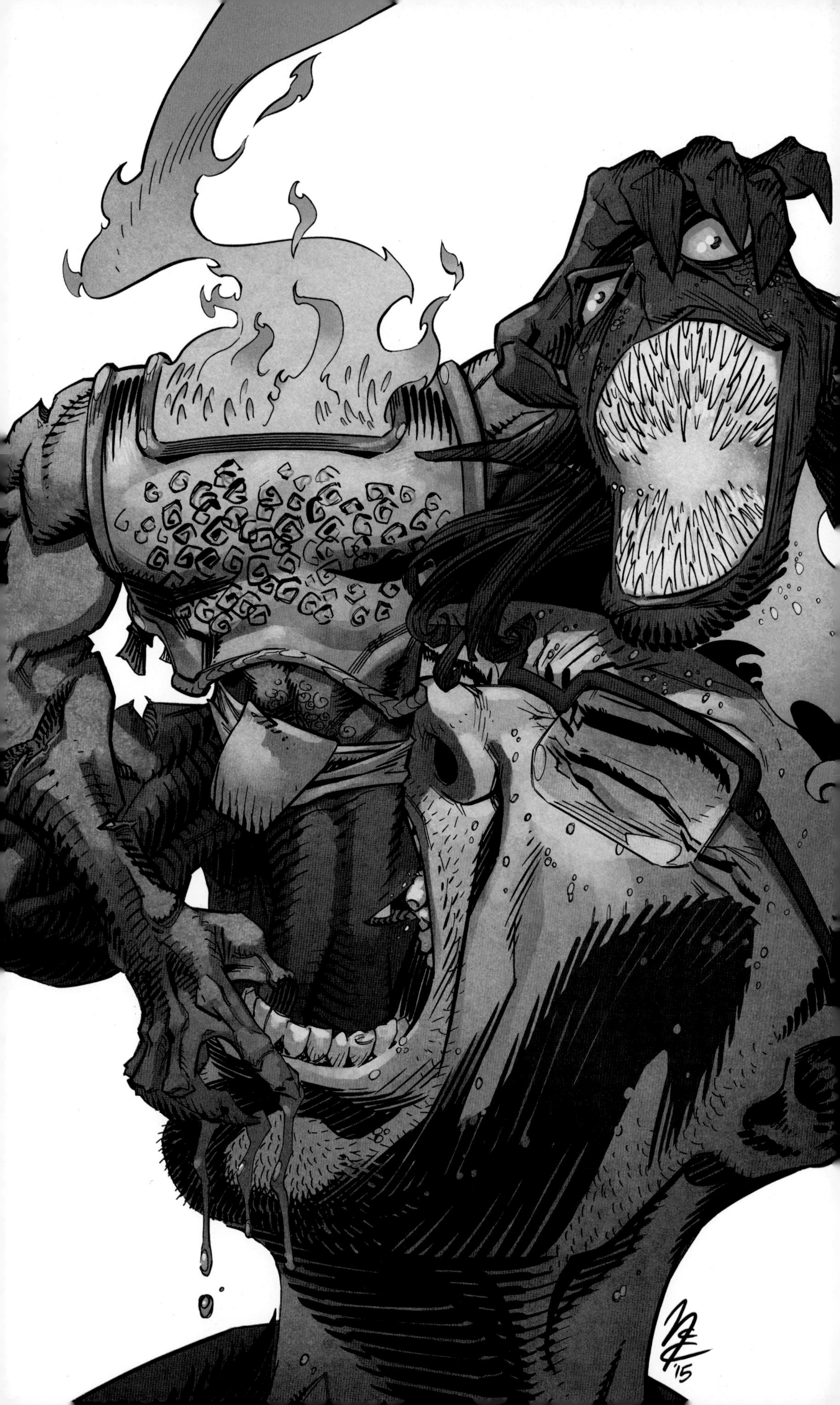

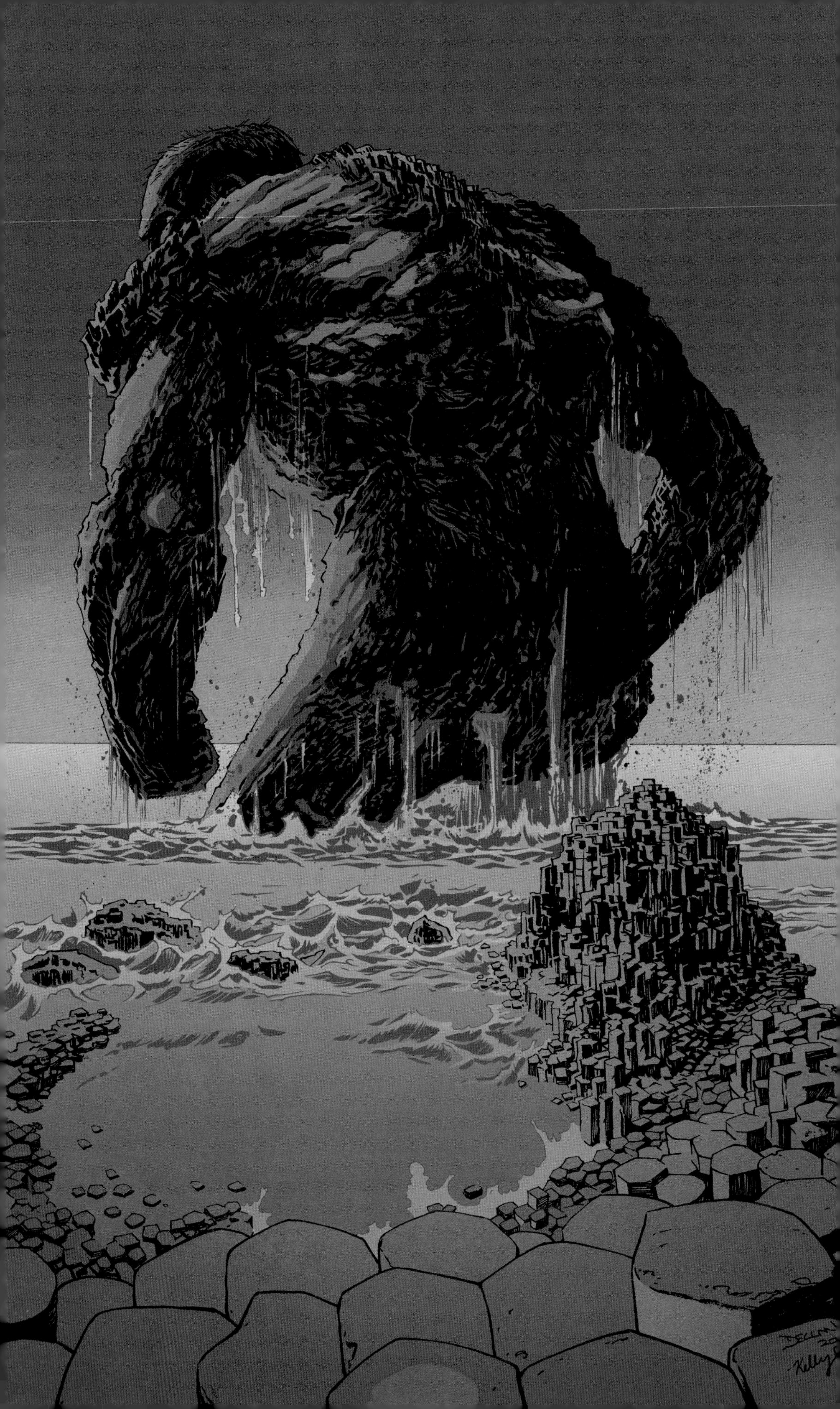

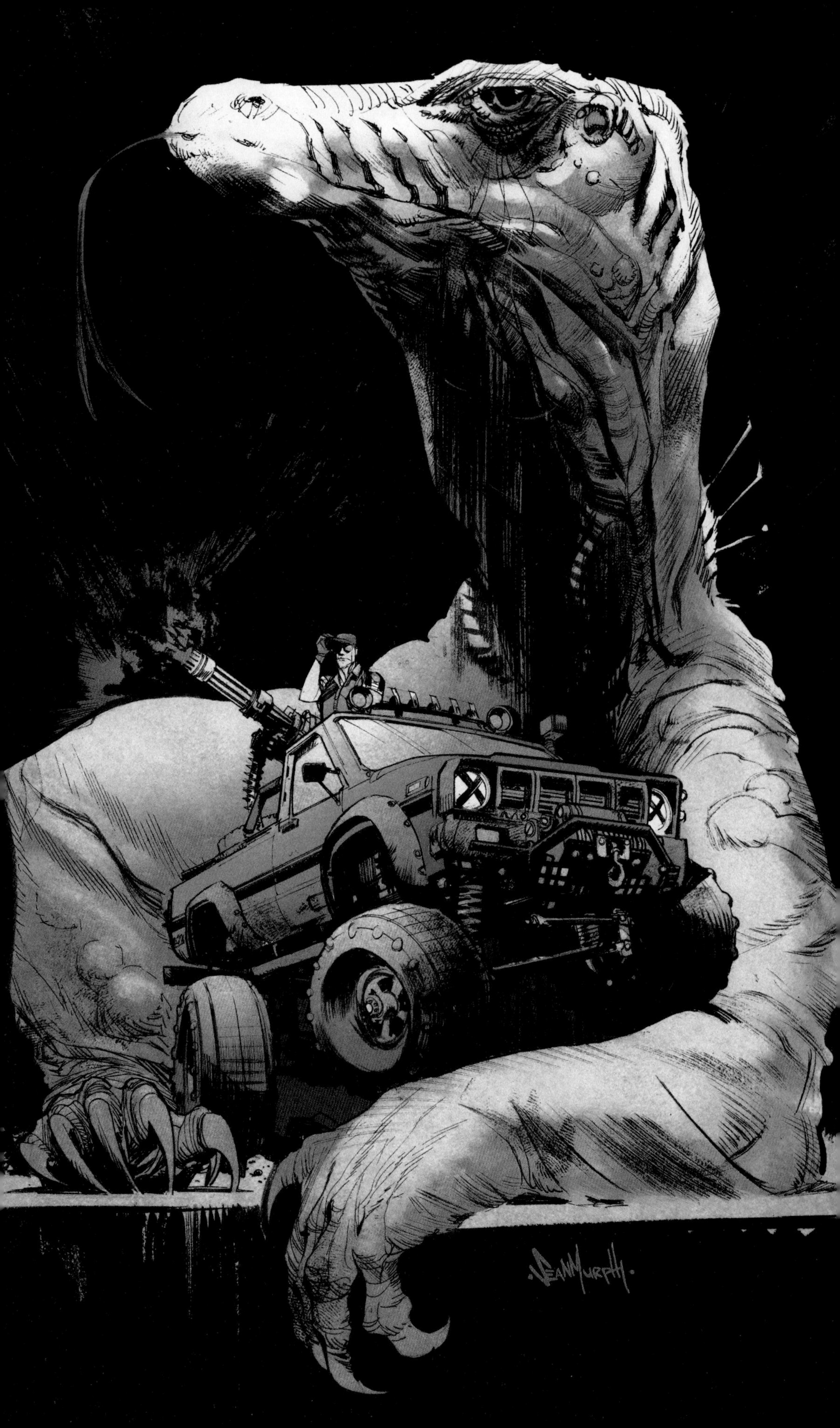
SEANMURPHY

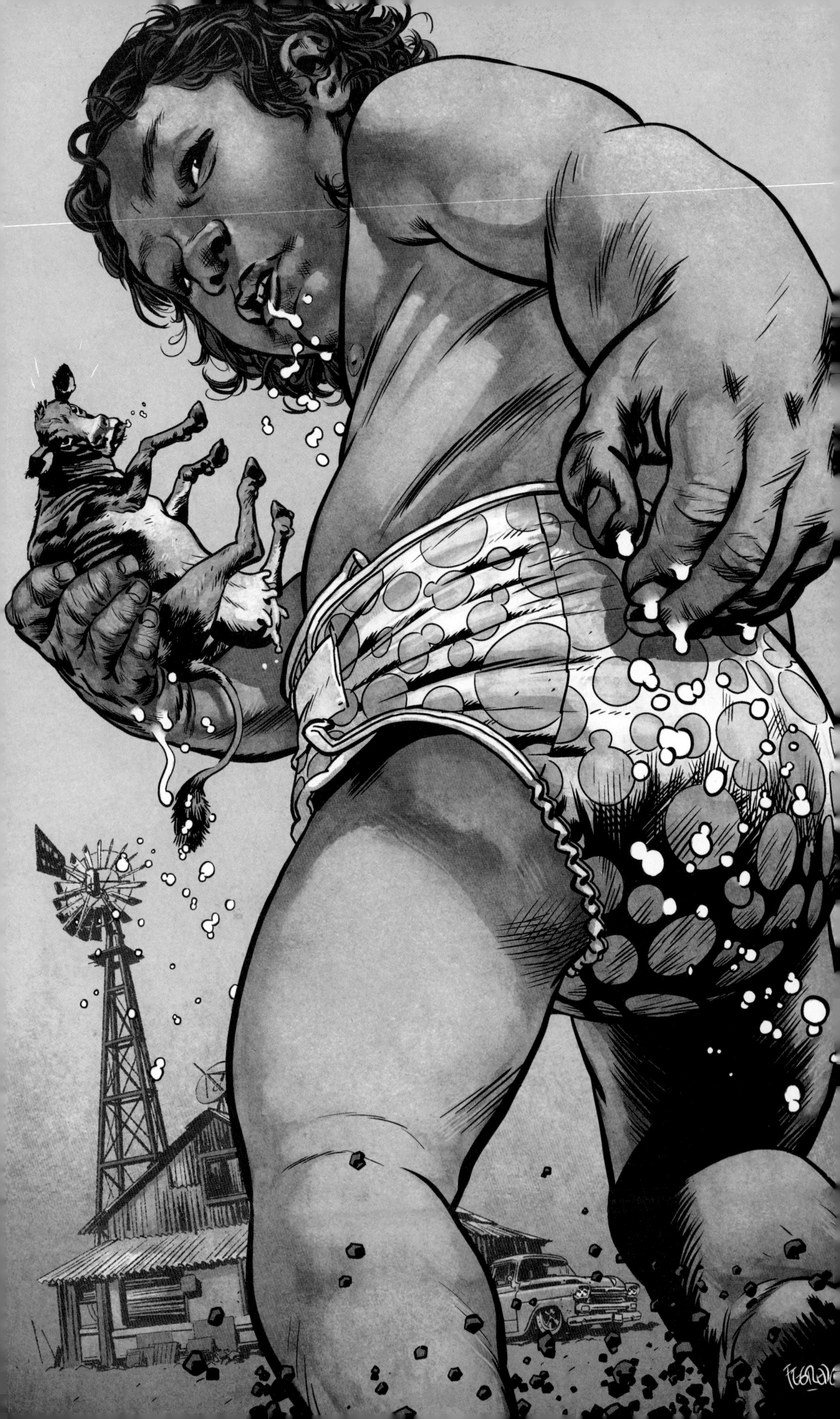

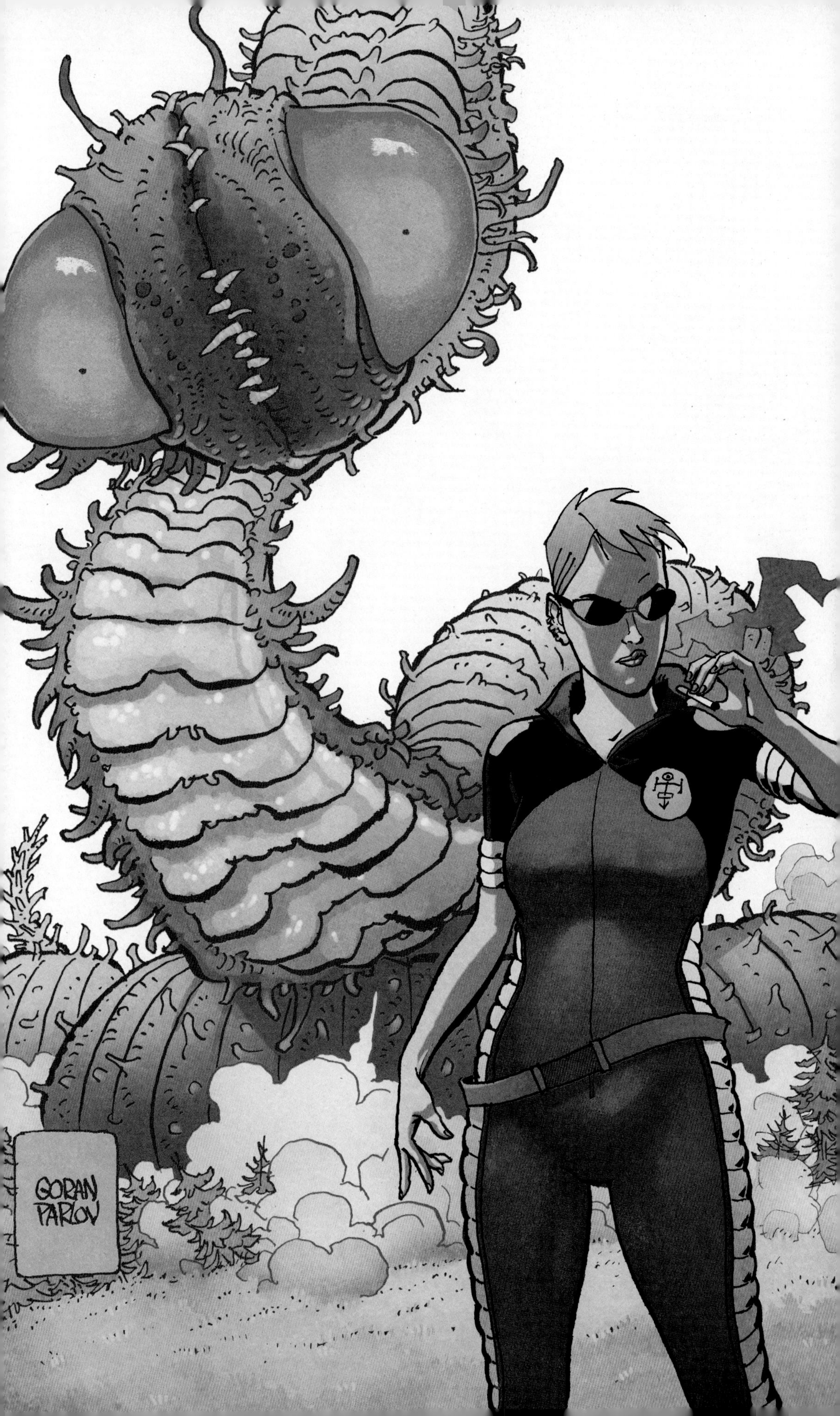
GORAN PARLOV

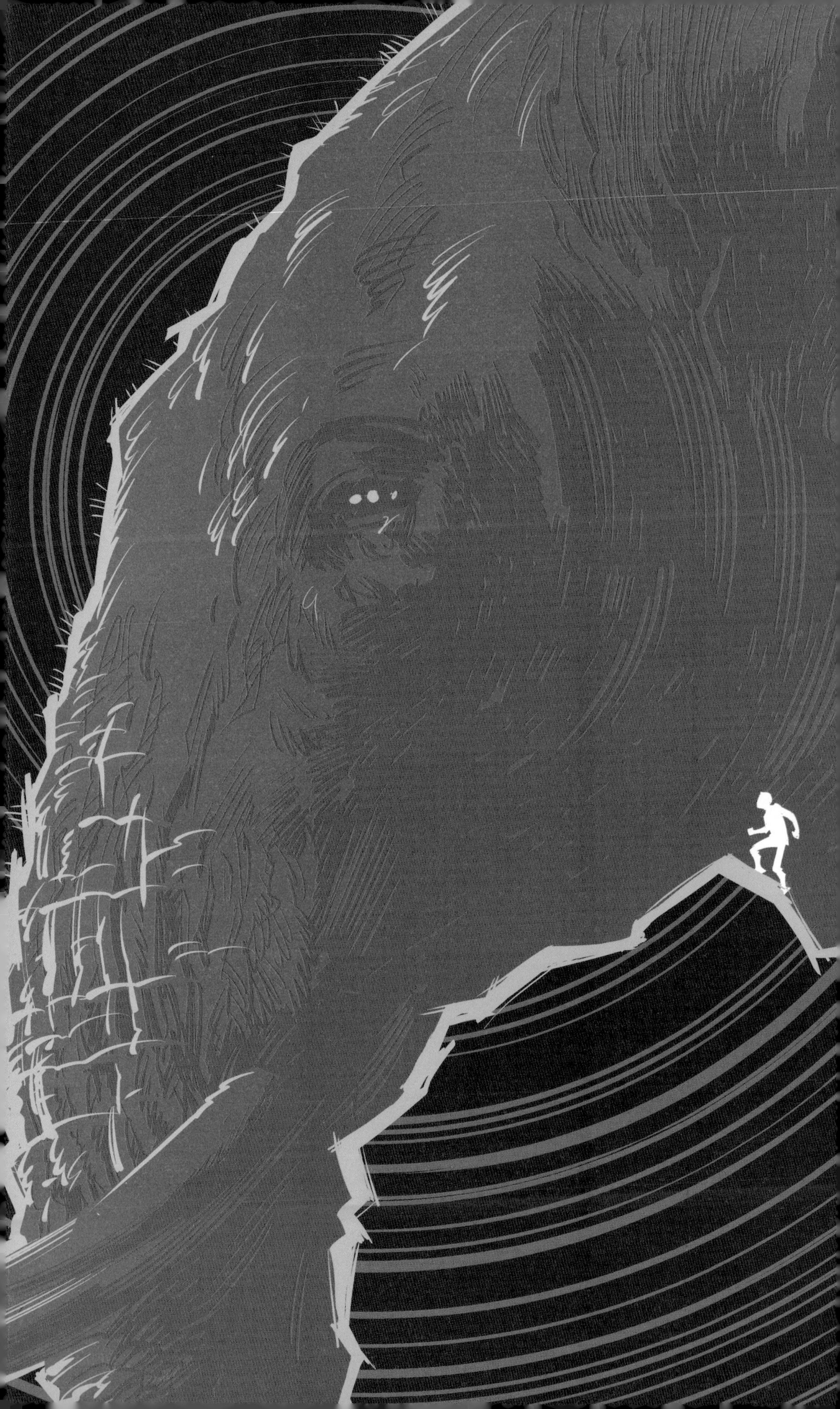

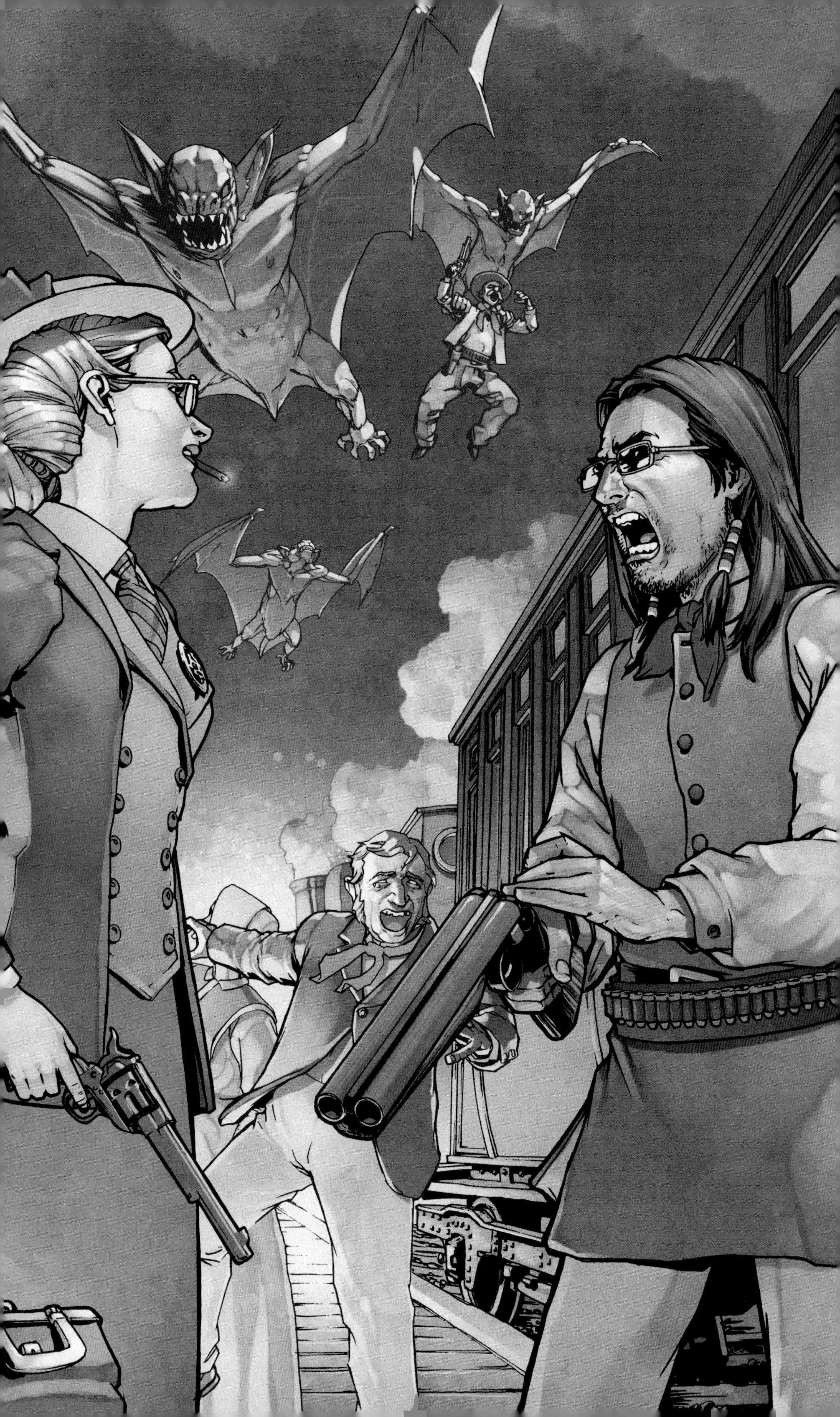

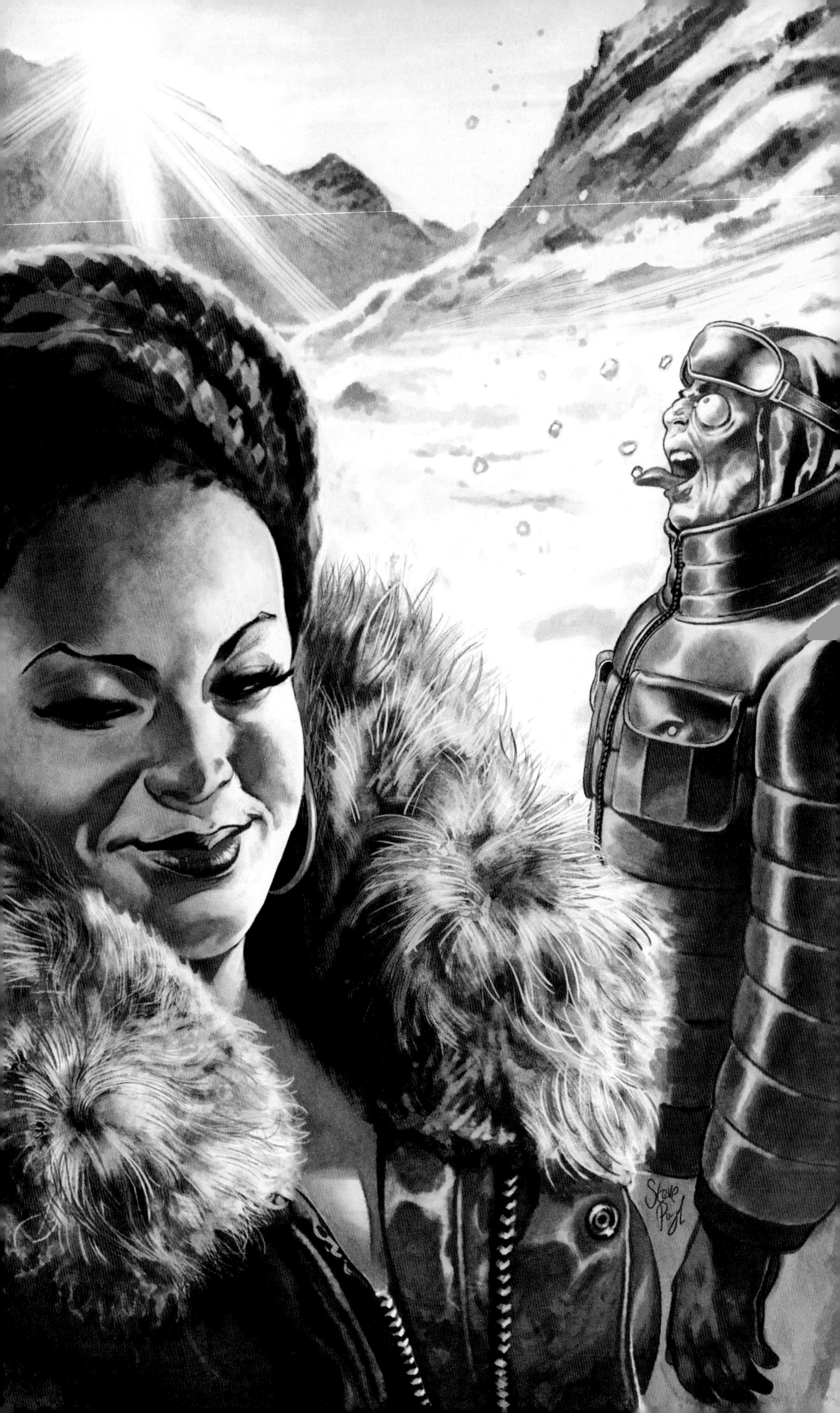

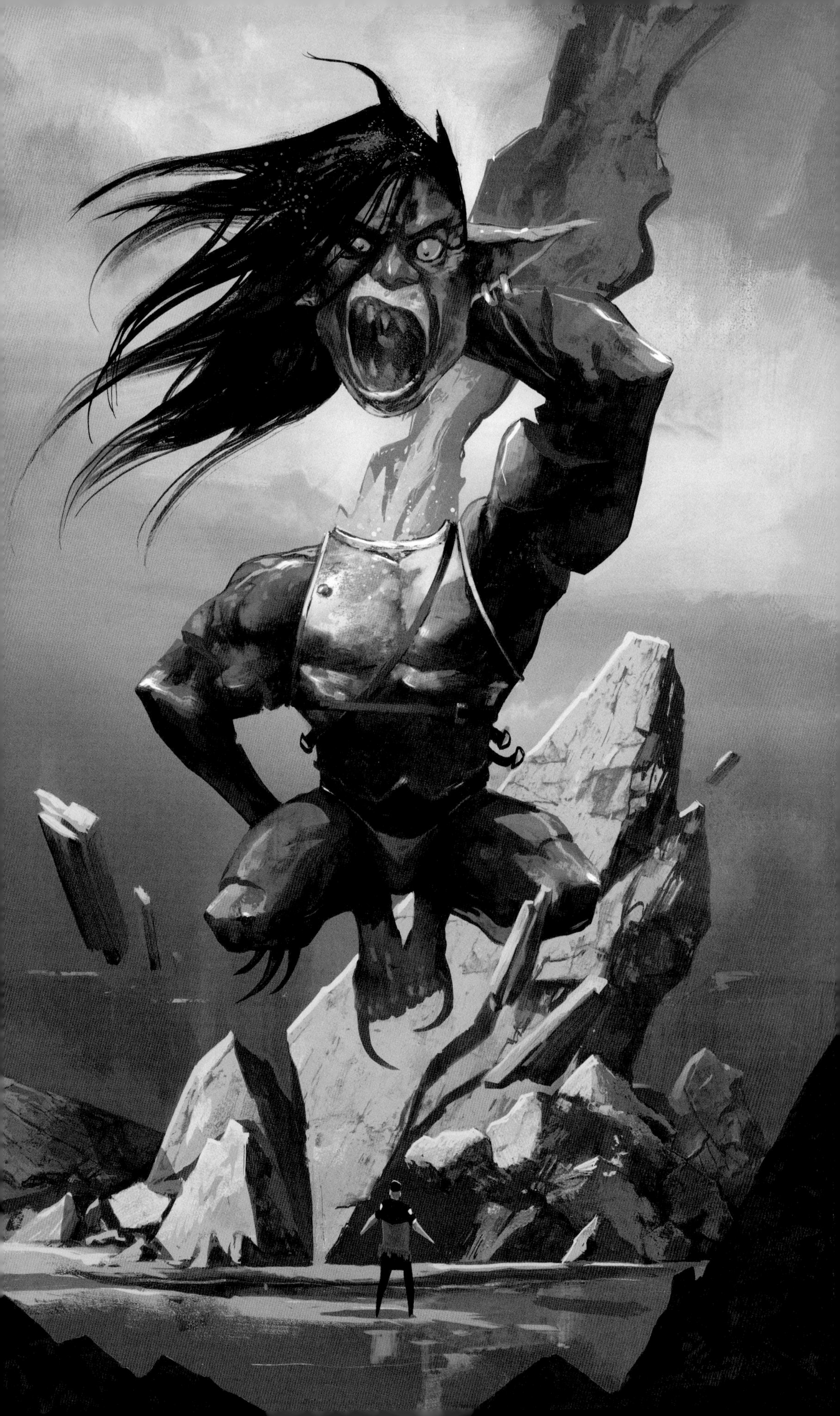

EXTRAS GALLERY
BEHIND THE SCENES OF MYTHIC

THE FOLLOWING PAGES TAKE YOU INSIDE JOHN'S
SKETCHBOOK, SHOWCASING HIS CHARACTER DESIGNS,
COVER ROUGHS AND STORY PAGES IN VARIOUS FORMS.
YOU CAN ALSO SEE SOME CHARACTER DESIGNS FROM
PHIL AND RIAN'S MANY BRILLIANT IDEAS FOR THE BOOK'S
LOGO AND TRADE DRESS.

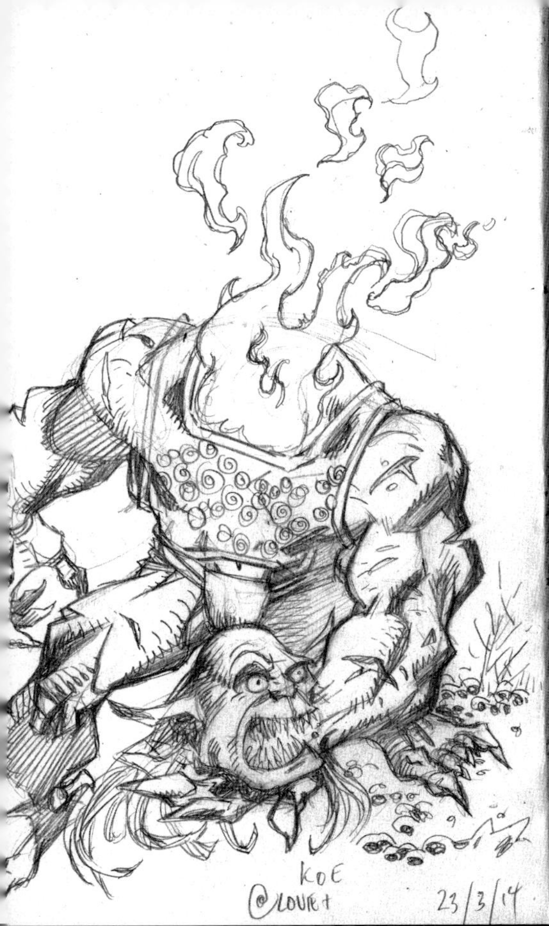
KOE
@LOUIE+
23/3/14

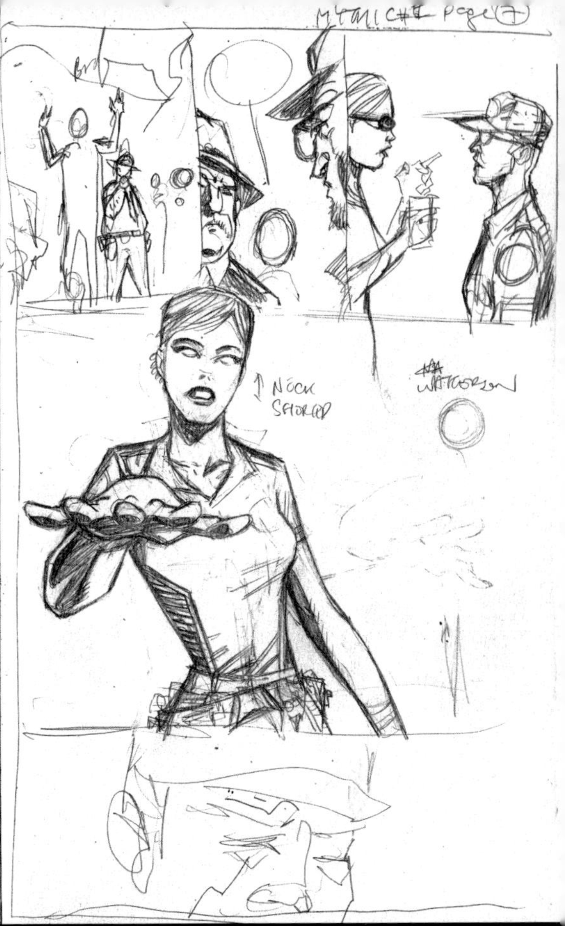
MYTHIC #1 page 7
NECK SHORTER
WATTERSON

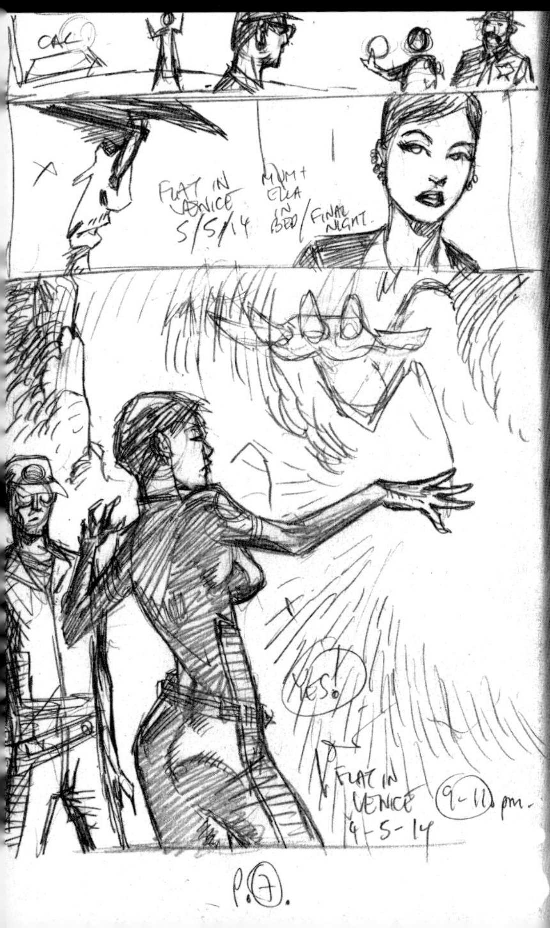
FLAT IN VENICE 5/5/14
MUM + ELLA IN BED / FINAL NIGHT.
YES!
FLAT IN VENICE 4-5-14
9-11 pm.
P. 7.

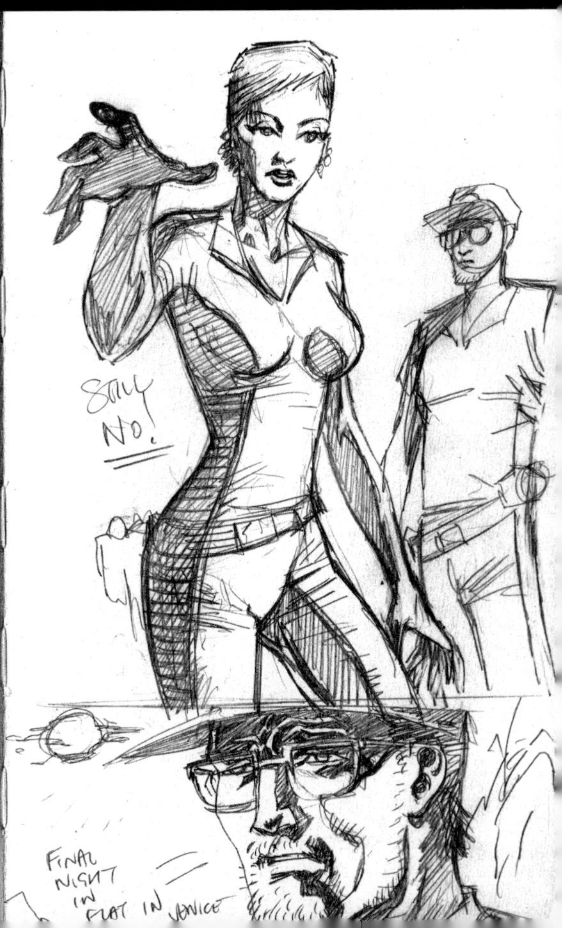
STILL NO!
FINAL NIGHT IN FLAT IN VENICE

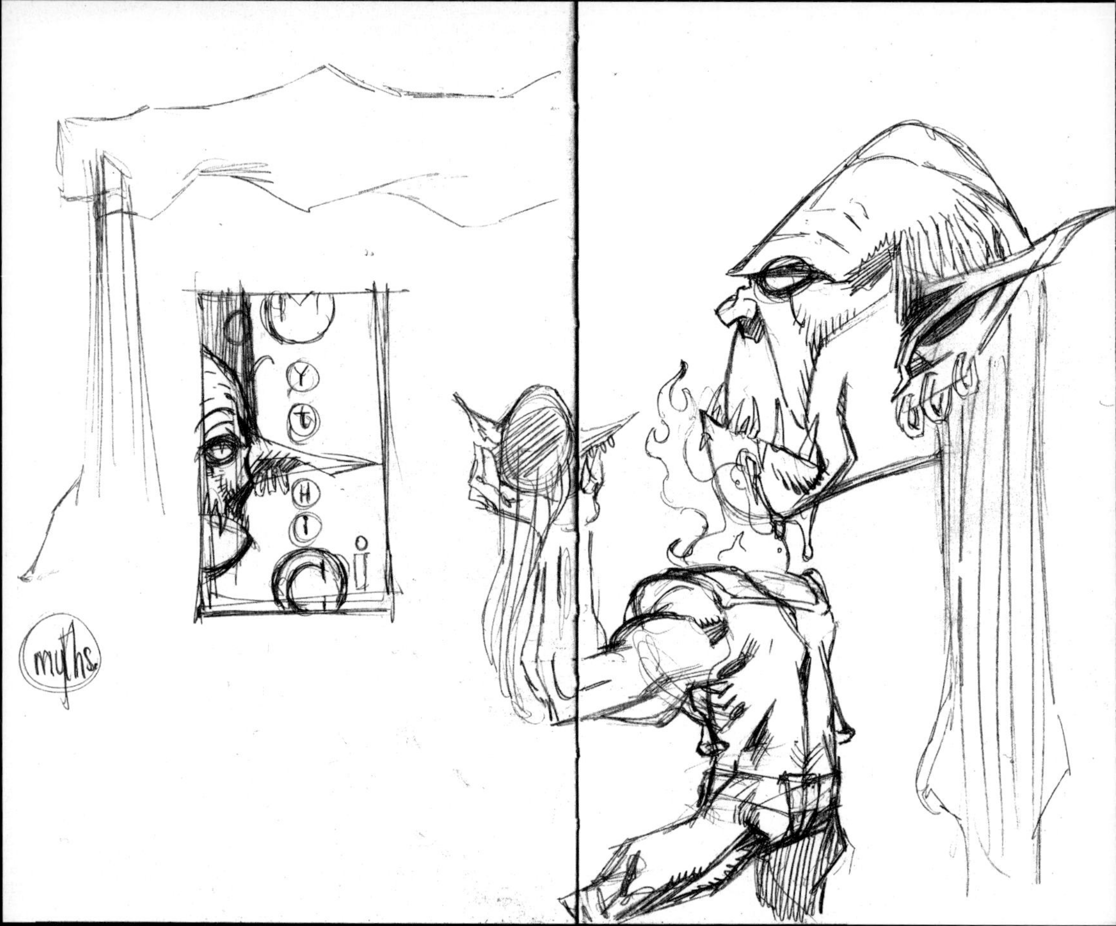
myths

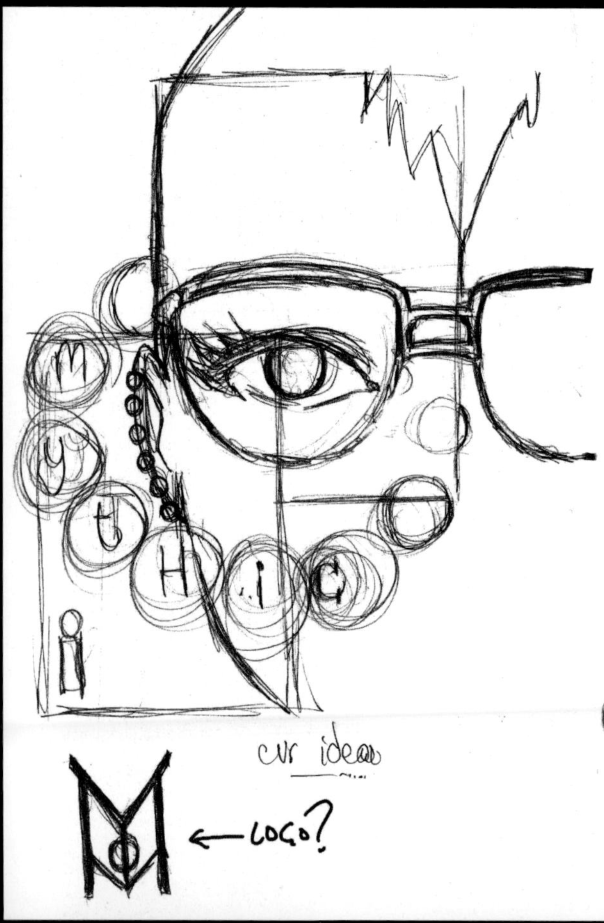
cvr idea
LOGO?

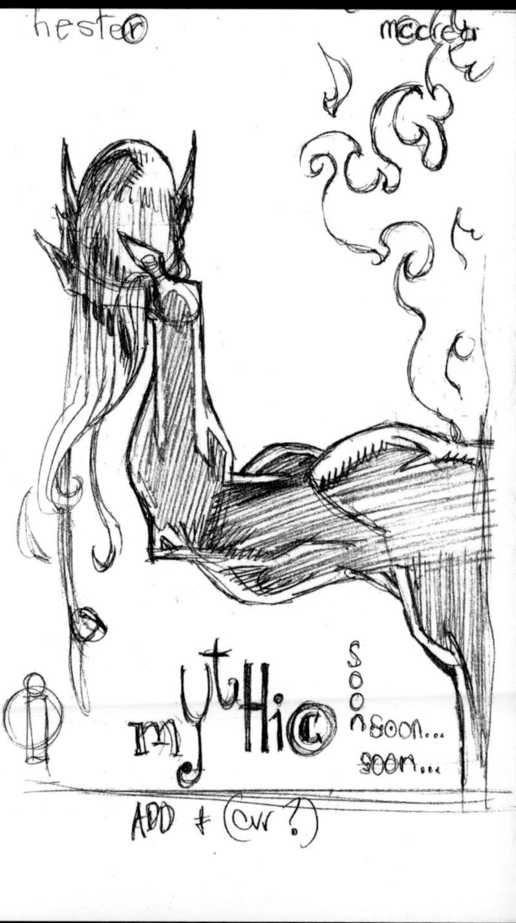
hester
mythic
soon soon... soon...
ADD + (cvr?)

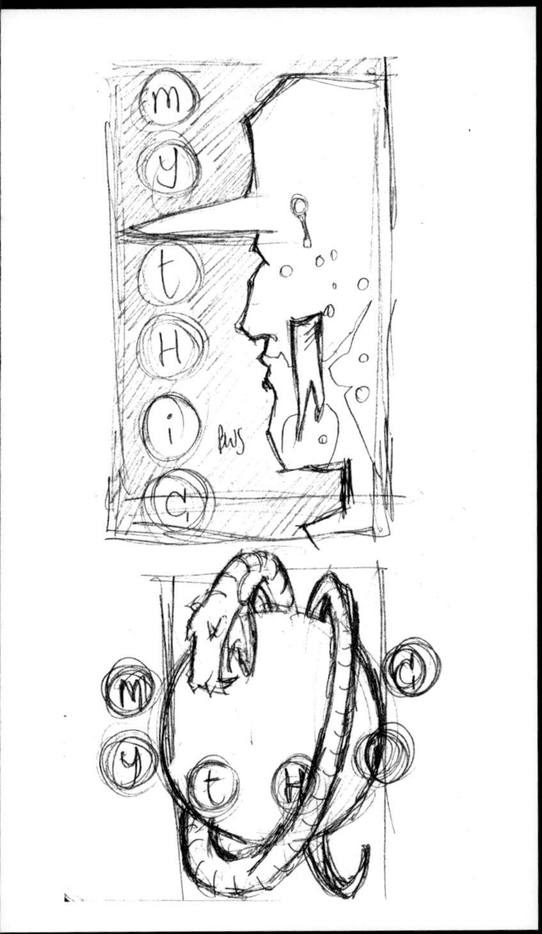
m
y
t
H
i
c
BWS
m
y
t
H
c

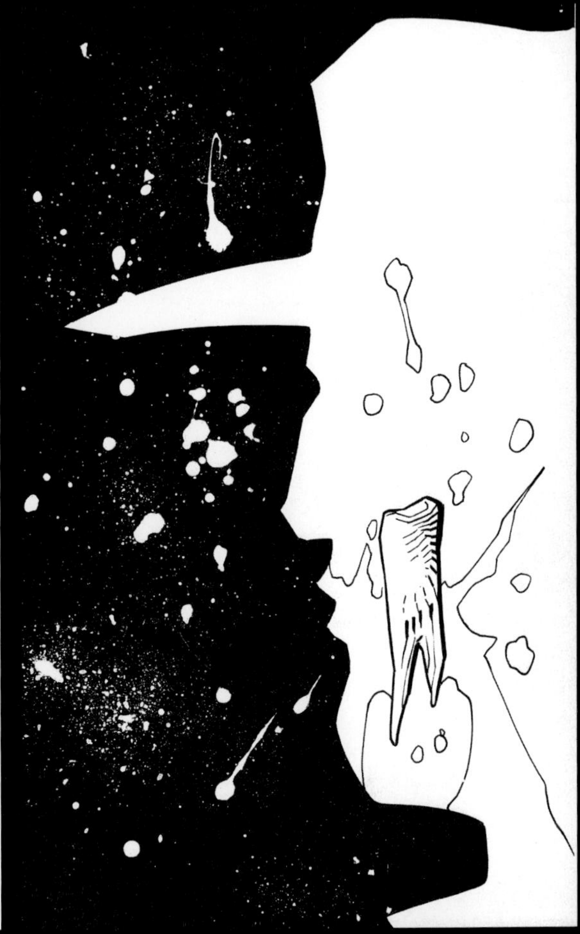

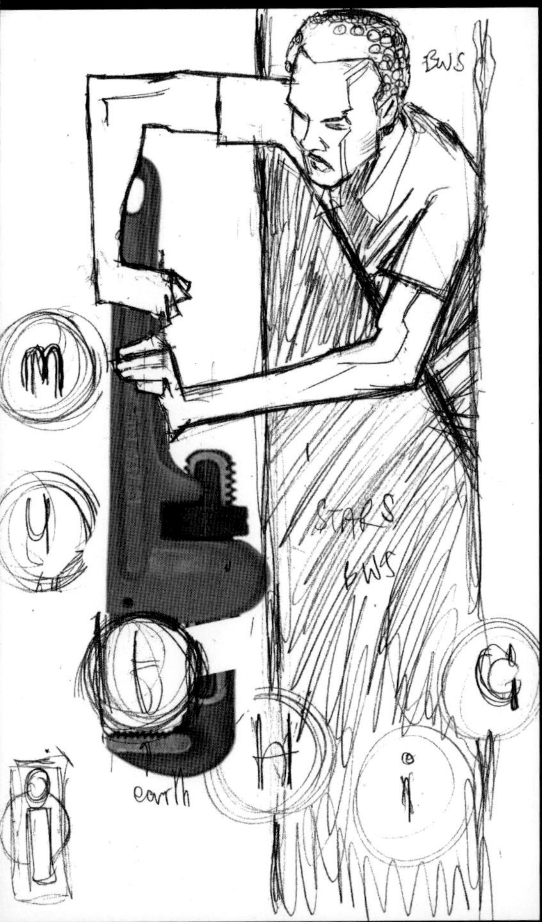
BWS
STARS
BWS
m
y
earth
i
c

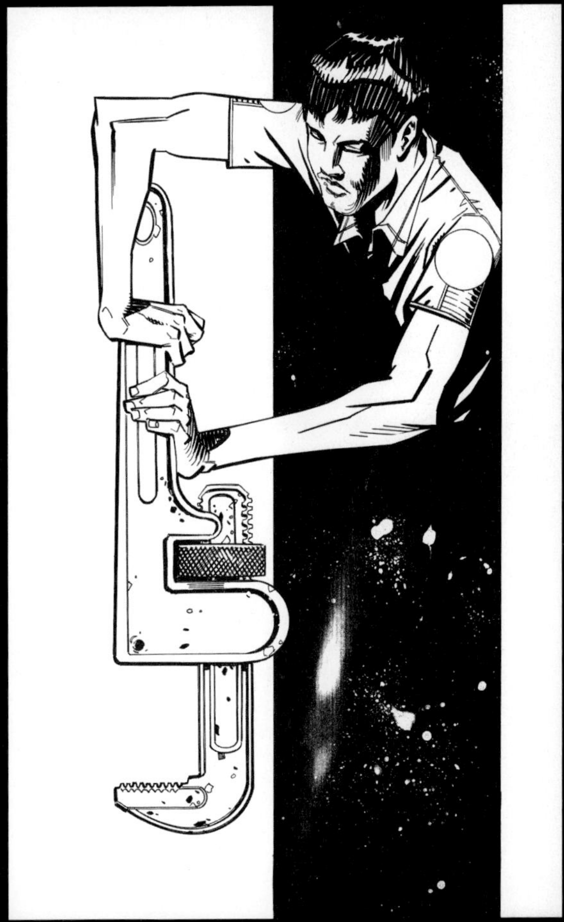

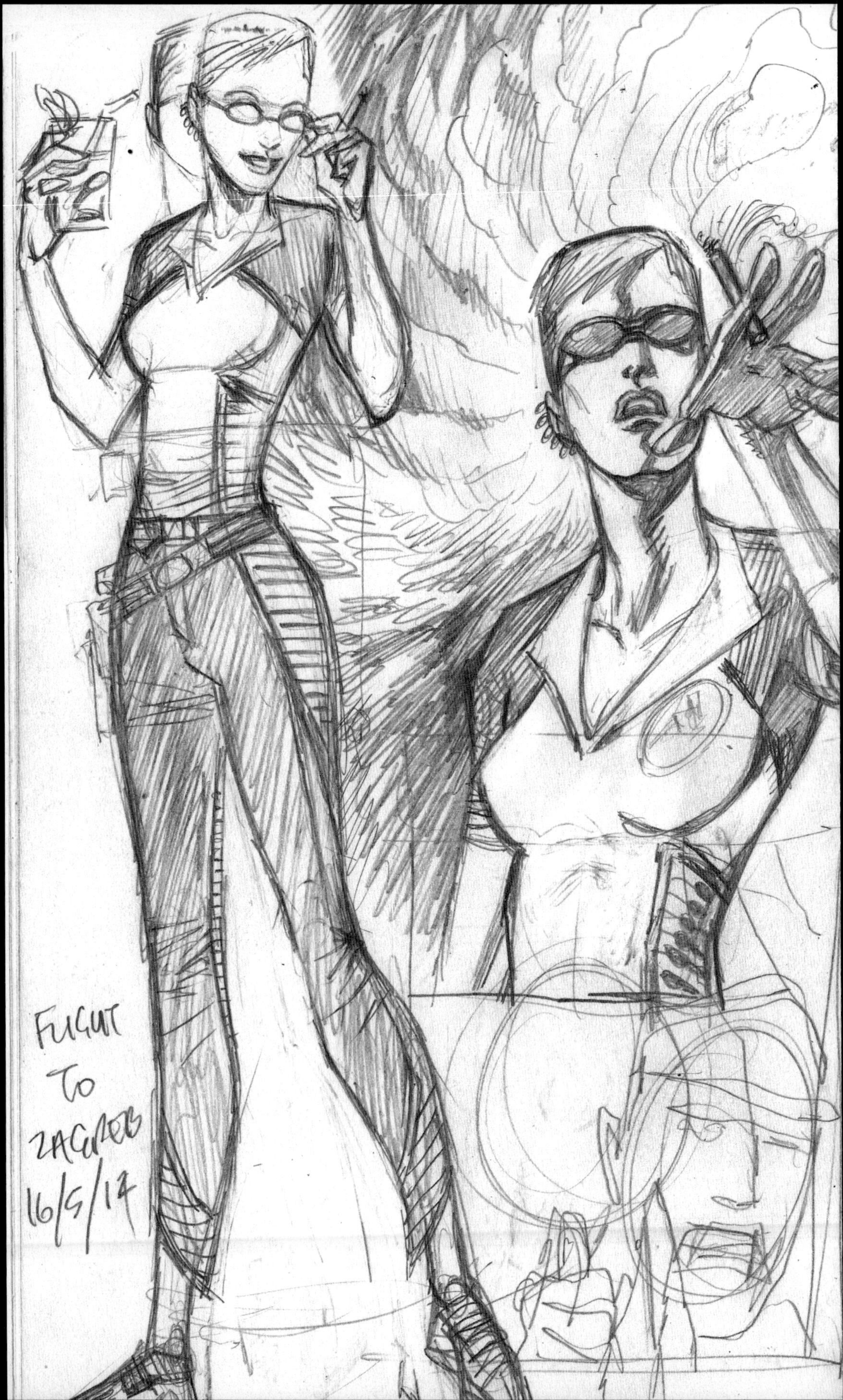
FLIGHT
TO
ZAGREB
16/5/14

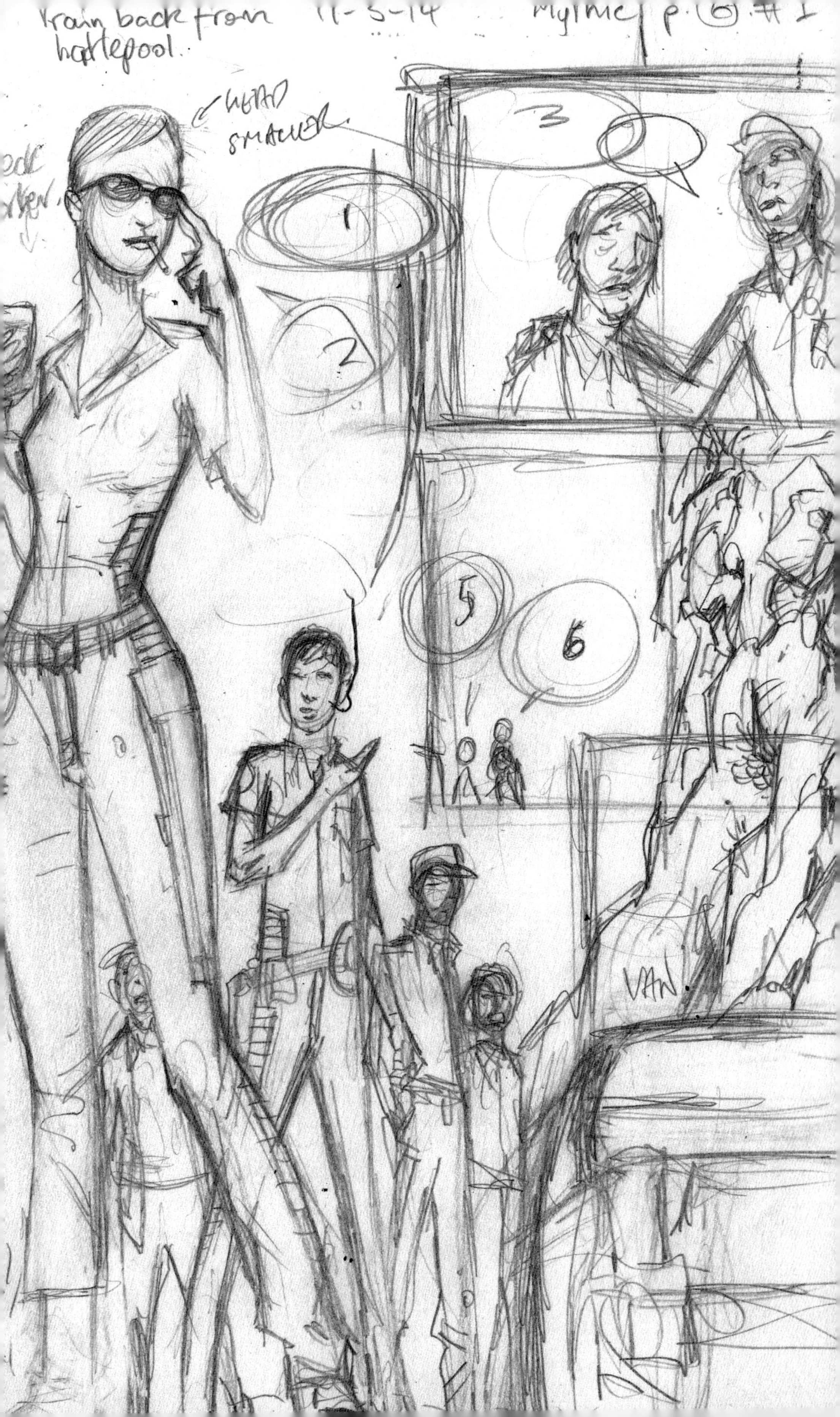
train back from
hartlepool.
11-5-14
HEAD
SMACKER
VAN.

MYTHIC P.13.
#1

11-4-14
AIRPORT
LOUNGE
TO DUBLIN

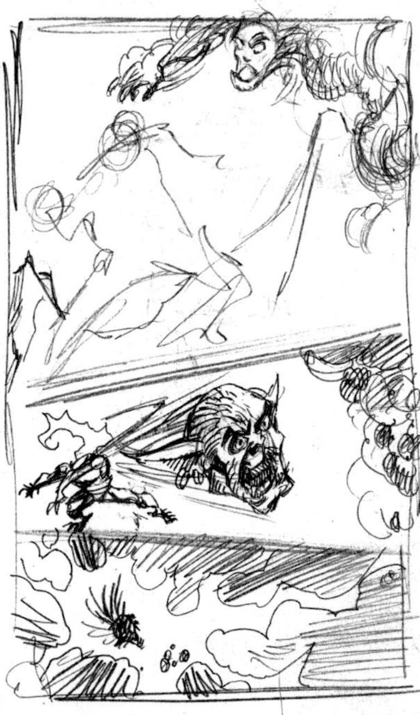

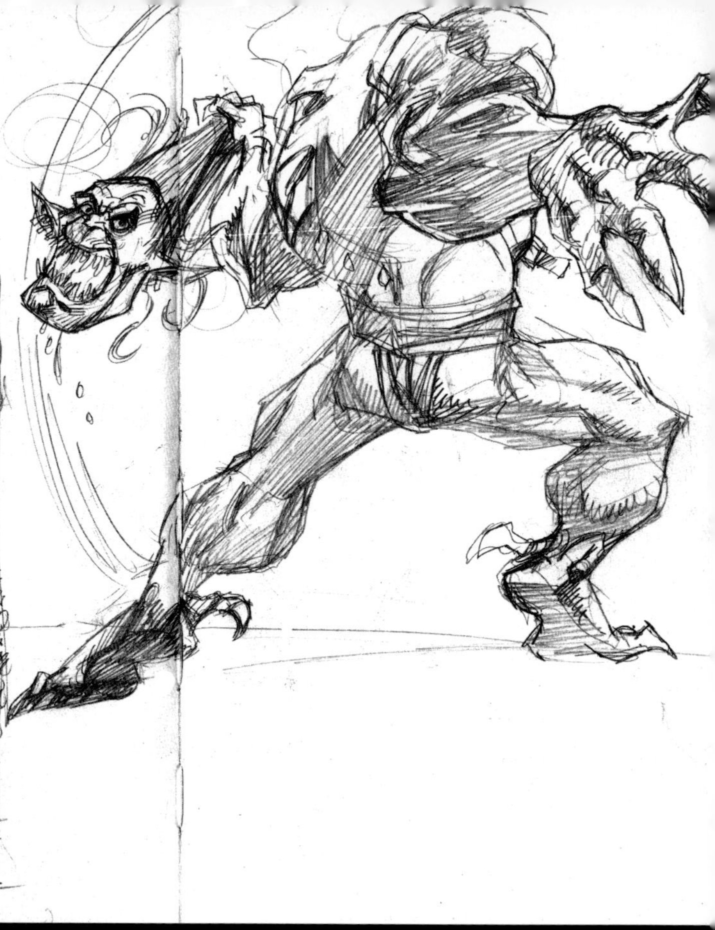

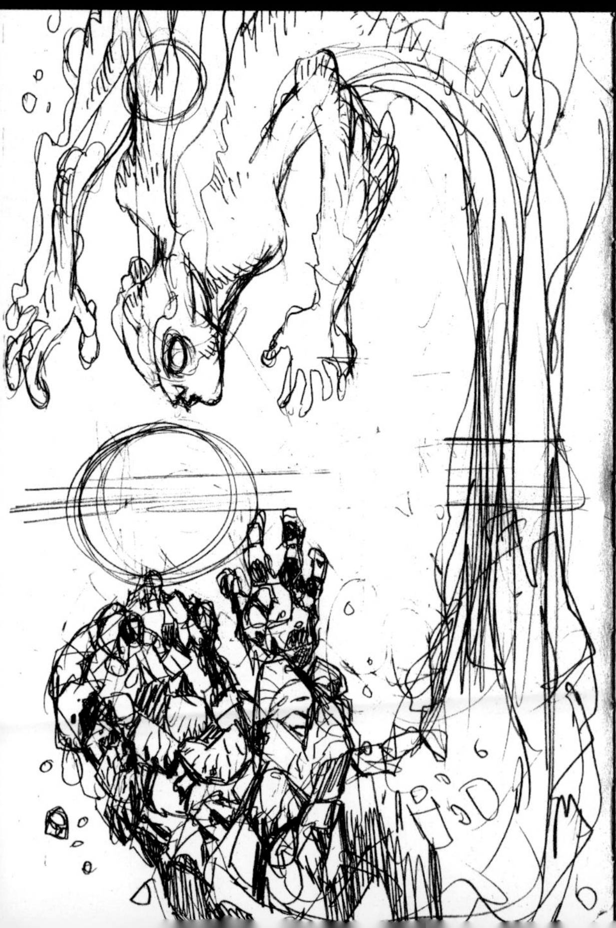

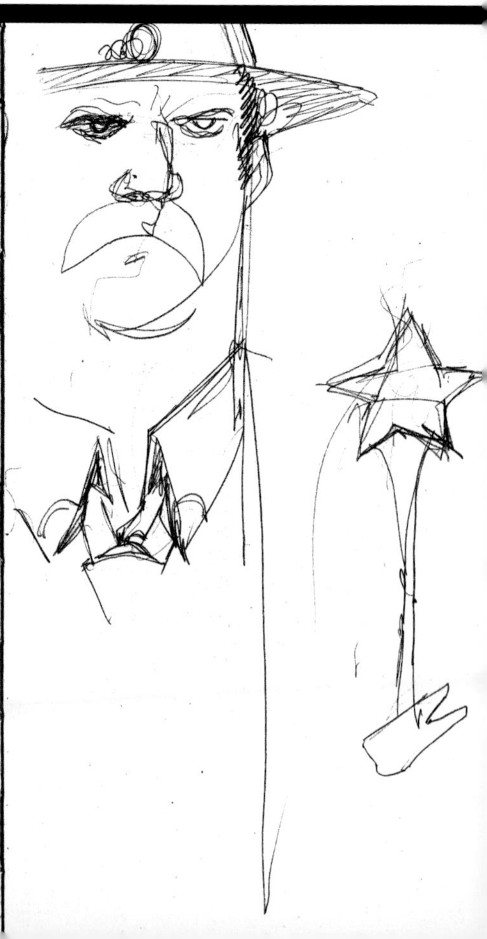

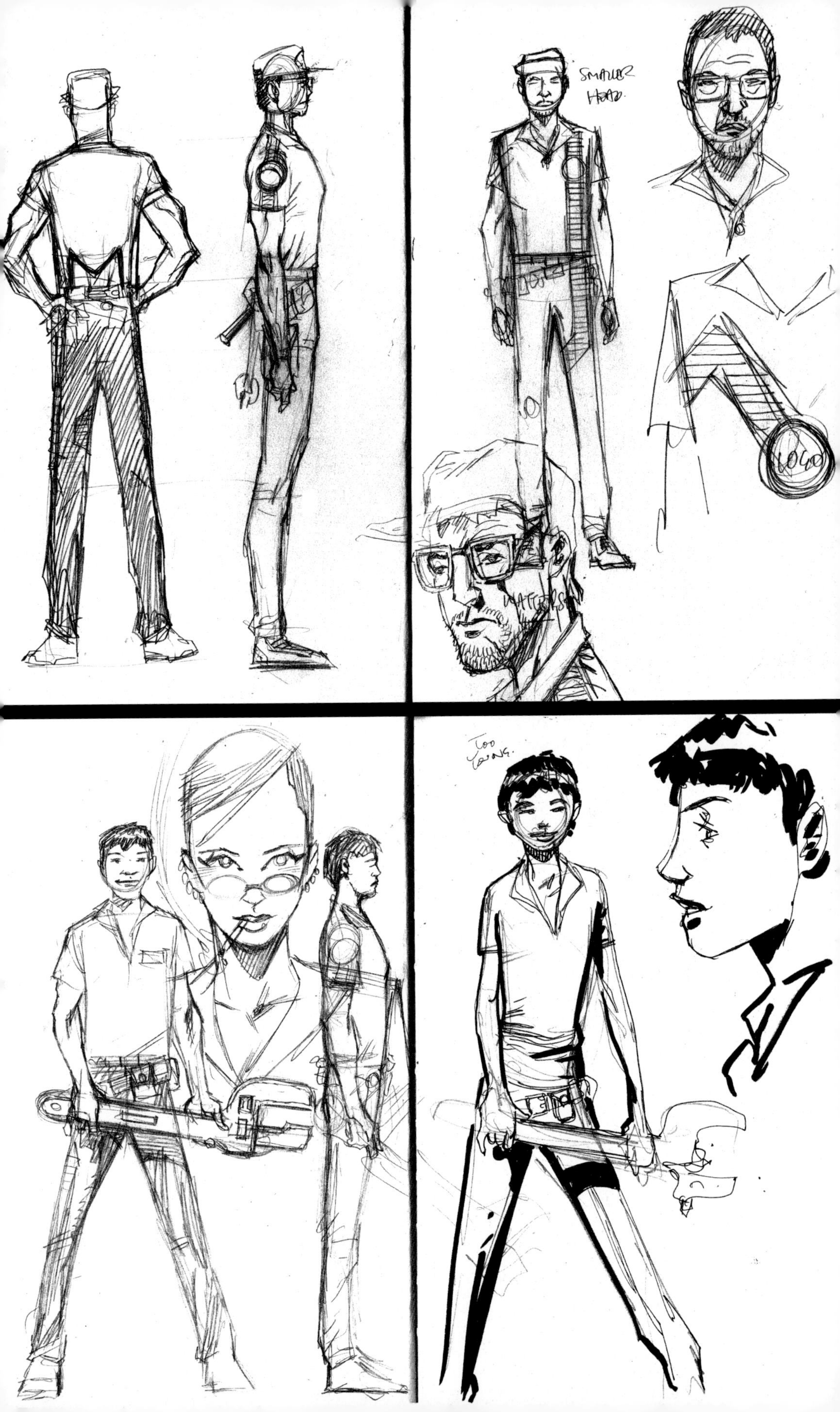
SMALLER HEAD.
LOGO
TOO YOUNG.

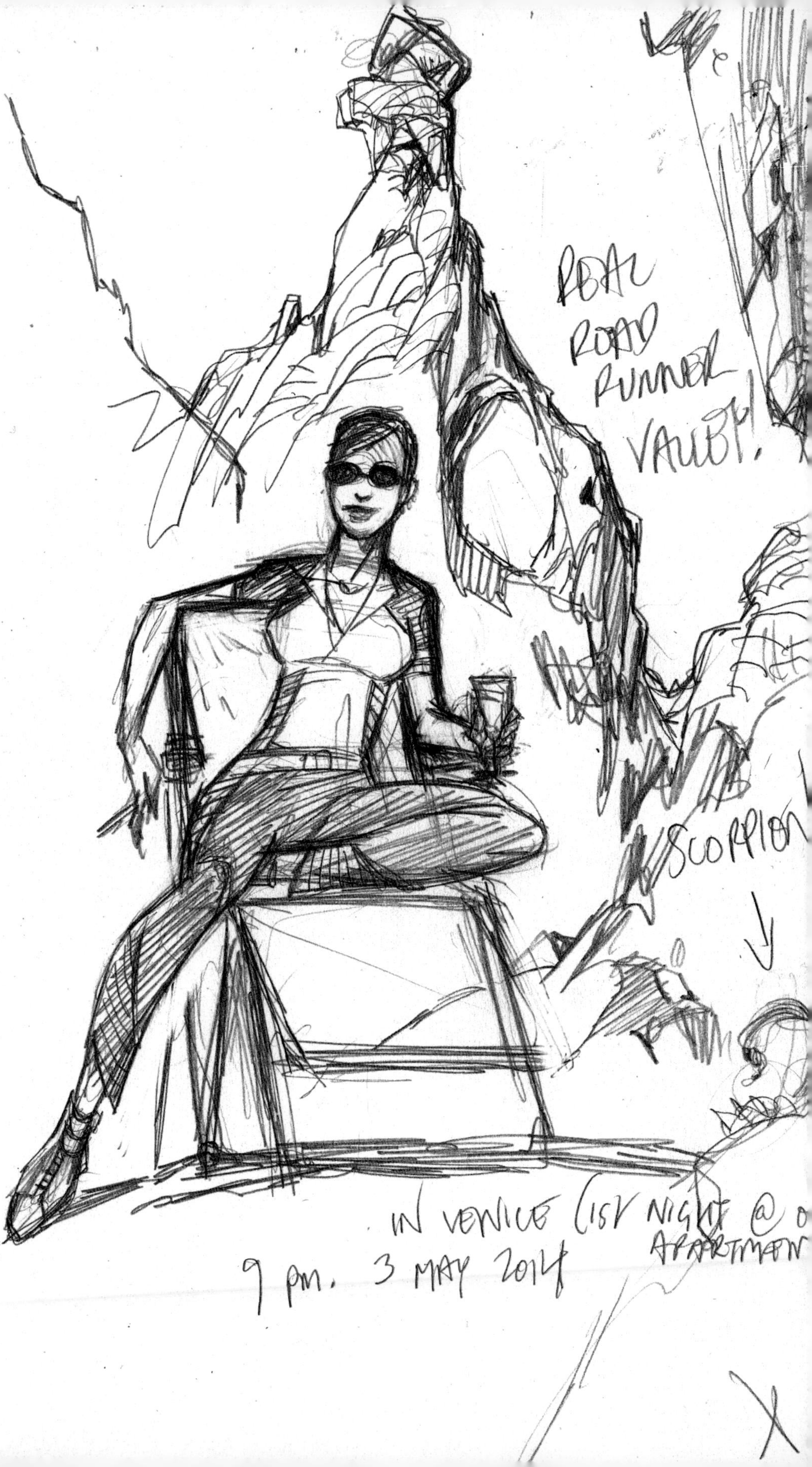
REAL ROAD RUNNER VAULT!
SCORPION
IN VENICE LAST NIGHT @
APARTMEN
9 pm. 3 MAY 2014

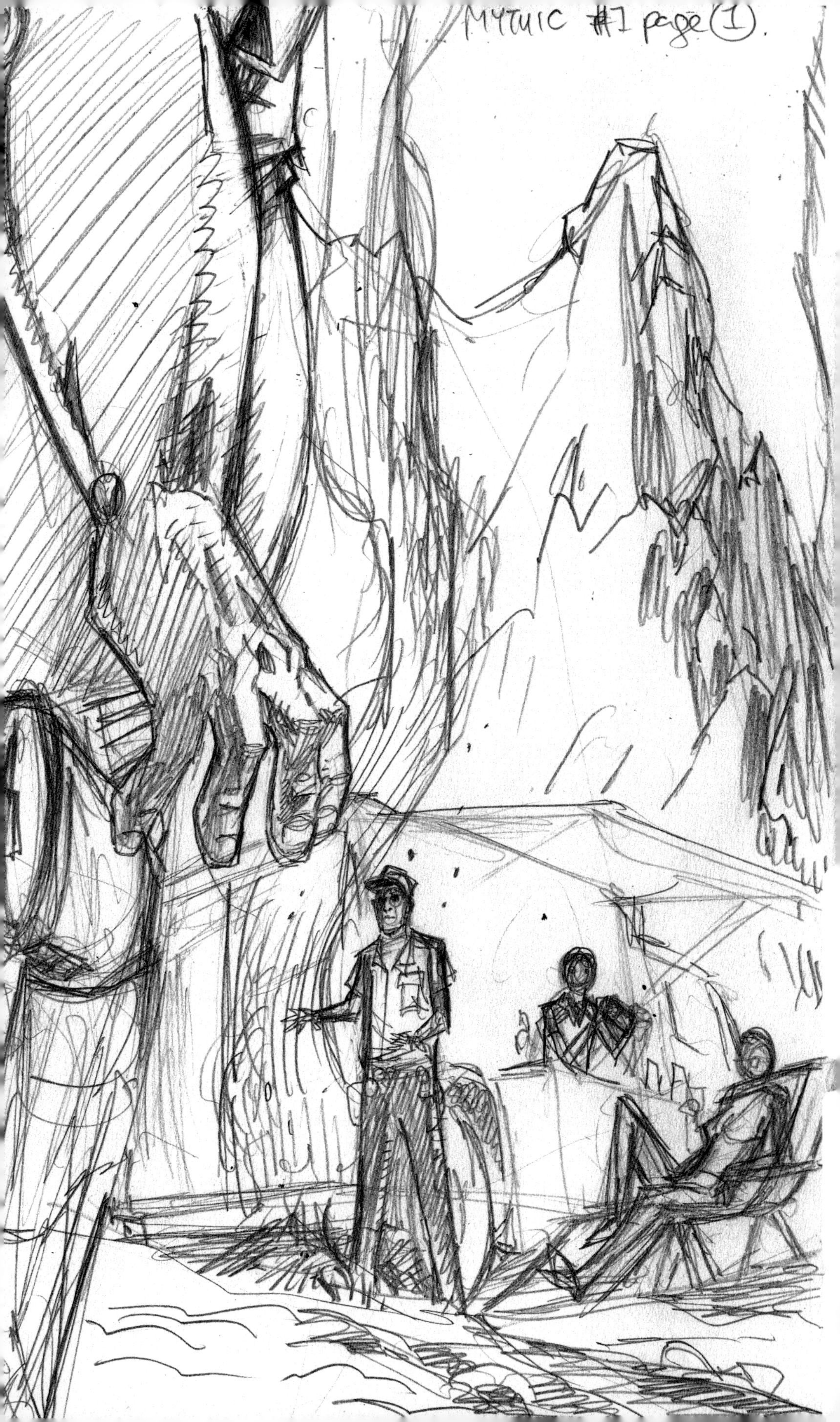
MYTHIC #1 page (1)

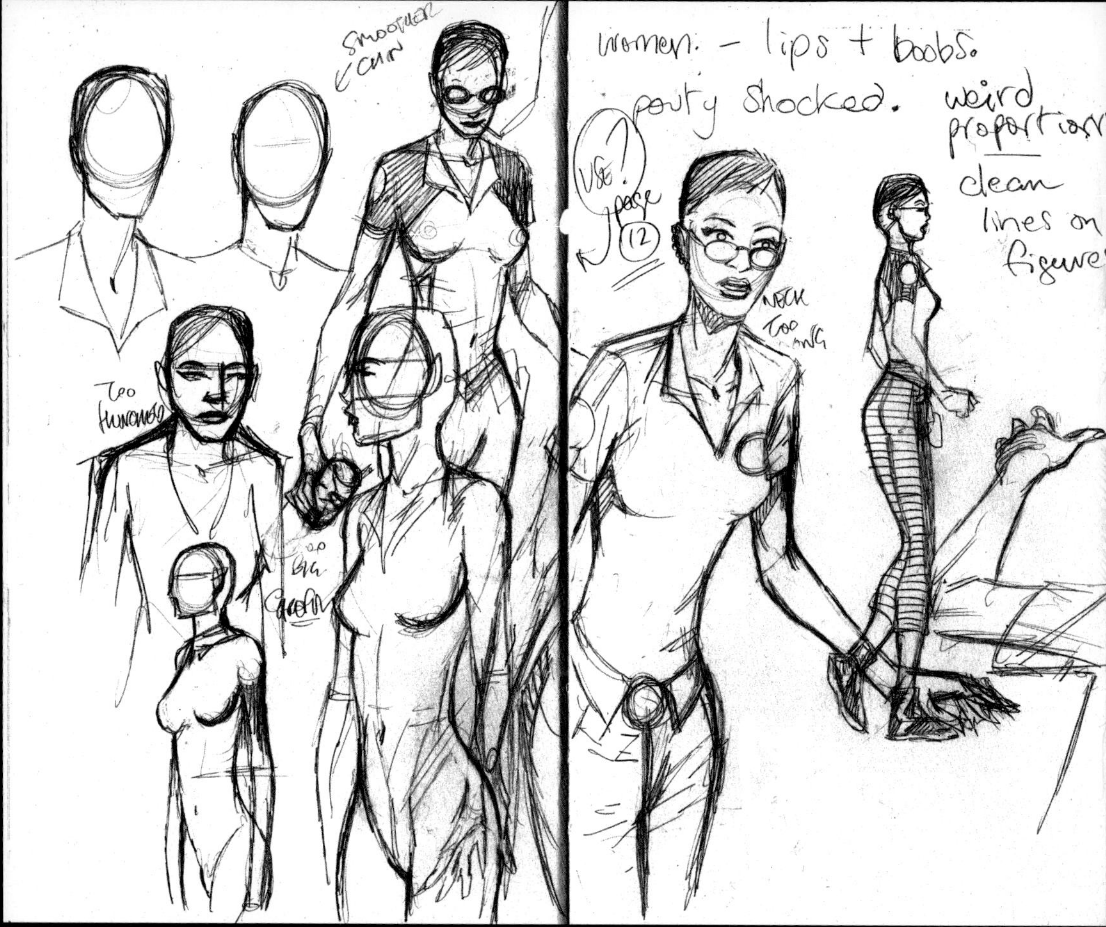

SMOOTHER CHIN
TOO HUNCHED
TOO BIG CHIN
women: - lips + boobs.
pouty shocked.
weird proportions
clean lines on figures
USE? page 12
NECK TOO LONG

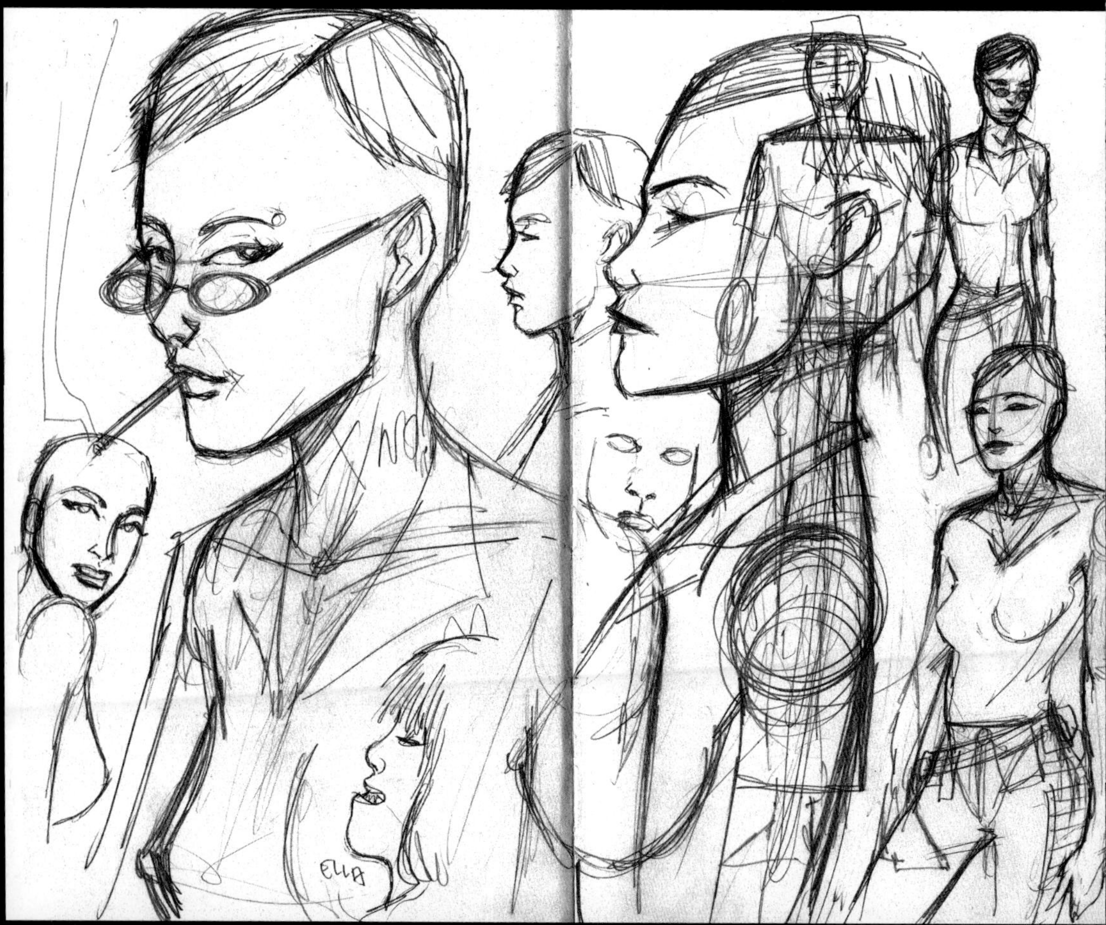

NO!
ELLA

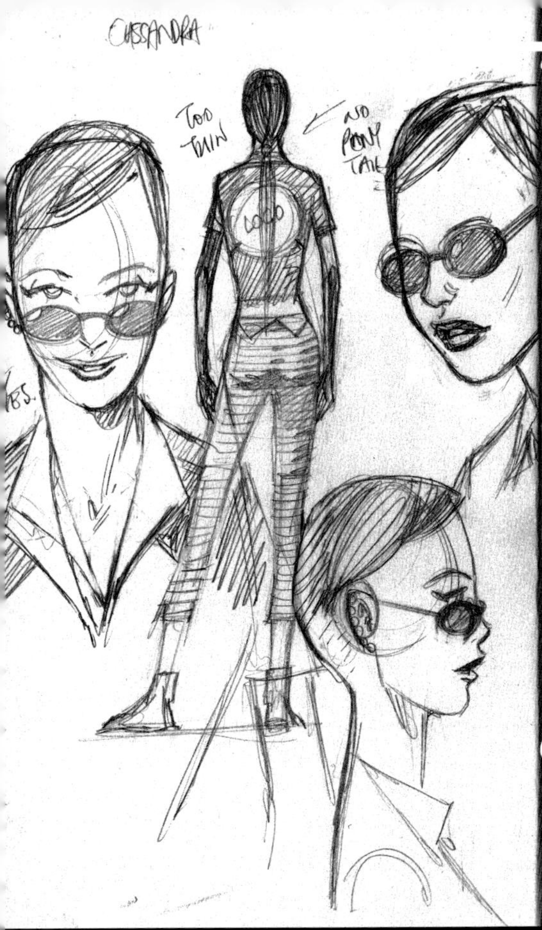
CASSANDRA
TOO THIN
NO PONY TAIL
LOGO

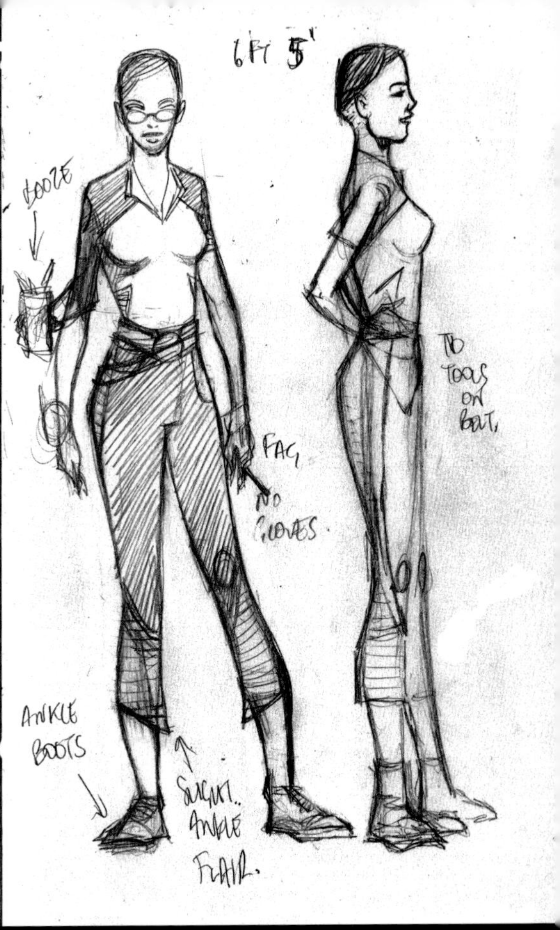
6FT 5'
BOOZE
TO TOOLS ON BELT.
FAG,
NO GLOVES
ANKLE BOOTS
SLIGHT.. ANKLE FLAIR.

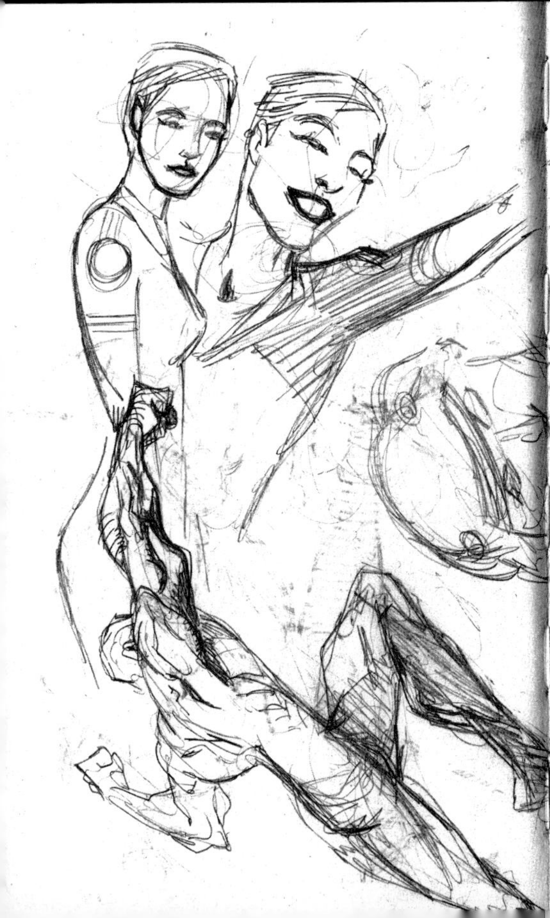

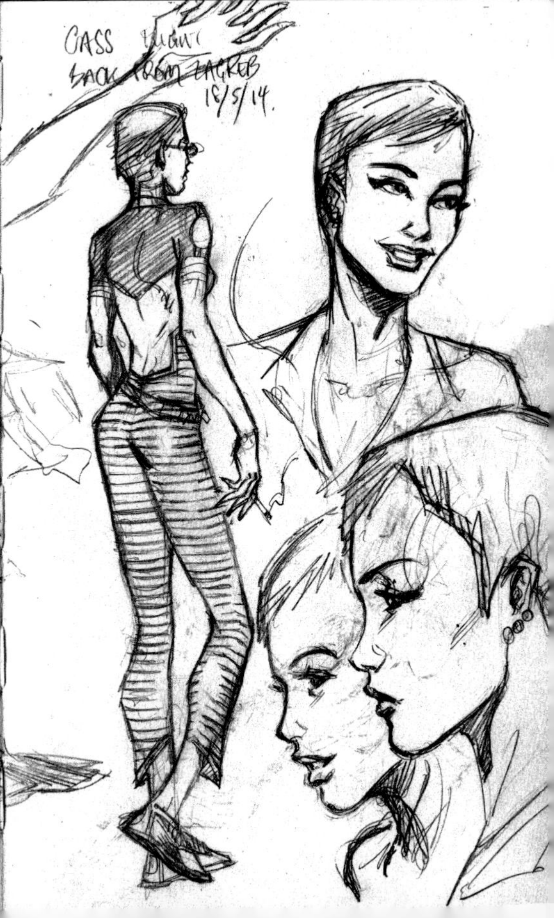
CASS
BACK FROM ZAGREB
18/5/14.

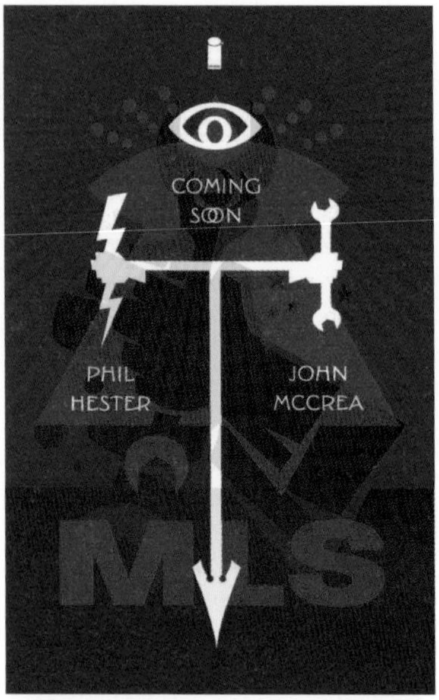
COMING
SOON
PHIL
HESTER
JOHN
MCCREA
MLS

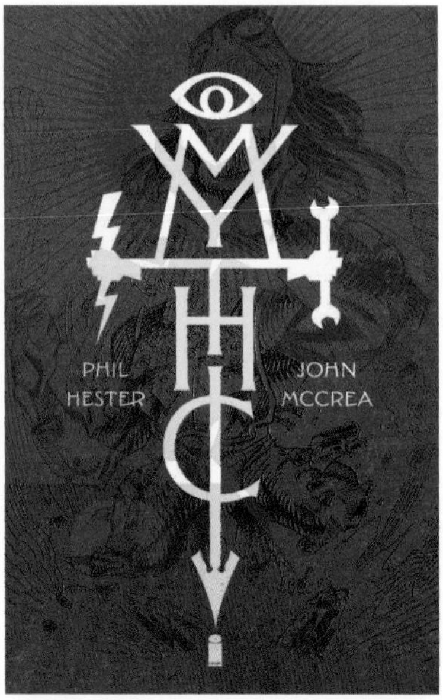
MYTHIC
PHIL
HESTER
JOHN
MCCREA

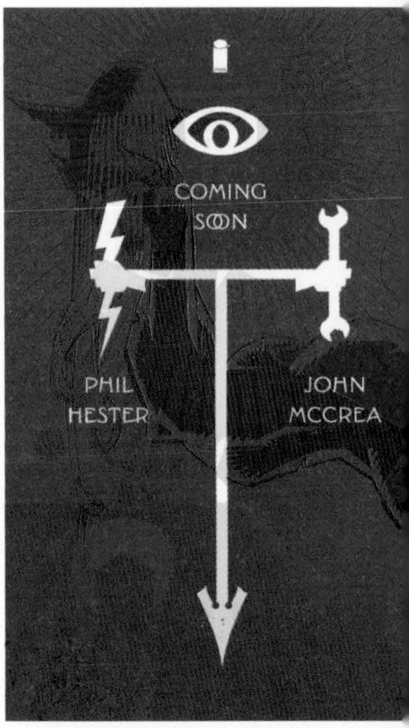
COMING
SOON
PHIL
HESTER
JOHN
MCCREA

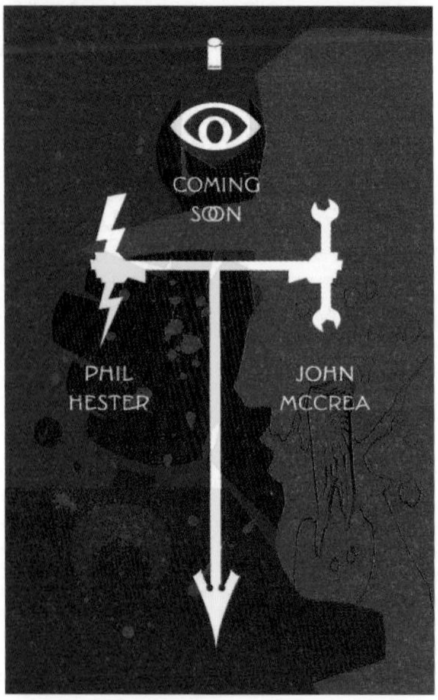
COMING
SOON
PHIL
HESTER
JOHN
MCCREA

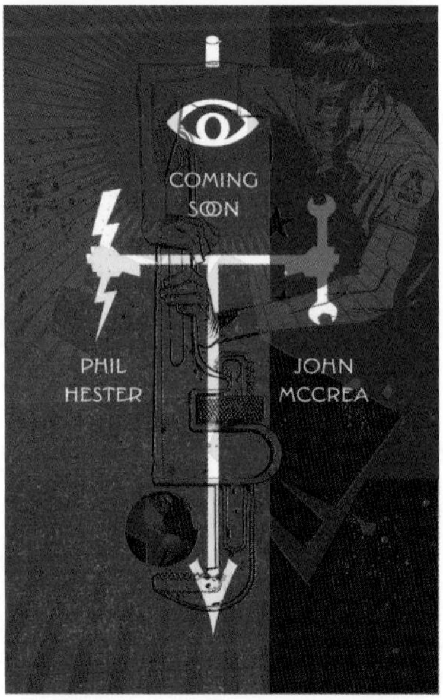
COMING
SOON
PHIL
HESTER
JOHN
MCCREA

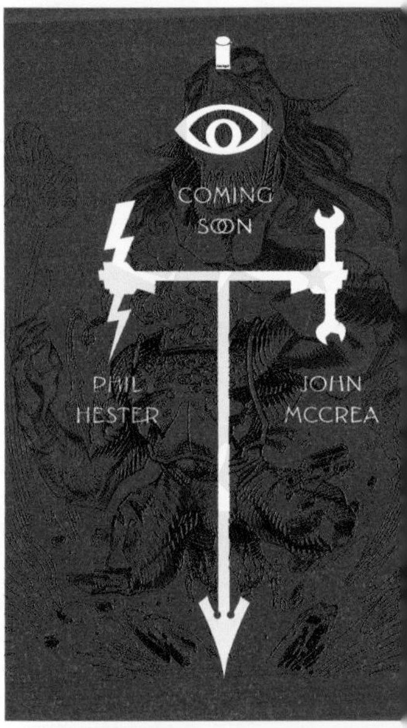
COMING
SOON
PHIL
HESTER
JOHN
MCCREA

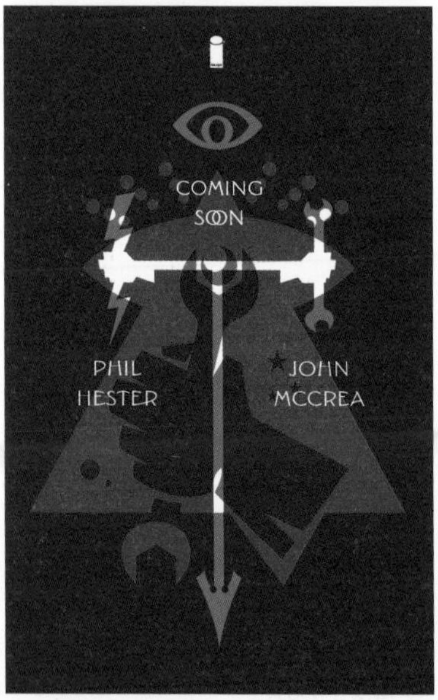
COMING
SOON
PHIL
HESTER
JOHN
MCCREA

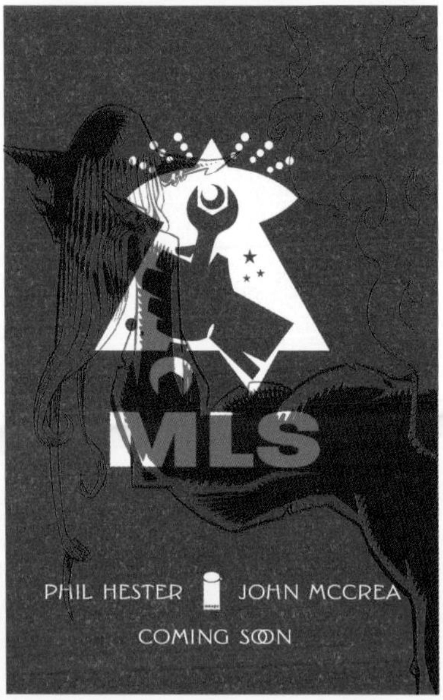
MLS
PHIL HESTER
JOHN MCCREA
COMING SOON

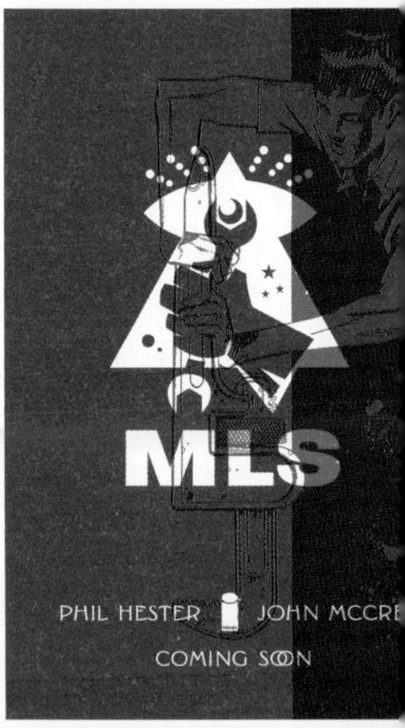
MLS
PHIL HESTER
JOHN MCCRE
COMING SOON

MYTHIC
MYTHIC
Mythic
PHIL HESTER
JOHN MCCREA
PHIL HESTER
JOHN MCCREA
PHIL HESTER
JOHN MCCREA
PHIL HESTER
JOHN MCCREA

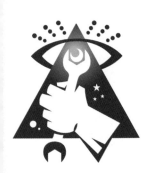

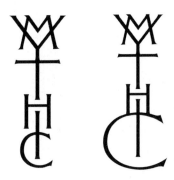

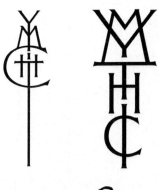

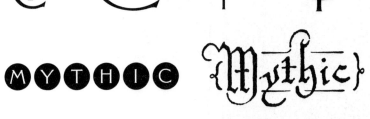

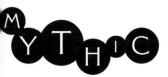

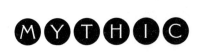

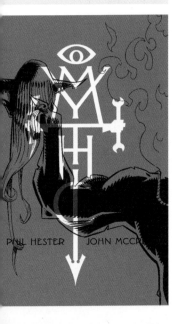

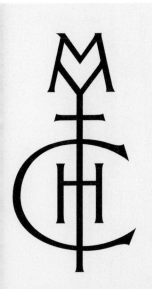

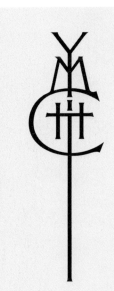

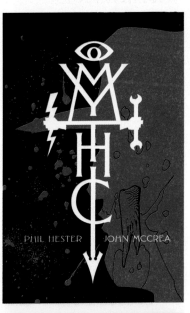

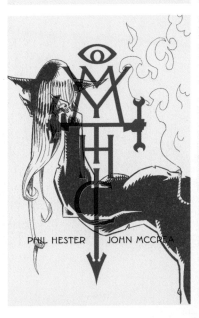

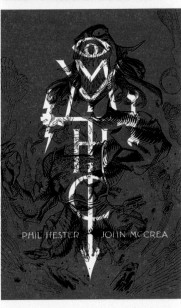

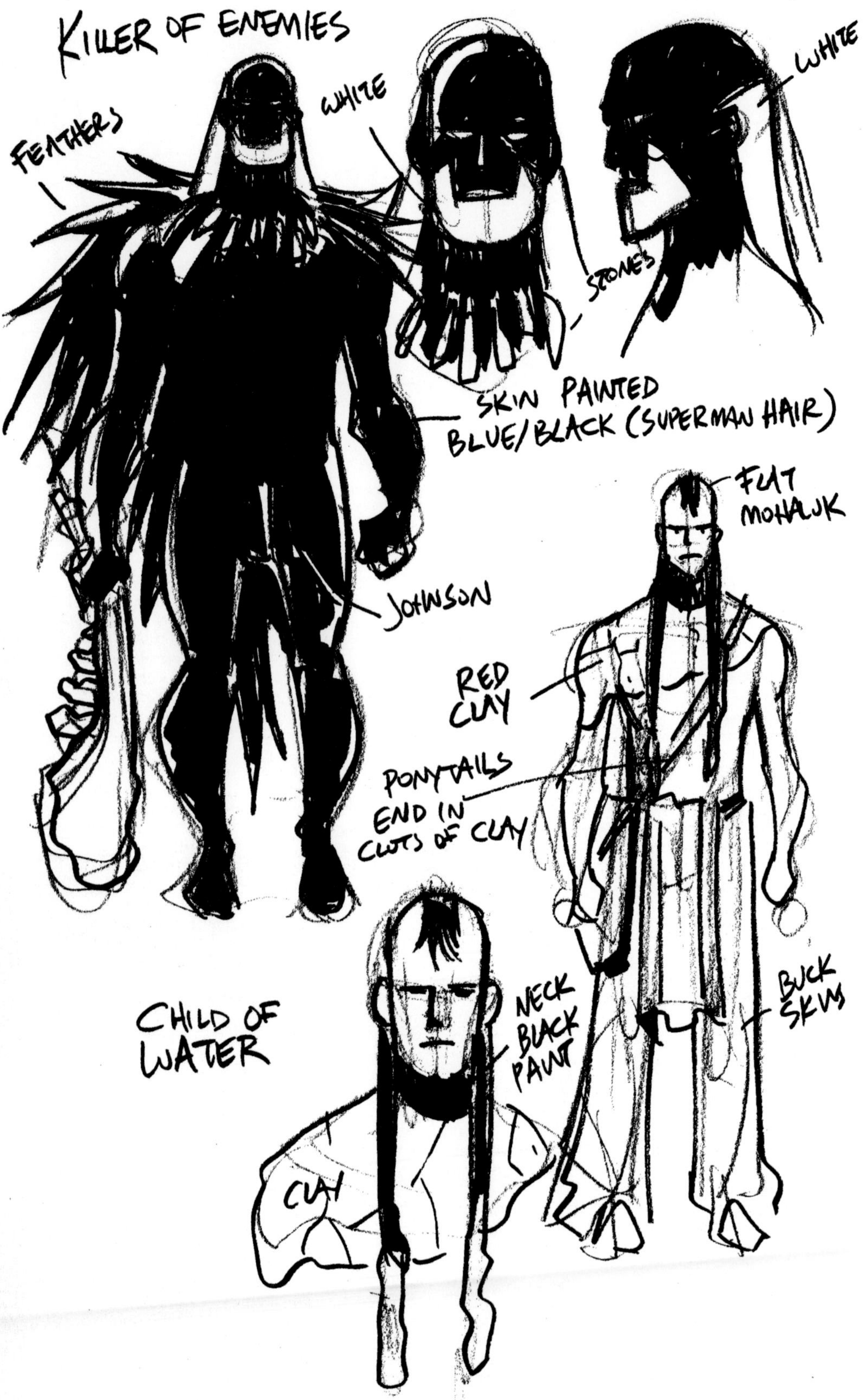
KILLER OF ENEMIES
FEATHERS
WHITE
WHITE
STONES
SKIN PAINTED
BLUE/BLACK (SUPERMAN HAIR)
JOHNSON
FLAT
MOHAWK
RED
CLAY
PONYTAILS
END IN
CLOTS OF CLAY
CHILD OF
WATER
NECK
BLACK
PAINT
BUCK
SKINS
CLAY

BIOGRAPHIES
THE MYTHIC CREW

John McCrea was born in Belfast, N. Ireland, John has been a Marvel zombie since the age of 4. He opened N. Ireland's first comic shop, *Dark Horizons,* at 19 (with pal Fred Collier and the help of Terri Hooley, N.I.'s punk guru). It was there he met Garth Ennis . . . and that was that . . .

Phil Hester has been writing and drawing comics since the dawn of time. After doing tons of black and white indie comics, he broke into the mainstream as penciler of DC's *Swamp Thing* with writer Mark Millar. He wrote and drew the Eisner Award-nominated series *The Wretch.* Phil drew Kevin Smith's revival of DC's *Green Arrow* with long time inker Ande Parks. He wrote *The Coffin* with artist Mike Huddleston for Oni. At Image Comics he created *Firebreather* with artist Andy Kuhn, which became an Emmy-winning animated television feature for Cartoon Network.
His work, as both artist and writer, has been featured in hundreds of comics, and includes such titles as *The Darkness, Wonder Woman, Ant-Man, Ultimate Marvel Team-Up, Nightwing, Invincible Universe, Batman Beyond, The Flash: Season Zero,* and many more he's trying to forget. Phil lives in rural Iowa with his family.

Willie Schubert started lettering comics before computers and became the third letterer to produce digital lettering. He met John while working on *Hitman* at DC Comics. After spending some time away from comics, John hunted him down with an offer to letter *Mythic.* Now he's having a blast and thanks John for inviting him back into the pool.

Michael Spicer is a south Florida based artist, and has been coloring comics since 2007. Husband to an amazing wife, father to a beautiful son, Daddy to an stubborn dog. He likes pizza, burgers, beer, and wine . . . AND COLORING FRIGGIN COMICS! Seriously, its the best! Mike has worked for several publishers including DC, Vertigo, Valiant, Image, IDW, and BOOM! on titles like *Suicide Squad Most Wanted: Deadshot, Mad Max Fury Road, Mythic, Head Lopper, Dead Drop, Silent Hill* and *Sons of Anarchy.*

Rian Hughes is a graphic designer, illustrator, comic artist, author, and typographer who has produced hundreds of logo designs for Marvel, DC and many other comic companies for titles such as *Batman, X-Men, James Bond* and *Spiderman,* and recently wrote and drew a *Batman: Black and White* tale. His comic strips have been collected in *Yesterdays Tomorrows* and *Tales from Beyond Science,* and his burlesque art in *Soho Dives, Soho Divas,* all available from Image.

Rob Levin is a writer, editor and creative consultant. He broke into comics with Top Cow Productions, becoming VP - Editorial and overseeing such titles as *Witchblade,* *The Darkness* and pioneering the innovative Pilot Season initiative. Since founding Comic Book Consulting he was worked on a variety of projects including other Image Comics books *Nailbiter, Mind the Gap, Severed* and *The Last of the Greats.* His writing credits include *Bushido, Netherworld, 7 Days From Hell, Broken Trinity: Pandora's Box* and *Abattoir.* You can find him in Los Angeles and on the Internet.

PJ Holden is a Belfast based comic artist. He's best known for his work on 2000AD drawing *Judge Dredd, Rogue Trooper, Sinister Dexter* and much more. He's the co-creator of *Dept. of Monsterology* and *Numbercruncher.* He likes drawing monsters and people hitting them. He is the shortest of the Belfast giants.

Brian Churilla is a comic book writer/artist currently drawing *Godzilla: Oblivion* for IDW Publishing. He's best known for his work on *Big Trouble in Little China* and *Hellbreak.* He's currently studying web development at Epicodus. His psychedelic, red-scare alternate-history yarn, The *Secret History of D.B. Cooper* (Oni Press) is really awesome. Past credits include: *Secret Wars Too, The Avengers* and *The Infinity Gauntlet* (Marvel), *Plants vs. Zombies, Dark Horse Presents* (Dark Horse), *The Sixth Gun: Sons of the Gun* (Oni), *The Anchor* (BOOM!), *We Kill Monsters* (Red 5), and *The Engineer* (Archaia).